W9-AZJ-143

"The author's remarkable literary achievement here is that she has created the distinct voices of three very different characters who belong to, and who express, the traditions and the values of their own rich cultures. . . . Like the best historical novels, [it] takes readers into a remote time and place, and like them, it also shines a light on the present."
—*The Press Democrat*

"Breathes life into the story of one Chinese man who achieved much in American agriculture but died an unsung hero in an unmarked grave."
—*Northwest Asian Weekly*

"Subtle . . . a novel of intriguing ambiguities and paradoxes. . . . It is epic in scope, spanning a century of history, two continents and one ocean, but it is, nevertheless, an intimate portrait."
—*Front Row Critics' Circle*

"A worthy tale of landmark events in a Chinese-American's remarkable life—and hard times—in two cultures." —*Kirkus Reviews*

"Her skillful balance of individual stories and social history makes a poignant statement about the waste of lives." —*Publishers Weekly*

"McCunn's precise ear for dialect and her lyrical, totally original prose style make each of her 'voices' convey a character as believably real and clearly drawn as Lue Gim Gong himself." —*Nichi Bei Times*

"The reader learns something about Lue's work and is given the opportunity to think about cultural conflict, the evils of racism, and the opportunities lost to blind prejudice." —*Library Journal*

RUTHANNE LUM McCUNN was born in San Francisco's Chinatown. She grew up in Hong Kong but returned to San Francisco to attend college. She has worked as a teacher, librarian, and writer, with books that include the novel *Thousand Pieces of Gold*, the highly acclaimed *Chinese American Portraits: Personal Histories 1828–1988*, *Sole Survivor*, and a bilingual children's book, *Pie-Biter*. She lives in San Francisco and is currently working on a new novel.

WOODEN FISH SONGS

Ruthanne Lum McCunn

A PLUME BOOK

PLUME
Published by the Penguin Group
Penguin Books USA Inc., 375 Hudson Street, New York, New York 10014, U.S.A.
Penguin Books Ltd, 27 Wrights Lane, London W8 5TZ, England
Penguin Books Australia Ltd, Ringwood, Victoria, Australia
Penguin Books Canada Ltd, 10 Alcorn Avenue, Toronto, Ontario, Canada M4V 3B2
Penguin Books (N.Z.) Ltd, 182–190 Wairau Road, Auckland 10, New Zealand

Penguin Books Ltd, Registered Offices: Harmondsworth, Middlesex, England

Published by Plume, an imprint of Dutton Signet,
a division of Penguin Books USA Inc.
Previously published in a Dutton edition.

First Plume Printing, May, 1996
10 9 8 7 6 5 4 3 2 1

Copyright © Ruthanne Lum McCunn, 1995
All rights reserved

 REGISTERED TRADEMARK—MARCA REGISTRADA

The Library of Congress has catalogued the Dutton edition as follows:

McCunn, Ruthanne Lum.
    Wooden fish songs / Ruthanne Lum McCunn.
        p.   cm.
    ISBN 0-525-93927-X (hc.)
    ISBN 0-452-27346-3 (pbk.)
    1. Lue, Gim Gong, 1858 or 9–1925—Fiction.   2. Chinese Americans—Florida—
History—Fiction.   3. Citrus fruit industry—Florida—History—Fiction.   4. Women—
United States—History—Fiction.   I. Title.
PS3563.C353W66   1995
813'.54—dc20
                                                    94–42797
                                                    CIP

Printed in the United States of America
Original hardcover design by Leonard Telesca

Without limiting the rights under copyright reserved above, no part of this publication may
be reproduced, stored in or introduced into a retrieval system, or transmitted, in any form, or
by any means (electronic, mechanical, photocopying, recording, or otherwise), without the
prior written permission of both the copyright owner and the above publisher of this book.

BOOKS ARE AVAILABLE AT QUANTITY DISCOUNTS WHEN USED TO PROMOTE PRODUCTS
OR SERVICES. FOR INFORMATION PLEASE WRITE TO PREMIUM MARKETING DIVISION,
PENGUIN BOOKS USA INC., 375 HUDSON STREET, NEW YORK, NY 10014.

For
my Hong Kong family
now scattered in this world and beyond.

And for
Don,
who has been at the heart of my life in America
almost from the beginning.

AUTHOR'S NOTE

The lives portrayed in this novel were reclaimed with the generous assistance of the many individuals and institutions named in the Acknowledgments. The interpretation of the facts recovered, however, is mine alone, and as in any historical novel, fact and fiction are closely woven together.

I did write two factual profiles of Lue Gim Gong, which may be found in *Chinese American Portraits* (San Francisco: Chronicle Books, 1988) and *Chinese America: History and Perspectives* (San Francisco: Chinese Historical Society of America, 1989). But in my view, the deeper mysteries and truths of Lue Gim Gong's life lie here, in the stories—the wooden fish songs—of the women who were closest to him.

History is a novel that has been lived.
—*Edmond & Jules DeGoncourt*

Who has the right to speak for whom?
—*Anna Deveare Smith*

SUM JUI

Toishan, China
1842—1870

I was marked by ghosts in my seventh winter. One ghost. My grandfather's.

He'd been driven to his bed by old age and the spitting-blood disease even before I was born, and from the time I could crawl, I became his legs. Puffed up with self-importance, I toddled after his tobacco and helped pack the bowl of his long bamboo pipe. When he complained about the heat, I fanned him. When he felt chilled, I crawled under the quilts to rub warm his feet and hands. And when coughing turned his face purple and the veins on his forehead bulged and pulsed as if they would leap through his skin, I pummeled his back with my tiny fists. He called me Sum Jui, Heart's Pearl.

Each autumn, when the wind from the river turned sharp, his cough worsened; his skin, yellow as old ivory, flushed with fever. My mother said it was because the wind, pressing through the cracks between the bricks, stole into his body: he must be forced to sweat so the wind could seep back out through his pores.

For three or four days and nights, she piled all our quilts and winter clothes on top of him. She fed him soups of ginger and garlic. Slowly, his skin cooled. His eyes lost their glassy stare. And when he told me to fetch his pipe and I heard the familiar *tap-tap* of its bowl against the smoke-blackened wall, I knew my grandfather, my Yeh Yeh, was himself again.

In my seventh year, this fever struck just after the Moon Festival. The harvest had been unusually good, and the largest landlord in the district had hired an opera troupe and acrobats to celebrate. Everyone had gone to the performance, even Yeh Yeh. Since he could not walk, he went in a chair. My brother, six years older than I, was almost as tall and strong as my father, and he and my father carried the chair between them. As soon as the cymbals crashed and the hero stalked on stage, Yeh Yeh grinned, baring his toothless gums. But it was the acrobats who captured my heart, and for days after, I tumbled on top of Yeh Yeh's quilts, imitating them with teetering handstands and somersaults.

I was too young to realize that Yeh Yeh was more seriously ill than before. Even after the whites of his eyes turned yellow and beads of sweat glistened on his forehead, I did not fret. Hadn't our water buffalo looked far worse, with thick, sticky saliva hanging in transparent strings from its mouth? All winter its mournful bellows had kept the entire village awake, but by spring it had been back in the fields, cured by my mother's brews.

My mother's remedies had never failed, and I knew nothing of the rituals for a person close to death, so I was pleased when my mother dressed Yeh Yeh in new clothes. My father and brother took a half-dozen boards and set them on two trestles in the main room, not far from Yeh Yeh's bed, between the family altar and the front door. Then they laid Yeh Yeh down on the boards. Though he panted for breath in little shallow bleats, I felt certain he'd be asking for his pipe soon.

That same day I discovered a nest of wild kittens in the weeds by the river. Their playful tumbling made me laugh, and I wanted to share my pleasure with Yeh Yeh. Carefully I tucked one under my jacket and took it home.

As I burst into the house, my mother said, "Hush, Yeh Yeh is in his big sleep." Still I sensed nothing unusual; Yeh Yeh often drifted in and out of sleep during the day. Thinking only of my surprise, I ignored my mother and ran to him. As I reached his side, the kitten wriggled out from under my jacket and leaped onto his chest. Yeh Yeh jerked upright. The kitten, startled, jumped off. There was the clink of coins dropping onto the floor.

My mother gasped, pushed Yeh Yeh back down. "Forgive Sum Jui," she cried. "The girl didn't know the kitten would pull your spirit back into this world."

Too astonished to speak or move, I stared blankly as my mother picked up two pieces of copper cash from the floor and placed them on Yeh Yeh's eyes, weighing down the closed lids, then secured the knot on a strip of cloth that bound his face from chin to forehead. But when she snatched the kitten from the corner where it was hiding and hurled it across the room, its terrified mews woke me from my stupor, and I chased after it.

My mother grabbed me by the collar. Kicking the kitten through the door, she scolded, "Don't you know cats are dangerous creatures with demonic powers?"

As always when I needed help, I shouted for Yeh Yeh. My mother slapped me. "Ancestors, have pity on this ignorant girl," she pleaded.

Swiftly dragging me over to the altar, she sprayed me with a mouthful of holy water, lit a handful of incense, and pushed me down onto my knees. Once, twice, three times she knocked my head against the hard dirt floor, all the time crying, "Ancestors, guide Yeh Yeh's spirit to the Yellow Springs."

Blood spurted out of my nose. "Yeh Yeh," I wailed. "I want Yeh Yeh."

My mother, her face rapidly turning red then pale again, dragged me back to Yeh Yeh. A brisk wind was blowing through the door, chilling. But he did not have one of his coughing fits. He did not so much as shiver. He was without breath, completely still.

"Don't you see your Yeh Yeh's dead?" my mother asked, her voice, her touch suddenly gentle.

The only dead I'd seen were the mosquitoes and flies I squashed flat on hot summer evenings, the pigs and chickens slaughtered before a festival. Who would dare kill Yeh Yeh? And why? More frightened and confused, I cried louder.

Squatting down low, my mother pinched my nostrils until the flow of blood stopped. She cleaned my face with the edge of her underjacket and hugged me close until my sobs quieted into whimpers. Then, gripping my shoulders, she held me at arm's length. "Your father and brother will be back with the coffin soon. You must not tell them about the kitten breaking Yeh Yeh's journey."

My mother's warning puzzled me, but I did not dare chance another outburst. So I said nothing. Sighing, she continued, "The first hours of death are important because the spirit is reluctant to let go. We the living must encourage the spirit to leave and help guide it to the afterworld. Otherwise the person cannot go on to his next turn in the wheel of life."

Her grip tightened and her eyes bore into mine. "The kitten's life force brought Yeh Yeh's spirit back. Now his spirit may get lost, and if he doesn't find the Yellow Springs, he will wander like a ghost that belongs nowhere and bring trouble on us all. Be silent and no one will know you are to blame." She shook me lightly. "Do you understand?"

I did not. But when she shook me harder and asked again, I nodded yes.

My father and brother placed Yeh Yeh in the coffin. They hoisted a paper stork above the house to carry his spirit to the Yellow Springs. They scraped off the strips of faded lucky red papers pasted on either side of the door, replacing them with white. They lit a Heavenly lantern, a pair of mourning candles. My mother draped the altar with unbleached sackcloth; she gave us sackcloth to wear over our jackets and pants.

While the village priest studied the almanac for an auspicious burial date, we kept vigil beside the coffin, rolling out our sleeping mats beside it. The house, without Yeh Yeh's tortured breathing and fits of coughing, seemed strangely quiet. The flames of the mourning candles, small as beans, flickered in the drafts gusting through cracks, casting ghostly shadows. The coffin loomed in front of the altar like a dragon crouched, ready to pounce.

I thought of Yeh Yeh inside. My mother had removed the cloth binding his head. But his face was strangely stiff and stern, darkly foreboding. Because his spirit had left? The kitten had brought it back once. If I opened the coffin and climbed inside, could I bring it back again?

Under the paper stork, the priest had posted a paper with detailed instructions to guide Yeh Yeh's spirit to the Yellow Springs. We had fed his spirit offerings of rice, chicken, fruit, and tea for the journey. And we had burned paper clothes, houses, money, and servants for his use when he arrived. So perhaps it was too late. But even if his spirit was gone, didn't his hands and feet need me to warm them?

I started to rise from my sleeping mat. My mother pressed me back down, and in the force of her hand against my chest I felt all the fire of her earlier outburst. Frightened, I lay silent. Eventually, sleep came. But with it came dreams. Dark, terrible dreams of Yeh Yeh butchered, his bowels ripped open by four-eyed dogs, a stump where once he had a tongue.

Yeh Yeh in Hell, thrown on a mountain of knives.

Yeh Yeh flattened on a lake of ice, the King of Hell pouring boiling copper down his throat . . .

Shrill cries, shouts woke me. Before I could collect my wits, my mother scooped me into her arms.

"Go back to sleep," she told my brother.

"What is it?" my father insisted.

"Nothing," my mother said, holding me tight so I could not speak.

I realized then that the shrieks had come from me, the shouts from my father and brother, and I shuddered, remembering what had made me cry out. Awake, the horrible images of Yeh Yeh in the Courts of Hell frightened me even more. Despite my mother's fierce hold, I shook so hard my teeth clattered, and I wept huge, silent tears that soaked her to the skin.

Every day during the forty-nine days of mourning, my father burned ingots made of gold and silver paper to bribe the officials in Hell to lighten Yeh Yeh's punishments. Every night in my dreams, Yeh Yeh underwent new and increasingly terrible tortures. Unable to bear the sight of his suffering, I began to fight sleep. My head drooped with heaviness. My eyes became red and swollen. An angry rash ringed my mouth. I had no appetite. Nor could I swallow.

Thin and pale, I clung to the hope that somehow Yeh Yeh would return. When his burial robbed me even of that, I lost my senses. Later, my mother told me I had thrown my arms around the coffin. When she tried to pull me off, I'd fought with a strength that was clearly not my own. As the clods of earth showered down, sealing his grave, I screamed as if I were mad, and during the night, I became delirious with a raging fever.

"You were no longer mistress of yourself. Something else was directing your will. You see, Yeh Yeh, confused by the kitten, was still not fully aware he was dead. His spirit must have been wandering around looking for his own body. When he could not find it, he took possession of yours."

Hiding my real problem from my father and brother, our neighbors, and all the village, my mother tried to pacify Yeh Yeh, vowing to build a small shrine by his grave if he would go on to his life in the next world rather than try to reenter this one through possession. Since Heaven watches over the good and does not approve of killing animals, she promised Gwoon Yum, the Goddess of Mercy, that for the rest of our lives she and I would both keep from eating meat. Then, afraid to share her fears with the priest yet unable to read the almanac to find the right charm to help me, she burned the entire book and mixed the ashes with water for me to drink.

Vaguely, I recalled feeling parched, as if my lips and tongue were about to crack, the relief of soothing drops of moisture, then jerking bolt upright like Yeh Yeh. "After that your fever broke," my mother said, "and I knew you were yourself again. But you must be careful not to tell *anyone* you've been marked by a ghost, or the matchmaker will never find a groom for you."

My father liked a smoke as much as Yeh Yeh. Sometimes, after he lit up, I would close my eyes and pretend it was Yeh Yeh I heard drawing on the pipe. But my make-believe was as hopeless as trying to hold water in a bamboo basket. Nothing was the same.

Before Yeh Yeh's death, the household had turned around him, and since I was the heart of his life, around me. My mother complained that Yeh Yeh, in favoring me instead of my brother, had turned Heaven and Earth upside down. It was my brother who would feed them in their old age and their spirits when they died, not me; I would belong to my husband's family. "You must learn your proper place," my mother told me, "begin your training in a woman's work."

Though Yeh Yeh had eaten little more than soups and rice gruel, he'd always topped my bowl of rice with a sliver of salt fish or preserved egg. At festival dinners he'd taken the pearls of flesh from either side of the chicken back and dropped them on top of my bowl of rice, chuckling, "Pearls for my Sum Jui, my Heart's Pearl." Now I ate only after my father and brother were finished. If on the few occasions we sat together as a family I was foolish enough to reach for a choice morsel, my mother swiftly rapped my wrist with her chopsticks, forcing me to drop it.

The little services I'd performed for Yeh Yeh had been more like play than chores. And he'd been generous with praise and real rewards: a dried plum to sweeten the tongue, a handful of crunchy peanuts or lotus seeds, a tickle, a story. As I worked under my mother, my ears rang from her impatient cries: *"Ai yah,* you useless rice bucket, you dead girl, you clumsy dolt."

Her tongue never seemed to stop. Guiding my hands on spindle and wheel, her voice would rise over the dry, musical hum, "Remember how hard your clothing is to make." Showing me how to care for seedlings, to graft and prune, she would say, "When you eat your food, remember it's not easy to grow." She permitted no rest between tasks. "You must prepare things before you need them. Don't wait until you're thirsty to dig a well."

Fearful I might carelessly reveal the truth of my illness, she kept me constantly by her side. Since I sometimes called out in my dreams, she set up a makeshift bed for me next to the one she shared with my father. That way she could reach out and cover my mouth before I betrayed myself. In my longing for Yeh Yeh, however, I began sleepwalking back to his bed.

My mother tied my feet to the sawhorses beneath the planks of my bed. "If you're startled awake while you sleepwalk, the cord joining body to soul might snap."

Struggling against the bindings, I began to cry. Her fingers brushed my cheek in a brief caress. Startled, my tears stopped. "There was once a girl who walked in her sleep just like you," she began. "Only she walked out of her house and village—right into the lair of a fox ghost with dazzling white fur and flaming red eyes—"

"If that happened to me, I'd spit," I interrupted. "Yeh Yeh said ghosts are afraid of spit and will run."

She pulled the quilt up to my chin. "This girl did spit. But a fox ghost is not so easily frightened."

"Then I'd call for help from Jung Kwai, the giant. Yeh Yeh said he eats three thousand ghosts just with his morning rice!"

"Jung Kwai was too far away to hear the girl's cries. So she shouted for her father, 'Ba Ba! Ba Ba!' Her father chased after the fox. 'Release my daughter,' he ordered. Swiftly the fox turned, pierced the father with its poisonous glance—and vanished."

"Just like Ba Ba would save me," I breathed, relieved.

My mother shook her head sadly. "The fox ghost cannot injure a strong man. Its venom went past the father and into the girl. Her blood dried up and she died."

* * *

In time I persuaded my mother to let me try sleeping without the bindings. The first few nights I willed myself to stay awake so I could not sleepwalk. When the ghost-white mosquito net around my bed billowed in a draft, I stuffed my fist into my mouth to keep from crying out. Gradually I gave in to snatches of thin sleep that grew longer, and my mother put away the cloth ties. I thought then that the weight on my heart would also disappear. Instead, it grew heavier with each passing year.

The summer my little red sister came, making me a woman, smallpox invaded our village. The heat was terrible, and mosquitoes and flies swarmed in droves, sounding like thunder. My mother smoked the house with a dried plant that kills disease. She spread lime powder in dark corners and under our beds.

Every day she checked my brother and me for watery-looking pimples, lit incense in thanks when none appeared. Many fell ill and died that year; the ones who survived were covered with pockmarks as big as soya beans. Pointing to the girls, my mother sighed, "What kind of a match can they hope for?"

"At least *their* mothers-in-law will know exactly what they're getting," I wanted to say. "Unlike me, those girls can never be blamed for hiding the truth. They never have to worry that their marks might bring sickness, madness, poverty, failure, or some other terrible misfortune to their families. They're free."

But by then I was too well schooled in silence to speak out loud. So I simply lit the incense as my mother instructed and loudly thanked the Gods and our ancestors for my safe delivery, keeping in my heart the prayer that they would please spare me from bringing anyone harm, my gratitude for the release that came when I worked in our family's orchard.

In our village, men labored in rice fields, women in orange orchards. My mother could produce better and larger quantities of fruit than even the richest landowners, and she taught me her secrets to increase my value as a bride. What I soon discovered, however, was that when nursing seedlings into tender sprouts, transplanting them into moist, warm soil, or selecting the right branches to graft and prune, I could lose myself in the pleasure of such work, forgetting the burden of my ghost mark for a morning, sometimes an entire day.

My mother could not. But she hid her worry well, speaking in front of Old Auntie, the matchmaker, as glibly as any vendor at market. "Look!" she demanded, thrusting my hands up at the shortsighted old woman. "Feel how strong they are. And they're as skilled at sewing and cooking as they are at fruit cultivation."

Dropping my hands, she pointed out the absence of blemishes on my face, the breadth of my hips. "She'll have many children and ease in bearing them. And she'll be a dutiful daughter-in-law. She's obedient. Doesn't indulge in idle gossip. Since she was seven, she's not eaten meat. Such virtue will surely bring blessings on her husband's family as it has on ours. We were spared the smallpox, you know."

Once we were alone, my mother brooded over my invisible but terrible mark. "There isn't a family in the village that doesn't have more eyes than a sweet potato. Even their chamber pots have ears. Anyone might know your secret and just be waiting for the time when we can be hurt the most to strike." Sewing little squares of red cloth onto the insides of my collars for luck, she fretted over my fate, whether Old Auntie would find a suitable groom, any groom.

When Old Auntie brought news of a fine young man from a good family in the Lue clan, my mother could not trust the claims made by the groom's matchmaker. Hadn't her own avowals of my perfection been less than true? Then, after Old Auntie convinced her, swearing that she spoke with her own eyes as witness and not from hearsay, my mother worried that the groom's and my horoscopes would not match. When they did, she agonized over the offers and counteroffers for betrothal gifts, settling at last for eighty-eight catties of rice, twelve catties of salt fish, six chickens, two pigs, a pair of good-omen candles, and two bottles of *ng ga pei,* a fine medicinal wine.

For the next three days my mother scarcely breathed as she watched for signs that the match should be given up. When nothing in the house broke and no chickens died, she and my father received the gifts and burned three incense sticks down to the root, sealing the betrothal.

As the last bits of ash crumbled from the incense sticks, I felt a spurt of hope. Perhaps my mother's claims to Old Auntie were true. Perhaps my ghost mark no longer mattered.

But this hope did not, could not last. That same night I dreamed of pig traders. Human-pig traders. And they were going after my betrothed.

I was very young, not more than a year or two out of split-bottomed pants, when I first heard about the human-pig trade. Almost every family in the village raised pigs in their courtyards, and I was down by the river watching the men ship their prize porkers to the market in Sang Sing. Each animal lay in a wicker cage the exact size of its own body, with its snout sticking out at one end, its tail at the other. My father and brother were carrying the cages up the gangplank to the boat; our neighbors, Baldy and Fish Eyes, were stacking them on the deck. Listening to the pigs squeal, I could sense their fright, the suffocation and pain the ones at the bottom must feel from the pressure of those above, and I wondered out loud if they could survive the journey downriver.

"*Hnnnh!* Don't waste your pity on pigs," Baldy snorted. "Foreign ghosts fill the holds of their great ships with our men in just this way."

"Why?"

"To work on their ghost farms on the other side of the world," Baldy said.

"Is that farther away than Sang Sing?"

The men laughed. My brother pinched my cheek kindly. "Yes, Little Sister. Much farther."

"And the men don't die?"

"Certainly they do," my father said. "Sometimes by the hundreds."

"Often by their own hands," Fish Eyes added darkly.

"How?" my brother asked.

"Down in the holds, those who can find a sharp bit of wood stab themselves. If they're brought up on deck for exercise, they throw themselves over the side of the ship."

Horrified, I gasped, "Why?"

Fish Eyes leaped ashore, grabbed an empty basket, and dropped it over me. Startled, I began to cry even before he latched it, tossed me onto his shoulder, and trotted up the gangplank. By the time he laid me on top of the pigs, I was screaming.

Baldy quickly freed me, but I continued to cry. Over my wails, I heard Baldy scold Fish Eyes for frightening me.

"She should understand why men traded like pigs will take their own lives," Fish Eyes said.

My father took me from Baldy. "The ocean is full of their hungry ghosts."

"Yes," Fish Eyes agreed. "And those who don't die are forced to work night and day on the foreign-ghost farms. They're whipped and underfed. What kind of life is that?"

Though my father patted me on the back and rocked me gently, I could not be quieted. At last, losing patience with my tears, he told my brother to carry me home.

Back with Yeh Yeh, my sobs dwindled into whimpers, then disappeared, and I sank into a deep, dreamless sleep.

When I woke, I felt again the terror of my brief imprisonment. Fish Eyes had trapped me easily because I was a small girl. Baldy had said the human-pigs were grown men. How did they get snared?

I asked Yeh Yeh.

"The men go willingly," he said.

Astonished, I blurted, "Why?"

Yeh Yeh reached for his pipe. While he packed it with tobacco, I jumped off the bed, lit a taper from the incense on the altar, and brought it to him. He drew deeply on the pipe, began to cough. Quickly, I crawled up behind him and pounded his back. When his coughing quieted, I climbed back down and poured him a bowl of hot water from the teapot in the padded basket. Laying his pipe aside, Yeh Yeh took the bowl in both his hands. He started to raise it to his lips, stopped.

"Look!" He nodded down at the bowl of water. "We grow tea. But after the officials take a portion to cover our taxes for the scrap of land we own, the landlord collects his share for the fields we rent, and the middlemen who sell for us take their bite, we can't even afford to keep the sweepings, the dust from drying leaves. We have to drink water.

"It's the same or worse for most of our people. No matter how hard we work, we have as much chance of living well as a blind man has of catching an eel. That's why we're easy prey."

Closing his eyes, he sipped the water thoughtfully. When he finished, he set the bowl down beside his pipe. "I once saw a birdman capture cranes. He used a decoy that had its eyelids sewn shut and its feet fastened in a net. In the same way, foreign ghosts trap our men with the promise of good wages. But unlike birds, men can talk. Already word of the foreign ghosts' treachery is spreading. Soon they will not be able to fill their ships."

As Yeh Yeh had foreseen, our men could not be gulled forever. But when they refused to go willingly, the foreign ghosts hired sea robbers to attack villages along the coast and capture them. Any resistance was so much dust thrown into the wind. Like turtles trapped in a pot, villagers could not escape. Soon rival clans and families took up arms against each other, hacking down their enemies as heedlessly as if they were slicing melons, selling prisoners to the foreign ghosts. Bands of thieves stole upriver, seizing young men in shops and in rice fields.

We were far enough inland to be safe. My betrothed, Lue Hok Yee, was not. That was why I'd seen human-pig traders chasing him in my dream, though I did not know it until Old Auntie beat on our door late one evening.

A squat dumpling of a woman, she tumbled in too breathless to speak, but only trouble would have brought her out during the third watch. My mother, trying to hide her fear, plied Old Auntie with hot water and meaningless prattle. My father, also concerned, told my brother and me to fan her.

Finally Old Auntie took a deep breath and began. "The day of the betrothal, the *very* day, Hok Yee's father sent him to a neighboring village with their water buffalo. A cousin wanted to borrow it for spring plowing, you see. Now, it's only a half-day's walk and Hok Yee set out early, but somehow the buffalo got loose and Hok Yee had to chase it, so he was still on the road when the first star rose. It was a new moon, you remember—it's only a quarter moon now—and there wasn't much light, but knowing the way well, he wasn't worried.

"Then, suddenly, he saw torches snaking through the darkness not far from him, a burst of light as they joined and flared into a circle of fire. Dogs began barking, and from the screams and shouts that followed, Hok Yee realized his cousin's village was under attack and the dogs' alarm had come too late. Tying the buffalo to a tree, he turned and ran back to his own village to give warning."

As the words spilled out of Old Auntie, I saw my mother pale, her eyes darken. My own head whirled. Were Hok Yee and his family safe? Had Old Auntie placed special emphasis on the day of my betrothal because she'd guessed I was the cause of Hok Yee's trouble? Had she come to break the contract?

"Hok Yee's village was not attacked. Not that night. Not yet. But those sons of turtles captured his cousin, and you can be sure they'll come again. What if they take Hok Yee next time? Heaven forbid, they could take his brothers too! And the family has no grandsons yet! So you can understand, they don't dare wait three or four years for Sum Jui to reach the more common age of marriage. They want the wedding on the earliest auspicious date the priest can find in the almanac."

"The girl's only thirteen," my father said.

Old Auntie leered. "She's already a woman. Her betrothed is sixteen, a man."

My mother pulled my father aside. "We cannot refuse the Lues."

"Why?"

"If we deny them this opportunity for grandsons, Heaven might deny us, too."

The priest selected the third day of the third moon for the wedding, leaving my mother and me less than two moons to sew all the bedding and clothing I would need to take to my new home.

She offered counsel with each stitch. "Be dutiful to your new parents, your husband, and your brothers. Never bring dishonor on your father."

In the kitchen peeling bamboo shoots, she pointed out how each layer we pulled back revealed yet another layer underneath, each tightly bound to the next. "Your betrothed is an adopted son. His older brother has been married four years, but so far, his wife has borne no son. There are two younger brothers, who will each take wives in their turn. Such a large family has as many layers as these shoots, and you must tread carefully."

Even on the morning of the wedding, while Old Auntie combed my girlish braid into the knot of a married woman and dressed me in bridal red, my mother's flow of advice did not cease. But when the matchmaker fastened the last button on my satin jacket, my mother's tongue suddenly stopped.

For years I had prayed for just such a silence. Now I found myself unnerved by the unnatural quiet, and as Old Auntie stepped back to survey her handiwork, I looked over at my mother. She turned away deliberately and left the room. Tears sprang unbidden from my eyes, coursed down my cheeks. Paying no attention, Old Auntie went on with her work, draping the red silk veil over my face, setting the headdress firmly in place, leading me from my parents' bedroom to the family altar in the main room.

Blinded by my tears and veil, I stumbled. Old Auntie held me steady, guided me in paying respects to Heaven and Earth, in taking leave of my ancestors, my father and mother. Then she led me outside, thrust me into the enclosed bridal chair, slammed shut the door, and locked it.

The chair was windowless. Trapped in its suffocating darkness, I was overcome by the same panic that had struck when Fish Eyes had thrust me into the pig basket, and my wails soared. But this time no one unlatched the door. No one comforted me. How could they when custom decrees that a bride show her reluctance to leave her parents by crying? Tears were expected. No, required.

I fumbled for my handkerchief as the bearers turned my chair around three times, then began the long walk to Lung On village in a hail of firecrackers. The chair swayed back and forth like the bobbing of a boat, and I thought of the men captured for the human-pig trade stuffed into the holds of foreign-ghost ships. How different was my fate from theirs?

Though I wasn't crossing an ocean, I was going to live among strangers, and I knew from watching the families in our village that daughters-in-law were often worked like slaves. Bad-tempered mothers-in-law were commonplace. As the saying goes, ninety-nine out of every hundred are terrible. Husbands who beat their wives were no less unusual. So, to signify my hope that my husband and I would live and grow old together in harmony, I was bringing a pair of shoes to exchange with him. But that was a custom all brides observed. I might still be beaten.

Suddenly I realized how much I'd relied on my mother to keep me safe. When Yeh Yeh's spirit took possession of me, she had persuaded him to leave. She had protected me from the smallpox and secured a husband for me by hiding my secret and teaching me well. Only the day before, over my father's objections, she had slaughtered and roasted our best pig so it could be carried at the head of my wedding procession, before the drummer and men beating the gongs, to feed any hungry ghosts who might wish to harm me. Without her, I would be as helpless as a slender reed torn from the protection of a strong tree.

The weight of my headdress made my neck ache. Wedging my elbows on either side of the bridal chair, I shifted it, easing the pressure. My veil slipped, clung to my tear-streaked face, smothering. Gasping for breath in the steamy darkness, I understood why brides and human pigs sometimes arrived at their destination as ghosts.

Ghosts. We would not reach Lung On before nightfall. What if the village was attacked before my arrival? If Hok Yee was captured, I would have to marry him through a substitute. If he was killed, I could be forced to marry his ghost. His family would surely, probably justly, blame me for his death, and their treatment could be cruel.

My fears churned like troublesome spirits. I felt as if I were sinking in an unclean pond, my head pressed under by the ghosts of those who had drowned and wished me to take their place. Choking, I remembered the time my mother had shuttered all the windows and locked the doors because ghosts would be walking through our village.

So the ghosts would not suspect our presence, we'd sat inside and kept very quiet. The whole village was quiet. Not even the dogs or chickens made a sound. Then, after a while, we heard heavy footsteps in a steady rhythm as the walker of the dead, who had special powers, led the ghosts away.

I imagined the man carrying the roasted pig at the head of my wedding procession was the walker of the dead. The footsteps I heard were foreign ghosts marching out of our country back to their homes at the other side of the world. Old Auntie was releasing me from this cage because my betrothed was no longer in danger. . . .

From what seemed like a great distance I heard strings of firecrackers explode, the sharp rap of knuckles against wood, a latch unfasten. I felt a gust of fresh air, a shaft of light from a lantern held high.

Squinting against the sudden glare, I sucked greedily at the air. A woman's face bore down on mine. With practiced ease, the woman straightened my headdress, pulled me into the chill night, and tossed me over her back. Through the soles of my shoes I felt the sharp, burning heat of coals. . . .

I realized then that some time before we reached Lung On, I must have lost my soul, that the slow charcoal fire, burned at a groom's threshold to destroy any evil influences a bride might carry, was bringing it back.

I became fully sensible as Old Auntie slid me down her back to my feet. "Kneel," she whispered. "Prostrate yourself before your betrothed."

Through the red haze of my veil, I saw the shape of a man seated on a high stool. Sinking to my knees at his feet, I knocked my head against the floor. Old Auntie grasped my elbows and helped me up. The man reached out. Instinctively I shrank back. Old Auntie's grip tightened, forcing me to remain still. Eyes downcast, I felt the man remove my veil, my face burn bright, and I was grateful for the strands of pearls that dangled from the front of my headdress, shielding me like a beaded curtain.

Guided by Old Auntie, we carried out the rituals to make us husband and wife. We prostrated ourselves to Heaven and Earth, his ancestors and parents, now mine. We sipped honey and wine from goblets tied with red thread. We took a bite each out of a sugar cock and pieces of dried fruit.

Not once did I dare lift my eyes from the floor. Even seated side by side on the edge of our bed in the bridal chamber, I kept my head low. Guests crowded close, loudly discussing the shape of my feet, my ears, my nose. They tested my temper by ordering me to pour tea for my husband, to guess at lewd riddles.

At home, watching brides squirm under this teasing, I had giggled. Now, struggling to keep a steady smile while being pinched and insulted, I could not think what I had found so amusing, and it seemed to me the guests would never leave.

As the door closed behind the last of them, however, I had to bite my lips to keep from calling them back.

As everyone knows, a man who has plenty of money and no children cannot be reckoned rich; a man who has children and no money cannot be considered poor. Yes, my husband's parents, Ba and Ma, hoped I would increase their holdings with my skills in cultivation, and in my wedding trunk my mother had packed seeds she'd saved from delicious oranges; these I planted in a piece of land Ba rented for me to develop into an orchard. But above all else, Ba and Ma wanted me to give them a grandson who would feed their souls after they died.

Like all brides, I had embroidered luck-bearing pictures on the bedding I would share with my husband: mandarin ducks nestled among lotus blossoms; phoenixes and unicorns with babies on their backs; the Celestial Fairy who grants sons and grandsons. And on our bed and all over our room, Ma had pasted long strips of red paper with couplets wishing us one hundred sons and one thousand grandsons. All the same, I was as ignorant and shy as any respectable bride.

Hok Yee's fumblings revealed he knew little more than I. Yet he was so gentle and kind that he filled my heart with warm feelings. Before long, he discovered how to make those warm feelings leap into flames. I learned to please him as well, and night after night we enjoyed the pleasures of fish in water, our souls flying away over the Heavens. Nevertheless, my little red sister continued to arrive as usual.

I could see that Elder Sister, still barren after four years of marriage to my husband's elder brother, was relieved when she saw me washing out my bloodied cloths. Ma was disappointed, though too tenderhearted to scold. Quietly she boiled more lotus kernels with rock sugar for Elder Sister and me. "Sons will come one after another," she encouraged. "We must be patient." But the blackened hills surrounding Lung On, burned to destroy the coverts of raiders and prevent a surprise attack, belied her words, and concern clouded her eyes.

Ba was openly bewildered. My husband, as his protruding teeth signified, was a man of luck. Before his adoption, Ma had successfully borne only one child after ten years of miscarriages and stillbirths, and when this son had nearly died from cholera in his eighth year, Ba had adopted Hok Yee to assure himself of an heir. In the next three years, Ma had given birth to two more sons though she was almost past the age for childbearing. Clearly Hok Yee had brought them these sons. Why wasn't he bringing grandsons?

At home and at the temple, I lit incense to the Gods, Hok Yee's ancestors, my own.

I prostrated myself before the Queen of Heaven.

I made offerings to the Celestial Fairy.

I pleaded with the Goddess Gwoon Yum for mercy, placed a small shoe at the foot of her statue as a pledge of my trust that she would give me a child.

I fasted.

I studied my dreams and watched for signs.

Just after the Moon Festival my little red sister stopped coming. By New Year I could feel the life in my belly.

Ma, remembering her own misery when childless, was careful not to show me any favor. But Elder Sister ate vinegar just the same. How could she not? In almost five years her belly hadn't once swelled with child. She couldn't even produce a girl, and the fortune-teller Ma had called in to examine me had divined that I was carrying a boy.

In the afternoons while Ma was resting, Elder Sister would order me to bring her a bowl of herbal soup, let it stand until it grew cold. Then, complaining it wasn't fit to drink, she would fling the contents at me and demand another bowl. At morning and evening rice she slyly gave me the burned scrapings from the bottom of the pot. She searched for opportunities to bump against me, to pinch my arms and legs.

But I was no soft-shelled egg. My mother had seen to that. *Hnnnh,* Elder Sister's petty cruelties troubled me as little as the pinpricks I felt when Ma plucked out the hair on my forehead by catching each strand in a twist of thread. In truth, I pitied her.

Where my husband was broad and strong and brown as a cup of old tea, Elder Sister's husband was scrawny and jaundiced, forever scratching his head and feet like a moulting chicken. Hok Yee never failed to beat the dust of the fields from his clothes before entering the house; Elder Brother was always covered with dirt, his feet caked in smelly manure. Hok Yee's well-shaped face wore a ready smile. He thanked me for the smallest service and brought me sesame cakes, sweet roasted peanuts, and crunchy chestnuts from market; he picked fragrant blossoms to put in my matron's bun. Elder Brother's thin, long face was ever scowling. He treated Elder Sister with the arrogance of a landlord; his gifts to her were bruises.

She was beautiful, with soft curves, fair skin, kingfisher eyebrows, and tiny feet arched like new moons. And she was expert at spinning and sewing. Yet Elder Brother would shout as he hit her, "You're useless as a piece of wood! You've less value than a pig ready for slaughter!"

No one stopped him. Nor did Elder Sister ever cry out loud. She knew she was at fault in failing to give him a son. So I held my tongue when she tormented me. As the saying goes, when you have meat, you should share the bone.

A ten-month baby is best. My son began his struggle to enter the world at the end of seven. Ma hung balls and tassles, bringers of sons, on the posts at the head of the bed.

"Push," she instructed.

Curling my fingers into fists against the pain, I took a deep breath and pushed, thrusting my belly, arching my whole body off the bed in my eagerness to greet my son.

"Harder," Ma urged. "You must push harder."

Straining, I tried again.

Once, twice, over and over, I felt my son forced forward as I squeezed—only to have him retreat when I panted for breath. Sweat poured from me. Still I kept heaving myself up for another push until, finally, the torment of failed effort and unrelenting pain ground me down, and I fell back weeping.

"Don't cry," Ma begged, pasting paper charms on my belly. "These will ease the pain and bring my grandson."

But they did neither.

One by one the charms slipped from my belly onto the bed, shredded as I writhed in helpless agony. The stench of blood, my blood, filled my nostrils. I could not breathe. Sweat-soaked, chilled yet flushed with fever, my cries weakened into whimpers, my pants into faint huffs.

Gray with fear, Ma picked at the broken, bloody talismans that littered the bed. "Heaven's will is sometimes extreme," she murmured. "But we must not complain."

Elder Sister led her to a chair in the corner of the room. "Sit a moment, Ma, and rest. I'll take care of Sum Jui."

Wiping my face roughly with a hot cloth, she leaned close and hissed, "You're sinking into the bloody lake. That muddy swamp which devours the souls of mothers who die in childbirth."

"No," I mewled, tasting blood. "No."

Pretending to soothe, Elder Sister said, "Hush, let me change you."

As she peeled off my soiled jacket and tugged on a fresh, she deliberately twisted and wrenched my arms. I flailed feebly. Elder Sister, her eyes narrowed, her lips parted in a secret smile, pushed me down.

Too late I saw her little pointy teeth, her fox-colored eyes, the fine hair covering her hands and face. Too late I recognized Elder Sister was a fox ghost in the form of a woman.

No. It was not too late. Hadn't my mother said a man can fight fox-ghost venom? That was why Elder Brother could overpower and beat her. Then surely Hok Yee could as well.

But men are never present at a birthing. No, not even a husband.

Yet Hok Yee was the one the Old Man in the Moon had bound me to with his invisible red thread. He was the one who would rescue my soul from the bloody lake if I should die. Why shouldn't I call on him to save me? Why shouldn't I call on him to save his son?

"Hok Yee," I sobbed with the last of my strength. "Hok Yee."

Outside the door I heard voices raised in argument.

Elder Sister snickered. "Hok Yee won't come. Ba won't let him."

I tried to call again. But Elder Sister clamped a rag over my face, muffling my already weak cry, making it impossible for me to draw breath.

Suddenly the door slammed open and Hok Yee rushed in. Elder Sister slipped the rag off my face, backed away. At that same instant Ma leaped from her chair.

I thought she meant to stop Hok Yee from coming any farther into the room. Instead she ran toward me. "There's a hand, yes, an arm poking out." Turning to Elder Sister, she ordered, "Bring some rice!"

As Elder Sister left, Hok Yee reached down, pulled me from the lake, and held me close.

Ma took the rice Elder Sister brought, placed a few grains in my son's tiny hand. Murmuring, "Here, little one, eat," she gently tucked his arm back in to my womb, forced her own hand in and turned him around.

And then she was ripping her grandson out into the world, I was tearing grotesquely, and she was moaning, "Oh, child, what evil wind has blown on you?"

The puny creature Ma dragged out of me was as yellow-black as a preserved egg and no bigger than Hok Yee's hand. His little face, sunk between his shoulders like a turtle, was wrinkled and sad, already tired of life. But I was determined he would live.

His skin was too tender to bear even a cloth worn soft by many washings, so I slit open my winter jacket and pulled out swathes of cotton batting, which I wrapped around him in a fleecy cocoon. He sucked too feebly and briefly for proper nourishment, so I squeezed milk from my breasts into a bowl, pulled feathers from the rooster's tail, and while he slept, fed him drop by drop through the quill.

By year's end, my son was as long but not as fat as a piglet. His ears were delicate and pink as peach petals, his fingers dainty as spring bamboo buds. Ba named him Wai Seuk: Preserve Brightness. Hok Yee made him a tiny bamboo chair that had a board in front that slid back and forth, serving as both a table to hold playthings and a lock to keep him safe.

Propped up in his little throne, Wai Seuk ignored the toys and studied me as I kindled a cooking fire, made a meal, or cleaned ashes out of the stove for fertilizer. When I sewed, his eyes, bright as lanterns, darted back and forth, following needle and thread. If I began to spin, his whole head turned. Then, as I drew a fine thread out from the roll of cotton and wound it on the spindle, the rhythmic humming would slowly lull him to sleep and he'd droop like a morning glory in late afternoon.

Elder Brother said Wai Seuk resembled a lump of rice. Elder Sister sneered at his wisps of hair, the way he gulped air, his inability to talk, even to call me Mama. But I only cared that he was alive.

And Elder sister and I were both with child.

We delivered the same night. My second son, Wai Yin, leaped out of my belly like a young tiger. When I put him to my breast, he suckled with a force that shook my very soul. Quickly I pierced his left ear with an earring so jealous Gods would see him as a worthless girl. If only I had known how to protect him from a jealous fox ghost.

Elder Sister's son, his umbilical cord tangled around his neck, was stillborn. Elder Brother, scraping his foot over the floor like a cock impatient for a fight, lashed out at his wife. She accused Ma of exchanging babies.

There was no doubt that the dead child was Elder Sister's. But Ma directed me to give her Wai Yin. "Ba has decided. He's already told Hok Yee."

My heart split open, I hugged my son close.

"You have Wai Seuk, and Heaven will grant you more sons. Elder Sister has none. She's crazed with grief. Just now, when Elder Brother kicked her, she flew at him and clawed his face raw."

I should have spoken out then, exposed Elder Sister as a fox ghost. I tried. But the words choked in my throat: Elder Sister might somehow know my secret, and if I told hers, she would surely reveal mine.

Ba would be furious at Old Auntie's deceit. Not only had he paid a good bride-price for damaged goods, but I could bring calamity on the family as well. He would almost certainly return me to my father, my father from whom my mother and I had hidden my ghost mark, my father who could refuse to take me back.

If I were banished, would my husband go with me? Yes, he had defied his father for me before, and though Elder Brother had made Hok Yee's devotion the brunt of village jokes, my husband continued to treat me tenderly. But if he knew about my ghost mark, would his deep feeling for me be the same? Would he turn his back on his family, the Lue clan?

And our sons. Would Ba allow us to take his grandsons?

I could lose both my sons, not one. My husband and my family, too. No. My possible losses were too great. I could not speak.

But Elder Sister would have killed Wai Seuk and me if Hok Yee had not destroyed her venom by coming when I called. She had since ignored the boy only because she was convinced Wai Seuk would not live to manhood. And she'd not meddled as I grew large with Wai Yin because her own belly bulged like a small hill. How could I give such a woman, a fox ghost, my son?

Ma called for Hok Yee. Kneeling beside me, he said, "If we try to keep Wai Yin, Elder Sister will surely do him harm. As his mother, she'll protect him."

I knew he spoke the truth. Still I clung to our son.

Tenderly but firmly Hok Yee pried him out of my arms. "We must be generous," he said. "Like my mother, who gave me to Ma."

I sought comfort in the orchard. I had transplanted my mother's orange seedlings the year before. Now I made cuttings, which I grafted onto rootstock, taking care not to bind them too tight or too loose, too high or too low.

Always before I had kept Wai Seuk strapped to my back while I worked so that I would lose no time in running if we were set upon by raiders. But for some time there had been talk the foreign ghosts had found gold in their land, gold that leaped out of the earth as soon as feet touched the ground. The same men and boys who had fled the human-pig traders were flocking to the ports begging for passage. There were no more attacks on villages, and Wai Seuk could safely play at my feet.

Hok Yee had made him a rattle by sucking a large duck's egg empty, then dropping in a few peas and closing the opening with a paste of cooked rice. When Wai Seuk took out the peas and planted them, I thought he had accidentally broken the egg and was aimlessly poking the peas into the dirt. After Hok Yee made a new rattle, however, I saw Wai Seuk break the egg deliberately and plant the peas one by one.

Yes, Wai Seuk was clever. He was the stem of my heart, gaining strength and health with each day. And Elder Sister was the kindest of mothers, doting on Wai Yin's every whim. But when she suckled him, my own breasts leaked milk. In truth, watching her raise my second son, I felt like a hungry cur at a dog teaser, one of those wooden cages that people sometimes put over chicken feed: the bars are spaced wide enough for chickens to eat but dogs can only look.

I said nothing to Hok Yee. I did not want him to know I had such a small heart. Yet he understood. "I'll ask Ba to set us up in our own house," he said.

Lung On village had six rows of houses separated by five alleys. Ba's house, the middle one in the alley closest to the well, was like all the others. It had a central room where we ate and Third and Fourth Brothers laid out their bedrolls at night, a sleeping room on either side. Ba had partitioned one of these for Elder Brother and Sister, Hok Yee and me, keeping the other for Ma and himself. During the preparations for Third Brother's wedding, Ba leased a second house in the last alley near the temple and river for Hok Yee, Wai Seuk, and me, giving our old sleeping room to Third Brother and his bride.

Since Elder Sister had robbed me of Wai Yin, Elder Brother had stopped beating her. Instead, the two worked together at stirring up trouble. If I turned my back for a moment while cooking, Elder Sister would purposely throw in extra salt, even a handful of sweepings. When I spread out rice in the courtyard to dry, she would slip in a chicken to scatter the grain. Then she would place the blame on me by saying, "Sum Jui, you should be more careful," in honeyed tones.

Of course, Ba's temper would flare, and he would scold me soundly. Then Elder Brother would say, "Ba, your health is too important for you to get so angry. Calm yourself." And Elder Sister would quickly brew a special tea to soothe Ba's throat.

I expected Elder Sister and Brother to object to Ba giving Hok Yee and me our own house, to demand one for themselves. Instead they praised Ba loudly for his generosity and helped us move our few belongings.

Hok Yee was not fooled. "They want to stay where they can best influence Ba."

Too young to be wise, we did not understand the hardships this would cause us.

Though we now lived separately, the family continued to eat and work as one. Hok Yee labored in the fields with his father and brothers; I cultivated the orchard. For a short while, Ma sent Third Brother's bride to assist me. She was cheerful and willing, but Wai Seuk, not yet four, had more understanding of the soil, more of a feel for the trees in our care. In truth, Third Sister made so many foolish mistakes I was relieved when the birth of twins, a son and a daughter, kept her home.

As soon as the trees reached a height of three feet, I uprooted them carefully and cut the taproots. Wai Seuk helped with the replanting. While I held each tree straight, he inserted a piece of tile beneath the stub of root. Then together we plunged our hands into the piles of cool mud Hok Yee had hauled from the river, packing the richness solidly all around.

The trees grew vigorously, and when they came into bearing during my seventh year in Lung On, they gave an abundant harvest of large, sweet fruit. Hok Yee and his younger brothers brought in the crop. Ba and Elder Brother took the oranges to market, fetching an excellent price.

Before we could take any pleasure in our success, however, the landlord sent word that he would not renew the lease for the land where I had planted the grove. Ba suggested the landlord take back another piece of land. When he refused, Ba offered a generous share of the next crop of oranges above the rent. Again the landlord refused: of course, he wanted it all.

Ba exploded with anger. But what could we do except bow our heads and keep on working? As the saying goes, water flows down, mankind oppresses the weak.

The landlords in our district were all the same, drawn to money like flies to blood. If I started a new orchard on another piece of rented land, we would only be robbed again. But we didn't have sufficient silver to buy a suitable piece of land, and Fisherman Low, the moneylender, was a bloodsucker, too.

Hnnnh, people called him a fisherman because few borrowers could shake him loose any more than fish, once hooked, can escape: he charged enormous interest, kept careful records of every copper cash, and accepted no excuse for failure to pay. That was why Ba had rented land for our orchard instead of buying. He didn't want to get caught.

"Let me go to Gold Mountain," Fourth Brother begged. "A man has only to step off the boat to stuff his bags full of gold." Elder Brother and Sister, excited by the promise of riches, encouraged the boy and added their own pleas.

Ba dismissed their entreaties. To buy Fourth Brother's passage, he would have to borrow from Fisherman Low. And though people said the foreign ghosts who lived in Gold Mountain were different from the human-pig traders, we knew they could also be cruel. Sing Gei in the next village had come back from his sojourn in Gold Mountain on two stumps, his toes and much of his feet eaten away by lye water foreign ghosts had poured over them. Helpless as a woman with bound feet, he could not walk even a short distance without support.

Then Scarface came home. Scarface had been among the first in the district to chase the foreign-ghost gold, buying his passage by selling himself into temporary bondage. His family was so poor his mother couldn't even get together enough cloth to make him a proper pair of trousers, and he had left home wearing the short pants of a boy though he was a man past twenty.

He returned like gentry: dragging a long silk gown, seated in a sedan chair carried aloft by four bearers. And he invited every single person in the entire district to a nine-course banquet! It took a dozen hired men one full day just to set up the tables: the men's section covered nine fields, the one for women and children another twelve.

While his guests feasted on crispy roasted pig, smooth bird's nest soup, and other rare delicacies, Scarface strutted from table to table. He reminded us of his poverty, how he had been so weak from hunger as a young man that he couldn't hold up a bucket of night soil to fertilize the fields without help, how he couldn't afford a wife. Then he tossed handfuls of copper cash onto the damp earth, laughing as even the toothless graybeards among the men fell to their knees and scrabbled for the coins in the dirt, among the broken roots of harvested crops. Fingering the puckered flesh that pulled the left side of his face crooked, he brazenly stroked the smooth cheeks of young girls. Leering, he ordered the matchmakers to bring him their very best.

The house he built of fine blue brick roofed with glazed red tiles was the largest and grandest in the district. And its fortified towers, one at each corner, served as reminders to all of the wealth within. Dazzled by Scarface's success, families who had no sons or husbands in Gold Mountain pressed them to go. Elder Brother and Sister finally succeeded in persuading Ba to risk all.

"Our lives are comfortable," Ma pleaded. "We eat twice a day. We manage to have new clothes at New Year, to make offerings to the Gods and our ancestors. Let's be content with what we have."

But Ba's desire to build for his sons and grandsons ran deep, and though his back was still straight, his chest high, he was old in years. Fearful he might not have another opportunity, he borrowed from Fisherman Low and bought passage for Fourth Brother.

At the farewell feast, Ma picked the choicest, tastiest pieces from each dish for Fourth Brother. Her voice hoarse with unshed tears, she cautioned, "Protect yourself against cold winds. Eat well. Look after yourself in all ways, and return quickly."

"Avoid games of chance," Ba advised. "And may Heaven shower you with blessings."

Elder Sister pinched Fourth Brother's ear fondly. "Hurry and send those gold-eagle coins home."

The following Dragon Boat Festival, I gave birth to my third son. Ba named him Gim Gong, Double Brilliance. To me, after five barren years, Gim Gong did in truth shine bright; Ba meant the name to signify his hopes for Fourth Brother in Gold Mountain.

There was nothing to fuel these hopes. Fourth Brother had discovered that gold did not leap out of the ground, and the foreign ghosts had passed laws making it difficult for our people to dig for it. He was drifting from town to town, taking work wherever he could find it. His letters home were empty of money, and our family's debts began to mount.

Heaven had been kind, sending no drought to prevent sowing at the right time, no floods to wash away the crops, no pests to attack the trees in our orchard, and season after season we were bringing in good harvests. But the interest Fisherman Low extorted was so unreasonable that after paying him, we could never quite endure until the next harvest without borrowing a little more.

Each time Ba went back to the moneylender, the hook he had swallowed with the first loan pierced deeper and pricked more sharply. Yet he stubbornly insisted we had no cause for concern. He even paid tuition for Wai Yin at the village school because Elder Brother and Sister had convinced him the boy would one day bring rank and honor to our family as a scholar just as Fourth Brother would bring wealth.

Of course I was glad of this opportunity for Wai Yin. Wasn't he my son? But what about my other two sons and Third Brother's children? And Elder Brother's daughter, born a few months after my Gim Gong?

Hnnnh, for years I had fretted that Elder Brother and Sister would make Wai Yin's life a misery if she birthed a child of their own. Though my husband kept his feelings over his adoption almost as well wrapped as I hid my ghost mark, Third Brother had told me how Elder Brother would beat Hok Yee, shouting, "I'm the real son. You're adopted. It's right that I scold and hit you." And I saw for myself how Hok Yee always gave in to his brothers, how they sometimes balked at orders from their parents while he never could.

Since Elder Brother and Sister's child was a daughter, however, they continued to dote on Wai Yin. Ba and Ma both favored the boy as well. They had never expected Wai Seuk to live, so they'd held back their affection. Then we'd taken Wai Seuk to live with us.

Wai Yin was the first grandson Ma had held in her arms and sung to sleep. He was the first son of Ba's first son. "Ba, look at how Wai Yin's forehead bulges like yours," Elder Sister would flatter. "He'll be smart like his grandfather," Elder Brother would add. Is it any wonder Wai Yin was first in Ba's heart though the boy did no work?

By morning rice, Wai Seuk would have already weeded or hoed a field. Third Brother's son would have taken the water buffalo out for grazing. Wai Yin, just getting up, would come to table with sleep in his eyes. Yet he was the one Ba brought candy for from market, the one still eating meat while everyone else was eating boiled sweet potatoes and watery rice gruel, famine food.

Hok Yee and I could clearly see that one stroke of bad luck—a runaway water buffalo trampling our seedlings, thieves stealing ripening shoots, too much rain or not enough—and we might not be eating at all. Nevertheless, Ba continued to dismiss our misgivings, waving them off as if they were pesky flies. "Endure, and these hardships will fade. Fourth Brother will bring us ease and plenty."

We could not quiet our doubts as easily. Yes, some men in Gold Mountain were sending money home, and a few had come back rich, though none as wealthy as Scarface. More remained absent; some had been away as long as ten years. Worse, there were those like Old Lue's son who had come back as bones in an urn, others who had died but whose bodies had not been recovered. These dead, without anyone to put them at rest, honor their spirits, or see to their needs in the next world, were now hungry ghosts. Lonely and bitter, they were wandering the earth seeking vengeance for their misery. What if they came back to Lung On?

Of course Bo Gung and Bo Poh, the friendly spirits who lived in the old banyan tree by the temple, would try to keep them away. And the footpaths that divided the fields wound in and out to confuse any evil spirits that might try to cross them. Moreover, every family in the village made donations to the priest to pacify hungry ghosts at the Festival of Dead Souls each spring. In the past, Ba's contributions had been generous. For the last two years, however, he had given almost nothing. Would the ghosts punish us for our neglect? Would they harm Fourth Brother, prevent his success?

And what of the foreign ghosts? Hok Yee had seen one during a trip to market in Sun Ning, the district capital. The ghost had been standing on a corner calling out, "Good news! Come listen to the good news," and Hok Yee, curious, had joined the crowd gathered around him.

He was big, so tall that Hok Yee, though near the back, clearly saw the ghost's face, red as Guan Gung, the God of War, his shaggy hair and beard the color of fire, his eyes green as a cuckold's hat. Hok Yee was glad he was no closer. The men pressed nearest the ghost complained that he stank of tainted flesh.

"*Ai yah!* Everything about him was repulsive," Hok Yee told me. "Especially his news. I thought at first I'd misunderstood because he spoke our language so peculiarly. Surely he could not be shouting, 'God, the Great Lord of Heaven, killed His son to wash you in His blood.' Then he began passing out pictures of this murdered son. Look!"

The white chest under the son's mournful, hairy face was carved open, and a coil of thorns pierced the heart, which was dripping blood. What chance could Fourth Brother have among such ghosts? Ghosts who worshiped a God that killed his own son and then wanted to wash our people in his blood. Ghosts who called this good news.

Hnnnh, what chance did we have with Fisherman Low? When our near neighbors had failed to pay Fisherman Low the interest they owed, the moneylender had seized their fields, including the crop they were about to harvest. Then he forced them to indenture their oldest boy, Little Turnip, to him to cover the debt. After he worked Little Turnip so hard and fed him so poorly that the child fell ill, he demanded the family sell one of their daughters to pay for a laborer to take Little Turnip's place. In the end, both their girls were sold, the boy died, and Fisherman Low drove the rest of the family out barehanded to live in the open.

That could happen to us. Thinking to keep the family from Fisherman Low's hook, I had sold my wedding bracelets and hairpins to help Ba buy a strip of land for a new orchard before Scarface bewitched him. Since then, Ba had signed over as security Ma's and Elder and Third Sisters' wedding jewelry, the house, land, farm tools, water buffalo, and pigs, even the chickens. There was nothing left for Ba to borrow against. If he faltered on a single payment, Fisherman Low would pull in his catch.

We could not depend on Fourth Brother to rescue us; we had to save ourselves. Two lutes tuned in harmony, Hok Yee and I formed a plan: we would work for landlords with large holdings during the day and cultivate our own land at night.

Ba and Ma were of course too old to hire out, Elder Brother too proud. His fox-ghost wife liked to pretend her tiny feet were the golden lotus of a wealthy lady; we had never seen her in the fields, not even when we needed extra hands at harvest. Wai Yin, grown tall and strong, was a scholar, not a laborer. Wai Seuk was too thin and weak, Third Brother's son too young. Third Brother and his wife would both be willing, but Third Sister was so clumsy no one would buy her labor.

With only Third Brother, Hok Yee, and myself hiring out, our wages could not possibly pay off our debt. Nevertheless, our daily meals would be provided, and we would be more certain of covering the interest due Fisherman Low.

For the plan to work, however, Ba had to agree. So Hok Yee presented it after evening rice, when Ba was at his most mellow.

"There's no need for it," Ba said testily. "Fourth Brother will send money soon."

"We have to pay Fisherman Low his interest now," Ma reminded.

Ba shot up, knocking over his stool. "There's no need, I tell you."

As usual, when Ba stamped his foot, the noise he made was like thunder. Yet Ma did not retreat, as was her habit. "We can lose everything," she said quietly.

Kicking aside his stool, Ba paced the length of the room from altar to front door, all the time insisting, like a monk repeating his mantra, that hiring out was not necessary, that Fourth Brother would send money soon. But for once Elder Brother and Sister were silent, and Ma stood her ground, patiently, firmly wearing him down.

At last Ba gave his reluctant approval. I felt Hok Yee, seated across from me, nudge my feet with his: now the family, our sons, had a chance against Fisherman Low.

Ba wheeled around abruptly to face me. "You're not to work for anyone else. I'll not have a landlord benefiting from your skills."

Taken aback, I stammered, "We need all three wages if we're going to meet the payments to Fisherman Low."

"What about Wai Seuk?" Elder Sister suggested, her voice pulsing with spite.

My bowels twisted. "He can't. You know landlords work their laborers hard, and you've said yourself that he's scrawny and feeble."

Swiftly Elder Sister pasted a false smile on her face. "He has spirit. More strength than we credit."

"He's shorter than Wai Yin," Hok Yee argued, "and sickly."

"Sickly only as a baby," Elder Brother said. "Now he can handle a hoe as well as a man. Isn't that so, Ba?"

"Yes, he's a good worker. Any landlord would be glad to hire him." Ba took a glowing incense stick from the altar and lit his pipe, drawing deeply. "That's it. Let Wai Seuk take his mother's place."

Red-faced, Hok Yee countered boldly, "Is the family to be saved at the cost of my son?"

Ba slammed down his pipe, scattering hot ash, unsmoked tobacco. "Do I have to remind you that a man's son belongs to his father? Wai Seuk is mine!" he roared.

For a moment no one dared speak. In truth, my chest felt so tight I could scarcely breathe. Then Elder Sister picked up Ba's pipe, packed the bowl with tobacco, and handed him a taper to light it.

"Fourth Brother will send money soon," she soothed as Ba

puffed out a steady stream of acrid black smoke. "Meanwhile, it is only fair that we sacrifice equally. So Elder Brother and I will give up our daughter."

Elder Brother, clearly caught by surprise, grunted deep in his throat.

"She's pretty enough to fetch a little something for the family," Elder Sister continued, "and we can get a newborn for nothing. I'll nurse the babe and bring her up as a bride for Wai Yin."

Elder Brother's face brightened with understanding. The sale would not bring much, but the savings in a bride-price when Wai Yin was ready to marry would be great. And if the family did not recover financially, Wai Yin would still be assured of a wife. He smiled. "An excellent plan."

Elder Sister drew her eyebrows together in the slightest of frowns. Immediately, Elder Brother pulled his face long, pretending grief. She turned to Third Brother. "Won't you make the same sacrifice?"

Third Brother and his wife paled. Unlike Elder Brother and Sister, they cherished their daughter. But they could not match the fox ghost's cunning any better than Hok Yee and I could. Before a new moon rose, Ba had sold our family's daughters and found two babies suitable for raising as daughters-in-law; he'd hired out Hok Yee, Third Brother, and Wai Seuk as laborers.

Ba could no longer stoop to plant or wield a hoe or scythe. Third Brother's son, at six, could do even less. Elder Brother broke sweat only when giving me orders.

Alone, I cut sugarcane into short lengths, steeped the joints in water until young shoots showed, then planted the cuttings in long rows.

Alone, I set out slips of sweet potato vines.

Alone, I sowed rice, flooded the paddies in preparation for transplanting, regulating the levels as the grain ripened.

No, not alone. Not entirely.

Fertilizing, watering, weeding, or bringing in the crops, I took my youngest with me just as I had taken Wai Seuk to the orchard when he was a baby. Unlike his brother, though, Gim Gong did not sit quietly. The moment I looked away, he darted off, scrambling over ridged furrows and vegetable beds or up terraced hillsides of tea bushes.

One day, leaning over the edge of a paddy to play in the water, he tumbled in. The water in the paddy was not deep, but he must have fallen headfirst and sunk into the soft mud, for he did not call out. And he was unable to pull himself out. Nor did I hear him fall. In truth, if not for the sudden flight of the paddy birds, the frightened quacking and splashing of ducks, I would not have turned in time to save him from drowning. As it was, the shock brought on a high fever that burned his face red as a pig's liver, his skin so hot I could scarcely touch him.

Just before the fourth watch, he fell into a stupor in which he cried in tiny choked whimpers. I knew then that the same hungry ghost which had tried to drown him was trying to steal his soul. By morning rice, Gim Gong was almost gone.

Quickly Hok Yee pawned our winter jackets for spirit money so we could make offerings to the Gods and our ancestors. Then we went out into the courtyard. Holding Gim Gong's jacket up to the four winds, I called, "Gim Gong, come home."

"I'm coming," Hok Yee answered for him.

"Gim Gong, don't be afraid," I assured him. "Your father and mother are here."

"I'm not afraid. I'm coming home. I'm coming now."

Hurrying back inside, I wrapped the jacket around Gim Gong and cradled him. When my arms grew stiff and sore, Hok Yee took him. Then, when he tired, I held the boy again.

Finally, late that afternoon, our son's soul completed the journey back, and he drifted into real sleep.

"Let me mind Gim Gong for you," Ma offered.

"We'll watch him carefully," Third Sister promised.

"Yes." Elder Sister smiled.

But I noticed how Third Sister's son avoided his aunt, the way the two child-brides whimpered when she came near though she was the one who suckled them. Except for Wai Yin, no one escaped Elder Sister's ill will. I could not risk leaving Gim Gong where she could harm him. Yet how could I keep him from injury in the fields?

I tried tying him to my leg with a soft cloth. But he fought against the binding, and in his struggles I felt my own unhappiness when my mother tied me to my bed. Then I tried strapping him to my back in a *meh dai*. Almost out of split-bottomed pants, he had grown too big, too heavy to be carried like a baby. The square of cloth sagged under his weight; the bands dug into my shoulder, the tender flesh above and below my breasts. When the weather turned hot, I developed a rash that soon rubbed painfully raw. But he did not cry. And he was safe from the fox ghost.

Not so my firstborn.

Hnnnh, what landlord doesn't try to squeeze every ounce of strength, every drop of sweat, from his laborers? And Wai Seuk was an undersized boy of ten summers. Full buckets of water were too heavy for him, so he had to carry half-buckets, making twice as many trips from well to house, river to fields. To make up for time lost, he had to run where others would walk. By nightfall, his legs trembled from weariness; he could hardly stand. Nor could his father or Third Brother help him; each worked for a different landlord.

A less filial son would have given in to his weakness. But Wai Seuk never complained or asked his grandfather to release him. Instead, he pushed himself to work harder. Yet he could not please his master, and he would come home with his ears swollen red, blue-black bruises on his arms and legs.

Night after night I stuck medicinal plasters on his bruises and massaged his legs with liniments. I scoured the hills for herbs, brewing soups to build his strength. Nevertheless, he woke exhausted. What little flesh he had fell from his bones. Only Heaven had the power to save him from Little Turnip's fate, and I begged the Goddess Gwoon Yum for mercy.

Despite all our efforts, Ba barely managed to meet the payments on the interest we owed. There was never a spare copper to put toward the debt itself. Nor would that have changed when the second orchard I'd planted came into bearing. Yes, the trees yielded generously. But I'd had so few pieces of wedding jewelry and Ba so little money saved that the land he'd bought was a mere patch, the profit too small to rescue us from Fisherman Low.

How, then, did we escape? The foreign ghosts in Gold Mountain saved us. Yes. The foreign ghosts! They decided to build a long iron road across river and streams, through mountains and forests. Bridges had to be raised, tunnels dug, trees felled, and the ghosts sent for our people to do the work. Fourth Brother, already there, was among the first hired. He did not forget us.

The first money he sent allowed us to make thanksgiving offerings to the Gods and our ancestors, to bring Wai Seuk home and begin rebuilding his broken body. The next year we were able to hold back a pig from market for the family's eating. Then, after Fourth Brother joined together with some other men to open a store, Hok Yee and Third Brother stopped hiring out. Ba paid off Fisherman Low and even bought a few *mau* of land.

"You see," Ba said. "I told you Fourth Brother would bring us ease and plenty."

Plenty, yes. Ease, not exactly. Fourth Brother never became another Scarface, and we continued to cultivate our own fields and orchards. I did not regret that. In truth, I was glad. Even now that I am old, I cannot be idle. At that time, I was young and strong.

During the years I'd toiled in our fields, however, I'd found Elder Brother a harsher taskmaster than the worst landlord. So, to shield Wai Seuk and Gim Gong from him, I convinced Ba I needed both boys to help me plant more trees, to improve the ones we had.

I showed them how to make cuttings from good straight branches as thick as a grown man's thumb, then insert them into taros and plant the two together; how to take a brush and transfer pollen from the flowers of one tree to those of a slightly different variety. Wai Seuk always followed my directions precisely and without question. Gim Gong, having never felt the bruising hand of a harsh master, often went his own way.

Hnnnh, that boy had a mind of his own in all things. Everyone in the village threw stones at thieving dogs; Gim Gong petted them. Wai Seuk and his friends set bird traps by propping up a big threshing basket with a short stick and scattering husks of grain underneath; Gim Gong lay in wait to foil their plans. His behavior won him no friends, but he did not seem to care. Instead of playing with other children, he played with flowers.

While he was still strapped to my back, I had kept him happy for entire mornings by giving him a flower, a few leaves to hold in his hand. Turning the blossom or leaves in his tiny fingers, he had looked at them seriously, then showered me with questions. What was that stickiness oozing out of a stem? Why were the petals pointed or curved, the fragrance of one flower different from another, one leaf thick and smooth, another fuzzy?

No sooner was he off my back than he tried planting different seeds, using mud from old swallows' nests as soil. He slipped seeds under laying hens to hasten their sprouting. He planted seedlings in broken bits of pots to bind the roots and keep the grown trees small.

Only those too old to farm had time to fool with flowers for their own sake, and Gim Gong begged cuttings from them. Where they planted flowers and vegetables separately, however, Gim Gong mixed New Year lilies with cabbage sprouts in a single pot, covering the dirt with bits of charred wood so the blackness of the coal made the white of the cabbage and the jade green stems of the lilies stand out. He turned our gray brick courtyard wall into a bright screen of flowering vines and hyacinth beans. He arranged his plantings so that before one flower faded another was in blossom, and each season in our courtyard seemed like spring.

Like an overfond parent, he pampered his flowers, daily sweeping away the fallen petals and leaves, watering and talking to each plant in turn, sealing any broken stems with mud. If a storm sprang up, he brought in the plants that were in pots, crowding them into the kitchen. If the sun blazed strong, he sprinkled the flowers with water from a whisk. And when I killed a chrysanthemum by accidentally splashing it with boiling water, he wept as pitifully as I had when Elder Sister claimed his brother.

The wealth of scents from Gim Gong's mass of colorful blossoms was thick and sweet as honey, smothering the foul odors from our privy, and on warm evenings it became our habit to linger in the courtyard where a cool breeze blew from the river. Cicadas sang in the fields. Occasionally a duck or waterbird hiding in the tall river weeds cackled, a dog barked. Neighbors called out to one another; there was the shrill laughter of children. The dried grasses under the family's water buffalo rustled as it shifted. The chickens, penned in for the night, scratched at their feed. Sharing a companionable silence, Hok Yee smoked his pipe while I mended, Gim Gong fussed with his flowers, Wai Seuk fixed the handle of a hoe or honed the edge of a scythe.

Our firstborn was as clever with tools as our youngest was with flowers. While we still owed money to Fisherman Low, our plow's side-peg handle, the bit that changes the depth of the furrows, had broken during spring plowing, and neither Ba nor Elder Brother could fashion a peg to replace it. Hok Yee and Third Brother might have, but they were so overworked by their landlords that they had no chance to try.

When Wai Seuk said he could fix it, Elder Brother sneered. And if Ba had not been desperate for us to complete the plowing, he would have scoffed as well. But he reluctantly agreed to let Wai Seuk whittle a new side-peg, and it fit perfectly. Since then, Ba had entrusted Wai Seuk with the upkeep and repair of all our tools, and it seemed to me the boy's hands were never still.

In truth, he could no longer rightly be called a boy. Short and narrow-chested but sturdy, Wai Seuk was, at fifteen, already older than I had been when I'd given him birth, only a year younger than Hok Yee when I'd come to Lung On as his bride.

After so many years, my husband's face, weathered by sun and wind, had lost its youthful smoothness. So had my own. Where he'd become leaner, however, I had thickened. Where he smelled of smoke and tobacco, I smelled of the blossoms he continued to pick and place in my bun.

The hangings around our bed had faded from many washings, the colors of the embroideries run together so that the pairs of mandarin ducks had become one. And it seemed to me the pleasure Hok Yee and I found in each other ran so deep that we, too, were one.

I had failed to keep Wai Yin from Elder Brother and Sister's grasp, to protect Wai Seuk from their spite. Now Gim Gong became their victim. Elder Brother made him into the village laughingstock for his fondness of flowers, his kindness to animals. Elder Sister stirred up trouble for him in school.

Having Wai Seuk and Gim Gong join their brother in school had been our heart's hope, and Hok Yee finally persuaded Ba to pay Lo See to teach them. The opportunity came too late for Wai Seuk. He chafed at being indoors, at being treated like a child when he was almost a man, and he remained only long enough to learn a few characters, to write his name. When Gim Gong recited, however, he rolled the phrases around in his mouth like other children roll sweets, and he soon became the teacher's favorite.

I knew Lo See's affection for Gim Gong must have stuck in Elder Sister's belly like a dagger. But she cloaked her true feelings in kindness, cautioning Elder Brother to stop making fun of "our little sage," pretending an interest in the boy's flowers.

Visiting our courtyard, she listened attentively as Gim Gong explained why he planted duckweed and smartweed together, how he forced a bloom, kept a tree small.

"You know so much about flowers," Elder Sister flattered.

Pleased, he confided proudly, "Mama says the garden is so pretty the Gods walk down from the sky to see it."

"How do they do that?"

Shading his eyes against the glare of the setting sun with one hand, he pointed up at the roof with his other and told his aunt what she already knew. "See how the corners of the roofs curve? They make a highway for the Gods."

"Have you ever seen them here?"

He shook his head.

"What about the Earth God and his wife who live in the pavilion near the paddies? Have you seen them walk?"

"No," he said, his voice suddenly small and unsure.

"We make our offerings right in front of them," I pointed out. "Why would they walk?"

"We're just foolish women," Elder Sister simpered. "Gim Gong, why don't you ask your teacher to explain?"

"Lo See doesn't allow questions, not even about the lessons."

Hok Yee, coming out to empty his pipe of ashes, said, "Of course! The Five Classics have been the foundation for all behavior, all thought for centuries. They must be memorized without question."

With Hok Yee in the courtyard, too, Elder Sister said no more, and I was fooled by her silence. Afterward, when it was too late to repair the damage, I discovered that she had assured Gim Gong privately, "Lo See does like questions. But he's an old man and hard of hearing. You must speak up. Then, if he still doesn't answer, you must shout louder."

Gim Gong had no shortage of questions, and he posed them noisily, relentlessly, until Lo See denounced him as a troublemaker and banished him from the school.

"The shame of it!" Ba scolded.

"Never mind," Elder Sister soothed gleefully. "Wai Yin will restore the family honor."

Gim Gong, wounded and confused, wondered why his aunt had tricked him, why her honeyed tones had vanished, why he was again the butt of Elder Brother's jokes. How could I explain that his aunt was a fox ghost? That I, too, was responsible for his suffering because of my ghost mark?

Day and night my mind spun, winding and turning like a reel of thread, trying to unravel a way to deliver my youngest from harm. Unexpectedly, Fourth Brother brought the answer when he came

home to marry and rest for a few moons before returning to his
store in Gold Mountain.

From the first Gim Gong attached himself to his uncle like a disciple to a master, gulping down Fourth Brother's tales whole.

"In the Big City where I have my store," Fourth Brother said,
"every day is like a holiday, every night a festival." He described
lofty buildings; houses with kitchens in which you could turn on
water at will; stoves that made the inside of houses feel like spring
though bitter winds blew outside. He told of the iron road he had
helped build through forests of pines so tall they pierced the clouds;
the fire-eating wagons that thundered up mountains without men
or beasts to pull them.

His eyes round and big as ladles, Gim Gong pleaded, "Take me
back with you, Uncle."

Fourth Brother tweaked the boy's queue. "I do need a helper in
my store, and it would be good to have a family member I can
trust. But you still smell of mother's milk."

Springing up from the ground where he'd been squatting, Gim
Gong pulled himself up to his full height and puffed out his chest.
"I'm ten."

Fourth Brother laughed. "Aren't you afraid of foreign ghosts?
Those savages who spear their meat with sharp pieces of metal and
behave so wantonly that men and women sit together in public and
touch lips like fish drinking water?"

"I want to see them. I want to see everything."

"What about your garden?"

For a long moment, Gim Gong hesitated. Then he said, "Mama
will take care of it until I come back."

My mother had taught me to graft fruit trees by taking a very fine
saw and cutting off the rootstock one foot above the ground, then
splitting the bark and inserting a shaped slip into the stock, cautioning, "If you slice too deep or fail to match slip and stock, you'll kill
the plant." I could see that a sojourn in Gold Mountain was just as
risky. Yes, it could better the lives of men and their families. But it
could also kill. How could it be otherwise when the foreign ghosts
were so different from us?

To have Gim Gong risk the dangers of Gold Mountain was therefore not a path either my husband or I would have chosen freely for our son. As much as we feared what might happen to our son among foreign ghosts, however, we feared what Elder Sister might do to him more. Besides, Fourth Brother had proved himself as skilled in dealing with the dangers of Gold Mountain as that long-ago scholar who had outsmarted ghosts.

That young man, bow and arrows at his waist, had been riding through a forest in the north when he noticed a dozen or so men with loosened hair gambling in a clearing. Since it was night and there was no moon or fire giving him light to see more than a few feet, he knew the men must be ghosts. Boldly he rode closer, drew his bow, and shot at them.

They vanished instantly, leaving behind piles of Hell money, a large jade bowl for rolling dice. The money crumbled when the scholar touched it. But the bowl was from this world, and it made him a rich man. Likewise, Fourth Brother's boldness had also won him wealth, wealth that gave him security against Elder Sister.

How disappointed she had been with the foreign goods Fourth Brother brought home: a box that made music when you opened the lid, a machine that marked foreign-ghost time with little tick-tock sounds and had a bell to jangle people awake in the morning. What did we need with that bell when we had roosters? What did we need with foreign-ghost time? Or that useless box? Why hadn't he brought more gold eagles instead? But Elder Sister swallowed her dissatisfaction: insult, annoy, or anger Fourth Brother and there would be no more gold-eagle coins. Just so, when Gim Gong returned, Elder Sister would not dare offend him.

On the morning of Fourth Brother and Gim Gong's departure, Hok Yee told our son, "You're still a child. There are vices of which you are not even aware. Obey your uncle in all things, and discipline yourself with virtues. Bring no dishonor on the Lue clan."

Unable to speak, I silently hung around Gim Gong's neck a little red bag of ashes from incense burned before Lui Kung, the Thunder God, to keep him safe. The boy, eager to be gone, could not stand still.

Once on the path out of the village, he did not look back. I gazed after him until he disappeared in the clouds at the edge of the sky.

Hok Yee and I had hoped that in giving Wai Yin to Elder Brother and Sister, we would keep him from harm. But man's wishes are not equal to those of Heaven.

We could not blame Elder Brother or Sister altogether for Wai Yin's temper. That he might well have got from his grandfather. Where Ba had been a tireless worker, however, going back into the fields after evening rice to trim a windbreak, build up the banks between our paddies, or repair a fence, Wai Yin was lazy like Elder Brother and Sister. He had their arrogance and cruelty as well. Wrinkling his nose, he would strut back and forth like a general. Or he'd chase the chickens or Bik Wun, his little child-bride.

Between Wai Yin and Elder Sister, that poor girl didn't know a moment's peace. If she wasn't feeding the pigs and chickens, she was carrying water from the river, gathering brush from the hills, washing clothes, or sewing. And if Elder Sister caught her resting for even a moment, she would call, "Bring Ba some tea," or "Pour me a basin of water," or "Grind some ink for Wai Yin."

Ma, slipping Bik Wun rock sugar to take away some of the bitterness, would say, "You must be paying for wrongs in a previous life." Perhaps she was. But Wai Yin was surely paying for my wrong, my ghost mark: petted and spoiled, he grew ungovernable as a calf without a peg in his nose, and Elder Sister took to calming him with opium.

Ba might have stopped her. Only Elder Sister was careful, lighting the pipe in her room, burning incense to smother its sickly sweet odor, so he did not notice. Neither would Ma let us tell him. He was often ill, and she did not want to risk damaging his health further with an explosion of temper.

When I fretted, Ma assured me, "Elder Sister says she just gives Wai Yin a puff or two. She'll stop as soon as he gets old enough to quiet with reason."

Back in our own house, I wept. "Wai Yin is not a child. He can be, he must be, properly taught *now.*"

"Since Wai Yin can grasp learning, there will come a time when he can reason," Hok Yee comforted. "We must be patient."

By the time Gim Gong left for Gold Mountain, Wai Yin had studied with Lo See for almost ten years, longer than any other boy in the village, and he boasted the pale skin and soft hands of a scholar. He read Fourth Brother's letters from Gold Mountain to the family; he wrote Ba's replies. And when Gim Gong's first letter arrived, Elder Sister set it in front of Wai Yin, crowing, "What money we save by having our own letter reader!"

Wai Yin picked up the letter. Preening like a rooster, he pushed back his sleeves, cleared his throat, and began to read. " 'Writing respectfully, beloved grandfather, kneeling at your feet, I beg you not to worry about me. When you read this, you will know I am well. I wish you and every member of our family health, strength, peace, and safety. Enclosed is three dollars. Please check the sum. It is at your disposal.

" 'On the ship . . .' " Frowning, Wai Yin stopped. His eyes narrowed. He wiped his face with his sleeve.

Suddenly, he crumpled the letter and hurled it across the room, shouting, "I can't read the rest! Gim Gong's made too many mistakes!"

Elder Sister shook her head. "What a waste school fees were for Gim Gong."

Ba bit down on each of the three gold eagles Gim Gong had sent. When they proved true, he smiled broadly. "Not wasted. Not entirely. The boy is filial."

As we left, Wai Seuk edged over to the corner where the letter had fallen, picked it up. Then, while we were walking back to our house, he smoothed out the paper, handed it to Hok Yee. "Maybe Lo See can read it."

The teacher read the letter easily. "The problem is Wai Yin," Lo See sighed. "That boy has never applied himself and is barely able to read."

"But he's always read Fourth Brother's letters," Hok Yee said. "And he read part of Gim Gong's."

"He can manage stock phrases, the kind Fourth Brother's letter writer uses, the kind Gim Gong started with. But when Gim Gong was describing his journey and Fourth Brother's store in First City, he wrote more freely, using characters Wai Yin doesn't know."

Lo See sighed again, more deeply. "I've told your elder brother over and over that his son is worthless, that I feel like a thief taking your father's money. But he pleads so strongly for Wai Yin that I always end up agreeing to keep him as a student."

We did not tell Ba or Ma. They were both old, and we wanted to spare them the disappointment. I could not, would not, hold my tongue any longer with Elder Sister, however.

"Wai Yin is young. Stop the opium, discipline him, and he may yet succeed."

Elder Sister's eyes flicked fire. "How dare you blame my son for the faults of yours? Have you forgotten what happened at the rounding of Wai Yin's first year? When Ma placed pen, cash, abacus, and rice stalks on the tray for him to choose, he reached for the pen. To be a scholar is his destiny." She twisted her lips into a satisfied smile. "Gim Gong is the one you should be worrying about."

Could Elder Sister be right? Not about Wai Yin. I had seen her tip the tray so the pen had all but rolled into his hand. But when Ma had set the tray in front of Wai Seuk, he had ignored it, preferring to play with an old lock he'd found under our bed instead, and he was certainly clever with tools. Gim Gong, trying to grab at everything, had upset the tray, losing all. Was that why he'd been blind to his aunt's guile and his teacher's anger and lost his chance at study? Because that was his fate?

Through Lo See, we reminded Gim Gong to obey his uncle in all things, to avoid foreign ghosts, to work hard.

Still Gim Gong began to grumble through his letters: *Fourth Un-*

cle promised me a feast of wonders but I have seen as little of Gold Mountain as a blind man.

Fourth Brother also complained. *The boy has no head for business. He notices neither customers nor thieves and can be cheated even by simpletons.*

Of course we asked Lo See to instruct our son that he must swallow his discontent. Nevertheless, Gim Gong answered a call for workers at a foreign-ghost shoe factory on the other side of the gold mountains. And though Fourth Brother refused him permission to go, Gim Gong raised his own desires above those of family and ran away.

Fourth Brother was justly angry. Ba's fury made him so ill he was forced to take to his bed. Hok Yee and I worried. Gim Gong was a child, the factory in a place of deep frost and snow. Without Fourth Brother, who would make our son the special soup that prevents chills? Who would shield him from foreign ghosts?

By then a pair of foreign ghosts had opened a worship hall in Toi Sing. If Hok Yee and I went to see them, could we discover a way to protect Gim Gong? Ma, speaking for Ba while he was ill, gave us permission to try.

On the long walk into town, the fields stretching out on either side of the footpath and the clusters of gray brick houses looked much the same as those in Lung On. But it was my first time out of the village since coming as a bride, and beneath my concern for Gim Gong, I felt the excitement of a New Year morning.

Gim Gong had written that the section of First City in Gold Mountain reserved for our people was very much like Toi Sing. And the streets and shops were every bit as full of people and noise and smells as he'd described.

The market crackled with the same loud heat as strings of firecrackers. I was accustomed to peddlers who carried all their goods in the two baskets at either end of their poles. In those days, a whole moon would sometimes pass without any coming through the village. There were never more than one or two at a time. A few *clack-clack*s of their bamboo rattles would set dogs and children into a frantic round of barking and shouting. *Hnnnh,* before a peddler had a chance to cry out what he had to sell, half the village would be crowded around him, giving him their whole attention.

In Toi Sing my head spun like a child's top, and still I could not see all the kettles and pots and crocks and toys and bolts of cloth spilling out of the stores. But my need to see foreign ghosts for myself, to determine how we might protect Gim Gong from the ones in Gold Mountain, overrode my desire to linger. Hurrying after Hok Yee, I pressed through the crowded streets without stopping until we reached the worship hall.

The foreign ghosts, a giant of a man and a big-boned woman, were as ugly as I'd expected, their behavior more barbaric. Mounting a raised platform, the ghost man called for silence, then shouted and howled, flinging his arms and twisting his body so furiously that his unhealthy white skin soon blotched red. Sweat poured from him. Yet he did not have the sense to take off his jacket or loosen the sash tied peculiarly around his neck instead of his waist.

I was not surprised. From what I could understand of his broken Chinese, he was denouncing our Gods, even Gwoon Yum, the tenderhearted Goddess of Mercy, praising the foreign-ghost God, the one who'd murdered his own son. Clearly the ghost man had lost his reason. Could Gim Gong, living among them, have lost his as well?

Then, just as suddenly as the ghost man had started his ranting, he fell silent, nodded at the ghost woman. Immediately she began making strange music by pounding and pumping a large boxlike instrument with her fingers and feet. Her lips moved, so I guessed she was singing, but I could hear no voice.

"Louder," someone called out.

"How can she sing louder?" the woman beside me snorted. "She's bound her waist so tight it's a wonder she can breathe, let alone sing!"

"Yes," I heard someone else say. "She has to be carried everywhere in a sedan chair like a bound-foot woman."

"But her husband speaks out against foot binding."

"What husband?"

"That ghost man, of course. Who else?"

Listening to the buzz of talk around me, I realized that many of the people had been to the worship hall before, some more than once.

"Watching these ghosts is like going to the theater," the woman behind me laughed.

In opera, however, the colors painted on the actors' faces clearly reveal heroes and rogues. From the chatter I was picking up, these foreign ghosts, white as any villain, were confusing. Though they'd come to live among us, they were keeping their own clothes and customs, rudely rebuking us for ours. Yet they'd also opened a free school and regularly gave away medicine to the sick.

Were they perhaps a little crazed but sincere in doing good? Or were they devils working out some evil design? Not knowing for certain, mothers covered the faces of their babies and ordered their children to hide when the foreign ghosts finished their worship and came near.

If only Hok Yee and I could have protected our son as easily. But separated from Gim Gong by sea and mountains, we could not hide him. And he refused either to return to Fourth Brother or to come home.

FANNY

North Adams, Massachusetts
1870—1875

I begin my story at the heart, my heart, with Lue Gim Gong's arrival in North Adams.

I will never forget that day. My sister Phoebe had just left for a long-planned holiday at the shore with friends, leaving me in charge of Father's comfort, and I'd sent Bridget, our hired girl, out for some calves' liver, to which he was particularly partial. She returned empty handed and wildly excited, crying, "Chinamen! Mr. Sampson's bringing Chinamen to break the strike at his shoe factory!"

The month before, Mr. Sampson had brought in forty-five men from North Brookfield. Every one of his three hundred and fifty laborers had gone to the depot to meet the train. Shouting, "Scabs!" they had thrown some of the new arrivals into the river, broken the ribs of others, and made the rest run for safety as best they could.

Mr. Sampson, furious over the debacle, had vowed to break the shoemakers' union, the Secret Order of the Knights of St. Crispin. He'd hired carpenters to erect a high board fence around the factory, then met with Father and other merchants. Soon after, covered wagons began making deliveries and there was the scrape of saws and pounding of hammers from the rear of the factory.

Rumors flew. But those in Mr. Sampson's confidence met inquiries with resolute silence. When I pressed Father, he said, "Would you have me betray a friend?" Ashamed, I'd retreated.

Now the secret was out. Revealed, Bridget said, by newshounds who claimed Mr. Sampson and his Chinamen—seventy-five of them—would be on the afternoon train. Eager to see my first Chinese, I hurried on bonnet and shawl and set off for the depot at the other end of Main Street.

The Crispins had packed the depot with strikers, and the noise from men shouting oaths and imprecations and the smell of rum in the close, stale air was overwhelming. Then the whistles in the cotton mills, print works, and shoe-and-boot factories shrieked dismissal, and laborers—men, women, and children—swept in like a rush of mighty water to lend their support. Those unable to squeeze inside swarmed in the streets surrounding the depot, pressing close, hanging through open windows. Faith, if Father's position as owner of the largest mercantile establishment in the Berkshires had not afforded me a view from the stationmaster's office above the platform, I might have bolted.

The stationmaster's office was small, the crush within no less than that below, the heat worse. Since there were only ladies present, however, there were no foul odors, no choking smoke from cheap tobacco. And stalwart gentlemen, escorts for some of the ladies, guarded the stairs between us and the boisterous mob.

Many in that mob were the same people who sat by my side at church, tipped their caps, bobbed their heads, or smiled shyly at me in Father's store. But today their pinched, chalk-white faces were blanched with hate, and anxiety rose in me as if I were a fearful child rather than a woman on the edge of middle age.

Burly town officers and state constables stood with arms linked, forming a human cordon between those on the platform and the tracks. Directly in front of these guards, the Crispins' chief, a tall, hard-looking French Canadian, was mobilizing his people like a general rallying troops for battle. In thickly accented English, he warned that if Mr. Sampson succeeded in bringing in Chinamen who'd work for less, other manufacturers would follow suit, driving wages still lower. He reminded them of their previous victory over Mr. Sampson, concluding, "We got rid of those scabs. We can make the yellow scabs fly too!"

Cheering wildly, the crowd chorused, "Make the yellow scabs fly!"

Their voices revealed the desperation I'd seen while distributing food baskets with Phoebe in their tenements, and I felt a sudden warmth, a surge of accord with their cause. Then their chief raised his fists, and they pushed forward, pressing hard against the human cordon. A few of the constables, obviously alarmed, broke ranks and drew out their nightsticks, wielding them freely. But that only intensified the jostling, and as the chanting turned into an ugly, ominous roar with cries of "Blow up the train!" my sympathy dissolved in a chill wave of fear.

"Let us pray," our pastor's wife, wedged in the corner farthest from the door, suggested.

At that same moment, the earsplitting whistle of the 5:15 from Troy pierced the crazed shouting, eerily silencing, immobilizing. With a final wail and shriek of brakes, the train labored into the station, puffing steam in every direction, and it seemed to me all heads—constables and Crispins, those around me and those below—turned as one to the final "immigrant" car.

The door swung open. Mr. Sampson, his ruddy face flushed, stepped out. Short but compact, he stood ramrod straight, staring out at the mass of people jammed into the depot. His jacket bulged oddly.

Behind me, a voice breathed, "Pistols."

Swiftly the pastor's wife shrilled a plea to the Almighty for the stationmaster's office to be a sanctuary for us, His children. "We pray this in Jesus' name."

"Amen," we said in unison.

The crowd below remained silent, but I noticed a hand closing over a crucifix hanging from its owner's neck, another making the sign of the cross, the faint rustle of rosary beads. Clearly they were praying, too.

"Stand aside," Mr. Sampson boomed. "I've hired these men to work for me, and I'm bringing them off the train."

No one moved. No one spoke.

Mr. Sampson's flush deepened to a fearful red-purple. His eyes narrowed, swept the crowd. The neck muscles above his starched collar bulged. Thrusting his chin forward, he said firmly, "I mean to take these men to my factory. Make way."

"Take them heathens back where they come from!" the Crispins' chief yelled.

The trance cast by the train's arrival snapped, and many in the crowd erupted in a savage chant: "Take them back or we'll break their backs!"

Mr. Sampson threw open his coat, gripped the pistol strapped to his side. Swiftly the officers and constables also drew arms, and the Crispins' chief fell mute, the chant faded raggedly.

Leaping down the steps, Mr. Sampson clapped his free hand on the Crispins' chief. "Make way," he repeated. "I'm bringing my men through."

Behind him, the Chinamen stepped down from the train one by one. The first wore boots, suit, and hat of American manufacture, the rest thick-soled cloth shoes, flowing trousers, and loose jackets of blue calico fastened by frogs and shiny brass buttons. The front of their heads were shaved close, while down their backs hung jet black queues that reached almost to the ground. Their beardless faces suggested they were mere boys of twelve or thirteen. Each carried a bundle or bag upon his shoulders, and as they spilled across the platform in a steady stream, I had the bewildering sensation of watching the figures painted on a willow-pattern dinner service leaping off their plates in a great escape.

The Crispins' chief stood aside. The crowd parted like the Red Sea had for Moses. The Chinamen, flanked by officers and constables, padded through the opening on their silent slipperlike shoes. Though small and slight, they were wiry, emanating a certain strength, and the firm tread of their walk denied what might otherwise have been considered womanish grace.

Their faces, with eyes so narrow they seemed half shut, betrayed no dismay at their hostile reception, no fear. But I kept my own feelings too well hidden to believe that these creatures, albeit degraded heathens, had none. And years later, Lue confirmed what I had then suspected: the Chinamen had been terrified.

The San Francisco agency which had handled their hiring had made no mention of a strike in its advertisement or during the interviews. Only when Mr. Sampson boarded the train as it approached North Adams did they learn that they had been hired to break a strike. By then it was too late to turn back: they had signed three-year contracts, contracts Mr. Sampson adamantly refused to revoke.

Lue tried to reassure himself and his companions by recalling how their foreman and interpreter, Charlie Sing, had ejected an Irishman who had forced his way into their car at gunpoint in Omaha. How Charlie had seized the fellow's pistol hand and held

it harmlessly aloft with his left hand while drawing his own re-
volver with his right. How the Irishman, struck speechless, had
backed silently out of the car. But even as he spoke, Lue recognized
that Charlie had defended them from one man, a drunk. They
would likely be facing a mob.

Neither did Mr. Sampson's success in quieting the crowd at the
depot dispel Lue's fears. He thought it another trick. Indeed, marching through the jeering crowds lining the streets, Lue was as frightened of the armed guards as he was of the men who yelled, even the
ones who boldly threw stones, clods of mud. And he believed that
the factory's high board fence—so new he could smell the rawness
of the wood—had been erected, not to protect him and his fellow
Chinese, but to keep them from running.

That day at the depot, I little suspected I would come to know one of the Chinamen intimately. Or that he would change my life forever. Likewise, when Father lost his factory in my tenth year, I'd had no notion his ruin would give me my heart's desire, even lead to my salvation.

My earliest memory is of myself hiding under the kitchen table while Mother was teaching Phoebe, two years my elder, the alphabet. How happy I was the day Mother gave in to my pleadings to join them! But the half hour of instruction each morning did not satisfy; it whetted my appetite for more.

When I asked Mother to enroll me in the school we passed on our way to market, she said, "Every penny of your father's wages is already spoken for. Besides, you must learn to be useful in the home."

Under Mother's tutelage, Phoebe cooked jellies bright as amber and made samplers of unrivaled beauty. Cynthia—four years my junior—baked light, flaky biscuits. I had difficulty warming milk or bringing a piece of patchwork into conventional shape.

Mother, scrubbing yet another pan I'd scorched black or consigning more of my needlework to her ragbag, would purse her lips tight as the opening of her reticule. "Fanny, you don't love Jesus. If you did, you'd make more of an effort."

Scarlet with shame, I would hang my head and beg forgiveness. I would listen and watch more carefully when she demonstrated, but the stockings I knitted continued to be narrow where they should be wide, my bread refused to rise. Only after Father turned the parlor into a small satinet factory with one other laborer did I finally prove helpful, for I could calculate the cost of materials and wages owed against possible profits more swiftly and accurately than he could.

With me to do his figuring, Father could devote his every moment to operating his machine and supervising his laborer. Gradually he expanded the number of machines and laborers in his service, moving them into the cottage on the other side of our vegetable patch.

There was money then to pay school fees. But Father refused my request. "You already know more than enough mathematics to count your children, sufficient geography to find the different rooms in your home. Where you fall short is in the kitchen."

Indeed, my puddings did still separate, my pickles turned soft and yellow. So I pressed down my dreams of school and indulged in the pleasure of books only when illness banished me to bed.

Then Father's factory failed during a financial panic. Mother bore the loss bravely. "You were a laborer when we married, and what we built together once, we can do again," she comforted.

Father, slumped down in his chair by the back window, stared out at the cottage that had housed his factory. "No. It's gone. Everything's gone."

Hoping to lift his spirits, Cynthia climbed on his lap and smoothed out the anxious furrows creasing his forehead. Phoebe sang his favorite hymns. I cudgeled my brain for means to recover his losses, rhymes and riddles to make him smile. But Father was too deeply sunk into gloom to notice.

When not even a spark of recognition brightened his eyes, Mother, bent on restoring Father, sent us to live with her younger brother in Culloden, Georgia.

Looking back at our six years with Uncle John's family, I see endless fields of cotton under blazing skies, mighty oaks hung with streamers of gray Spanish moss. I smell the perfume of colorful tropical blossoms. I feel the warmth of affection freely given, approbation justly earned, the thrill of a challenged mind.

Education was the great business of Uncle John's life, and he and his wife, Aunt Julia, had established an academy where children were taught through play: staging mock battles from history, writing and mounting elaborate dramas, searching out constellations in the night sky.

All knowledge was meat and drink to me, but studying nature was my chief delight. Uncle John was preparing a botany of the southern states for use as a reference text. Aunt Julia, a writer and artist, assisted him, and I doubt there was any tree or flower they could not recognize and call by name. Yet they rarely answered any question directly. "Accept only that which is the product of your own reason and intelligence," Uncle John would say.

He showed me how to dissect a plant, to make drawings of the various sections and accurately identify them. He encouraged me to collect my own specimens. When shortness of breath prevented me from going into the woods to search them out, he threw away my stays. I threw away the ribbons and pins that bound my long, brown hair into thick, heavy braids as well.

Where I had frequently been sick in North Adams, I did not know a day of illness in Culloden. Nor can I recollect a moment's unhappiness. Indeed, I confess I gave little thought to the trials my parents were enduring. And when Uncle John solemnly told us that caring for Father had crushed Mother's health, bringing on consumption, I was so shocked I scarcely understood what he was saying: Father, fully recovered from his mental collapse, wanted Phoebe and me to return home to keep house for him and to nurse Mother, to care for a new baby on its way; we were to leave the morning after Phoebe's graduation from the academy.

Father had, after two years of labor for others, bought a small drugstore. He was gradually expanding its inventory to include hardware, mill supplies, and building materials.

Phoebe suggested he employ a housekeeper so I could return to Uncle John's academy. But Mother explained that was impossible: the loss of Father's factory had left him in severe arrears. Since it was the failure of others that had caused his ruin, he had no legal obligation to repay these debts. Nevertheless, he had claimed them as his moral duty, and until all his creditors were fully recompensed in principal and interest, Father had vowed that the family would live as frugally as if he were destitute.

Mother, praising Father as a man of firm character and unim-
peachable integrity, gladly supported his stand, although it was the
demands of his integrity that had weakened her. I should have been
glad to help as well. But I did not yet understand that great sacrifices can turn into even greater compensations, and in a letter to
Uncle John I poured out my burning desire to return to Culloden to
complete my studies and then to teach.

He reminded me that his own education had been interrupted
when his father died, throwing upon him the cares and responsibilities of the family. "So I worked in the old fulling mill during the
day and studied at night. Even at my machine, my books were always open and ready for a spare moment. You can do the same."

There is, of course, no place to prop a book when sweeping,
making beds, doing laundry, filling lamps, building and tending
fires. So I exercised my mind with mathematical problems while
baking; I revised Latin declensions while cleaning. But my bread
came out of the oven sour and heavy; I tripped over scrub buckets
or covered myself in stove blacking. Then I attempted to squeeze
out spare moments by taking shortcuts. Father—kind and genial
unless crossed—criticized me for keeping a disorderly house and
providing comfortless suppers.

Where Uncle John's week at the mill had ended with a half day
of freedom, mine closed in a push to complete the baking for Sunday as well as Saturday. Nor could Phoebe help me. If she was not
plying Mother with draughts that promoted expectoration, syrups
to soothe her throat, or prickly-pear tea to lower her fevers, then
she was reading to her, trying to keep her cheerful. Or she was making mustard whey to stimulate Mother's appetite, brewing chicken
broths and sago gruels for nourishment, peppermint tea to improve
digestion.

Every time Dr. Waterman came to bleed Mother, he assured us
she would rally after the delivery. Instead, the damps of the tomb
settled on her and she went home to Jesus less than a fortnight after
Baby Julia's birth. I confess I envied Mother her release.

Since Father would not hire a wet nurse, Phoebe and I tried to
hand-raise our sister with a sucking bottle. But sweetened cow's
milk proved indigestible, and preparations of arrowroot or sago
and tapioca flour did not satisfy. A single feeding could take an
hour of coaxing. Then she would spit up almost as much as she had

swallowed. Hungry, she would whimper yet refuse the bottle, or suck so hard she flattened the goose-quill nipple, blocking the flow. Lacking sufficient nourishment, she was weak and fretful, frequently ill, requiring our constant attention.

Discouraged, I pleaded with Reverend Sandler to intercede and insist that Father hire a wet nurse. He counseled me to turn to our Father in Heaven. "Don't you see? He has deliberately placed salt on your tongue out of love for you. So you will thirst for Him."

On the eve of my seventeenth birthday, I pledged my allegiance to Jesus as King of Kings and Lord of Lords. Reverend Sandler led the Saints and myself from the First Baptist Church to the river's edge. We were robed in white, the trees in autumn crimsons and golds. A gentle breeze chased off the few clouds in the sky, and the sun blazed down, warming.

"Let us all unite in singing 'What a Friend We Have in Jesus' followed by 'Blessed Be the Ties That Bind,' " Reverend Sandler called out.

While the Saints raised their voices to the Almighty, I followed Reverend Sandler into the water. Its chill startled. Nevertheless, I forged forward, clenching my teeth to stop their chatter, to steady myself against the pounding of my heart.

For a moment my robe ballooned out despite the weights sewn into its hem. Then it sagged, clinging, dragging against my ankles, my legs. Still I pushed on. One step. Another. And another.

When the water lapped Reverend Sandler's waist, he turned, signaled for me to remain where I was. Already chest deep, I was only too glad to stop, to see him reach out. But then he gripped my shoulders with one hand, laid his other on my head, and pressed me down.

As the icy waters swirled over me, my arms shot out in panic. His hold tightened so that I could not shake loose, and he forced me deeper and deeper into the river's suffocating darkness until I felt my very lungs would burst and I would die.

Suddenly, Jesus rose before me though my eyes were squeezed shut.

"Be of good faith," He said. "I will save you."

Smiling, He took me into His arms. Oh, the unspeakable sweetness, the ecstasy of His embrace. Lightning darted through me, transporting my soul to Paradise. And as He lifted me out of the water with His mighty power, I shouted out my joy, my love for Him, my thanks for this mark of His grace.

Afire with love for the Master, my life quickened. And had my thwarted desires not held me fast, I might indeed have found Jesus all-satisfying, as I should. But despite daily, almost hourly prayer, my heart burned for a larger usefulness than household toil. Soon throbbing headaches and nervous weeping laid me low.

"Illness and tears are part of the discipline necessary to make us pliable in our Lord's hands," Reverend Sandler said kindly. "Faith will make you strong."

His words brought back the comfort of the Master's promise when He'd lifted me from the icy waters of the river. "Be of good faith. I will save you." I thought, too, of my first year at Culloden.

There had been a spiritualist among the senior boarders who'd claimed that if we had sufficient faith, we could pick a girl up from the floor and raise her over our heads with a single finger of each hand. We'd done it, too. Not on the first few attempts, but after the spiritualist had weeded out the girls whose giggles betrayed their lack of faith.

I had been one of the girls the spiritualist had singled out for banishment, but I'd pleaded so earnestly for another opportunity that she'd allowed me to remain. The Master was even more forgiving. For as dull days stretched into dull years and then dull decades, my faith proved too weak to resist temptation, and I came to rely on the balm of the opiate laudanum more than prayer to ease my distress, to feel again the warmth of His embrace. Nevertheless, the summer of my forty-second year, He sent me Lue.

I met Lue through the Sunday school that our town's pastors organized in the Chinamen's quarters at the factory.

During a special meeting, Reverend Sandler explained that although Baptist doctrine forbids secular learning on the Sabbath,
this Sunday school would offer an hour of English lessons followed
by an hour of worship—English lessons being the net necessary to
draw in the Chinamen. Mr. Sampson's Chinese foreman, Charlie
Sing, had found Jesus through just such a school in San Francisco,
and, except for his queue, he'd become a completely civilized
Christian.

Pounding the pulpit, Reverend Sandler thundered, "We have the
opportunity—nay, the obligation—to lift up seventy-four more be-
nighted heathens from dark superstition to the bright light of Truth.
Remember, practical charity is the very heart of Christianity, and in
saving these heathens, we will be affirming our own faith."

When he called for teachers, I leaped to my feet. Nor was I alone.
In all, nine gentlemen, four children, and fifty-three ladies volun-
teered from three churches.

Not one volunteer was a laborer or a member of a laborer's family. Union leaders had been printing and distributing bills calling the
importation of coolies under contract a modern version of the slave
trade, accusing Mr. Sampson of being to labor what Jefferson Davis
was to slaves. Operatives at all the factories had gone out on strike
in sympathy, and the Crispins had celebrated this victory with a

torchlight rally and fireworks display at the head of Main Street, directly across from our garden.

Father, his bushy, snow-white eyebrows and side-whiskers twitching with anger, snapped, "What do they know of their employers' burdens? What do they care?"

I understood that his show of temper sprang from concern over the loss of trade his store would suffer during the strikes, for the more successful Father had become, the more he seemed to fear he might again lose all. Nevertheless, his wrath set my temples to pounding.

If Phoebe had been home, she would have distracted him with a few well-chosen words or soothed him with a prayer. I did not share her talent for setting Father to rights, but I could—and did—close our windows against the speakers' tirades, the laborers' chants of "Stop Sampson and his Chink scabs now!"

As I shut the final window, I pressed my forehead against the glass, felt it cooling me. Rockets, then roman candles and pinwheels, soared above the eerily lit human sea. The clouds in the night sky glowed bright as flames. Quickly I pulled the drapes so Father would not see.

The Chinamen locked in Mr. Sampson's factory would have seen nothing of the rally. But they must have heard the crowd's angry roar, the explosions. Had they thought the fireworks gunfire, I wondered. Had they been frightened? Or were they, like Father and the Crispins, angry and desperate?

Mr. Sampson himself escorted the pastors and Sunday school teachers to the factory in closed carriages. As we alighted inside the gate, he pointed to his fleet of guards patrolling the perimeter of the fence and assured us that we would be safe. Then Charlie Sing stepped forward and greeted us.

This was my first close look at a Chinaman, and I stared at his flat nose, large teeth, and dusky skin. Charlie did not seem to mind. Faith, when one of the little girls remarked loudly on his lack of facial hair, he laughed, "American men have whiskers. Chinamen have queues."

Taking off his hat, he uncoiled his pigtail from the crown of his head and held it up like a specimen for our examination. "See, we both grease and comb and brush our hair, only we grow it in different place."

He laughed again, and as we followed him down the gravel path to the rear of the main building, his face remained wreathed in a broad grin, and he praised the spacious grounds, the modern building. "Look how many windows Mr. Sampson's factory have. Inside is bright and airy. Mr. Sampson give us a number-one good place to work."

Leading us up the stairs to the Chinamen's quarters, he praised us for our willingness to teach without compensation. "Learning English and accepting Jesus is very good for Chinamen, very good," he gushed.

But the dining room, where we were to meet our scholars, was empty. Uncertain how to proceed, we massed awkwardly near the doorway. Acrid smoke scratched at my throat. A report, sharp and short as a pistol shot, jarred my ear, setting troops of wild fancies whirling into my brain.

"Come in," Charlie urged. He waved expansively at the tables spread with surprisingly clean white cloths, curious teapots, and small bowls. "See, everything ready."

My eyes warily following the sweep of his hand, I saw what looked like a pagan altar with gaudily painted wood idols, a pair of thick red candles, and a handful of incense sticks at the far end of the room, the source, I realized, of the pungent smoke irritating my throat. Suddenly a door near the altar flew open. I braced my nerves—for what I was not sure.

There was a burst of noise like the shrieking of crows. Charlie called out a string of meaningless sounds. Immediately the strange shrieking stopped. A tall Chinaman wearing a long, filthy apron stalked in, ostentatiously replaced some burned-out stubs of incense from the altar with fresh sticks, lit them.

Charlie spewed more prattle. He was still grinning, but there was a deadening in his face, a harshness to his tone. If he was rebuking his charge, the tall Chinaman paid no heed. Slowly, deliberately, he bowed to the idols, then turned, reached for one of the teapots, drank from its spout, setting off a ripple of horrified muttering among the volunteers.

Charlie, abandoning his pretense that all was well, barked what had to be a command. The tall Chinaman withdrew, a cluster of

Chinamen edged in. Reverend Sandler, his hand extended in the age-old gesture of friendship, headed toward them. Blanching like fainting girls, they dodged behind pillars, back into what I guessed was their sleeping room.

Their fear made me bold, and I would have followed. But the incense smoke had thickened and I was overcome by a fit of coughing.

There was a gentle tug at my sleeve. Startled, I turned, found myself face-to-face with a Chinaman, a lad of eleven or twelve. He was holding up a steaming bowl of tea, shyly miming for me to drink.

As I reached for it, Mrs. Sandler warned, "He poured it from the pot that Chinaman drank out of."

My stomach revolted, my throat seized, and I dropped my hand. Swallowing hard in an effort to stop my coughing, I began to choke. Desperately, I grasped the bowl, lifted it to my lips, took as small a sip as possible.

The tea, smoother and more delicate than that offered at American tables, coursed down my throat, soothing. Faith, it was marvelously delicious, and I smiled with honest pleasure as well as gratitude.

Clearing my throat, I pointed at the pale green liquid. "Tea."

The boy hesitated a moment. "Tea?"

I nodded, tapped my finger lightly on the rim of the bowl. "Bowl."

"Bo?"

"Bowl," I repeated.

With a laborious motion of the lower jaw and tongue, he imitated the sound correctly. I nodded, pointed to myself. "Miss Fanny Burlingame."

"Mis-see Fah-nee," he said.

I shook my head. "Miss. Miss Fanny."

"Missmiss Fah-nee."

Again I shook my head. "Miss Fanny."

His jet black eyes flashed understanding. "Miss Fanny."

Smiling approval, I pointed to him. "Your name?"

He reeled off a string of sounds. I caught only the first. "Louie?" I queried.

He nodded so agreeably I assumed I was correct, but his given name is, in fact, Gim Gong, meaning Double Brilliance. I was calling him by his surname. Further, I was mispronouncing it. By the time he felt comfortable enough to correct me, however, calling him "Louie" had become habit. Moreover, despite numerous attempts, I could not twist my tongue to duplicate his articulation of either his given name or his surname. Finally, he kindly assured me he did not mind "the American way," and Lue, pronounced as Louie, he has remained.

It seems inconceivable to me now, looking back, that for weeks I could not distinguish Lue from the other Chinamen. Then, however, even the small number of men in their twenties and thirties who refused to participate in the Sunday school and the boys in their teens who were our scholars looked as alike as so many peas. Nor could the boys pick out their particular teachers until they were seated in their appointed places at the pine tables. Only Lue had no trouble singling me out from the start, and I confess the way he ran to greet me flattered my pride.

Precisely thirty years my junior, Lue was my same height. His queue was longer than the brown braid coiled around my head, and his tawny complexion made mine seem pale, almost ghostly. In contrast to my inability to mimic his name, he had a knack for imitation. During our first hour together, he learned the words for everything in the dining room, even the heathen altar and incense. At our next meeting, he recited the entire list with perfect accuracy, then drew me into the Chinamen's sleeping room and inquired about the words for the bunks arranged in four tiers like the illustrations of an emigrant ship's steerage in *Harper's Weekly,* the ladders, and bedding. After he had these memorized, he would have led me to the kitchen, but the tall Chinese who had been so rude on our initial visit was the Chinamen's cook, and I felt his menace too keenly to follow.

Object teaching—dictated by the gulf of language and culture—is the dullest of methods. Yet Lue's enthusiasm and mental vigor gave the work interest. Understanding would brighten his face like a swift, rising light. When he made a mistake, chagrin would color his cheek. If his memory fell short, he would tug at his queue.

Some of the Chinamen made an awful job of writing. Lue grasped the alphabet readily and took an innocent delight in drawing out the letters on the slate I brought him. He was wonderfully well mannered for a heathen, holding his hands and bowing to the waist to thank me for the smallest gift—and, Charlie explained, to show his respect for me as his teacher and elder. Faith, Lue made himself so agreeable that I sometimes almost forgot he was uncivilized.

Since all the Sunday school volunteers employed the method of object teaching, the din during the hour of study was fearful. But the instant Charlie struck the bell for worship, every sound was hushed. Then one of the pastors, with Charlie serving as tongue and ears, taught the entire assembly a Scripture phrase, a little prayer, one or two cardinal truths of the Christian faith, a Gospel song.

Lue always delayed my departure with questions I was sure he saved for that purpose. And I sensed the enthusiasm with which he worked my arm up and down like a pump handle upon my arrival was at least as much for the outside world I brought him as for me. When I gave him a kite, he teased it into the air, then released the string, teared when it crashed.

I prayed Lue's imprisonment would soon be over. But two long months passed before the Crispins admitted defeat. Even then, the terms of the settlement—a further ten percent cut in wages—were so harsh that when Mr. Sampson threw open the factory gate, Lue and his countrymen were forced to remain in their quarters or risk attack.

At a meeting of the Sunday school volunteers, I suggested we give our scholars protection by inviting them into our parlors. Many spoke against it. Some claimed we would be petting the boys unwisely. Others opposed the social mixing of the races. But when Reverend Sandler spoke in support of the idea, I knew Father would not object if Lue came to supper. Nevertheless, I waited until Father was in Boston on business before I brought Lue home. I was never certain what would set Father to breathing fire, and I wanted nothing to mar the boy's first visit.

* * *

Lue rubbed his face against the softness of the velvet curtains in our parlor, the red plush covering the love seat and sofa, even the carpet. He worked the bellows and turned the handles that opened and closed the blinds in the deep-set windows. Darting from one thing to another, he picked out tuneless melodies on our small ebony piano and played with Father's glass paperweight, shaking it upside down, sideways, and all around to produce falling snow in the miniature village it contained.

Watching him, I thought of my excitement the first time I had entered Uncle John's academy. If propriety had allowed me to show my curiosity and pleasure as openly as Lue, I would have run from chalkboard to cabinet, examining the books on the shelves, twirling the globe on Aunt Julia's desk, unrolling the maps on the walls, and sniffing the bottles of paste and ink. Instead I had sat stiffly on my bench, feeling what Lue was saying out loud, "This heaven."

At supper he attacked his food before I had a chance to sit, spearing the bread with his fork, slurping spilled tea from his saucer. He took the little dish of green pickles I'd set in the middle of the table and upset it into his oyster stew. Then he alternately harpooned an oyster and a piece of pickle until there was nothing but liquid left. Seizing his dish with both hands, he raised it to his lips, bringing it down empty.

Too astonished even to make a pretense of eating, I thanked God for Father's absence and signaled for Bridget, our maid, to clear the table. She was shaking too hard from suppressed laughter to pick up our plates.

I would not have her make sport of such a gentle creature. Excusing myself from the table, I directed Bridget into the kitchen.

"When you came to us, you didn't know a soup tureen from a washbasin," I reminded. "Lue will learn too."

Ordering Bridget to hold dessert, I showed Lue how to draw back a lady's chair, how to handle our teacups and saucers and spoons. Finally I declared, "Let's show Bridget what a little gentleman you can be," and we approached the table as if for the first time.

Although Lue fancied sweets, he did not fall on the chocolate whips, fairy gingerbread, and nut creams as he had his supper. Instead, he moved my chair for me and placed it properly before taking his own seat. Neither did he lift a fork until I had done so. Like a well-bred boy, he ate without making any noise, and he solemnly echoed my amen when I thanked the Father for our abundance. At my signal to rise, however, he began emptying the leftover confections into his pockets. When I remonstrated, he misunderstood my meaning, pulling out his handkerchief to wrap the cakes more neatly. Bridget, unable to stifle her giggles, swung open the door and hurtled into the kitchen.

Blackie, Phoebe's beloved mother cat, sauntered through the open door, the runt of her litter close behind. Lue was too busily engaged with the confections to notice the creatures. Before I could call out a warning, the kitten seized Lue's queue, which was dangling temptingly behind his chair.

As the kitten clambered up, Lue shrieked and leaped to his feet, vigorously shaking his head. The kitten clung more tightly. Its mother hissed, jumped to the sideboard, scattering plates and silver. Instinctively I reached out in hopes of catching them, failed, and there was the horrible crash of breaking crockery. Bridget, who was peeking through the hatch, slammed it shut. The kitten meowed plaintively.

Lue, realizing at last what was caught in his hair, ducked his head, swinging his queue forward so he could reach it. Murmuring soothingly, he gently untangled its claws. Then, cuddling the freed kitten close with one hand, he petted Blackie, still on the sideboard, with his other. Blackie purred, lifted the root of her tail. The kitten crept up to Lue's shoulder and nuzzled his neck. Its amber eyes all innocence, it blinked, yawned pinkly, and relaxed into sleep.

On Lue's next visit, Phoebe, back from her holiday at the shore, greeted him kindly. Father, relieved at the restoration of trade at his store and eager for the Chinamen's patronage, laid himself out to be agreeable, taking Lue on a tour of the garden.

As far back as I can remember, Father had cultivated a garden; he claimed the deferred hopes and blighted expectations that are the lot of every gardener gave him the patience and philosophy necessary to endure the toilsome portions of his life. And when he had finally become prosperous enough to pay off the last of his debts and build a house of his own, his one indulgence had been to surround it with an acre of flowers, shrubs, vegetables, and trees, a greenhouse of tropical blooms and fruits.

Inside the warm damp of the greenhouse, I would close my eyes and inhale the fragrances and almost believe myself back in Culloden. Lue said the greenhouse reminded him of his garden in China. He, too, had grown flowers in pots, and most of the plants were familiar.

A few were new, and Lue's excitement over these discoveries awakened the thrill I used to feel searching for new specimens for Uncle John. When I brought out Uncle John's book on southern flora, Lue's eyes grew as large as a child's on Christmas morning. "You really know man who make this book?"

I nodded, pointed out the plants I'd found for Uncle John. Lue, lightly tracing the shapes of the petals and leaves with a finger, sounded out the botanical as well as common names beneath each drawing. He asked about their colors, textures, and fragrances, when they bloomed and for how long.

Lue's hunger for learning was as great as mine had been, and I wanted to employ Uncle John's philosophy in teaching him. According to Charlie Sing, however, rote learning was the method by which scholars study in China, and as the Chinamen had advanced beyond object teaching, Reverend Sandler had instructed the Sunday school teachers to follow this strategy, with the New Testament and *Webster's Spelling Book* as our principal tools and the boys declaiming sentences, conjugating verbs, and reciting multiplication tables from cards posted on their dining room walls. Even this rote learning was difficult to accomplish in the confines of the Chinamen's quarters, for the cook and his cronies, heathen to the core, squatted in a corner, chatting noisily while our scholars studied— sometimes during the hour of worship as well.

The pastors had hoped that in time these renegades would come to feel our sympathy and join the Sunday school. Instead they continued to puff on their long, malodorous pipes, laugh boisterously over games of chance, and light fistfuls of pungent incense, loudly chanting incantations before their idols. Charlie lashed out at them more than once. But the dining room being a part of their quarters, the wretches boldly stood their ground, becoming increasingly rowdy and hostile.

The cook seemed the most malevolent. Making no effort to hide his animosity, he twisted his lips in a perpetual sneer of contempt, and I was not sorry when the dry hacking cough I suffered each winter returned, forcing me to remain indoors and Lue to come to me.

"Not on the Sabbath," I told him. "You must continue to attend the factory Sunday school. But during the week. After work."

"Every day?"

I smiled at his eagerness. "Yes, every day if that is your wish."

"I do wish. I wish learn everything. Everything!"

In the quiet of our parlor, I brought out our stereoscopic collection to illustrate lessons in geography. I gave Lue the order forms in mail catalogs for practicing lettering and calculating, a journal in which to set down his thoughts. I encouraged him to follow his own bent in learning, to ask questions, to try and find his own answers.

Instead of blossoming under these alterations as I'd expected, Lue wilted. Where he had been frank and artless, he began to weigh his every word and deed. Where he had been lively and inventive, he turned stiff and dull as Sunday.

The more I pressed Lue to set his own course, the more he waited for me to lead. Deeply disappointed, I suffered a storm of racking headaches, and on those days I was in too much pain or my brain too dulled by laudanum to teach, I heard Lue asking the rest of the family sprightly questions. Why did Father greet him with "This is nice weather" or "Lovely" on days quite clearly the opposite? Why did Phoebe salute women by bringing their lips into contact? Why did Bridget's church display encased bone fragments?

That Lue still spoke freely with them although he'd fallen all but mute with me was an added thorn. When I called him on it, he flushed, pulled at his queue. "You are my teacher."

"All the more reason you should question *me,*" I said sharply.

Lue cringed at my rebuke, and I repented my show of impatience. Yet I was in too much of a fret to soften my tone or to stop pressing my case.

For a long time Lue retreated into silence, as I did when Father was in a temper. Finally, his every feature stiff with resolve, he asked in a barely audible whisper, "Why you want trick me?"

"Trick? What trick?"

"In China, my teacher made me leave the school because I speak out like my aunt tell me. Like you say I should do with you. I don't want lose this chance for study, too."

Lue did not have the vocabulary to reveal the details of his expulsion. But his voice and face proclaimed his pain, his belief that he'd been unjustly treated. Listening, I felt a spark of kinship, for I had felt the same when Uncle John had insisted I obey Father and quit the academy. Quietly I shared this old wound with Lue.

My long years of silence coupled with the need to choose only the simplest of words made my delivery so halting I feared he would not, could not, grasp my meaning. Nevertheless, I persevered, and it seemed to me that as I spoke, his anxious, injured look lifted a little.

When I finished, I sank back into my chair completely drained. Lue, animated as he'd not been for weeks, leaped to his feet and thrust out his chest.

"Look, Miss Fanny." With both hands he pointed to each of his eyes and nostrils, his mouth. "In my front are five openings." He wriggled his ears. "On my sides are two more." He leaned close. "From now, I open *all* for learning."

"Yes," I laughed. "Oh, yes."

Teaching Lue was work I could put my whole heart into, and I gave it my all. No teacher ever boasted a more rewarding pupil. Faith, there wasn't one scholar in the Sunday school who could match Lue in originality or breadth of inquiry. He was not, however, alone in replacing heathen garb with civilized dress: American hat, shoes, stockings, shirt, and suit. Many of the Chinese also seemed as comfortable as Lue with knife and fork and the high culture implied in their exclusive use. Some even read, wrote, and spoke English with his same fluency.

"Our Chinamen have become gentlemen," I exulted.

"They only *seem* like gentlemen," Phoebe corrected. "They've acquired the veneer of civilization, not the heart. Now I know why God has kept me in North Adams."

While we were children, I had played at teaching, Phoebe at preaching, faithfully carrying out all Baptist practices, singing hymns and calling up mourners, baptizing believers through immersion by substituting sweet-smelling hay for water. And when Father had finally repaid his debts and given us permission to hire a maid, Phoebe had applied for service to the American Board of Foreign Missions. The Board—explaining that they did not think single women could be brave, steady, or contented far from home—had turned her down, and she had since been teaching Sunday school, distributing tracts to the destitute, proselytizing in rum shops.

Having been away when the Chinamen arrived, she was not one

of their teachers. Nevertheless, Phoebe became convinced she was to be God's instrument in saving them, and she believed the key to their conversion lay in the reading of God's word in their own language. Lue warned her that most of the scholars had so little, if any, schooling in China that many could already read English as well or better than they could Chinese. I told her the pastors had long ago presented each Chinaman with the Gospels in English. She sent for seventy-four copies of the New Testament in Chinese from the American Bible Society anyway.

The very hour the Bibles arrived, she enjoined me to help her carry them to the factory for distribution. The Chinamen were about to sit down for supper, but they listened politely to Phoebe's announcement that she'd brought food for their souls. Lue leaped up to help us, and as we cleared a table and arranged the Bibles in neat stacks, the Sunday scholars crowded close.

Suddenly I noticed Lue stiffen. Glancing up, I saw one of the older men slipping into the kitchen. That the cook was being informed of our presence could only mean trouble, and I whispered to Phoebe, "We should leave."

"No," she said. "This is what the Almighty has called me to do, and I will do it. Don't worry, He will protect us."

Scooping up a pile of Gospels, she began to pass them out. At that moment the cook stalked out of the kitchen yelling and capering in fantastic style. Charlie barked something incomprehensible. The cook, ranting even louder, stormed across the dining room, bearing down on us, the Bibles piled on the table. Phoebe walked toward him, her step firm. The Sunday scholars scattered, flapping and chattering like frightened magpies—except Lue, who ran in front of Phoebe, trying to ward off the cook.

I hurried after him. But we were as helpless as sparrows against a hawk. Brutally knocking Lue aside, the cook plunged past Phoebe and me and flipped over the table. Above the crash I heard cries of terror. The cook, swooping like a bird of prey, snatched a Bible from the heap on the floor, spun around.

"Come!" he commanded.

His knowledge of English surprised me. What else had he been hiding? What was his ploy now?

"You afraid?" he sneered.

Ignoring him, I leaned down to check if Lue was badly hurt. He was already picking up Bibles, shards of broken crockery.

"Praise Jesus you're all right."

Red-faced, he apologized, "The cook shames us all."

"No, only himself," I assured Lue.

Straightening back up, I looked for Phoebe. She was following the cook into the kitchen, Charlie and a gaggle of Chinamen close behind. I chased after them with Lue tugging at my skirt, urging me to leave the cook to Charlie, Phoebe to him. Together we squeezed through the horde of Chinamen massed noisily at the door.

Inside the kitchen all was strangely quiet. Startled, I stared at Phoebe, the cook. What had happened? I wondered. Although the cook had demanded she come to the kitchen, he was standing to one side while Phoebe was stirring soup in the cauldron, tasting it, nodding approval. He looked taken aback, she as composed as if she were at her own stove. Charlie hovered uncertainly between them. And if any of the three noticed Lue or me, they gave no sign.

Utterly perplexed, I watched Phoebe lift the lid from another pot, releasing a plume of steam, the stench of burned rice. She turned to the cook. "I'm sorry. I've been inconsiderate." Smiling, she reached for the New Testament still in his hand. "The Good News will keep for another hour—your rice won't."

The cook frowned. His grip on the Gospel tightened. "Your foreign God powerful?" he asked.

"*All*-powerful," Phoebe said. "He is everywhere present and knows all things."

"He see us here?"

"He is watching."

Swiftly, unexpectedly, the cook opened the door to the stove and hurled the Gospel into the fire. "Then ask your God save book."

Despite the burst of heat from the open stove, I shivered. Phoebe closed her eyes and folded her hands in prayer. Lue leaped for the tongs, Charlie for the cook, who felled both with well-aimed blows.

Giving Lue my hand, I helped him to his feet, all the while silently pleading with the Almighty to make a miracle, to show the Chinamen His mighty power by saving His word. But inside the stove the Bible buckled, twisting the gold cross stamped on its cover.

As the pages curled and charred, vanished in the flames, I saw in Lue's face a disappointment that reflected my own.

"Where your God? Where power?" the cook scoffed.

Charlie, rising to his feet, opened his mouth, closed it, looked over at me, then at Phoebe. I, too, turned to her. Behind me, the Chinamen's chatter became muted, stopped.

Phoebe, her eyes shining with faith and love, calmly explained that God could have saved the Gospel, that in letting it burn He was showing us He had other plans. "What these are we cannot see since the Almighty moves in a way unknown to men and can outride any of our ideas. Nor do we need to know. We have only to accept and trust."

I knew she spoke the Truth. Yet I felt defeated. How, then, could she convince the Chinamen? How could I persuade Lue?

A miracle like the one I had prayed for in the Chinamen's kitchen was, of course, possible. This I knew from my Bible and my brother-in-law William Dumville.

William, a Union veteran, had married my sister Cynthia shortly after the War of the Rebellion. Although six years younger than Cynthia, he was hollow-eyed and wasted. His chestnut whiskers were already graying, his hair thin, and a tremor in his left hand indicated the onset of palsy. His condition was the result of his imprisonment in Andersonville, where shelter was a hole scraped out of the ground, the daily ration no more than a handful of beans and cornmeal, and the single source of water served as sewer too. Yet it was in that Secesh Valley of Gehenna that William witnessed the saving hand of our Heavenly Father. For when the men held a great and earnest prayer meeting in which they cried out to God to send them water, He heard their parched whispers and ripped open the heavens in a terrible storm. Lightning flashed. Thunder rolled loud as heavy cannon. Rain poured down in torrents, hewing deep gullies in the sandy soil. In the morning, a pure spring spurted from one of those excavations. Nor did the stream dry while prisoners abided there.

"That stream was a miracle," I told Lue. But Lue, having not seen the stream for himself, would not believe it. Indeed, just as the Master's own disciple, Thomas, had demanded visible proof of His claims, Lue and his countrymen clamored for the pastors to demon-

strate Jesus' power, to prove He is Lord. And when the pastors refused, so many scholars refused to stay for worship after the hour
of study that the pastors disbanded the Chinamen's Sunday school.

Some of the Chinamen accompanied their teachers to church services out of loyalty. These our pastors made welcome, inviting them
to enroll in Bible-study classes and prayer groups, to take part in
ice-cream socials, picnics, and entertainments. Not a few in our
congregation protested. But Reverend Sandler insisted on their com-
pliance: "Just sitting down by the side of a Chinaman will be teaching him Christianity."

Lue joined Phoebe's Sunday school class. He and I continued
his lessons on weekday evenings, and as his vocabulary developed, I came to see that he possessed wonderful intuitive and
reflective powers. Yet he could not seem to understand that questioning me during study was good, challenging Phoebe in Bible
study unacceptable.

At first, Phoebe told me, she had been lenient. When Lue had
asked, "Why didn't God stop Judas from betraying Jesus?" she had
patiently explained that without Judas's betrayal, there would have
been no crucifixion, no redemption. But when Lue had persisted,
"If God is all-powerful, why does He allow evil?" she had spoken
more sternly.

"We must not blame God for sin. And we must trust Him to
bring good out of calamity. Look at the enslavement of the African.
That was evil. Yet it brought him to America for Christianizing just
as the greed of capital brought you. It was also the opium trade that
truly opened China to missionaries. So you can rest assured the Almighty will always triumph."

Lue, apparently unmoved by either Phoebe's reasoning or her
consternation, had parried, "Like a tyrant triumphs." Then Phoebe,
appalled at his blasphemy, had admonished, "God is not an earthly
ruler, and reason cannot be applied to Divine mystery."

Long ago Reverend Sandler had used these same words to stem
a flood of similar questions from me. Lue, however, was not
swayed. Yet it seemed to me there could be no one more capable
than Lue of entering the spirit of Christ.

As fond of animals as Phoebe was, he built little doors into the
baseboards of our first-floor rooms so her cats could move freely in
and out of the cellar and thence outside. He helped her devise clever

ruses to render useless the traps I set for mice. He nailed a "birdboard" outside the attic windows so the birds that swooped down to feed on the cracked corn we put out in winter would not fall prey to the cats.

I could, on account of weak lungs, walk but slowly. Yet Lue accompanied me on walks in the wooded hills that surround our valley, and to keep me from tiring, he would suggest we rest in rocky nooks shaded with hemlocks and white birches or near fragrant jungles of wild roses, where we could enjoy the song sparrow's clear, penetrating trill, the goldfinches' warble.

Having his arm to lean on, I ventured farther with him than I had ever dared on my own. Lue, acutely observant, discovered the tiny lavender-tinted red sandwort that I'd seen only in books. When I took a pair of small scissors from my reticule to snip a specimen, he stayed my hand and gently pried loose a few for transplanting in Father's garden instead.

Likewise, when I admired a patch of rough-leaved purple asters or some white rock saxifrage, Lue would not pluck bouquets for a vase but would dig them up and transplant them whole. Faith, he was so tenderhearted that he surrounded Father's spring flower beds with rows of sticks lest sprouting seedlings be crushed by careless feet. He devised a mixture of root and wood ashes that drove away—but did not kill—the black bugs which would otherwise have turned the leaves of the tomato plants into lacework.

Noticing how eagerly Father waited for the first corn of the season, Lue germinated seeds in a pan of shallow water before planting so they would have a head start and be ready for harvest weeks earlier than usual. Neither did he forget Bridget.

God had reminded Father too frequently of the uncertainty of life for him to be loose with his purse, and the wages he paid were so meager the girl could not satisfy either her vanity or her morbid curiosity. Lue, however, was as open-handed as Father was closed, and he bought Bridget the ribbons and bits of trimming that she coveted. He took her to see the circus, a visiting Japanese troupe walk barefoot up ladders of sharp-edged swords, a minstrel show.

Yet Lue's kindnesses would not ransom him from Hell should he die unsaved, and I fretted, "Why can you recognize and satisfy everyone's needs except your own need for Jesus?"

"Because I *don't* need Jesus. *You* are the one who came to the factory when I was imprisoned. *You* freed my body by inviting me to your home, my mind by teaching me. *You* make my happiness, not Jesus, and you make me so glad that I want to make you and your family glad, too."

As Lue's teacher and elder, I should have explained that all happiness comes from Jesus, that earthly happiness, however great, cannot equal the joy awaiting us in Heaven. Nor can we rely on any mortal. But never before had anybody warmed my heart with such a pretty speech, and I could not give it up for Truth any more than I could stop stoking hot my love for the Master through laudanum.

In other Chinamen, the seeds sown by the pastors in the factory Sunday school gradually sprouted and ripened. Two in Phoebe's class confessed Christ openly, another came forward as an upright inquirer, and a half dozen from other classes and churches were baptized.

Lue never missed a Sunday of worship. But he continued to bow before the pagan altar at the factory, to honor the Chinese sages whose writings he had studied in his village school. Faith, when Phoebe rebuked a convert she discovered practicing the pagan ritual of ancestor worship, Lue defended the Chinaman, arguing that the ancestral tablet was no different from the tombstones in our cemeteries, the incense the boy lit before it had the same significance as the flowers we lay on graves, the deep bows he made reflected nothing more than respect, like the bows gentlemen make to ladies.

Neither Phoebe nor I could make Lue recognize that his reasoning was false, and I began to fear not only for Lue's immortal soul but for his mortal happiness, my own. What if Phoebe, becoming weary, accused him of being insincere in seeking Truth, of attending Sunday school solely to insinuate himself into our family? What if Father were to make Lue unwelcome or forbid our lessons?

Sharing my fears with Lue, I begged him to temper his speech. He could not have looked more wounded had I boxed his ears, and I knew he was remembering his China teacher's betrayal.

"I will never betray you," I assured him. "But I'm dependent on

Father. That's why you must guard your tongue with him and with Miss Phoebe."

"I understand," he said.

But his expression was as mournful as if I had broken faith with him. And on the cover of his journal, which he'd previously shared with me, he wrote: *For Lue Gim Gong's eyes alone.*

That fall our pastors organized a revival. The fortnight of meetings, though held at the Baptist church, were of a nondenominational character. Mr. DeWitt, a forceful exhorter, came from Boston to lead the services, and a choir of more than one hundred singers and dozens of church helpers, like Phoebe, assisted the preacher by raising the spirits of worshipers and laboring with the unredeemed.

So that everyone might have the opportunity to benefit, manufacturers closed their factories, merchants their stores. Families from outlying farms came in wagons filled with provisions and set up makeshift tents of sheets or quilts, living on the ground. Some stayed in the open.

During his first sermon, Mr. DeWitt sounded solemn notes of warning on the certitude of eternal damnation for the unsaved, thundering with such energy that his face swelled red, his eyes bulged, and sweat poured from him in rivulets although the windows were wide open, the morning unusually brisk.

At his sharp hits and pointed illustrations, many of the unsaved fell to the floor wailing, "What shall I do to be saved?" Others sobbed, "I yield! I yield!" I became tormented by thoughts of Lue burning in the fires of Hell. I could feel the heat of its flames licking, scorching the soles of his feet, smell brimstone, his roasting flesh, and I groaned in agony. Lue, seated beside me, remained absolutely still.

In meeting after meeting the struggle for souls went on. Worshipers held up dozens of prayers simultaneously. There were inspiriting Gospel songs, prolonged, heart-searching testimonials, recitations of favorite Bible verses. Mr. DeWitt, coming down from the pulpit, encouraged and instructed seekers in the joy of salvation with fiery, unrestrained exhorting. Ever more frequent were the shouts of "Praise Jesus," "Hallelujah," and "Glory," from penitents—their faces radiant and their clothes askew from their exertions—crossing over into Beulah Land.

On the third day I, too, was felled by the Holy Ghost. Lying prostrate in the aisle, I wept with sorrow and shame for my weak faith; my inability to be all-satisfied by Jesus; my use of laudanum to keep the mark of God's grace burning bright, to find the peace which should have come from the promise that happiness deferred on earth would be mine for all eternity. But even as I wept I hungered for the joy and peace laudanum gave.

With laudanum I felt afresh the otherwise dimly remembered thrill of Jesus' embrace. With laudanum I courted dreams. Dreams in which I refused to leave Culloden. Or in which I did leave but chose loyalty to self instead of family, returning to southern sunshine before the bitter cold of northern winters pulled me down. Or in which I did fulfill my duty to Father and Julia but was not robbed of my health.

Always, always in these dreams I matriculated from Uncle John's academy and became a teacher like him. And now I was just such a teacher with Lue. Still I was not content. Still I sought and found relief in laudanum more than prayer.

"Weep! Weep for mercy!" Mr. DeWitt urged. "Howl! Howl out loud, for your miseries have come upon you."

Springing to my feet as by an altogether supernatural impulse, I cried, "Forgive me, Lord. Oh, forgive me." And when Mr. DeWitt asked those who wanted to be God's children to manifest that wish by going to the altar, I dropped onto my knees and crawled toward it as a humble penitent.

At the altar I renewed my pledge of allegiance to the Master, publicly acknowledging, "You are King, your authority absolute," silently vowing, "Save Lue and I'll give up laudanum."

Too overcome to rise, I remained on my knees in prayer. Suddenly Jesus came to me as He had in the river and lifted me up, restoring my strength.

Praising His name, I walked back to my seat, saw Lue had left our pew for the mourners' bench and was weeping in red-hot earnest. Thoroughly aroused, I clapped and called out, "Yes, Master. Take him. Take Lue now."

Church helpers, led by Phoebe, crowded around to labor with him. Entreating and admonishing, they warned Lue that an upright life was not enough to save him from hellfire, that trying to work out his salvation through merit was the same as if he fell into a river and tried to save himself from drowning by clinging to his own queue.

"The only remedy is Jesus Christ," Phoebe pressed. "Open your heart so He can enter and drive out Satan."

Lue, turning deathly pale, rolled on the floor, pounding his chest, moaning over and over, "I'm a sinner. I'm a sinner."

Quickly Mr. DeWitt directed the choir to sing "He leadeth me."

Falling down beside Lue, I implored, "Accept Jesus. Own Him as Master."

Above us Mr. DeWitt called for the Holy Ghost to enter Lue.

Turning my face to Heaven, I cried, "Yes, Lord. Give Lue the Spirit."

Phoebe and the church helpers added their pleas to mine.

Lue, writhing on the floor, moaned, "Come. Come into me. Come now." Then, in wonder, "I feel it. Yes! Yes, I feel the Holy Ghost. I repent. I do believe. I do."

His face glowing with the light of Truth, Lue leaped to his feet speaking in tongues. Burning with a zeal clearly not his own, he swayed backward and forward, dancing up the aisle to the altar, where he made of himself a living cross, crying, "Jesus, I want Jesus to save me, to wash me white."

I shouted out praise for the triumph of faith over sin, for the miracle of joy through Jesus and Jesus alone.

Over two hundred souls, many of them Chinese, were saved during this wide and deep awakening.

At the love feast that ended the revival, Mr. DeWitt spoke of how our community's special ministry to Mr. Sampson's Chinamen brought to mind John Sergeant's work among the Mohican Indians, who had once roamed our hills. "He also used consecrated families to raise rude pagans into the condition of polished people by transmitting Christian virtues through personal contact. Then, when the Mohicans were removed from their land, Mr. Sergeant's civilized primitives became the source for greater work by spreading the True Doctrine to heathen Indians in their New York reservation. So may the Chinamen you have raised up one day witness for Christ in dark China."

On every side I heard hearty amens, Phoebe's the heartiest of all, since a missionary is not content with a single convert but wants to found churches. My amen died unspoken in my throat, for I believed God had a different purpose for Lue.

SUM JUI

Toishan, China
1875—1876

Gim Gong's letters were full of praise for the foreign ghosts. They had generously opened a free school at his factory. His teacher was kind, encouraging questions, inviting him to her house. Their Jesus God, unlike any of our Gods, was all-knowing.

Hnnnh, what kind of a school has women for teachers? What kind of teacher permits questions from a child? And if that Jesus God is all-knowing, how was he caught and killed? Remembering how easily Elder Sister had gained Gim Gong's trust with her flattery, how she'd then tricked him, I feared the foreign ghosts were doing the same.

Hadn't Fourth Brother accused Gim Gong of following foreign-ghost ways when he ran away? *Here in Gold Mountain,* he'd written, *blood kin often demand independence and fly their own way. So, too, has Gim Gong.*

Yet Gim Gong never once failed in his duty to family. At each festival he sent money home. And, as was proper, he directed these gifts to his grandfather.

Ba added to the family land. His good humor restored, he arranged a marriage for Wai Seuk. He bought the house we lived in and gave Hok Yee the deed.

Then Ba died. Because of his age and poor health, his death was not unexpected. Likewise, Hok Yee and I knew Elder Brother would inherit all Ba's land, chattel, and authority; tradition decreed it. And with Elder Brother and Sister so empty of heart and liver, we braced ourselves for trouble.

We buried Ba shortly after spring plowing. They waited until we safely brought in the harvest before Elder Brother announced, "We will no longer work as one family."

A just man would then have shared the land, farm tools, and livestock equally among the brothers. But Elder Brother was the kind of person who borrowed polished rice and repaid it with un-threshed grain. He kept everything except the fields and orchards. These he grudgingly divided among Third and Fourth Brother and himself, taking care to keep the largest and best for his own use. He gave nothing to Hok Yee.

The shock I saw in my husband's face was a reflection of my own: to be excluded entirely was a possibility we had not considered.

We were gathered in Ba's house, now Elder Brother's. As on any other day, smoke, chopping and sizzling noises, and cooking smells drifted in from the kitchen where Third Sister's daughter-in-law and Bik Wun were preparing the evening rice. I could hear Wai Seuk's wife, Moon Ho, in the courtyard singing to our grandson, Little Tiger, while feeding the livestock, their laughter rising over the chickens' eager scratching and pecking, the pigs' messy splashing. The rest of the family was assembled around the table in the central room. Was there one among them who would speak for Hok Yee?

Not Third Brother or his wife. The one tall and thin as a bamboo pole, the other short and narrow as a bamboo leaf, they'd long ago learned to sway with the wind. And they'd taught their son and daughter-in-law to do the same. Living under the same roof as Elder Brother and Sister, they'd had to or they would have snapped and died. Nor was it possible for them to move, though Elder Brother had given Third Brother a share of the land; they needed Elder Brother's buffalo, plow, and harrow to work it.

Fourth Sister was safe because of her husband in Gold Mountain. When I raised my eyebrows questioningly, however, she looked away. She'd been cool to us since Gim Gong had offended Fourth Brother. She would not support us now.

My firstborn's rage was clear in the awful grinding of his teeth, the veins in his temple pressing against his skin, pulsing. But since his marriage and the birth of Little Tiger, Elder Brother and Sister hated him worse than ever. Aware anything he said would likely provoke rather than help, Wai Seuk would force himself to remain silent.

The son I'd lost would be silent, too. Grown into a large, pale man with fish eyes and a fish mouth, Wai Yin was too full of opium to be anything else. He and Bik Wun had been formally married the same year as Wai Seuk and Moon Ho, but Wai Yin had no son. Neither was he likely to father one soon. I'd seen Bik Wun weeping at the temple, overheard her choked whispers to the Celestial Fairy that her husband could not lie with her as a man.

And Ma? In the moons since Ba's death she'd shrunk, becoming even quieter, more fearful of hard words.

It was she who broke the silence, however.

"What about Hok Yee?" she asked.

Like a cat that had finally snared a long-chased mouse, Elder Brother purred, "He's adopted."

Ma's grip on her cane tightened. "All that's missing in Hok Yee is the ten moons in my belly." Pushing down with both fists, she hoisted herself up from her chair, stumped across the room, took the family's book of names from the altar, and shook it at Elder Brother. "Ba wrote Hok Yee's name in the *ga bo*. He's family and entitled to a share."

She hobbled back to the table, thrust the book in front of Third Brother. "If not for the luck Hok Yee brought this family, you and Fourth Brother wouldn't have been born." Dropping heavily onto her chair, she turned to Fourth Sister. "You wouldn't have a husband."

Red-faced, Third Brother clutched his stool as if he'd otherwise fall. Fourth Sister fussed with the chopsticks and bowls on the table.

Elder Sister curled her lip. "Ma, don't worry your heart. Hok Yee has an inheritance. He has a house."

"They can't eat bricks," Ma said tartly.

Were we to stop eating together as family too? Swiftly I counted the chopsticks Fourth Sister was clicking together in a nervous fidget. Four pairs were missing. My belly churning with panic, I drew in my breath with a hiss, catching Hok Yee's eye, then glanced down at the chopsticks, the sacks of rice stacked against the wall, the dried turnips and sweet potatoes stored in the loft above the altar. He understood. All the harvest was here; our house was empty.

"I sweat for this harvest," he told Elder Brother. "So did my wife and son. You must give us our share."

Elder Brother hesitated.

"We've been feeding you all these moons," Elder Sister said. "And Wai Seuk eats enough for three men."

Like an actor on a stage, Elder Brother picked up his cue. "Yes, Moon Ho is a rice bucket too. Besides, Third Brother's daughter-in-law and mine were free; yours cost the family plenty. I'd say between your house, your daughter-in-law's bride-price, and your son's wedding banquet, you've received more than your share."

Hok Yee, slow to anger, snapped. "Everything was paid for with Gim Gong's earnings. And you know Moon Ho cost very little because Elder Sister made certain Ba asked the matchmaker for a plain girl. The wedding banquet was only five tables. You're just eating vinegar because Wai Yin had none. But that's because he was marrying a child-bride. And whose fault was—"

Seeing Elder Brother and Sister darken with rage, I interrupted, my teeth clenched to force back my own anger, to keep my voice low and humble. "At least let us have the land Ba bought with Gim Gong's money and my wedding jewelry."

"Gim Gong's money? Wedding jewelry?" Elder Brother and Sister echoed.

"Don't pretend ignorance," Ma scolded.

"Ma," Elder Brother cautioned sharply. "Now that Ba's gone, it's not for you to command but to submit."

Ma's eyes filled with tears. Yes, a woman's three obediences are to her father, her husband, and then her son. But only a snake would press his right rather than yield to his mother's age.

"Better to have no son than a bad one," she cried.

Fourth Brother's wife poured Ma a bowl of tea, presented it respectfully with both hands. "Hok Yee can work Fourth Brother's fields as a tenant," she said.

A packet of money from Gim Gong for the Moon Festival and then New Year, husbanded carefully, brought us through the winter. Our meals were not much more than rice porridge or noodle soup with pickled vegetables. But eating in our own house, free of Elder

Brother and Sister's carping, was like being released from a harsh taskmaster. In truth, we knew happiness despite our mourning for Ba and worries for our future.

Though I was a grandmother, my blood still ran hot for my husband; the fire in his belly burned fierce for me. Wai Seuk lingered near his wife, stealing glances like a lovesick calf instead of a man two years married; Moon Ho's round face, broad cheeks, and large, honest eyes beamed her warm feelings for him. The two were well matched, their characters as sturdy as their bodies. And Little Tiger tottered, laughing, among the four of us, weaving strong ties of pride and pleasure.

In the spring, Hok Yee and I hired ourselves out to landlords, leaving Wai Seuk and Moon Ho to work Fourth Brother's land. Fourth Sister pressed Elder Brother until he permitted Wai Seuk the use of his buffalo and tools. Gim Gong sent another packet of money to see us through to the harvest.

Under normal conditions we would not have needed more. But there was almost no rain that year, and the drought reduced the harvest so that our share of Fourth Brother's crop was too small for us to live on. Worse, insects had attacked the orchards, and the landlord who hired us counted against my wages each tree I failed to save. He also deducted double for every little mistake, even if the fault, like the hoe Hok Yee broke because of the hard soil, was not ours.

With that kind of accounting, we received no wages but owed money instead. *Hnnnh,* if Moon Ho had hired out too instead of working Fourth Brother's land with Wai Seuk, we would have been even deeper in debt.

Is it any wonder we lit incense in thanksgiving for Gim Gong in Gold Mountain?

FANNY

North Adams, Massachusetts
1875—1877

When I'd vowed to give up laudanum to save Lue's soul, I'd known I would be sacrificing the dreams and peace it brought. I never suspected that its loss would cause me to become so agitated I could scarcely see or breathe, that I'd shake as one in a palsy.

Claiming I'd been felled as usual by the onset of winter, I stumbled to my bed. There, hidden from prying eyes, I surrendered to uncontrolled shivering and long, violent fits of weeping, moaning and twitching and flailing like a creature caught in a trap. My agony was truly awful, and I confess my strength to endure came not from the desire to do right, but from fear. Fear that if I gave in to my need and broke my vow, Lue's soul would yet be lost.

Long after I rose from my bed, my nerves jangled with weary irritation. One day, while distributing temperance tracts with Phoebe, we saw some cadets from Father Matthew's Total Abstinence Society seize a barrel of intoxicating liquor, empty it onto the street. As the liquid ran into the gutter, men and boys dropped to their knees and lapped it up. Phoebe gasped at their debasement. Recognizing in them my own neediness, I bowed my head in shame.

Haunted by unrest, I was too abstracted to tutor Lue beyond a half hour at a stretch. I had to wedge my feet under my chair to keep from leaping up and fleeing the parlor when Reverend Sandler stopped for a long pastoral visit.

"You will, of course, replace your pagan name with a Christian one," Reverend Sandler instructed Lue, as he did all baptismal candidates.

"No," Lue said.

Reverend Sandler's wild, gray brows shot up disbelievingly. "No Chinaman has ever refused."

Quickly I assured our pastor that Lue's refusal was not an indication of paganism or breach of respect but a reflection of his attachment to his home country. I explained how, during our first winter together, I'd noticed Lue studying the Chinese views in our stereoscopic collection with an application almost painful in its intensity, discovered he knew scarcely anything of China or its people outside of his own small village.

"So I showed him Phoebe's *A Missionary's Guide to China*. He had to look up most of the words, but he read every page." I smiled with feigned cheerfulness, frank teacherly pride. "He's since read all the books on China in the town's lending library."

Reverend Sandler returned my smile, but his was one of pity at a woman trying to understand something beyond her ken. Sternly he insisted that a new life in Christ called for a new, Christian name.

Locking my fingers to stop their trembling, I begged Lue to surrender.

Lue, however, was firm. "Our Father in Heaven wants my soul, not my name."

Even after Reverend Sandler catapulted off his chair, drew himself up to his full height, and lectured Lue, the boy held his ground. And although every drop of blood left his face when Reverend Sandler turned him down for baptism, Lue did not yield.

Phoebe suggested that Lue prove his sincerity by touring the valley's Sunday schools and churches in native attire, singing hymns in Chinese, and testifying.

"Be exhibited and petted like a tamed monkey?" he cried. "Never."

Two livid spots blossomed on Phoebe's cheeks. Leaning forward, I caught Lue's eyes, flashed him a look of warning.

"Miss Phoebe," he said more quietly. "Didn't Jesus tell us He came to fulfill, not to destroy?"

The spots on her cheeks darkened. But Phoebe, utterly honest, acknowledged that Lue's reasoning was Truth, and she invited him to join her Wednesday evening prayer group.

Through powerful exhorting, Lue brought two inquirers in the group to own Jesus as Savior. He also canvassed diligently for our church renovation fund and for subscriptions to establish a reading room to counteract the evil influence of the dramshops.

Reverend Sandler, won over by these good works, finally acceded to Lue's desire, baptizing him as Lue Gim Gong. I praised Jesus for His mercy.

The name Gim Gong, Lue had told me long ago, signified his family's hopes for gold, and he faithfully, uncomplainingly sent them generous remittances several times a year. To me, however, the meaning of his name—Double Brilliance—reflected Lue's mental riches, his genius with plants. Faith, Lue played with plants the way other boys try their skills in games, mixing pulverized charcoal into the earth around Father's petunias, tinting the white blossoms with red veins, the violet with irregular spots of bluish black.

The Chinese lilies Father grew had one or two small, fragrant blossoms at the end of each slender stalk. The ones Lue raised boasted thick stems with double rows of heavily scented blossoms so extraordinary in size and beauty that Mr. Hurd asked Father's permission to photograph them for stereoscopic views.

Neighbors and friends with cuttings that wouldn't root came to Lue for advice as if he were an elderly professor and not a boy of seventeen. Lue, naturally curious, delighted in the challenges they brought him, and in a corner of the greenhouse that I called his sanitarium, he patiently, skillfully nursed their sick plants back to health.

Lue attributed his aptitude in the garden to his mother. "She grows the best oranges in our village," he told everyone proudly. But her skills must have been instinctive, for he had not known the inner workings of plants until I'd dissected one for him and explained the function of each part.

He'd been fascinated, as he was by all knowledge, and in time it occurred to me that Lue's intuitive affinity with nature combined with scientific knowledge could be formidable. So I began giving him books written by plant improvers in Europe. Despite the difficulty of the texts, Lue studied them eagerly, and through pointed questions and extensive discussions together, he gradually came to grasp the ideas their authors presented, to connect them to what had before only been play.

For such brilliance to be shackled to a factory bench rankled. Nor did Lue make any secret of how much he preferred his work with plants to the repetitiveness of his labor in the factory, the quiet of the garden to the noise from the belt-driven pegging machines, the open air to a closed room where whirling cylinders of sandpaper constantly spewed choking dust.

"If not for my desire to continue studying with you," he confided when his three-year contract with Mr. Sampson expired, "I would quit the factory like I did my uncle's store." And I told him, "If I were my own mistress, I would free you." But I was not.

Faith, when Mr. Sampson told his Chinamen they would be working on an equal basis with the Crispins—receiving an hourly wage and boarding outside the factory—I could not even invite Lue to live with me. He was then still in the thralldom of superstition, and I knew Father would never permit a heathen to join our household.

But the Almighty moves in mysterious ways, His wonders to perform: the failure of a New York banking house plunged the country into a depression, and our manufacturers, including Mr. Sampson, reduced the hours of labor for their operatives, freeing Lue to work out in experiments with plants the ideas he had been developing through reading and close conversation with me.

Lue was intrigued by Thomas Malthus's theory that favorable variations are preserved, unfavorable destroyed, thereby forming new species. And, like the British scientist Charles Darwin, Lue wished to apply Mr. Malthus's observations on heredity, selection, and crossing to the development of plants. Only where Mr. Darwin was experimenting in order to discover and set down laws, Lue wanted to make experiments that would result in something useful.

From his mother, he had learned how to help nature bring about improvements by taking the pollen from one plant, placing it upon the pistil of another, then screening the blossom with a bit of gauzy material to prevent its fertilization by insects. Using these techniques, he crossed Father's best-looking raspberry with a wild berry that had a small, ugly, yellowish fruit but was very sweet.

Carefully, Lue and I examined and discussed each fruit that resulted from this cross, harvesting seeds only from the ones we agreed were both sweet and at least somewhat attractive. These seeds Lue then planted in oblong flats he made for this purpose.

As the seedlings thrust their tiny heads above the soil, Lue and I studied them, noting those which grew quickly or slowly. While the berries were developing, we observed them for size, color, and shape. When they ripened, we picked and tasted them, discussing what we liked, what we thought was wrong.

The process was long—Phoebe said tedious—but Lue and I found it exciting in the extreme. And I became convinced that just as God had kept Phoebe in North Adams to help save the Chinamen, He had kept me there for Lue.

As the depression deepened, manufacturers reduced hours and wages so that even laborers lucky enough to have employment were earning less than a dollar a day. Unemployed men and women crowded our streets; there were so many poor the work farm could not accommodate them, the lockup had to be turned into a temporary shelter.

Father's store lost most of its customers. Lue could not meet his obligations to his family or his landlady except by borrowing from his countrymen. Where Father stormed, however, Lue stayed cheerful: the fewer hours of labor Mr. Sampson offered his operators, the more time Lue had for experimenting and study; and since Mr. Sampson had promised to restore wages as soon as there was an improvement in trade, Lue was confident he would be able to repay his mounting debts.

Only when his father lost his land did worry weigh Lue down so that even in the greenhouse his step lost its bounce, his face its happy glow. Determined to ease his burden, I turned to Father the very hour after Lue was baptized and begged permission for the boy to board with us. That way he could send home what he was giving to his landlady or he could borrow a little less.

Father, as I'd feared, stormed that his losses were too severe. But Lue's need gave me courage, and instead of cowering in retreat, I pressed my claim, I persuaded Phoebe to throw her influence to my support.

When we finally won Father's approval, I would have cheered had it not been Sunday. Lue, moving into the room adjoining mine, danced up the stairs with his belongings. Laughing, he slapped the backs of the Chinamen who were helping him and tickled their ears.

The Chinamen showed none of Lue's relief or joy. And when we were alone, Lue reluctantly admitted that they considered his decision to live with us a betrayal. Indeed, they charged him with rejecting his people and being overly ambitious, of aspiring to a society and grade in life to which he'd not been born.

What would they say, I wondered, if they knew the full extent of my aspirations for Lue?

All the first-generation fruit from crossing the wild berry and raspberry had been ugly. Undaunted, Lue and I had laid our heads together and discussed the qualities of each fruit, the traits they suggested, any curious habits we'd observed.

How my heart beat quicker, Lue's breath grew unequal, while he was harvesting seeds from the berries we'd agreed were best. And, oh, the flutters of expectation as we looked for new seedlings. Tears were audible in Lue's voice when he had to weed out the weak from the strong. But nursing timid sprouts into bold, bearing vines, he chirped and trilled like a skylark.

The canes and leaves were dark, the flowers pale, and when Lue took their pollen for crossing with the first-generation bushes, I felt as if he were gathering stardust from moons in a night sky. Watching the fruit grow, Lue's eyes flashed pleasure at their beauty. Their taste, however, turned the smiles that wreathed our faces into grimaces.

So we started anew, discussing each berry, culling seeds, and raising new seedlings. Only, now, with Lue a member of our household, we no longer had to abandon our discussions just as crude, undigested ideas were taking shape. We could—and did—talk late into the night, then rise at dawn to talk some more, to check the progress of a promising seedling or fruit.

Lue's memory was a marvel. He needed no written records, keeping the progress of each plant in his head. Moreover, he seemed to have an ability not only to observe the most minute characters in a seedling but to match them with those that would likely appear in the next generation. If Lue was to develop and hone these God-given gifts, however, I would have to free him from any labor except with plants.

Having no means of my own, I planned to secure his freedom through Father—by convincing him to pay Lue for the gardening the boy was doing without compensation. Of course, I could not approach Father until a revival in trade allowed him to redeem the losses he'd been incurring. But the minute the red ink in Father's ledgers turned black, I'd take up the cudgels for Lue and win his freedom.

Just thinking about it made my heart quicken. Faith, I began building air castles in which Lue was not only free but already winning acclaim for extraordinary horticultural feats. "When did you first know you were nurturing genius?" people would ask. In answer I would show them the photograph Lue and I had taken to commemorate his baptism, the one with me seated and Lue standing behind, one hand resting trustingly on my shoulder. I would point out the boy's youth, the pride visible in the set of my lips, my chin. "Even then," I would say. "Even then."

And so real to me were these air castles that I never once gave thought to what would happen if the manufacturers again broke their pledge.

With the long-awaited revival in trade, four-wheeled carts began rattling across our brick pavements, hauling raw materials and manufactured goods between the depot and factories. Stacks belched black smoke from seven in the morning until five in the afternoon, sometimes later, and there was the constant hum of machinery. But there was no rise in the laborers' pay, and outraged union leaders called for work stoppages at all the factories.

Lue burst into the parlor with the news. "The Chinese are joining the Crispins in a walkout at Mr. Sampson's. The vote was unanimous."

Taken by surprise, I bolted upright on the chaise where I'd been resting and said stupidly, "Walkout? Unanimous? But Mr. Sampson and Father are good friends."

Lue cocked his head to one side. "Pardon?"

Breathing deeply in a desperate effort to remain calm, I explained, "If you go out on strike, Father will be furious. You're his guest. He'll feel you've betrayed his trust, his hospitality. He'll turn you out."

"Laborers are the ones who've been betrayed," Lue came back hotly. "How are we supposed to live?"

"You don't need to worry, you have a home here."

"I have debts. And my family needs more money. Besides, the strike will fail unless we stand united."

Fear for Lue and my plan made me blunt. "The strike will fail regardless."

"No."

"Wait," I said, holding up my hand. "Listen to me. Yes, Mr. Sampson has been unfair. Yes, the reasons for the strike are good. But the same was true for the strike you and your countrymen were instrumental in breaking."

Lue bristled. "We didn't know."

"That's my point. The French Canadians that Mr. Sampson brought in to break an earlier strike didn't know either. Mr. Sampson even got them to sign pledges never to join a union. But every one of them ended up a Crispin. They were the ones at the station trying to keep you out. Did they succeed? No. Now you and your countrymen are joining them, but you can't win either. Because Mr. Sampson and the rest of the manufacturers are too powerful."

"Maybe," Lue conceded. "But shouldn't we at least try?"

"Let the others try, not you."

"I've already given my word. I'll explain to Mr. Burlingame. He'll understand. . . ." Lue paled, broke off. I knew why. He'd been around Father long enough to know that for him the strike would be like a red rag shaken before an angry bull. He would *not* understand. He *would* turn Lue out, forbid him access to the garden and greenhouse.

Lue turned, looked out the window at the greenhouse. The fruit from the last cross had come up a lovely salmon color and had a sweet, translucent pulp, and we'd been talking of developing a cherry currant by crossing currant and grape pollen.

"You're my teacher," he said. "What should I do?"

I trembled at the responsibility he put on me, but I would not shirk it. Crossing the room, I stood beside him. "Keep your promise to go on strike. Just say nothing about it to anyone and refuse to picket. That way Father won't know. He won't expect you to go to the factory as a scab. It's too dangerous."

SUM JUI

Toishan, China
1877

In reply to our plea for help, Gim Gong sent barely enough to pay off our debt to the landlord. Work in Gold Mountain had become scarce, he wrote. His factory had been closed more than open. "So you cannot rely on me. I am not a bottomless measure. The money I'm sending you has been borrowed."

Had he been borrowing from our own people, I wondered, or from foreign ghosts? Perhaps his ghost teacher. He had sent us a picture of them together. She looked exactly like the ghost woman in Toi Sing: her nose was large, her waist tightly bound, and her long, melon-seed face had the same mildewed eyes. Gim Gong, too, seemed like a ghost to me: though I searched, I could not find the son I had carried under my heart for ten moons, the son I carried there still.

Of course Gim Gong had left home a boy. Yet it was not the missing years that made the man in the picture a ghostlike stranger. Nor was it the tight-fitting foreign-ghost jacket, the sash tied foolishly around his neck. A mother's eyes are not so easily deceived. No, it was Gim Gong's hand placed brazenly on his ghost teacher's shoulder.

She was, he'd written, older in years than I. Yet she had no husband. And from their shameless display of intimacy in the picture, I feared she was using Gim Gong as one. Had she seduced him with her ghost scent or by lending him money? Or had she snared him through that ghost religion?

In the worship hall in Toi Sing, men and women sat separate, as is proper. But returning Gold Mountain guests said that in their own country, ghost men and women threw away decency and sat side by side, that those who agreed to follow the Jesus God were subjected to all kinds of improper rites, customs that were not lawful. Could the ghost teacher have bewitched Gim Gong?

In the red faces of my husband and son and daughter-in-law, I saw my same fears. But our thoughts held too much dishonor for us to give them voice even between ourselves. How then could we speak frankly to Lo See? How could we show him that shameful picture and ask him to direct Gim Gong back to the right path? Nor could we try persuading Gim Gong to come home and take a seemly, carefully chosen bride. We were depending on his Gold Mountain wages.

Then Moon Ho, returning home from gathering brush with Bik Wun, brought news of more trouble. Fourth Brother had written that the foreign ghosts in First City were blaming our people for their lack of work. They were punishing ghost employers who hired our people by refusing to buy from their stores or eat in their restaurants. They were attacking our people as well, and Fourth Brother was selling his store and coming home.

If he took back his land, how would we live?

In his letters, Gim Gong had stopped asking about his flowers long ago. He wrote instead of his ghost teacher's garden. How it was larger than our biggest field. How there was so much variety and beauty in Gold Mountain plants. Still I had continued to care for his flowers. And while watering, plucking off dead blossoms and withered leaves, I would silently tell him, "The orchid you call Monkey has bloomed." Or, "The bamboo has sprouted three new shoots." "The chrysanthemum blossoms are as large as soup bowls."

During the dry summer, though, the soil had gradually pulled away from the rims of the pots, choking the roots, turning supple green stems into brittle brown stalks, killing fragrant blooms. Not one plant had survived, and I would have avoided the courtyard if I could. Since we lived too sparingly to burn bean oil for light, however, we were forced to pass our evenings outside until complete darkness drove us to bed.

Squatting near the privy, I turned out the soil from Gim Gong's pots, brushed them clean, then stacked them against the wall. Hok Yee, seated on the bench near the trellis, puffed on his pipe. Just outside the kitchen, Moon Ho washed our few bowls from evening rice. Wai Seuk, cradling Little Tiger in his arms, paced between us, lulling the child into sleep. Fretting over our troubles, we did not speak. In truth, we were like turtles shrunk into our own shells.

Then, one night, Wai Seuk suddenly stopped his pacing and blurted out, "I must go to Gold Mountain."

I dropped the pot in my hand. Its loud shattering wakened Little Tiger and he began to cry. Quickly Hok Yee set aside his pipe and reached for the boy. "There's no work to be had there," he said.

Wai Seuk passed Little Tiger to Hok Yee. "According to Fourth Uncle and Gim Gong. But look how many families are still receiving money from their men in Gold Mountain."

He sank down on a stool beside his wife. She nodded encouragingly, and I realized Wai Seuk was not speaking on a whim. He had discussed his leaving with Moon Ho and they were in agreement.

My throat tightened and I unfastened my collar to knead it. "Maybe they're borrowing like Gim Gong."

Hok Yee patted Little Tiger, soothing.

"Gim Gong and Fourth Brother might be exaggerating to serve their own interests," Wai Seuk pressed.

"Gim Gong perhaps," I acknowledged reluctantly. "But Fourth Brother wouldn't be coming back unless there really was no more money to be made."

"He has no son," Moon Ho said softly. "And Fourth Aunt is near thirty. Bik Wun says that in every letter Wai Yin writes for Ma, she has been urging Fourth Uncle to come home without delay."

Just as Hok Yee and I had once tried to convince Ba to accept our plan, Wai Seuk and Moon Ho were pushing us to act on theirs. But how could we risk sending Wai Seuk, the last of our sons, into known danger? Yes, returning Gold Mountain guests said that only the ghosts on Fourth Brother's side of the country were attacking our people, that those on Gim Gong's side were kind. But if Wai Seuk avoided the cruelty of the savage ghosts by going to Gim Gong's side of Gold Mountain, might he not fall to ghost enchantment as well?

Suddenly our circumstances did not seem quite as desperate as before. "We have no debt," I pointed out. "We have our own house."

"And Fourth Brother has not farmed in twenty years," Hok Yee added. "Surely he won't want to work his land himself."

"Even if Fourth Uncle doesn't reclaim his fields, we don't have enough food to last until the next harvest," Wai Seuk said. He pointed to Little Tiger asleep on Hok Yee's lap. "What will your grandson eat?"

"Gim Gong will send a packet of money for New Year," I assured him.

Hok Yee agreed. "Yes, he always does."

"What if his factory doesn't reopen or he can't borrow what we need?" Wai Seuk countered. "Hasn't he warned us we can't rely on him?"

I thought for a moment. "We can take apart a section of the house and sell the bricks."

"Do that *now* and buy my passage to Gold Mountain," Wai Seuk urged.

For a long time the only sound was our breathing, faint as the rustle of cicadas' wings. Slowly the light faded until I could only see shadows, the occasional flicker of a firefly. From far away a dog began to howl in long, drawn-out wails.

Sensing Hok Yee turn toward me, I went to sit beside him. In the darkness his hand, rough as the bark of an old yet familiar and well-loved tree, closed briefly over mine, showing me his heart. Silently, I eased Little Tiger onto my lap, drew him close for comfort. Hok Yee fumbled for his pipe, the sack of tobacco in his pocket. Moon Ho brought him a fragrant stub of incense. A moment later, his tobacco smoke curled around me, our grandson.

The new moon rose, its thin light cool and pale. Crickets chirped. There was the whine of a mosquito, a sharp slap, from Moon Ho or Wai Seuk I was not sure. Our neighbor's water buffalo lowed. Finally Hok Yee, his voice choked with emotion, said out loud what his touch had already told me.

"You're right, Wai Seuk. Our family is no different from a man standing up to his neck in water. The slightest ripple will be sufficient to drown us. We must take the long view and send you to Gold Mountain."

*   *   *

The morning Wai Seuk left, we rose in the chill darkness that comes before cockcrow, when the moon has gone down but the sun has not yet risen. Rain, the first in more than half a year, began to fall, promising good fortune, and as the sky slowly turned silver then copper, a gust of wind drove the clouds so that the lucky drizzle followed our son.

Yet that night, and the nights that followed, I dreamed of leaves falling from a tree, a bird flying into our house, an empty town. These, I knew, were signs of danger.

FANNY

North Adams, Massachusetts
1877

The town's manufacturers, determined to drive the unions out of North Adams, replaced the strikers with newly arrived immigrants from Europe willing to work for less. The manufacturers also combined to refuse employment to strikers at any of the factories.

Lue, with Father's support, could easily have persuaded Mr. Sampson that he had not been on strike. But then he would have revealed his duplicity to the Crispins. As it was, his countrymen had seen through his excuses for not picketing, his strained silences when Father spoke out against the strikes, and they abused Lue as cruelly as if they were Phoebe's cats tormenting a trapped mouse: those who were leaving North Adams demanded Lue repay his debts; the few who were remaining turned him away when he asked to join them in the small groceries and laundries they were starting.

Even before the strike, the Chinamen had been warped in their minds against Lue—first for leaving their colony, then for cutting off his queue. No, not that exactly, for Lue was not alone in residing outside the tenements on Brooklyn Street where most of the Chinamen boarded, only in making his home among the captains of industry; likewise, he was not alone in dispensing with his queue, only in his reasoning, the manner in which he'd done it.

He had, Lue confided, tried to persuade his countrymen that they should *all* cut their queues, not because they would not be returning to China but as a symbolic declaration of independence from feudalism. Reminding them of the suffragist who had bobbed her hair in the park while reciting the Declaration of Rights for Women published by the National Women's Suffrage Association, he'd urged, "We can do the same. All of us together. But in place of the Declaration, we should have a constitution for establishing a Chinese Republic."

The older men accused Lue of treason, the younger of exhibitionism. Nevertheless, with the same high-hearted courage with which he'd stood up to our pastor, Lue pursued his own course: he drew up principles for a form of government modeled mainly after that of America, boldly read the document out to passersby on Main Street, then cut his queue in one swift stroke of the knife.

I led the small crowd gathered around him in warm applause. But for weeks afterward his countrymen berated Lue for confounding conceit for self-respect. How they had reviled him! Yet he had held his head high and defended his actions hotly. Now he hung his head and pleated his lips. If he made confidences, they were to his journal.

At night, long after I had turned off the gas in my room, light from Lue's streaked under his door and across my floor; I would fall asleep to the scratch of his pen. In the morning, he came to breakfast wan and heavy-eyed.

"You are not dependent on your countrymen," I comforted. "You're educated. You can secure more suitable employment than they can offer."

Lue, at nineteen, was familiar with the best poets and writers of criticism. He could solve different problems in mathematics and had a more than competent view of history, a good foundation in chemistry. Moreover, he had a dignity in his demeanor and a consideration for the feelings of others that reflected a maturity well beyond his years. Since he'd cut his queue, he hardly looked like a Chinaman. Faith, if he was not a gentleman, I did not know one. Still he found every door closed to him.

Phoebe declared the sum of these rejections a sign from God. "Remember the slave whose freedom our congregation purchased?" she asked me brightly.

Turning to Lue, she explained how that Negro, a man of letters, had also been unable to find employment, so he had joined a missionary society, which had sent him to Africa to save the heathen. "This must be God's will for you as well," she concluded. "It's Mr. DeWitt's prophecy coming to pass. Look at how many of the Chinamen are making plans to go home."

"No," I wanted to cry. "No." But Phoebe's proposal had shaken my nerves too severely, and no voice came. Dumbly I gripped the arms of my chair.

Lue, scarcely more calm than I, chafed in his seat by the window. "The Chinese are leaving because they can't find work and because it's too risky to start over elsewhere. . . ."

Afraid he would upset Phoebe if he said any more, I forced out a faint but sharp, "My sister knows that."

Lue reddened, looked down at his feet. Phoebe, riffling through the stack of newspapers in the far corner of the parlor, made no acknowledgment. But how could she not know? According to the newspapers, politicians in the West had been blaming Chinamen for the country's hard times, and violent men were assaulting Chinese all across America, driving them out of towns. Every week I read of new atrocities.

Pulling out a paper, Phoebe showed us a passage she had marked, a passage on mission work in China: "Sons bring their fathers to Christ, husbands their wives, families their clans. Thus the Good News of the Savior's love is passed on from mouth to mouth, from village to village, and churches have been opened in places where, a few years ago, the name of Jesus was unknown."

Her face radiant with joy, she said, "Lue, won't you take the Good News to your family?"

"There are souls to be saved here," I protested. "Souls you yourself have said Lue has been instrumental in bringing to the Master."

"Yes, but the moral debasement of pagans in China is fouler by far," Phoebe countered.

"There are already missionaries near my village," Lue said dully. "Nor would my family be able to feed me. The whole district is suffering from a drought, and my brother has been forced to leave home and look for work in San Francisco."

That Lue's inability to find work was, as Phoebe said, a sign from God I, too, came to recognize. But I believed it was a sign I should enact my plan to free Lue so he could fulfill the Almighty's purpose by developing his God-given gifts.

Father, nearing eighty, was feeling the burden of his years. He had taken on a partner to run his store, and it was not difficult to convince him to hire Lue formally to undertake full responsibility for the garden. Only Father growled that the prolonged loss of trade had cut deeply into his capital, that taking on a partner had meant halving his income, doubling the time required for recovery, and he offered Lue a salary that was not much more than an allowance: there would be no money for either Lue's debts or his family.

Of course I knew that when Father was in a fierce mood, it was worse than folly to take him on. Since there could be no delay, however, I plucked up heart and tried to reason with him. Surely he could not be as badly off as he claimed. Hadn't he enjoyed years of profit before his losses? Didn't we live among the town's wealthiest citizens in a spacious, handsome house? Weren't we still pleasured by snug fires and good dinners?

My questions unleashed a fury in Father such as I had never seen, and I swiftly withdrew lest he retract his offer altogether. But Phoebe could yet succeed where I had failed, and I begged her help. She refused to intervene. That way, she said, God's will would be made manifest, not hers or mine or Lue's.

When I told Lue, I saw in his face the same dismay I had felt when I had been forced to leave Culloden. His eyes swept the greenhouse, his little "sanitarium," the boxes where he birthed and nursed seedlings, the bench where we sat and discussed their progress, the salmonberry bush he'd created, the jar that held the seeds he'd harvested. "Miss Fanny, how can I give up my work with you?"

How could I? Before Lue had come into my life I had spent more days in bed than out. There was no reason to rise. My winter coughs, frequent inflammation of the lungs, and reliance on laudanum had prevented any hope of useful employment. And I confess good works were for me like the charity food baskets I distributed with Phoebe: they staved off hunger for the moment but could not satisfy.

Teaching Lue, however, my rusty faculties had sharpened. Working with him on his experiments, I was at last using all the brain God had given me; I often felt the deep contentment I'd known in

Culloden. Indeed, my days were so filled with joyful purpose that I no longer even felt the want of laudanum.

Certain I was carrying out God's will, I reached up to my collar, unfastened the garnet pin Uncle John and Aunt Julia had given me on parting, and told Lue, "A short distance from Culloden, there was a school almost as fine as Uncle John's, a school that allowed the best of their senior students to cover their board and tuition by helping out with the younger children. I could have quit my family and gone there. All I needed was train fare, train fare I could have had by selling this pin. Only, as you see, I never did sell it because it was my obligation to stay with Father and Julia and Phoebe."

I pressed the pin into Lue's hands. "Selling this will help you meet your obligations to your lenders. You have no other obligations except to the gifts the Almighty has bestowed on you."

While I was speaking, Lue's expression had turned hopeful, then eager. As his fingers started to curl over the pin, however, his face darkened, and he stared down at the garnet stones as if they were drops of blood.

"My family . . ." A spasm seized his throat, and he could not continue.

At his distress, my own throat dried. But the Master held me up so I did not falter.

Fixing my eyes on his, I said, "Your family is in the hands of our Father in Heaven, not yours, and He has already guided them to send your brother to America to work in place of you. Is your faith strong enough for you to believe that, for you to trust in God and God alone?"

For a long time Lue neither spoke nor moved. Then slowly, ever so slowly, his fingers coiled over the pin.

"Yes," he said gravely. "Pray God, yes."

SUM JUI

Toishan, China
1877—1879

For the first time Gim Gong sent no gold eagles at New Year. He was no longer at the factory but working in his ghost teacher's garden, he wrote, and his earnings were too small, his debts too large, for him to send us any.

Yet we began the year with hope. Fourth Brother had written his wife that he was opening a store in the provincial capital, Sang Sing, and we should continue to farm his land on shares. We believed Wai Seuk, unusually blessed by Heaven, would send what was necessary to see us through to harvest. Perhaps he could even reclaim Gim Gong from that ghost teacher.

People's destinies, however, cannot be separated from the times in which they live. Returning Gold Mountain guests said the troubles Fourth Brother had run from had grown worse: villainous foreign ghosts, determined to drive our people out of their country, were robbing them, pelting them with stones, even killing them. We received no word, no money from Wai Seuk. And Lung Wong, the Dragon King who lives in the Eastern Sea and gives us rain, sent none.

Of course we carried water up from the river. Nevertheless, many seedlings withered in the unyielding heat. Moreover, Fourth Brother's paddies were too scattered for us to keep a constant watch on them all. As soon as we left one, some other farmer, desperate to save his own crop, would steal our water.

With no relief from the blazing sun, the soil began splitting and

cracking in everyone's fields, stunting the sweet potatoes and turnips, killing the rice. In truth, all I saw growing was Moon Ho's
belly, a sight that should have filled me with joy. But with no rain
or reserves of food or money, how could I welcome another mouth?

By early summer we'd already sold our stools, table, and beds.
Fourth Brother, home to fetch Fourth Sister to Sang Sing, saw how
we'd taken apart all but the main room of our house. His eyes
darted from the two thin quilts that served as all our furniture to
the small hill of Moon Ho's belly. And although all his capital was
tied up in starting his new store, he said, "No need to pay rent this
harvest. We'll settle up in a better year."

We were glad of his kindness. And of the handfuls of rice and
dried sweet-potato slices Bik Wun and Ma slipped us when they
could. But we needed more, and Hok Yee asked Lo See to write
Gim Gong.

"Tell him it will be four moons before harvest, that there will
probably *be* no harvest. Tell him we can stretch what we have on
hand for less than a moon, that we have nothing of value left to
sell."

*The Jesus God has promised He will provide. But He works in
mysterious ways,* Gim Gong replied. *You must trust in Him as I do.
Good will come.*

Lo See, reading the letter, shook his head. Hok Yee tore it into
shreds. Then we heard that the two foreign ghosts in Toi Sing were
offering rice to those who entered the gates of their religion. Could
this be what Gim Gong meant?

On the long walk to the worship hall in Toi Sing, heat rose up
through our straw sandals, burning our feet. Hot winds carried dust
from the dried-out fields high into the air, stinging our eyes, filling
our parched mouths with grit. Sweat beaded our foreheads, then
our backs, soaking through our thin cotton jackets and pants, clinging. Although Moon Ho, Hok Yee, and I took turns carrying Little
Tiger, he grew heavier with every *lei*. After we told the ghost man
we accepted the Jesus God, however, he marked our heads with water and gave us rice.

We wanted to go and collect rice every day. But the ghosts only
gave it out at the end of their worship meetings, and these were
held every seventh day. This day, the ghost man told us, was special,

one where we should perform no labor. Why then did he choose that day to hold his meetings? Moreover, the way the ghost man leaped about on his platform and his wife pounded on her music box was anything but restful.

Hnnnh, it seemed to me the ghost man often went against his own words. First he told us his God commanded us to honor our fathers and mothers, as is proper. Then he ordered us to stop feeding our ancestors. And when Big Dumpling's father refused him permission to enter the Jesus religion despite the gifts of rice, the ghost man directed the boy to give up his father, his family.

Explaining that the bit of bread he handed out during worship became the flesh of the Jesus God in our mouths, the ghost man warned us not to bite down or blood would spurt from it and we would be punished by the Jesus God's father. I had not eaten meat since I was seven, and not wanting to break my vow, I slipped my piece to Little Tiger, cautioning him to take care. Too hungry to listen, he fell on it as if he were a tiger. But there was no blood when he chewed. Nor did the bread become meat.

Some men began wondering out loud if the ghost man was deceiving us deliberately because he was an agent for his country, which was not Gold Mountain, as I thought, but one that had sent soldiers to attack our people in the past and might again. Others, claiming foreign-ghost eyes had the power to pierce the earth, said the ghost man intended to steal treasure out of the ground.

The ghost man insisted he and his wife had come to save us. But I had not forgotten the pig trade, and it seemed to me that their gifts of rice could be a decoy, that they might be deliberately driving away the rain clouds. After all, before the drought, they had failed to convince any of our people to enter their religion. Now, because we needed their rice, we numbered in the hundreds.

The rice, so important to us, was nothing to them. Their cook said they were eating meat three times a day. He said they were wasteful: when the taste of a dish did not suit, they ordered him to make it over; they also made him throw away food that was just a little spoiled.

The amount of rice they allowed us was one bowl for each man and woman, a half bowl for a child. Even watering our allotment down into the thinnest gruel, we could not make it last the six days between worship meetings. Since the rice was unthreshed, however, we were able to grind and boil the husks for eating as well.

In truth, what we needed, what we wanted, was rain, not charity.

The number of Jesus followers swelled until the ghost man had to hold six meetings on worship day. To avoid the worst of the heat, we started out from Lung On before sunrise, attended the second meeting, then left as soon as the ghosts gave us rice. The trouble began at the end of the sixth meeting.

Though we were not there ourselves, those who were talked about it for many moons. And from what we heard, the ghosts were at the front of the worship hall handing out the last of the rice when Big Dumpling's father rushed in, charging, "You ghosts, you devils, you told my son Jesus is the only God."

Of course the ghost man had said that many times during every worship meeting, and the ghost woman sang songs about it too. Listening to that nonsense was part of the price we paid for the rice. Big Dumpling's father knew that. What upset him was that his son had come to believe the foreign ghosts' foolish talk and had smashed the Gods and the ancestral tablets on their family altar.

"Friend," the ghost man said. "Listen to your son."

"A father listen to a son!" Big Dumpling's father shouted. Turning to the people gathered around, he stormed, "This ghost upsets the proper order. He teaches our sons to insult our Gods and ancestors. No wonder Lung Wong won't send rain!"

His words acted like fire on oil. Everyone started to yell against the ghosts.

"Yes, he's the cause of our troubles."

"He turns Heaven and Earth upside down."

"He's poisoning our children."

"His wife steals girl babies."

"*Ai yah,* she bewitches them, their mothers too."

"The ghost man cut off my brother's leg and wouldn't give it back."

"He has a box of human bones."

No one spoke for the ghost. Yet he refused to back down. "Jesus only God is. Jesus only one with power rain make. Not Dragon King. No Dragon King is!" he shouted, kindling the flames.

People outside the worship hall, hearing the disturbance, surged in, adding more fuel, and there were cries of "Kill the foreign ghosts!"

The ghost woman shrilled, "We not afraid. God with us stand!" And her husband, curling his hands into fists, shot his arms high above his head, calling on their God for help.

But it was their cook who saved them by running to the magistrate and bringing back soldiers who escorted them out of Toi Sing.

That same moon, all the villages in the district joined together in a huge procession to honor Lung Wong. At the head was Lung Wong himself, his long, scaly body borne aloft by a dozen men. Then came creatures of the sea and storms, colored banners of yellow and white to symbolize wind and water, black and green to represent clouds.

Leaping and prancing, Lung Wong circled the fields, kicking up clouds of dust that stuck to our sweaty, dirt-streaked skin and caught in our throats. His attendants sprinkled cooling water from willow branches onto us and the parched earth, crying, "Come rain, come!" Young men crashed cymbals together and beat on gongs. Elders exploded long strings of firecrackers, filling the air with shredded red wrappers, the smell of gunpowder.

Priests fed crackling hot bonfires with sacrifices of spirit money. And as the smoke from our offerings climbed up to Heaven, Teen Mo seared the sky with lightning, Lui Kung hurled thunderbolts so fierce the earth shook in deafening rumbles. Still Lung Wong refused us even one drop of rain.

With the ghosts gone, we had no rice, either.

Before the ghosts were driven out of Toi Sing, Wai Seuk had raised our hopes with a letter assuring us he had finally found work and we would be receiving money soon. But nothing had come. Not even another letter. And as his silence stretched longer and longer, our hopes for help from him grew wings and flew away. Worry for his safety pressed our hearts. Hunger clawed ever more fiercely at our bellies.

Moon Ho had come to our family fat. During her bridal teasing, guests had laughed at her roundness, twitting lewdly, "When you buy a chicken, you want it plump." Now her belly and breasts hung like melons on a stick frame. Hok Yee and I, never stout, were all sharp points, our skin wrinkled and muddy as dried bean curd. How could it be otherwise when the sum of what we ate was thin soups of herbs and wild grasses we gathered from the hills? Only Little Tiger, pulling and sucking mightily at his mother's breasts, had any flesh. But he was past three, his appetite increasingly hard to satisfy. How could Moon Ho make enough milk for him *and* a baby?

Elder Brother's household had ample stores of rice. Each time Ma asked him to share their reserves with us, however, he snapped, "No one knows how long the drought will last. We cannot risk running out." *Hnnnh,* why would he feed us when he called his own mother a useless eater and Elder Sister ordered Third Sister to give Ma the scrapings?

Nor were Elder Brother and Sister any more openhanded with the dead. At Ching Ming, when we went to sweep and repair the family graves, they offered our ancestors only a few sticks of incense, a thin packet of spirit money, coarse grain in place of meat. Ma said that was why Heaven was denying Elder Brother and Sister a grandson to feed their spirits after they died.

The first year of the drought, Bik Wun had blurted out during one of Elder Sister's scoldings, "Don't blame me for being childless. Your son can't raise his manhood."

Wai Yin had blustered that his wife was lying, that he mounted and rode her every night, that she was the one at fault. Of course Elder Brother and Sister yelled at Bik Wun for not pleasing their son. But they also put a stop to Wai Yin's eating opium.

For days Wai Yin howled so loudly the whole village heard him. Raging like a wild demon, he broke furniture and beat Bik Wun until her ears were discolored with bruises and clotted blood. Then, too weak to lash out anymore, he curled tight as a cooked shrimp, sweating and shaking, begging in broken whimpers for just one smoke. Elder Sister wept. She cradled him in her arms as if he were a baby again. But she did not relent. And his habit was finally broken.

While chasing the dragon, Wai Yin had been gaunt, his skin sallow, his eyes sunken. After he stopped, his eyes gradually lost their blank stare. His skin began to gleam with restored health. But a tree planted crooked can rarely be straightened, and Wai Yin's character remained lazy, selfish, and bad-tempered, his manhood limp.

Elder Brother consulted the best doctors in Toi Sing. Digging up taels of silver, he bought Wai Yin expensive herbs guaranteed to give hardness and strength. When even the ground testicles of deer failed, Wai Yin again blamed Bik Wun. "How can I lie like a man with a piece of dead wood?"

But the artful skills of courtesans could not arouse him either.

From the shape of Moon Ho's belly, Ma was certain the baby would be a boy. "I've spoken to Elder Brother. He's agreed to give you a year's supply of rice and sweet potatoes in exchange for a grandson."

The price was too generous not to have been hard-won, and Hok

Yee, his shoulders hunched, his face pinched with misery, thanked Ma. I swallowed my protest until my husband and I were alone in the hills.

"Elder Sister will destroy this child just like she did Wai Yin."

"What choice do we have?" He pointed to the grass we were cutting, the way I had to kneel like an old woman because I'd become too weak to squat. "We're no less trapped now than when we were forced to give up Wai Yin."

I shook my head, refusing defeat. "Perhaps we should take apart the rest of the house and sell it."

"And sleep out in the open?"

"We can clean out the shed where we used to keep the family buffalo."

"And after we sell the last brick?"

"The Dragon King won't deny us rain for a third year."

Though I'd tried, I'd not kept the doubt out of my voice, and Hok Yee squinted up at the cloudless sky. "We cannot know that for certain."

"Neither can we know for certain that Moon Ho's child will be a boy. What if it's a girl?"

"We'd have to sell her."

Plucking excess blossoms is necessary for healthy, vigorous fruit: if Moon Ho tried feeding a baby as well as Little Tiger, neither would live. Since the new baby would be the smaller, weaker blossom, that should be the one plucked; in that Hok Yee and I agreed. Where we differed was in what to do if Moon Ho gave us a grandson.

When selling Elder and Third Sisters' daughters, Ba had been careful to find them good homes, ones where they would be treated kindly. And if Moon Ho's child was a girl, we would have a chance to do the same. But if the baby was a boy, Hok Yee insisted we must give him to Elder Brother.

Denying my pleas to sell Moon Ho's child whether she gave us a granddaughter or a grandson, Hok Yee repeated over and over that we must honor Ma's agreement, that no one else would give us as much for the boy. Would he say the same if he knew Elder Sister was a fox ghost?

I had not revealed the secret of the fox ghost to save my son. Could I do it to save my grandson?

No. Even if Hok Yee and Ma believed me, I would never convince Elder Brother, so nothing would be gained. And if Elder Sister revealed my secret, my ghost mark, my losses now would be even greater than before.

Hok Yee was right. We were trapped.

Unless. Unless there was no child to give.

Moon Ho's struggle to push the baby out began in midafternoon. Since we had only the one room, Hok Yee took Little Tiger out into the hills to look for herbs. When they returned at dusk, the baby still had not come, and they went out to the old buffalo shed in the courtyard to pass the night. In truth, Moon Ho had already become so weak, I wondered whether Little Tiger would wake to find his mother gone from him, how we would feed him then.

When I finally drew the baby out of Moon Ho, the shaft of moonlight through the window was fading. In the gloom, she was white as mourning, the baby blue. Neither moved while I cut the cord, and I thought them dead. Then Moon Ho, grunting feebly, pushed out the afterbirth, sank into exhausted sleep. I picked up the baby, felt it squirm. Holding it close, I saw it was a boy, and my heart quailed. Did I have the strength to carry out my resolve to kill the baby and claim he was stillborn?

Killing any living thing is an offense against Heaven. And because I did not eat meat, my mother and then Ma had always made certain I would not have to butcher the pigs and chickens at festivals. Having never taken an animal's life, how could I take a child's, my own grandson's?

But if Wai Yin had been destroyed as I believed, wasn't he the same as dead? Surely, then, the Gods would agree that knowingly placing the baby in a fox-ghost's lair would be the true offense, that it was kinder to give him another chance on the wheel of life.

Crouching deep in the shadows farthest from Moon Ho, I slid my grandson under my cotton jacket. Still slick with his mother's blood, he was soft and warm, small, not much larger than his father, my firstborn, had been at birth. Wriggling in search of a nipple, his mouth caressed. His nails, small and razor sharp, grazed my skin. The smell of blood was hot and strong.

I heard a whimper, almost dropped him. Was Moon Ho awake? Could she see me despite the darkness? No, her breathing was soft and regular.

Another, louder mewl broke the quiet. It was the baby. What if Moon Ho or Hok Yee heard him? How would I explain? Sweating yet shivering, I pressed my grandson's face firmly into my breasts, stifling his cries, his breath.

With a strength I did not think possible, the baby wailed in protest, fiercely drumming my arms and ribs with his tiny fists and feet. Weeping, I clenched my teeth to stop their chattering and hugged him tighter, then tighter still.

Slowly, very slowly, his muffled cries became fainter.

His kicking weakened, stopped.

By first light, he was cold and stiff.

Like most people in our district, Hok Yee and I had experienced spring hunger, that time when the last of the winter stores has been eaten and none of the new crops are ready for harvest. While caught in Fisherman Low's stranglehold, we had felt hunger in fat years and lean. Until the Dragon King denied us rain, however, we had never known starvation.

By the third summer, the hills were stripped bare of herbs and grasses; people were dying on every side. Landlords and Gold Mountain families still receiving gifts of money did not suffer, of course. Elder Brother's household, too, was still eating rice. Had I not tried to bend Heaven's will to mine, we would have had our chopsticks clattering against full bowls as well.

Except for myself, no one accused me. No one even showed the least suspicion. But Hok Yee's heart knew mine too well for him not to sense what I had done, and though he never said a hard word, I felt his horror and sorrow no less than my own.

We endured the winter by selling the roof beam, timber, tiles, and bricks from our remaining room. In the spring, we took apart the buffalo shed and exchanged those bricks for seed potatoes, receiving enough to sow a single field.

We barely had the strength to plow and harrow and hoe. And when the Dragon King did not send rain, we were too weak to carry sufficient water from the river to keep alive more than a few rows.

Ma and Bik Wun could no longer help by slipping us scraps from Elder Brother's stores. Ma had become too unsteady on her feet to leave the house. Bik Wun was held captive by chores and her adopted son, Sesame, an unusually lively boy in split-bottomed pants whom Elder Brother had bought for two strings of cash.

From our own sons in Gold Mountain, we received silence. But a cousin of one neighbor and the brother of another had seen Wai Seuk. He had been fired unfairly and cheated out of wages due him, they said. Last they saw, he was in rags, hungry, on the road looking for work. Unable even to feed himself, how could he help us?

Nor did the Goddess Gwoon Yum grant us mercy. So we slept out in the open without even mats to lie on. When lucky, we discovered a root or two we could dig up, we found a tree that still had a few leaves, a bit of bark. Otherwise we ate dreams, dreams of young leafy vegetables and golden-brown bean curd atop steaming white rice, slippery noodles flavored with crunchy jade green peppers and coarse salt, peanut porridge with crispy fried doughnuts and fermented soybeans.

Moon Ho made less and less milk. Little Tiger's flesh melted like wax from a candle. Soon her breasts were dry as the earth. He became so thin his bones all but stuck through his skin. Only his belly, swollen with worms, stayed falsely fat.

Hok Yee and I knelt before Elder Brother and Sister. Knocking our heads on the ground, we begged for food, money for medicine. "Not for us," Hok Yee assured them. "For the child." And Ma added her own pleas. But all that snake and his fox-ghost wife gave us were curses.

Helplessly we held Little Tiger as worms, whole basins of worms, crawled out of him.

Even after he was dead, they kept coming.

Ma took her revenge on Elder Brother and Sister by hanging herself from their bedpost.

The two, justly afraid, quickly tried to make their peace. Where they had buried Ba with scarcely any ceremony, they hired priests to say prayers night and day for Ma. They bought her a fragrant sandalwood coffin of the best quality and slaughtered their fattest pig and chickens for offerings. They made no objection to Hok Yee,

Moon Ho, and me coming back to honor Ma, to pray for her soul's successful entry into the world beyond.

But Ma's forgiveness, freely given in life, was not easily bought in death, and her ghost punished Elder Brother and Sister relentlessly, knocking them off their bed, snatching rice bowls out of their hands, upsetting chairs and stools from under them, tearing down their bed hangings, forcing open doors they closed.

Always striking when Elder Brother and Sister were by themselves, Ma also made clear that they alone were her victims, and no one else was frightened. *Hnnnh,* Elder Brother and Sister began clinging to the rest of the family like shadows. They even changed their sleeping arrangements: Elder Brother hid under Wai Yin's quilt, Elder Sister under Bik Wun's. No sooner did they fall asleep, however, than Ma's ghost pursued them in their dreams.

Shuttering windows and doors could not keep her out.

Neither did placing willow branches under the house eaves draw her away.

At last, unable to sleep or eat, Elder Brother called in a diviner to explain what Ma wanted.

The diviner, a small, chicken-breasted man in a long blue gown, arrived beating a gong. There was no farm work to occupy anyone, and it seemed as if all the village followed him to Elder Brother's, swarming around the front door and hanging over the courtyard walls with the same noisy excitement as when crowding into a mat-shed theater for a show.

Placing his gong and bundle on the table, the diviner called for the family to stand close, men on his left, women and children on his right. Then he set out a lamp with an iron stand and a large incense burner; a jar of black oil, which he poured into the lamp; incense sticks, bigger and longer than ordinary ones, which he placed in the burner.

Lighting the lamp and incense, he struck his gong and intoned, "Oh, departed one, do you wish to speak?"

He set down the gong, threw a soul cash onto the table. The copper coin, fastened to a string, which he held, landed head up. "The departed one says yes."

Repeating the same ritual as before, he asked, "Do you wish your eldest son and his wife to make right a wrong?"

Again Ma answered yes.

Pursing his lips until they looked like a water chestnut, the diviner peered down his long, narrow nose at Elder Brother and Sister. "What is the wrong?"

Elder Sister smoothed her hair with her hands. Elder Brother tugged at the corner of his jacket. The rest of the family stole glances at those closest to us or studied the ground. Out of the corner of my eye, I looked for Hok Yee, found him standing half behind Elder Brother. Moon Ho, beside me, nudged my leg with her knee, tilted her head slightly toward the crowd jamming the open door: Thin Dog, our neighbor, was squeezing forward.

Boldly pointing to Elder Brother, Thin Dog told the diviner, "That scoundrel's cheated his second brother."

Elder Brother bucked like an angry buffalo. "That's not true."

But other voices outside yelled their support.

"Yes, the second brother was cheated."

"After their father died, the second brother didn't get a fair share of the land."

"Fair share? Hok Yee got none!"

And when the diviner asked Ma, "Did your first son cheat your second?" the soul cash landed head up.

From those nearest the table to those outside, gasps, whispers, and angry muttering spread like ripples in a pond. Then other villagers began to call out accusations.

"They beat their daughter-in-law."

"They haven't plastered their father's tomb."

"Their second brother is starving."

"Their nephew's son died of starvation."

Elder Brother, his fingers curled into fists, stalked over to the door, slammed it shut. But the smoke from the lamp and incense was thick, and the diviner, coughing, ordered, "Leave it open."

One by one, the diviner posed the charges from those outside to Ma.

Each time she answered yes.

The diviner cocked his head and stroked his beard thoughtfully. "The departed one wishes you to pay proper respect to your ancestors; to rebuild your second brother's house; to feed him, his wife, and daughter-in-law," he told Elder Brother and Sister.

"I'm not made of gold," Elder Brother cried. "I can't, I won't, re-build Hok Yee's house."

Through his plaintive wail, I heard the sharp *clink-clink* of coins. Turning, I saw six gold eagles dancing on a little pile of earth next to a shallow hole in the floor by the altar.

Sesame laughed. "Look!"

As the rest of the family turned, Elder Brother threw himself on top of the coins. "No, Ma. No."

The villagers surged into the house. "What?" "What is it?"

The diviner held up both hands. "Back! Back! You're interfering with the dead."

Grumbling, those in the front pressed back against those shoving forward. Sesame stamped his little feet. "I want! I want!" Bik Wun, scooping him up into her arms, tried to quiet him with a candy.

Still on his belly, Elder Brother begged the diviner, "Tell my mother I'll do everything she asks."

"Yes, everything," Elder Sister echoed.

"I was not finished," the diviner told them sternly. "The departed one also desires better treatment for your grandson's mother. There must be no more beatings from either of you or your son."

"Yes, yes, even that," Elder Brother and Sister agreed.

Now that Ma had shown her power to reveal their hidden gold, would they dare deny her?

FANNY

North Adams, Massachusetts
1877—1880

When Lue stopped sending his family remittances, their letters ceased. Since most of the Chinamen in North Adams were from his vicinity, however, he knew from them that the drought had worsened, all but destroying the district's harvest.

For a while, a missionary couple near his village handed out relief, and many Chinese—including, praise Jesus, Lue's parents, a sister-in-law, and a baby nephew—were baptized. Then idolaters drove the missionaries out.

"How will my family eat?" Lue fretted.

I understood his concern, but I said lightly, "Uncle John's family often went hungry during the War of the Rebellion. When Aunt Julia had nothing to cook, the family sat at table anyway; they listened to her read recipes out loud; they gave thanks that they could eat their fill in their imaginations. And when Union soldiers burned them out of their home, leaving them without so much as one particle of food, they scoured the ground where the soldiers had picketed their horses, gathered up bits of corn which had been dropped, and ate that, all the while praising God for His mercy."

Lue released a small, penitent sigh. "Yes, God is just even if man is not. And I do trust in Him. I do."

The sale of my garnet pin had failed to cover all Lue owed. To pay off the Chinamen who were leaving, he had been forced to borrow more from those who stayed. Now these men began pressing Lue for repayment in the name of their families.

Once again I petitioned Father to raise Lue's salary. But Father, confusing old losses with new, had become even more mistrustful of his circumstances. Faith, he'd come to prize his ledger as much as his Bible, and he was so implacable I might as well have been a serf entreating the czar of Russia.

Still I was hopeful that Phoebe, who delighted Father with her clever economies—saving grease to make soap, the fingers from threadbare gloves to cover cuts—could somehow wheedle him into doing right. When I turned to her for help, however, she shook her head, repeating what she'd said before, "God's will be done."

While telling Lue, a sick headache seized hold of me, and I buckled under its onslaught. But what was the pain from its fierce grip compared to Lue's suffering? Praying for strength from the Master, I labored on.

"Perhaps you can repay your countrymen by helping out in their laundries and stores. I could shield your absence from Father."

The wrinkle in Lue's forehead deepened. "I already asked. They won't have me. They say I should quit North Adams and seek work that will allow me to repay them *and* send money home."

"We've been over that. Your brother can send your parents money. Maybe he already is. Your place is here."

Lue plucked at his collar the way he used to tug at his queue. "If only God would tell me Himself that His purpose for me is here, that He wants me to stay with our work in the greenhouse. Then I could be sure."

"God *is* telling you," I assured him. "He's speaking to you through your success with the plants."

On Lue's face hope rose, battled doubt.

Leaning forward, I pressed my point. "The bushes of your salmonberry are more early bearing and productive than the ordinary raspberry, and your development of a cherry currant shows promise. If you continue to develop your gifts, you have the possibility of making discoveries that may benefit many people, your people."

"Do you really think so?"

"Absolutely."

That same day Lue began to explore the development of new varieties that could withstand drought. Although student had by then surpassed teacher, Lue floated his every idea with me. "You help me find my way," he said.

Together we spun vague notions into possibilities, wove possibilities into ever more concrete plans. And while we were talking—indeed, so long as we were in the greenhouse—indomitable purpose kindled Lue's eye. Despite obstacles, he fairly glowed with confidence. He was commanding, manly, and spirited.

While he was raking or burning leaves, digging snow, splitting kindling, or polishing Father's boots, however, Lue's whole air changed. It was as if he'd walked from sunshine into shadow. When he thought himself alone, I would sometimes hear a pensive sigh, notice spasms of agony, doubt, even anger cross his face. And since Lue never put on airs, it could not have been the lowly nature of the chores that upset him, but the burden of his family.

My annual clothing allowance from Father was meager. But by wearing boots that leaked and making over my dresses and cloaks to cover worn spots instead of replacing them with new, I had been able to turn it over to Lue in its entirety. Had the Chinamen not forced Lue to repay them, he could have again sent these few dollars to his family.

He was, however, too honorable to deny his debtors' claims, and since he could only meet them by turning to a usurer, my clothing allowance and every penny of Lue's small salary—outside of what he tithed—had to go to that viper. Yet when Charlie Sing heard through a cousin that Lue's brother had disappeared in the West and his two nephews had succumbed to starvation and his grandmother had died as well, the Chinamen placed all the blame on Lue.

Lue, head bowed, accepted their charge. His tone low, rapid, and full of pain, he recalled his grandmother's many kindnesses: the little treats she had slipped him when he'd visited, her stout-hearted defense when he'd been expelled from school, her praise for his flower garden. "I might have saved her. I might have saved my nephews who have lived and died without my ever seeing them. . . ."

"We cannot save those whom God has marked for death," I reminded softly. "Remember what I told you about my sister Julia? How she was born with God's claim already stamped on her brow? How she went home to Jesus after five years of struggle and suffering? Yet her short life and death had purpose, for it was through Julia that I came to Jesus."

Lue clasped his hands as if in prayer. "I know my family's suffering has been ordered by Providence for good reason. I know that although I cannot yet see or understand what that reason is, 'He doeth all things well.' But . . ." His voice broke. "Miss Fanny, it is hard to bear."

Touched to the heart, I confessed, "When I first came home from Culloden, I also said, 'It is too hard, Lord. I cannot endure.' " I forced a smile of encouragement. "But with the Master's help I did. You will, too."

Indeed, Lue never did weep or rail but was wonderfully brave and faithful: at least twice a week he fasted in his family's name; night after night he continued to raise the burden of their suffering to the Almighty during prayer in the parlor.

Always he would begin in a voice so low I had to strain to hear. Then slowly, in a manner that thrilled my every fiber, he would work himself up until finally he was shouting loud and sweet as an angel's trumpet call, lifting my very soul to Heaven.

More than once Phoebe told Lue, "You have a gift for prayer that could be used in preaching." Not a day passed that she did not ask the Almighty to help Lue see that his true work lay in China.

I dared not speak my prayer out loud.

I reached the half century just months before Lue came into his majority, and we marked these two milestones with a photograph.

Lue's image was that of a man of strong mettle. Almost a head taller than I, he stood straight and slender as a pine. His face, still beardless, was well defined, his complexion golden. He had a thick head of gleaming black hair. His hands, clasped loosely before him, emanated strength. There was an air of earnestness and hidden care that added to his years. Indeed, strangers often mistook him for a man past thirty.

My image was a blow. Never handsome, I seemed even plainer standing beside Lue—a dull winter sparrow beside a bright spring robin. And yet . . . Phoebe said that I looked more like a woman of forty than fifty, that my neck had a pleasant curve, the braids circling my head an almost regal elegance.

What Phoebe did not remark on, what she could not see, was the procession of feelings—vague yet intense, strange yet delightful—that were roiling inside me. It was as if a subtle music had stolen into my heart and nestled there—except I also churned in a curious state of unrest.

Before, only Jesus had made my blood dance. Now that Lue had become a man he did too. Just the sound of his footfall would set my flesh to tingling. When his shadow fell near, there would be a pull on my heart. Leaning on his arm while walking, my throat would throb with a pleasurable aching. At his smile, I'd melt as if I had drunk a strong cordial.

Frightened, I would lock myself in my room, fall on my knees, and beg the Master's help in living down these dangerous feelings. But even as I prayed, Lue's pitcher would clink against his basin or his bed would creak, and my heart would swell until it threatened to burst.

As a child, I had never been free of Mother's scolding except when I was ill. Then she had been amiable and tender, holding me close, telling me stories, feeding me syrups and broths. To entertain me while she was busy, she would give me a case of Bible pictures that moved over rollers I manipulated with a key. Or I would ask for the family Bible so I could read and reread my favorite chapters: Pharoah's daughter saving baby Moses; Ruth forsaking her family and people for the man she loved; Delilah outwitting Samson. So long as I was confined to bed, Mother would not refuse me, and I welcomed the onset of winter coughs that brought these proofs of her affection. Then, too impatient to wait for winter, I began feigning illness, complaining of feeling chilled though the summer sun shone bright and hot.

Now, when my head ached or I was hot with fever, Lue would bathe my temples with cool water. When I was felled by harsh winter, he would smooth out my quilts and plump my pillows. His hands, though callused, were gentle. Well washed, they yet smelled of tobacco from the pipe he had taken up, the earth and plants he loved so well, and at his slightest touch, the fire shut up in my bones would leap into flame.

I wanted nothing more than to minister to Lue as he did me. When his forehead beaded with perspiration or his hair fell forward, however, I clenched my hands to keep from reaching out and drying him with my kerchief, brushing back the fallen lock. Only when Lue fell to coughing in winter did I dare give in to my longing: I plied him with tonics; I unraveled my warmest shawl and knit a long, thick muffler that he wrapped around his neck, his mouth.

Each night I fell asleep vowing, "My feelings must be conquered." But my attempts to suppress them seemed to increase their strength, and I began to wonder whether I might be wrong in battling them as if they were sent by the Prince of Darkness, whether they were instead a gift from the Master that I could embrace.

So I started preparing for my strolls with Lue with special care: tying a fresh bow onto my bonnet, tucking a fallen blossom in my sash, wearing my smart Sunday slippers in place of patched boots. My hair being my only true adornment, I also tried different, ever more becoming arrangements. Once, while in the greenhouse, I confess I let it fall loose as if by accident.

If Lue noticed, he gave no sign. Wouldn't he have if Jesus did indeed want me to have an earthly soother as well as a friend in Heaven? Having read little of love and heard and seen even less, I was not certain. Nor was there any person in whom I could confide. Not here on earth.

Turning to Jesus, I prayed, "Give me a sign. Please, give me a sign."

The sign, I believed, would come through discovering how Lue's heart lay, and this would surely be revealed in his journals, which he left on top of the desk in his room. But he had continued to write *For Lue Gim Gong's eyes alone* on their covers, and honor forbade my reading them.

Forced to look elsewhere, I rearranged the furniture in the parlor, setting my chair where it would command the best view of Lue in his. Then I studied him as carefully as he did his seedlings and fruit. Faith, I weighed his every word, his every action; I examined my every memory.

And, oh, the heart quakes and spirit sinkings.

Yes, Lue flew at my least sign of want. But he also treated Father with little attentions, Phoebe with gentle courtesies.

Yes, when Lue grasped my hand to help me cross a stream, he did sometimes let it linger. But was he showing concern or affection?

Yes, Lue's face glowed with passion when we talked of his plants. But was any of that passion for me?

No, he was not paying court to any other woman. But that was true of almost all his countrymen. Of course, several had left wives in China, and a few were already promised to women chosen by their families, women who were waiting for their return. Then, too, more than one of the Chinamen was open in his disapproval of any woman who was not Chinese. Charlie Sing, however, had been charmed sufficiently by Miss Ida Wilburn, a visiting Virginian, to offer her his hand. And Thomas Ah Num, a Chinaman in Lue's prayer group, had married a young woman with the reputation of being fast. Indeed, rumor had it that she was the one who'd proposed. Was it possible that Lue shared my yearnings but was too shy to speak?

"Let it be, kind Heaven," I prayed. "Let it be."

SUM JUI

Toishan, China
1879—1882

Even today, I have only to crumble hot, dry soil in my hand to feel again the awful hunger and helplessness we endured during the drought. Likewise, a single dewdrop sparkling on a reed or the smell of damp earth is enough to bring back the relief that washed over me, over us all, when Lung Wong finally soaked our fields with rain.

Yes, Elder Brother had already rebuilt our house and was feeding us two meals a day as Ma had demanded. Nor was that any more than Hok Yee's due. As the saying goes, however, it is easier to move a mountain than to change a man's character: Elder Brother and Sister gave so grudgingly it seemed they counted every brick, every grain. In truth, we were eager to be free of them. Besides, what farmer can be content without seeds to sow, fields to weed, crops to harvest?

The rain came just before spring plowing. And as any child knows, plowing wet soil causes stubborn clods that will remain hard for years to come. But without a buffalo of our own, we were forced to borrow from Elder Brother, so we could not wait for the fields to dry; he made certain of that.

When the surface of the soil turned pale, we had to draw a toothed rake over each field to break up the clods. Where it should have taken us two days' labor to prepare one *mau,* we were not ready after six. The planting, too, took longer than was usual. We had not yet recovered our strength, and after each row, we had to rest, to lift our heads and straighten our backs to ease the strain.

There is, of course, always wild grass seed mixed in with the rice, but that year it seemed to me the wild grasses grew faster than the seedlings. If we weren't weeding, we were applying manure or watering. By day's end we could barely shuffle to Elder Brother's for our evening meal, then home to bed.

Despite our exhaustion, sleep did not come easily for either Hok Yee or me. Our dead grandsons lay between us, and we could not draw comfort from each other as before. We tried. How we tried. But their loss and my part in their deaths was too painful, the wounds too fresh and deep. Neither could there be any healing so long as we had no sons to make more, and I lit incense morning and night for the Gods to give us back Wai Seuk and Gim Gong.

Wai Seuk returned that autumn. He was yellow and thin as a parched weed. Not one of us recognized him until he called out to his father. And he told us a tale so terrible I would not have accepted it as true from anyone else.

Who could have believed that boys, even ghost boys, could be so heartless as to drag an old, defenseless man off his wagon by grabbing and pulling at his queue? Worse, tie him to a wheel and whip the horse into a gallop so that the old man's head pounded repeatedly into the hard dirt street, finally falling off and rolling into a ditch like a broken, bloody ball?

Surely the outrage of our people who witnessed this horror was just. Yet Wai Seuk said that when a few of our people fell on the ghost boys, beating them with the old man's horsewhip, it set off a riot.

For the ghosts to storm the quarter where our people lived, to loot stores and hurl bricks and torches into homes, would have been bad enough. But as our people fled the burning buildings, Wai Seuk saw ghosts with guns shoot at men young and old, women with babies on their backs and in their arms, even children hiding behind their mothers' pants.

Faced with such savagery, is it any surprise our people scattered like hunted animals, each person acting on his own and without reason? Some, trying to dodge bullets, ran into the street and fell under the hooves of crazed horses or into the arms of ghost men with knives. Others, screaming, plunged back into the flames. Wai Seuk, trapped inside his rooming house, looked for escape through an underground room.

The room turned out to have no outer door, and though Wai Seuk clawed desperately at the walls, he could not pry loose a single brick. Nor could he go back up the stairs. Flames licked the door at the top. Thick, choking smoke and the terrible smell of scorched human flesh seeped under it.

Moments later, or much later, Wai Seuk could not be sure, a falling beam smashed through the charred door. As it splintered, red flames leaped through the gaping hole, devouring the stairs, and he felt his skin blister from the fierce heat. Above him he heard glass shattering, more timber fall. But the ceiling held. The fire that swooped down the stairs died.

Wai Seuk said the fire died because the room was empty and there was nothing to feed the flames. I believe it was the special protection of Heaven that saved him: no one else in that rooming house survived; Wai Seuk left the underground room with gold.

Yes, scrambling over the charred wreckage, Wai Seuk felt the hot prick of metal, the sharp edges of a tin, the smooth roundness of a padlock, heard the rattle of coins, knew he'd tumbled onto treasure. When no one came to claim the gold eagles, he took them for his own and set sail for home.

We did not speak of what we would do with the gold until one evening, after Wai Seuk had been back for almost half a moon.

"Shut the front door and the door to the courtyard," he told Moon Ho. "The window shutters, too." Turning to Hok Yee, he whispered, "I want to tell you my plan. To show you what is in that crate I brought back."

When the house was sealed, however, Wai Seuk made no move to bring the crate out from behind the altar where he had hidden it. Nor did he reveal any scheme. Instead he began to speak on the absurdity of ghost clothes, how they were too warm for summer yet not warm enough for winter, how they bound body and limbs. And I wondered if Wai Seuk was perhaps more deeply affected than we realized by the horrors he'd experienced, the loss of his sons.

The room became stuffy, overheated. Hok Yee took off his jacket, used it to wipe sweat off his face. I poured water in our bowls from the pot on the table, signaled Moon Ho to stir the air with a fan. Still Wai Seuk rambled on.

"Ghost beds are uncomfortable, too. Instead of good hard boards and wood pillows, they stuff cloth sacks with feathers you sink into, and their food is tasteless." Suddenly he leaned forward. "They also have things that are very wonderful. Lights that turn the darkness of night into the brightness of day. Machines of iron and steel that spin cotton and silk and push boats and do other work as well." Jumping to his feet, he dragged out the heavy crate. "Inside is a machine that can raise water."

Hok Yee frowned. "A waterwheel?"

Wai Seuk laughed softly. "No, this machine doesn't need men to work it. And unlike a waterwheel that can only draw water out of rivers or streams, this machine can raise water out of a well."

"So will a bucket at the end of a rope," Hok Yee said.

"Only with a person at the end of the rope. Once this machine is started, it works by itself, and it gives a steady flow of water."

He came back to the table. "You know I didn't bring back enough gold eagles to buy good bottomland. But there's that hill just west of the village, the one that has never been cultivated because it's too far from the river. We can buy that cheap and plant an orange orchard. The biggest orange orchard in the entire district."

"Except there's no well on that hill," Hok Yee said.

"I will dig one."

"What if there's no water?"

Wai Seuk looked over at his wife. Flushing red, she lowered her head, hid her face by raising her bowl to her lips.

"Moon Ho has the gift for divining water. And since I've come home, we've walked that hill several times with Moon Ho holding a divining rod. Whenever we near the top, the rod has turned in her hand, so there's water all right, water that can be drawn up by the machine and then spread out to trees on every side of the hill."

As always when he wanted time to think, Hok Yee picked up his pipe, filled it with tobacco. Moon Ho brought him a taper from the altar. I picked up the fan she'd dropped on the table, waved it in little worried jerks. Yes, Wai Seuk's plan was clever. He was cunning with his hands, a serious worker. But no man, however vigorous, could dig a well or set out a whole hill of trees on his own, and Wai

Seuk was thin and weak. We were, too. Moreover, it seemed that each time we'd reached out for more than the Gods gave, we'd slid just short of disaster. Attempt a scheme of such ambition when we were already having difficulty farming Fourth Brother's fields, and the Gods might push us over the edge.

Hok Yee clearly shared my concern. "It's not good to be greedy. We have enough to eat now; we have no illness."

"And no grandsons," Wai Seuk said.

I bit my lips. Hok Yee flinched as if he'd been struck.

"Heaven may yet grant you sons," he said quietly. "Or we can buy a boy, just as Elder Brother bought Sesame."

"Isn't that why we say human resolution can overcome Heaven's destiny? And by following my plan, never again will a child in this house die of hunger."

As he spoke, I studied my husband's face. Hok Yee could not fail to notice that where Wai Seuk had once been silent, he was now speaking openly, even boldly. But did Hok Yee understand that if he ruled against Wai Seuk, our son might not give in as he should?

"Resolution is not enough," Hok Yee sighed. "Nor is gold or your machine. We must also have the necessary strength. But where there is opportunity, danger always lurks. We must take the chance."

Of course any mountain, however small, has a dragon that can be aroused if the earth is disturbed. So before clearing the land, we hired the village priest to make certain the dragon in our hill would not flick its tail in anger.

Carefully the priest cut the comb from a live cock and dipped specially inscribed bamboo sticks in the blood that dripped from the severed comb. He covered several dozen pots with lucky red paper, placed five of the bamboo sticks in each, distributed them at different points on the hill.

At each place we lit incense and made offerings of food and wine to the dragon who lived in the hill and then to the Earth God, begging them to turn away evil. When we finished, the priest told us we could safely open up the ground.

Why, then, did I feel so uneasy?

So many people had died during the drought that the village elders had extended the Festival of Dead Souls for soothing ghosts from three days and two nights to five days and four nights. Every little thing was done correctly. Black-robed priests brought huge paper statues of the King of Ghosts and Goddess of Mercy to watch over the proceedings and lead the ghosts out of the village. They made the cleanest and purest of offerings—rice, bean curd, wine, special buns—and performed rituals to open the narrow throats of hungry ghosts, to flick sweet water into their mouths, thus quenching the fires in their bellies. They scattered flowers to rid us of any remaining difficulties and beat their gongs and set fire to the paper statues, bidding solemn farewell to them, the ghosts. Nevertheless, not all the ghosts left as they should—although we did not know it until a neighbor's boy was attacked and killed the same moon we began preparing the land for our grove.

The boy had been playing a hiding game with his friends not far from our hill. When they could not find him, they called for him to come out. Hearing their shouts, we added our own. Still he did not show himself. Then, on our way back to the village, Wai Seuk noticed his body in a gulley.

There was no sign of a struggle. No part of the boy had been gnawed at or eaten. But his throat gaped wide open, his back was gouged by deep scratches, and hunters hired by the village elders agreed the jagged tears of flesh and claw marks pointed to a cat as the killer.

Scouring the foothills surrounding Lung On, the hunters found more than one. But the animals vanished when fired upon or pressed too close. One hunter, standing on top of a boulder, swore that a ring-tailed cat under his feet had disappeared as he'd leveled his gun. Another reported shooting a big hole through a black-spotted cat, after which it had run all the faster. Yet another had shot through a striped cat without making the slightest impression on it. Realizing then that these had not been flesh-and-blood animals but spirit creatures, which cannot be killed, the hunters quit the chase.

Our village priest offered special sacrifices, and there were no further kills. But women and children gathering fuel in the foothills heard rustling in the underbrush, the sound of tongues lapping water from small streams. The night watch reported ghostly wails and anguished, drawn-out howls.

Each time a watchman lifted his lantern, everything fell silent. Nor did anyone ever find tracks. And the village elders issued warnings against venturing out except in the company of others and in the bright light of day.

The labor during the first few years of establishing a grove is hard. We had the work of clearing an entire hill, digging for water, laying out bamboo pipes to carry that water to every part of the grove, and farming Fourth Brother's fields as well. And though we were neither brave nor foolhardy, we set out in the gloom before cockcrow, while trees still floated in gray-white mist, dew soaked our pants, birds were yet silent in their nests. To further stretch our day, we did not go back to the house for our morning rice but carried it with us.

When working together, we would drop our hoes and sit in a shady spot to eat after the sun rose. We would take turns drinking from a pot of boiled water. Then Wai Seuk and Hok Yee would pull out their tobacco pouches and light their pipes, and along with the smoke swirling up to the birds twittering overhead, I would feel the tiredness in my bones drawn out into the air, disappear.

Most days we worked apart, however. Then we did not stop for more than a moment to swallow our rice. Wai Seuk did the heavy labor, Hok Yee and I the skilled; Moon Ho washed our dirty clothes, prepared our food, collected our fuel. Even taking no time out to rest, dusk would have deepened into night long before we returned home for our evening rice, and coming from different directions, each of us would be forced to risk walking alone. I took as a sign of Heaven's favor that no ghost or spirit creature ever disturbed us.

Hnnnh, because the boy had been killed close to our hill, we were able to work without prying eyes. People saw, of course, that we were digging a well and planting seedling oranges. But they watched from such a distance, they could not hear the ghost machine's steady hum. We were also careful, shielding it and the bamboo pipes with prudently placed mounds of soil and brush.

Since I had chosen the sour Saangut, which can survive on very little water, and Lung Wong was especially generous with rain, people did not ask why our seedlings grew. Instead, they called us fools.

Some—like Thin Dog, who had spoken out for Hok Yee to the diviner—spoke kindly. "Don't you know if you rely on your own idea rather than the order of nature, your efforts will be futile? Give it up."

Others mocked us.

"You may as well be looking for fish up on that hill."

"Or trying to roll a ball up a slope."

Elder Brother, throwing wide the doors to his house so all could see and hear, bowed before Ma's soul tablet and said loudly, "Don't blame me for Hok Yee's stupidity. Only a wooden head would try to cultivate land that far from the river."

My mother used to say, "When a tree blooms, it's like a mother giving birth to a baby. That's when the work begins. There cannot be too many flowers or the fruit will drop. While the oranges are growing, the roots must be fertilized frequently, the leaves trimmed so they won't take food from the fruit. Except the last leaves. Those must be left to feed the next year's fruit." For us, however, the hardest work came sooner, in the third year, when we had to graft the seedlings.

The best time for grafting—lying as it does between the moment the leaf buds begin to swell and when they actually unfurl—is brief, and we had a thousand seedlings, only four pairs of hands. Four pairs of hands and three pairs of legs.

Moon Ho, too large with child to bend, had to kneel to trim the seedling down to its trunk, make the cuts, insert the slips, bind them with mud and grass. Then, unable to rise without help, she had to half crawl, half drag herself to the next tree.

She could not even finish one tree for every five that one of us completed. Yet I did not regret the child in her belly. In truth, I believed the child as necessary to us as the slips we were setting into the trees. For just as the Tonkan and Ponkan grafts would ensure that the Saangut would give sweet fruit, we needed new life to restore ours, to bring us joy.

Since the drought, our hair—which had fallen out in handfuls during those hard years—had come back. Despite our long days of heavy labor, we'd put on flesh. Our eyes were no longer sunken into our heads. But we'd become increasingly sunken into our selves, breaking silence only to discuss chores.

Alone in the darkness of my silence, I saw Moon Ho clasping tight Little Tiger's cold, dead body; I felt the weight of the grandson I had killed. Yes, I was haunted by my grandsons, though their ghosts never entered my body like my grandfather's or pursued me the way Ma's chased Elder Brother and Sister. And it was when Hok Yee and I reached out to each other by lying together that I felt their pressure the most.

More than once, when my soul took flight, it plunged into the underworld. Each time I called for my grandsons. Then I saw Yeh Yeh leaning on his cane, hobbling hurriedly toward me, ordering me to leave.

Next Ma came near. "Don't worry, I am taking care of Little Tiger, the baby, too." She pointed to a group of children. "See."

Little Tiger's only toy had been a clay rooster whistle, which we'd buried with him, and I recognized its shrill notes, saw him holding it in both his hands, its tail against his lips, his cheeks swelling out as he blew. At his feet his little brother, lively as a red pepper, tugged at Little Tiger's pants.

Both appeared happy. Yet when Yeh Yeh raised his cane and

waved me away, repeating, "Go back, go now," I stubbornly stepped forward.

Instantly the children disappeared, Yeh Yeh and Ma with them, and I felt such sorrow I did not think it possible I would see morning come again.

FANNY

North Adams, Massachusetts
1881—1885

Mother had taught Phoebe, Cynthia, and me that marriage is the summit of earthly happiness. But while Dr. Waterman was tending Mother through the final stages of consumption, he had warned me that my long neck, high shoulders, slender build, and winter coughs suggested weak lungs, a susceptibility to the disease. Frowning sternly, he'd concluded, "Since you've inherited the family weakness, you ought to be circumspect in your manner of living." I understood his meaning: unlike my mother—and her father before her—I should not marry and pass the disease on to another generation.

I might have argued that by living in a gentler climate, Uncle John and his children seemed to have escaped injury from the family weakness, that I had also been free of illness in Culloden. Instead, I nodded assent. By then I'd learned from Aunt Julia that married women—like idiots, felons, and minors—could not contract, buy, sell, or bequeath in their own names, that a woman could not keep her own child should her husband choose to take it from her. I had seen how even in Uncle John's household, a household in which the husband claimed woman was made equally with man for her own individual happiness, it was the husband who ruled, not the wife. Seething under Father's yoke, what I wanted was to rule myself, to hold the power of self-protection in my own hands. How could the bonds of matrimony attract me?

Now that I was past childbearing and had awakened to love, however, I wondered: How does a woman play at the game of hearts?

* * *

Phoebe, as lovely as I was plain, was never ill. Like Mother, she believed God had made man for himself, woman for him. And while we were yet in Culloden, she was wooed and won by Edward, a young man who had, like herself, heard the Master's call. Indeed, Edward had already been accepted for mission work in dark China, and the two made plans—plans sanctioned by the missionary society, Uncle John, and Father—to marry upon Phoebe's graduation, to turn the long journey to Edward's mission station into their wedding tour. Yet when Father had sent for us, Phoebe had not uttered a word of protest; she'd released Edward, vowing, "The heathen waiting for you to bring them the Good News will not be deprived of God's mercy for even a day on my account." She never did entertain another suitor. "Jesus is my best friend," she told those who sought her hand, "the only one I need."

Cynthia shared our eldest sister's good health but was as defiant as Phoebe was submissive: When Father instructed Cynthia to return to North Adams after her matriculation, she wrote back that she intended to take a teaching position she'd secured for herself in Saratoga Springs, New York. Father roared; Uncle John must have explained that if she lived at home and taught in the newly opened Drury Academy, Father would benefit from her salary, Phoebe and I from her assistance with household chores, nursing Julia. Nevertheless, Cynthia held to her resolve.

Where Phoebe's beauty came solely from an inner light, Cynthia had a majestic figure, perfectly molded; fine shoulders and arms; splendid auburn hair that glinted red in the sun. Is it any wonder her letters were filled with the antics of hopeful swains? Yet she, like any other woman, had no right of selection in a husband, only of refusal, and she'd turned suitors away for almost two decades before saying yes to William.

Many laughed scornfully, others in pity. All agreed, "She waited too long." Cynthia, tossing her curls, bravely ignored them. She loudly declared her admiration for William.

If William—hollow-eyed, gray, and palsied—had pleased Cynthia over troops of handsome, healthy men, why might I not find favor with Lue? And if the Master blessed me with that great mercy, would He not also give me the courage to withstand Father's certain disapproval, the gossips who would most certainly snipe at Lue and me?

* * *

Cynthia and William, seeking relief for his palsy, had purchased ten acres of rolling pineland in northern Florida, just outside DeLand.

You must come and experience for yourself the remarkable purity of air and water, she wrote. *You'll find the town agreeable as well. It has the snap and push of a California mining camp with none of the dangers. There are no hostile Indians, no wild men armed with knives and guns, no saloons. Water oaks line wide streets paved with pine needles and sawdust from the mills. Modest cottages stand beside fine residences, families living in camping-out style, business buildings of brick and stone.*

In subsequent letters, Cynthia wrote glowingly of improvements in William's health, improvements that gave him the vigor to supervise the development of an orange grove. Father growled the enterprise was foolish, and Cynthia acknowledged, *Raising oranges in this narrow peninsula is yet an experiment, one involving considerable money and labor.* Nevertheless, she airily dismissed Father's worries. *The town's founder—a Northern baking manufacturer—has such confidence in the area's genial climate and kindly soil that he has been advertising a money-back guarantee for anyone willing to set out a grove.*

Faith, so widely did Mr. DeLand distribute his call for settlers, it seemed Lue and I could not open a newspaper or magazine that we did not see it. Soon Cynthia wrote that orange fever was spreading like mining excitement had in the West, that strapping young men and invalids, poor folk as well as rich, were pouring into the state from all over the Union and beyond. Then northerners, including people from our vicinity, began wintering in DeLand, leaving as soon as sharp frosts tinted our hills red and gold.

Long before Lue had raked and burned the last autumn leaves, I would be coughing; even with the house tightly shuttered and the furnace and fire stoked high, my lungs would become inflamed. Nor did Lue's constitution seem any better adapted to our bitter climate than my own. He never complained. But I noticed his stern winter pallor, the rustle as if of dry leaves in his chest when he coughed, his sometimes labored breathing; and I prayed God that Lue and I could visit Cynthia and William, perhaps even resettle in the idyll she described.

I knew without asking that Father would refuse any such request. He could not keep me from dreaming, however, and I built air castles in which Lue and I also exchanged the damp, penetrating snows and raw winds of Massachusetts for Florida's warm sunshine and soft breezes. In the roseate-hued mist of my imaginings, I confess, Lue and I also exchanged tamped-down feelings for lives fully shared.

Was I doing wrong? Day after day, month after month, I asked the Master for a sign. Did it signify that Lue's face brightened at my approach? That his voice sometimes faltered when I leaned on him while walking? That almost every night I heard his restless marching on the other side of my door?

Hope cried, "Yes." Still I could not be sure. Not until the day Lue learned the drought was over, his brother restored. For on that day, Lue—caught up in a whirlwind of joy—threw open a window to his heart.

"Charlie Sing said my brother is safe at home. Not only that. He gave our parents money to buy land. Oh, God *is* good! He *does* answer our prayers." Lue paused, took a deep breath. "Miss Fanny, I've not only been praying for my family but for us, for the chance to take our work to DeLand."

My soul singing thanks to Jesus, I pulled my shawl tight to hide the rioting in my bosom. "That's been my dream too!"

Too excited to sit, Lue paced before me. "DeLand's climate matches that of my home district. I could experiment with the kinds of plants that farmers raise there."

"You could also expand the scope of your experiments."

"Yes. I won't have to keep everything in a greenhouse."

I smiled. "All of Florida is a greenhouse."

He laughed. "I could—" He stopped, laughed again. "Not could, but *will*. As soon as the Almighty answers this prayer too."

"Will what?" I prompted.

"I'll experiment with plantings that can restore exhausted soil. My people need that as much as they need crops that can withstand drought."

Bending our heads together, we drew detailed plans for enlarging Lue's experiments, setting out a grove and garden, building a well-appointed house—nay, not a house but a home, a sanctuary in which love would reign.

In anyone less true than Lue, Father's miserly tyranny would have crushed all charitable impulse. But when Father was felled by a stroke that left him lying flat and limp where he'd been tall and strong, bleating where he'd thundered, dependent where he'd ruled, Lue nursed him devotedly.

Neither Phoebe nor I had the strength to lift Father. I fear Lue overrated his strength when he did. Indeed, it seemed to me that during the long months Father lingered, Lue's flesh melted; he grew wan and haggard.

He would not yield to fatigue, however. And in reply to my warnings against doing himself harm, he said, "I never had the chance to care for my grandfather or grandmother or nephews. Your father I *can* help; in comforting him I bring myself ease."

The doctor told us Father was capable of opening his eyes, but he never did, and while feeding him, I frequently noticed tears seeping out from between the closed lids. I thought then he was weeping out of misery. I wept, too, out of pity. Only after the Angel of Death freed him did I realize he'd more likely been crying repentence.

The extent of Father's assets confirmed what I had long suspected: there had been no need for his close-fisted ways. According to his partner, the store yielded an annual income which—even divided among Phoebe, Cynthia, and myself—was substantial, more than enough to answer the prayer Lue and I had been raising to our Father in Heaven. Not yet, though. Father had left no will, and although Phoebe, Cynthia, and I were in accord, the lawyer to whom we entrusted the settlement of the estate explained that processing the necessary papers would require a minimum of twelve months. Meanwhile, he agreed to an allowance to meet our household expenses. Since Phoebe and Cynthia made no objection, he also agreed to forward out of my portion a sum equal to the salary Father should have paid Lue.

Lue, after tithing to the church and paying off the usurer, sent his parents every penny of the back wages I gave him.

"Every penny?" I gasped. "But from what Charlie told you, they don't need it. Besides, you haven't heard from them directly in years."

His face clouded. "I haven't written them, either. I couldn't. Not until I could send them something more than words." A broad smile of satisfaction broke through his gloom. "Finally, because of you, I could. So I did."

Faith, there never was a man more true.

I knew from loving Jesus that love breeds love. Still I trembled at the power of my feelings for Lue. How I longed to express them! But of course I could not speak out until he did. And Lue, being a gentleman, would never declare himself unless he could support a wife.

My brain burned for a solution to this conundrum. Making Lue a man of independent means by giving him my inheritance was an obvious answer. But how to broach the subject with the lawyer? How to protect the estate from Lue's generosity?

Phoebe, as innocent as I was of worldly machinations, could not help. Besides, she was yet praying for Lue to hear God's call. It was my hope, however, that Cynthia and William would show me a way to make a heaven on earth for Lue and me as they had for themselves.

In a fever of impatience, I counted the days until the estate was settled—and then to our departure for DeLand. Lue was on thorns as well. Should he hand-carry the seeds from his crosses or pack them? Should he hold out the drawings he'd made of our plans so we could continue to discuss and adjust them? Should he pull back out the books on raising citrus so we could consult them while we talked?

Several times a day he would say to me, "Pray God October fifteen will come soon."

Each time I would reply with a loud, "Amen."

Yet when the gray light of that morning crept through a break in my curtains, there was not a single sound of stir from Lue's room. Nor did he reply to my inquiring knocks, my calls. He could not. He was in a stupor.

Dr. Haven verified the frightening conclusion I'd drawn from the blood soaking Lue's pillow, bedclothes, and nightshirt; the ghostly white of his skin; my inability to rouse him: Lue had suffered a severe hemorrhage of the lungs.

"How long before he regains consciousness, before he recovers sufficiently for us to travel?"

"Don't you understand, Miss Burlingame? Lue has galloping consumption. One lung is gone and the other affected seriously. The only journey he'll be taking is to his Maker."

As nearly as I can recall, Dr. Haven said nothing more. But I cannot be certain since my chest seized and I suffered such shortness of breath he had to administer salts.

"There has to be something you can do," I insisted as soon as I recovered sufficiently to speak.

Dr. Haven snapped his bag shut. "No, Miss Burlingame. There is not."

During family prayer that night, Phoebe murmured, " 'The Lord giveth, the Lord taketh away. Blessed be the name of the Lord.' "

She had raised up this same verse in prayer when Dr. Haven had told us Father could not live. But Father had been an old man whose work was done. Lue, not yet thirty, was in his prime. His work lay before him.

Kneeling by Lue, I vowed, "You *will* recover. You *will.*"

At the sound of my voice, his eyes opened wide, his mouth gaped, and there was a terrible rasping.

I bent my head close to his. "What is it?"

Blood bubbled at his lips. My hands shaking, I reached for a cloth—knocked over the bottles on the table. The bottles fell onto the floor and shattered. Lue jerked as if flayed by a whip. Tears spilled from my eyes, splashed on his cheek. Moaning, he twisted and flailed.

From behind me Phoebe reached down, took the cloth from my hands, gently wiped Lue clean. His muttering quieted. He ceased his flailing. When she closed his eyes with the tips of her fingers, he offered no resistance but released a soft, almost melodious sigh through the ugly gurgling in his throat.

Phoebe had ever been soothing where I was awkward. Nevertheless, watching her minister to Lue and seeing him relax under her touch, I confess that jealousy wrung my heart. Ashamed, I struggled against its awful pull and yielded to Phoebe's gift for nursing.

I could not, would not, yield to her pronouncement, however, and I called in a specialist from Boston. He confirmed Dr. Haven's prognosis. "The illness has been creeping up on the man for a long time. Now it has him by the throat. There is nothing any mortal can do to save him."

SUM JUI

Toishan, China
1882—1885

Moon Ho gave us not one grandchild but two—twin grand-daughters. We were, in truth, sorry they were not boys. Girls, belonging as they do to other people when they marry, are blessings that have to end, goods on which a family is bound to lose capital, and we had none to spare.

Nevertheless, Hok Yee could not hide his pleasure when he pinched and nibbled their fat little cheeks, his pride when he crowed over their loud suckling. I prepared celebration food: red-dyed eggs of happiness to give to family and neighbors, long-life noodles for us.

At the meal's end, my husband's foot touched mine. "I have names for our granddaughters," he said softly. "Bo Jun, Truly Precious, and Lin Hei, Link Happiness."

The twins were small enough to fit into a single *meh dai*. And since Moon Ho carried them everywhere, they were with her when she was set upon.

"*Ai yah*," she gasped. "I was washing clothes down by the river. Stooped over. Pounding a pair of pants against a rock. The animal lunged from behind."

She paused, took a deep breath, a gulp of hot water. "I tell you, if it had not misjudged and leaped over my head, landing in the river, it would surely have killed me and the babies."

From the flash of fur Moon Ho caught out of the corner of her eye as the animal scrambled out of the water and slunk into the tall weeds crowding the opposite bank, she thought it was a fox rather than a cat. But she had fallen flat against the rock as it swooped over her, so she could not be certain. Neither could we find tracks for a cat or fox or any other earthly animal.

Could Elder Sister be working her evil again? I wondered. I could see she was not abusing Bik Wun. Nor were Elder Brother or Wai Yin. And Bik Wun, generously laying aside their previous ill treatment, was teaching Sesame to be filial to his grandparents and father. We had no grandson, no earnings except our shares from Fourth Brother's fields, nothing Elder Sister could possibly envy. Surely there was no reason for her to risk stirring Ma's anger by making trouble?

That there were spirit creatures lurking in the area, however, there was no doubt. And Hok Yee agreed with me that regardless of any work we might have to leave undone, we had to take the attack on Moon Ho as a warning from Heaven that none of us should go anywhere alone.

Our trees were so green we had to cut the bark to force them to flower. By then, Bo Jun and Lin Hei had grown too big to be carried comfortably in one *meh dai*. But they were as adventurous as their uncle, Gim Gong, had been, so Moon Ho and I each worked with one of the babies tied to our back. Even after both feel asleep in the steamy heat of the late afternoon sun, we did not dare put them down. Since Moon Ho had been attacked, there had been too many reports of ghostly creatures.

While my hands busied themselves, I thought of Gim Gong, the letter and gold he had sent. No, he had not forgotten us. He had, he wrote, never stopped praying to the Jesus God on our behalf. And through his work in his teacher's garden, he had been looking for ways to help our people.

"His ghost God didn't save my sons," Wai Seuk had said bitterly. But wasn't that why Gim Gong had stopped writing until he'd had gold to send? Because he knew that, too, and was ashamed?

That he had been holding us in his heart all these years warmed mine. Remembering the flowers he'd raised in our courtyard, I wondered what marvels he might be making in his ghost teacher's garden, what he would say about our orchard.

Suddenly, the straps of the *meh dai* tugged sharply, as they did whenever Bo Jun's head fell backwards in her sleep, jerking me out of my musings. Quickly I tilted forward so the cloth would not cut into her neck and wake her. My eyes drawn from the branch I was working on, I noticed a gathering of men farther downhill, near Hok Yee.

"How is it possible your trees are so green?" Thin Dog was asking. "Lung Wong hasn't even sent enough rain for them to live."

Hok Yee finished the cut he was making. "We have a well."

Thin Dog frowned. "I saw Wai Seuk digging it. But I've never seen you draw water out."

"Or carry water to the trees," Elder Brother added.

Hok Yee waved in the direction of the river, the two men treading the wheel, slowly drawing water up into irrigation drains alongside the footpaths. "We do the same."

Shielding their eyes against the glare of the setting sun, Elder Brother, Thin Dog, and the other men studied our hill.

"There's bamboo pipes all right, but I don't see any wheel."

"Nor I."

"Is it behind that pile of brush?"

"You'd see the top if it was."

"And the men working it."

"Besides, all four of them are here and they don't have anyone working for them. Who's doing the treading?"

Pressed, Hok Yee stopped cutting, held up his hand for quiet, and explained Wai Seuk had brought back a ghost machine that raised water by itself.

Elder Brother turned to our neighbor. "*Ai yah,* was it a ghost from that machine which killed your son?"

Our neighbor's sun-browned face paled. He sank onto his haunches.

Hok Yee quickly offered him water from our pot. "The ghost machine has no ghost in it. Moreover, the machine was still in our house when the boy was attacked."

"The ghost could have followed the boy," Elder Brother suggested.

Our neighbor nodded. Others did, too. And there was a muttering of agreement. Bo Jun began to whimper. As I undid the ties and rocked her in my arms, I heard Hok Yee remind the men that the hunters had said a cat attacked the boy.

"That's what they saw when they went into the hills. And not just one cat but many."

"Foreign ghosts are clever," Elder Brother insisted. "They can change into different forms. And the machine might hold many ghosts. How else can it draw up enough water for the whole hill?"

Again heads nodded, and there was a second, louder round of muttered agreement.

Wai Seuk stepped forward. Even from a distance of more than ten, twelve trees I could see he was angry. Yet his voice, when he spoke, was reasoned. "If I brought the ghosts as you claim, why did they attack my wife?"

Elder Brother smirked. *"Because* you brought them."

"If there are ghosts in our ghost machine, then it follows there must be ghosts in the ghost music box Fourth Brother gave Ba and in the machine that marks foreign-ghost time. Both are still in your house."

Wai Seuk turned to our neighbor. "Didn't you bring back an iron tailor from Gold Mountain? And, you, Thin Dog. Don't you have foreign-ghost goods, too?"

Looking steadily at each man, he continued, "At the very least, one house in five in this village, in this district, holds something from Gold Mountain." His eyes rested on Elder Brother. "Are you willing to accuse every person with ghost goods, yourself as well?"

Elder Brother bristled and blustered, backed down, the other men with him. But we knew we'd not heard the last from them. Now that it looked as if our trees might bear, they would search for a way around Wai Seuk's reasoning. Nor could we rely any longer on fear of spirit creatures to protect our ghost machine.

FANNY

North Adams, Massachusetts
1885—1887

Phoebe accepted the Boston specialist's prognosis for Lue just as she had Dr. Haven's. I searched the papers for advertisements of new elixirs, stories of miraculous cures.

There was, I discovered, a homeopathic physician in south Berkshire who boasted of success with purges. In answer to my letter of inquiry, he wrote: *Diseases of the chest are caused by tapeworm much more frequently than is generally believed. I've observed tapeworms insinuate their heads as high as the chambers of the nose, occasioning violent catarrh attended with the copious defluxions of mucosities and blood that you describe in your patient. Enclosed is my receipt for a cure.*

Carefully following his instructions, I made up worm clysters of aloes, castor oil, linseed, rose leaves, and bay salt. I persuaded Phoebe to administer a dose once a day with an enema syringe as prescribed. But Lue, weakened by his loss of blood, could not bear the effects of the remedy.

I then engaged a doctor who claimed cures through hanging his patients from rings suspended from the ceiling, swinging them backward and forward, sideways and in a circle. Lue, uttering queer little cries and panting for breath in strangled gulps, resisted the treatment, clutching at Phoebe's skirt, her hands, twisting this way and that until he exhausted what little strength he yet retained and there was only the faintest flutter of breath between his lips.

For the rest of that day and all the next, his eyes did not close but gazed about wildly. He cowered like a frightened fawn from anyone who came near, even Phoebe. When the doctor arrived for another treatment, I sent him away.

Decoctions of sarsaparilla and pomegranate root, frictions with camphor pomatum, and alcohol compresses also failed, and Lue's attempts to draw breath into his congested lung grew ever more labored, the rattle in his chest louder. Although I burned papers and threw pungent vinegar onto red-hot coals to purify the air in his room, I could not drive out the sick, cloying smell that heralds the Angel of Death. And in the fearful wail of the wind, I heard the harsh, determined flap of his wings.

So desperate did I then become that when I read of a doctor who was said to have cured a widow's consumptive son by exhuming the body of a sister who had recently died from the same disease, taking out all the organs where blood could be found and burning them, I confess that only the absence of a suitable corpse prevented me from sending for the quack.

It aches me yet to recall Lue's swift sinking, his distress since fever had driven away his reason, perhaps his faith as well.

"Even the most civilized African retains his savage animal nature," Aunt Julia used to say. And Phoebe had more than once sighed and said the same was true of her Chinese converts. "They are never entirely rid of their superstitions."

"Not Lue," I had protested vehemently. "He is the genuine article—a civilized Christian gentleman right down to his very soul." When Lue fell into delirium, however, my certainty wavered.

Father, at the approach of the Angel of Death, had shed all signs of misery and unease. Indeed, with the knowledge that Heaven awaited him, he'd turned radiant with joy. Lue twitched in terror. Sweat soaked his nightshirts. He reverted to his native tongue.

Yet Phoebe could still calm Lue by taking his hand and humming a hymn or raising a prayer. Would that be possible if he had slipped back into the thralldom of superstition? I recognized, of course, that the answer likely lay in Lue's mutterings. Nevertheless, I hesitated to call in Charlie Sing to interpret. Despair had not yet murdered all my hopes for Lue's recovery, and I feared Charlie might discover thoughts and feelings Lue preferred to keep private—as he did his writings in his journals. How, though, would I answer Lue in the life to come if his faint but desperate mutterings were last messages for his family, pleas to stop the Devil from repossessing his soul?

My every nerve strained to the utmost, I sent for Charlie.

He claimed Lue's tortured breathing was too loud, his whisperings too soft. "I cannot make anything out."

But Charlie's air of satisfaction betrayed him.

From the other side of Lue's bed, I accused, "You *have* understood something."

Charlie, with cool possession, insisted he had not. When I pressed, he stood on his dignity.

Quietly, Phoebe, standing beside me, reminded Charlie that he was a Christian, that his Christian duty was to tell the truth. "You need have no fear."

"It is not me who is afraid but Gim Gong," he blazed. "He talking to his grandma and baby nephews. No, he not talking. He *begging*. Yes, he begging them to forgive him."

"He bears no blame for their deaths," I said hotly.

Charlie shrugged.

Phoebe placed her hand over mine. "If only Lue had answered God's call and gone home, they could have enjoyed the gift of life eternal."

Withdrawing my hand from hers, I repeated, "Lue bears no blame." I fixed my eyes on Charlie. "Tell Lue. Tell him he bears no blame."

Phoebe shook her head. "Tell Lue that although blame does lie at his door, he has been washed clean of it by the blood of the Lamb."

Slowly Charlie began to speak. What he said, however, we could not know.

In the days that followed, Lue gradually became more easy. His eyes lost their wild, woeful look. He ceased his feeble flailing, the muttered ravings of a disordered mind. His skin, colorless as a wax doll's, cooled. His chest no longer rattled like earth falling down on a coffin.

Dropping onto my knees, I prayed the Master as I had never prayed before that He would raise Lue up to a full recovery. The next afternoon, Lue wakened from his long stupor—only to sink back into a faint. He breathed more softly and regularly, then gasped in violent fits of coughing that turned his lips blue. He rallied wonderfully. He suffered fierce relapses.

In brief, he mended, then faltered. But each time it seemed he would fail altogether, the Master lifted Lue in His arms, pulling him back from the borders of the grave. And at last the day came when victory was sure.

Oh, how I thanked Him and praised His name!

I never suspected He would launch yet another bolt, and soon.

For weeks Lue was so wasted and feeble that the least exertion made him feverish. His first time out of bed, he tottered, rolled, and pitched like a baby learning to walk. Even talking brought on a hectic flush, and he passed the better part of each day in sleep.

While Lue was awake, I would read to him. Or we would sit in that silent communion between friends that can be as satisfying as speech. Gradually he improved, and I found myself surrendering once again to the reckless pleasure of daydreams.

When his eye finally grew bright, his color good, his voice clear, I exulted, "You'll soon be strong enough for us to leave for DeLand."

Looking down, Lue studied his quilt. He plucked at its threads, the collar of his nightshirt. His response startled. Was it possible his feelings for me and for his work had changed? Uncertain what to say or do, I gazed at him in bewilderment.

"While I was sick, I saw them," he said with mournful tenderness. "My grandmother and nephews. They were falling into hellfire, and they kept calling out to me, begging me to save them. But when I reached out, Satan pushed me back with his pitchfork, and they fell screaming into the flames."

Lue shuddered. Gooseflesh prickled my arms, the back of my neck.

"Miss Fanny, their skin blistered and peeled off in strips, their mouths became dark pits without sound, and the smell was so terrible I couldn't breathe."

Lue's lips trembled, his voice trailed into a thin whisper. "Had I only listened to God more carefully, I would have understood my true duty, and they could have been safe in the Master's arms." He paused, took a deep breath, released it resolutely. "But God is good. He has restored me so I can go home and save the rest of my family, the people in my village and district."

The shock was terrible. Could I have been so mistaken in what I had believed—nay, still believed—was God's purpose for Lue that I had directed him onto the wrong path? Or had I muddled right and wrong in my feelings for him? Perhaps the Master had been testing me and found me wanting. Was that why He was taking Lue?

My thoughts swirled. The room swam. Wrestling for control, I could not speak. Lue, plainly exhausted, sank back onto his pillows, closed his eyes.

"Miss Phoebe once thought she heard the call, but she was wrong. Perhaps you are mistaken, too," I said at last.

Lue raised his eyes to meet mine. "Remember when you told me God was speaking to me through my work with plants? I did not hear Him then. I cannot say I have heard Him now. But I did hear my grandmother and nephews, and I believe He was speaking to me through them."

I argued that Lue's dream was a nightmare born of his fever, something Charlie Sing might have said. Phoebe proclaimed it a vision.

Letters from her Chinese converts who had returned to China told of a school one had opened, improvements in hygiene another had instituted, an entire village brought to Jesus. None of these Chinamen was as educated or talented as Lue, and Phoebe spoke of his coming mission as the crown on Mr. DeWitt's prophecy. I protested otherwise.

From everything Lue had told us, his village was primitive and filthy, the people ignorant. And although he was on the mend, consumption is the most deceitful of diseases. A great improvement can be followed by a sudden decline. If he were to suffer a relapse, how would his family care for him?

Moreover, since Chinese planning to return to China kept their queues, Lue—with his neatly trimmed hair and western suit—would be as conspicuous in his village as an ultraist with bobbed hair and bloomers in North Adams. Faith, even in civilized Massachusetts, ultraists sometimes had mud and stones flung at them, and they were denounced so vehemently that suffragist leaders like Miss Susan Anthony had been compelled to abandon the practical bloomer for the traditional long skirt although it drabbles in the mud and becomes caught in carriage wheels. How would Lue fare in dark China?

Of course, replacing his queue would be possible—though he was so high minded he might refuse. In any case, it was because of what they called Lue's "peculiar ideas," not his lack of a queue, that the Chinese in North Adams shunned him. What if his family, his village, abused him, too? Where could he go?

Returning missionaries said Chinese officials had become so bitterly antiforeign that some of them secretly paid mobs to attack foreigners and westernized Chinamen. Clearly Lue could expect no help from his government. And Washington, bowing to public opinion, had passed a law of exclusion against the Chinese that would prevent him from returning to America. Ever.

To all of these concerns, Phoebe said, "Lue will do his best and leave the consequences to the Lord." When I raised them with Lue, his gaunt frame shook, but he said with dogged courage, "I entrusted my family to the justice and mercy of God. So must, so *do* I entrust myself."

Lue's society was dear to me. A future without him was no future. But Phoebe had surely felt as strongly about Edward, and she had not held him from the Lord's work. How could I stop Lue?

Taking Phoebe as my polestar of right, I buried my dreams of a life with Lue; I subdued my desires and directed the bank to release the necessary funds for him to purchase passage for China.

Where Phoebe, a model of earthly goodness, had freed Edward cheerfully, however, I confess I felt inclined to howl. And throughout Lue's long convalescence, my heart burned with the selfish hope that he would tell me he was mistaken after all, that God's purpose for him was not to take the Good News to his family in China but to work with plants in DeLand with me.

Lue, too noble to shirk what he believed his duty, did not speak the words I longed to hear. Indeed, he withdrew from close conversation with me as he had from my nursing, turning ever more to Phoebe.

Watching them put their heads together over his mission as he and I had over plants, I was struck by the same waves of abandonment and uselessness that had swept me into deep waters during the long, lonely years before the Master sent Lue to me. And, oh, how the temptation to ease my distress with laudanum molested me. But I knew that if I fell from grace, I would lose any hope for reprieve from the Master, and that stayed my hand.

As the day set for Lue's departure neared, I became certain that he, too, was praying for a reprieve.

Where before he had always hummed cheerily while in the greenhouse, he now worked soberly, transplanting his hybrids, touching their leaves, even scraping mold off his boots with melancholy tenderness.

Night after night, I'd hear his tread on the stairs, see his ghostly figure glide out the kitchen door to the greenhouse. He never entered. Instead, raising his arms high, he'd embrace the cold panes of glass, then slowly sink to his knees, his body shaking with what seemed like silent weeping.

When I suggested he might have misgivings regarding his mission, however, he insisted he did not. When I remarked on the state of his eyes, he claimed they were swollen and discolored on account of neuralgia.

The morning he was to leave for China, my head throbbed with misery, my throat choked with tears. But, recognizing Lue was troubled for all he was playing the stoic, I would not add to his burden by revealing I was ill. So I forced myself to eat a hearty breakfast. I smiled and spoke lightly when I gave him the basket of comforts I had prepared.

Phoebe, always joyful in the Lord, gaily suggested we commemorate the beginning of Lue's service for the Master by each opening the Bible and reading a verse from wherever our fingers should fall.

"I'll begin," she offered.

As the Good Book fell open, she beamed, sang out a strong,

"Yes, Lord. This is Lue. Psalm 66, verse 10. 'For you, O God, have tested us; you have refined us as silver is refined.' "

Faith, Lue *had* come out of his illness handsomer, truer, and so beloved that I again cried out in my heart to the Master, "I cannot bear to let him go." And again back came the hard answer, "Lue is not yours to keep."

Phoebe passed the Bible to Lue. He accepted it and opened it with a smile. But he could not prevent a traitorous huskiness from creeping into his voice as he read, "Psalm 3, verse 7: " 'Up, Lord, and help me.' "

I, too, was unsuccessful in hiding my true feelings. Despite my best efforts, my fingers trembled as I took the Bible from Lue, my voice faltered and I stumbled through the final words of Job 42, verse 2. " 'I know that thou, Lord, canst do all things, and that no purpose of thine can be thwarted.' "

Lue, leaning so close his breath brushed my cheek, closed the Bible, set it on the table. His fingers touched mine like a benediction, and before I could prevent it, hope scorching my breast yet again.

"Now," I told myself. "Now the Master will grant us our reprieve."

But He did not.

We traveled to the depot in silence.

About to board the train, Lue turned—and again hope blazed. But as he started across the platform, the stationmaster shouted warning.

Lue froze.

"Come," my heart cried.

Bowing his head, he spun on his heel, leaped up the steps of the train.

I covered my mouth to keep from calling out.

Unable to remain where every room held reminders of Lue, I arranged to visit Cynthia. But Lue was never far from my thoughts. Indeed, on the train to New York and then on the boat to Jacksonville, my imagination was so filled with his image and voice that when transferring to a small steamer at the mouth of Florida's St. Johns River, I took a stranger's arm thinking it was Lue's. The mistake chilled my heart with renewed loss, and I studied the scenery in the first stretch of the river through a mist of tears.

Like a vast lagoon, the shores on either side rose in a series of bold bluffs and declivities covered with towering forests of pines, cabbage palms, hickory, sweet gums, and willows. Spanish moss draped live oaks in funereal festoons. Carolina asters and brilliantly hued trumpet vines spiraled around feathery tipped cypresses. Wily lynxes, foxes, wildcats, and white-tailed deer bounded through the trees in tawny streaks. In my longing for Lue, I foolishly thought I saw him as well.

The land was thinly settled with only an occasional cabin, an orange grove, a few razorback hogs or cattle penned in a fenced clearing. Even the settlements where the steamer stopped were no more than a cluster of cabins near a store and a pier.

Each time the boat prepared to dock, the captain sounded the horn twice, triggering a flurry of activity on land. Settlers arriving at the last minute to trade cracked long, snakelike whips at their horses, driving them to the limit. Men rolling barrels of fish and kegs of syrup onto the pier hollered at each other to hurry. Barefoot children ran, yelling, down to the riverbank with packs of dogs chasing after them, yelping and barking. Negro deckhands unloaded and then loaded cargo while passengers hurried down the gangplank to visit with those ashore. If Lue had been with me, we would have gone exploring. Alone, I sought refuge from the stir and bustle, going below until we were underway once more.

Upriver, jungle vegetation turned the water a dark coffee color. The course narrowed and twisted, becoming so tortuous I gasped and reached for Lue each time the boat turned a curve. But of course he was not there.

Like a kaleidoscopic view, the scenery changed constantly. Alligators, often ten or more together, sunned themselves on dark logs. Some, disturbed by the gentle chug of the boat's engines, slid down into the water to float, becoming invisible except for the tops of their heads. Ducks of all varieties splashed in the bayous. Ospreys swooped fearlessly to grab fish in their talons.

Near the shoreline, sandhill cranes honked melodiously and the cypress came alive with snowy egrets. Tall flamingos poked delicately in thickets of tropical grasses and reeds or stood in motionless meditation, rising and wheeling gracefully into the distance whenever the boat came too close. High above, red-shouldered hawks whistled to their mates.

In the afternoon, several passing showers washed the already wonderfully varied greens, reds, yellows, and purples to a dazzling brightness. The rich perfume of enormous blossoms and the tang of resiny pine gladdened my senses so that I fancied myself transported to the original Eden. Later, as luminous apricot sunset gave way to dark night, the horrible, terrifying screams of panthers destroyed this vision. The Negro deckhands' soul-stirring camp-meeting hymns, the most sorrowful of all earthly music, reminded me that Paradise has been lost to us this side of the grave, and I wondered how I could ever have harbored the hope of happiness with Lue.

SHEBA

DeLand, Florida
1866—1876

Listen. I ain't got the blessing of book learning. But I got eyes for seeing, ears for listening, and a good memory to call upon. And, no, I ain't ever stepped out of Florida. But I seen and heard a heap anyways cause people the world over, even Chinamens, come here. Some—like the first white folks I cooked and kept house for, Miss Cynthia and the Major—come for the strong ground, and they make themselves new homeplaces. Others—like Miss Cynthia's sister, Miss Fanny—is snowbirds running from cold to our hot sun. Then there's the old people—the ones white folks stole from Africa to do for them—and the Africans' childrens and grandchildrens, colored folks like my man Jim and me.

My mama and daddy, now, they was born in slavery.

"Slavery days was dog days," Mama'd say. "Soon as a girl began her misery, Old Master'd make her take a man so he could get himself more slaves. And whoever Old Master took a notion to, that body was his."

He used Mama's mama, Grandma Sue, for a wife, and it was clear to anyone with eyes Mama was crossbreeded: her skin, the color of cooked cane syrup, and her hair, even lighter and very fine and straight, gived it away. But Old Mistress, she couldn't do nothing cept pretend she ain't noticed.

Day Old Master died, howsomever, her true feelings jumped out. She ain't even laid him out decent before she sent for the trader and told him to sell Grandma Sue down the river.

Mama was just a little bit of a gal, no more than four or five, but ain't nobody too young to feel. In Grandma Sue's arms, she was happy as if she was in Diddy-Wah-Diddy where nobody knows sorrow, the streets play tunes when walked on, and all shoes have songs in them. Nights she had to lie alone cause Old Master come to the cabin and fall on Grandma Sue, Mama couldn't get warm. She shook hard as the bed rocking under her mama and daddy, her teeth chattering apace with the cornshucks rustling in the mattress.

The trader carried chains and a whip, frightening Mama even more than Old Master did, and she clung to Grandma Sue like a limpet.

"The pickaninny too?" the trader asked.

"No," Old Mistress said. "She stays."

Course Grandma Sue wept and begged mercy, but Old Mistress didn't think no more of selling a baby from its mother than taking a heifer from a cow. Huh, slaves was less than dust to her, and she ordered Aunt Mattie, the woman what minded the slave children, to take Mama.

Mama, her throat plugged with terror, couldn't say nothing. But she tightened her hold round Grandma Sue's neck so Aunt Mattie couldn't tear her off. Took the trader's whip to do that. Even so, Mama no sooner fell in the dirt than she scrabbled after Grandma Sue.

Aunt Mattie scooped Mama up and held her close. "Give it up, child," she whispered. "Give it up."

In time Aunt Mattie healed Mama's outside hurts with salve. But she couldn't do nothing about the inside hurts cause she couldn't bring Grandma Sue back, she couldn't change the way things is.

Stead of playing in the kitchen at the big house while Grandma Sue cooked, Mama got to go out to the fields at first light to work as a scarecrow, chasing birds from the shoots of corn just poking up their heads. She got no shoes, and long before sundown, her feets hurt so bad she couldn't hardly walk.

Before, Mama'd eaten from the same roasted meats and cakes Grandma Sue made for the people in the big house. Now she got to fight a mess of children, even dogs, ducks, and peafowl, for her share of the buttermilk and crumbled cornbread or greens and bones Aunt Mattie poured into a wooden trough in the yard twice a day.

"Wasn't for your daddy taking up for me," Mama'd say, "I'd have gone hungry."

Mark it down, Daddy wasn't much bigger than Mama. Unlike Mama, howsomever, he'd come up in quarters. He never did know who his mama or daddy was. Old Master'd brung him home one day with a passle of younguns what he'd gived to Aunt Mattie for raising. Anyways, Daddy knowed how to grab for himself. He got to. And he and Aunt Mattie learned Mama how, too.

Aunt Mattie, now, she was from Africa. And every night, when she put Mama and Daddy and all the other childrens down for the night, she'd tell them, "Africa been a land of magic power since the beginning of time. Moses conjuring his rod into a snake shows it, and there's plenty others what got his gift. Some is born with the power. Others get it through learning."

Well, Aunt Mattie wasn't born with the gift. She never got the chance to learn, neither. Why? Cause she was just a gal when she was fooled aboard a slave ship.

She was playing on the beach, see, when a slaver done slip up to the water's edge in a boat what had a pretty piece of red flannel hanging over the side. Being a curious gal, she went close to look at what she ain't seen before, and quick as a flash of lightning, the slaver grabbed her.

A heap of younguns was tricked the same way, not only Aunt Mattie. And when their folks went looking for their little chaps, they got caught too. They never got the comfort of being family again, mind. The slavers, separating the mens from the womens and herding the younguns into pens by themselves, made sure of that.

Mark it down, the slavers treated the Africans worse than awful from the get-go. But chained in the holds of the slave ships, the Africans could only fret. Soon as they was turned into the fields, howsomever, folks what possessed the magic power got together and commenced to move in a ring.

Round and round they went, stomping the ground faster and faster. Huh, their feets got to thundering, and they raised so much dust the overseer come running with his whip. But that lash never touched them. No. Cause the Africans, stretching their arms out, took wing.

"We going home to Africa," they said, rising up like birds. "Goodie-bye, goodie-bye."

Aunt Mattie was right there in the field, and she seen them. Yes, she seen them Africans fly with her own eyes. And she told my mama and daddy, what told me, just like I'm telling you.

Aunt Mattie learned Mama and Daddy every little thing she could remember about Africa. But she couldn't pass on what she ain't got, so neither one knowed any magic. All the same, Daddy was powerful. To me, anyways.

He was a double-strengthed man, see, strong outside and in. His back was a sight—scarred up and brittled from whippings. But the lash never did cut the starch out of him. No. During the Freedom War, he got him a yearling calf by the tail and lit out with it, stepping on its droppings so the hounds'd lose track. Huh, he dodged them hounds all the way to the Yankees and fought in the Gospel Army.

"Your daddy fought hard," Mama'd tell me. "Hard and strong."

Come Surrender, Daddy figured he'd crossed over the River Jordan and received deliverance. Tossing the slave name he and Mama was born under, he took him the freedom name of Jordan. And when Mama birthed me the next year, she named me for King Solomon's queen.

First thing in the morning and last thing at night, she'd say, "You black and you beautiful like that queen." Or, "You is a queen, a queen born in freedom."

Daddy told me the same, adding, "When we was coming up and the overseer or Old Mistress was meanly, Aunt Mattie'd tell us, 'Don't you fret. Bottom rail will rise to the top someday.' Well, we ain't at the top. Not yet. But we got us our freedom and a farm. We got us a start, a right good start." Then he'd laugh and swing me up over his head. "You the top rail already."

Flying high, I tell you I did believe I was the top rail, a queen.

Now Daddy'd saved most every penny of his army wages, and when he'd come back from the fighting, he'd bought a stretch of good bottomland from Old Mistress and her grandson, Master Gillian.

"They was mighty glad to sell," Mama said. "Old Mistress'd lost all but her youngest grandson, Master Gillian, to the fighting, her stock and silver to the Yankees what passed through, most of her stores as well. Last year of the war, we couldn't even get salt for our cooking or oil for our lamps. Slaves kept disappearing. And the day the Freedom man come and read the President's paper what said we was free, everybody what wasn't feeble or sickly or waiting for somebody—like I was for your daddy—everybody picked up their heels and took off. Ain't knowed where they was going, just wanted to see about something else, somewhere else.

"Anyways, Old Mistress and Master Gillian ain't never worked a lick in their lives. They lived off other folks' labor. So when they seen your daddy's cash—real cash, not worthless Confederate trash—their eyes bulged big as fists, and they snatched it right quick. Then they bought a few mules and brung in freedmens to work the plantation on shares, with Master Gillian furnishing quarters, grub, seed, and use of his mules and tools in exchange for half the crop and deducts from the rest.

"Sound all right, could've been all right, but Master Gillian was the sorriest piece of a man, fit for nothing. He weasled out of the war by paying a Cracker to fight in his place. And he fixed the deducts so that come August, when the cotton was picked and sold, the folks doing the work owed *him* money. He was scared they'd leave him, see, so he held them down. Then he spent so much on corn liquor he couldn't furnish them the fertilizer he oughta.

"Huh, you put nothing into the soil, you get nothing out. Your daddy and me knowed that, and we plumped up our soil with fertilizer, bent our backs, and fell on our hoes."

*   *   *

Mama and Daddy learned me how to work with them, and together we was turning that bottomland into a right fine farm. But
the Ku Klux, they was against that.

Mark it down, there wasn't nothing they hated more than seeing
Colored rise. When the Bureau, the Freedmen's Bureau, built a
school for colored children, the KK burned it down, so I never did
learn me how to read. They shot to pieces the Yankee what was telling colored folks they oughta take forty acres and a mule from their
old masters. And they come after my daddy.

I was a sizable gal already, but I don't mind telling you when I
was wakened by galloping, looked out the window, and seen a
whole army of ghosts busting across the fields, I was scared. Ain't
no need for Daddy to say, "Get down." I was down already, down
and shaking.

Daddy started out the door, Mama after him. He turned round,
touched her shoulder gentle, and said real quiet, "Stay with Sheba."

Standing in the moonlight, Mama looked like something hunted
what don't know which way to turn. I leaked a whimper I couldn't
swallow. She cocked her head, spinned her eyes on me, Daddy, and
the Ku Klux thundering close. Then she reached up, took Daddy's
hand what was on her shoulder, pressed it against her face, let it go,
and come in, shutting the door behind her.

All that happen quick as anything, mind, but Mama was just
dropping down beside me when the hoofbeats stopped. Listening to
the scuffling of hooves in our yard, my skin prickled and my heart
leaped like a hooked fish. Only fear for my daddy gived me the dar-
ing to peer out a knothole and look for him.

The Ku Klux was by the well, the mens looking ten feet high, the
horses big as elephants, all robed in white. I counted eleven, heard
a bullwhip crack, hiss through the air like water on a red-hot iron,
then another and another and another. Wherever them whips
snapped and snaked, a dark shadow jumped. I'd found my daddy.

At every crack, every leap, Mama jerked. I stuffed my fist into
my mouth to keep from crying out. Way after a while, the leader
held up his whip. Directly, the others followed. The cracking and
snapping stopped. The shadow what was my daddy stilled.

"We're just up from Hell, and I'm feeling pretty dry. Draw me
some water," the leader hollered in a strange, put-on-like voice I
recognized was Master Gillian's.

Daddy limped over to the well, filled a bucket, and toted it over. Master Gillian lifted the bucket under his hood, then brung it down empty.

Making a loud smacking noise, he told Daddy, "Sure is hot in Hell. You don't want to find out how hot, you get off what ain't yours."

SUM JUI

Toishan, China
1885—1888

When Gim Gong was a boy, his favorite story had been the one of Muk Leen, the Buddhist saint.

"Muk Leen's mother did not believe Buddha's teachings," I would begin.

His eyes wet with tears, Gim Gong would continue, "So she was imprisoned in Hell where she got nothing to eat."

"Right. Then Muk Leen, seeing she was hungry, sent her a big pot of rice gruel."

"But her jailers ate it all."

"Muk Leen could have given up. He could have told himself he'd tried. Knowing filial piety is the root of all virtue, however, he looked for another way to send his mother the gruel."

Quickly Gim Gong would rub his eyes dry with his little fists, break into a smile, and finish all in a rush. "Muk Leen took a lot of red jujube, longans, sesame seeds, black sugar, and peanuts and mixed them into the gruel, and the jailers, thinking it was muddy soil, gave it to his mother, and she was saved."

It seemed to me Gim Gong was not unlike Muk Leen. Yes, his first attempt to help us had failed. Yet he had not abandoned us. And having replaced his worthless prayers with gold, he made it possible for us to build a fortified tower of gray brick around the well and ghost machine, to buy two ghost guns.

Wai Seuk taught his father, his wife, and me how to use the guns. Then, as warning, we each fired once out in the open; we spoke loudly of how there would always be at least one of us in the tower keeping watch.

We thought, we hoped that would be enough to prevent any attempts at attack. But late one night, I noticed the flicker of torches approaching the base of the hill. Immediately I poked my gun barrel through a cleft in the tower wall. Behind me I heard the rasp of metal against brick, knew Hok Yee, on the opposite side, had done the same, and realized we were surrounded.

That those carrying the torches intended to set fire to the orchard was clear. Why else would they betray their presence with light? And although there were too many and they were too distant, moving too swiftly for me to take proper aim, I pulled the trigger.

The force of the explosion knocked me down. Scrambling back up, I reloaded, fired a second shot, a third. Hok Yee's gun likewise roared over and over.

Soon the sharp, bitter smell of gunpowder filled the air.

Smoke stung my eyes, blinding.

Still I continued to fire.

Now, looking back, I cannot say for certain how many shots we fired that night. Nor did we ever discover who the attackers were or whether anyone was hit. What I can tell you is that when the smoke cleared, the lights were gone—and none of us had to fire a gun again.

Whenever a knot of people gathered, however, Elder Brother would shake his head and sigh, "It's guns that allow the foreign ghosts to force opium on our people."

"*Ai yah,*" Elder Sister would cry. "That poison almost killed our son. Those ghosts have no morality."

There was always a returned Gold Mountain guest or someone from a Gold Mountain family who would leap at their bait.

"It's not that the ghosts have *no* morality. Rather, their morality is not fixed. They say they love what is good, that they especially love justice. Yet their treatment of our people is outrageous."

Others, of course, would jump in.

"That's right. Look how they got us to open the doors to our country by saying we could go freely to theirs. Now they're shutting us out."

"The ghosts see us as weak. They like to side with the strong."

"*Hnnnh*, they are who made us weak."

Relentless as a dog gnawing on a bone, Elder Brother would repeat, "It's guns that allow the ghosts to enforce their will."

"Yes," Elder Sister would agree. "We've seen for ourselves how loudly guns can speak."

With each word the suspicion and jealousy Elder Brother and Sister had planted grew. But so cunning were they in twisting truths that we could not openly accuse them of wrongdoing, not even to Ma.

Before Wai Seuk brought back the ghost machine, we had, like everyone else, planted our fruit trees in small, dense plots of land unsuitable for growing rice, or mixed them in with vegetables and other crops. So our thousand-tree grove on the hill was an amazing sight people came from a distance of many *lei* to see. In truth, I never tired of looking at it myself. Even the talk against our ghost machine and ghost guns, the fortified tower looming above the trees could not spoil its beauty to me.

When the trees came into bloom, their sweet fragrance reached our house. Then there was the pleasure of watching the flowers turn into fruit. The loose-skinned Ponkan mandarins ripened close to the autumn Moon Festival. The Tonkan we stored on the trees for delayed harvesting between New Year and Ching Ming. Each tree yielded forty to forty-five catties of fruit, and in the first year alone we were able to repay Fourth Brother all of our back rent, to hire guards to take our places in the tower.

The following year, we bought a buffalo and several pigs and chickens, a few good fields. We might have bought more. But to quiet the talk against us, we made Elder Brother and Sister a gift of silver. To show our gratitude to Heaven, we gave generously to the village priest. And to honor those who came before us, we contributed a large sum to building an ancestral hall for the Lue clan.

Soon after, Moon Ho's belly swelled with child, and in the spring, we celebrated the arrival of a grandson with a banquet for every person in the village. Hok Yee named the baby Hei Oi, Wanted Happiness.

Each morning Wai Seuk carried Hei Oi into the kitchen where the shelves, once bare, were crowded with crocks of pickled vegetables, jars of oil. Sacks of rice rose in neat stacks from the floor all the way to the Kitchen God's altar. Baskets of dried stores and bundles of salt fish hung from the ceiling.

"Look," Wai Seuk would say. "You'll never starve like your brothers."

Stepping out into the courtyard, he would lift Hei Oi high above the wall and point to our hill orchard. "See the pretty fruit on the trees? They're the same as gold. You'll never have to hire out as I did."

Of course no parent wants to see their child eat bitterness. But just as gold is purer after passing through heat and jade is more precious after careful polishing, man is stronger after overcoming trouble. Wai Seuk was proof of that.

Even Elder Sister recognized it. Why else would she hold her tongue when Bik Wun scolded Sesame and gave him chores? Where Wai Yin had never dirtied his hands, not even with ink, Sesame labored beside Third Brother's sons in the fields. He helped his mother cut wood and collect dry leaves and branches for fuel. He gathered dung and prepared it for fertilizer, spreading it out to dry in the sun, beating and sifting it into powder.

Sometimes I would see Wai Yin watching Sesame with what looked to me like regret and envy. Then I would feel I had been right to speed my second-born grandson on to his next cycle of life. At the sight of Sesame laughing, running along the footpaths between the fields, however, the wrong I had done weighed heavy.

Likewise, the photograph of Gim Gong and his ghost teacher had made me wonder if Hok Yee and I had wronged our youngest son in sending him to live among foreign ghosts. But when Gim Gong wrote that he was coming back to live under our sun and sky, I told myself my fears for him had been exaggerated.

Gim Gong's absence had lain like a shadow on my heart for twenty years. On nights I could not sleep, I had gone out to the courtyard and stared up at the Heavenly River that flowed between us. I'd arranged and rearranged the words of welcome I would say when he returned. Yet the moment I saw Gim Gong approaching our house with a grandfather's shuffle, stopping every few steps to rest and wipe beads of sweat from his forehead, all my carefully prepared phrases died unspoken in my throat.

From his letters I knew he had been gravely ill with the spitting-blood disease. But my mother had kept Yeh Yeh, an old man, alive for years with her brews. I was sure I could do the same for Gim Gong. Neither did I have to rely on her soups alone. The herbalist at the Long Life Medicine Shop in Toi Sing had sold us a prescription guaranteed to remove congestion from the chest. So, no, it was not Gim Gong's illness that made my thighs tremble, my legs so weak I had to lean against the doorpost instead of running to greet him.

Nor was it his foreign jacket and pants and leather shoes, the shrill cries from the children who surrounded him, taunting, "*Mo been yun*, man without a queue." There had been other returning Gold Mountain guests who had dressed like ghosts or lost their queues to villains, and I could give Gim Gong his brother's clothes, make him a false braid to wear until his hair grew again.

What, then, pinned me to the threshold and tightened my tongue?

A flash of feeling that had come before thought: this man, although my son, was a stranger.

Moon Ho brought water for Gim Gong to wash away the dust from his journey. Bo Jun and Lin Hei poured tea for their uncle. Someone—Gim Gong or his father or brother—must have spoken. Yet I remember no words, only Gim Gong's eyes, sad as dark autumn pools.

At last, enough strength returned to my legs so I could fetch a bundle of incense from behind the altar. When I tried to hand it to Gim Gong, however, he pushed it away, and in a strained whisper, told us between coughs that worship belonged to the Jesus God and His Father alone.

Wai Seuk jabbed the air in front of Gim Gong with his fingers. "Where was your Jesus God when my sons were starving? Where was his father when I was attacked by ghosts in Gold Mountain?"

Hok Yee, stepping between our sons, placed his hand on Wai Seuk's arm, Gim Gong's shoulder. "Gim Gong," he said quietly. "The Queen of Heaven doesn't begrudge our worship of other Gods. Why should Jesus?"

"Because He's the one true God."

Hok Yee shook Gim Gong's shoulder gently. "Come now, only a son with no heart would refuse a father's just request."

"But that's it," Wai Seuk exploded. "Jesus followers *don't* have hearts."

Wrenching free of his father, Wai Seuk seized Gim Gong by his hair and pulled him to his feet. "When the foreign ghosts stormed our quarter, I saw the woman ghost who talked loudest about that Jesus taking things from our dead. There were others from their worship hall who cheered and clapped whenever one of us fell. Most of us who survived were protected by courtesans and native people. People you Jesus followers condemn."

Gim Gong clasped his hands together and shut his eyes as if in prayer. "I cannot, I will not, bow to idols."

Even Elder Brother at his worst had not dared to deny our Gods and ancestors. Gim Gong persisted in his refusal to either thank our Gods for his safe return or honor his ancestors, and my old fear that he had been bewitched returned like a gust of cold wind.

In the end, Hok Yee and Wai Seuk had to drag Gim Gong in front of the family altar, pitch him forward, and knock his head to the ground while I lit incense on his behalf. As the smoke rose, I tried to recall the boy who had wept for a flower, the boy who had returned eggs his brothers stole to the birds' nests. But these memories, so clear through Gim Gong's long absence, flitted through my mind like shooting stars, dying before they could fully form.

Over the years I had, like all women, saved my hair from combings for my old age when I would need to fill out my thinning bun. During Gim Gong's first days back, while he was too weak to rise from his bed, I fashioned this hair into a queue for him.

As I worked, I tried to bring back the son inside the stranger by reminding Gim Gong of the stories he had loved: Muk Leen, the Buddhist saint; Nui Wa, who had melted colored stones to seal a split in Heaven's floor.

"The Jesus God's father, not Nui Wa, made the rainbow," he said.

I laughed. "You mean that story the foreign ghost man in Toi Sing told us about the man Noah and his ark?"

"Not a story. The truth." Lifting himself up with great difficulty, he leaned forward, grasped my hand. "When I first heard the Jesus doctrine, I did not believe, either. For years I argued with my teacher and her sister, the priest as well. Then the Holy Spirit entered me and I saw the Truth."

Lue's words hit my chest with the force of pounding fists. Still I tried to hide from what my heart had whispered for so long. Surely Gim Gong's crazed talk was caused by the fever clouding his mind. Surely he was not bewitched.

When I attempted to calm him, however, he spoke even louder and more intensely about how this "Holy Spirit" had come to lodge in him during some kind of strange worship meeting where there was dancing, tongues gone wild. And although Gim Gong was feeble, lighter even than a sheaf of rice, he suddenly had the power to stop me from pressing him back down. He was, in truth, possessed by this spirit, this ghost.

My mother had saved me from Yeh Yeh's ghost by burning the almanac and mixing the ashes in water for me to drink. I had heard the village priest say that washing in water heated with pomelo leaves cleansed a body of ill humors. But neither treatment worked on Gim Gong. I could not even persuade him to keep his possession a secret.

"Don't you see?" he cried, tears streaming down his face. "That is why I gave up my work in Gold Mountain. Because the Jesus God told me to bring you this Good News. So you, so everyone in the family, the whole village, even the district, can be filled with the Spirit, too."

Having hired labor, we did not need Wai Seuk's. And so that he, Moon Ho, and our grandchildren would not be harmed by the ghost in Gim Gong, Hok Yee sent them to Fourth Brother in Sang Sing.

We were certain of their welcome. As a token of our gratitude for Fourth Brother's generosity during the drought, we had continued to farm his fields but had taken no share of his crops since our orchard's first harvest. Each spring, when he came back to honor our ancestors, he would invite us to visit him in Sang Sing.

"On your way," Hok Yee told Wai Seuk, "stop in Toi Sing. Find the diviner, the same one who spoke for Ma's ghost, and instruct him to come after dark, so no one will see."

The diviner, puffing out his chicken breast, assured us he had experience expelling ghosts through cabalistic formulas and charms. He explained that he would wait until Gim Gong was asleep. Then he would place a jar and stopper by Gim Gong's head. "After I draw out the ghost, it will go into the jar, which I will then seal."

To avoid waking Gim Gong, the diviner lit the room with a single lamp in the corner farthest from our son. He muttered his incantations so quietly I could scarcely hear them, though we were separated only by the length of the bed, he at its head, I at its foot, beside Hok Yee. But of course ghost hearing is sharper than ours, and the diviner was also using charms and incense to entice the creature.

In the dim light, my eyes clouded by anxiety and incense smoke, I could not see clearly. Then I felt Hok Yee lean lightly against me, and I leaned forward, saw what looked like a wreath of gray smoke curling into the jar, knew from the diviner's satisfied expression it must be the ghost.

Hurry, hurry, I silently urged the diviner.

Deftly setting down incense and charms, he reached for the stopper. As he was pulling the pig's bladder over the mouth of the jar, however, Gim Gong woke—whether from the incense smoke, the diviner's chanting, or loss of the ghost I do not know. Neither did I nor my husband know what to do since the diviner had not prepared us for this possibility.

The diviner did not seem to share our confusion. "Have no fear," he told Gim Gong soothingly. "I have captured the ghost in this jar. It cannot escape."

Crying, "Devil!" Gim Gong snatched the jar from the diviner, threw it onto the floor.

Since Gim Gong was weak and the jar sturdy, it did not break. But it must have cracked, for as the diviner swooped to pick it up, I noticed thin, misty wisps seeping out.

Swiftly the diviner cupped both hands around the jar. But how could his fingers stem the leaks? Setting down the jar, he turned to Hok Yee. "Your son's fate has been decreed. Nothing I can do will change it."

Where did Gim Gong's ghost go? Back inside him. No, I did not see it. Nor did Hok Yee. But what else could have happened since Gim Gong himself said, "I am filled with the Spirit. You have not taken it from me."

Yet he seemed sound enough when asking about our orchard. Or in discussing its development, in telling us of his own work in his ghost teacher's garden, how he had created new and better fruit.

In truth, our son's methods were so well reasoned that sometimes, listening to him, Hok Yee would throw me looks full of pride and hope. But even as I smiled agreement, Gim Gong would say something foolish such as, "People can be improved the same way," or, "The strength of the ghosts in Gold Mountain comes not from guns but from mixing together different peoples and new ideas."

He claimed that unlike Wai Seuk, who had brought back a machine which benefited us alone, the beliefs and ideas he had brought would improve the lives of everyone. *Hnnnh,* you can't eat ideas. Ideas won't put clothes on your back or keep you warm on a cold day. And we had already found the Jesus God wanting, his teachings against ours.

But Gim Gong had ever gone his own way. That was how he had fallen into the rice paddy as a child and almost died. Now he seemed determined to pull us down with him.

His queue, he told us proudly, had not been cut by villains, as we supposed, but by himself. To show that he renounced the Emperor and desired a government where everyone expressed their own inner feelings and opinions.

What dangerous foolishness! If each person had his way, there would be no end of confusion and abuse. To have harmony we must have masters, and the proper order begins with a son obeying his father and honoring his ancestors. Then all else flows naturally, with the father respecting the elders of the village, the elders venerating the district magistrate, the magistrate bowing to the viceroy, and the viceroy kneeling to the Emperor, the son of Heaven.

But Gim Gong had already refused our ancestors their due. And despite his father's warning that the Emperor had spies everywhere and men had been killed for saying less, Gim Gong insisted on his "right" to speak his mind.

As long as Gim Gong did not have the strength to rise from his bed, we were safe. Hok Yee had paid the diviner generously for his silence. Gim Gong's voice was too weak to carry through the walls, and we kept the window in his room shuttered, the door closed.

He had few callers. Only ten when he'd left for Gold Mountain, he had been absent twenty years, and he'd never been well liked. The curious and the greedy came, of course. Elder Sister even brought over a pot of nourishing soup.

Pouring it into one of our own pots, I rinsed hers clean, placed a fat packet of lucky money inside, thanked her for her concern. Then, although every person in the village already knew that Wai Seuk, his wife, and children were gone, I repeated what I had told the callers who'd come before her, what I would say to those who followed.

"Did you know Hok Yee sent Wai Seuk, our grandchildren, and their mother to stay with Fourth Brother in Canton? Yes, Gim Gong is that ill. He cannot see anyone."

Where the diviner had failed to rid Gim Gong of his ghost, my mother's brews and the prescription from the Long Life Medicine Shop restored his health. Inside of a moon, his cough disappeared, his skin regained its color, his bones put on flesh, he walked with a firm step.

Laying our heads together, Hok Yee and I convinced Gim Gong that no one would ever get a chance to hear his ideas if he spoke out against the Emperor and was arrested. That he must exchange his foreign suit for our own clothes and wear a false queue or no one would trust him and children would shout him down with cries of *"Mo been yun."* But we could not prevent him from acting like the foreign ghosts our people had run out of Toi Sing.

Those ghosts had lived among us for years, yet they had never really known us. How could they when the beams of conceit in their eyes were so big? Gim Gong, likewise blinded, found fault not only with our Gods but with everything we did.

As if he were a magistrate issuing proclamations, he declared that our laborers should not work longer than the span of three watches in a single day and should rest one day in seven. Instead of carrying baskets of oranges and bundles of grain on their backs or by means of poles, they should use wheelbarrows. Instead of flailing the rice to thresh it, they should use a machine.

He told mothers they should cover their babies' bottoms with thick layers of cloth instead of split-bottomed pants. It was unhealthy, he said, to let the village dogs eat the babies' droppings, to blow our noses with our fingers or spit into the street.

When people called Gim Gong a humbug or a trader in wind, Elder Brother and Sister would try to hide their pleasure by placing their hands over their mouths and saying soothing words. If people did not lose their tempers and treated him kindly, however, their faces would cloud over and they would cunningly prolong Gim Gong's senseless talk by asking him to make clear some nonsense he had said, such as why it was cruel to eat dogs and cats but not chickens and pigs.

After only a few days, Gim Gong could not leave the house without being jeered at and deliberately jostled. And late into the night, I would hear him mumbling in his room. I could not understand what he was saying. Since he was on his knees, however, I guessed he was asking that Jesus God for help. Whether that God tried but was too weak to succeed, or whether he paid Gim Gong no mind, I do not know. But this I can tell you: nothing got easier for my son.

Standing on top of the wall outside the temple or on an overturned bucket by the well, Gim Gong would begin, "We are all sinners. You may not know it yet. Just as a man with a fever doesn't know he is sick when he is delirious. All the same, he needs medicine. And so do you. Yes, you need the medicine Jesus brought us from Heaven. The medicine of faith."

"Here," someone would shout, throwing a clod of dirt at him. "Here's some medicine for you."

Others would join in, and Gim Gong would soon become splattered with mud. Still he would go on with his prattle until the baiting became too loud for him to be heard or someone knocked him down. Then, the next day, he would start right up again.

Watching him, I was reminded of how, as a child, he had stubbornly continued to stand up against the boys trapping birds even though they had chased him with sticks and made him cry. When I'd asked him why he'd persisted, he had said, "The birds need me. I have to save them."

Now, when his father and I pleaded with him to stop his talk and work in the orange orchard instead, he shook his head sadly. "Don't you think I want to? But I must obey God's will, not yours, not mine. Besides, if I am silent, how can Jesus speak through me? How will you be saved?"

One afternoon, he was cornered by some village toughs. Thin Dog, who rescued Gim Gong and brought him home, told us the ruffians had pummeled and kicked him brutally. And Gim Gong's breath caught like a sob in his throat as I rubbed salve and placed plasters on his dark bruises. Yet Thin Dog said Gim Gong had not tried to run or defend himself. He'd merely lain on the ground where he'd been thrown, not once raising his voice against his attackers.

He was, Gim Gong explained, following the teachings of that Jesus. "If we are struck on our right cheek, we should offer our left." After he recovered sufficiently from the beating, however, he took to slipping out for walks in the early morning, before the village woke, otherwise staying indoors.

The danger from spirit creatures was even greater than that from people, of course. But Gim Gong refused to believe us.

Fear for him made me impatient. "Are you deaf? Didn't you hear me say your own sister-in-law was attacked? And just last winter, one of the night watch almost had his breath sucked out by a fox ghost that leaped down from the eaves of his hut. Only by chance was he able to stab the creature with his stave and drive it off."

"A Jesus follower has nothing to fear from creatures or people," Gim Gong insisted.

"How can you say that?" Grasping our son's wrist, Hok Yee pushed back the sleeve, revealing ugly purple weals. "Look."

Gim Gong winced, his voice trembled. Still he maintained that he was not afraid, that he was safe with Jesus.

FANNY

DeLand, Florida
1888

From their letters, Lue and I had imagined Cynthia and William in Arcadia. And DeLand did indeed possess every element a cultured or refined person could seek. Moreover, their property—a half-hour's ride from town—was beautifully situated amid pines and oaks alive with songbirds, chattering squirrels.

Their white clapboard house, built in the southern style, was remarkably like the one Lue and I had planned for ourselves. Raised on blocks some distance from the ground, it had no cellar. Spacious verandas ran clear across the front of both floors. A breezeway separated the kitchen from the dining room. A long hallway ran through the center of the downstairs, opening on to rooms on either side.

Within, every room was bright and airy, the walls neatly plastered, the woodwork a lovely curly pine resembling burl mahogany, the whole comfortably and tastefully furnished by Cynthia and impeccably maintained by Sheba, a Negress with an air of alert patience, who served as cook. Outside, the garden and grove laid out by William was meticulously tended by Sheba's husband, Jim. And since the rich soil and warm climate enabled the growing of everything peculiar to semitropical conditions, a stroll in any direction resembled a visit to a botanical garden or horticultural museum.

But of course perfect happiness in this weary world is not possible: without Lue, DeLand could not be Arcadia for me; and William, in spite of the vicinity's year-round sunshine and frequent bleedings and blisterings by the doctor, was no longer on the mend but failing, losing the strength he had reclaimed and more.

Faith, the effects of William's palsy were becoming so severe that he had difficulty in controlling his twitching sufficiently to speak. Visibly shrinking, he lacked the strength to cross even the smallest room without pausing to rest, and his left arm and leg were rapidly losing their cunning.

Cynthia, still beautiful and lively, had lost none of her eagerness for gaiety, however.

"The cordiality of the people is DeLand's chief charm," she had enthused the day I'd arrived.

"And th-th-they are the r-r-right s-s-s-sort of p-peo-p-ple."

As William slowly forced out each word, Cynthia smiled encouragingly, but her fingers drummed the table so impatiently that he soon abandoned the struggle, and she swiftly picked up where he'd ended.

"There's Mr. DeLand himself; Mr. Stetson, the Pennsylvania hat manufacturer; Father's friend, Mr. Sampson . . ."

To me a list without Lue's name could hold no interest. And in the dark mood that had possessed me since his departure, I could find no head for polite conversation, no heart for society. Although I was included in their invitations to oyster roasts, croquet parties, and formal dinners, I declined them all, preferring to occupy myself in writing letters to Lue or reading and rereading his to me; recalling our happy, tranquil hours at study and work, his many kind acts, familiar scenes.

Indeed, so vividly did Lue yet live in me, I could, when alone, enter into the make-believe that he'd not left. If I'd had the gift of prophesy, however, I would have followed William's brave example and accepted every invitation.

I boasted of Lue's successes to Cynthia and William: the bushes of his salmonberry were more early bearing and productive than the ordinary raspberry; his cherry currant grew on thrifty plants with dark, thick foliage; he'd also created an improved variety of tomato that resisted drought and produced large clusters of hardy fruit on vines frequently fifteen feet in length.

My creation, although I did not say it, was Lue. For Lue— wonderfully lettered, cultivated, and strong in spirit—was, it seemed to me, as much of an improved variety of Chinaman as his salmonberry, cherry currant, and tomato were of plants.

His last words to me before boarding the train had been, "Gim Gong is going back to China. Lue will stay in America with you." What he discovered, however, was that in people, as in plants, a hybrid once created cannot be separated. In his first letter from his village, he wrote, *I was foolish to think I could leave Lue behind. Lue Gim Gong is one. And, oh, Miss Fanny, he feels estranged from his people, his father and mother and brother, even himself.*

I had asked Phoebe to arrange for Lue to break the long, rigorous journey back to his village with a week's rest at a mission in Canton that her Sunday school class helped support, and its director, a Mr. Randall, had replied: *Lue Gim Gong will be heartily welcome. The Devil has been making a mighty struggle against the Holy Spirit in the Chinaman's home district, dooming every attempt by foreign missionaries to establish work there. Since he is a native, they will be more accepting of him, and he may well be God's instrument in defeating the forces of evil there.*

But Lue admitted in his letters to me that he was proving less successful than the foreign missionaries had been. *The people in my village, including members of my family, vie with one another to see who can invent the best plan to vex me. The only comfort I have are your letters, the only peace I know is the hour before dawn. Then I walk the hills unmolested and pray for guidance, the strength to endure another day.*

And the Master did give him strength equal to each day. But I knew from sore experience that endurance is a thin gruel. It sustains life; it does not nourish.

How I longed to help Lue. Separated by a continent and an ocean, however, I could do nothing except add my prayers to his and send words of encouragement.

Phoebe counseled patience. *I have reminded Lue of how long he resisted Truth,* she wrote me, *and of how it was through work in the greenhouse that he developed his gift with plants. With practice, he will become more skilled at preaching. Indeed, our Father in Heaven surely foretold this through Lue's naming by his fathers on earth and his insistence on retaining that name—Gim Gong, Double Brilliance—at baptism, for he can save his people through teaching them improvements in farming as well as winning their souls for Jesus.*

But Lue confided to me that despite his best efforts he was failing at teaching, too. *Miss Fanny, when I try to raise my people up as you did me, they insist their backward ways are superior. How can I help them if they refuse to listen?*

Faith, the abuse those pagans heaped on Lue showed such want of feeling that my mind became occupied with every possible horror. And I could not forget that the Jews, also pagans, saved the thief Barabbas and crucified the One who had come to give them life.

SHEBA

DeLand, Florida
1876—1878

You ever hear tell of Little John, that slave what bargained with his master for freedom?

Little John was small as his name and weak besides. But he had a wanting for freedom what was big and strong, too big and too strong for him to give it up. Well, his master had him a fierce wildcat spoiling for a fight. So he told Little John, "You want freedom, you whup that cat." And Little John, he wanted his freedom so bad he agreed.

The fight was set for sundown. Long before that, howsomever, folks was pouring into the yard, staring bug-eyed at the wildcat roaring and thrashing about in its cage at one end and Little John on his knees praying at the other.

Suddenly, his master made a sign. But Little John, his head bowed in prayer, ain't seen it. He ain't seen the five mens what jumped out of the crowd at that sign, neither.

Lickety-split the mens fell on Little John and tied his feets at the ankles and his hands behind his back. I tell you, they trussed him up like a hog. Then they digged a hole in the middle of the yard, dropped him in standing, and heaped dirt down on him till only his neck and head was showing.

Mark it down, Little John's face turned white as the folks crowded round him, the folks what was laughing and slapping his master on the back for being so smart, the folks calling for the fight to begin. Even so, Little John never hollered. He never whined or groaned. No.

Only short to the time his master done turn the wildcat loose—and the beast, snarling and hissing, pounced across the yard—did Little John open his mouth. He opened his mouth, grabbed the cat's tail between his teeth, and bit down. Huh, he bit so hard the critter yowled. Little John's master, too.

"You want your freedom," he howled, "you better fight fair!"

I tell you straight and I tell you true, Master Gillian and the Ku Klux was meanly as Little John's master. Mama knowed that, and she pushed for us to give up the farm and run north.

Daddy shook his head no. "Master Gillian and the Ku Klux is devils all right. They ain't fit to go to Hell. But how free is free if we still got to run? Besides, people is the same everywhere—there is good ones and bad ones."

I was too much of a youngun yet to understand. Fact is, I thought North and Diddy-Wah-Diddy was the same and Yankees was angels. Wasn't till I was working for Yankees like Miss Cynthia and Miss Fanny I caught Daddy's meaning. So I was crying and begging loud as Mama for Daddy to run.

He shook his head at me the same as he did Mama. "During the Freedom War, I ran *to* the fighting, not away, and there's fighting still to be done."

I looked down at his feets, all ragged and raw from the KK's whipping, then at Mama, hoping she'd tell him, "Give it up," like Aunt Mattie done told her.

What come out of Mama's mouth was a soft, "How you going to fight evil?"

"Soon as I whittle me a pair of helping crutches, I'm going over to the Bureau and make a complaint."

A fresh flood of tears rolled down Mama's cheeks. "Them folks can't save their own people from the KK's devilment. How they going to help you?"

Daddy wiped her eyes with the back of his hand and pulled her close. "I don't know."

The Bureau stopped the KK from killing Daddy outright. But Master Gillian wasn't willing to let Daddy go no way, and he got Daddy arrested for stealing Old Mistress's land.

Well, you know a Negro got no standing in the court and no testimony according to the law. Not then. Not now. So the sheriff paid no mind to Daddy saying he gave Old Mistress cash or to the paper what showed it.

All the justice in the world ain't fastened up in the courthouse, howsomever. When the Pharoahs was meanly to the Israelites, Moses saved them with conjure. And Mama and me, we done run to a two-headed doctor for help.

The conjure man wrote Master Gillian's name on a paper and put it in a can what he set in a bucket of ice. Then he took soot and ashes from our chimney and mixed them with salt, stuck pins crosswise in a pair of candles, and burned them at a good hour, all the while reciting the One-hundred-and-twentieth Psalm, you know the one: "In my distress I cry to the Lord that he may answer me, 'Deliver me, O Lord, from lying lips, from a deceitful tongue.' "

Even so, the Judge gave Master Gillian our farm, Daddy prison.

Master Gillian wasn't satisfied with dragging Daddy through the hackles and stealing our farm. He took every little thing in our house.

"For court costs," he said.

"For meanness," Mama said.

Scuffling down the road with only the clothes what was on our backs, I kicked at the dirt and dreamed out loud. In my dreaming, Mama and me wasn't dragging ourselves to a cabin she'd found in the woods, a cabin what was bare-bones empty, with cracks so wide there wasn't no need for windows. We was flying. Daddy, too. Yes, we got us back our power to fly, and we done rise and rise in the sky till we got to Diddy-Wah-Diddy.

Mama took me by the hand. "We done lost the power to fly, but we got the power to work, and we going to use it to get back your daddy."

White folks could buy a man's jail time, see, and Mama and me, we tasked ourselves to raise the cash. There was always a call for baskets—great tall ones for carrying cotton to the gins, flat ones for carrying clothes—and while Mama cut splints from oak saplings, I wove them, then stitched them together with scrub palmetto. We also took in washing. I declare, we had tubs and baskets in every corner of our cabin. We crisscrossed lines all over with sheets, collars, wristbands, pants, and shirts. We boiled water and heated irons till it was so hot in the cabin it was a pity.

Huh, we dripped like the wash and couldn't hardly breathe. But weaving the splints for baskets or fetching the dirty wash and carrying back the clean, I'd recollect the handsome times we'd had before the KK brung on Misery.

We'd rock on the porch swing evenings, see. Daddy'd shade my eyes from the setting sun with his hand and say, "You know, the sun is a mama what can see all you do. She got a voice pretty as your mama's, and she sings all the day long cause she's so happy she got nothing to do cept shine." Then Mama'd start up a sinner song or a hymn tune, and Daddy and me, we'd join in. Or Daddy and Mama'd commence hug-dancing. Or they'd turn the work of hulling peanuts into a game, inviting folks over and making like it was a corn shucking.

Without Daddy, work was just work. There was no rocking or dancing or singing at the end of the day. No end of the day at all for Mama—I fell asleep and woke to the slap of her irons.

The morning Mama figured we got us the cash we needed to buy back Daddy, howsomever, we was right joyful. We sang with the rising sun. Fact is, we was so laughing glad we forgot the old people's warning: If there's singing before breakfast, crying will fill the mouth before sunset.

SUM JUI

Toishan, China
1888—1889

In trying to prevent Gim Gong from walking alone in the hills, Hok Yee and I had been thinking only of our son's safety. We should have known Elder Brother and Sister would find a way to use Gim Gong's recklessness to harm us as well. *Hnnnh,* they were probably responsible for the actions they blamed on our son.

From what the night watch said, all had been peaceful until just before dawn.

"Old Lui and I were patroling the southern edge of the village," Old Wong began. "The sun had not yet risen, but the sky was bright enough for us to see without the lantern. So I'd set it down and was bending over to put out the light, when I heard a rustling off the path, in the grass."

"I heard it, too," Old Lui interrupted eagerly. "Of course, I lashed out with my stick, and straightaway there was this whirring. Like a swirl of wind. Nothing else."

Old Wong shook his head in puzzled agreement. "Even raising our lantern high, we didn't see anything or anyone. But after the sun came up, we went over the area again, this time on our hands and knees, and we discovered this paper figure smashed into the earth."

The paper figure, torn into three ragged pieces, seemed rotted, as if it had long ago been cut by a child for play and carelessly dropped and trampled on. But Old Lui said it was one of those paper forms that can come to life and roam about doing harm, and Old Wong credited him with having crushed it.

Likewise, Elder Brother's buffalo, found dead in its stall the same morning, had been old and near death. But Elder Brother, forcing Third Brother to act as witness, claimed the opposite. Pointing to the paper figure, he added, "That creature could have killed it."

"Foreign ghosts make creatures from paper forms," Elder Sister said, "and Gim Gong has lived among them for so long, he must know this magic. Perhaps that is why he dares walk alone when our night watch patrols in pairs. They say he goes into the hills which they—and even bandits—avoid."

That Gim Gong had been poisoned by foreign ghosts the whole village—no, people in every village from here to Toi Sing—knew. He had made certain of it with his rash talk. And though he'd stopped holding forth in the street, he was still reading from those books of his that were marked with the death cross.

But Gim Gong's feelings for animals had not changed from when he was a child. To avoid upsetting our brood hens, he removed their eggs with one hand while scratching their necks with his other and making clucking noises deep in his throat. He was as patient and tender in feeding our runt piglet as I had been with Wai Seuk.

Both Hok Yee and I would have staked our lives that Gim Gong had not harmed Elder Brother's buffalo, and we believed our son too forthright to have anything to do with those paper figures. Yet we did not ask him to come out of the house and deny Elder Sister's charge. The danger that he would offend rather than soothe was too great.

Sometimes, looking back, I wonder what would have happened if we had taken that risk. With Gim Gong standing before them, would the night watch, honest men, have suddenly remembered—as they did under Elder Sister's sly prompting—that they'd seen our son walk past and drop something just before they'd heard the rustling? And without that change in their report, would our village elders have come to the decision that we owed Elder Brother compensation for the buffalo?

This decision condemned us along with our ghost son, giving rise to renewed mutterings against our ghost machine. Of course, the diviner had warned, "Your son's fate has been decreed. Nothing I can do will change it." But what of our fate? Could we, should we, have separated it from Gim Gong's?

After the foreign ghosts had been driven out of Toi Sing, people had avoided those among us who'd continued to worship the Jesus God, refusing to speak to them, even to sell them rice or let them draw water from wells.

In one family, a father had shrunk from expelling his son though the boy had made no secret that he was a Jesus follower, and they had both drowned in an overturned ferryboat. "See," people had said, "Heaven is showing its anger."

In another, the son, learning that his elderly parents had burned their ancestral tablets in the name of Jesus, had thrown them out of the house with only the clothes on their backs. Yet no one had called him unfilial.

Nor would anyone have blamed us for abandoning Gim Gong. In truth, we would have been praised. But where would he have gone?

If not for the protection we gave him, he would not have survived in our village although it was his own, and in spite of our increased wealth, our influence did not stretch beyond. Perhaps Fourth Brother would have given him another opportunity, but we did not have the face to ask.

The letters between Gim Gong and his ghost teacher were frequent. But he could not go back to her, not with the gates of Gold Mountain sealed against our people. Besides, how could we send our son back to that treacherous ghost? If not for her, he might have come back whole.

Late at night, within the curtains of our bed, my husband and I searched for a way to make happiness possible for Gim Gong.

"A wife," Hok Yee said, wrapping his arms around me as if I were a bride. "Gim Gong needs a wife."

My head pillowed on my husband's chest, I sighed, "You know Gim Gong claims a person with the spitting-blood disease should not marry. That's why his ghost teacher has no husband."

"That ghost teacher and her foolish ideas! If he has no wife, who will warm his bed? If he has no son, who will weep for him at his death? Who will feed his spirit and take care of his grave?"

"He also says that in Gold Mountain, men and women marry only for love."

Hok Yee's arms tightened around me. "Love begins after marriage, not before. And if love doesn't blossom, husband and wife can still enjoy the satisfaction that comes from raising sons, sharing happiness and sorrow. Don't worry. Once married, Gim Gong will be lacquer, his wife glue, and all his foolishness will stop."

But Gim Gong, on his own, was not a groom any matchmaker could honorably recommend. He had brought home no gold, no useful machine, not even any curiosities; only his disease, a head filled with dangerous ideas and beliefs, a loose tongue, a ghost.

Since family is more important than the groom, however, we were not without hope. Moreover, our hill orchard was an asset few would ignore, and the matchmaker was careful to look for a suitable bride in villages at the farthest reaches of our district.

Before another moon passed, we were exchanging betrothal gifts.

According to the matchmaker, Gim Gong's betrothed was skilled at cooking, spinning, and weaving, as lovely in shape and as bright as a mountain flower. Her face required no powder, her eyebrows no blackening. Best of all, she had wide hips that promised plenty of sons.

The girl's name—Oi Ling, Beloved Brightness—showed her parents' affection for her. Yet she had not been spoiled. During the day she helped her mother at home or earned wages for the family by working for others, making ritual money, preparing and drying olives, planting rice seedlings, bringing in the harvest. Then, after evening rice, she went to a girls' house for the night.

"The family house is small," the matchmaker had explained, "and there's no sleeping room for Oi Ling. If she didn't go to the *nui jai nguk,* she might see her father or brothers using the chamber pot at night or hear embarrassing sounds. Staying with other girls, she's been able to keep her modesty."

Although there were no *nui jai nguk* in the villages near Lung On, they were not uncommon, so Hok Yee and I had heard of them. Nor did we disapprove of girls grouping together in this way. Because we were choosing a wife for our son, however, we were careful to ask about Oi Ling's house, whether the members were known to her parents, whether the girls behaved too freely.

"All eight are cousins or sisters," the matchmaker assured us, "and I've never seen cleaner, neater, or better-disciplined young women. Newcomers wait on older members, fanning them, boiling water for tea, washing the cups, sweeping the floor—in the same way a new daughter-in-law serves the rest of the family—and if any girl leaves a mess or has a little dirt or even a stray thread on her person, she has to pay a fine.

"They're never idle, either. Each girl teaches the others what she knows. That's how Oi Ling learned to read the three-character classics. She can even write a little."

Yes, everything the matchmaker told us about Oi Ling was good. So good that Hok Yee had willingly agreed to the bride wealth of four hundred silver dollars her father had demanded. And when the matchmaker handed Gim Gong a betrothal cake and leered, "Eat this so you'll enjoy a good relationship with your bride," he did not refuse, as I had feared, but ate it in three bites. Neither did he make any objections to his father asking the priest to find the earliest possible auspicious day for the wedding.

Can you see why Hok Yee felt it safe for Wai Seuk, Moon Ho, and our grandchildren to come home although Gim Gong stubbornly persisted in his early morning walks? Can you understand why I believed my husband's good luck had overcome not only my ghost mark but also Gim Gong's ghost?

The afternoon before the wedding, Wai Seuk brought a good-luck man to set the marriage bed in place. So that Gim Gong would have many sons, I covered it with dried dragons' eyes, red jujubes, oranges, lotus seeds, and pomegranates. Then Moon Ho called in some children who were playing on the other side of the courtyard wall to scramble for them. When they left, Hok Yee had our grandson sleep in the bed to further ensure Oi Ling's fertility, the birth of sons.

Finally, we made offerings of chicken and wine to Gwoon Yum, the Goddess of Mercy, and Guan Gung, the Warrior God, to protect the bridal procession from harm. Should we have also laid our sleeping mats across the doors that night and prevented Gim Gong from going out? Or failing that, should we have raised the alarm when Gim Gong did not return for his morning rice?

I had heard Gim Gong lift the crossbar to the front door. Hok Yee had also been awake. Neither of us could say whether Gim Gong had left earlier or later than usual, however. A strange, milky

fog spilling through our bedroom window had blocked out that
small square of sky, and in the damp chill we'd burrowed deeper
under our quilt, given ourselves up to warmth, to joy. Then, when
Gim Gong had not come back as expected, we'd told each other
that he'd become lost in the fog, that he'd stopped somewhere and
was waiting for it to clear.

Only when the sun had swallowed the last traces of gray did we
sound the alarm. By then, all that could be found was Gim Gong's
false queue caught in a thorny thicket of bamboo, some snags of
cotton thread that were the same blue as his jacket, signs of a body
being dragged.

One of the watch remembered sighting what might have been a
blue fox slinking in that direction. But he was not sure. "The fog
was thick and dark as smoke. Even with two lanterns I couldn't
make out anything more than a shape, a bit of color—something
blue and long and low." He nodded at his partner. "Ping, here, saw
nothing at all."

Ping tugged at his ears, scratched his chin. "Now we come to
talk about it, maybe I did hear a growl. No, not a growl, a cry. Yes,
a man crying out from deep in his throat."

My husband's neck flushed red as the sun, I felt heat rise in my
own: while our son had been attacked, we'd been lying together.
Hok Yee had whispered, "This time tomorrow Gim Gong will find
his bed too filled with pleasure to leave." I'd laughed softly at our
happiness, the happiness our son would soon know.

Had Gim Gong been crying for help then?

Was it too late to save him now?

Offering gold as a reward, Hok Yee persuaded some of the night
watch and the guards from our orchard to mount a chase into the
hills. But at dusk, when the blowing of conch shells and beating of
gongs signaled the end of the search, we still had nothing more of
Gim Gong than his false queue and a few blue threads.

The wedding proceeded as arranged with a live cock taking Gim
Gong's place.

This was the very ceremony I had once feared would be mine. Oi
Ling's hands, presenting me with the ritual bowl of tea, were steady,
however, her face beneath the beaded curtain of her headdress calm.
Beautiful, too.

The matchmaker had not exaggerated in her praise. And as she guided Oi Ling in completing the rites, there was a ripple of flattering murmurs from family and guests commenting on the shape of Oi Ling's feet, her hands, her hips—her hips which were, in truth, made for bearing sons.

My belly, reminded of the joy that comes from life growing within, twisted in sorrow.

Sorrow for my ghost son.

Sorrow for his wife who would lie alone, her only embrace grief, her only child bitterness.

SHEBA

DeLand, Florida
1878—1883

If the Lord tied warning rattles on to the wicked like he does to diamondback snakes, Mama would've knowed the white man she picked to take our cash to the courthouse was a two-faced devil. Mark it down, that captain what grinned and said yes to buying Daddy, that captain didn't buy Daddy for us but for himself. He dragged Daddy to a turpentine camp in chains, turning him back into a slave in all cept name. And when Daddy made a run for freedom, the captain shot him.

Mama said Daddy'd found the power to fly and was gone to Diddy-Wah-Diddy. His chains throwed off, he was dancing on them golden streets. Chitlins, possom pie, sweet potatoes, and every good thing was in his mouth.

Course everybody in Diddy-Wah-Diddy is mirthful. So I knowed Daddy got to be glad. Mama said we should be, too. What I was feeling, howsomever, was my heart strings snap. And Misery was writ all over Mama's face.

I recognized she was mooded to go to Daddy. Even so, the first few times the screech owl come shivering round the cabin crying death, she hushed it. Yes, Mama jammed a shovel into the fire till it got red hot. She sprinkled salt on the blaze. She turned up her shoes on the floor with the soles against the walls.

Studying on it now, I reckon Mama was doing like them Africans what'd younguns here. The womens Aunt Mattie said got the power to fly but never did, not till they was done raising their childrens. The womens what'd fly to visit with their mens in Africa but was pulled back to their childrens here.

The day I got my misery and become a woman, see, the screech owl called again. This time Mama poked a small gold ring through my right ear.

"It'll brighten your eyes for seeing ghosts," she said. "For seeing me."

Bawling like I was a little chap, I pulled on her dress. "Take me with you. I want to be with Daddy too."

She cradled me gentle. "Hush. Hush now. It ain't your time. And I ain't going to stop with Daddy." She tapped the ring in my ear. "Look sharp. I'll be near."

That night she had me set a dish of salt on her chest to stop what was in her from coming out. Then she turned her face east so she'd go easy.

We'd no light in the cabin, and the quarter moon wasn't giving none neither. Shivering and crying like the old screech owl himself, I grabbed on to Mama's hands what she'd folded on her belly.

Bit by little bit, her hands cooled. And the more they cooled, the more they got hard and lost their comfort, the more I shivered and cried.

Way after a while, a hotness growed near my face. Hanging even tighter on to Mama with one hand, I pulled loose the other and reached up.

My fingers brushed a shadow the color of moonlight.

"Mama?" I squeaked.

"Yes."

Our old neighbors done come out to the cabin to bury Mama. Kneeling beside her, I heard them lining out hymns before I seen the light of their fat pitch-pine torches through the cracks in our cabin.

Daddy's good friend, King David, come in leading the mens what was carrying shovels, a pine coffin, and a death drum. The womens brung bread and a three-legged spider of coffee what they boiled up while the mens digged the grave.

So long as Mama was lying on our bed of cured moss like she was sleeping, I stayed strong. My eyes was dry even when one by one folks touched Mama light on her nose and ears, whispering, "Don't call me, I ain't ready to go." Soon as King David lifted her into the coffin and started hammering it shut, howsomever, cold lonesome gripped my heart.

Stepping out into the steamy hot night behind the mens carrying the coffin, I looked for the pale shadow what'd said, "Yes," when I'd called out, "Mama?" the night before. But all I seen was yellow streaks of light and pitchy gray smoke from the torches the womens was holding high.

King David beat the death drum. Down his hand done fall, then rise, then fall again, long and slow like our feets circling the grave. And when we done gone round, the mens dropped the coffin in.

They was heedful. Even so it scraped and banged something terrible.

"Mama," I wailed.

"Don't cry." Mama's voice slid over me like warm honey. "I ain't gone."

"You ain't here, neither."

King David set aside the drum. "What you say?"

"Careful," Mama warned. "Don't nobody see or hear me but you."

"What should I do?" I asked her.

"Bring me your dishes," King David said.

Digging my fists into my eyes to stop their watering, I looked over at Mama. She nodded for me to do it, and I brung the two we got out from the cabin. He throwed them down hard, busting them into little pieces. I jerked back, falling into the floating haze what was Mama.

King David's wife, Sarah, crowded her fleshy arms over me like Mama wasn't there. "Don't you fret, you safe now. King David done broke the chain of death." Her tears splashed hot on my neck. "If only your daddy'd run, you wouldn't be no poor orphan child."

King David and the other folks shook their heads and clicked their tongues.

"Jordan done killed his wife all right."

"Broke her heart."

"He was too prideful."

"He should've gived up his land."

Their words cut me sharp and deep as a lash. Pushing hard, I broke free of Sarah and run into the woods.

"Come back!" Sarah called.

"Let her go," King David said. "That gal's hard-headed and prickly as her daddy."

Brush crackled under my feets and slashed my legs. Low-hanging branches and moss whipped my face and arms.

Mama floated up ahead of me. "They ain't calling your daddy down, child. They just afraid of trouble, bad afraid. They is plumb wore out by it, and they need all the grit they has for making-do. They ain't got nothing left over for fighting against the rulings of white folks. Ain't many folks do."

Closing my ears with my hands, I stayed running.

While running that night, I fixed on staying in the woods. Mama'd learned me how to pick out roots and berries what was good eating. Daddy'd learned me how to fish good—how to beat the ground with a switch so worms'd figure it was raining and wriggle out, how to find the best places to drop a line, even how to braid a line out of sweet grass and make a hook out of a thorn.

I figured I could keep myself in rations easy. And I did. Fact is, I caught and ate so many fish my belly rose and fell with the tide. There was a few times I lingered uncertain over a plant, mind. But then a heat'd come to me, and Mama'd be by my side, telling me if what I was studying was poison or safe.

Yes, my belly was satisfied all right, but not my *kra*, my dream soul. It was fighting every night in my sleep, fighting so hard stars'd blaze in my head like the Great Day of Judgment'd come.

Many a night my arms and legs was scraped raw from thrashing about in the brush. Sometimes I shouted out loud, waking myself so sharp I bruised my *kra*. Even when I woke natural, I'd feel a heaviness, and I got to dragging so low all I wanted was a hole for hiding in.

Mama said my spirits'd rise if I got back with people, and she pushed at me to quit the woods. I tell you, she never let up for a minute, not till I got my feets on a cow trail. Following it, I come out in DeLand.

* * *

I can't rightly say how long I was in the woods. I never did count the days, and I paid little mind to the moon. But I was a growing gal then for all my misery coming each month marked me a woman, and my dress'd got short on me and powerful tight round the arms and chest.

Mark it down, the sides was splitting; the cloth was thin and the color faded from beatings against rocks during washing. Ain't no need for Mama to tell me to find a church where I could get another from a missionary barrel. My own good sense told me that.

Ain't no need for nobody to show me the way, neither. Folks was having them a shout, and I just followed the calls of "Come believer," "Shout, sister," "Now brother," "Yes, sir, King Jesus, yes."

Listening to them, my own feets stopped trailing and got to tapping, scuffing up balls of dust. And when the preacher started in singing that sorrow song, "You got a right, I got a right," and trumpeted, "Join, shouters," I did. Yes, out there in that dirt street, I clapped my hands, dipped my knees, slid and stamped my feets, and answered, "We all got a right to the tree of life."

At my shouting, dogs in their yards barked and pulled at their ropes, a fire lit in my chest. The flames streamed out, leaping through my throat into my head and down into my arms and legs, setting me to jumping and throwing my hands high. Short to the church, howsomever, something like a river mist clouded my eyes spite of the sun climbing in the sky, and I fell by the fence, groaning and crying.

Grandma Maisie—a big-boned, coffee-colored widow-woman—found me, and she brung me to her cabin.

No, Grandma Maisie wasn't no blood kin. I never knowed no blood kin outside of my mama and daddy. But it was plain to anyone with eyes Miss Maisie was getting up in years, and she was kindly as a grandma to me, so I claimed her for my heart kin.

She made a space for me in her bed, see, and nights my *kra* got to fighting, she'd wrap her arms around me and hold me tight like my own mama couldn't. Bit by little bit, she'd ease me into wakefulness by humming a hymn tune. Then she'd make me laugh with a bold sinner song.

She never made no complaint when I struck out in my sleep. She never pricked me with questions, neither. Huh, she'd stop folks what did. "I always wanted me a child," she'd tell them, "and the Lord done sent me Sheba." Or, "Sheba come to me like Baby Moses to Pharoah. Nothing else you need to know."

Now Grandma Maisie was cook to Miss Cynthia and the Major, and she got them to take me on as helper. "I'll learn you how they like their eating, and you can take my place when I can't do for them no more."

I already knowed how to cook some from Mama, and Grandma Maisie, she was a right fine teacher. But Miss Cynthia was high tempered and terrible particular about every little thing. If I spilled any of the water I was toting, missed a pin feather in plucking a chicken, or left any silk dangling on the corn I shucked, she'd call me down and call me down sharp. Wasn't no time before I was like a bird when a gunner's about, expecting a crack any minute.

The Major was hard as Miss Cynthia. He'd fought in the Freedom War and had terrible spells of sickness from suffering in a Rebel prison. Even so, when he gived orders to me or Grandma Maisie or any of the hired mens, you could hear a switch in his voice. Shucks, he'd rather have been friends with the worst Reb than the finest black man.

I seen then I was foolish for thinking North was Diddy-Wah-Diddy and Yankees angels. And I recognized why Daddy'd said, "Peoples is the same everywhere. There is good ones and bad ones."

"Pray Jesus soften their hearts," Grandma Maisie'd say every time Miss Cynthia or the Major got in an uproar. But they stayed the same. I was the one what changed. I changed on account of Jim.

Jim did the outside work for the Major, and he made me mindful of my daddy. He was the color of ginger cake where my daddy was black, blue black. He'd come up easy in slavery where my daddy'd come up hard. Like my daddy, howsomever, Jim was a man free inside himself. He was double-strengthed like Daddy, see. He was strong from being big and stout, and he got the power what come from having a head of his own and knowing his own self.

Huh, Jim lived the same as he ate cane, chewing it good, squeezing out every bit of juice, swallowing the sweet and spitting out the chaw. He made happiness whether he was setting out a tree or spinning music out of his gourd fiddle.

Shucks, he made me feel like that old hymn tune, you know the one: "I looked at the world and the world looked new, I looked at my hands and they looked so too, I looked at my feet, my feet was too." And spite of Miss Cynthia and the Major, my spirits done rise so high I could've washed my hands in a cloud.

Now everybody knows witches is people what's sold themselves
to the Devil. And Master William and the KK and the turpentine captain was so evil, I reckoned they was witches, the witches
what was riding me nights and fighting my *kra*. So I took to sleeping with Grandma Maisie's Bible under our pillow.

That drove them out of my head all right. Out of my head and
onto my chest. Huh, they jumped up and sat there and rode me till
I was coughing for air, coughing so hard I'd jerk awake and wake
Grandma Maisie, too.

Holding me tight, she'd pat my back. "Don't you fret. You all
right. You throwed off what was choking you."

Fact is, I never did throw them off. Not with the Bible. Not by
laying a broom across the door. Not by setting out a dish of sulfur.
Not even with Jim.

Mark it down, folks'd say a body could walk the world over and
not find two people more different than my mama and daddy. All
the same, they was fools about each other. Huh, they was sweethearts all the time, sweethearts what never wanted to make no
swaps.

So, yes, I was fifteen to Jim's near thirty. I looked on life like it
was a fractious horse, not the sweet cane he seen. I'd a quiet, home-
keeping heart, not one what chased after funning like his. Even so,
I rejoiced in Jim and Jim in me.

When he made admiration over me the way a gal likes, my knees'd go weak. Just the sight of him made me so glad my hips'd swing, popping my dress tail.

Grandma Maisie held him high too. "Jim ain't no reckless, flyaway person but he a fine man. The best what breathed outside of my own, God rest his soul."

Mama come to me and said the same. "Jim ain't stout in worldly goods, but he ain't trifling."

I could see for myself what was in Jim's mouth was also in his heart, and we jumped up and married after sparking less than a year.

Grandma Maisie picked a Wednesday for Jim and me to cast our lots together cause Folks say that's the grandest day for a wedding.

She made me a right fine dress of white cotton, threading it with blue so Jim'd be true. And while she was sewing, Jim and me, we papered over the walls of the cabin we'd be sharing; we planted sweet basil on either side of the doorstep and nailed a horseshoe over it for luck; we swept the yard and beat it down to a hard smoothness for good dancing.

There wasn't no woman in our church what ain't baked and cooked for us. I declare, our supper table was piled powerful high with biscuits, fried chicken, cakes, and every other good thing.

Miss Cynthia and the Major gived us their carriage and pair of horses for the ride from the church to our cabin. And when Jim and me got to bed, I tell you straight and I tell you bold, the loving we made was so joyful I reckoned I'd bust.

Even so, when I fell to sleep, them witches, they come riding. I'd told Jim about the devilment what killed my daddy and mama. When he seen how it pressed my mind, he cautioned me to give it up like Aunt Mattie'd done to my mama when the trader took Grandma Sue.

And while Jim was petting me, say, or we was kicking up with each other or laughing together or stamping our feets in a shout, I did forget. But then I'd be testing a red-hot iron with water, and in that hiss I'd hear the lash coming through the air, splitting my daddy's flesh. Smelling smoke from a pitch-pine torch, that turpentine captain'd rise like a haint. Setting salt on the table, I'd see Mama mooded to die over losing Daddy.

Then my insides'd get into a uproar, and Jim'd tell me again, "Give it up. We got our own living to do."

Grandma Maisie placed a heap of stock in stories. "Stories is my books. They has the learning of our people in them," she'd say.

There was one about a boy in Africa way back in the beginning of time what she told me for a warning.

That boy was walking by a river, see, when the Water God called out to him, "You want to help your people?"

Course the boy shook his head yes.

So the Water God said, "Then walk away from the river and never look back."

Well, the boy commenced to walking just like the Water God told him. Behind him he heard strange noises—mighty strange—and he fretted over what they could be. But he never looked back. No. Sticking out his chest and holding his head high, he stayed walking.

Soon them strange noises become a stomping what growed into a rumbling and then a thundering, a thundering so loud and fierce the boy was shaking. Still he marched his feets forward.

When the earth got to shaking, howsomever, the boy turned his head, and he seen a herd of cattle coming out of the river, following him.

"Mark it down, them cattle was a present from the Water God to the boy's people," Grandma Maisie said. "But the present wasn't near as big as the Water God'd fixed on giving, cause minute the boy looked back, the cattle stopped coming out of the water."

She shook her head slow and sorrowful. "Them people never did live good like they would've if the boy'd stayed looking forward."

Way I figured it, howsomever, if the boy'd not turned his head, the cattle coming after him would've killed him.

Looking forward, Jim wanted to raise a crop of younguns. Looking back, I could not.

So I got me some black haw roots from the woods, taking care to dig from the north and south sides of the plants, crosswise of the world. I got me some red-shanks roots the same way. Then I brewed them up in two pots.

While the black haw was boiling, I dropped in a small piece of bluestone. The red-shanks tea I mixed with red pepper and a teaspoon of gunpowder. Both I strained into quart jars what I hid careful from Jim.

Every time the moon changed, I drank a spoonful from each jar.

Every time my misery come, I shut my eyes to keep from seeing sorrow cloud the shine in Jim's.

FANNY

DeLand, Florida
1889

In our letters, Lue and I shared an even deeper intimacy than we had before his illness. Indeed, so frankly did he write that I flattered myself he was honoring me with free outpourings of the thoughts and feelings he had previously reserved for his journals. Yet it was through Phoebe—who had the news from Charlie Sing— that I learned of Lue's betrothal. And I am ashamed to own that although I had wrestled down my wrong feelings for Lue, tears welled unbidden into my eyes and my fingers shook like aspens in the wind as I read her letter. Nevertheless, with the Master's help, I forced my lips to form the words, "Thy will be done."

What I did not then know was that far away in dark China Lue had been likewise distressed when his father and mother told him they'd selected a heathen he'd never seen as his bride, and he had turned to the Bible for guidance. It fell open at Matthew 10.

His thumb, he thought, marked verse 23: "When they persecute you in one town, flee to the next."

Or was it the previous verse?: "You will be hated by all for my name's sake. But he who endures to the end will be saved."

A person less scrupulous than Lue would have simply chosen as duty his desire for escape. Lue, the mirror of Truth and constancy, prayed for the Master to make His will plain.

One day passed and then another and another, he wrote, *and still the Master did not answer. Finally, on the eve of my wedding, I ran away to Mr. Randall's mission, and there, after long fastings and prayer, I heard God's voice.*

Yes, Miss Fanny. Our Father in Heaven spoke to me. Not through plants. Not through my grandmother or nephews. But directly. And you were right! He does not want me to give my life for the growth of His Kingdom in China. His work here will be carried out by others in His own way and in His own time. My work is with plants.

So much more that was dark to me before is now clear, not least of which is that the ties of spirit, affection, and need are deeper than those of blood. Yes, my mother gave me physical life, but you gave me my intellectual life. I retain her physical characteristics, but I bear the stamp of your thoughts, your beliefs. Oh, Mother Fanny, bring me back to my rightful work, my rightful place with you.

Holding Lue's letter close, I whispered, "Yes. Oh, yes, Lord. Yes."

I wanted nothing more than to have Lue back with me. Faith, I had never wanted him to leave. But the exclusion law against Chinese forbade his return.

To me the law was dishonorable, however. Why, then, should I feel bound to obey it any more than my mother had abided by the shameful edicts of slavery when a runaway female slave had burst into our kitchen crying, "For God's sake, save me!"?

I was only five. The few colored people I had seen had all been free. But I knew of slavery from our prayers at church and from Old Testament stories, and I instantly recognized that the poor creature pleading with my mother was a slave. Like one of the women in a picture I'd seen of Jews laboring under the whip in Egypt, her face bore the ugly marks of a lash. Moreover, her underlip was torn, her arm dripped blood from an ugly wound.

Swiftly Mother seized the shawl covering Cynthia, a mere babe in her arms, gave it to the panting fugitive to staunch her wounds, and shepherded the woman out of the kitchen, the house, all the time issuing orders to Phoebe and me to bolt the doors, to open them to no one except herself.

My desire was to run with Mother. But overcome by excitement and fear, I could not move. Rooted at the window, I stared helplessly as the two men who had been chasing the slave bore down on their quarry, on us.

Behind me, Phoebe bolted doors, called out reports on Mother's progress from a window in the rear. Mother and the slave had reached Father's factory at the bottom of the garden by the river. Father was covering the slave with his cloak. Mother was running back. Father and the slave had disappeared. Cynthia was crying.

Her sobs covered the sharp scrape of metal as Phoebe shot back the bolt for Mother, who arrived at the back door just as the slave-hunters began pounding on the front, demanding the colored woman they'd seen enter. Breathless, Mother hugged Cynthia tighter, pulled Phoebe and me to her, opened the door, and boldly invited the men in, saying, "Find her if you can."

Cellar, attic, woodshed, all were searched—and thoroughly. But the Negress was not discovered.

And just as Mother had saved the runaway slave, could I not rescue Lue?

William had been working with southern planters eager to repeal the exclusion law so they could import Chinese laborers to take the place of Negroes grown arrogant as freedmen. "The exclusion law is not ironclad," he explained. "It allows entry to diplomats, teachers, students, merchants, and travelers."

I fidgeted with the reticule I carried everywhere, the letters from Lue within. "How can those exceptions help Lue?"

"Because he can pretend to be one of them," Cynthia laughed.

Of course! Not a diplomat. He would have no credentials to produce. Nor could he pass himself off as a teacher. Having never received any formal schooling, he had no diplomas. Moreover, William said the law barred the return of any Chinaman with previous residence as a laborer, so Lue would have to pose as a newcomer.

"What about a student or traveler?" Cynthia suggested. But Lue had no talent for deception, and William said all Chinese had to pass rigorous interrogations at their points of entry.

I shook my head. "I doubt Lue can fabricate answers which will satisfy."

"Disguise him as a merchant," William said.

"Yes," I decided. "Having merchandise speak for him will be the least risky."

Thinking it through, a thousand questions reared their heads. After Lue purchased the necessary assortment of lacquer boxes, embroidered silk shawls and scarves, fans of carved sandalwood and ivory, jade ornaments, and porcelains—all the lovely and fantastic geegaws Charlie Sing sold in his store—where should he ship them?

William, recognizing his time was near, wanted to say good-bye to his family. And, hoping to be of assistance to Cynthia, I had already made arrangements to accompany them north. From Phoebe's letters, however, it seemed the winter had been as harsh as ever, and Lue had only one lung. How would he manage? Unless I remained in DeLand, as Lue and I had once dreamed. William had advised Cynthia to hold on to their property as an investment, and Jim had already agreed to stay on and manage the grove. When I asked Cynthia whether she would leave the house open for me, she said, "Gladly." And Sheba was pleased to stay on rather than seek a new position, one away from Jim.

That settled, there was another, less easily resolved complication. Although more than twenty years had passed since Emancipation, the sentiments associated with the doctrine of slavery persisted in every sphere. And the southern eye clearly viewed Chinamen as Colored, fit only for labor. What if people somehow failed to see Lue as different from ordinary Chinese, deserving of a place in society, a place beside me? Racial feeling would then proscribe us from sharing a house as we had once planned.

Should we try and flout convention? Without asking, I knew that Cynthia, in my place, would. But wasn't that why the Almighty was taking William from her? Because she had tried to make a heaven here on earth? All pain of heart and confusion of mind, I raised this burden to the Master as Lue had raised his.

He gave me Isaiah 11:13, "I the Lord thy God will hold thy right hand, saying unto thee, Fear not, I will help thee."

Trusting our future to the Lord, I sent Lue the money to make the necessary purchases, instructing him to ship the merchandise to North Adams but to come to DeLand. And when the Master guided me to a neighbor who agreed to sell me five acres with a two-room shotgun house suitable for Lue, I took it as a sign of His Grace.

Waiting for word that Lue was safely landed, however, doubts ugly as the grotesque cone-headed Florida grasshoppers flitted through my head.

What if Phoebe, believing Lue was abandoning his duty, exposed him to the authorities? Or if Mr. Randall, disapproving of my ruse, betrayed Lue? Or if Lue's own rectitude disclosed his disguise?

No. Lue would succeed. Wasn't his return ordained by the Almighty? Didn't I have His pledge?

I thought of Charles Gates, a boy in North Adams who had enlisted in the war over his parents' protests and simply vanished one morning after taking the cows to pasture. Three years later, he had reappeared at evening cow-time and driven them home. Perhaps Lue, intending to surprise me, was already on a train bound for Florida.

I jumped every time I heard a carriage or the knocker.

I wore out the road with my gaze.

Still he did not come.

SUM JUI

Toishan, China
1889

Oi Ling mourned Gim Gong as a wife should. She asked what his favorite foods had been so she could send them to him in offerings. Taking no food herself, she wept day and night until her face swelled red as a radish, her eyes became small as sesame seeds, her mouth foamed, and she had no voice.

Since his body could not be found despite further searches, however, we could not give him a proper burial, proper rest. And to prevent Gim Gong's ghost from wandering in search of a body to inhabit—as Yeh Yeh's disturbed spirit had long ago taken possession of mine—we paid the village priest to perform special rites.

Holding a three-sided dagger with two bells on the brass handle, the priest stabbed spirits that might wish our ghost son ill. Then he set up a ceremonial tree with candles on its four leafless branches and led each of us around it in a circle while he recited prayers and the rest of the family stood back and wailed. He burned paper goods: a boat to help Gim Gong sail across to the Yellow Springs, bats to bring him good luck, a wedding bowl for marital happiness.

But people complained that protecting them from Gim Gong's ghost was not enough, that they were still in danger. And one evening, while we were finishing our evening rice, Elder Brother led a group of men from the seven villages surrounding Lung On into our house.

They claimed to be petitioners. But their faces were black as the night outside, and they made no greeting, no attempt at courtesy.

As they strode in, Moon Ho and Oi Ling backed into the kitchen with the children. Wai Seuk and Hok Yee started to rise—to do what, I don't know. Softly I cautioned, "Beware," and they sank back down onto their stools.

Forcing a smile, I offered wine to Elder Brother, the men crowded near. Like actors uncertain of their cues, they looked at Elder Brother for guidance. He glared a withering no at them and dismissed my offer with an arrogant wave.

Then, clearing his throat, he pushed back his sleeves, declared, "I speak for every man here," and plunged into a lengthy tirade against Gim Gong, the Jesus God, and foreign ghosts. Blaming Hok Yee and Wai Seuk anew for bringing spirit beasts to Lung On, he accused them of disturbing the dragon who lived under our hill orchard and demanded that they remove these creatures by uprooting our trees.

With each word, I felt my breath, my life, drawn out of me. Hok Yee lost more color, becoming white as the mourning we wore. Wai Seuk reared off his stool. *Hnnnh,* were the men not pressed so close, he would have overturned stool and table both.

"Destroy the orchard?"

Elder Brother's lips curled, hissed a satisfied, "Yes."

The men squeezed inside chorused, "Yes, chop down the trees."

Those jammed in the doorway and spilling into the alley also took up the cry.

Hok Yee gripped the table, pulled himself onto his feet. "We made peace with the dragon before we broke ground," he shouted above the roar. "And the orchard's success is proof of his approval. . . ."

Elder Brother cut him off. "The dragon is angry. That's why he swallowed Gim Gong."

"The watch said it was a blue fox," Wai Seuk snapped.

"A blue fox sent by the dragon. Just like he sent the fox that attacked your wife." Elder Brother looked over at our neighbor. "And the creature that took your son."

"No," I wanted to cry. "Elder Sister, the fox ghost is responsible."

But the words choked in my throat. How could I accuse her without betraying myself?

* * *

Inside the Ancestral Hall we had helped build, the Council of Elders affirmed that the loss of Gim Gong to the spirit beasts proved we were to blame for their presence. They accused us of showing disrespect for our ancestors.

Scolding Hok Yee as if he were a boy and not a grandfather, they told him we should not use new things to take the place of old. They commanded the destruction of the ghost machine and the orchard to bring back peace.

The branches of our Ponkan trees were heavy with fruit that would soon be ripe, fruit we'd already sold to pay for Oi Ling's bride wealth and for Gim Gong's wedding—turned funeral—banquet.

"At least give us a stay that will allow us to harvest the Ponkans," Hok Yee pleaded.

Quick as lightning, Elder Brother said, "You would keep the whole village in peril just to fill your purse?"

The Council of Elders, agreeing the threat of another attack was too great, lectured Hok Yee on duty and ordered the trees cut without delay.

Of course, chopping down trees carries its own risk since the spirits in them can be offended. Before Hok Yee and Wai Seuk raised their axes, they apologized to our trees, asking pardon for the pain they would cause.

The trunks, thick as human necks, were not easily severed, however, and I felt each blow as if the ax were sinking into my flesh.

Our hill could not be cultivated. Neither could we sell it. Who would buy? Yet we had to pay taxes on the land. We had to pay for the fruit we'd been forced to destroy, wages for our guards and laborers, Gim Gong's funeral rites. As the saying goes, succeeding is like a turtle climbing up a mountain; failing is like water running downhill.

No, we did not go hungry. But we had to sell most of the fields we'd bought during our few years of plenty.

Wai Seuk and Hok Yee blamed Gim Gong as much as Elder Brother: had Gim Gong not angered everyone with his talk, they said, Elder Brother would not have succeeded in fanning people's jealousy into the typhoon that toppled our orchard.

Nor did I disagree.

And yet.

And yet, lying awake at night, turning over Gim Gong's talk like a farmer turns soil, I began to wonder. Was he at fault, had he been wrong, as we believed? Or had he been a golden carp leaping upstream, scales shimmering in the sun, while the rest of us were catfish, willing to wallow in the mud at the river's bottom?

"Open your ears and listen," he had said. "You condemn foreign ghosts for their treatment of our people. But what about the suffering of our people here? Here in our own country. Our own country where we are ground under the iron heels of landlords and officials so that we cannot support our families except by leaving them to live and work among the ghosts you hate."

Wasn't that what my Yeh Yeh had said? "No matter how hard we work, we have as much chance of living well as a blind man has of catching an eel."

That was why so many of our men had fallen prey to the pig traders, why they had to go overseas still. Because, in truth, nothing had changed for our people since Yeh Yeh had been forced to drink hot water though our family grew tea.

Sesame said that in school his teacher would unroll maps of our country whenever a student misbehaved.

"Look," he would say. "See how the colors change year by year as our nation loses more and more land to foreign ghosts. If we are to be saved, we must throw them off. And how do we do this?"

"By practicing traditional virtues," every student in the school had to answer. "By obeying without question."

Gim Gong had urged the opposite. "We not only can change, we must. We must take the money from surplus harvests, the money you now borrow for funerals and weddings, and spend it on fertilizers, better seed, and improved tools that will bring advancement."

Of course, spending on funerals and weddings is not money wasted but our obligation. But what about our surplus harvests? Should people, could people, really do something with a surplus other than convert it into coins, which can be buried? Or was that yet another foolish ghost idea? Or an idea that worked for them but not for us?

Where houses in Gold Mountain might have large windows at eye level, even on outer walls, as Gim Gong had claimed, we had to make the windows in our houses small and set them high beyond the reach of thieves. Where crops in Gold Mountain might safely ripen unguarded, our people had to arm themselves with knives and sticks and remain in the fields all through harvest to protect their grain and fruit from neighbors as well as strangers. Wasn't that why we'd had to build the watchtower in our orchard and hire guards? Even then, neither tower nor guns had saved it.

No, only buried coins were safe. Anything else could be stolen. It would ever be thus so long as men like Elder Brother wielded power. And when people are unjustly treated, what can they do except endure?

SHEBA

DeLand, Florida
1883—1889

I ain't lying before God when I say putting on an apron makes a body invisible, able to see and hear every little thing. You don't believe me, ask any cook or maid or washwoman, don't matter their color, they'll say the same: not a word passes what escapes our listening ears, and we use our tongues as well.

Now I started in as Grandma Maisie's helper. But Miss Cynthia, seeing I was an orderly gal, brung me into the house for other work—serving at table, say, or polishing the brass and silver, or making the beds.

They'd a maid, Sarah. But she was slow and I was quick. Fact is, while dusting one morning I heard Miss Cynthia tell the Major she was fixing to let Sarah go. Only Sarah got the jump by quitting.

Sarah was disgusted with Miss Cynthia's red-hot temper and skint wages, see. And Miss Cynthia was close with her cash, all right. She had me take Sarah's place and stay on helping Grandma Maisie without adding a nickel to my wages.

When Grandma Maisie's rheumatics got so bad she got to stop cooking, Miss Cynthia called me in to say I'd be taking over and she'd give me a rise to full wages. Even so, it was full wages for one job, not two.

Back in the kitchen, I snapped, "Miss Cynthia tests me, she do. I've a mind to quit."

"No use running from bad to worse hunting better," Grandma Maisie cautioned.

Wasn't for my wanting to be near Jim, howsomever, I'd have drawed up my grit and done it.

Anyways, working like I done in every corner of that house, I seen a heap and I heard even more.

Take Miss Cynthia's daddy and her sister, Miss Phoebe, they never did visit. All the same, I can tell you her daddy was always fretting the sky'd fall on him. Miss Phoebe, she was working on being an angel.

Or take colored mens having the power to vote. I can tell you Miss Cynthia and the Major hated that something terrible: Miss Cynthia wanted the power for herself and wanted it bad; and the Major, he reckoned colored mens overestimated themselves on account of it.

Mark it down, the Major was working with other mens on bringing down our people by changing the law. Not only the law what gived colored mens the power to vote, but the one what was stopping growers from getting themselves gangs of mens from China.

Grandma Maisie laughed over that till her belly shook and her eyes watered. "Don't that beat all?" she whooped.

Directly after the Freedom War, see, when the itching heel got ahold of so many Folks, her old master'd got him a passle of Chinamens.

"He treated them meanly as he did us. Shucks, he was more kindly to his mules. But them Chinamens was like the Africans. No, they didn't look nothing alike. Them Chinamens was small and yellow, and their hair was long and plaited like women's.

"Even so, Chinamens is like folks from Africa, cause they also got the power to fly. Huh, them Chinamens Old Master brung in wasn't there a month before they disappeared—every one of them together—and Old Master was shouting himself hoarse over their flying."

Jim and me, we didn't laugh, howsomever. If there was Africans what couldn't fly and lived in slavery, there got to be Chinamens what ain't got the power neither, and they'd be the ones white folks'd use to bring us down.

*   *   *

Miss Cynthia, now, she said her sister, Miss Fanny, was training up a Chinaman. And from her talk, it looked to me Miss Fanny held him high—high as Jim's Master Alex did Jim during slavery.

Jim was gived to Master Alex in payment for a debt. Master Alex's own boy, Master Nigel, was about the same size as Jim, the two of them just crawling babies, and they slept in the same room and ate from the same table. Only Master Nigel lay on the feather mattress while Jim got a hard pallet. Master Nigel sat at the table while Jim squatted on the floor waiting for scraps like a pet dog.

"I *was* a pet to my white folks," Jim told me. "A pet nigger."

Master Nigel wouldn't let Master Alex work Jim like the other younguns what had to tote kindling and water and help feed the stock. He wanted Jim for playing, climbing trees and shooting marbles in the yard, and fishing in the creek. Their games was of Master Nigel's choosing, howsomever, and if Master Nigel should fall or get angry or unhappy, Jim was the one blamed. So Jim reckoned he was tasked anyways. He was tasked to keep Master Nigel safe and happy.

Well, when Master Nigel got to playing, he didn't want to pay no mind to where he was. And he didn't have to. But Jim couldn't follow him off the plantation without a pass. So Master Alex pinned a sign on Jim's cap, warning: *Don't bother this nigger or there'll be hell to pay.*

Come Freedom Day, Jim was maybe twelve, no more than thirteen, and Masters Nigel and Alex both wanted him to stay on with them in the big house. But Jim'd been hungering for freedom too long to give it up for ease. So he told them no, he'd be cutting loose.

Miss Fanny's Chinaman, Lue, done took off too. And Miss Fanny, she grieved so hard over losing him, she come down to DeLand to stop with her sister.

Miss Cynthia and the Major recognized he was failing, and short to the time the squinch owl got to hooting for him, they fixed on going back north, shutting up the house and making Jim overseer for the grove.

Huh, they was only giving a name to what Jim'd been doing from the get-go. He was the one what'd hired the mens to clear the land and set out them orange trees. He was the one what laid out the work every day and got the trees to bearing good, making a heap of cash for the Major and Miss Cynthia, cash they wasn't wanting to give up.

But fox does always want to know what rabbit's doing. So Miss Cynthia and the Major was mighty glad when Miss Fanny took a notion to stop on. I was joyful, too.

I'd got to wanting a baby, see, wanting one bad. Could be I was born with the Wanting like most womens, only Fear'd pressed it down so deep I ain't knowed it was there. Or maybe Wanting'd come from Jim loving me. Fact is, Wanting done rise so high I could feel it strong, strong as Jim himself.

I still did take them teas for stopping a baby, mind. Wanting ain't beat out Fear. But mark it down, the fighting between Wanting and Fear closed my throat so I could scarce swallow the teas, and when my misery'd come, I'd sorrow hard as Jim.

Jim, seeing my sorrow, brung home a bucket of water what'd bathed a new baby. "Conjure man say for us to use it like a lotion—me smoothing it over you, you over me. Then we can catch us a baby."

From listening to my mama's whispering with womens, I knowed the teas I was taking ain't only for stopping a child from coming but for washing away one what's growing inside its mama. Even so, when I dipped my fingers in that water and brushed them over Jim, Wanting got me to believing we was starting on a baby. And when Jim got to stroking me, I pulled him deep inside me, so deep I could feel him under my heart like a growing baby.

"Conjure man say you the one he got to see," Jim told me Sunday after my misery come.

We was sitting at the table in our cabin. Making like I ain't heard him, I scraped back my chair and forced my feets to take me to the stove, my hands to stir the pot of hominy, so I could hide my face, my fear the two-headed doctor'd recognize through Hoodoo what Jim ain't seen.

"He puzzled in his mind over that water failing," Jim said.

Shaking something terrible, I squeezed out, "Conjure failed for my daddy too."

Jim jumped up and wrapped his strong arms round mine, holding me till my shaking eased. "Ain't nothing in this world what don't fail some of the time. But a body what don't keep trying is a body what's gived up on hoping, and that body is same as dead."

Wasn't hoping, howsomever, what got me to the two-headed doctor but Fear. Fear of losing Jim if I disencouraged him by saying no.

Conjure man ain't recognized my secret anyways. He wasn't birthed with a caul, so my heart was blind to him spite of Hoodoo. And the charm he gived me for wearing round my neck? That charm ain't got the power for stopping me from looking back, so how could it help me make a baby?

Then Miss Fanny got a letter from Lue what said he'd run from his kinfolks and was claiming her for his mama. And Miss Fanny, I declare, she was high on a mountaintop one minute, deep in a valley the next.

She was powerful glad to be his mama, see. Only she wanted him by her side. And that law what stopped growers from getting themselves gangs of Chinamens? That law was stopping her from getting her wanting.

Walking home with Jim, my own feets dragged. "Miss Fanny moaning something terrible over Lue."

"Don't you be fretting on her account," Jim said. "White folks always get their wantings."

"Not always. The Major, he been working on busting that law about Chinamens for the longest, and he ain't done it yet."

"Praise Jesus."

I squeezed Jim's hand for amen. "Miss Fanny ain't looking to drag down colored folks. She looking to raise Lue up."

"Remember Uncle George?"

In the moonlight poking through the clouds, I seen Jim smile, showing he knowed I ain't forgot the man what was kind to him in slavery, showing he was funning.

"Well, after Surrender Uncle George cropped for Master Alex, and the Ku Klux done deviled him."

Weak-kneed like always at talk of Whitecaps, I stumbled. "Why?"

Jim caught me. "No reason. You know they don't never need no reason cept they has the power and they wants to show people they has the power."

I started my feets going again to keep Jim from worrying.

"Anyways, Uncle George dreamed of silver money the night before they come, so he knowed to expect trouble. And that old man, he was white-headed as cotton, but he had grit. When he seen night creeping in, he toted his hunting musket and chewing tobaccy up onto the roof of his cabin, made himself a comfortable place by the chimney, and waited. Sure enough, come dark he heard horses."

My heart was pounding loud as them horses. Turning my face to Jim, I buried it in his chest. He stopped, kneaded my neck and back, all the time talking.

"Uncle George, he seen the Whitecaps charging brassy as tacks down the road, aiming for his cabin. Spitting out his chaw, he hollered for them to turn back or he'd shoot and shoot to kill. But they ain't believed him. They was too used to scaring people and having their way. Even after he blasted the lead rider off his horse, they kept coming. They commenced shooting as well. Only Uncle George, being on the high ground, had the advantage. None of their shots marked him. And when he knocked down another KK, they wheeled round and kited off hollering like stuck pigs."

Laughing fit to kill, Jim told how Uncle George hot-footed to Master Alex and explained what he'd done. "Huh, Master Alex fixed everything so no KK or lawman ever bothered Uncle George."

I tipped my head back and looked up at Jim. "How'd he do that?"

Jim shrugged. "Master Alex was powerful before Surrender and after. What he wanted was the thing done."

Mark it down, Miss Fanny got what she wanted, too. Yes, she figured a way round the law for Lue just like Master Alex done for Uncle George.

Studying on it, I reckoned if Miss Fanny knowed how to fight for Colored and win, she could keep a youngun safe for Jim and me.

FANNY

DeLand, Florida
1889—1893

The suspense of whether Lue's disguise would succeed put me in a fever. Even after I received his telegram with the welcome word LANDED! and the time of his arrival ten days hence, I could not rest easy, I was too wildly excited. And when that glorious morning dawned at last, I ordered Jim to take me to the depot long before Lue was due.

As the time for the train crept closer, the day turned hot, and I regretted wearing my best black silk. Then the depot began to fill with men, women, and children in crisp white linens and cool muslin prints, and I turned glad, for if my eyes, wearied by long, sleepless nights of waiting, failed to seek out Lue, he would surely notice me.

When his train pulled in at last, I squinted eagerly at the blur of windows streaking past.

"Mother Fanny."

Turning toward the call, I thought I saw Lue leaning out of the last carriage. But the train was yet puffing and steaming, its wheels grinding, and I could not be sure. Not until he slipped past the conductor at the door, leaped off, and ran toward me, his arms outstretched.

Waving, I hurried forward. But as we drew close, I became aware of the stares and comments we were exciting; I saw that Lue's face was streaked with soot from leaning out to greet me, his black broadcloth was wrinkled and shiny with travel stains.

At his next "Mother Fanny," a sudden shame seized me, and I stood rooted to the platform. My arms, raised for an embrace, straightened my bonnet and dress instead, then fell. Lue also dropped his outstretched arms, and we came together in an awkward silence.

"Your baggage, Mister Lue?" Quietly, diffidently, Jim took charge, introducing himself to Lue, suggesting I rest on a nearby bench while they attended to the baggage.

Lue nodded with what looked to me like relief. Unnerved, I too acquiesced.

Fewer than fifty yards separated Lue's little house from Cynthia's, and we shared our meals, our days as before—except the unease that had sprung up between us at the depot remained.

Snatching covert glances from behind raised teacups and newspapers, I studied Lue. He was thin but seemingly healthy, the last traces of his cough apparently vanquished by the same tropical sun that had bronzed his complexion into a golden glow. His mustache—grown as a disguise in the days after his escape from his village—suited, as did the threads of gray in his hair although he was only just past thirty.

There was courage and resolution in the set of his lips—the same courage and resolution I had recognized and admired when we had been strangers in the factory dining room. Then, however, he had been an eager student bright with hope. Now he had the bruised look and melancholy cadence to his speech of a veteran maimed in a brutal war.

I had long realized that no veteran of the War of Rebellion had survived that carnage intact, even those who'd lost no limbs and suffered no illness, and there were few who would share what they had endured with those outside their brotherhood. Lue, likewise, met with silence any question I posed about China, his family, his betrothed.

"You're home," I told him over and over.

"Yes," he'd say.

But his face stayed dark with hidden sorrow. Nor could I find any sense of homecoming in his awkward manner, his forlorn smile of gratitude.

* * *

That Lue would be the only Chinaman in DeLand I, of course, knew. For many, however, he was the first they had seen, and whether we were driving, shopping, or worshiping, I noticed men, women, and children—native and foreign born, masters and servants, white and colored—gaping at Lue.

Remembering my own fascination during my initial encounters with Chinamen, I could not fault people for their curiosity. But it seemed to me that they looked on Lue as if he were not made of the same flesh and blood or sent into the world by the same Creator as they. And when a half hour of refined and elevated conversation clearly proved Lue a man of culture and fine taste with feelings as acute, judgment as sound, and interests as dear to him as those of his inquisitors, yet they continued to act as if it were incomprehensible that a Chinaman could be educated and cultivated, then my heart burned.

There was never a hot word spoken or even a fierce look, only a cool air of displeasure when Lue walked into First Baptist to worship as an equal, abrupt pauses in conversation when we approached people in the social hour that followed, bows so slight they had the air of a rebuff when I introduced him.

Under this abuse, Lue withered, and I heartily repented my failure to embrace him at the station, the invitations I had refused, the opportunities I had lost to prepare a better welcome for him.

So that Lue would feel his own master, I told him my five acres were his to develop as he wished. And, recalling how I had hated petitioning Father for money, I made certain Lue would not have to suffer the same indignity.

Placing one hundred dollars in a jar on the buffet in Cynthia's dining room, I assured him, "Spend as you see fit. This will never be empty."

He did not abuse the privilege. Rather, he was too thrifty: after deciding to clear the land for an orange grove, he did not hire a gang of laborers but set out to do the work himself, rising while it was yet dark to work in the cool before dawn.

Previously the only sounds had been from birds and other small animals, the occasional muted whistle of a distant riverboat or train. Now there was the rasp of Lue's saw and ax ripping through timber as he felled trees, the resounding echo of his hammer as he fenced the property against marauding foxes, deer, wildcats, cattle, and razorbacks.

Listening, watching from behind cabbage palms and palmettos, I worried that he was risking his restored health. That countermanding him would undermine his already shaken confidence. That speaking out might lead to a misunderstanding, exacerbating our discomfort with each other.

Faith, I fretted until my brain ached. Finally I swore Jim to secrecy and made a private arrangement with him to help Lue.

Orange trees are greedy and must be well fed. Lue's improvements called for the wise use of natural materials at hand rather than expensive implements and fertilizers. He and Jim prepared the soil for planting by hauling muck out of a nearby lake. They made composts of leaves, mulch, and barnyard waste. They grew cowpeas and velvet beans for green manure.

While the surface soil was loose, it was underlaid with sand clay and lime rock, making any labor grueling. Yet the light breezes wafting through the open windows often brought great claps of laughter: Lue's, Jim's, sometimes Sheba's as well.

With me, however, Lue remained sadly sober. Nor could we seem to recover the intimacy that had bound us while he was in China, the ease we had known before his illness.

In settling Father's estate, Cynthia, Phoebe, and I had agreed we would always share his house equally among us. So when Florida's summer heat and rains became as oppressive as its people, Lue and I returned to North Adams, leaving the groves and houses in the care of Jim and Sheba.

We took up residence in our old rooms. Cynthia, installed in Father's former bedroom since losing William, paid Lue little mind. Phoebe, although she did not reproach him for quitting his work in China, could not hide her disappointment. At their cool reception, Lue seemed to shrink even further into himself, further from me.

Clearly, though, it was with his own people that Lue had the most difficulty, for they made no effort to hide their snubs. When I remarked on it to Phoebe, she explained that several in the Chinese colony had heard from relatives in China that Lue was dead, mysteriously killed on the morning of his wedding; they were angry with him for deceiving his family, the woman to whom he'd been betrothed.

Lue, I knew, was too dispirited to defend himself. So I tried to win sympathy for him through the Chinamen who had chosen wives for themselves: Thomas Ah Num and Charlie Sing. They listened to me politely. But when Thomas arranged a dinner to celebrate the birth of a son, he deliberately excluded Lue. Neither would Charlie sell the merchandise Lue had purchased.

Phoebe had already unpacked the crates, and all manner of curiosities crowded every shelf and cabinet in the parlor. Lue, intending to recoup the expenses I had incurred, tagged each article with a price and invited callers to buy. He was too generous to succeed: presenting them with anything they admired, he sold nothing.

I did not care a whit whether Lue recovered a penny of the money I had expended for his return; I would gladly have used my entire inheritance. What tormented me was his unhappiness, the distance between us.

Lue's name for me—Mother Fanny—was in everybody's mouth. Used as a salutation in his letters from Mr. Randall's mission, it had thrilled. Hearing people make a game of it, I own I almost asked Lue to return to Miss Fanny. Instead I fixed my mind on proving myself worthy of the title.

My chief ambition was to prevent Lue from being forcibly returned to the cruel heathens he had fled. Any one of the Chinamen in North Adams might betray him by revealing his illegal reentry to the authorities, and so long as Lue remained a Chinese citizen, he could—indeed, would—then be deported. But the exclusion law forbade Lue's naturalization. Nor was there any hope of the law's repeal; according to the newspapers, politicians in the western states were pressuring Congress to pass more restrictive legislation against Chinamen.

I had, however, successfully circumvented the law once. Why should I not do it again, this time with the assistance of my two sisters?

Phoebe agreed that exclusion was unjust. Nevertheless, she shrank from breaking the law. Cynthia, who had willingly helped me scheme for Lue's return, opposed his becoming a citizen as vehemently as William used to speak against the enfranchisement of Negroes.

"Why should Lue have the vote when we do not?" she demanded.

Swallowing the expressions of indignation choking my throat, I said quietly, "I am not seeking enfranchisement for Chinamen. I only want to secure Lue's place here with me."

I reached across the small table between Phoebe's chair and mine, covered her hands with my own. "An application for naturalization requires two character witnesses. All I'm asking is that you testify to what is true—that you've known Lue for more than five years, that he is of good character and attached to the principles of the Constitution."

I twisted around to face Cynthia, seated on my other side. "We will need a sympathetic judge to receive our testimony and declare Lue a citizen. William told me his commanding officer was a strong abolitionist, and I've heard he's now a superior court judge in Boston. Won't you please put in a word—just a word—with him about Lue?"

Before Cynthia could answer, Phoebe said, "Let's ask the Master."

They bowed their heads; I fell on my knees. They sought direction from the Master; I pleaded with Him to remind them that God Himself had ordered Lue back to America.

At our prayers' end both Phoebe and Cynthia, salving over our differences, agreed to throw their support to Lue.

Lest my plan fail, I did not tell Lue of our application on his behalf, and when his citizenship paper arrived in the post, he stared at it disbelievingly.

I smiled. "It's true."

While Phoebe, Cynthia, and I explained what we'd done, Lue tugged at his mustache with one hand, traced the words on the certificate with his other—not once, but over and over. At each new reading, it seemed to me his back grew straighter, his head more erect. Finally, he tore his eyes from the paper, found his voice, and offered his thanks, vowing, "I'll use my vote to get you yours."

Registering as a Republican, Lue enthusiastically attended party rallies and caucuses; at his urging, I delayed our return to DeLand so he could exercise his franchise. If only his citizenship could have won him his rightful place in society as well.

*   *   *

While still in North Adams, I'd noticed that Lue conducted himself as if he were still in Father's employ. At social gatherings, he edged uneasily around the fringes, helping to serve or clear away, assisting the elderly, entertaining small children, or performing some other service. Unless questioned directly, he did not speak. Then, avoiding talk that was personal, political, or dogmatic, he would converse only in general pleasantries.

Back in DeLand, he was even more withdrawn. And no wonder! His presence no longer elicited rude stares, but people continued to greet him with disdainful sniffs, a politeness so cold he could not but feel himself held in contempt.

It seemed to me that people might be slighting Lue because they mistook him for my servant, although he called me Mother Fanny. The land he was developing was mine, and Lue, ever obliging, often helped Jim in Cynthia's grove, Sheba in her kitchen garden, further confusing his position.

Carefully I explained to Lue that if he expected people to accept him as a gentleman, he must act like one. "You must stop inviting Jim and Sheba to smoke or take cool drinks or visit at your house. You must see that they go back to addressing you as Mister Lue."

I had no sooner begun than Lue's brow had furrowed in distress, smiting my heart. To relent, however, would have been to shirk my duty as his mother and protector. Bringing out his letters to me, I showed Lue where he had written, *Miss Fanny, you have ever advised me right*. Then, *If only my mother advised me as you do, I could obey*. Then, *Mother Fanny, I will obey you on earth as I obey our Father in Heaven*.

Step by step I brought Lue around to doing as I bade him. Jim and Sheba, understanding that they had overstepped the boundaries of servants, put up no protest; both went back to addressing Lue as Mister. When Sheba was serving, she showed the same deference to him that she did me. And although Lue could not seem to give Jim directions except in the form of gentle suggestions, the man followed them to the letter, continuing to fertilize the trees with muck hauled out of the lake, planting cover crops to serve as green manure.

Under Lue's direction, each of Cynthia's trees yielded seven boxes of oranges—one box more than the average for other growers. The fruit was also more attractive and smoother-skinned than before.

Instead of stenciling a single shipping address on a box, as was the standard practice, Lue asked Jim to mark every end so the address would always be in sight, thus preventing the fruit from being bruised by the box being roughly turned over. When Cynthia received the box I sent her along with a full accounting of her increased income, she was so well pleased that I easily persuaded her to name Lue manager in place of Jim.

Lue feared Jim would resent the change even though he would retain the salary. I insisted the adjustment was necessary for squelching the persistent whispers that Lue was not only a servant but working under a Negro.

As I'd expected, Jim yielded the title without argument.

Still people refused to acknowledge Lue as an equal.

Thoroughly disheartened, I nevertheless presented a cheerful face to Lue. Taking out the plans we'd made before he'd fallen ill, I suggested he go back to his search for improvements.

For the first time since his return, his eyes sparked fire. But he shook his head at the papers I proffered, saying, "I have a new idea."

His voice pulsing with excitement, he explained that the decimation of the tall pine forests in northern Florida for settlements and groves would, he believed, affect the weather, causing increasing cold.

I felt my heart quicken. "So you want to produce a hardier orange."

"Exactly." He beamed. "One that will resist frost."

His previous experiments had proved Mr. Darwin's rule that crossfertilized plants are superior to those which are self-fertilized, and we discussed the characteristics of the varieties in the vicinity—those that were cultivated, the ones growing feral in hammocks—different crosses he might attempt, and their possible results.

Faith, so caught up did we become that when Sheba announced supper, we did not stop but continued our talk while we ate. Long after the moon rose over the cabbage palms, we were still at it.

And, oh, how my heart sang!

Lue was not alone in the search for improvements. Mr. Codrington, editor of the *Florida Agriculturalist*, had planted a grove with over fifty varieties of citrus in order to assess their relative merits, and his paper reported numerous experiments—some noteworthy, many amusing—by parlor naturalists and garden enthusiasts. But even old-timers could recall only one freeze severe enough to damage fruit, and there had been few frosts, and those very mild, since. So people, including those from North Adams who knew firsthand of Lue's talent and skills with plants, laughed at his proposal for developing a frost-resistant orange.

Of course, the originators of things useful to mankind are often denounced. As I told Lue, learned men had laughed at Benjamin Franklin's idea of extracting electricity from the clouds, regarding his experiments with a kite as child's play. Nevertheless, he had persisted.

Lue likewise ignored the ridicule directed at him, crossing two of the most vigorous trees in Cynthia's grove: a Hart's Late, the standard late orange grown in Florida, with a Mediterranean Sweet.

As the oranges from this crossing ripened, Lue and I examined them for size, texture, and taste. Since sampling too many acid fruits gave me a sour stomach, Lue would pick an orange, taste it. Then, if it pleased him, he would cut a slice for me and we would discuss its virtues and weaknesses.

Good judgment is the very core of plant breeding, and Lue's natural acumen combined with his fertile imagination and powers of reasoning—further honed through years of close observation and our ongoing exchange of ideas—had become akin to a gift of prophecy. After a series of lively discussions, he chose a single orange from which he harvested eighteen seeds that he planted in flats.

Together we studied and debated the characters of each seedling, ever on the alert for those that would serve as clues to each plant's ultimate value. In all, Lue selected twelve to transplant and raise, and as soon as the trees grew tall enough to allow the removal of budwood, he decided to cut off tiny twigs and graft them onto older trees so he could obtain fruit within a year or two instead of waiting six or seven.

The trees were then dormant, the bark too dry and tight to slip the tiniest slice of budwood into a limb. Lue, undaunted, dug the soil away from the roots, which had enough sap for him to force back the bark and insert the budwood without damaging either.

When budding citrus on limbs, the incision is wrapped with waxed cloth to protect it against drying out. Lue fastened his buds to the roots with tacks and paper, then covered them with soil. Contrary to doleful predictions of disaster by naysayers, these grafts not only took, they started growing much sooner than buds on limbs.

Mornings, while Lue crawled on his hands and knees, inspecting the scions, searching out any signs of weakness in bark or leaves, I would go over menus with Sheba and attend to the accounts with Jim.

Lue, eager to make further improvements in the groves, proposed scouring the country for selections of improved varieties, and in the late afternoons, we would go on delightful drives through piney woods and orange groves, under moss-draped oaks and lacy chinaberry trees, past shimmering lakes, palms, and flowering shrubs. If the weather was wet, we would stay indoors and write letters, enjoying the patter of rain on the roof.

On cool evenings, Lue would build a fire in Cynthia's parlor, and we would listen to its sharp crackle and savor its warmth while we read out loud to each other from scientific journals, histories, newspapers from New York and Jacksonville, the *Watchman*. More often, we would linger on the veranda long after sunset, reluctant to leave the rich medley of fragrances from flowering shrubs and trees.

Most satisfying were our conversations in which we shared the excitement of thoughts budding, expanding unchilled, the intimacy of common purpose. In the interest of the subject, we talked as easily as before and often forgot the hour. More than once Lue, thoroughly aroused, exulted, "This, this is why our Lord brought me back to you." I felt the reserve between us crumble, the closeness we had once enjoyed, restored.

Long after we parted for the night, however, the smell of tobacco from Lue's pipe would waft across the fifty yards that separated us. Or, if we were in North Adams where his room adjoined mine, I would hear him tossing in his bed.

He never shared with me what kept him awake. Nor did I ever tell him of the dream that haunted my sleep.

In DeLand, as in Culloden, lacy garlands of Spanish moss hang from the gnarled branches of oaks.

"What is that?" I had asked Uncle John.

Reaching up, he had plucked a few strands, handed them to me. "Long ago a bride and her lover were killed on their wedding day and buried beneath an oak. Following the custom of the time, the bride's hair was cut and hung on a branch above the grave. People say that over the years, it's turned from black to gray and spread from tree to tree, becoming the moss."

Touched to the heart, I had mounted the spiky gray-green tangle in a shadowbox above my bed. And years later, during the long, hard months I was burying my wrong feelings for Lue, I had lain pale, rigid, and stony cold, staring up at the brittle tendrils as if I were the dead bride.

Now, in my dream, Lue was the dead lover, and the hair hanging on the branch above his grave was his queue.

SHEBA

DeLand, Florida
1889—1892

Directly I quit trying to stop a baby from coming, I gived in to my feelings for younguns, fussing over them every chance I got. Shucks, I was borrowing babies from their mamas just to feel them in my arms and on my hip.

Heisting a little chap onto my shoulders, I recollected how Aunt Mattie'd counseled my mama and daddy, "Bottom rail will rise to the top someday." How Mama'd taken it for a comfort, Daddy a star to aim at. How my heart'd rise high as a flying African when Daddy swung me over his head, singing, "You the top rail."

Back in our cabin, I dreamed out loud to Jim. "I want for our younguns to be top rails."

Jim dropped down on the bench beside me. "There can't never be no top rails without rails below, and that don't make for good living."

"Unless you the top rail."

Jim shook his head. "You know during slavery I was tasked light and got meat stead of bones, pretty clothes stead of guano sacks—everything folks in quarters wanted for themselves and their younguns. I was top rail to them, and they hated me for it. Wasn't for Uncle George, I'd been cold lonesome."

I reached for his hand. "Them folks was meanly on account of slavery."

"They was meanly on account of envy, envy what come from fences and top rails and bottom rails." Jim took both my hands.

Laughing, he pulled me onto his knees. "My wanting for our younguns is funning and loving."

Lue, now, he was top rail to Miss Fanny and no mistake. Short to the time he come back to her, she bought a piece of land longside Miss Cynthia's just for him. And when he fixed on clearing it for a grove, Miss Fanny couldn't stand to see him straining his lungs out. She gave Jim wages over what he was drawing from Miss Cynthia to help Lue.

We was right glad of the cash. Jim liked to put by a little every month for the younguns we was hoping for, see. But we was keeping Grandma Maisie like we oughta, and without no rise in our wages for the longest, stretching out what we got was terrible hard.

Jim wasn't the kind what waited for cash before helping a body, howsomever. He'd jumped in beside Lue from the get-go. Only Miss Fanny, she never knowed it. Staying close to the house, there was a heap she ain't seen. And Lue wasn't confidential with her. Fact is, cept for talking about plants, she and Lue was mighty quiet.

Mark it down, plants was what Lue prized over everything, and he asked Jim to learn him the signs colored folks go by. When he seen I could read the woods like he read books, he asked me to learn him that, too.

Bit by little bit, Jim told Lue about the signs his Uncle George'd told him. I showed Lue how to pick out roots and berries and herbs what was good eating—just like Aunt Mattie'd showed my mama what'd showed me.

Huh, Lue swallowed learning the way other folks swallow rations. He wasn't a body what accepted everything he was told, mind. He never would try planting potatoes on dark nights. Or purge trees with Epsom salts. But he listened for the whooperwill before planting peas in Miss Fanny's truck garden. He waited till dogwood was in bloom before planting corn.

I declare, he got so he could prophesy weather good as Jim: heavy dew for fair skies, red sunset for chill, whirlwind for dry. When Lue prophesied winters with bitter cold was coming, howsomever, that was from his own figuring, not signs.

Jim and me, we wasn't settled in our minds over what to make of Lue's prophecy. Miss Fanny, she told Lue he was right smart. And when he got a notion to make a better orange—one what'd come through a cold spell without being hurt—she crowed he was like his name in China talk: Gim Gong, Double Brilliance.

She was the only one singing praise. Growers scoffed Lue was thin-brained. Not just growers, neither. Snowbirds, Crackers, and Colored, they was all calling Lue a fool. Course they'd been against him from the day he come to DeLand.

Jim'd carried Miss Fanny to the station to fetch Lue. So Jim'd seen for himself how folks stretched their eyes when Lue jumped off the train shouting, "Mother Fanny." And Sarah, what'd quit Miss Cynthia's and was maid to Miss Fanny's preacher, she said her white folks was red hot over a Chinaman calling a white woman mother. Shug and Ruth and Minty, their white folks put the blame on Lue. They—Shug and Ruth and Minty, I means—did too. Huh, they was buzzing and stinging worse than bees.

"That Chinaman above himself."

"He got high ideas, all right."

"What Lue hold high is our ways, Africa ways," I cut in. "He look on us with respect."

Jim called out to the hired mens what sweat and strained longside him and Lue. "Nate, Jethro, Ben, you seen how Lue is!"

"He too swelled up to eat with us."

"He talk like white folks."

"Act like them."

"Only cause he got book learning," Jim come back.

"He ain't nothing like the Chinamens Old Master brung in," Grandma Maisie said. "Lue small and yellow like them. But he ain't got their freedom spirit."

Louella, what was in slavery with Grandma Maisie, sucked her teeth. "Maybe he done cut it off with his hair."

Folks was snappish, terrible snappish. But Lue never once put a bad mouth on them. Not to Miss Fanny. Not to Jim or me. There wasn't no complaining in Lue, see. He swallowed his feelings the same as he swallowed learning. Even so, Misery was writ all over his face.

Well, Miss Fanny, she was falling down on her knees and calling for God to make white folks look kindly on Lue. When they stayed meanly, she told Lue white folks looked down on him on account he was too friendly with Jim and me. She told Lue he should be overseer over Jim. She even fixed it with Miss Cynthia.

I was pouring morning coffee for Lue and Miss Fanny when she started in, and I tell you, I was hard angry at her for overlooking Jim. Lue, seeing me fold my lips, picked at his napkin. Miss Fanny, she pressed on, making Lue her straw bossman for notifying Jim.

Now Lue wasn't drawing no wages, so he got nothing of his own. He was relying on Miss Fanny for the chance to make his orange, for every little thing. But he spoke up for Jim.

I scarce heard Lue, he was speaking so soft. Miss Fanny took on something powerful anyways. She wasn't wanting to hear no cross talk, soft or loud. No, not even from Lue.

Directly he recognized that, Lue gived in.

Jim, recalling how he was hated in slavery, made his calling down easy for Lue. Shrugging, he said, "That's white folks for you."

All the same, Lue dropped his head, studied the ground, and shuffled his feets. My eyes, they started watering.

"Hush," Jim said. "Ain't nothing changed."

Fact is, howsomever, I'd recognized Miss Fanny got no feeling for nobody outside of Lue, I'd recognized she'd never keep a youngun safe for Jim and me.

SUM JUI

Toishan, China
1889—1893

What mother fails to teach her daughters to gaze at the ground when a man is near? Even so, we say that girls of marriageable age are as dangerous to the peace of a family as smuggled salt. But what of women young and soft and tender who lose their husbands to death or Gold Mountain or some other calamity? Don't they present the same danger?

Although the punishment for a woman caught in adultery is death by slow strangulation, who has not heard whispers about widows who, cold and lonely, take men under their quilts? Women who, betrayed by swollen bellies, take their own lives, the lives growing inside them. So when it had become clear that Bik Wun was a widow in all but name, Elder Sister had forced her to bind her breasts tighter, to wear her clothes looser.

Then, when Ma's ghost stopped Wai Yin from beating his widow-wife, and Bik Wun's face, no longer swollen or discolored by bruises, was revealed as beautiful, Elder Sister wanted her to stop plucking her hair from her eyebrows and forehead. But Elder Sister was too frightened of Ma's ghost to forbid her daughter-in-law outright.

Bik Wun, emboldened by her mother-in-law's fear, not only refused to stop but began working resin from wood shavings into her hair, then combing it until it shone like black satin. She also left her husband's bed, laying out a pallet on the floor for herself and Sesame. And when a storyteller passing through the village told of women in the district of Sun Duk who refuse husbands and live together as sworn sisters in spinster houses, *gu poh nguk,* Bik Wun asked so many questions that more than one wag called out to Wai Yin, "Better watch out." But Bik Wun continued to serve Elder Sister and Brother, Wai Yin, and Sesame as she should, and she was praised in the village as a dutiful daughter-in-law, wife, and mother.

It was my hope that Oi Ling, my ghost son's wife, would earn similar approval, thus redeeming our family in some small measure from the dishonor Gim Gong had brought on us in his few moons home.

I'd not forgotten how, as a bride, I'd stolen glances at my husband's legs in the fields when he had his trousers rolled up above his knees. Oi Ling hitched her trousers so the hem was high above her ankles. She ornamented her glossy black bun with fragrant *bak lan* blossoms and polished her gold tooth until it sparkled. *Hnnnh,* there was no man so old, so sick, or so occupied that he did not turn his head when she passed. She, however, did not seem to see them.

Acknowledging her place in our house as below Moon Ho's, Oi Ling rose before cockcrow to light the fire, wash and cook the rice. She took our dirty clothes to wash in the river, then carried them home, hanging them over bamboo poles in the courtyard to dry. She fed our buffalo and chickens and pigs.

In the spring, she helped with the sowing, in the autumn the harvest. When she was not out in the fields herself, she was ready with hot water for Hok Yee and Wai Seuk at the end of the day.

At her suggestion, we exchanged one of our good rice fields for several *mau* of poor land where we cultivated hemp. This we bleached and washed white, then spun into slender threads, which we wove into cloth, cloth Hok Yee sold at market, adding to the family income, cloth we made into clothes for ourselves. And so skillful was Oi Ling in cutting out garments that other women— even Elder Sister—would come and ask for her help.

Nor did Oi Ling work with a long face. In the *nui jai nguk,* she said, the girls told stories or sang while they sewed and spun and wove, and she made our evenings lively with the tales and songs she had learned from them, stories she read out loud from books.

The stories she favored, however, were the wooden fish songs that lament the absence of husbands and lovers in Gold Mountain, warning young women of the loneliness that is the lot of most Gold Mountain wives. As she chanted these sad tales, one or other of the twins would beat out the rhythm on a wooden fish, and it seemed to me the hollow *bok-bok-bok* of mallet on fish echoed the emptiness of Oi Ling's heart.

When she thought no one was looking—when she was feeding the fire in the kitchen stove or pouring mash for the pigs—I'd sometimes see her wiping her eyes, her nose. Yet she did not eat vinegar over Moon Ho's good fortune in having husband and children.

The very first thing Oi Ling made was a beautiful stomach purse for Moon Ho. Shaped like the seedpod of the lotus, it was delicately embroidered in many colors, with twenty or thirty tiny, closely set buttons. Moreover, when the twins became too old to stay in the same room as a husband and wife, Oi Ling willingly took the girls into her bed.

That, of course, should have been my duty as their grandmother. But then Hok Yee and I would have had to sleep apart, and we could not bear it.

If I, at fifty-five, did not want to be separated from my husband, how could my heart not leap with happiness for Oi Ling when Fourth Brother told Hok Yee that Gim Gong might not be dead? And had Fourth Brother only said Gim Gong had escaped from spirit creatures or bandits and was on his way home, I could have also rejoiced for a son lost but soon to be restored. The word from a returning Gold Mountain guest at Fourth Brother's store, however, was that Gim Gong had tricked us, his own family and people, then gone back to live among foreign ghosts.

I swallowed hard. "The man must be mistaken. Haven't foreign ghosts sealed their gates against our people?"

Fourth Brother shifted uncomfortably on his stool. "You know there are ways around that ban."

"But Gim Gong was without guile or gold. How could he have managed it? And why?"

"It must have been that spirit, that ghost inside him," Hok Yee said.

Wai Seuk snorted. "More likely his ghost teacher was the rope that pulled him away."

But if Gim Gong had intended to go back to his ghost teacher, surely he would have refused the betrothal. Or would he? Certainly Gim Gong the child would not have deliberately trapped a woman into a ghost marriage. That boy had set free birds that others had snared. But the ghost man he had become was without heart, without morality, a stranger capable of who knew what.

My soul shaken, I sought an answer from Tin Hau, the Queen of Heaven, at the temple. Taking two pieces of bamboo root, each with one side cut flat, the other round, I passed them through the warm, fragrant smoke spiraling above the sandalwood-scented incense on the altar, then knelt and tossed them onto the floor in front of her. They spun a moment, fell with soft thuds.

In the dim light of the candles on the altar, it seemed to me both pieces of root had landed the same way, and I felt a tangle of relief, regret, renewed grief: Gim Gong was in truth dead; he had not dishonored the family.

As I picked up the pieces, however, I realized they were lying with one round surface and one flat exposed: Tin Hau had not answered my question but thrown it back like an echo from a deadened wall.

While the Queen of Heaven kept her own counsel, people did not. The talk from Fourth Brother's store soon spread into our district, and Gim Gong became the subject of street gossip and slanderous remarks.

No tongues labored faster or longer than those of Elder Brother and Sister.

Over and over she would say, "What if Gim Gong takes a ghost wife and fathers a ghost child? He'll disgrace our ancestors."

Then Elder Brother would gloat, "He already has, and the Code of Conduct in the *Clan Register* is clear: 'If any male commits a serious offense against lineage rules, his name must be struck from the clan genealogy.' "

His threat drew gasps and righteous nods from all who heard it. For if Gim Gong was struck from the *ga bo,* he would, of course, forever be an outsider, rootless as the duckweed floating in the village pond, a no-name man, a hungry ghost.

Outside the curtains of our bed, Hok Yee hotly defended our ghost son, winning a ruling from the elders in the Lue clan that Gim Gong would not be condemned on the basis of idle talk. There would first have to be a witness, someone who had actually seen him, someone who could give solid proof of deliberate wrong.

Alone, however, Hok Yee and I admitted to each other that the blue fox the night watch had seen shrouded in mist might have been our ghost son crouched over and running low to the ground. That Gim Gong might have playacted his own death.

And Oi Ling. What did she think? Going about her work, she continued to light incense before Gim Gong's stone tablet and send him offerings. But when Moon Ho gave us another grandson and we suggested Oi Ling raise the child as her son so he could feed Gim Gong's ghost, she refused. At the Feast of Lanterns, when would-be mothers went to the temple carrying lanterns painted with the Goddess leading a little boy by the hand or the characters "make haste," I saw Oi Ling slip out and follow them. I guessed she was praying that Gim Gong was alive and would come home to father his own. I could not have been more wrong.

New Year is, of course, the most important feast. But when I was a child, the Double Seven celebration of the Cowherd and the Weaving Maid had seemed more weighty, since this was the night my mother and I invoked the celestial lovers' help in finding me a husband.

Long before the seventh day of the seventh moon, we would begin our preparations, sewing seven pairs of little shoes, making seven sets of small-scale furniture out of bamboo slats, decorating them with embroidery, intricate designs of sesame seeds. Closer to the festival, we would cook little dumplings and cakes.

While we worked, my mother would tell the story of the Cowherd and Weaving Maid, who were so in love that they neglected their duties in Heaven and were separated by the Gods, one on each side of the Heavenly River—except for once a year, when magpies form a bridge across the river so they can meet.

"Mothers and daughters everywhere will be pleading for the blessing of handsome and good husbands," she would caution. "So the offerings we make must be the very best." And if a single stitch was uneven or a sesame seed was slightly crooked, she would make me take apart the entire shoe or chair or table and start over.

On the actual night the lovers met, we would, like everyone else, set up a temporary altar in our courtyard with red candles and smoldering incense, the delicacies we had prepared, sweets and fruit, a paper tray with the shoes and furniture, paper flowers, a comb and fan. My mother boasted our offerings were the best, and I had always believed that the reason the lovers had granted me such a fine husband in Hok Yee.

Yet Oi Ling claimed the girls in her *nui jai nguk* had not only made the usual offerings but embroidered dragons and phoenixes spangled with colored beads and sequins on red satin as a special covering for their altar. They had used the money they had collected from their fines to hire carpenters to build a stage, musicians and players to perform for the pleasure of the lovers and the entire village. Why, then, had the Weaving Maid and Cowherd given Oi Ling a ghost husband?

Was it because the girls in her *nui jai nguk* had aroused the Weaving Maid's jealousy by honoring her sisters as well? I had even overheard Oi Ling telling Moon Ho and Bik Wun, "The sisters are luckier than the Weaving Maid. She enjoys only one day of happiness a year while they enjoy happiness every day."

"How can that be?" Moon Ho had asked. "The sisters have no husbands."

"They have one another," Oi Ling had said.

"Like sworn sisters in a *gu poh nguk*," Bik Wun had breathed.

"Exactly."

Had the Weaving Maid matched Oi Ling with our ghost son as punishment? Or was Oi Ling's destiny so deeply entwined with Gim Gong's that even the celestial lovers could not change Heaven's will? Or was my ghost mark to blame?

The year after Fourth Brother told us Gim Gong might be alive, two Gold Mountain men with family in the area made the same charge in letters home. Both had worked with Gim Gong in the shoe factory, so they could not have mistaken a stranger for him. But one wrote that our son was laboring for his ghost teacher as an unpaid servant, the other that Gim Gong was living as her son and calling her mother.

In truth, these accounts reminded Hok Yee and me of the rounding of Gim Gong's first year when, wanting everything, he had grabbed at the pen, cash, abacus, and rice stalks Ma had placed before him, upsetting the tray, losing all. But in front of the clan elders, Hok Yee insisted the letters were nothing more than rumor, too fantastic, too at odds to be accepted as proof that Gim Gong was alive.

And the elders, holding to their earlier judgment, once again ruled against Elder Brother's desire to expel Gim Gong from the clan.

Clearly, however, Gim Gong, if alive, could never come home. Neither could we send his wife to him. For I recognized too late that it must have been the marriage we were arranging that had pricked our ghost son into running.

"What else did I fail to see?"

"You have no reason to reproach yourself," Hok Yee soothed. "None of us do."

"Gim Gong alone is responsible," Wai Seuk agreed.

And since our orchard had been condemned in the belief that Gim Gong had been snatched by spirit creatures, Wai Seuk argued that the Council of Elders would grant permission for us to restore it if we'd acknowledge Gim Gong was alive.

My eyes widened in horror. "Strike him from the *ga bo*?"

"Why not?" Wai Seuk said bitterly. "When did Gim Gong last think of us?"

"Even so, why make him a no-name man?" Hok Yee said. "In any case, Elder Brother destroyed the ghost machine and the hill can't be cultivated without it."

"I've rebuilt the machine."

"That's impossible," Hok Yee and I burst out in one voice.

Wai Seuk barked a short laugh that held no joy. "Sesame was with his grandfather when Elder Uncle and his friends broke the machine, and he showed his mother where the parts were buried. Then Bik Wun, Moon Ho, and Oi Ling dug them up, hid them in their bundles of brush, and brought them to me a bit at a time."

At the other end of the room, the spinning wheel whirred, the loom clicked in a steady rhythm. Moon Ho and Oi Ling, their faces blank, gave no sign that they were listening to our talk. But, then, they had concealed an entire machine.

I thought of Bik Wun and Sesame. They had been as quiet, as careful as my daughters-in-law. What other secrets were the four hiding? Did they know of Elder Sister's, of mine?

Beside me, Hok Yee fumbled with pipe and tobacco. But as I rose to fetch him a light, he shook his head, set down both, turned toward the courtyard door. Following his gaze, I saw our hill in the distance, its barren soil changing from dull brown to blood red beneath the setting sun.

"There've been no spirit creatures since we were forced to do away with the orchard," he said heavily. "Why would the Council of Elders allow us to start over?"

"Because Elder Sister, the fox ghost, invited the creatures to Lung On, then dismissed them," I might have said. But I'd held my secrets too long to break silence so easily, and although they pressed down on my shoulders and choked my neck like a prisoner's cangue, I swallowed the words with my spittle.

For what seemed a long time, the only sounds came from our breath, the loom and wheel, the children playing under the banyan tree on the other side of the courtyard wall. My shoulders hunched down farther. Keeping my secrets had already cost the happiness of my second and third sons in this life and caused the death of two grandsons. But if Wai Seuk insisted on striking Gim Gong from the *ga bo,* he would have nothing in his afterlife either, nothing for all eternity. Could I still hold on to my silence then?

I studied Hok Yee's wind-chapped face, the wrinkles at the corners of his eyes and lips. I breathed in his special smell of soap and sun mixed with tobacco. Without him to share my pillow, I . . .

Suddenly Wai Seuk sighed, "You're right. There cannot be another orchard. Elder Brother would never allow it."

In a giddy rush of relief, I closed my eyes, whispered a prayer of thanks to Gwoon Yum for sparing me, my ghost son. When I opened them, Hok Yee's forehead was creased with pain. Confused, I looked over at Wai Seuk, realized he was asking permission to take Moon Ho and the children to Fourth Brother's in Sang Sing, pleading, "Can't you see? The loss of our grove is like a leech that has been broken off with its head still buried in my flesh. Maybe if I don't have to look at the barren hill, I can pluck it out."

The priest chose an auspicious day for their departure. And it was a time when the days were already lengthening, when it was warm enough to remove our padded jackets. But what fastens to the heart strings and pulls on the liver are sons and grandsons, so that even when Hok Yee and I held each other close, we felt cold.

Taking his rough, work-stained hands in mine, I said, "Our first-born is a farmer, not a storekeeper. He'll not stay away long."

My husband forced a smile. "Our grandsons will be back, too."

Still we shivered. Still the fire in our bellies turned to ash.

FANNY

DeLand, Florida
1894—1895

Lue's family, blinded by their paganism, had failed to see his vir-tues. The Chinese colony in North Adams, fixed on Lue's repu-diation of a heathen stranger for a bride, continued to reject him. There were also fools and knaves in DeLand who could not, would not, acknowledge Lue as an extraordinary Chinaman deserving of a place in society. But Lue's unremitting civility in the face of barely concealed contempt was a reproach that pricked the consciences of true Christians, gradually earning him their regard.

By our sixth winter in DeLand, he was as warmly greeted at Sun-day worship here as in North Adams. When we went on drives, we received few sharp looks or derisive sniggers, many warm waves, invitations to stop and take tea or play a game of croquet, and in the sunshine of people's approval, Lue opened up like a morning glory at dawn.

He reserved his brightest, softest looks for his seedlings, however. His first thoughts in the morning and his last at night were for them, he confided, and he enjoyed nothing more than discussing their growth, the characters he observed in them, the grafts he'd made. Faith, he nursed each tree with the patient tenderness of a mother for her young. Whether watering or crumbling loam around their roots, his joy spilled out in cheerful whistling. And although he did not put on airs, he could not conceal his pride when showing them off to visitors.

Never idle, he developed a large, juicy, and delicious scuppernong grape during our summers north. He made improvements to Father's fruit trees so that our apples ripened thirty days prior to any in the vicinity, and Phoebe and Cynthia enjoyed peaches from the greenhouse as late as Thanksgiving.

A reporter, learning of the increase in yield in Cynthia's grove, sent some muck from the lake for analysis in a laboratory and found it, as Lue claimed, equal to commercial fertilizer, even superior in some components. The article spurred other growers to try it. Some also followed Lue in applying tobacco stems to the soil around their orange trees in order to clear out insects and add essential nutrients that made their fruit more attractive for market.

Still, people—like Noah's neighbors, who insisted there would be no need for an ark—dismissed the necessity for an orange that could withstand frost. Then the Big Freeze struck.

December was like spring, the anniversary of our Lord's birth, so sunny and mild I told Sheba to serve dinner on the veranda.

Over the years, Lue had made over Cynthia's garden. Along the drive he had set out a double row of pink-and-white oleanders. Back of the house he had created deep shaded arbors. On either side of the steps, he had planted my favorite Cape Jasmine bushes; all along the sides of the house were roses of every color. Honeysuckle vines trailed over the railings of the veranda, and while we ate, our senses were pleasured by the blossoms' delicious perfumes as well as the succulent turkey and trimmings Sheba had prepared.

Afterward, Lue and I went for a drive. Pine needles covered the sand roads, and the tang of bruised needles under the surrey's wheels was fresh and sharp. Laughter and music floated out to us from open windows. Chattering cicadas greeted the dusk. And the night was so warm, the moon so bright, that I was wakened more than once by mockingbirds bursting into song.

But a cold northwesterly wind swept in like a thief in the night. By late Friday afternoon, the thermometer beside the front door had dipped below forty, and we knew there would be a freeze.

We had no means for calling back the laborers we had released for the holidays. So Sheba, large and strong as a man, went to help Lue and Jim pile brush and pine between the rows of trees, while I—struggling against the wind stinging my eyes, whipping the blankets and quilts, my skirts, the ropes, tangling all—wrapped Lue's twelve precious seedlings, grown almost as tall as I.

By eleven o'clock the mercury was plunging below twenty. But the fires were belching thick plumes of gritty, choking smoke that enfolded the trees in life-giving warmth. Above, the wind-ripped clouds in the night sky unfurled like brightly glowing torches. Moonlight flashed, and from the snug comfort of the parlor I saw Lue and Jim, stumbling from fatigue, hauling in more pine, Sheba feeding the hungry flames.

I longed to join them, to be useful. But I was too exhausted from wrapping the seedlings. Faith, my limbs were shaking as if they were in a palsy, my heart was creaking and thumping loud as a riverboat, I could not draw breath without a painful grating in my chest and throat.

As the night wore on, I became faint with weariness. Yet I could not sleep. The howling wind was forcing pitchy smoke through the cracks in the windows, and my nose curled at the stench, my eyes streamed. Even wrapping shawls around my head, I could not shut out the smoke, the steady thud of oranges, frozen hard as bullets, falling to the ground.

By morning my lungs were so inflamed that I was threatened with pneumonia. Confined to bed, I coughed great ugly clots of black phlegm laced with blood, I suffered sharp pains in my sides as well as chest, a raging fever.

My only concern was whether the seedlings had survived. Lue, black as Sheba from the smoke, assured me they had. Our relief was short-lived, however. Within a few days, they—like many of the trees in the area—were almost completely denuded of their leaves.

I was too ill to have an appetite. Worry over the damage to his seedlings, Cynthia's grove, and mine robbed Lue of his. But Sheba—barking, "You don't eat, how you going to get well, how you going to work?"—insisted on bringing up Sunday supper to my room.

Pushing my poached quail around my plate, I sought to distract Lue. "Was Reverend Dole in good form today?"

"He said we are like little children taking our first steps. When we are successful a few times, we become overconfident in our abilities and try to walk alone, forgetting we are poor creatures dependent on our Heavenly Father. That's why He sent the freeze. To remind us He is Lord." Lue sighed, pushed away his plate, any pretense of eating. "Pray God His hand has struck lightly."

In the days and weeks that followed, it seemed our Heavenly Father had answered Lue's prayer. A portion of Cynthia's crop was ruined for market—my own grove was not yet bearing—but none of his seedlings or Cynthia's trees or mine had suffered severe wood damage. Lue and Jim did little more than prune them lightly, and as the weather turned warm and moist, the branches began budding out.

There were, of course, some growers whose trees were more seriously injured, and these had to be cut back to the trunk. But as the cambrium layer of bark became deluged with sap, they, too, started putting out vigorous new shoots.

I was not as resilient. Although my fever eased and I did not fall to pneumonia, my lungs remained so congested I could not breathe unless I was sitting up. Even then the strain set my heart to a queer, irregular hammering. Nor could I recover my strength. Indeed, when the mercury sank again in February, I was still bound to my bed.

Too weak to walk to the window without someone to lean on, I listened for Lue's step above the howl of the wind, the pounding in my chest. As often as he could, he would burst in as if blown, mend my fire, issue a staccato report.

"I've hired on more laborers."

"We can't haul enough pinewood to keep the fires burning steady."

"The older trees in Miss Cynthia's grove are doing all right. The ones sheltered by windbreaks, too."

"The young trees, your trees, are taking it hard."

For three days the temperature did not once rise above twenty. In the bitter cold, Lue fought to save the trees without pause. When it was over, he sank into the chair beside my bed and cataloged the destruction in a voice tight with fatigue and barely contained grief.

Vegetable crops had been immediately destroyed. Large turtles had become so numb they were floating on the surface of the river. Schools of fish had frozen, washing ashore in such large numbers they would have to be buried in deep trenches. The sap in trees caught in the full flush of new growth had turned to ice, rupturing bark, girdling trunks in death grips.

"Look."

Lue, his face grim, helped me out of bed and across the room to the window. Mute with horror, I stared out at Cynthia's grove, mine: every tree had its bark split the entire length of its trunk and was standing black and bare and gaunt, the ground beneath it golden with fallen oranges.

"The fruit is leathery, tasteless pulp. It will have to be buried like the fish." Lue bit his lips, unable to go on, to answer the question I'd dared not ask.

"The seedlings?" I prompted at last in a hoarse whisper.

"Killed to the ground. The grafts I made as well."

SHEBA

DeLand, Florida
1892—1895

Jim and me ain't held what Miss Fanny done against Lue. And Lue, he never strutted or was bullying like a nigger driver. When Grandma Maisie got terrible poorly and I was wanting to run home afternoons to sit with her, Lue freed me by taking Miss Fanny on long drives. When I told him Grandma Maisie's time was near, he fixed it so he and Miss Fanny stopped for a week at Lake Helen.

But Lue couldn't change who Miss Fanny is, and I couldn't look on her without feeling the emptiness in my belly. So when Sadie what was cook at the Putnam told me her son up north was sending for her, I jumped at the chance to quit Miss Fanny.

"That hotel is always needing outside mens," I told Jim. "We can both go."

He took a length of cane from the stand by the stove. I spread a newspaper on the floor to catch the shavings.

"You forget what Grandma Maisie said about running from bad to worse hunting better?" Jim asked, his knife stripping the cane swift and sure. "You only cooking for two here, and Lue's learning me a heap about raising oranges."

My feets scuffed at the purple peelings falling pitter-patter onto the paper. "Your learning only make Miss Cynthia richer."

Jim leaned forward. "It don't matter whether we is at the Putnam, or with Miss Fanny or Miss Cynthia and the Major, our heads is under yokes. What we got to do is paddle our own boat."

"How?"

Smiling wide, Jim cut off a piece of cane for himself, another for me. "By getting a place of our own."

His words closed my throat. Unable to chew, I held on to the cane.

"Everybody got happenings in their lives they can't get over and can't forget," Jim said, soft. "But your daddy and mama is gone, and we got to rock along best we can."

"Best for Colored is what we can grab for today. Try for anything else, it'll be taken away."

Swallowing the sweet juice, Jim spit out the chaw. "Making us live for today is how white folks keep colored folks down like we's still in slavery. We got to start believing in and working for tomorrow or we'll never get free."

Well, my believing'd died. But Jim, he couldn't be disencouraged. No, he wouldn't let up about how our younguns could be free of living under a yoke like we been doing; all we got to do was add on to the money we been laying by for them till we got enough to buy a bit of land where he could set out a grove. How everything he was learning from Lue was important for when we strike out on our own, so we got to stay with Miss Fanny.

When I dragged on saying yes, Jim started in talking admiration the way he done when we was sparking, praising my blackness, my fullsome nose and lips and nappy hair. Huh, he took up his fiddle and sang I was more comely than King Solomon's Sheba. He followed his praise-song with strong loving.

Wasn't his loving I said yes to, howsomever, but his hoping.

I couldn't kill Jim's hoping. But I never figured on him getting what he was dreaming, neither.

Directly Lue'd cleared Miss Fanny's land and set out a grove, see, she'd stopped Jim's extra wages. And doctoring Grandma Maisie and giving her a right fine send-off done swallowed up most of what we'd laid by. So we was near starting over.

Only white folks could buy land anyways. That wasn't the law, mind. Just the way things is. Like them colored soldiers from the Freedom Army what started Eatonville, that town for Colored down the road a piece? They'd the cash, but wouldn't nobody sell to them. Wasn't for a Yankee willing to do their buying, there wouldn't be no town.

Come bad times, howsomever, white folks ain't so fussy. Look at how quick Old Mistress and Master Gillian sold their good bottom-land to my daddy. And bad times, they done come to DeLand.

Mark it down, there was a Big Freeze just like Lue'd prophesied, and the winds what brung that freeze was so powerful, they throwed all the oranges and grapefruit and tangerines to the ground. Every one of them fruits was tasteless leather what couldn't be saved. Mens digging trenches night and day couldn't bury them fast as they was rotting, and their stink was everyplace.

That freeze ain't only killed the fruit but a heap of trees, killed them root and branch. Mens what wasn't burying oranges was cutting down dead trees and burning them. I declare, a body couldn't breathe for the smoke, and the sky, it was black as the long hours of the night even when the sun was high.

Anyways, the price of land dropped to near nothing. White folks, they was on the run, green the only color they could see. And Jim, he was busting at the chance to make good his dreaming.

"If we buy close to Miss Fanny's, we can set out a grove while drawing wages for our living and improvements and taxes," he said.

But even with a gang of hired mens, Jim'd been straining his lungs digging and sawing and burning in Miss Cynthia's grove. And Miss Fanny'd fallen terrible sick and was running me ragged with her fussing.

"How we going to squeeze in more working?" I said.

"We can do it," Jim said. "We got to."

Now, you know my mama and daddy was tasked hard in slavery, and there was folks in quarters what said an old African'd brung a magic hoe with him, a hoe what could cultivate a field without no-body touching it. Course Mama and Daddy wanted that hoe, and they asked Aunt Mattie what she knowed about it.

She pulled close Mama and Daddy and all the other younguns in her charge. "Back in Africa, Spider done seen Porcupine got a hoe what worked his crop all by itself. Porcupine'd just stand it up and say, '*Gyensaworowa, kotoko, saworowa,*' then sit himself under a tree while the hoe done all the work.

"Well, Spider wanted that hoe. He wanted it so bad he done steal it, and directly he got it, he put it to work in his own fields, sticking the hoe in the ground and saying, '*Gyensaworowa, kotoko, saworowa.*'

"Spider ain't even closed his mouth back up and that hoe, it commenced hoeing. It cut this way and that, up one furrow and down another. Shucks, it was going so fast it finished the field in no time.

"So Spider called for the hoe to stop. But that hoe, it just cut and slashed some more cause Spider ain't got the words for stopping it.

"Lickety-split Spider jumped on the hoe. But the hoe, it stayed hoeing. Spider called out all the words for stopping he could think of and then some. Ain't one of them done the trick.

"Pretty soon, the hoe done cut down the crop Spider was saving for winter. Still it ain't stopped. It never did stop, neither, till everything Spider got was gone."

Mama and Daddy, telling me about that magic hoe, always said, "Better to rely on yourself and keep inching along like a poor inchworm than wish for magic."

But I tell you straight and I tell you true, when Jim pushed for buying land after the Freeze, I prayed for a magic hoe and I prayed hard.

FANNY

DeLand, Florida
1896—1902

After the Big Freeze, no one disputed the possibility of further frosts, the need for a hardy orange. And when shoots sprouted up from where the twelve seedlings had stood, I viewed the miracle of their rebirth—from roots the Great Creator had, in His mercy, spared—as confirmation of my long-held belief that Lue's brilliance would one day benefit others.

I shall not see that day, however. Years of work yet lie ahead for Lue, and the time remaining to me in this world is limited.

Away from the unhealthy, stuffy conditions northern people live under during the long winter months and breathing the soft, healing air of DeLand, neither Lue nor I had fallen to any hard spells of sickness before the Big Freeze. And, praise God, Lue's one lung was not affected by the bitter cold, pitchy black smoke, or lack of rest he'd suffered then—or by the way he drove himself in restoring the groves as if he were Hercules bent on completing the twelve labors.

I, however, mark my steady decline from the one night I braved the Freeze's terrors. I never could throw off the cough or reclaim my strength, and although the following winter was mild, I was afflicted with strictures of the chest and shortness of breath, attacks of asthma so severe the doctor declared it was not safe for me to pass my nights alone.

Sheba, while attending me through my previous illnesses, had revealed that where she was a capital cook and housekeeper, she possessed neither the sympathy nor the education necessary to make a satisfactory nurse, the refinement to serve as a pleasant companion. When in a pet she slammed doors and exercised her tongue, which could be sharp as a sword. When in good humor she belted out laughs so loud my every nerve tingled with irritation. Nor would she stay with me through a night.

Lue was as patient as Sheba was brusque, as gentle as she was rough, as warm and kindly as she was cold. Had I asked, he would surely have nursed me willingly and tenderly. But I would not take him from his work. Moreover, there were then already periods when I required comforts that only a woman could give.

When I asked the doctor for a recommendation, he suggested I hire LaGette Hagstrom, a girl from Pierson, the Swedish colony just north of DeLeon Springs. "She's neat and clean and from a good family that lost all but one of their trees in the Freeze. They could use the help, and you'll be well satisfied."

LaGette does possess the qualities the doctor promised. More. Though small, she is strong. Though well endowed by nature—she is blue-eyed and fair, with flaxen hair, skin soft and creamy as the petals of Cape Jasmine—she knows nothing of artifice or affectation. Thoroughly sensible, gentle, and considerate, she steps lightly, reads aloud well, sings sweetly, and possesses a cheerful temper. In short, she has all the quiet, patient ways Lue boasts and Sheba lacks.

In the weeks immediately after LaGette joined our household, Lue's face burned and flushed like a bashful boy's each time she entered a room. Even when she was not present, he walked about as one in a dream. And although neither said anything untoward, I own I suffered flashes, not of jealousy, but of something kin to it, which cut me to the bone.

Ashamed, I resolutely shut my heart to these ill feelings, my mind to cold suspicion, the Devil's work, making not only LaGette but her family welcome. On our way north for the summer, I arranged to stop in New York so she could fulfill her desire to see Castle Garden, where her father and mother first marked American soil, to climb Lady Liberty. Once in North Adams—where my sisters could help in attending me—I did not deny her permission to attend the circus, a minstrel show with Lue. Nevertheless, always to be three where we had—for the most part—been two, has not been easy.

In the six years LaGette has been in my employ, my most pleasant hours have remained those I have passed in Lue's company alone. And I confess that during our summers north, I encourage LaGette to form friendships with other girls, to go with them on excursions to points of interest; while we are south for the winter, I often excuse her for visits with her family.

Where Lue—forty to LaGette's twenty—has become like an uncle to her, he has been for me the son of which every mother dreams. When I feel sufficiently well, he wraps me in shawls and carries me out to mark the progress of his seedling trees, the new buddings he has made. Knowing I feel chilled even on warm days, he closes the windows and doors and builds a fire, choosing my comfort over LaGette's, his own. Seeing me pick at my food, he tempts my appetite by asking Sheba to prepare special delicacies. He gathers up fallen yellow jasmine or orange or honeysuckle blossoms, the petals of roses, and scatters them across my quilts like fragrant stars. He is ever ready to fly at my least sign of want.

Not once has Lue complained that my age burdens his youth. Not once have we had words between us. Every day I thank God for the comfort Lue gives me. Every day I pray for Lue's.

In working with plants, Lue has been fulfilling God's purpose; it is a duty he has always performed with his whole heart, a happiness I sought to secure for him after I am gone.

His seedlings and grafts are, of course, in Cynthia's grove. And I am confident that Cynthia, well pleased with Lue's management of her property, will never take that from him. But to complete his work in developing a hardy, frost-resistant orange, Lue needs not only the plants but time, freedom from financial care. So I thought to make him a man of independent means by leaving him my five acres, my inheritance from Father, reasoning that if Lue were to dip into it with the same thrift that he takes money out of the jar I keep in Cynthia's dining room—a few dollars for buying a journal at the start of each year and a few toilet articles, tools for the grove—he would never be in want.

I could not, however, forget how he sent his family every penny of the back wages I gave him after Father died. And although he's had no contact with his family since he ran from them, I have noticed that whenever anyone chances to speak of China, a shadow flickers across his face as if he is struggling with some strong impulse. How, then, could I be sure he would not commit some other foolishness? How could I prevent it?

This was the burden I raised to the Almighty. He answered me through the prayer Lue has made daily since he realized his seedlings survived the Big Freeze: "Lord, forgive me for my lack of trust. Know that I have learned my lesson, that I thank Thee for the past, praise Thee for the present, and trust Thee for the future."

I confess I listened to the prayer for years before I heard what the Almighty was trying to tell me. And then it was not in the prayer itself but in something Phoebe said during a summer in North Adams that all was finally made clear.

I had been feeling myself sinking and was fretting more than ever over how best to secure Lue's future. Faith, a most fearful insomnia had taken hold of me, and where calomel and Godfrey's Cordial succeeded in easing the worst of my cough, bromides clouded my mind without bringing any real sleep. In hopes of warding off heavy thoughts, I'd asked Phoebe to read to me. She'd chosen the Book of Ruth.

When she finished, I mused, "Lue has cleaved to me as faithfully as Ruth to Naomi."

"Yes. He has risen far from his ignoble beginnings. His nightly prayer resonates with earnest, whole-hearted faith."

As Phoebe spoke, all the blood in my body rushed to my head, and I suddenly understood that I, who had been Lue's teacher, should now learn from him: there was no need to fret over his future without me, for he was not—and had never been—in my hands but those of the Almighty, the Almighty who is ever victorious over the powers of darkness, whose mercy is everywhere manifest.

That night I slept like a suckling baby.

But I own I am weak where Lue is strong.

Once again my brain aches with dark thoughts.

Oh, I am afraid, so afraid, for Lue.

SHEBA

DeLand, Florida
1895—1904

Miss Fanny never did recognize Jim or me as people. For all she held Lue high, she never gived him the freedom of a dog. Outside of his working in the grove and their hours of sleeping, she made him stay by her side. If he dragged even a speck when she crooked her finger at him, she'd pout out her lip to quicken his step.

But I believe in praising the bridge what carries a body over. So I got to tell you Miss Fanny did give Lue a chance to mess with plants any way he liked, and she took on his wanting to make a better orange like it was her own, straining longside him over books and papers on growing, talking with him hour by hour, fixing on trying one thing and then another.

Lue nursed his seedlings tender as a mama her younguns. Miss Fanny watched over them just as careful. When the first freeze come, she run out and bundled them in blankets like they was little chaps. And when it looked like the cold done killed the seedlings in the second freeze, she cried loud as Lue.

She was so enfeebled from trying to save them seedlings, she couldn't get out of her bed. But did she call on the Lord to raise her up? No. She hollered for Him to make Lue's seedlings rise. Lue, he was calling out the same.

Every day he was on his knees studying the ground. The morning he seen shoots pushing up from the seedlings' roots, he danced a jig all across the grove and garden and up the stairs to Miss Fanny. She clapped her hands and sang, "Praise Jesus," strong as folks at a shout.

Mark it down, that orange Lue'd fixed on making was dear as life to them both. Freedom was the thing dear to Jim. Chasing it, he'd cut loose from Master Alex. Still looking to grab it, he pushed for us to buy a patch on the other side of Miss Fanny.

I never did believe Jim could get it. Freedom, I means, not the land. The folks what was selling them four acres was running. I was fixing to run myself. Not a tree on that patch was living. We'd have to dig up every one, then get us new trees, set them out, and graft them when they was ready.

"How we going to do all that just working nights?" I fretted. "And another freeze'll kill any new trees we plant."

"You got to have faith," Lue jumped in. "My family lost their land in a bad drought. But when I was back to see them, they'd a thousand-tree grove."

"From what I seen, the Devil's always outsmarting God," I come back.

Jim pressed for me to give in to his wanting anyways, and while he was speaking, a heat come up in my face. First I thought Mama was near. Then I recognized the heat I was feeling was shame, shame cause I was coming at Jim like the folks what'd called Daddy down for striving at freedom. Mama'd said them folks was afraid of trouble. And Fear was woven into me all right, woven in too deep for me to throw off. Even so, I pulled up my grit and told Jim to buy the land.

Huh, Jim was laughing glad. Lue, he said, "I'll help." He did, too. He was like the magic hoe, bending his back for us, not only at night when we was there but afternoons while Jim was working in Miss Cynthia's grove, I was in Miss Fanny's kitchen, and Miss Fanny was sleeping.

One by one we dug up the dead trees and burned them. One by one we uprooted sour seedlings from the swamps and set them out, then grafted them with slips from Miss Cynthia's best trees and Lue's own special seedlings. We also planted cowpeas and velvet beans for green manure; beans, tomatoes, and corn to bring in cash.

Many a night we was so played out we could scarce lift a bucket or hoe between the three of us. When the Moon Regulator failed to bring on light, the onliest way we could water was by feeling our way from tree to tree, furrow to furrow. But Lue, he never wavered.

Laying by our first crop of oranges after seven long years sure was a big time for Jim and me, and we had us a gathering for sharing our happiness. I cooked a feast. Jim played his fiddle. We ate and sang and danced and shouted the night through.

Come cockcrow, Preacher beat the drum. Nate and Jethro rattled dry gourds. Jim and me asked for folks to honor Lue. Directly there was some growling. But Jim and me marched a circle round Lue anyways, shaking our hands and stamping our feets. Most folks followed, shouting and kicking up the dust. Lue, smiling ear to ear, turned red as the rising sun.

Now Lue never could've helped us cept Miss Fanny stayed ailing from the Big Freeze on, sleeping a heap and scarce rising from her bed.

Course she was old, and wasn't nothing no doctor or nobody else could do about that. But I could've eased her cough with tansy in honey and her fevers with juice from mashed peach leaves. I could've settled her stomach with tea brewed from parched rice and bay leaves. Only she turned her face from everything cept what the doctor gived her.

Anyways, she got so poorly the doctor found her a waiting maid, Miss LaGette, to watch her day and night. That gal was trained up by the doctor himself, and she was right fine, never complaining when Miss Fanny got peppery.

Well, Miss Fanny lingered for the longest. The doctor, he was powerful surprised. Way I figured it, there couldn't be no Diddy-Wah-Diddy for Miss Fanny without Lue in it, and she was fighting Death.

She was too enfeebled to win, howsomever, and come the time she sunk real low, Miss LaGette got scared about being alone with her nights while Lue was in his cabin and Jim and me was at our own place. So she asked her sister, Miss Eleanora, to stop with her.

When Miss LaGette sent Miss Eleanora down to tell me Miss Fanny'd sat up and asked for my fried chicken and cornbread, I knowed her time was near, and I called Lue in for saying goodie-bye.

"It's good Miss Fanny wants to eat," he laughed. "I'll get you a chicken."

"No. Go to Miss Fanny. It ain't her but Death what's asking to be fed."

Come nightfall, she was dead. Lue started in weeping like Miss Fanny *was* his mama. But I was too embittered in my feelings to grieve for her. Jim never shed no tears for Miss Fanny, neither. He did go tell the trees she was dead so they wouldn't rot, mind. I set Miss LaGette and Miss Eleanora to turning all the pictures in the house to the wall and stopping the clocks so they wouldn't run to nothing. Then I done the laying out. That was how I seen Miss Fanny foam at the mouth during the washing and knowed she'd died without speaking her mind.

Yes, she called out plenty to God, "Take care of Lue. Take care of my Lue." But she never did help the Lord none by writing out a will or nothing. Fact is, Miss Fanny ain't looked out for Lue any more than my mama's Old Master looked out for Grandma Sue.

Aunt Mattie said Old Master'd promised to free Grandma Sue, see. Mama, too. Only he never gived nobody a paper to show it. Aunt Mattie reckoned that's why folks smelled Old Master's soul prowling round the plantation, giving them the cold chills worse than when he was alive. Cause wouldn't God or the Devil take him in.

At the start of every year, Lue'd get himself a big notebook. Late at night—or in the early hours of morning—I'd see him at the table near the window of his cabin, scratching a pen across the pages, filling them one by one.

First time I seen him crouched there was the morning after he'd come back to Miss Fanny. He looked so terrible sad, I made up a pot of the tea he'd brung her, carried it over to him, and poured out a cup.

Lue wrapped his hands round it like he was cold and breathed in the steam.

"What you writing?" I asked just for something to say.

He spoke so soft, all I heard was "spilling my heart." Well, I couldn't catch the meaning of that. But I recognized from my own trouble dreams some devilment was riding him. So I gone on, trying to drag him out of that lonesome valley like Grandma Maisie done with me.

He sipped at the tea, saying nothing. After a spell, I seen Miss Fanny's light go on. She wasn't one what waited quiet if I was late getting her tea, so I run back to the kitchen.

Looking over at his cabin, I seen Lue'd picked up his pen and started in writing again.

Turning Lue's words over and studying them out in my mind, I figure a body'd have to read them notebooks of his to know his deep heart feelings, cause he never did talk a heap to folks cept about plants. The orange he was striving after, say. Or the garden he'd made when he was a little chap. Or the water buffalo his people use for plowing stead of mules. He did talk lively and long about them.

There was a few times he let loose something confidential after Jim and me cultivated a friendship with him. Like when we was setting out our trees? He let slip his folks'd lost their thousand-tree grove on account he run from them. And once, when Jim and me was funning together, he looked at us mournful and groaned he ain't done right by the gal he run from, and his people hated him like poison. Minute we said anything back, howsomever, he blew on us cold.

He never said nothing confidential about Miss Fanny or her sisters to us, neither. Not ever. So I can tell you on every anniversary of Miss Fanny's passing, Lue'd send a blanket of her favorite Cape Jasmine to Miss Cynthia and Miss Phoebe to set on her grave, and he'd make up a box of his best oranges for them as well. But whether he sent them cause he stayed faithful spite of their treating him worse than awful or cause he never recognized them for what they is, that I can't rightly say.

Anyways, Lue and Miss LaGette both took Miss Fanny north for burial. After the send-off, Miss LaGette, figuring her service to Miss Fanny was over, went back to her folks. Lue stayed on like he done every summer.

His letters to Jim was the same as always, asking about the horses and his special trees. But Miss LaGette'd told me Miss Cynthia was bothered over Lue voting when she could not. And Sally— that gal what cooked for the shoe man, Mr. Sampson—she heard talk about that other sister, Miss Phoebe. How she ain't never got over Lue coming back to Miss Fanny stead of sticking it out as a preacher to his people.

I reckon everybody what worked for a snowbird from North Adams knowed neither one of Miss Fanny's sisters was partial to Lue. And when the snowbirds come back down that winter, they was buzzing, saying Lue was selling—they called it stealing—berries and vegetables out of the sisters' garden.

Jim figured Lue must've run out of cash money, and we sent him

some of our own, making out it was owed Miss Fanny. Back come
a letter saying he was right glad of the cash and he'd be late returning on account of "business."

Piecing together a story here and a whisper there, I suspicioned
the "business" was making a claim for Miss Fanny's property. But
with Miss Fanny gone, Miss Cynthia and Miss Phoebe showed their
real feelings, telling Lue he got no rights since he wasn't true blood
kin. Shucks, they must've pressed that man till he feared he was going to lose the chance to finish making his orange and have to start
over from the stump. There ain't no other reason he'd have tried
storying, giving the sisters what he said was Miss Fanny's will.

Lue's hand and hers was real close, mind. But Miss Cynthia was
sharp, sharp and flinty. She seen right off the paper was false. That
put a fire in her belly, and she sent for her cousin, Mr. Darby, to run
Lue off.

Always before Lue'd talked humble to them. This time he ain't
slinked away like they expect. Stead, he told them stout and he told
them strong if he wasn't no kin, the family owed him fifteen years'
back wages.

Course they liked to have had a fit, and they dragged up all what
Miss Fanny done for him.

"What about your passage back from China?" Miss Cynthia
said.

Miss Phoebe done point at the things Lue'd brung from China,
the things he was spozed to sell and never could. "You bought these
goods with Miss Fanny's money."

"There's also your years of free lessons," Mr. Darby told him.
"All your doctor bills, too."

They was on him like white on rice. But Lue, he just turned his
back on the lot of them, walked to the open window, and folded his
hands in prayer.

"O Lord," he called out so people in the street turned their heads
to stare. "O Lord, you know these people are unfair. Praise Jesus
I'm not a sinner like them."

Miss Cynthia, about to bust, sent Mr. Darby to fetch their lawyer. Minute he was out the door, the sisters say, Lue flew at them
with a knife.

Huh, Lue was so gentle he wouldn't poke out a razorback sow
what broke under his cabin for giving birth and set fleas jumping

up through the floorboards something awful. He never would set out traps for mice, neither. And if Miss Fanny's horses stopped while he was driving them? He never did ply no whip. He got down from the surrey or wagon or whatever they was hitched to and fed them lumps of sugar till they was willing to start up again.

Tell me, would a man like that pull a knife on two old womens? And if he did, would those womens have gived Lue their property in DeLand and twelve thousand dollars besides?

Yes, Lue did win what he was wanting—the chance to finish making his orange. And Jim and me, we got our two-room house, a right fine grove, brood sow, and passel of chickens, so we figured we could breathe along on our own the way Jim been wanting.

Like the old people say, howsomever, watch out when you get all you want, fattening hogs ain't in luck.

"Work, hard or easy, was a slave's whole life," my daddy told me. "We was trained up for it. But there was very few slaves what knowed anything about how to depend on their own selves for a living. No master learned us to do that."

Mark it down, Miss Fanny never did learn Lue. Whatever she said was what Lue done. He never got the chance to figure or plan nothing cept with his plants. He was absolutely unfitted for life on his own.

Take what Jim told me when Lue come back from burying Miss Fanny. "I picked him up from the dock like always, and he come off that boat with twelve thousand dollars. But twelve hundred is gone already. We stopped at the bank, and Lue fixed for them to send five hundred to his homefolks in China, three hundred and fifty to the church he and Miss Fanny gone to regular up north, and the same to First Baptist down here."

Course from all the talk while Lue was yet north, there wasn't nobody in DeLand—Yankee, Cracker, or Colored—what ain't knowed he'd come back with a heap of cash. Huh, he wasn't home a week when out come three specks of white trash trying to pass for mens, inviting Lue to join in a sawmill. Jim recognized right off they was doing nothing more than offering to part Lue from his money, and he said as much. Lue just laughed and told Jim he was hunting trouble.

Fact is, that trash run like deer the minute Lue gived them what they was asking for. And when other scalawags bothered him to join in a factory or a feed store or some other made-up business, Lue did listen more careful to Jim's advisements. But if the tongues on those devils dripped enough honey, they'd fool Lue spite of Jim's counsel.

The folks what hit Lue hardest, howsomever, was Yankee friends of Miss Cynthia and Miss Phoebe. They was angry at a colored man outsmarting their own kind, I reckon, and they put a bad mouth on Lue, spreading the word just before orange-picking season they didn't want nobody working for him.

Now Yankees is powerful, cause working folks in DeLand, Cracker and Colored, depends on winter wages from snowbirds to see them through summer. So ain't nobody dared go against them.

But oranges got to be picked careful. If you pull straight from the twig, you can jerk off flesh, and plugged fruit rots easy; every orange got to be cut a little ways up the stem. Then there's sorting, washing, and wrapping each one in special slick paper, and packing. After all that, the trees got to be trimmed. We is talking two, three weeks' work for a mess of laborers.

Ain't no need for Jim to say, "No way Lue can do it all alone." I knowed that. But if we was to go up against the Yankees and help Lue, we could lose everything. Just like my mama and daddy.

Lue was the one what gived us something to lose, howsomever. There was plenty what bought land after the Big Freeze, then lost it to taxes. Plenty more what hung on but ain't got none of our improvements. Onliest reason we wasn't still scratching was all the help Lue gived us. How could we hold off from helping him?

Wait, you say. Them people what was after Lue was Yankees. So why was you scared? Yankees don't wear white caps like Crackers. And that be true. But a body ain't got to hide behind no cap to do ugly. Them people what made Jim Crow the law, *they* wasn't the Ku Klux. And wasn't the Yankees in DeLand dictating to us just the same? I tell you, they watched us like roosters watching for worms, fretting me so when I asked Jim what we was going to do, I was whispering spite of us being alone in our own kitchen.

"Way I figure it, we got to have us a body like Master Alex to help us over our trouble," Jim said.

"You know my mama tried that for my daddy," I fussed. "But

the captain what made out he was willing to help turned out to be a devil. How can we see clear so the body *we* get won't be another devil?"

"Cause we going to do like Uncle George. We going to ask a body we know to act for us. We going to ask Miss LaGette."

Settling into my chair, I chewed on Jim's plan. Miss LaGette was a little thing, no taller than a broom. Huh, she looked like pretty china what'll break at a touch—her skin was white as hickory ash, her hair pale and fine as cornsilk. All the same, she ain't come from no flower bed of ease. No. Her daddy was one of them Swedes the Union brung to mine coal during the Freedom War, and after he made him a family, he homesteaded ten acres up in Pierson, where all them other Swedes round here live.

Ain't nothing harder than breaking in land covered with saw palmetto: the leaves cut sharp as razors, the roots grow in twisty tangles what stick to the soil like burrs in fur. Miss LaGette was only eight then, too much of a youngun to help with the sawing and grubbing what strains a body full growed. But her daddy said if she wasn't toting water or piling up brush for burning, she was helping her mama with the babies. And I seen for myself how she was never still, how the younguns in that family was stuck on her.

Master Axel, the youngest, was yet a little shaver when Miss LaGette hired out to Miss Fanny, and he cried so hard for his sister, their daddy carried him down for a visit. Not just that little chap either, but the three older chaps, two gals, and mama as well, all of them piled into a wagon with enough grub to make a party satisfying as a hog killing.

Miss Fanny was powerful prickly about strangers and receiving people she ain't invited. But she recognized she couldn't get by without Miss LaGette. And Miss LaGette's kin never did overlook Lue like other folks. They was too kindly, laughing, and happy in their souls to stretch their eyes at anybody. Yes, they was joyful. They made everybody round them joyful. Even Miss Fanny.

They was people what respect a body's feelings, too. Miss Fanny, now, she treated Miss LaGette like she was equal. Told her she could invite her brothers and sisters to stay when she got the urge. Well, Miss LaGette knowed *I* ain't any voice, though I was the one the extra work fall on. But she asked me polite for permission every time anyways.

Course I gived it. Those younguns never did act unruly. They was easy to control. Master Axel followed Lue round the place like a puppy. His brothers too. And Miss Adele and Miss Eleanora was right handy and willing in the kitchen. Shucks, they pleasured me, they pleasured us all.

They wasn't the kind what only sticks together for the good times, neither. Look at how Miss Eleanora stayed by Miss LaGette all the while Miss Fanny was dying.

So I reckoned Jim was right. Miss LaGette *would* be willing to do for Lue what Master Alex done for Uncle George. Only Lue was hiding his head from facts like a groundhog hiding in a hole, telling Jim, "I'll get pickers. You'll see. They just busy now." How was we going to get him to ask for help?

When I put that to Jim, he said, "You got to talk up for Lue."

For Jim and me as well.

Cause the Yankees was watching, I couldn't go up to Pierson. But Miss LaGette got a uncle, Mister Carl, what was a teacher learning woodworking at the university in DeLand, and it wasn't nothing unusual for me to take him eggs from our hens or something from our cash crops. So I run over with one of my baskets, and when he asked me to sit on the porch and visit like always, I let him know about the uproar over Lue. How he couldn't get no workers to pick his oranges and trim his trees. How Jim and me'd bring trouble down on us if we was to go against the Yankees and help Lue.

Mister Carl caught my meaning. Before the week was out, Miss LaGette and her whole family come flying into Lue's grove, tackling tasks one after another. Huh, Lue run to Miss LaGette, then her daddy, her brothers, her mama, and sisters, thanking them over and over. He praised God and grinned like a possum while he was working.

The Yankees, they burned red hot. They was mad as hornets. Wasn't nothing they could do, howsomever. No, Miss LaGette's family wasn't big in the county like Master Alex was in his. But Swedes rely on other Swedes, not on snowbirds. Yes, their gals, like Miss LaGette, sometimes hire out to Yankees. But most times their wages is for their own selves, not their families, and soon as they marry, they quit working out.

Wasn't nothing Miss LaGette and her family left undone for Lue, neither. I tell you, Lue was sailing high, and he asked me to cook a great pot of cane syrup for a candy pulling. Then he partnered himself to Miss LaGette, making sure the lump of syrup he took was big enough for a mighty long spell of pulling.

The first time their fingers touched, I can't rightly say who turned redder, Lue or Miss LaGette. Even so, they both did race to make their fingers touch some more. There was no mistaking the feelings what spilled out of their eyes, neither. Shucks, them two was kneading and pulling on that candy like they was woofing about love.

SUM JUI

Toishan, China
1894—1904

As everyone knows, daughters must marry out, but the presence of sons is a blessing that does not have to end. Our sons were scattered like clouds before a bitter wind.

Yes, Wai Seuk returned each year for Ching Ming, sometimes for New Year, the Mid-Autumn Festival as well. And while he was home, he would examine the fields and talk to us closely about rainfall and proper irrigation, the rotation of crops, the payment of taxes and rent. But he never once spoke of taking up his hoe again, and in his fourth year away from Lung On, he left Fourth Brother's and started his own business, an inn, just outside Sang Sing.

Although the inn became a success, Wai Seuk took no joy, no pride, in it.

"If I'm not giving orders to a servant, I'm bargaining with a guest," he would complain.

"Come home, then," Hok Yee would urge.

And Wai Seuk would say, "I will."

But he did not.

Even after more than ten years had passed, Wai Seuk seemed to feel the injury of our loss as keenly as if it were fresh, to fear further losses should he come back to farm.

"You're like a man who has been bitten by a snake and ever after shudders at the sight of a straw rope," Hok Yee accused. "There's no danger for you, for any of us now."

I was not so sure. Not with Elder Brother and Sister keeping alive the talk that we'd endangered the village by disturbing the hill dragon. Not with them continuing to insist the clan elders should banish Gim Gong. Not with my ghost mark.

Yet when Hok Yee suggested that our grandson, Hei Oi, stay on with us instead of returning to Sang Sing, I pushed down my doubts. And when Wai Seuk, too filial to refuse outright, tried to put his father off with, "Soon as Hei Oi is a little older," I pressed, "He's twelve. You were younger by far when Ba hired you out."

"Really? Yes, well—"

I cut my son short. "Surely you've noticed that your father has begun to stoop even when he's not carrying a load, that his stride has become short and stiff, that there's a trembling in the swing of his hoe near the end of a day. The same is true for me. Oi Ling doesn't complain, but the slower we get, the more she's burdened."

Of course, Hei Oi was a child, a city boy without skills. And when Wai Seuk gave in to our pleadings, I knew he understood it was not help with chores we needed. Otherwise he would have offered to hire us a laborer.

Hei Oi, a long-necked, oversized duckling, was full of song and laughter. Popular with the village boys, he was included in all their games, he made play out of what they called work: drawing water, weeding, taking the water buffalo out to graze.

Like Gim Gong, Hei Oi was full of questions. He also shared his uncle's special feeling for the soil, the kind of good judgment that comes from within and cannot be taught. As clever as his father with tools, he attached a plate with many nails onto a long bamboo pole and dragged it through the paddies, efficiently uprooting the wild grasses that spring up with the rice.

Too spirited to stay in one place for more than a moment, Hei Oi was, like sunlight, everywhere at once, brightening, warming our days. In truth, as one year slid into another, Hok Yee and I felt almost as if Gim Gong and Wai Seuk were restored to us in our grandson, and the happiness we found in him and in each other was deep.

Then, after fifteen years of silence, Gim Gong sent us a letter. A letter that offered no explanation for his running away, no acknowledgment of his wrong. A letter that untangled none of the rumors we'd heard. A letter that declared his marriage void.

Oi Ling's hands shook so that the paper crackled, her voice sounded like a broken gong. "He says I will be receiving five hundred gold eagles in compensation through Fourth Uncle's store." She looked up at Hok Yee and me. "There's nothing more."

My own hands shaking, I took the letter from Oi Ling. "We must make certain no one finds out Gim Gong shows no remorse."

"How can we hide it?" Hok Yee sighed. "Everyone knows we got a letter. Elder Brother has already called a meeting of the clan elders for tomorrow and ordered me to bring it."

"You'll take a letter, but not this one," I said, crumpling it in my fist. "Oi Ling, quick, bring out the ink stick and brush."

Her forehead creased in a puzzled frown. "I . . ."

"You must write another letter. One that begs forgiveness and offers the gold eagles to the clan elders as a token of Gim Gong's repentance, a vow to right his wrong."

"The gold is mine, compensation for . . ."

"Don't worry," I assured her. "The seven outs for a man from marriage are clear. A wife must be barren, jealous, or diseased; disobey or neglect her husband's parents; lie with another man; steal; or talk too much. Gim Gong has no grounds to set you aside."

"But a woman has no outs she can declare, and I want to be free."

Hok Yee and I stared stupidly at our daughter-in-law as her true thoughts poured out like a flood after years of drought. She had not wanted to marry, but to live as a sworn sister in a *gu poh nguk*.

"These women don't have to suffer childbirth or the responsibility of bringing up children. They look after no one except themselves. Neither are their movements controlled or restricted by others. They earn their own rice, and they govern themselves."

Hnnnh, Oi Ling's desires were no less strange than those of our ghost son! She had even run away, as he had. Only her parents, more vigilant than Hok Yee and me, had caught her and locked her up. Then the matchmaker had tricked her into eating the betrothal cake.

"When my mother told me what I'd swallowed, I cried. What else could I do? Then I remembered the Goddess herself resisted marriage, and I prayed to Gwoon Yum for mercy. When she gave me a ghost to marry, I began to hope. That's why I refused to adopt a son. And now Gim Gong has set me free. He's even given me the means to go to Sun Duk and live as I wish. I won't give it up. I won't."

Smoke from our neighbors' evening cooking fires drifted through our doors and windows. But neither Oi Ling nor I rose to start ours. Hok Yee, hunched between us, also sat unmoving, not even reaching for his pipe.

"Hei Oi will be coming in to eat soon," I said at last. "He will not refuse to write another letter for us."

Oi Ling sucked in her breath.

Waiting for her reply, I felt my own breath catch.

Finally, looking down at the table, she said slowly, "One hundred gold eagles should cover the expenses of travel and buy me a place in a *gu poh nguk*. The rest can be used to persuade the clan elders to deal kindly with Gim Gong."

I questioned Hok Yee with my eyes.

He shook his head. "A new letter, even gold eagles, will not save Gim Gong if Oi Ling brings shame to the clan."

Oi Ling colored. "We can say I'm joining my husband."

"Sooner or later people will find out, as they did with Gim Gong. Unless you remain with us as his wife, he'll be struck from the *ga bo*."

"Am I in the *ga bo?*" She turned to face me. "Are you?"

"Oi Ling, you know the names of daughters and wives are never entered," Hok Yee said quietly. "Nor do they need to be, since they depend on their parents before marriage, their husbands after. But if Gim Gong is banished from the clan, there will be no spirit tablet for him when he dies, no one to feed his ghost. And if Gim Gong is a no-name man, a hungry ghost, you—as his wife—will be a no-name woman and a hungry ghost as well."

Gripping the table, Oi Ling raised herself up. "*I* will have a name. *My* ghost will be fed. My new family, my sworn sisters in the *go poh nguk,* will see to that."

Whether it was the ghost in Gim Gong, my ghost mark, or Oi Ling's stubborn will, I cannot say. But we could not stop Oi Ling from leaving, and without her, we could not save Gim Gong.

Elder Brother and Sister gloated over their victory. Hok Yee and I bowed our heads in sorrow and shame.

But Hei Oi said, "If no-name aunt can redeem herself by getting a new host for her spirit in Sun Duk, maybe no-name uncle can do the same in Gold Mountain. Maybe he already has."

And although his grandfather and I scolded him for talk that turned Heaven and Earth upside down, Hei Oi's words released in our hearts the seeds of hope.

SHEBA

DeLand, Florida
1904—1915

God Himself got to be colored. Why else was His son brown? And the first people God made—Adam, Eve, Cain, Abel—they was all black as jet. Yes, they was. Then Cain killed his brother Abel with a great big club.

"Cain, where your brother Abel?" God asked.

Cain pouted out his lip. "I don't know. What you asking me for? I ain't my brother's keeper."

That riled the Lord. It did. Stomping on the ground, He shouted, "Cain! You, Cain! Where your brother Abel?"

Well, Cain turned white as bleached cambric, and his younguns and their younguns done carried that color right on down till today. Leastways that is what spirit-filled black mens preach. And what I believe.

When I was coming up, howsomever, Folks was always shaking their heads and talking sorrowful over my being dark like my daddy stead of light like my mama. Cause, fact is, the shade of Fear and Sin is the one favored by most people over the color of God.

White folks is the ones with the power, see. No use asking why. They just is. So, yes, Jim and me got our patch and was paddling our own boat. But Crackers ain't stopped forcing me off the sidewalk into mud. Jim still got to tip his hat to white boys wet behind their ears and call them Mister. We still got to crowd below decks on the riverboat spite of the cabin upstairs being near empty. And when Wanting said, "Now you is free of living under a yoke. Now

you can fill the emptiness in your belly, the emptiness in your arms
and Jim's." Fear come back, "You willing to raise your younguns to
live uneasy, to look down stead of up?"

"You and Jim can wrap them in your loving," Wanting answered. "You and Jim can help them rise."

"Huh," Fear snorted. "Look at Lue."

Lue ain't throwed down his hoe over having a heap of money. He
ain't moved into the big house. He ain't whooped and hollered over
outsmarting Miss Fanny's sisters or the Yankees in DeLand.

White folks took on anyways. There wasn't one what ain't acted
hard-handed and high-tempered to Lue. Huh, they cut him dead on
the street and changed the name of the watering hole on his land
from Round Pond to Chink. They even froze him out of First Baptist, the church he done gone to with Miss Fanny for fifteen years,
the one he done gived all that money to.

Lue tried going over to First Methodist. But them people ain't got
any more filling between the crust of their religion than the Bap-
tists. And folks in our church, they held too much envy for Lue to
welcome him like they oughta.

Lue overlooked each new trespass. He made himself a prayer garden in his grove, setting up orange boxes for a pulpit inside a nest
of trees what'd branches thickly locked into a roof and walls of
leaves. He invited preachers to come preach.

The one at First Methodist did. He'd done mission work in
China, and he told Lue he was missing Chinamens. Lue was right
pleased. But the preaching that man done for Lue was the kind
what's long on the meek inheriting the earth, the kind what keeps
colored folks on their knees praying for better.

"That what you want for your younguns?" Fear hissed.

"No," I cried. "No."

I swallowed my wanting. Lue, he run after his. Not only his
wanting for a better orange but for Miss LaGette.

Mark it down, once the deep feelings he got for her come out
during that candy pulling, there was no pushing them back in. No.
Mornings I stopped by his cabin with a pan of cornbread or pot of
mush, he'd be writing in them notebooks of his, and I tell you, I
ain't never seen writing like that before or since.

He'd made inks out of pokeberries, roots, and bark, and he was drawing words with flowers and birds scrolling in and out. Nobody what seen them could've failed to recognize Lue was sick with loving. Loving and Wanting. Loving and Wanting so deep they done drive everything else away, even sleep.

Night after night, he'd take a lamp across to the big house and just sit in Miss LaGette's room. Watching him from our cabin, Jim and me'd hold each other close. And when I did fall to sleeping, Lue's wanting and not having'd mix into mine.

First Lue's face'd come to me. Tears rolled from his eyes. Tears of wanting. Tears what become eyes. The eyes of the babies I washed away every month with my teas, my misery.

One by one they called out, "Mama," to me. One by one they called out to be born. One by one they turned back into tears, tears red as my misery. Spilling out of my eyes, they formed a stream, a river, a flood. A flood so hot with wanting my skin split open and babies tumbled out.

Jim and me, we recognized Lue's wanting all right, and we got plumb weak in the knees for him and the trouble his wanting could bring down on himself and on all Colored in DeLand. Cause the same white mens what act trifling with colored womens, they raise the very devil if a colored man even looks at a white gal, and they done made crossmarrying against the law.

So I cooked up a mess of pig's feet the way Lue liked and Jim called him over. After eating, we sat out on the porch—Lue with his pipe, Jim with his chewing tobaccy—and while we was watching the Moon Regulator raise his light over the tops of our trees, we talked on the oranges we'd laid by, the corn we'd be planting soon.

Slowly, ever so slowly, Jim and me brung the talk round to signs and how masters tried to stomp out our Africa ways. Then we remarked on how Swedes is people what stick to their own selves, keeping the language, grub, and ways of their home country, even learning them to their younguns. All the while, Lue laughed and nodded, saying Chinamens is the same.

Only when I said, "Swedes marry their own," did Lue catch our drift. Then he swelled up like a pot of hominy and started in on how Miss LaGette was birthed in America, how he'd throwed off everything from his homefolks cept for their ways with plants.

"Sheba and me, we ain't got but a few Africa ways," Jim said real quiet. "All the same, we got the color of its people. Just like Miss LaGette got her people's color and you got yours. And there's no throwing off color, no getting round it—not with money or land or nothing."

Maybe Wanting blindfolded Lue. Or maybe he was looking for better in people like he was with plants. Anyways, he said his wanting and winning Miss LaGette wasn't no different from her daddy wanting and winning her mama.

Mister Gustave met Miss Margaret at church in the old country, see, and he found her right smart, sweet as honey in a comb. Well, church is for praising Jesus, and Jesus was a carpenter. All the same, Mister Gustave's family told him he couldn't marry Miss Margaret cause his family got land and money while her daddy was in the same line of work as the Lord, and that ain't good enough.

They never did use them words, mind. No, they tippy-toed with fancy talk the way people trying to hide ugly always do. But that was their meaning. Only Mister Gustave favored Miss Margaret too much to give her up. So he quit his family and his easy life in Sweden, selling his muscle to a Yankee sharpee for a new chance in America.

Took Mister Gustave ten years of straining in coal mines to pay off that Yankee for his passage and buy a ticket for his gal. But the two stayed faithful to each other, and when Mister Gustave sent for Miss Margaret, she come flying.

Now everybody know Swedes put more store on land than money, cause in their home country few people got the chance to own any. And Lue, he tried to raise himself up in Mister Gustave's eyes by buying one hundred more acres spite of having trouble working the fifteen he got, spite of what Jim'd said.

Then Lue took the train up to Pierson. What passed during this visit not Lue or nobody else ever told. But he left home looking like he was on a mountaintop, and he dragged back deeper than if he was in a valley.

Minute he landed home, he asked Jim to help him board up the big house. It was like they was nailing a coffin. And all the while they was pounding their hammers, tears rolled down Lue's face and he moaned low. I cried my own apron limp.

Lue was powerful cut up. But he pushed down his grieving and throwed himself into his work, spinning ideas with Jim like he'd done with Miss Fanny.

When Lue tasked himself to make a better grapefruit top of finishing his orange, Jim was right there working longside him. And when Lue made his orange, Jim laughed, "You got Double Brilliance like your China name, all right. Maybe triple."

Yes, Lue made his orange. He did. And it turned out just the way he dreamed. The tree don't look a heap different from most—it got a well-rounded head and low-spreading branches. But the fruit, the fruit is something else—a fair size, full of juice, and tasty. It ain't got many seeds and is a good keeper and shipper. It ripen late in the season, too, at a time when oranges is few and the price high. Best of all, it's hardy, hanging on to a tree through winter cold and summer rain without hurting none.

Well, nurserymens was always sniffing round groves looking for something new, and there was one what got eyes sharper than the rest. Huh, his eyes bulged big as fists over Lue's orange.

"You give me the budwood to raise," that nurseryman said, "I'll name the orange *Lue Gim Gong*. I'll make you famous in Florida, in America, and all the world. Famous and rich."

Mark it down, that nurseryman poured it on, promising the moon with a fence round it. Lue's eyes, they got to shining bright

as when he was pulling candy with Miss LaGette. He wouldn't hear
no contrary word from Jim or me.

"Yes," Lue told the nurseryman. "Yes."

While the nurseryman was yet raising the *Lue Gim Gong* trees,
he put the orange up for a big prize. It won, too, just short to the
time the trees was ready for selling. Yes, a big medal. One called
the Wilder for best new fruit of the year.

Nineteen and eleven that was, a date I won't soon forget. The
nurseryman made sure news of the medal got floated round good,
and Lue was writ up in newspapers and magazines everywhere. One
look at them, Jim say, and you can see clear how plain folks, big
growers, and powerful government men all was buzzing.

I tell you, they was calling the orange "a marvel," "rare and
good," Lue "a genius," "a plant wizard," and more. Fact is, they
bragged so big the wanting for *Lue Gim Gong*s caught and spread
quicker than a fire.

People from all over the world commenced to send Lue letters,
and his grove spilled over with folks coming to make admiration
over him and his orange. Them river excursion boats even made his
place into a stop.

Lue put out a book for people visiting to sign their names, and
Jim counted more than two thousand in a single year. That don't include younguns, neither—the ones what come with their folks or
with teachers what brung their classes.

Lord, how Lue prized them visitors. For the longest, he ain't had
nobody cept Jim and me, laborers, and scalawags. Now even them
Yankees what'd called Lue down come smiling like they'd never
parted ways.

Well, I tell you straight and I tell you bold, I hold what Master
William, the KK, and that turpentine captain done to my daddy
against them still. But Lue, he was a forgiving man. Them Yankees
done licked his spirit raw as the whip what laid open my daddy's
feets. Even so, Lue spoke kind to them. He spoke kind to everyone.

Anyways, people coming to visit made Lue powerful glad. I declare, he'd be welcoming them at his gate before they'd a chance to
ring his bell.

Course everybody was in a almighty hurry for a close look at the
Lue Gim Gong. But Lue'd take his time getting to the mother trees,

stopping to show folks the way he done his grafting or how he use palmetto roots and cuttings for fertilizer. If there was a heap of younguns, he'd draw them down to Round Pond and show them how the fish jump up and eat out of his hand. He'd call out March, the rooster he'd saved from a chicken hawk and raised for a pet. He'd tell them stories about coming up in China.

Way after a while, he'd get to his *Lue Gim Gong* trees. But he'd not let on. No, he'd point a distance to oranges from other trees what'd dropped to the ground on account of rain or cold. Then he'd remark on how there was no droppings under the tree he was standing by, draw himself up right tall, and say, "This is the *Lue Gim Gong.*"

Now *Lue Gim Gong* oranges can hold on after ripening while the tree blossoms and bears new fruit. So Lue'd have one-year, two-year, three-year oranges hanging on the same trees. Only he'd know their age, and he'd cut off a sampling of each kind, then lead people to his "cathedral."

That was what Lue got to calling his prayer garden, see. He'd planted wild yellow jasmine and Cherokee roses at his south fence so the smell from them'd spill into where he was praying. He'd let the branches of the trees grow so thick, they kept out all but the heaviest rain. Jim done made some benches and set them front of the orange-crate pulpit, and Lue's visitors, they'd crowd onto these and sit more hushed than if they was in a real church.

Soon as they was settled, Lue'd stand at his pulpit and offer up a prayer for every good a body could want. Then he'd call on six people to come up and stand them in a circle facing the crowd. When they was set, he'd cut open the *Lue Gim Gongs* one at a time and hand the six people sections to taste.

Always they'd smile and fuss over the orange being juicy, free of seeds, and sweet. Always they'd make over the last piece most. Lue'd let them go on for a bit. Then he'd tell them the last orange was the one what been hanging for three years, and everybody'd clap their hands and ask him how he done it.

Just like a preacher giving a sermon, Lue'd start in on how people from countries all over the world come to America looking for gold.

Yes, somebody'd call out. In her home country, she'd believed the leaves of the trees here was gold and people only got to go into the woods and pull off armfuls of golden leaves to buy anything they wanted.

Directly, somebody else'd say he was told people in America could just hit rocks with a stick and rum'd come spilling out.

By and by, Lue'd come back with how he'd aimed for learning, not gold or rum or whatever else people been saying. How he wanted to do good with his learning. That was how he'd come to dream of making his orange. "The rest was work. Hard work."

Sometimes folks'd call out their dreams. Dreams they'd made true. Dreams they'd gived up. Had Lue ever been disencouraged, they'd want to know.

Yes, he'd tell them. But he'd called on the Lord to give him faith. And the Lord done answered his prayers, holding him up when he was down and guiding him to the finish.

Lue was preaching all right. The white folks, they was hanging to his every word. It was a sight to see. And the change their admiration made in Lue was the same as between hail and sunshine. He swelled right proud. He never did put on airs, mind. But he got all lit up, and there was a pertness to his walk.

Visitors left with the sun, howsomever. And they never did invite Lue to worship at their churches. There was no invitations to their homes, neither. When Lue called on folks anyways, they ain't turned him away like before. But nobody asked him *in* to a house. Few offered refreshment, even a glass of cool water. Most they'd generally do is come out on their porches to visit.

Lue was like that Conjure Man from Africa, see, the one what run from his slavers in Georgia and joined up with the Indians here in Florida. Made himself a good life too—till the government sent soldiers to drive the Indians off their lands.

Course Conjure Man and the Indians fought the soldiers, fought them fierce and fought them smart. But there was a heap more soldiers than Indians. And the government was mighty powerful, too powerful for the Indians and Conjure Man.

Those people the soldiers ain't killed the government done drove out of their homes and out of the Territory. Cept Conjure Man.

When the soldiers come for him, the wind was blowing rash and the moon shining dim. Conjure Man, slipping in and out of the shadows, led the soldiers a fine chase. Then he changed into a alligator and slid, laughing, into Lake Belle.

Wasn't long before he quit his laughing, howsomever, cause having the shape of a alligator is not the same as being a alligator, and Conjure Man got terrible lonesome. He is lonesome still. Nights you hear bellowing from the lake, you is hearing him cry.

Lue cried in the night, too.

So many people was crazy for *Lue Gim Gong* trees, the nursery couldn't keep up, and folks was begging Lue to sell them budwood from his mother trees, offering him enough cash to make him prosper more than the nurseryman done promised. But the nurseryman done fixed Lue's contract so only the nursery could sell them trees and nobody could sell the budwood.

Course that paper ain't got no justice in it. After thousands of trees was sold, Lue's portion added up to scarce two hundred dollars. And the nurseryman told Lue there'd be no money from the ones the nursery'd go on selling. Like my mama said when Master William stole my daddy's farm, "The colored man works, the white man gets."

Now Lue ain't no spender cept for grain for his horses and books for himself. He dress plain as Jim—shirt and overalls for working, cotton jacket and pants for Sunday best. His grub is what I make or what he grow.

He ain't the kind pleasured by riches, neither. When he lost the last of his twelve thousand dollars from Miss Fanny's sisters to a man what made out he was a kind of money manager or something, Lue just shrugged.

But his plants was the one place he'd always run his own affairs. Even Miss Fanny'd never dictated to him there. So it wasn't the money Lue was losing what got him in a white heat over the nurseryman's ruling. It was what the nursery was doing with the *Lue Gim Gong* orange.

The *Lue Gim Gong* tree was costly, see, the most costly tree the nursery sold. People was willing to pay cause the orange was so special. They *got* to pay cause there was no place else to buy it.

Well, that nursery was prospering a heap and aiming to prosper more. Folks blamed Lue, howsomever, not the nursery. Chinamens is sly, they said, slanty like their eyes.

Mark it down, I ain't never seen nobody leave Lue's grove without a gift of oranges, not even when he was counting over four thousand visitors a year. And them oranges he give is his best, not culls. Tell me, would a man like that set out to cheat folks?

Anyways, Lue commenced giving visitors *Lue Gim Gong* budwood. That forced the nursery to drop the price of the trees directly, and the top of the nurseryman's head, it flew off. But there was nothing in Lue's contract about giving, there was nothing the nurseryman could do to stop Lue. No.

When it come to plants, Lue ain't never quit looking for a way round what is, he ain't never quit looking for better. Huh, he mix pollen and budwood like I mix grub in my kitchen: in that tangle by Miss Fanny's house is a rosebush what got seventeen kind of roses in seven colors, all from a single root; beside it is a tree what got grapefruit, tangerines, and oranges hanging on it.

Plants is what Lue hold dear all right. Younguns is what Jim and me cherish. Even so, I never could find me enough hoping to birth babies. Jim held on to his hoping till I slid past forty and lost my misery.

The wanting we shared for babies still burned something terrible, howsomever. I seen Jim's in his eyes every time he carried a little chap or swung one high. Mine, it done ride me in my trouble dream and ride me hard.

Course there ain't no dream what ain't got a meaning, and I studied on mine: the cries of my unborn babies, the hot river of wanting what split me open, the babies what tumbled out. I declare, I turned every little thing over and over in my mind for the longest till I done puzzled it out: them babies what tumbled out, they was mine, only they wasn't birthed by me.

* * *

Now there ain't nobody with eyes what ain't seen the younguns of working folks what can't pay for a body to mind them, the younguns what snowbirds give pennies to for swallowing raw eggs and joining pie-eating races and other foolishness, the younguns coming up wild. After I figured the meaning of my dream, it come to me Jim and me could satisfy our wanting by watching them younguns for their folks.

"We can help raise them," I said to Jim.

"Yes," Jim laughed. "Yes."

Folks was powerful glad over my notion. Wasn't no time at all before Jim and me got us a crop of little chaps, most coming to us day by day, some week by week, a few month by month. And them younguns, they pleasure us. They do.

Shucks, there ain't no end to the fine times we make together. Easter we color eggs for hunts. Halloween we make haints out of Spanish moss. Christmas Jim gets himself up as Santy Claus, giving out little cloth sacks of cakes and goobers.

What the younguns like best, howsomever, is stories. The stories about Africa passed down from Aunt Mattie and Grandma Maisie. The stories from Lue about China. Ain't only our younguns what ask for them stories neither, but the younguns what come to Lue's grove with their folks and teachers, then come back on their own and follow him over here.

I tell you, the faces turned up at us for stories is like the roses on that bush Lue done made. They is a mess of colors, their skins soft as petals and smelling as sweet. Looking at them, a new dream come to me: a dream of better. Not with plants, mind, but with people. Yes.

Epilogue

Before his death in 1925, Lue Gim Gong perfected a hardy grapefruit and a perfumed grapefruit. His obituaries estimated his contributions to the citrus industry in the millions, and his work was honored in the Florida Pavilion at the 1933 Chicago World's Fair and the 1940 New York World's Fair.

Lue Gim Gong the man, however, was not acknowledged in death any more than in life. His extensive library was sold, his personal papers largely destroyed. Even his grave was left unmarked until George A. Zabriskie, president of the New York Historical Society, chanced to visit DeLand and made arrangements for a simple plaque.

In the late 1980s, I learned that one volume of Lue's diaries had survived. But while I was still trying to pinpoint its location, the person in possession of the diary offered it to a university archive. Told the diary had no value, the person burned it.

Acknowledgments

I have accumulated many debts while researching and writing this book, and it is my pleasure to acknowledge them here.

Him Mark Lai turned over his extensive files on Lue Gim Gong to me. He also introduced me to Lew Yao Huan, who shared his memories of Lue Gim Gong and his brothers and wrote letters of introduction for me to the Lue clan in Lung On village.

Flower City Publisher in Guangzhou, the China International Exchange Centre, and the Overseas Chinese Affairs Office of Toishan funded a research trip to Lung On that was meticulously organized by Tsai Nuliang, then director of the Foreign Language Department of Flower City. Regretfully, lack of space prevents me from naming all the people who helped make this journey a success, but I would be remiss if I did not recognize my special debts to Chen Wen Jun for his hospitality; Lue Duk Sum for making his grand-uncle, Lue Gim Gong, come alive for me and for giving me a copy of the Lue clan's *ga bo;* Leung Mao Wah for explaining orange cultivation in Toishan; Tsai Nuliang for making my quest hers.

In North Adams, Lisa Jarisch made available the public library's archival collection while I was there. She also later trusted me with reel after reel of the *North Adams Transcript,* and she introduced me to people in the community who were familiar with the town's history. Audrey Sweeney drove me to Vermont to meet Burlingame descendant Sanford M. Plumb who, together with his brother John H. Plumb, gave me copies of family documents. Dan Connerton introduced me to Tim Coogan, who has provided an answer for every one of my seemingly endless questions about North Adams for the past seven years. Also helpful were Ruth Browne, Lorraine Leonard, Betty Marsico, and Stephen Ning.

In Florida, Bill Dreggors, Jr., and Alice Van Cleef shared their memories of Lue Gim Gong with me; Theresa Lupica Poss made my husband and me welcome in Lue Gim Gong's former home; Helena Friese shared her extensive files on Lue Gim Gong; Sidney Taylor helped me locate and understand court documents. Maxine Turner's honesty about human relations provided valuable insights. She also introduced me to Ruth Hagstrom, who shared family photographs and documents and her extensive knowledge of family and regional history not only during our interview but through a voluminous correspondence in the years since. George E. Pozzetta shared his research on Chinese in Florida. Harold Cardwell, Sr., Blanche Mercer Fearington, and Amy Jean Hanscom were also helpful.

I was aided moreover in no small measure by the scholarship of academics in a host of fields. Their work—published and in manuscript form—provided me with necessary context and insights. Individuals in institutions all across the United States assisted me in accessing these works as well as raw data: Wei-Chi Poon, Asian American Studies Library at University of California, Berkeley; Kathleen M. Reilly, Berkshire Athenaeum; Jill Erickson, Boston Athenaeum; Ruth Marshall and James Merrick, Boston Public Library; Paula Batten and Celia Jones, Deland Public Library; Keith Sheldon, Florida Department of Citrus; Joan Morris and Juanita Whiddon, Florida State Archives; Jack Hearn, Horticultural Research Laboratory, Orlando; Patricia Redd, Massachusetts State Library; Elizabeth Alexander, P. K. Yonge Library of Florida History; S. Broomall, Orange County Library, Florida; Loren D. Tukey, American Pomological Society; Janice S. Mahaffey, Putnam County Archives; Jo Waterhouse, Putnam County Library; Michael J. Costello, Rhode Island Historical Society; Roberta Griefer, Carol Small, and the many librarians and clerks who staff the reference and interlibrary loan departments at the San Francisco Public Library; Beverly Byrd, State Library of Florida; Dorothy Minor, Stetson University; Tom Joyner, Virginia Military Institute; Corawayne Wright, Wesleyan College.

Friends and colleagues read drafts of the manuscript and provided criticism that helped shape it: Catherine Brady, Dorothy Bryant, Tim Coogan, Deng Ming-Dao, Rita Drysdale, Lorraine Dong, Ann Edelstein, Marko Fong, Peter Ginsberg, Robin Grossman, Ruth Hamel, LeVell Holmes, Marlon Hom, Yvette Huginnie, Kee Huo, Steven Kahn, Harry Lawton, Jean Lim, Lillian Louie, Felicia Lowe, Cathy Luchetti, Valerie Matsumoto, Drummond McCunn, Teddi McCunn, June McLaughlin, Susan Moldow, Carol Olwell, Peggy Pascoe, Shifra Raffel, Walter Reuther, Ruth Sasaki, Jay Schaefer, Tsai Nuliang, Jan Venolia, Susan Weinberg, Stan Yogi, Ellen Yeung, Judy Yung.

Others contributed to this novel in diverse ways: Chu Moon Ho with powerful descriptions of ghosts and village life; Marlon Hom by introducing me to *muk yu goh* (wooden fish songs), refining the translation of Lue Gim Gong's name, and not only translating the Lue clan's *ga bo* but making elaborate, color-coded charts that illuminated the complicated family relationships; Charles McClain and Laurie Wu McClain with their knowledge of the law; Dr. Chih Meng by sharing his papers on Lue Gim Gong; Walter Reuther with his expertise in matters horticultural; the staff at Sam Tung Uk Museum in Hong Kong with a slide discussion of ghost rituals; Ellen Yeung by formulating a policy for the romanizations. Any errors that remain are mine.

It is no exaggeration that without the generous assistance of those named above, there would be no book, and I am profoundly grateful. I also wish to thank Peter Ginsberg for being the kind of agent I thought existed only in writers' dreams, Rosemary Ahern, for her sensitive, insightful editing.

As always my largest debt is to my husband, Don, who has worked with me in every capacity. Of his many contributions, I am most grateful for his understanding of Aristotle, Stanislavski, and the human heart; his extraordinary ability to analyze and to create; his absolute honesty; and his continuing support. Thanks.

DUTTON **PLUME**

COMPELLING NOVELS

☐ **SINGING SONGS by Meg Tilly.** Written by the acclaimed actress, this novel explores how one family lives, centerless, caught in a flux of emotion and violence that touches and transforms each of its members. It is the masterful realization of a young girl's journey to adulthood in a chaotic, abusive, and fragmented world— an affirmation of a child's ability to use her judgment and imagination alone to light her way. "A triumph . . . absolutely believable, completely irresistible." —*Chicago Sun-Times* (271657—$9.95)

☐ **THE BOOK OF REUBEN by Tabitha King.** Reuben Styles has spent his entire life in Nodd's Ridge, Maine trying to do the right thing according to the standard American success story. While nothing turns out as he expects, his incredible spirit and strength keep him struggling to become the man he envisioned. Capturing the searing, gritty reality of small-town America of the '50s, '60s, and '70s, this stunning, deeply involving novel touches a common nerve and casts a light on our own lives. (937668—$22.95)

☐ **RIVER OF SKY by Karen Harper.** This magnificent epic of the American frontier brings to vivid life one woman's stirring quest for fortune and happiness. This is Kate Craig's story—one of rousing adventure and heartbreaking struggle, of wildfire passion and a wondrous love, as strong and deep as the river itself. It will sweep you into an America long gone by. (938222—$21.95)

Prices slightly higher in Canada.

Visa and Mastercard holders can order Plume, Meridian, and Dutton books by calling
1-800-253-6476.
They are also available at your local bookstore. Allow 4-6 weeks for delivery.
This offer is subject to change without notice.

Ⓟ **PLUME**

SIZZLING READING

☐ **THE AMERICAN WOMAN IN THE CHINESE HAT by Carole Maso.** Abandoned by her lover of ten years, and devastated by the painful death of her brother, an American writer named Catherine comes to live and heal her wounds on the French Riviera. With passionate abandon and detachment, she pursues her own destruction through brief but irresistible sexual encounters until she meets Lucien. "Gorgeous . . . an outpouring of passion."—*San Francisco Chronicle*
(275075—$10.95)

☐ **FEAR OF FLYING by Erica Jong. With a New Introduction by the Author.** The most delicious, erotic novel a woman ever wrote. . . . Flying to Europe with her brilliant psychiatrist husband, Isadora Wing makes an adulterous bolt across the continent in the most uninhibited sexual extravaganza that is no longer for men only. "Extraordinary . . . wildly funny and very wise. It is the devastating, disarming, explicit exposure of the very core of a woman."—*Los Angeles Times*
(274796—$12.95)

☐ **HOW TO SAVE YOUR OWN LIFE by Erica Jong. With an Afterword by Anthony Burgess.** This tantalizing sequel to *Fear of Flying* pushes the boundaries proscribing women and sex in print still further as its protagonist, Isadora Wing, continues her mythic journey to self-discovery. Spurred by a friend's suicide, Isadora chooses to face her fears, leave her marriage, and search for sexual fulfillment. "Shameless, sex-saturated and a joy."—*People* (274540—$11.95)

☐ **THE AUTOBIOGRAPHY OF MY BODY by David Guy.** This provocative novel is a startingly explicit exploration of a man's sexual life that plumbs the forbidden zones of sexual desire and fantasy. Charles Bradford is drawn into an erotically charged relationship with a woman whose sexual insatiability creates a dangerous but irresistible bond between them. "Lusty . . . compelling . . . a tale of discovery and intimacy that can be read by both men and women."—*Houston Post*
(274532—$12.95)

Prices slightly higher in Canada.

Visa and Mastercard holders can order Plume, Meridian, and Dutton books by calling
1-800-253-6476.
They are also available at your local bookstore. Allow 4-6 weeks for delivery.
This offer is subject to change without notice.

℗ PLUME   **DUTTON**

OUTSTANDING MODERN NOVELS

☐ **DEPTHS OF GLORY: A *Biographical Novel of Camille Pissarro* by Irving Stone.** Camille Pissarro led all others in a style of painting that would bring new boldness and freedom to art—and plunged into a love affair that would put him outside respectable society's bounds. Now in this brilliant biographical novel, we see how Pissarro and his circle were driven to the depths of poverty and forced to the brink of despair even as they founded the great French Impressionist School of Art. "Impressive."—*New York Times*
(275016—$14.95)

☐ **NIGHT SHALL OVERTAKE US by Kate Saunders.** The lives of four extraordinary women are bound together by a shared past and a secret vow. But their friendship is tested and finally betrayed by a forbidden passion. This gripping novel recreates the sights, sounds, and textures of turn-of-the-century England—and the heartbreak of World War I. But most important, it is a celebration of relationships—of love lost and love won.   (937641—$22.95)

☐ **HEROES AND LOVERS by Lucy Kavaler.** An extraordinary story that is at once a gripping historical saga, a fascinating exploration of sexuality, and a tantalizing mystery. Sweeping through the mists of time and place—from the vanished era of old New York society to the slums of London to the frozen world of the Antarctic to the present—this novel focuses on the dark secret that drives two vibrant, strong-willed women, who live decades apart, toward their separate yet hauntingly intertwined destinies.   (93815x—$22.95)

Prices slightly higher in Canada.

Visa and Mastercard holders can order Plume, Meridian, and Dutton books by calling
1-800-253-6476.
They are also available at your local bookstore. Allow 4-6 weeks for delivery.
This offer is subject to change without notice.

Ⓟ PLUME

CONTEMPORARY FICTION

☐ **RAMEAU'S NIECE by Cathleen Schine.** This delightful literary romp spoofs the cultural elite, taking contemporary fiction to new levels of comedy. Margaret Nathan is the brilliant though mortifyingly forgetful author of an unlikely bestseller celebrated as much by feminists as deconstructionists. She seems blessed until she finds herself seduced by an eighteenth-century lascivious novel she has discovered. "Witty, erotic, hilarious."—*People*　　　　　(271614—$10.95)

☐ **DISH!** *A Single Woman's Confessions on Food and Sex* **by Juli I. Huss.** This deliciously sexy adventure exposes the consuming passions that drive today's single female. With wit, insight, and all the juicy parts left in, this bawdy confessional tale follows the intricate ups and downs in the lives of four modern women. Equal parts Xanax and pasta, meatloaf and Wonderbra, it includes suggestions for foods to ease every crisis in a girl's complicated love life. "Hilarious, trashy, truthful and informative."—*New York Daily News*　　　　　(274508—$10.95)

☐ **CHINA BOY by Gus Lee.** "A robust, startling book . . . hilariously poignant . . . a fascinating, evocative portrait of the Chinese community in California in the 1950s, caught between two complex, demanding cultures."—*New York Times Book Review*　　　　　(271584—$11.95)

☐ **GO by Holly Uyemoto.** A hilarious, irresistibly fresh novel that imbues a unique experience with universal truth. Wil is one week away from her twenty-first birthday, but she wonders if she'll ever see the day. Depressed by a breakup with her politically correct boyfriend and fortified with a prescription for lithium, she returns from college to her family . . . back where all the trouble started. "Succeeds with humor and style, in ways that are all Uyemoto's own."—*San Francisco Chronicle*　　　　　(271975—$10.95)

☐ **MATRICIDE by Carla Tomaso.** This novel is a darkly delicious concoction of secrets, lies, and unconditional love—and loathing. Every woman has considered murdering her mother, at least once. The quirky, verse-scribbling, passion-seeking narrator, however, has actually tried it. "Hilarious and heartbreaking . . . A roller-coaster ride of the emotions."—Lisa Alther, author of *Kinflicks* (271118—$9.95)

☐ **BALLS by Gorman Bechard.** It's the year 2000, and baseball has changed dramatically. The Supreme Court has ruled that women can play in the major leagues. As firstbaseperson for the expansion Manhattan Meteorites, Louise "Balls" Gehrig is about to break baseball's gender barrier and change America's pastime forever. Loaded with sassy wit and social satire, this wonderfully fresh and original novel blends suspense, romance, and excitement into one grand slam.
　　　　　(272947—$10.95)

Prices slightly higher in Canada.

Visa and Mastercard holders can order Plume, Meridian, and Dutton books by calling
1-800-253-6476.
They are also available at your local bookstore. Allow 4-6 weeks for delivery.
This offer is subject to change without notice.

W9-ATB-191

NOLS
Wilderness Medicine

0 11557 03306 9

NOLS
Wilderness Medicine

Tod Schimelpfenig

Illustrated by Joan Safford

A Publication of the
National Outdoor Leadership School
and
Stackpole Books

Text copyright © 2008 National Outdoor Leadership School
Illustrations copyright © 2006 by Joan Safford
All rights reserved.

Published by
Stackpole Books
5067 Ritter Road
Mechanicsburg, PA 17055
www.stackpolebooks.com

All rights reserved, including the right to reproduce this book or
portions thereof in any form or by any means, electronic or
mechanical, including photocopying, recording, or by any
information storage and retrieval system, without permission in
writing from the publisher. All inquiries should be addressed to
Stackpole Books, 5067 Ritter Road, Mechanicsburg, PA 17055.

Printed in the United States of America
10 9 8 7 6 5 4 3

Cover photo by Brad Christensen

This book was printed using responsible environmental practices by
FSC-certified book manufacturers. The Forest Stewardship Council
encourages the responsible management of the world's forests. The
Rainforest Alliance works to conserve biodiversity and ensure sus-
tainable livelihoods by transforming land-use practices, business
practices, and consumer behavior.

Library of Congress Cataloging-in-Publication Data
Schimelpfenig, Tod, 1954-
  NOLS wilderness medicine / Tod Schimelpfenig ; illustrated by
Joan Safford.
    p. cm.
  "A Publication of the National Outdoor Leadership School and
Stackpole Books."
  Previous editions had title: NOLS wilderness first aid.
  Includes bibliographical references and index.
  ISBN-13: 978-0-8117-3306-9
  ISBN-10: 0-8117-3306-8
  1. First aid in illness and injury. 2. Outdoor medical emergencies.
I. Schimelpfenig, Tod, 1954-   . NOLS wilderness first aid.
II. National Outdoor Leadership School (U.S.) III. Title. IV. Title:
Wilderness medicine.

RC88.9.O95S35 2006
616.02′52—dc22

2006010138

THE AUTHOR

TOD SCHIMELPFENIG

As a wilderness educator since 1973, and a volunteer EMT on ambulance and search and rescue squads for the past thirty years, Tod Schimelpfenig has extensive experience with wilderness risk management. He has utilized this valuable experience by conducting safety reviews as well as serving as the NOLS Risk Management Director for eight years, the NOLS Rocky Mountain School Director for six years, and a member for three years on the board of directors of the Wilderness Medical Society (WMS), where he received the WMS Warren Bowman Award for lifetime contribution to the field of wilderness medicine in 2001 and was elected a Fellow of the Academy of Wilderness Medicine. Tod is the founder of the Wilderness Risk Managers Committee, has spoken at numerous conferences on pre-hospital and wilderness medicine, and has taught wilderness medicine around the world. He has written numerous articles on educational program, risk management, and wilderness medicine topics, and currently reviews articles for the *Journal of Wilderness and Environmental Medicine.* Tod is also currently the Curriculum Director of the Wilderness Medicine Institute of NOLS.

To the students at NOLS. I hope this text helps you to be better outdoor leaders.

To all NOLS instructors, who on a daily basis teach and practice first aid and safety in the wilderness and are the source of the practical experience that is the foundation of this text.

To Betsy, Sam, Dave, Mark, and Emily for their support and patience during the time I devoted to this project.

To the St. Michael's College Rescue Squad, where I first learned quality patient care.

QUICK-REFERENCE INDEX

CONTENTS

PREFACE

Traditional first aid programs are designed for the common medical problems, telephones, ambulances, and hospitals of urban areas. In wilderness medicine we take these practices and make them relevant to the medical problems we experience in the outdoors and the available equipment, transportation, and communication systems. Wilderness medicine training has become the standard for outdoor professionals, and the relevant training for the outdoor recreationist. When the first edition of *NOLS Wilderness First Aid* appeared on bookshelves in 1991, the concept of wilderness medicine seemed clear. Today, its very definition, at least in North America, has blurred.

In 1991, the traditional definition of medical care in remote locations, with improvised gear and challenging environmental conditions, applied to many wilderness areas. Today, technology and the growing popularity of outdoor pursuits has managed to effectively "shrink" many wilderness areas. Multiday evacuations with improvised litters are less common, largely replaced by helicopters. Communication technology now offers the chance of quick transport from remote areas to urban medical care, and many wilderness visitors have come to expect such service. In fact, much of what we call wilderness medicine is really a simple extension of modern emergency medical services into the wilderness by cell phone and helicopter instead of into a city by telephone and ambulance.

This doesn't mean wilderness medicine is obsolete. There are still areas where a radio or a cell phone will not work and where quick rescue service is not available. Weather and terrain can still hamper rescue. True wilderness medicine means we don't have the advantages of modern medicine. We don't have access to medications, diagnostic equipment and procedures, rapid transport, and specialty care. In reality, a medical emergency in the wilderness is a grave situation.

For over forty years, students and instructors on NOLS courses in remote locations around the world have received top-notch wilderness medical training in the outdoors. This book is an extension of those years of practical experience. It uses the insights and experience of NOLS instructors, who among their many talents must occasionally assess patients and make decisions about medical treatment and urgency of transport. Using the experience of our staff—who volunteer as members of the Fremont County (Wyoming) Search and Rescue—and our experience with NOLS instructors leading expeditions and evacuating people from all over the world, we can learn how skilled outdoors people, who are not medical professionals, make decisions. We can use our NOLS database of field risk management incidents—the most extensive in the industry—to look at what decisions wilderness leaders make. We gain insights into how and what we should teach and how to craft our decisions. The treatment and evacuation guidelines in this text are consistent with the same guidelines that guide the decisions of NOLS instructors in the field.

NOLS Wilderness Medicine reflects the changing field of wilderness medicine. In 1991, for example, there was no Wilderness Risk Managers Committee. In 1992, that group was started by this book's author, Tod Schimelpfenig. Today, it has combined wilderness leadership, risk management, and wilderness medicine into one of the most important conferences of its type.

Another very important move by NOLS in the past decade was the acquisition, in 1999, of the Wilderness Medicine Institute. One of the nation's leading wilderness medical trainers, WMI of NOLS is the foremost wilderness medicine training center in the western United States. WMI of NOLS provides wilderness first aid, first responder, and emergency medical technician training to more than 10,000 students each year.

Practical experience. Innovation. Vision. These are qualities that have made NOLS and this text a success. But no medicine is better than prevention. The prevention theme runs throughout this book. You'll read about it in chapters on hygiene, gender, and cold injuries. You'll also read about it in the chapter on leadership, teamwork, and communication for small groups. A foundation of wilderness medicine must be competence in basic outdoor skills and leadership. You can't learn this from a book. You need to go on your own wilderness trips or take a NOLS course.

John N. Gans
Executive Director

ACKNOWLEDGMENTS

I would like to thank the following people for their assistance in the preparation of this edition:

Shana Tarter of the Wilderness Medicine Institute at NOLS.

NOLS Field Program Supervisors Allen O'Bannon, Missy White, Pete Absolon, Kathy Brown, and Gary Cukjati for reviewing the chapters on cold injury, gender, and hygiene and helping to assure the text reflects what really happens in the wilderness.

Karl Weller, long time NOLS Rocky Mountain chef, for his advice on hygiene and foodborne illness.

Molly Doran for her review of the chapter on leadership, curriculum, and teamwork.

Herb Ogden, M.D., NOLS Medical Advisor and Chair of the NOLS Risk Management Committee, for review of the new sections of the text and his advice and support of NOLS instructors and students.

Louise Collins, M.D., for her assistance with the chapter on gender-specific concerns.

Wilderness Medicine Institute instructor Mike Ditola for his review of this edition.

Linda Lindsey, Human Resources Director for NOLS, who coauthored the first three editions of this text. Linda's career in wilderness medicine includes extensive field work as a NOLS instructor. As the former coordinator of the Colorado Outward Bound first aid program, she has five years' experience as a staff nurse in obstetrics and neonatal intensive care. She served six years as a board member of the Wilderness Medical Society. Linda's work on the early editions of this text is deeply appreciated. You'll see her touch in much of the book, especially the gender-specific, respiratory and cardiac, heat, and altitude illness chapters.

INTRODUCTION

Wilderness has no handrails, no telephones, and no simple solutions for complex emergency situations. It does have dangers. Some are obvious: rock fall, moving water, stormy weather, avalanches, crevasses, and wild animals. Others are subtle: impure water, dehydration, cold and damp weather, altitude illness, and human judgment.

Although these risks can be minimized with skill, experience, and judgment, outdoor leaders know that despite their best efforts, accidents and illness will happen. Leaders prepare for the challenge of providing emergency medical care in remote and hostile environments with limited equipment and long and arduous transport to a hospital.

This book is designed as a text to accompany the wilderness first aid curriculum presented on NOLS field courses and the Wilderness First Responder (WFR) course taught by WMI.

Chapters one through eight cover fundamental topics in first aid—patient assessment, shock, soft tissue injuries, burns, fractures and dislocations, and chest, head, and abdominal injuries. Chapters nine though fifteen present environmental medical problems—heat, cold, water, altitude, and poisonous plants and animals.

Chapters sixteen through nineteen cover medical topics—cardiac, respiratory, diabetes, allergies, anaphylaxis, and gender-based medical problems. The final section discusses a variety of topics pertinent to expedition medicine—water disinfection, hygiene, hydration, flulike illness, and dental problems, as well as leadership, stress, and legal topics. These concerns may not threaten life or limb, but they are the everyday medical experience of the wilderness leader.

The NOLS leadership skill curriculum has been woven together with current research in human factors in accidents to discuss the critical topic of leadership, teamwork, and communication among rescue groups. This chapter is unique within wilderness medical texts and curricula and sets this text apart from others in the field.

Many of the changes in this version are organizational and designed to fit the structure of the Wilderness Medicine Institute courses. Two new chapters have been added to discuss common non-urgent medical problems and medical legal concepts. The evacuation guidelines have been highlighted to help the reader understand key points in deciding whether or not to evacuate a patient.

NOLS Wilderness Medicine may also be used as a text for any wilderness medicine course, as an information source for outdoor enthusiasts, or as a resource to tuck into your pack or kayak. This text covers the material commonly taught by reputable wilderness first responder (WFR) instructors or listed in the Wilderness Medical Society's recommended minimum WFR course topics. People using this as a WFR textbook should seek supplementary background information on cardiopulmonary resuscitation (CPR); obstetrical, psychological, and behavioral emergencies; oxygen use and mechanical aids to breathing.[1]

Simply reading the text or successfully completing a NOLS course does not qualify a person to perform any procedure. The text is not a substitute for thorough, practical training, experience in emergency medicine and the outdoors, critical analysis of the needs of specific situations, or the continued education and training necessary to keep skills sharp.

The majority of the first aid practices discussed in this text are common and accepted. Wilderness medicine expands the scope of practice beyond what may be routinely done when we are close to a hospital or physician. For example, in remote settings it is appropriate to attempt to reduce dislocations, clean wounds, and consider clearing a potential spinal injury. Wilderness leaders often make decisions on whether or not to seek the advice of a physician; decisions that are not made by ambulance personnel who routinely transport all patients; decisions that may end an expedition or place rescuers in jeopardy. The wilderness practices presented in this text are consistent with wilderness medicine protocols for NOLS Instructors and those taught by the Wilderness Medicine Institute of NOLS (WMI). People leading trips or managing wilderness programs should be aware of the medical legal issues in wilderness medicine and consider utilizing written medical protocols, such as the *Practice Guidelines for Wilderness Emergency Care*[2] developed by the Wilderness Medical Society, and a physician medical advisor to guide the wilderness protocols specific for their program.

In addition to first aid, a NOLS course gives invaluable experience in critical areas of wilderness medicine: fundamental wilderness living and travel skills, expedition planning, prevention through risk management, and leadership and judgment. To care for your patient in the wilderness you first have to care for yourself.

The most effective first aid is prevention. Wilderness medicine training should prepare the student for serious illness and injury. It should also discuss prevention and treatment of common wilderness medical problems such as infected wounds, hygiene-associated illness, and treatment of athletic injuries. You will find prevention to be a recurring theme in this text.

Tod Schimelpfenig
Lander, Wyoming
October 2005

---

[1] Wilderness first responder recommended minimum course topics. (Wilderness Medical Society, 1999).

[2] Wilderness Medical Society, *Practice Guidelines for Wilderness Emergency Care*, ed. Wm. W. Forgey, M.D. (Merriville, Indiana: ICS Books, 2005).

PART I

Patient Assessment

CHAPTER 1

PATIENT ASSESSMENT SYSTEM

INTRODUCTION

Imagine yourself kneeling beside a fallen hiker, deep in the wilderness. As you examine the victim, thoughts of your remoteness, the safety of your companions, the incoming weather, evacuation, communication, and shelter possibilities swirl through your brain. The telephone, the ambulance, and those images and expectations we have of prompt advanced medical care don't apply to this situation. You are about to make decisions and initiate a series of events that will affect the safety and well-being of the patient, your group, and outside rescuers.

In the city, the patient could be quickly transported to a hospital. In the wilderness, patient care may be your responsibility for hours or days. You cope with improvised gear and inclement weather and take care of yourself, the other members of your group, and the patient. The rescue or evacuation may be strenuous and can jeopardize the safety of the group and the rescuers.

You need information to help you determine how to best care for and transport the patient. You will gather that information during the patient assessment, the foundation of your care.

SCENE SIZE-UP

Patient assessment begins immediately as you arrive on the scene. Your observations of weather, terrain, bystanders, and the position of the patient are your first clues as to how an injury occurred, the patient's condition, and possible scene hazards.

Scene Safety
Look for danger to yourself, bystanders, other rescuers, or the patient. Your top priority is the well-being of yourself and your fellow first responders. A patient can be served only by healthy rescuers, not by more patients.

Driving cold rain may make constructing on-the-spot shelter an immediate priority to avoid hypothermia. Falling rock or avalanche may dictate a move out of the path of danger. Protect your patient by protecting yourself.

Mechanism of Injury or Illness
Assess the mechanism of injury or illness (MOI). Look around. Your observations of the scene and questions of bystanders can give clues about what happened. Is the patient ill or injured? If ill, gather a short history of the illness. If injured, what is the mechanism? If the patient fell, find out how far and if he or she was wearing a helmet. Did the person land on soft ground, snow, or rocks? Did he or she fall free or tumble? Mechanism can give us critical information about the location and severity of injuries.

Find out if you have more than one patient. If so, a quick initial assessment may tell you who needs your immediate attention and how best to use your companions to organize the scene and care for the patients.

Body Substance Isolation
Health care workers practice body substance isolation (BSI) to protect themselves against infectious disease. It's impossible to know for sure if the patient is germ free. All body fluids and tissues are considered infectious, and appropriate precautions are taken as standard practice by health care workers. Protect yourself by washing your hands; using gloves, eyewear, and face masks; properly disposing of soiled bandages, dressing, and clothing; and avoiding needlestick injury.

Disposable latex, vinyl, or other synthetic or natural rubber gloves should be in your first aid kit (people allergic to latex will need nonlatex gloves). Wear them when there is a chance you may contact a patient's blood, other body fluids, mucous membranes, or broken skin, or if you handle bandages, clothing, or other items contaminated with blood or other body fluids. Hands should be thoroughly washed, ideally before and certainly after contact with a patient.

Long-sleeve shirts and pants and pocket masks for mouth-to-mask ventilation are recommended in situations in which splashes of blood and other body fluids are likely to occur. If there is splashing blood, vomit, or other fluids, wear a protective mask and glasses, or at least a bandanna over your nose and mouth. Wear your sunglasses or rain gear if nothing else is available. Items such as gloves and bandages that are contaminated should be placed in sealed plastic bags and labeled as a biohazard or incinerated in a hot fire.

Scene Size-up

- Identify hazards to self, other rescuers, bystanders, patient.
- Determine mechanism of injury.
- Form a general impression of seriousness.
- Determine the number of patients.
- Protect yourself with body substance isolation.

INITIAL ASSESSMENT

The initial assessment is a ritual performed on every patient to find and treat life-threatening medical problems. Besides attending immediately to vital functions, it provides order during the first frantic minutes of an emergency. You check, stop, and fix problems in the vital respiratory and circulatory systems. You assume disability and protect the spine. You assess and treat for environmental hazards.

Establishing Responsiveness

As you approach the patient, introduce yourself and ask if you may help. You're obtaining consent to treat, being polite, and finding out if the patient is responsive. If there is no response, attempt to arouse the patient by saying hello loudly—the person may just be asleep.

If this fails to arouse the patient, try a painful stimulus—pinch the shoulder or neck muscle or rub the breastbone.

At this point, if there is any mechanism of injury, control the cervical spine (neck). Place hands on the head to prevent unnecessary movement of the neck.

If the patient is awake and talking, the airway is not obstructed; the person is breathing and has a pulse. If the patient is quiet, you need to check the ABCs (airway, breathing, and circulation) immediately. In both responsive and unresponsive patients, you proceed through the entire initial assessment, and make a decision about possible disability, environmental threats, and hidden major injury.

ABCDE

The initial assessment checks the airway, breathing, and circulation, plus possible serious bleeding and shock. The airways are the mouth, nose and throat, and trachea. Oxygen is exchanged between the air and the blood in the lungs. Circulation is a function of the heart, the blood vessels, and the blood, which contains vital oxygen. We use ABCDE (airway, breathing, circulation, disability, environment, expose, examine) as a memory aid for the initial assessment sequence. ABC is familiar as the initial phase of cardiopulmonary resuscitation (CPR).

Airway. The airway is the path air travels from the atmosphere into the lungs. An obstructed airway is a medical emergency because oxygen cannot reach the lungs. If the patient is awake, ask the patient to open his or her mouth and check for anything, such as gum or broken teeth, that could become an airway obstruction. If the patient is unresponsive, assess the airway by opening it with the head-tilt–chin-lift method or the jaw thrust and look inside the mouth. If you see an obvious obstruction—a piece of food, perhaps—take it out.

If you can see, hear, or feel air moving from the lungs to the outside, the airway is open. A patient making sounds is able to move air from the lungs and past the vocal cords. This indicates that the airway is at least partially open.

Signs of an obstructed airway are lack of air movement, labored breathing, use of neck and upper chest muscles to breathe, and pale gray or bluish skin. If you discover an airway obstruction, attempt to clear the airway before proceeding to assess breathing. The appropriate techniques are those taught in CPR for treating a foreign body–obstructed airway.

Breathing. If the patient is awake, ask him or her to take a deep breath. If the patient's breathing is labored or painful, expose the chest and look for life-threatening injuries. If the patient is unresponsive, assess breathing using the "look, listen, and feel" format taught in CPR classes. Look for the rise and fall of the chest as air enters and leaves the lungs. Listen for the sound of air passing through the upper airway. Feel the movement of air from the patient's mouth and nose on your cheek. If the patient is not breathing, give two slow, even breaths, then proceed with a check for a pulse.

Circulation. Check for the presence or absence of a pulse. Place the tips of your middle and index fingers over the carotid artery for at least 10 seconds. The carotid is a large central artery, accessible at the neck. Other possible sites are the femoral artery in the groin and the radial artery in the wrist (preferable for a responsive patient).

It may be difficult to feel a pulse if the patient has a weak pulse from shock, is cold, or is wearing bulky clothing. Finding a pulse is not always easy. If you are unsure about the presence of the carotid pulse, try the femoral or the radial pulse.

If the patient is moving or moaning, he or she must have a pulse. If there is no pulse, start CPR. If there is a pulse but no breathing, start rescue breathing.

Look for bleeding. Severe bleeding can be fatal within minutes. Look for obvious bleeding or wet places on the patient's clothing. Quickly run your hands over and under the patient's clothing, especially bulky sweaters or parkas, to find moist areas that may be caused by serious bleeding. Look for blood that may be seeping into snow or the ground. Most external bleeding can be controlled with direct pressure and elevation of the wound. Chapter 7 ("Soft Tissue Injuries") addresses bleeding control in detail.

Disability. Initially assume a spinal injury in any accident victim. Since moving a spine-injured patient poorly can cause

The Initial Assessment

- Obtain consent to treat.
- Assess for responsiveness.
- Control the spine.

A—Assess the airway
- Open the airway.
- Look in the mouth and clear obvious obstructions.

B—Assess for breathing
- Look, listen, feel.

C—Assess for circulation
- Check pulse at the neck.
- Look for severe bleeding.

D—Assume disability
- Observe spine precautions.
- Avoid moving the patient.
- Consider the jaw thrust to open the airway.

E—Protect the patient from the environment
- Expose and examine major injuries.

paralysis, move the patient only if necessary and as little as possible. An airway opening technique for an unresponsive victim or an accident victim is the jaw thrust. It does not require shifting the neck or spine. See chapter 4 ("Brain and Spinal Cord Injuries").

Environment/Expose. Without moving the patient, expose and examine for major injuries, which may be hidden in bulky outdoor clothing. Quickly unzip zippers, open cuffs, and look under parkas.

Assess and manage environmental hazards. It's not uncommon in wilderness medicine to need to protect the patient from extreme environments. You may need to move your patient off snow and onto an insulating pad, or out of a river onto dry ground.

THE FOCUSED EXAM AND HISTORY

Now pause a moment to look over the scene. The initial assessment is complete. Immediate threats to life have been addressed. Take a deep breath and consider the patient's and

The INITIAL ASSESSMENT

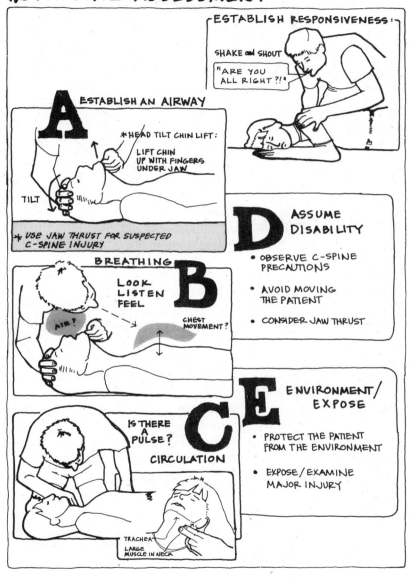

FOCUSED ASSESSMENT and HISTORY

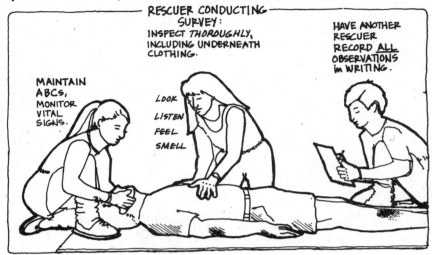

RESCUER CONDUCTING SURVEY:
INSPECT *THOROUGHLY*, INCLUDING UNDERNEATH CLOTHING.

HAVE ANOTHER RESCUER RECORD ALL OBSERVATIONS in WRITING.

MAINTAIN ABCS, MONITOR VITAL SIGNS.

LOOK
LISTEN
FEEL
SMELL

the rescuers' needs. If the location of the incident is unstable—such as on or near loose boulders or a potential avalanche slope—move to a safer position. Provide insulation, adjust clothing, rig a shelter. Assign tasks: boil water for hot drinks, build a litter, set up camp, write down vital signs. Establishing clear delegation of tasks helps the rescuers by giving everyone something to do and helps the patient by creating an atmosphere of order and leadership. See appendix B ("Emergency Procedures for Outdoor Groups").

The focused exam and history is done after life-threatening conditions have been stabilized. It consists of doing a complete head-to-toe physical exam, checking vital signs, and taking a thorough medical history.

Head-to-Toe Patient Examination

The head-to-toe exam is a comprehensive physical examination. Begin the head-to-toe examination by first making the patient comfortable. Except in cases of imminent danger, avoid moving an injured patient until after the exam. Your

---

Focused Exam and History

PATIENT EXAM	VITAL SIGNS	MEDICAL HISTORY
• Look	• Responsiveness	• Chief Complaint (OPQRST)
• Listen	• Heart Rate	• SAMPLE
• Feel	• Skin	• AEIOUTIPS
• Smell	• Respiration	
• Ask	• Temperature	
	• Pupils	

---

hands should be clean, warm, and gloved. Ideally, the examiner should be of the same gender as the patient; otherwise, an observer of the same gender should be present during all phases of the exam. Designate a notetaker to record the results of the focused exam and history.

As you examine the patient, explain what you are doing and why. Besides being a simple courtesy, this helps involve the patient in his or her care. This survey starts with the head and systematically checks the entire body down to the toes. One person should perform the survey in order to avoid confusion, provide consistent results, and minimize discomfort to the patient. Also, with a single examiner, the patient will be able to respond to one inquiry at a time.

The examination technique consists of looking, listening, feeling, smelling, and asking. If you are uncertain of what is abnormal, compare the injured extremity with the other side of the body or with a healthy person.

Head. Check the ears and nose for fluid and the mouth for injuries that may affect the airway. Check the face for symmetry; all features should be symmetrical down the midline from the forehead to the chin. The cheekbones are usually accurate references for facial symmetry. Feel the entire skull for depressions, tenderness, and irregularity. Run your fingers along the scalp to detect bleeding or cuts. Check the eyes for injuries, pupil abnormalities, and vision disturbances.

Neck. The trachea, or windpipe, should be in the middle of the neck. Feel the entire cervical spine from the base of the skull to the top of the shoulders for pain, tenderness, muscle rigidity, and deformity.

Shoulders. Examine the shoulders and the collarbone for deformity, tenderness, and pain.

Arms. Feel the arms from the armpit to the wrist. Check the pulse in each wrist; it should be equal on both sides. Ask the patient to move his or her fingers, then check grip strength by having the patient squeeze your hands. Check for sensation by gently pinching the fingers or scratching the palm of the hand and fingers. If no injury is apparent, ask the patient to move each arm through its full range of motion.

Chest. Feel the entire chest for deformity or tenderness. Push down from the top and in from the sides. Ask the patient to breathe deeply as you compress the chest. Look for open chest wounds. Observe the rise and fall of the chest for symmetry.

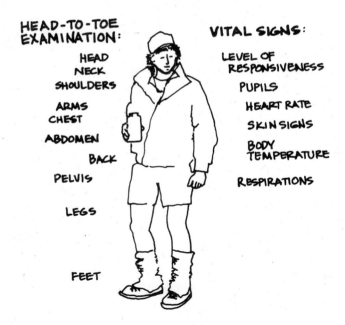

HEAD-TO-TOE EXAMINATION:

HEAD
NECK
SHOULDERS
ARMS
CHEST
ABDOMEN
BACK
PELVIS
LEGS
FEET

VITAL SIGNS:

LEVEL OF RESPONSIVENESS
PUPILS
HEART RATE
SKIN SIGNS
BODY TEMPERATURE
RESPIRATIONS

The Focused Exam and History: Head-to-Toe Patient Examination

- **Look** for wounds, bleeding, unusual movements or shapes, deformities, penetrations, excretions, vomit.
- **Listen** for abnormal sounds, such as crepitus and airway noises.
- **Feel** for wounds, rigidity, hardness, softness, tenderness, deformity.
- **Smell** for unusual odors.
- **Ask** if anything hurts or feels odd or numb.

Abdomen. Feel the abdomen for tenderness or muscle rigidity with light pressure. If there is tenderness, localize it into a quadrant. Look for distension, discoloration, and bruising.

Back. Feel the spine. Feel each vertebra from the shoulders to the pelvis. It is important to slide your hand as far as possible under the patient. There may be a hidden injury. If you suspect a spine injury, logroll the patient to palpate the spine and see the back.

Pelvis. Press first in from the sides, and then, if there is no pain or tenderness, press down on the front of the pelvis. Is there deformity or instability?

Legs. Check the legs from the groin to the ankle. Check the pulse in each of the feet; they should be equal. Check for sensation and motor function in the feet by touching the patient's feet and by asking the patient to move his or her toes and to push his or her feet against your hands.

Vital Signs

Vital signs are objective indicators of respiration, circulation, heart and brain function, blood volume, and body temperature. Checking the vital signs helps further evaluate the ABCs. Airway and breathing are checked by noting skin color and respiratory rate and depth. Good color and easy and regular breathing are signs our airway and lungs are working well. Circulation is evaluated by pulse, skin color, skin temperature, and level of responsiveness. Effective circulation gives us warm, pink skin and enough oxygen to keep our brain alert.

Focused Exam and History: Vital Signs

- **Level of Responsiveness**—Assess with AVPU.
- **Heart rate**—Assess pulse rate, rhythm, strength.
- **Skin signs**—Assess skin color, temperature, and moisture.
- **Respiration**—Assess rate, rhythm, strength.
- **Temperature**—Assess temperature with a thermometer.
- **Pupils**—Assess reactivity to light.

As a general rule, measure and record vital signs every 15 to 20 minutes—more frequently if the patient is seriously ill or injured. The initial set of vitals—responsiveness, pulse, respiration, skin signs, pupils, temperature—provides baseline data on the patient's condition. The changes that occur thereafter provide information on the progress of the patient.

Level of Responsiveness. Brain function, also known as mental status and reflected in how responsive we are to our environment, may be affected by toxic chemicals such as drugs or alcohol, low blood sugar, abnormally high or low temperature, diseases of the brain such as stroke, circulatory or respiratory shock, or pressure from bleeding or swelling caused by a head injury.

I have chosen to use the term "responsiveness" rather than the more common "consciousness" to describe brain function. Consciousness is a vague term and difficult to measure. The more specific responsiveness is a criterion we can evaluate on every patient and then describe with clarity and specificity.

When you assess responsiveness, first determine the initial state. Begin by approaching the patient, introducing yourself, saying "Hello," and asking if you can help. You're being polite as well as finding out if the patient is awake, asleep, or possibly unresponsive.

Then describe the stimulus you used to arouse the patient. If the patient opened his or her eyes and responded after a simple "Hello," the person may have been asleep or distracted. If you needed to shout loudly several times to arouse the patient, the person would be described as not awake but responsive to a verbal stimulus. If you needed to use pain to arouse the patient, the person would be described as not awake and responsive only to pain.

Awake. Normally, we are awake (or we wake quickly from sleep) and know who we are, where we are, the date or time, and recent events. This is described as A (awake) and O (oriented) times 1, 2, 3, or 4, depending on whether the patient knows who he or she is, where he or she is, what date or time it is, and recent events:

- A+O×4   The person knows person, place, time, and event.
- A+O×3   The person knows person, place, and time, but not event.
- A+O×2   The person knows person and place, but not time and event.
- A+O×1   The person knows person, but not place, time, and event.

A patient who is awake but not oriented to person, place, time, or event is described as disoriented. The spoken response may be incoherent, confused, inappropriate, or incomprehensible.

Responsive to Verbal Stimulus. The patient is not awake but responds to a verbal stimulus, such as the rescuer saying, "Hello, how are you?" If the patient does not respond, repeat louder: "Hey! Sir (or Ma'am)! Wake up!" The patient's response may be opening the eyes, grunting, or moving. Higher levels of brain function respond to verbal input, lower levels to pain. Test for responsiveness to verbal stimuli first, painful stimuli second.

Responsive to Pain. The patient is not awake, does not respond to verbal stimuli, but does respond to painful stimuli by moving, opening the eyes, or groaning. To stimulate for pain, pinch the muscle at the back of the shoulder or neck, or squeeze a fingernail.

Unresponsive. The patient is not awake and does not respond to voice or painful stimuli.

Report the patient's initial state, the stimulus you gave, and the response. For example: "This patient is awake and oriented times four." Or, "This patient is not awake, but is responsive to a verbal stimulus. When awake, the patient knows his name but is otherwise disoriented."

AVPU: Assessing Level of Responsiveness

- **A**wake
- Responsive to **V**erbal Stimulus
- Responsive to **P**ain
- **U**nresponsive

Heart Rate. Every time the heart beats, a pressure wave is transmitted through the arteries. We feel this pressure wave as the pulse. The pulse rate indicates the number of heartbeats over a period of time. For an adult, the normal range is 50 to 100 beats per minute. A well-conditioned.athlete may have a normal pulse rate below 50. Shock, exercise, altitude, illness, emotional stress, or fever can increase the heart rate.

The heart rate can be measured at the radial artery on the thumb side of the wrist or at the carotid artery in the neck. Place the tips of the middle and index fingers over the artery. Count the number of beats for 15 seconds and multiply by four.

In addition to rate, note the rhythm and strength of the pulse. The normal rhythm is regular. Irregular rhythms can be associated with heart disease and are frequently rapid. The strength of the pulse is the amount of pressure you feel against your fingertips. It may be weak or strong.

A standard pulse reading includes the rate, rhythm, and strength of the pulse. For example: "The pulse is 110, irregular, and weak." Or, "The pulse is 60, regular, and strong."

Skin Signs. Skin signs indicate the condition of the respiratory and cardiovascular systems. These include skin color, temperature, and moisture, often abbreviated SCTM.

Pinkness. In a light-colored person, normal skin color is pink. In darker-skinned individuals, skin color can be assessed at the nail beds, inside the mouth, palms of the hands, soles of the feet, or lips.

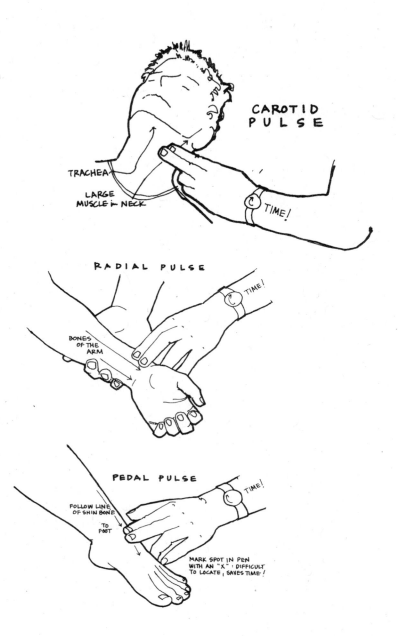

CAROTID PULSE

TRACHEA

LARGE MUSCLE in NECK

TIME!

RADIAL PULSE

TIME!

BONES OF THE ARM

PEDAL PULSE

TIME!

FOLLOW LINE OF SHIN BONE

TO FOOT

MARK SPOT IN PEN WITH AN "X" : DIFFICULT TO LOCATE , SAVES TIME !

Redness. Redness indicates that the skin is unusually flushed with blood. It is a possible sign of recent exercise, heatstroke, carbon monoxide poisoning, fever, or allergic reaction.

Paleness. Pale skin indicates that blood has withdrawn from the skin. Paleness may be due to fright, shock, fainting, or cooling of the skin.

Cyanosis. Blue skin, or cyanosis, appears when circulation to the skin is reduced or the level of oxygen in the blood falls. Well-oxygenated blood is brighter red than poorly oxygenated blood. Cyanosis indicates that oxygen levels have fallen significantly, or that the patient may be cold.

Jaundice. Yellow skin combined with yellow whites of the eyes—jaundice—is a sign of liver or gallbladder disease. The condition results from excess bile pigments in the blood.

Temperature and Moisture. Quickly assess the temperature and moisture of the skin at several sites, including the forehead, hands, and trunk. In a healthy person, the skin is warm and relatively dry. Skin temperature rises when the body attempts to rid itself of excess heat, as in fever or environmental heat problems. Hot, dry skin can be a sign of fever or heatstroke. Hot, sweaty skin occurs when the body attempts to eliminate excess heat and can also be a sign of fever or heat illness.

Skin temperature falls when the body attempts to conserve heat by constricting blood flow to the skin; for example, during exposure to cold. Cool, moist (clammy) skin is an indicator of extreme stress and a sign of shock.

A report on skin condition should include color, temperature, and moisture. For example: "The patient's skin is pale, cool, and clammy."

Respiration. Respiratory rate is counted in the same manner as the pulse: Each rise of the chest is counted over 15 seconds and multiplied by four, or 30 seconds and multiplied by two. Watch the chest rise and fall, or observe the belly move with each breath. Normal respiration range is 12 to 20 breaths per minute.

The patient's depth and effort of breathing enable you to gauge his or her need for air and the presence or absence of

SHAKE THERMOMETER BULB END DOWN
TO PUSH MERCURY DOWN BELOW TEMPERATURE MARKINGS:

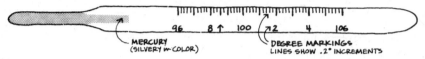

MERCURY
(SILVERY ᴍ COLOR)

DEGREE MARKINGS
LINES SHOW .2° INCREMENTS

PLACE UNDER PATIENT'S TONGUE FOR 3 MINUTES.
REMOVE, ROTATE THERMOMETER UNTIL MERCURY CAN BE SEEN;
READ TEMPERATURE BY NOTING WHERE MERCURY STOPS: NORMAL TEMP. READING below:

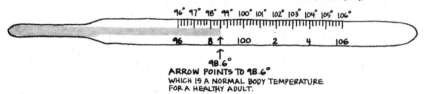

98.6°
ARROW POINTS TO 98.6°
WHICH IS A NORMAL BODY TEMPERATURE
FOR A HEALTHY ADULT.

chest injury. In a healthy individual, breathing is relatively effortless.

A patient experiencing breathing difficulty may exhibit air hunger with deep, labored inhaling efforts. A patient with a chest injury may have shallow, rapid respirations accompanied by pain. Irregular respirations are a sign of a brain disorder. Noisy respirations indicate some type of airway obstruction. Assess and, if necessary, clear the airway.

Smell the breath. Fruity, acetone breath can be a sign of diabetic coma. Foul, fecal-smelling breath may indicate a bowel obstruction.

Report respirations by their rate, rhythm, effort, depth, noises, and odors. For example, a patient in diabetic ketoacidosis may have respirations described as "20 per minute, regular, labored, deep. There is a fruity breath odor."

Temperature. Temperature measurement is an important component of a thorough patient assessment, but it is the vital sign that is least often measured in the field. It can tell us of underlying infection or of abnormally high or low body temperatures. Although a normal temperature is 98.6°F (37°C), daily variation in body temperature is also normal, usually rising a degree during the day and decreasing through the night.

Temperature can be measured orally, in the ear (tympanic), on the forehead (infrared), or rectally. Axillary readings—taken under the armpit—are the least reliable. Rectal temperatures are the most accurate indication of the core temperature available to first responders. Rectal temperature is sometimes considered necessary for suspected hypothermia but is rarely measured due to patient embarrassment and cold exposure. Diagnosis of hypothermia in the outdoors, discussed in chapter 9 ("Cold Injuries"), is often based on other factors, such as behavior, history, appearance, and mental status.

Many thermometers are now digital. If you have an older mercury thermometer, shake down the thermometer to push the mercury below the degree markings. This is essential for an accurate reading. Place the thermometer under the patient's tongue for at least 3 minutes. The patient should refrain from talking or drinking during this time. A report on temperature should include the method, such as "100°F oral" or "37°C rectal."

Pupils. Pupils are clues to brain function. They can indicate head injury, stroke, drug abuse, or lack of oxygen to the brain. Both pupils should be round and equal in size. They should contract symmetrically when exposed to light and dilate when the light dims. Evaluate pupils by noting size, equality, and reaction to light.

In the absence of a portable light source, such as a flashlight or headlamp, shield the patient's eyes for 15 seconds, then

PUPIL SIZE:

NORMAL SIZE
BOTH SIDES SAME SIZE

BOTH PINPOINT

UNEQUAL IN SIZE

BOTH DIALATED

expose them to ambient light. Both pupils should contract equally. When in doubt, compare the patient's reactions with those of a healthy individual in the same light conditions.

A patient whose brain cells are deficient of oxygen may have equal but slow-to-react pupils. A wide, nonreactive pupil on one side and a small, reactive pupil on the other side indicates brain damage or disease on the side with the larger pupil. Very small, equal pupils may indicate drug intoxication.

Blood Pressure. The concept of blood pressure is discussed in chapter 2 ("Shock"). Although blood pressure is always measured when professional medical care is being administered, accurate measurement requires a stethoscope and a sphygmomanometer—equipment rarely carried on wilderness trips. A strong radial or pedal pulse is a good sign and suggests the patient has a cardiovascular system healthy enough to pump blood to his hands and feet. The absence of a radial or pedal pulse, unless explainable by limb injury, suggests that blood pressure may be low. If this is the case, it's likely accompanied by other signs of shock.

Medical History

The patient's medical history provides background that is often relevant to the present problem. Gathering the history is an ongoing process that you typically carry out while measuring vital signs and performing the head-to-toe exam. Obtaining an accurate history depends greatly on the quality of communication between you and the patient. This rapport begins as soon as you approach the scene. Communicating clearly, acting orderly, and appearing to be in control make it easier to obtain an accurate history.

Chief Complaint. Obtain the patient's chief complaint—the problem that caused him or her to solicit help. Pain is a common complaint—for example, abdominal pain or pain in an arm or leg after a fall. In lieu of pain, a chief

Focused Exam and History: Medical History
• Chief Complaint (OPQRST)   • SAMPLE

complaint may be nausea or dizziness. A memory aid for investigating the chief complaint is OPQRST.

Onset. Did the chief complaint appear suddenly or gradually?

Provokes. What provoked the injury? If the problem is an illness, under what circumstances did it occur? What makes the problem worse, and what makes it better?

Quality. What qualities describe the pain? Adjectives may include stabbing, cramping, burning, sharp, dull, or aching.

Radiates. Where is the pain? Does it move, or radiate? What causes it to move? Chest pain from a heart attack can radiate from the chest into the neck and jaw. Pain from a spleen injury can be felt in the left shoulder.

Severity. On a scale of 1 to 10 (with 1 being no pain or discomfort and 10 being the worst pain or discomfort the patient has ever experienced), how does the patient rate this pain? This question can reveal the level of discomfort the patient is experiencing.

Time. When did the pain start? How frequently does it occur? How long does it last? Correlate the patient's complaints with the vital signs.

OPQRST: Assessing the Chief Complaint

- Onset
- Provokes
- Quality
- Radiates
- Severity
- Time

SAMPLE. This is a memory aid for a series of questions that completes the medical history.

Symptoms. What symptoms does the patient have? Nausea? Dizziness? Headache? Ask the patient how he or she is feeling, or if anything is causing discomfort. A symptom is something the patient perceives and must tell you about (e.g., pain). Tenderness, on the other hand, is a sign, something you can find when you touch an injury during a patient exam.

Allergies, Medications. Ask if the patient is currently taking any medications or has any allergies. If so, find out if he or she has been exposed to the allergen and what his or her usual response is. Ask about nonprescription, prescription, and herbal medications, as well as possible alcohol or drug use. Ask whether the patient is allergic to medications or has other environmental allergies to food, insects, or pollen.

Past History. The past history consists of a series of questions you ask the patient to discover any previous and relevant medical problems. (If the patient has a broken leg, for example, it's unlikely we need to know about childhood illness.) First ask these general questions: Has the patient ever been in a hospital? Is the patient currently seeing a physician? Next, ask about specific body systems. Avoid medical jargon. For instance, asking the patient about any previous heart problems may be less confusing than asking, "Do you have a cardiac history?"

Additional sources of information may include a medical alert tag or a medical information questionnaire. A medical alert tag is a necklace, bracelet, or wallet card that identifies the patient's medical concerns. It reports a history of diabetes, hemophilia, epilepsy, or other disorders; allergies to medication; and other pertinent information. Medical forms are common to many outdoor schools, camps, and guide services. The NOLS student medical history form is filled out by the student prior to the trip and is available for review by field staff.

Last Intake and Output. Ask the patient when he or she last ate and drank. This information may tell you whether the patient is hydrated or give you important history if, for example, the patient is diabetic. Also find out when the patient last urinated and defecated. Clear, copious urine indicates good hydration; dark, smelly urine suggests dehydration. A patient with diarrhea or vomiting may be dehydrated.

Recent Events. Recent events are unusual circumstances that have occurred within the past few days that may be relevant to the patient's present situation. Recent events might include symptoms of mountain sickness preceding pulmonary edema or changes in diet preceding stomach upset.

SAMPLE:
Assessing the History

- Symptoms
- Allergies
- Medications
- Past history
- Last intake/output
- Events

THE ASSESSMENT

The assessment is a review of the information gathered during the initial assessment and the focused exam and history. Examine the records of the head-to-toe examination, the vital signs, and the medical history. Think through OPQRST and SAMPLE.

Rule out possibilities as you assess. Many diagnoses are made by physicians on the basis of what a condition isn't rather than what it could be. Is chest pain a muscle pull or a heart attack? Does the patient have the flu, mountain sickness, or early cerebral edema?

The Assessment

- Review available information.
- Rule out other possibilities.

The Plan

- Prioritize and treat.
- Review and repeat exam.

The Plan

Next, prioritize the patient's medical problems and develop a treatment plan for each.

The initial exam provides a baseline. Periodically repeat the exam to judge the patient's response to treatment and any changes for better or worse. If there is any change or deterioration in the patient, return to the beginning and repeat the initial assessment.

SOAP Notes

You may find it helpful to write down the results of your assessment. You may also need to communicate with an evacuation or rescue party or the emergency room physician. Health care professionals commonly organize their medical notes into the SOAP format: subjective or summary, objective or observations, the assessment, and the plan.

Subjective or summary information is told to you by the patient or bystanders. It is the "story" of this event. It includes age, sex, mechanism of injury, chief complaint, and OPQRST findings.

Objective information is measurable or observable: vital signs and results, what we call "findings," from the SAMPLE history and the patient exam.

The assessment section categorizes the patient's medical concerns in a problem list. For example, a problem list might be "sprained ankle, mild hypothermia," or "chest pain, possible heart attack." There should be a plan for each problem.

EXTENDED PATIENT CARE

Emergency medical care in the wilderness may be prolonged over hours or days in isolated locations. Splints, shelter, and litters may need to be improvised. In addition to first aid, basic nursing care is necessary to manage the physical and emotional needs of the patient.

Daily Needs

Keep the patient warm, clean, and comfortable. Remove soiled and wet clothing, and wash the patient. An individual immobilized on a litter may need extra insulation to keep warm and occasional position changes to avoid bedsores. Hot water bottles, heat packs, or fires may be needed as sources of warmth.

Drinking and eating are not appropriate in patients with an abnormal level of responsiveness.

If the patient can drink, give water or clear soups and juices. Avoid lots of coffee, tea, or other beverages with high concentrations of sugar or caffeine. Excess sugar can delay fluid absorption; excess caffeine increases fluid loss.

Over a period of a few days, fluid intake is more important than solid food, as dehydration can complicate any existing medical condition. Dehydration is discussed in chapter 22 ("Hydration").

Arrange for the patient to urinate and defecate as comfortably as possible. These basic body functions are essential to overall well-being, despite embarrassment or temporary discomfort. The first responder's sensitivity to and support for the patient are essential here.

For male patients, a water bottle usually works well as a urine receptacle. For female patients, a bedpan can be fashioned from a frying pan or a large-mouth water bottle, or an article of clothing can be used as a diaper. Bowel movements can be managed by assisting the patient with an improvised bedpan.

Emotional Support

An ill or injured patient experiences a variety of emotions, including fear about the quality of care and the outcome of the injury or illness, the length of evacuation, loss of control and independence, loss of self-esteem, and embarrassment. To help the patient cope with such roller-coaster feelings, maintain your calm, respond promptly and clearly to questions, and treat the patient with respect and sensitivity.

Respecting your patient means using manners as you would in an average social situation. Introduce yourself, call the patient by name, and ask permission to give treatment. In doing so, you also begin to involve the patient in his or her own care. As you examine and treat the patient, explain your actions. Warn the patient if you might cause pain. Involve the patient in evacuation decisions.

Reassurance, concern, and sympathy are appropriate, but avoid making promises you are unsure of, e.g., "You're going to be just fine." It's healthy to allow the patient to discuss the incident. Talking about an accident begins the process of emotional healing. Do not critique the incident or lay blame on any party involved. This will only increase the patient's anxiety and agitation.

Anticipate a lull in your enthusiasm and energy as the initial excitement wears off, fatigue sets in, and you realize the amount of work required to care for and evacuate the patient. These emotions are a reality of rescue. They should not be communicated to the patient as a lack of concern. See chapter 26 ("Stress and the Rescuer") for more on rescue stress.

FINAL THOUGHTS—THE EVACUATION DECISION

An incomplete patient assessment system—failure to measure vital signs or review history and physical findings—has been the source of unnecessary and needlessly rushed evacuations. Helicopters have flown into wilderness areas for simple knee sprains and for hyperventilation misdiagnosed as a head injury. Rescue teams have hiked through the night expecting to treat serious injuries, only to find a walking patient with minor

NATIONAL OUTDOOR LEADERSHIP SCHOOL
FIELD EVACUATION REPORT

Name of Evacuee_____ Course/Section _____

Course Leader _____ Date & Time of Incident _____

SUBJECTIVE: Age _____ Sex _____ Location of Patient: Common name_____

Mechanism of Injury/Illness _____

_____

_____

_____

Chief Complaint (OPQRST*) _____

_____

_____

_____

OBJECTIVE: Vital Signs**

Date/Time	LOC	Pulse	RR	Skin	Pupils	T

Signs/Symptoms (patient exam) _____

_____

_____

_____

_____

Allergies _____ Medications _____

Past Medical History_____

Last Oral Intake _____

Events (recent, relevant)_____

ASSESSMENT: Problem list (prioritize)_____

_____

PLAN: Emergency Care Rendered/Changes in Patient's Condition _____

_____

_____

_____

Evacuation Plan (timetable, backup, pickup point) _____

_____

_____

_____

Instructor Signature _____ Date _____ Time _____

*OPQRST = onset, provocation, quality, region/radiation, severity, time sequence.
**LOC = alert x 4 (person, place, time, event), verbal, pain, unresponsive; pulse = rate, strength, and rhythm; RR = respiratory rate, depth, and rhythm; skin = color, temperature, moisture; pupils = equality, roundness, reactivity to light; T = temperature.

injuries. The patient, rescuers, and expedition members are needlessly put at risk.

Likewise, the same mistake has delayed evacuations. Life-threatening fevers have been overlooked because a temperature was not measured. Diabetic complications have been missed because no one asked about the patient's medical history.

A significant difference between urban and wilderness medicine is seen in the decision-making process. In the urban emergency medical services system, ambulance personnel rarely make a decision whether or not to transport a patient. If they are called to help, an ambulance crew either transports the patient or the patient signs a refusal of treatment form. In the wilderness, the leader must decide if a patient needs to see a physician, and if so, with what urgency. The patient assessment system is an invaluable tool for these decisions.

Throughout this text I will suggest evacuation decision points. I'll note the thresholds for when patients should be evacuated, and when they need to be evacuated rapidly. These are guidelines that you can use, in conjunction with your physician advisor, to develop a protocol for your expedition or program.

There are many stories of outdoor leaders who, though they lacked medical experience, performed a simple and methodical assessment, checked the ABCs for life-threatening problems, then followed the focused history and exam protocols. They used a checklist, took their time, and made a written record of their findings. The information gathered was the foundation for quality first aid. Good medical decisions and judgment made for a sound evacuation plan.

PART II

Traumatic Injuries

CHAPTER 2

SHOCK

INTRODUCTION

Shock is a simple name for a complex disorder of the circulatory system. Mid-nineteenth-century descriptions of shock as "a deadly downward spiral" and "a rude unhinging of the machinery of life" accurately portray a condition in which the circulatory system collapses in apparent disproportion to the initial injury. Shock is often the lethal component of burns, serious illness, fractures, injuries to the chest and abdomen, severe bleeding, and catastrophic injury. A first responder must anticipate, recognize, and treat shock.

THE CIRCULATORY SYSTEM

The circulatory system is composed of the heart, the blood vessels, and the blood. Its primary function is to deliver a constant supply of oxygen to the tissues, and an interruption causes cells and tissues to malfunction and eventually die. The circulatory system also transports carbon dioxide from the cells to the lungs, keeps the electrolyte environment stable, delivers hormones from their source to their place of action, and mobilizes body defenses.

The heart is a two-sided pump that propels blood through a system of pipes (arteries, veins, and capillaries). The right side receives blood from the veins and pumps it through the lungs for oxygen replenishment. The left side pumps the oxygen-rich blood from the lungs to the rest of the body. Blood leaves the

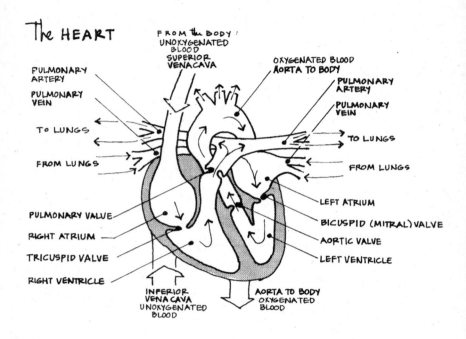

The HEART

heart through arteries, which narrow into smaller vessels called arterioles and eventually become a vast network of microscopic vessels called capillaries.

Capillaries are woven throughout the tissues. The exchange of nutrients and waste products from the blood to the cells takes place across capillary walls only one cell thick. Blood vessels leaving the capillary beds widen into veins, conduits for blood returning to the heart. The venous blood returns to the right side of the heart and then to the lungs to be replenished with oxygen. The circuit is complete.

The circulatory system adjusts automatically to our energy demands, activity level, position, and temperature. The rate and force of pumping, the diameter of the vessels, and the amount of fluid in the system vary to meet the requirements of exercise, stress, sleep, and relaxation.

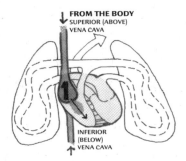

FROM THE BODY
SUPERIOR (ABOVE)
VENA CAVA

INFERIOR
(BELOW)
VENA CAVA

1
• BLOOD FROM BODY DELIVERED THROUGH VENA CAVA;
• ENTERS RIGHT ATRIUM;
• PASSES THROUGH TRICUSPID VALVE.

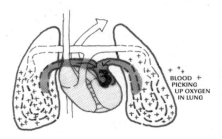

BLOOD
PICKING
UP OXYGEN
IN LUNG

3
• FROM LUNGS. PICKS UP OXYGEN;
• PASSES THROUGH PULMONARY VEINS;
• ENTERS LEFT ATRIUM.

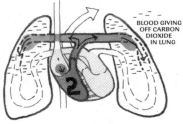

BLOOD GIVING
OFF CARBON
DIOXIDE
IN LUNG

2
• BLOOD ENTERS RIGHT VENTRICLE;
• PASSES THROUGH PULMONARY VALVE;
• THROUGH PULMONARY ARTERIES;
• TO LUNGS. GIVES UP CO_2.

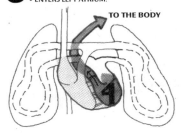

TO THE BODY

4
• PASSES THROUGH BICUSPID VALVE;
• ENTERS LEFT VENTRICLE;
• PASSES THROUGH AORTIC VALVE;
• PASSES THROUGH AORTA TO BODY.

SHOCK

Cardiologist and wilderness medicine specialist Dr. Bruce Paton suggests the following analogy for shock: Imagine the body as a healthy wetland with a river running through lush vegetation. The vegetation depends on the river's flow of pure, unpolluted water and the nutrients it carries. If the river dries up or the water becomes poisoned, the plants shrivel and die. The maintenance of a healthy, well-oxygenated flow of blood through the tissues is called good perfusion.

Shock is the inadequate perfusion of tissue with oxygenated blood. It is a failure of any or all of three basic components of the circulatory system—heart, blood vessels, and blood—to deliver oxygenated blood to the tissues. Insufficient

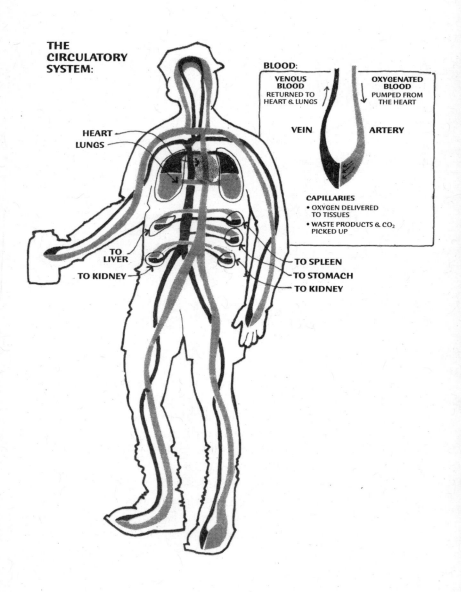

THE CIRCULATORY SYSTEM:

HEART
LUNGS

TO LIVER
TO KIDNEY

TO SPLEEN
TO STOMACH
TO KIDNEY

BLOOD:

VENOUS BLOOD
RETURNED TO HEART & LUNGS

OXYGENATED BLOOD
PUMPED FROM THE HEART

VEIN   ARTERY

CAPILLARIES
- OXYGEN DELIVERED TO TISSUES
- WASTE PRODUCTS & CO_2 PICKED UP

blood flow to the tissues causes inadequate oxygen and nutrient delivery and waste product removal. Shock is a state in which poor perfusion leads first to reversible then irreversible tissue damage. Bodily processes slow, and tissues begin to die.

Causes of Shock

Adequate blood pressure, like a healthy river flowing at a proper level into the wetland, is essential to maintaining perfusion of vital organs. Three factors influence blood pressure, and changes in any of them can have serious consequences. The three critical factors are blood volume, cardiac output (the volume of blood pumped per minute by the heart), and the state of constriction or dilation of the blood vessels (peripheral resistance).

Fluid Loss. Fluid loss is a major cause of shock. The primary causes of fluid loss are bleeding, infections, extensive burns, and metabolic disorders. Massive bleeding results in a reduced blood volume; blood vessels are inadequately filled, and blood pressure falls. Shock can also develop from fluid loss during watery diarrhea, from dehydration, from illness such as diabetes, or from hidden bleeding into fractures of the femur and pelvis.

The average adult has 6 liters of blood. A 10 percent loss (.5 liter) is enough to affect blood pressure. A 25 percent blood volume loss (1.5 liters) can cause moderate shock. A 30 percent loss (2 liters) is considered serious shock.

Decreased Cardiac Output. The heart muscle may become so damaged by a heart attack that it cannot maintain adequate output (pump failure). Shock secondary to a heart attack is referred to as cardiogenic shock.

Blood Vessel Dilation. Dilated blood vessels cause blood pressure and perfusion to decrease despite the extra pumping of the heart in response to the shock. Fainting, a mild form of shock, results when momentary dilation of blood vessels occurs in a person's body as a response to a strong emotional stimulus. As the volume of blood returning to the heart diminishes, blood pressure falls and the person may faint. If a spinal cord injury damages nerves controlling vessel diameter, they may widen and cause shock. Changes in blood vessel diameter, however, are generally not an important cause of shock, except in overwhelming infection in which there is widespread dilation of small vessels.

Assessment of Shock

A patient in shock has a rapid pulse rate that may feel weak, irregular, and "thready." The skin is pale, cool, and clammy. These signs and symptoms are due to our "fight or flight" response—our body's response to danger—wherein release of adrenaline increases heart rate, causes the skin to pale and sweat, and causes nausea and restlessness. Blood is routed away from the digestive tract and concentrates around the muscles and essential organs. These changes pump the blood faster, reduce the size of the blood vessels, and route the blood to essential organs, possibly enabling the body to compensate for the shock.

Most people, when frightened, injured, or ill, have a "fight or flight" or acute stress response. Your heart beats strong and fast; you sweat, become pale, and feel nervous. If you're not seriously ill or injured and your circulatory system is healthy, this response should abate in a short time. The heart rate slows, you relax, and the skin returns to its normal color. When you measure a series of vital signs over time, you may see this initial acute stress diminish as you recover from the initial fright. If the circulatory system is unable to adjust, a downward spiral of deterioration may begin in which first tissues, then organs, and finally entire systems fail from lack of oxygen.

Signs and Symptoms of Shock

EARLY CHANGES

• Rapid and/or weak pulse
• Rapid and/or shallow respirations
• Pale, cool, clammy skin
• Anxiety or restlessness
• Nausea, thirst

LATER CHANGES

• Decreasing level of responsiveness
• Slow-to-respond pupils
• Falling blood pressure

A progressively increasing pulse rate is a bad sign, indicating continuing blood loss or increasing shock. The skin becomes sweaty and pale, and the patient looks very ill. The patient may exhibit shallow, rapid breathing and be restless, anxious, irritable, and thirsty. Level of responsiveness is variable. If shock prevents the brain from being perfused with oxygen-rich blood, the level of responsiveness will deteriorate.

Treatment of Shock

Although shock is more likely with multiple injuries, serious illness, severe bleeding, dehydration, or a major fracture, initially you should treat every patient for shock. If the mechanism of injury is not serious and signs and symptoms stabilize or do not deteriorate, the patient is probably experiencing only a stress reaction.

Always assume that shock may occur, and begin treatment before signs and symptoms are manifested. Treatment begins with the triad of basic life support—airway, breathing, and circulation (ABC)—as well as control of bleeding and stabilization of fractures and other injuries. Thereafter, shock treatment moves to a second triad: temperature maintenance, position, and fluids.

Maintain Temperature. Protect the patient from excess heat and cold. Your goal is to maintain body temperature within normal limits. Insulate the patient from the cold ground, provide protection from wind and weather, and remove wet clothes and replace them with dry.

Elevate Legs. Unless the patient has a head injury, or injury to the legs or pelvis prevents it, position the patient with the legs elevated 8 to 10 inches. Whether this helps return blood to the heart is debatable, but it doesn't harm the patient. Whether we are treating for shock or simply providing long-term patient comfort, it is good to support the patient's low back by adjusting leg position. Even with

---

Treatment for Shock

- ABCs: open and maintain airway.
- Control bleeding, stabilize fractures.
- Maintain temperature.
- Elevate legs.
- Consider fluids.

TREATMENT FOR Shock:

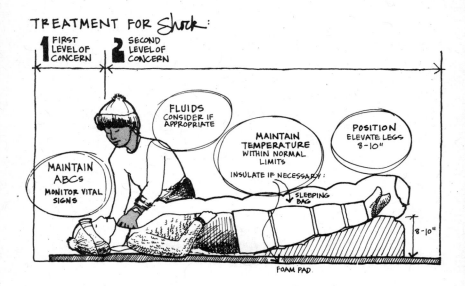

FOAM PAD

apparently minor injuries, this position can be used until you have assessed the problem and ruled out shock.

Consider Fluids. In the urban setting we rarely give the patient oral fluids. In the wilderness, fluids may be given if surgery does not seem likely, the patient does not have an altered mental status, and he or she can tolerate the fluids.

When giving fluids by mouth, plain water is adequate. Using one teaspoon of salt per liter is acceptable, as are dilute bouillon drinks. Beware of strong salty or sweet drinks.

FINAL THOUGHTS

Shock, an insidious and complicated disturbance in the circulatory system, is difficult to treat in the backcountry. Paramedics, nurses, and physicians in urban medical systems are trained to quickly assess, transport, and use technical medical procedures to fight shock. None of this is available in the wilderness.

The basic treatments of bandages, splints, and physical and emotional support, reinforced by temperature maintenance, position, and fluids, are all assets in the wilderness management of shock. The definitive treatment of shock in the backcountry, however, is evacuation.

Evacuation Guidelines
- Evacuate any patient whose vital signs do not stabilize or improve over time.
- Evacuate rapidly any patient with decreased mental status or deteriorating vital signs.

CHAPTER 3

CHEST INJURIES

INTRODUCTION

Chest injuries range from simple but painful rib fractures to life-threatening lung injuries. NOLS's incident data shows that rib fractures are most common. *Accidents in North American Mountaineering* has documented more than a few instances of mountaineers who've suffered serious chest and lung injuries from falls. Paddlers can experience chest injuries from impact with rocks or from blows by the bows of kayaks. Horsepacking and backcountry skiing are other wilderness activities in which there are mechanisms—falls and collisions—for chest trauma. In the backcountry, our role is to recognize the injury, support the patient, and make a sound evacuation decision.

CHEST AND LUNG ANATOMY

Chest injuries concern us because they can compromise the respiratory or cardiovascular system. The respiratory system provides oxygen to and removes carbon dioxide from the body. The cardiovascular system transports these gases as well as nutrients and waste products to and from the cells. Contained within the chest cavity are some of the structures responsible for these processes: the airway passages, lungs, heart, and major vessels—the vena cava and aorta.

The clavicles, rib cage, and diaphragm form the boundaries of the chest cavity. The rib cage consists of twelve pairs of ribs.

PARTS OF THE RESPIRATORY SYSTEM :

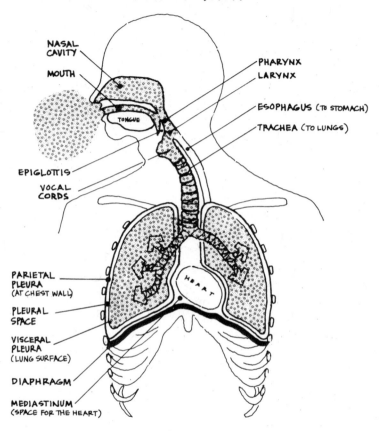

All the ribs are attached to the spine in the back. The upper seven pairs are attached to the sternum by cartilage; the next three pairs are attached to cartilage only; and the lowest two pairs ("floating ribs") are attached only to the spine.

The components of the respiratory system are the nose, mouth, pharynx, larynx, epiglottis, trachea, bronchi, bronchioles, and alveoli. The diaphragm and muscles of the chest wall move air in and out of the lungs.

The average healthy adult breathes 12 to 20 times per minute, moving half a liter of air with each breath. Respiratory rate increases with exercise, altitude, illness, or injury.

Nose, Mouth, Pharynx, Larynx. As air enters the nose or mouth, it is warmed and humidified by mucous membranes that line the respiratory tract. The mucus produced by the membranes and the cilia (hairlike structures) helps keep foreign material out of the lungs. Air passes from the nose or mouth into the pharynx, past the larynx, and into the trachea. The larynx consists of tiny bones, muscles, cartilage, and two vocal cords. Air forced past the vocal cords causes them to vibrate, producing sound.

Epiglottis. The epiglottis sits above the larynx and prevents food from entering the trachea by closing over the larynx during swallowing. If solids or liquids inadvertently enter the larynx, the vocal cords spasm, causing us to cough.

Trachea. The trachea is approximately 5 inches long and is composed of cartilage, which prevents the trachea from collapsing. At the bottom of the trachea, the tube divides into the right and left bronchi. After air enters the lungs via the bronchi, it follows smaller passageways called bronchioles until it enters the alveoli.

Alveoli. The alveoli are small air sacs surrounded by capillaries where red blood cells release carbon dioxide and pick up oxygen. Blood then flows into the pulmonary veins, which carry it to the heart and the rest of the body.

Lungs. The lungs occupy most of the chest cavity. Each lung is enclosed by a double-layered membrane called the pleura. The layer that attaches to the lung is called the visceral pleura, and the layer attached to the chest wall is called the parietal pleura.

Between the two layers is a thin film of fluid that lubricates the membranes and allows them to move freely. This area is called the pleural space, and under normal conditions, it is a potential space under negative pressure. If air enters the pleural space, as in a pneumothorax, the potential space becomes an actual space, and the lung collapses.

Inspiration is the active motion of breathing. The diaphragm moves downward, and the intercostal muscles (muscles between the ribs) move the chest wall outward. As the ribs move outward, the negative pressure in the lungs increases, and air is sucked into the lungs. When the pressure within the lungs and the atmospheric pressure are equal, air stops entering the lungs. At this point, the diaphragm and chest muscles relax, elastic recoil reduces lung size, and air is exhaled (expiration).

Diaphragm. The diaphragm is a specialized muscle that works both voluntarily and involuntarily. The level of carbon dioxide in the blood determines how fast and deeply we breathe. If the level of carbon dioxide in the blood increases, the respiratory center in the brain tells the diaphragm to increase the respiratory rate. If the level of carbon dioxide is too low, the brain tells the diaphragm to slow down. We can directly control the diaphragm by taking deep breaths or by holding our breath, but only for short periods of time, after which the involuntary control centers of the brain take over again.

RIB FRACTURES

The most commonly fractured ribs are ribs five through ten. Ribs one through four are protected by the shoulder girdle and are rarely fractured. The floating ribs—ribs eleven and twelve—are more flexible and will give before breaking.

Signs and Symptoms. Rib fractures cause deformity and/or discoloration over the injured area. The patient complains of tenderness over the fracture (point tenderness) when touched. Breathing or coughing causes sharp, stabbing pain at the site of the fracture. Respiratory rate increases as the patient breathes shallowly in an attempt to decrease the pain. The patient may clutch the chest on the fractured side in an attempt to splint it. Carefully observe rib fracture victims for other injuries.

Treatment. A single fractured rib that is not displaced (simple rib fracture) does not require splinting. Pain medication such as acetaminophen or ibuprofen may be all the treatment necessary.

Signs and Symptoms of Rib Fractures

- Point tenderness over the fracture
- Pain on inspiration, shallow breathing, coughing
- Shortness of breath during exertion

Treatment of Rib Fractures

- Tape the fracture site.
- Sling and swathe.

Tape the Fracture Site on One Side of Chest. If the pain is severe, tape the fractured side from sternum to spine with four or five pieces of 1- to 2-inch adhesive tape. This decreases movement at the fracture site and diminishes pain. Tape should never be wrapped completely around the chest, as this can restrict breathing. You may also find that a simple sling and swathe on the arm on the injured side limits movement and provides comfort. If the patient is not in respiratory distress, he or she may be able to walk out.

FLAIL CHEST

A flail chest occurs when 3 or more adjacent ribs are broken in two or more places, loosening a segment of the chest wall. When the patient breathes in, the increased negative pressure pulls the flail segment inward, and the lung does not fill with air as it should. When the patient breathes out, the opposite occurs, and the flail segment may be pushed outward. The flail segment moves in a direction opposite of normal breathing, thus the term "paradoxical respirations."

Signs and Symptoms. A flail chest develops only with a significant chest injury, such as a heavy fall against a rock. The patient may be in respiratory distress. Put your hands under the patient's shirt, and you may feel a part of the chest moving in while the opposite part of the chest is moving out. This may also be visible upon inspection.

Signs and Symptoms of Flail Chest

- Paradoxical chest movement
- Respiratory distress

Treatment. Stabilize the flail chest:
- Position the patient on the injured side with a rolled-up piece of clothing underneath the flailed segment.

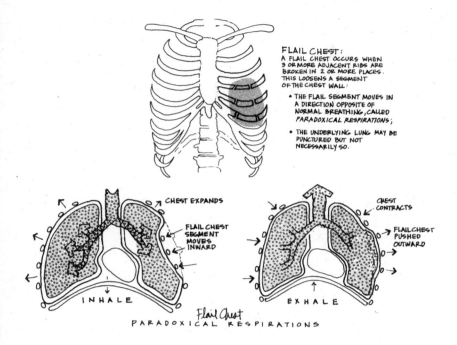

FLAIL CHEST:
A FLAIL CHEST OCCURS WHEN
3 OR MORE ADJACENT RIBS ARE
BROKEN IN 2 OR MORE PLACES.
THIS LOOSENS A SEGMENT
OF THE CHEST WALL:

• THE FLAIL SEGMENT MOVES IN
A DIRECTION OPPOSITE OF
NORMAL BREATHING, CALLED
PARADOXICAL RESPIRATIONS;

• THE UNDERLYING LUNG MAY BE
PUNCTURED BUT NOT
NECESSARILY SO.

CHEST EXPANDS

FLAIL CHEST
SEGMENT
MOVES
INWARD

INHALE

CHEST
CONTRACTS

FLAIL CHEST
PUSHED
OUTWARD

EXHALE

Flail Chest
PARADOXICAL RESPIRATIONS

- Apply pressure with your hand to the flailed area. This works only as a temporary measure, as it is difficult to hold pressure while transporting the patient.
- Tape a large pad firmly over the flail segment (without circling the chest).

Treat the patient for shock and evacuate.

INJURIES TO LUNGS

In addition to injuries to the ribs, the underlying lungs may be damaged. Blood vessels can be ruptured and torn, causing bleeding into the chest, and lungs can be punctured, causing air to leak into the chest.

Pneumothorax. This occurs when air leaks into the pleural space, creating negative pressure that collapses the lung. Pneumothorax can be caused by a fractured rib that lacerates the lung (traumatic pneumothorax), a weak spot on the lung wall

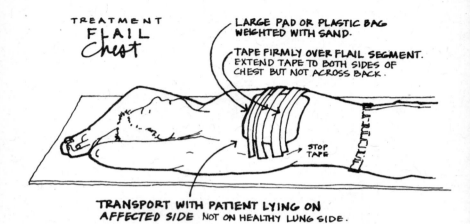

TREATMENT
FLAIL
Chest

LARGE PAD OR PLASTIC BAG
WEIGHTED WITH SAND.

TAPE FIRMLY OVER FLAIL SEGMENT.
EXTEND TAPE TO BOTH SIDES OF
CHEST BUT NOT ACROSS BACK.

STOP
TAPE

TRANSPORT WITH PATIENT LYING ON AFFECTED SIDE NOT ON HEALTHY LUNG SIDE.

that gives way (spontaneous pneumothorax), or an open chest wound.

Hemothorax. This occurs when lacerated blood vessels cause blood to collect in the pleural space. The source can be a fractured rib or lacerated lung. If more than 1 liter of blood leaks into the pleural space, a hemothorax may compress the lung and compromise breathing. The loss of blood may also cause shock.

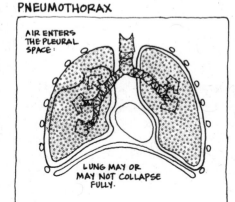

PNEUMOTHORAX

AIR ENTERS
THE PLEURAL
SPACE:

LUNG MAY OR
MAY NOT COLLAPSE
FULLY.

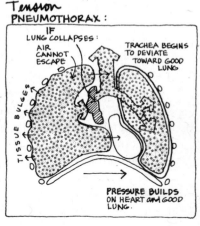

Tension
PNEUMOTHORAX:

IF
LUNG COLLAPSES:
AIR
CANNOT
ESCAPE

TRACHEA BEGINS
TO DEVIATE
TOWARD GOOD
LUNG

TISSUE BULGES

PRESSURE BUILDS
ON HEART and GOOD
LUNG.

Spontaneous Pneumothorax. A congenital weak area of the lung may rupture, creating a spontaneous pneumothorax. The highest incidence occurs in tall, thin, healthy men between the ages of 20 and 30. Eighty percent of spontaneous pneumothoraxes occur while the person is at rest. The patient complains of a sudden, sharp pain in the chest and increasing shortness of breath.

Tension Pneumothorax. If a hole opening into the pleural space serves as a one-way valve—allowing air to enter but not to escape—a tension pneumothorax develops. With each breath, air enters the pleural space, but it cannot escape with expiration. As pressure in the pleural space increases, the lung collapses. Pressure in the pleural space eventually causes the mediastinum to shift to the unaffected side, putting pressure on the heart and good lung. If the pressure in the pleural space exceeds that in the veins, blood cannot return to the heart, and death occurs.

As pressure builds, you may see the trachea deviate toward the unaffected side, tissue between the ribs bulge, and the neck veins distend. Respirations become increasingly rapid. The pulse is weak and rapid; cyanosis occurs.

Open Chest Wounds

If a wound through the chest wall breaks into the pleural space, air enters, creating a pneumothorax. If the wound remains open, air moves in and out of the pleura, causing a sucking noise.

The goal of treatment is to limit the size of the pneumoth-

Injury to Lungs

SIGNS AND SYMPTOMS
- Obvious chest trauma
- Shortness of breath
- Rapid, shallow respirations
- Cyanosis
- Shock
- Coughing up blood

Pneumothorax
- Sudden, sharp chest pain

Tension pneumothorax
- Tracheal deviation

Open chest wound
- Sucking noise

TREATMENT
- Seal open chest wounds.
- Immobilize rib fractures.
- Stabilize impaled objects.
- Position patient for comfort.
- Monitor for shortness of breath.
- Evacuate.

OPEN CHEST WOUND:
A WOUND THROUGH THE CHEST WALL THAT ALLOWS AIR
TO ENTER THE PLEURAL SPACE.

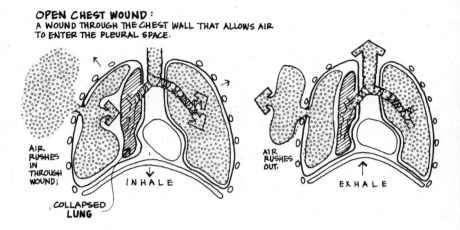

AIR
RUSHES
IN
THROUGH
WOUND;
INHALE

,COLLAPSED
LUNG

AIR
RUSHES
OUT.
EXHALE

orax. Quickly seal the hole with any nonporous material—a plastic bag or petroleum jelly–impregnated gauze, for example. Tape the dressing down on three sides to seal the hole, yet allow excess air pressure in the chest to escape.

RESPIRATORY DISTRESS

Respiratory distress is an overall term that covers any situation in which a patient is having difficulty breathing. Respiratory distress can occur after an injury, during an illness such as pneumonia, during a heart attack or an asthma attack, or after inhalation of a poisonous gas.

Signs and symptoms of respiratory distress are anxiety and restlessness; shortness of breath; rapid respirations and pulse; signs of shock, including pale, cool, and clammy skin and cyanosis of the skin, lips, and fingernail beds; and labored breathing using accessory muscles of the neck, shoulder, and abdomen to achieve maximum effort. The patient is usually more comfortable sitting than lying.

Respiratory distress is a frightening experience for both the patient and the rescuer. If the underlying cause is emotional, as in hyperventilation syndrome (see chapter 17), reassurance may be all that's needed to alleviate the problem. If a chest injury with underlying lung damage or an illness such as pneumonia or a pulmonary embolus occurs, treatment in the field is difficult. Evacuation is the course of action. The airway can be maintained, the patient placed in the most comfortable position for breathing, the injury splinted or taped, wounds dressed, and the patient treated for shock.

FINAL THOUGHTS

Chest injuries range from painful but not life-threatening simple rib fractures to serious injuries of the chest wall, lungs, and heart. Chest injuries are often complicated by other injuries as well.

Evacuation Guidelines

- The simple rib fracture does not necessarily need to be evacuated unless the patient is uncomfortable with pain, unable to travel, or has shortness of breath.
- Patients with shortness of breath following a blow to the chest, open chest wounds, or other obvious signs of serious chest injury will need to be rapidly evacuated.

CHAPTER 4

BRAIN AND SPINAL CORD INJURIES

INTRODUCTION

Head injuries range from simple scalp lacerations to life-threatening swelling of the brain. Spine injuries range from fractured vertebrae to actual spinal cord injuries that can result in paralysis. According to the data kept by NOLS, serious brain and spine injuries are rare in the wilderness, yet the urgency and care with which we must assess and handle these patients make them some of the more challenging problems to manage in remote areas.

CENTRAL NERVOUS SYSTEM

Together, the brain, spinal cord, and peripheral nerves monitor and control all body functions.

The brain governs thoughts, emotions, senses, memory, and movement, as well as basic physiological functions. The brain processes information from our senses, initiates motor responses, remembers, solves problems, and makes judgments.

The three main divisions of the brain are the cerebrum, the cerebellum, and the brain stem. The cerebrum is the largest part of the brain, the center for our "higher" cognitive functions: problem solving, memory, speech, hearing, sight, and so forth. The cerebellum, in the lower rear of the skull, regulates posture, coordination, and motor responses. The brain stem, at the base of the brain, maintains consciousness, heart rate, blood pressure, and breathing.

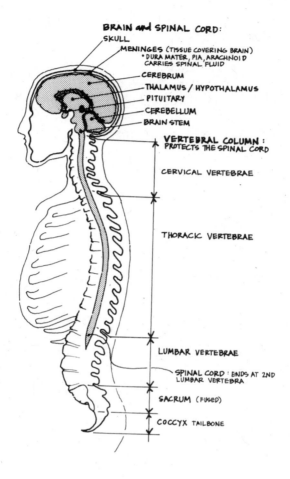

BRAIN and SPINAL CORD:
SKULL
MENINGES (TISSUE COVERING BRAIN)
 • DURA MATER, PIA, ARACHNOID
 CARRIES SPINAL FLUID
CEREBRUM
THALAMUS / HYPOTHALAMUS
PITUITARY
CEREBELLUM
BRAIN STEM
VERTEBRAL COLUMN :
PROTECTS THE SPINAL CORD

CERVICAL VERTEBRAE

THORACIC VERTEBRAE

LUMBAR VERTEBRAE

SPINAL CORD : ENDS AT 2ND
LUMBAR VERTEBRA

SACRUM (FUSED)

COCCYX TAILBONE

The skull houses and protects the brain. The brain is covered by three layers of tissue, known collectively as the meninges: the dura mater, the pia, and the arachnoid. Cerebrospinal fluid (CSF), nourishing and cushioning the brain, flows within these layers. Blood vessels are located within the brain and the meninges.

Central nervous system tissue is extremely sensitive to oxygen deficiency. Depriving the brain of oxygen for only a few minutes can result in permanent damage.

BRAIN INJURIES

Head injuries include scalp, skull, and brain injuries. Scalp and skull injuries can be serious by themselves, but we're more concerned with possible injury to the brain.

A large blood supply feeds the scalp, causing it to bleed profusely when cut. A bruised or lacerated scalp can mask underlying injury to the skull or brain. Examine scalp injuries carefully to see if bone or brain is exposed or if an indentation, which might be a depressed fracture, is present. Bleeding from the scalp can be controlled by applying gentle pressure on the edges of the wounds, being careful to avoid direct pressure on possibly unstable central areas.

The skull consists of 22 fused bones. The strongest are the bones forming the top and sides of the protective box encasing the brain. Fractures of the skull are not in themselves life-threatening except when associated with underlying brain injury or spinal cord injury, or when the fracture causes bleeding by tearing the blood vessels between the brain and the skull. Many serious brain injuries occur without skull fractures.

Skull fractures can be open or closed. Open skull fractures expose the brain to infection.

Brain injury can be fatal when it disrupts heartbeat and breathing. In the long term, a severe brain injury may leave the patient physically immobile or mentally incompetent, with severely impaired judgment and problem-solving ability or an inability to process or communicate information properly.

The brain can be injured by a direct blow to the head or by twisting forces, which cause deformation and shearing against the inside of the skull. Some movement between brain and skull is possible. A blow to the head can make the brain "rattle" within the skull, tearing blood vessels in the meninges or within the brain itself, stretching and shearing brain cells and the connections between cells.

A mild brain injury (also known as a concussion) is temporary brain dysfunction or loss of responsiveness following a blow to the head. There may be no or only mild brain injury in this case. Contusions (bruising of brain tissue) and hemorrhages or hematomas (bleeding within the brain) are more serious injuries that can lead to increased pressure in the skull. Encased in this rigid box, a swelling or bleeding brain presses against the skull; the body has no mechanism to release such an increase in pressure. As pressure rises, blood supply is shut off by compression of swollen vessels, and brain tissue is deprived of oxygen. The brain stem can be squashed by the pressure, affecting heart and lung function.

Signs and Symptoms of Brain Injury
Signs and symptoms of brain injury depend on the degree and progression of injury. Some indications of brain injury appear immediately from the accident; others develop slowly.

Changes in Level of Responsiveness. Loss of responsiveness may be short or may persist for hours or days. The patient may alternate between periods of responsiveness and unresponsiveness or be responsive but disoriented, confused, and incoherent—exhibiting changes in behavior and personality or verbal or physical combativeness.

Headache, Vision Disturbances, Loss of Balance, Nausea and Vomiting, Paralysis, Seizures. Headache, vision problems, loss of balance, nausea and vomiting, and paralysis may accompany brain injury. In serious cases, the patient may assume abnormal positions, with the legs and arms stiff and extended or the arms clutched across the chest. A brain-injured patient may have seizures.

Combativeness. A brain-injured patient may become combative, striking out randomly and with surprising strength at the nearest person. If the brain is oxygen-deprived, supplemental oxygen and airway maintenance may help alleviate such behavior. Restraint may be necessary to protect the patient and the rescuers.

Blood or CSF Leakage, Soft Tissue Injury to Skull, Obvious Skull Fracture, Raccoon Sign, Battle's Sign. Blood or clear cerebrospinal fluid (CSF) leaking from the ears, mouth, or nose is a sign of a skull fracture, as are pain, tenderness, and swelling at the injury site or obvious penetrating wounds or depressed

Signs and Symptoms of Brain Injury

MILD BRAIN INJURY
- Brief change in mental status or brief loss of responsiveness.
- Short-term amnesia.
- Temporarily blurred vision or "seeing stars."
- Nausea and/or isolated vomiting.
- Headache, dizziness and/or lethargy.

SERIOUS BRAIN INJURY
- Disoriented, irritable, combative, unconscious.
- Heart rate decreases and bounds.
- Hyperventilation, erratic respiration.
- Skin warm and flushed.
- Pupils become unequal (late changing sign).
- The patient may also experience a worsening headache, vision disturbances, protracted vomiting, lethargy, excessive sleepiness, ataxia, and seizures.

fractures. Two other signs of skull fracture—bruising around the eyes (called the raccoon sign) and bruising behind the ear (Battle's sign)—usually appear hours after the injury.

Slow Pulse, Rising Blood Pressure, Irregular Respirations. Changes in vital signs that indicate a serious and late stage brain injury are a slow pulse, rising blood pressure, and irregular respiratory rate. These contrast with the rising pulse, falling blood pressure, and rapid, regular respirations seen with shock.

Assessment for Brain Injury
Initial assessment of brain injury can be difficult. The symptoms of a mild brain injury are similar to those seen in more serious injuries. The assessment may also be complicated when the patient's mental status is affected by drugs, alcohol, or other traumatic injuries.

JAW THRUST AIRWAY OPENING FOR SUSPECTED C-SPINE PATIENTS :
- *DO NOT MOVE NECK OR SPINE.*
- *DO NOT TILT HEAD BACK*

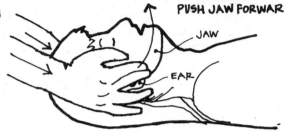

ONE HAND ON
EACH SIDE OF
HEAD :

PLACE FINGERS IN FRONT
OF EARLOBE.
PUSH JAW FORWARD AND UP.

JAW

EAR

Assessment of a brain injury begins by checking the airway, breathing, and circulation (ABC); bleeding; and cervical spine. A patient with a brain injury is at high risk for cervical spine injury. Avoid movement of the neck. If you suspect brain or neck injury, use the jaw thrust to open the airway.

After a thorough physical assessment, including vital signs, evaluate the nervous system. Note the level of responsiveness and the patient's ability to feel and move extremities. Use the AVPU (awake and alert, not awake but responsive to a verbal stimulus, not awake but responsive to pain, or not awake and unresponsive) system to assess mental status. Question the patient or bystanders as to a loss of responsiveness. Was it immediate, or was there a delay before the patient became unresponsive? Has the patient been awake but drowsy, sleepy, confused, or disoriented? Has the patient been going in and out of responsiveness?

Watch any brain-injured patient carefully, even if the injury does not at first appear serious. Let the patient rest, but wake him or her up every couple of hours and assess responsiveness.

Treatment of Brain Injury
Brain injuries can be difficult to assess, and some that appear initially benign may over time become serious. Thus, we have a

low threshold for evacuation. Evacuation is recommended for any patient who has become unresponsive, even for a minute or two, or who exhibits vision or balance disturbances, irritability, lethargy, or nausea and vomiting after a blow to the head regardless of whether they were knocked out. A patient who experiences loss of responsiveness but who awakens without any other symptoms may be walked out of the wilderness with a support party capable of quickly evacuating the patient if his or her condition worsens.

ABCs. An injured brain needs oxygen. Ensuring an open airway is the first step in treatment.

If Vomiting, Position Patient on Side. Brain-injured patients have a tendency to vomit. Logrolling the patient onto his or her side while maintaining cervical spine stabilization helps drain vomit while maintaining the airway. Use the jaw thrust to open the airway.

Control Scalp Bleeding. Cover open wounds with bulky sterile dressings as a barrier against infection. Although it is acceptable to clean scalp wounds, cleaning open skull injuries may introduce infection into the brain, so leave them as you find them. Stabilize impaled objects in place.

Do Not Control Internal Bleeding or Drainage. Do not attempt to prevent drainage of blood or clear CSF from the ears or nose. Blocking the flow could increase pressure within the skull.

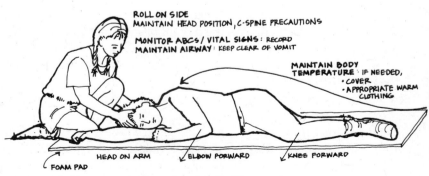

CARING FOR A BRAIN-INJURED PATIENT

Elevate head. Keep the patient in a horizontal or slightly head-elevated position. Do not elevate the legs, as this might increase pressure within the skull.

Record Neurological Assessment. Watch the patient closely for any changes in mental status. These observations will be valuable to the receiving physician. Record changes in your patient report.

SPINAL CORD INJURIES

As with head injuries, spinal cord injuries primarily involve young people, with most cases occurring in men between the ages of 15 and 35. An estimated 10,000 new spinal cord injuries occur each year in the United States, and because central nervous tissue does not regenerate, victims are left permanently disabled—half as paraplegics and half as quadriplegics. Motor vehicle accidents account for the majority of spinal injury cases, followed by falls and sporting injuries.

Treatment of Brain Injury
• ABCs.
• Assume cervical spine injury.
• If patient is vomiting, position on side.
• Control scalp bleeding.
• Do not control internal bleeding or drainage.
• Elevate head.
• Record neurological assessment.

The spinal cord is the extension of the brain outside the skull. A component of the central nervous system, the spinal cord is the nervous connection between the brain and the rest of the body.

The spinal cord is protected within the vertebrae, 33 of which form the backbone, or spine. A force driving the spine out of its normal alignment can fracture or dislocate the vertebrae, thereby injuring the spinal cord. There can be vertebral fractures or ligament and muscle damage to the backbone, however, without damage to the spinal cord. Fractured or dislocated vertebrae can pinch, bruise, or cut the spinal cord, damaging the nervous connections.

The smallest vertebrae with the greatest range of motion are in the neck—the most vulnerable part of the spine. From there, the vertebrae become progressively larger as they support more

---

Signs and Symptoms of Spinal Cord Injury

- Pain or tenderness on the spine
- Weakness in extremities
- Loss of strength or ability to move extremities
- Loss of sensation in extremities
- Tenderness on spine
- Numbness and tingling in hands and feet
- Incontinence
- Signs and symptoms of shock
- Shortness of breath

---

weight. The location of damage to the spinal cord determines whether the patient may die or be left paralyzed from the neck down (quadriplegia) or the chest down (paraplegia).

Signs and Symptoms of Spinal Cord Injury
Signs and symptoms of spinal cord injury include weakness, loss of sensation or ability to move, numbness and tingling in the hands and feet, incontinence, soft tissue injury over or near the spine, and tenderness in the spine.

Assessment for Spinal Cord Injury
Check for strength, sensation, ability to move, and weakness or numbness in the hands and feet. Ask the patient to wiggle fingers or toes, push his or her feet against your hands, or squeeze your hands with his or hers. Ask the patient to identify which toe or finger you are touching. If the patient is unresponsive, check for sensation by applying a painful stimulus at the toes and fingers (a pinprick or pinch) and watching the patient's face for a grimace.

Treatment of Spinal Cord Injury
Treatment for a spinal cord injury is to stabilize the spine to prevent further damage. Although it may be necessary to move a spine-injured patient, your first choice should be on-scene stabilization.

IMPROVISED CERVICAL COLLAR

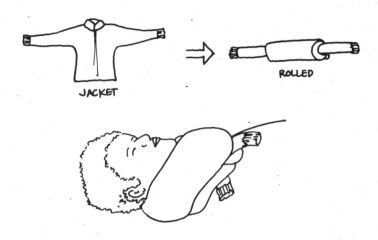

JACKET

ROLLED

Stabilize the Spine. If spinal immobilization devices are not available, one person should always be at the head of the patient, controlling the head and maintaining stabilization of the neck. A clothing or blanket roll may be used as an improvised cervical or neck collar to aid in stabilization, freeing rescuers for other tasks. A strap of cloth or bandage across the

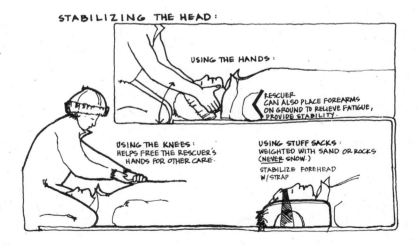

STABILIZING THE HEAD:

USING THE HANDS:

RESCUER CAN ALSO PLACE FOREARMS ON GROUND TO RELIEVE FATIGUE, PROVIDE STABILITY.

USING THE KNEES: HELPS FREE THE RESCUER'S HANDS FOR OTHER CARE.

USING STUFF SACKS: WEIGHTED WITH SAND OR ROCKS (NEVER SNOW.)

STABILIZE FOREHEAD W/STRAP

forehead secured with wrapped clothing stabilizes the head and neck.

Move with Logroll or Lift. Assume that the patient may have to be moved at least twice during the rescue—once to place insulation underneath the body to prevent hypothermia, and a second time to place the patient on a litter or backboard. Two common techniques for moving the patient are the logroll and the lift. Practice these under the guidance of an emergency care instructor.

A patient can be assessed and immobilized while lying facedown or on his or her back or side. Unless airway, breathing, or bleeding problems are present, you should take the time required to carry out the logroll or lift and explain your actions to the patient.

The Concept:

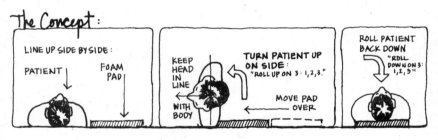

How to Perform a Four-Person Logroll:

1. The rescuers take positions:
   - Rescuer One maintains stabilization of the head throughout the procedure and gives the commands.
   - Rescuer Two kneels beside the patient's chest and reaches across to the patient's shoulder and upper arm.
   - Rescuer Three kneels beside the patient's waist and reaches across to the lower back and pelvis.
   - Rescuer Four kneels beside the patient's thighs and reaches across to support the legs with one hand on the patient's upper thigh, the other behind the knee.
2. The rescuers roll the patient onto his or her side:
   - Rescuer One, at the head, gives the command, "Roll on 3; 1, 2, 3," and the rescuers slowly roll the patient

Techniques :

RESCUER POSITIONS :

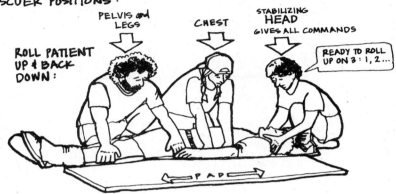

PELVIS and LEGS

CHEST

STABILIZING **HEAD**
GIVES ALL COMMANDS

ROLL PATIENT UP & BACK DOWN :

READY TO ROLL UP ON 3 : 1, 2 ...

P A D

toward them, keeping the patient's body in alignment. Rescuer One supports the head and maintains alignment with the spine. Once the patient is on his or her side, a backboard or foamlite pad can be placed where the patient will be lying when the logroll is complete.

3. The rescuers roll the patient onto his or her back:
   • When Rescuer One gives the command, "Lower on 3; 1, 2, 3," the procedure is reversed, and the patient is slowly lowered onto the backboard or foamlite pad while the rescuers keep the spine in alignment.

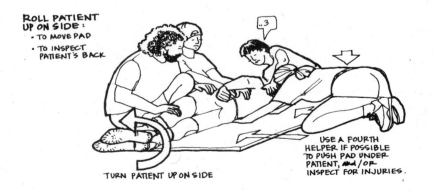

ROLL PATIENT UP ON SIDE :
• TO MOVE PAD
• TO INSPECT PATIENT'S BACK

..3

TURN PATIENT UP ON SIDE

USE A FOURTH HELPER IF POSSIBLE TO PUSH PAD UNDER PATIENT, and / or INSPECT FOR INJURIES.

THE LIFT
The Concept:

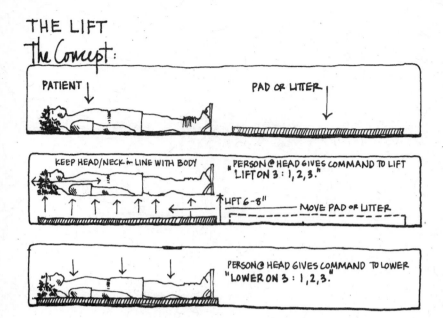

Lifting Technique. The patient can be lifted by four people, enabling a fifth person to slide a backboard, foamlite pad, or litter underneath. The rescuer at the head again maintains stabilization during the entire procedure and gives commands. The other three rescuers position themselves at the patient's sides, one kneeling at chest level and another at pelvis level on the same side, while the third rescuer kneels at waist level on the opposite side. Before lifting, the rescuers place their hands over the patient to visualize their hands in position under the chest, lower back, pelvis, and thighs. They then slide their hands under the patient as far as they can without jostling the patient. On the command, "Lift on 3; 1, 2, 3," rescuers lift the patient to a standing position, then lower him or her onto the pad or litter.

Immobilize the Spine. Ideally, the patient should be moved as few times as possible, and preferably after immobilization on a backboard, Kendrick Extrication Device, SKED litter, or other spine-splinting device, and with a cervical collar and head immobilization. Until such equipment arrives, insulate and shelter the patient.

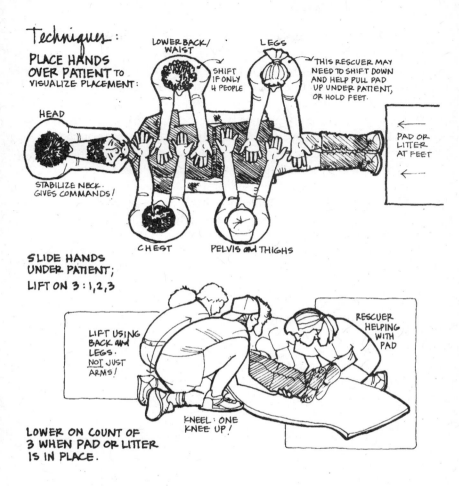

Techniques:
PLACE HANDS OVER PATIENT to VISUALIZE PLACEMENT:

LOWER BACK/ WAIST

LEGS

SHIFT IF ONLY 4 PEOPLE

THIS RESCUER MAY NEED TO SHIFT DOWN AND HELP PULL PAD UP UNDER PATIENT, OR HOLD FEET.

HEAD

PAD OR LITTER AT FEET

STABILIZE NECK. GIVES COMMANDS!

CHEST

PELVIS and THIGHS

SLIDE HANDS UNDER PATIENT; LIFT ON 3 : 1, 2, 3

LIFT USING BACK and LEGS. NOT JUST ARMS!

RESCUER HELPING WITH PAD

LOWER ON COUNT OF 3 WHEN PAD OR LITTER IS IN PLACE.

KNEEL : ONE KNEE UP!

Wilderness treatment may require caring for a patient during prolonged immobilization. It's uncomfortable to lie still on a hard surface for hours. Current advanced trauma life support (ATLS) curriculum recommends that patients on backboards be logrolled off the backboard approximately every 2 hours to prevent pressure sores on the back. Padding is important. A little bit under the lower back and behind the knees goes a long way to make the patient comfortable. Strapping over bony areas helps tie the patient down, but the straps should be padded and can be loosened when the patient is not being carried.

The Focused Spine Assessment. If a mechanism for a spinal cord injury has occurred, for example, from a fall from a height, a high-velocity skiing fall, a diving accident, or a blow to the head, initially assume the worst and control the head. If the mechanism is severe, or the patient has signs of a spinal cord injury, immobilize the spine. If the mechanism seems trivial and the patient has no signs of spine injury, you may consider performing a focused spine assessment to gather information to help you decide if immobilizing the spine is necessary.

After a thorough assessment, it is acceptable to consider "clearing" the spine of injury by using a method supported by the Wilderness Medical Society and other pre-hospital medicine experts to rule out spine injury. Without this protocol, we would unnecessarily immobilize all patients with insignificant mechanisms for injury. As with all wilderness protocols, support from a physician advisor is recommended.

Making a decision to not immobilize begins with a thorough patient assessment. Then proceed sequentially through this series of steps:

1. Is the patient A+O3/4 and sober?
   - If no, immobilize the spine. If yes, proceed to the next step.
2. Is the patient free from distractions (injuries, emotional distress)?
   - If no, immobilize the spine. If yes, proceed to the next step.
3. Is the patient free of pain, tenderness, tingling, or numbness on the spine?
   - If no, immobilize the spine. If yes, proceed to the next step.
4. Is the patient free of unusual or abnormal sensations in the extremities, such as numbness or tingling? Do extremities have normal circulation and movement?
   - If no, immobilize the spine. If yes, you can make a decision to not immobilize the spine.

If the patient fails any step in this process, or you're uncertain about the results of your exam, immobilize the spine. If at

PATIENT PACKAGING POINTS

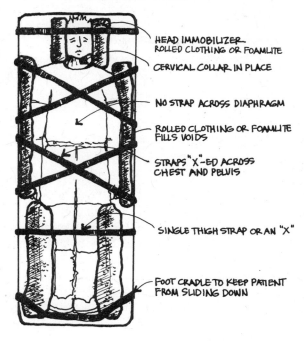

HEAD IMMOBILIZER
ROLLED CLOTHING OR FOAMLITE

CERVICAL COLLAR IN PLACE

NO STRAP ACROSS DIAPHRAGM

ROLLED CLOTHING OR FOAMLITE
FILLS VOIDS

STRAPS "X"-ED ACROSS
CHEST AND PELVIS

SINGLE THIGH STRAP OR AN "X"

FOOT CRADLE TO KEEP PATIENT
FROM SLIDING DOWN

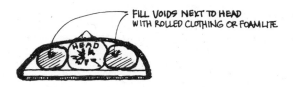

FILL VOIDS NEXT TO HEAD
WITH ROLLED CLOTHING OR FOAMLITE

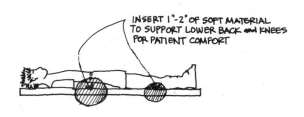

INSERT 1"-2" OF SOFT MATERIAL
TO SUPPORT LOWER BACK and KNEES
FOR PATIENT COMFORT

Treatment of Spinal Cord Injury

• Stabilize spine.	• Immobilize spine.
• Hands on patient's head.	• Cervical collar.
• Clothing or blanket roll.	• Backboard.
• Move with logroll or lift.	• Check CSMs before and after movement.

---

any time you're uncomfortable with this process, you can choose a conservative plan and immobilize the patient.

FINAL THOUGHTS
Airway maintenance, cervical spine precautions, and patient assessment are important treatments for patients with brain and spine injuries, but they are only stopgap measures. A quarter of all brain and spine injuries result in death or permanent disability. The cost of treating a serious brain injury is staggering. In urban settings, first aid for brain or spine injuries includes rapid transport to neurological care—an impossibility in a wilderness setting.

Prevention is the best treatment: Wear a helmet! Be careful out there.

Evacuation Guidelines
- Evacuate if the patient has:
  —A loss of responsiveness, even if he recovers to A+Ox3 or 4.
  —Headache, n/v irritability, or other s/s of mild head injury without loss of responsiveness and is not improving after 24 hours.
- Rapidly evacuate if the patient has:
  —Distinct changes in mental status (disoriented, irritable, combative).
  —Persistent vomiting, lethargy, excessive sleepiness, seizures, worsening headache, vision disturbances.
  —Signs of skull fracture.
- Evacuate any patient with possible spinal cord injury.

CHAPTER 5

FRACTURES AND DISLOCATIONS

INTRODUCTION

As recently as 90 years ago, a fractured femur was a deadly injury. Broken bone ends often did not heal properly. Open fractures frequently became infected, and amputation was a common unpleasant consequence. Modern emergency medicine, especially assessment and splinting in the field, has reduced these complications.

Fractures and dislocations are infrequent at NOLS, making up less than 7 percent of our field safety incidents. Among the general public, however, fractures and dislocations make up as much as 20 percent of reported wilderness injuries. NOLS instructors have cared for femur fractures in the remote backcountry of Yellowstone Park in the winter and at 16,000 feet on Denali. They've expertly splinted uncomplicated wrist fractures and walked patients 20 miles out of the wilderness. They've accurately diagnosed a complicated elbow fracture requiring an urgent helicopter evacuation.

THE SKELETAL SYSTEM

A bony skeleton shapes the body. From this scaffolding hang the soft tissues: the vital organs, blood vessels, muscles, fat, and skin. The skeleton is strong to support and protect internal organs, flexible to withstand stress, and jointed to allow for movement.

Bone is living tissue combined with nonliving intracellular components. The nonliving components contain calcium and

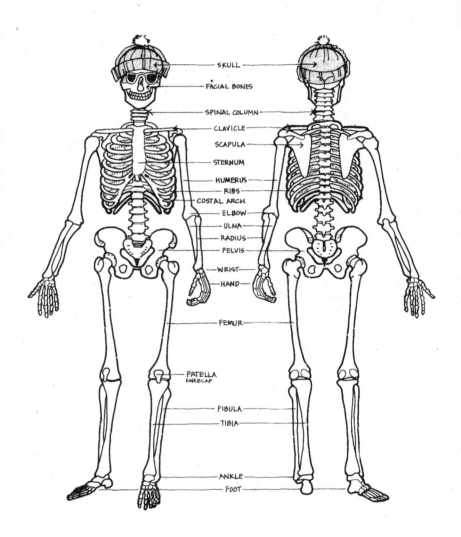

SKULL
FACIAL BONES
SPINAL COLUMN
CLAVICLE
SCAPULA
STERNUM
HUMERUS
RIBS
COSTAL ARCH
ELBOW
ULNA
RADIUS
PELVIS
WRIST
HAND
FEMUR
PATELLA
KNEECAP
FIBULA
TIBIA
ANKLE
FOOT

make bone rigid. Bones are connected by ligaments and connective tissue. An adult has 206 bones, ranging in size from the femur, or thigh bone—the largest—to the tiny ossicles of the inner ear.

The skeleton has axial and appendicular components. The axial bones are the pelvis, spinal column, ribs, and skull. Injuries to these structures—except for pelvic fractures—are

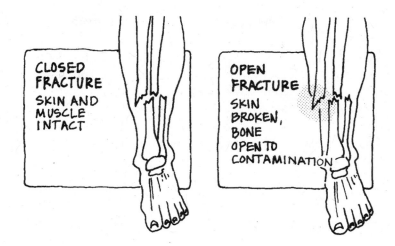

CLOSED FRACTURE SKIN AND MUSCLE INTACT

OPEN FRACTURE SKIN BROKEN, BONE OPEN TO CONTAMINATION

discussed in the chest and head injury chapters. This chapter covers injuries to the appendicular skeleton: the arms and legs.

The upper extremity consists of the scapula, or shoulder blade; the clavicle, or collarbone; the upper arm bone, or humerus; two bones in the forearm, the radius on the thumb side and the ulna on the little finger side; and 22 bones in the wrist and fingers.

The lower extremity consists of the pelvis; the thighbone, or femur; a small bone in front of the knee, the patella; two bones in the lower leg, the tibia and fibula; and 26 bones in the ankle and foot.

Bones connect at joints. Some joints are fixed; others allow movement. Joints are held together by ligaments, connective tissue, and muscle. Joint surfaces are covered with cartilage to reduce friction, and lubricated with joint fluid for smooth movement.

FRACTURES AND DISLOCATIONS

A fracture is a break in a bone. Fractures can be open or closed. With open fractures, the skin is broken, exposing the bone to contamination. Closed fractures are covered with intact muscle and skin.

Fractures can also be described as transverse, spiral, oblique, or crushed, referring to the type of fracture. This information is usually obtained from an X-ray and has little effect on first aid.

Fractures, in addition to causing pain, loss of function, and swelling, can be complicated by infection and damage to blood vessels and nerves. Fractured bone ends can pinch or sever blood vessels, blocking circulation or causing bleeding. Fractures of large, long bones, such as the femur, humerus, or pelvis, are often accompanied by blood loss that can cause life-threatening shock. Infection is a potentially severe complication of an open fracture.

A dislocation is the displacement of a bone end from its normal position at a joint. Dislocations damage the supporting structures at the joint. Blood vessels and nerves can be disrupted. The ball-and-socket joint of the shoulder is a common site for dislocation. Elbow, finger, and ankle dislocations are also possible. Less common are dislocations to the wrist, hip, and knee. Fractures and dislocations can occur together.

Signs and Symptoms of Fractures and Dislocations
Signs and symptoms of fractures or dislocations include pain and tenderness; crepitus, a grating sound produced by bone

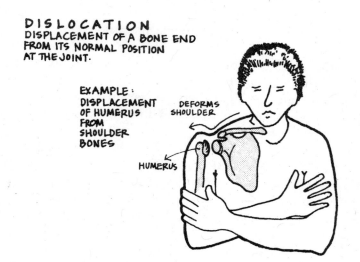

DISLOCATION
DISPLACEMENT OF A BONE END FROM ITS NORMAL POSITION AT THE JOINT.

EXAMPLE:
DISPLACEMENT OF HUMERUS FROM SHOULDER BONES

DEFORMS SHOULDER

HUMERUS

ends rubbing together (also a sign of instability and unnatural movement at the fracture site); swelling and discoloration, indicating that fluids are pooling in the damaged tissue; deformity of a limb or joint; and loss of function. Dislocations cause loss of function at a joint; fractures cause loss of function to a limb.

Signs and Symptoms of Fractures and Dislocations

- Pain and point tenderness
- Crepitus
- Swelling and discoloration
- Deformity
- Loss of function or range of motion at a joint (dislocation)
- Loss of function at a bone (fracture)
- Altered circulation, sensation, and movement (CSM)

Assessment of Fractures and Dislocations

Humans are bilaterally symmetrical animals, meaning that one side is the mirror image of the other. Comparing an injured with an uninjured limb can reveal a subtle angulation or deformity. The mechanism of injury also provides a clue to the extent and location of the injury. Particularly violent incidents, such as falls from a height or direct blows to a joint, are common fracture mechanisms in the outdoors.

Remove clothing if at all possible and visualize the injury. Look at the limb for deformity, swelling, or discoloration. Feel the limb for localized tenderness, abnormal bumps or protrusions, and swelling.

Assess for circulation, sensation, and movement (CSM). Assess circulation by feeling the radial pulse at the wrist or the pedal pulse in the foot. Impaired circulation may also be evidenced by cold, gray, or cyanotic extremities.

Assess sensation and movement by asking the patient to move fingers or toes. Test for

Assessment of Fractures and Dislocations

- Assess the bone or joint.
- Remove clothing; visualize the injury.
- Look for deformity, swelling, discoloration.
- Feel for tenderness, deformity, swelling.
- Assess circulation, sensation, and movement (CSM).

reaction to touch or pain. A blocked artery with loss of distal circulation is an emergency. After several hours, serious damage may result. Damage to a nerve is not as urgent, as the damage usually occurs immediately and may be irreparable.

Treatment of Fractures and Dislocations
Treat fractures and dislocations by immobilizing the injury. Immobilization prevents movement of bones, reduces pain and swelling and the possibility of further injury, prevents a closed fracture from becoming an open fracture, and helps reduce disability.

Immobilize the Injury. Any time there is loss of function to a limb or joint, the injury should be immobilized in a splint. If it is not clear whether the injury is a sprain or a fracture, immobilize. It is better to splint a sprain than to fail to immobilize a fracture. Immobilize the bones above and below a dislocated joint, and immobilize the joints above and below a fractured bone.

Clean and Dress Wounds. Clean and dress all wounds before splinting. Treat open fractures as contaminated soft tissue injuries and clean them thoroughly. Irrigate, but do not scrub, exposed bone ends and keep them moist with a dressing soaked in disinfected water. An infected fracture is a serious problem that can result in long-term complications.

Splint Before Moving. Splint the injury before moving the patient. A quick splint fashioned from a foamlite sleeping pad can stabilize the injury if you must move the patient off dangerous terrain or to drier, warmer conditions. Strap an injured arm to the body. Tie injured legs together.

Remove Jewelry, Watches, and Tight Clothing. Remove jewelry and watches and loosen clothing that might compromise circulation should swelling occur. If you are managing a splint in cold weather, hot water bottles or chemical heat packs tucked into the splint can provide warmth.

Elevate to Reduce Swelling. Elevate the injured limb a little (4 to 6 inches) to reduce swelling. RICE treatment, which is discussed in chapter 6 ("Athletic Injuries"), helps reduce pain and swelling and is appropriate for splinted fractures and immobi-

Treatment of Fractures and Dislocations

- Immobilize the injury.
  Bones above and below dislocations.
  Joints above and below fractures.
- Clean and dress wounds.
- Remove jewelry, watches, and tight clothing.
- Rest, ice, compression, and elevation (RICE) therapy.
- Assess circulation, temperature, and sensation before and after splinting.
- Assess for other injuries.
- Treat for shock.

lized dislocations. In warm environments where hypothermia and frostbite are not concerns, cold packs or ice or snow encased in a plastic bag and wrapped with a sock, or even a shirt soaked in cold water, may help reduce pain and swelling.

Assess Circulation, Sensation, and Movement. Before and after the splint is applied, assess circulation, sensation, and movement (CSM) to fingers or toes. Repeat this assessment periodically during transport as well.

Assess for Other Injuries. A fracture or dislocation warrants a full patient assessment for other injuries as well.

Treat for Shock. A fracture in and of itself does not cause shock. Damage to nearby tissues, organs, and blood vessels, however, may be a life-threatening problem. Splinting is the basic treatment for shock because it reduces pain and continued injury. Be especially alert for shock with femur and pelvic fractures, multiple fractures, and open fractures.

Angulated Fractures, Dislocations, and Traction-in-Line

Years ago, in basic first aid, we learned to splint fractures and dislocations in the position in which they were found. We were concerned that moving bones to straighten bent extremities would injure blood vessels and nerves. In practice, however, we found that gentle traction and straightening of any fracture reduces pain and makes splints more stable.

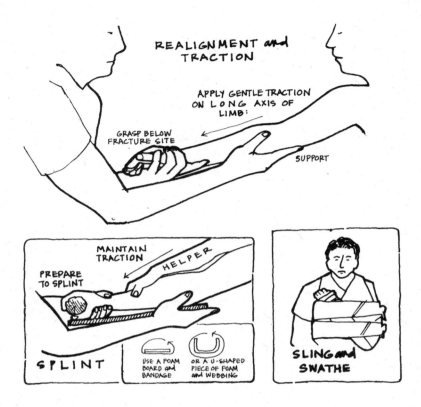

Medical opinion now favors straightening with gentle traction-in-line femur fractures, fractures that are difficult to splint or transport due to angulation, and any fracture or dislocation with impaired distal circulation, sensation, or movement. The current wisdom is that the danger of muscle, nerve, or blood vessel injury from gentle traction-in-line is less than the damage, discomfort, and pain from an injury splinted in an awkward position for long periods.

To straighten a fracture, apply gentle traction-in-line and realign the bone ends. To do this, grasp the limb below the fracture site while another person supports the limb. Align the limb with a gentle pull applied on the long axis of the bone. If resistance or pain occurs, stop and splint in the deformed position.

Dislocations. Consensus opinion in wilderness medicine supports reducing dislocations in the field if prompt transport is not possible or if circulation is impaired. The first responder should use judgment and discretion when transport to a medical facility is possible within a few hours. Early reduction decreases pain; is easier if done before swelling, stiffness, and muscle spasms develop; makes immobilization and transportation easier; and reduces risks of long-term circulation and nerve injury. Dislocations are relocated with a variety of traction-in-line techniques, depending on the location of the injury. We recommend that you contact a physician or a reputable wilderness medical program for advice and training on specific relocation techniques.

SPLINTING
In the wilderness, improvised splints are the rule, and they may remain in place for days. Splints should pad, support, and immobilize the limb and insulate the extremity from cold. They should be lightweight to make transporting the patient easier and allow access to feet or hands to check circulation. There are many commercial splints on the market, but in the backcountry, two commonly available items easily meet these specifications. They are the foamlite pad used for insulation under sleeping bags, and the triangular bandage.

Basic Splinting Techniques
Two basic splinting techniques cover most first aid situations. One is to make a foamlite tube to splint an arm or leg. The other is to fashion a sling and swathe to immobilize injuries to the upper extremities. The one exception is the case of a fractured femur, which is often immobilized using a traction splint.

Foamlite Tube. To make a foamlite tube, roll the foam sleeping pad into a U-shaped tube and trim to fit the limb. Secure with cravats (triangular bandages), bandannas, sling webbing, or tape. To make this supportive and comfortable, generously pad and firmly (but not tightly) compress it around the limb.

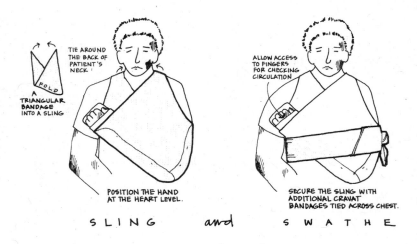

TIE AROUND THE BACK OF PATIENT'S NECK !

A TRIANGULAR BANDAGE INTO A SLING

POSITION THE HAND AT THE HEART LEVEL.

ALLOW ACCESS TO FINGERS FOR CHECKING CIRCULATION

SECURE THE SLING WITH ADDITIONAL CRAVAT BANDAGES TIED ACROSS CHEST.

S L I N G   and   S W A T H E

Sling and Swathe. The sling and swathe immobilizes arm, shoulder, and collarbone injuries using two triangular bandages, bandannas, or cravats.

First clean and dress any open wound. Then use soft material such as a pile jacket to pad the injury. Add a firm supporting layer outside the soft padding. Often this is a foamlite pad, Crazy Creek chair, or Therm-A-Rest pad. Sticks, tent poles, or the stays in soft packs can provide additional support. Secure with tape, webbing, or cord. Support the foot or hand, but provide access to fingers and toes to assess for CSM. Upper extremity injuries are often further supported with a sling and swathe.

Specific Splinting Techniques

Hand. The hand and fingers should be splinted in the "position of function": the position of the hand when holding a glass of water. Fingers can also be "buddy-taped" to each other to reduce range of motion yet still allow some degree of function. If the injury is confined to the fingers, the wrist need not be splinted. If the injury involves the bones at the base of the fingers, splint the wrist as well.

Qualities of a Good Splint

- Rigid; supports the injury
- Pads the injury
- Insulates from cold
- Lightweight
- Offers access to distal circulation

WRIST SPLINT

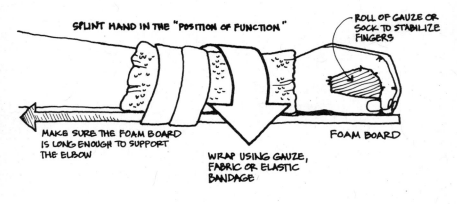

SPLINT HAND IN THE "POSITION OF FUNCTION"

ROLL OF GAUZE OR SOCK TO STABILIZE FINGERS

MAKE SURE THE FOAM BOARD IS LONG ENOUGH TO SUPPORT THE ELBOW

FOAM BOARD

WRAP USING GAUZE, FABRIC OR ELASTIC BANDAGE

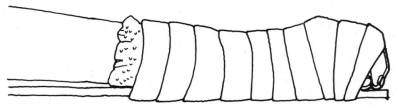

CHECK FINGERTIPS! OR LEAVE THEM UNCOVERED
• SWELLING?
• ADEQUATE CIRCULATION?

SPLINT MATERIALS

USE A FOAM BOARD and WRAP

OR A U-SHAPED PIECE OF FOAM AND WEBBING

USE WRAP TO HOLD IT ALL TOGETHER

CLOTHING 1"-2" THICK AS PADDING

ARM

FOAM BOARD

Wrist and Forearm. Splint injuries to the wrist and forearm with a foamlite stabilizer or a sling and swathe. Elevating the hand above the level of the heart helps reduce swelling and pain.

Elbow. An elbow dislocation is a serious injury. Several nerves and arteries pass around the complex elbow joint and may be damaged by displaced bone ends. The simplest splint for the elbow is the sling and swathe. Splint this injury in the position in which you find it. If the elbow is at an awkward angle, a sling and swathe will not work well. Try a foamlite pad stabilized with a tent pole or the stay from a soft pack bent to the angle of the joint. If possible, bandage the whole arm to the trunk for greater stability.

Upper Arm. The radial nerve and brachial artery lie close to the humerus and can be injured by a fracture. Damage to the artery is most common with elbow dislocations. Damage to the nerve is most common with midshaft fractures. Check the pulse at the wrist. The ability to bend back the hand tests the radial nerve. The humerus can be splinted with a combination of a foamlite splint and sling and swathe. Wrap foamlite on the inside of the arm, over the elbow, and up the outside of the arm for added stability. The patient may be more comfortable if the sling and foamlite cup the elbow without putting pressure on the humerus.

Shoulder. The humerus fits into a shallow socket in the scapula, forming the shoulder joint and allowing for a wide range of motion (ROM). This ROM makes the joint susceptible to injury. Most dislocations are anterior, with the head of the humerus displaced out of the socket toward the chest.

The signs of dislocation are drooping shoulder, a depression on the front of the shoulder, and loss of function or ROM at the joint. A sling and swathes provide a simple and effective splint. If the shoulder is immobile at an awkward angle, padding may be necessary to support the arm away from the chest.

Collarbone. The clavicle acts as a strut, propping the shoulder. It can be fractured by a direct blow to the shoulder or by a blow transmitted up an extended arm. A broken collarbone is a common mountain biking injury. Deformity and tenderness can often be found by feeling the entire clavicle from sternum to shoulder. Typically, a patient with an injured clavicle is unable to use the arm on the injured side. Splint with a sling and swathe, immobilizing the shoulder and arm.

Pelvis. The pelvis is a bowl-shaped structure consisting of three bones fused with the sacrum, the lower portion of the vertebral column. The upper part of the femur meets the pelvis at a shallow socket and forms the hip joint.

A broken pelvis is a serious injury. It takes considerable force to break a pelvis; such force can cause associated internal injuries, including rupture of the bladder and blood loss. Treat this patient as if he or she has a back injury, and immobilize the trunk and legs. A backboard, Stokes litter, or improvised litter is necessary to immobilize and carry the patient.

Femur and Hip. A dislocated hip is usually the result of a high-velocity mechanism, such as a fall from height. A leg with a dislocated hip is generally shortened, with the foot and knee turned in. If the hip is dislocated for more than a few hours, the blood supply to the head of the femur can be compromised, and permanent damage to the bone can occur. Splint hip fractures or dislocations with a U-shaped foamlite tube, immobilizing the entire leg.

Muscles surrounding the fracture of long bones may contract, causing the bone ends to override. This increases pain and soft tissue damage, as well as increasing the possibility of artery and nerve injury. Spasm of the large thigh muscles is of special concern in fractures of the femur. A femur fracture can bleed into the surrounding tissues, causing life-threatening shock. The leg may appear shortened and the thigh swollen.

Traction Splints. Traction is a common treatment for a midshaft femur fracture. Fractures close to the knee or the hip are splinted with a fixation splint. Traction splints place tension on the muscles surrounding a midshaft fracture, reducing pain and spasm and helping with realignment. Traction splints for femur fractures in the wilderness are a challenge to improvise, and the traction straps require constant attention to make sure they are not causing reduced blood flow to the foot.

Before you begin constructing the traction splint, splint the injury with a full-leg foamlite splint. The leg splint will provide support, insulation, and padding. Follow this by applying padding at the ankle. Ideally, you can promptly provide traction-in-line for the thigh and hold it while you are preparing the traction splint. This is not always practical, however, and you may need to apply a fixation splint, construct your traction splint, then apply traction.

1. To prepare for applying traction, attach traction straps over the boot or padded ankle. Fold two cravats into long, narrow bandages. Fold lengthwise, and pass one over and one behind the ankle, making sure the ends of each bandage are facing in opposite directions. Now pull the ends of each bandage through the loop in the other bandage. The bandages should fit snugly and flat against the ankle. The toes should remain visible or at least accessible for assessing blood flow and nerve function.

2. To construct the traction splint, place a ski pole, tent pole, or any polelike object a foot longer than the leg against the outside of the leg. Anchor the pole using a well-padded strap over the thigh at the hip.

3. Apply traction on the thigh by pulling the traction straps. Maintain traction by securing the traction straps to the end of the pole. Tie the traction splint to the leg splint.

Knee. Most knee injuries can be wrapped with an Ace bandage, taped, or stabilized with a foamlite splint in such a way that the patient can walk out without further damage. A grossly unstable knee with major ligament rupture is accompanied by severe pain, inability to move the joint or bear weight, swelling, and obvious deformity. This injury requires a simple splint and a litter evacuation. In some cases, it may be difficult to tell if the femur, the tibia, or the knee is injured. Assume the worst and splint the femur.

Lower Leg. The lower ends of the tibia and fibula are the prominent knobs on the sides of the ankle. The thin layers of skin over the tibia make open fractures common. Splint both the knee and the ankle in a roll of foamlite.

TRACTION

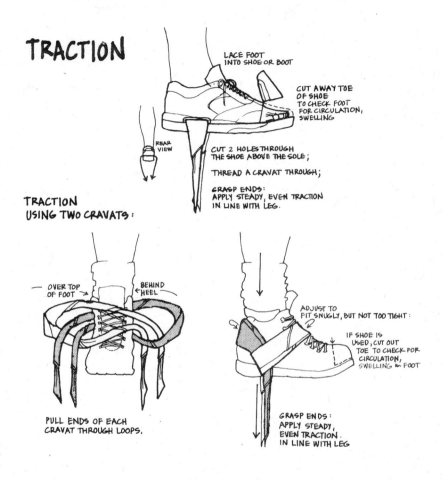

LACE FOOT
INTO SHOE OR BOOT

CUT AWAY TOE
OF SHOE
TO CHECK FOOT
FOR CIRCULATION,
SWELLING

REAR
VIEW

CUT 2 HOLES THROUGH
THE SHOE ABOVE THE SOLE;

THREAD A CRAVAT THROUGH;

GRASP ENDS:
APPLY STEADY, EVEN TRACTION
IN LINE WITH LEG.

TRACTION USING TWO CRAVATS:

— OVER TOP
OF FOOT

BEHIND
HEEL

PULL ENDS OF EACH
CRAVAT THROUGH LOOPS.

ADJUST TO
FIT SNUGLY, BUT NOT TOO TIGHT:

IF SHOE IS
USED, CUT OUT
TOE TO CHECK FOR
CIRCULATION,
SWELLING IN FOOT

GRASP ENDS:
APPLY STEADY,
EVEN TRACTION.
IN LINE WITH LEG

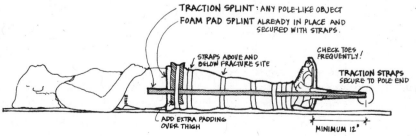

TRACTION SPLINT: ANY POLE-LIKE OBJECT
FOAM PAD SPLINT ALREADY IN PLACE AND
SECURED WITH STRAPS.

STRAPS ABOVE AND
BELOW FRACTURE SITE

CHECK TOES
FREQUENTLY!

TRACTION STRAPS
SECURE TO POLE END

ADD EXTRA PADDING
OVER THIGH

MINIMUM 12"

SIMPLE LEG SPLINT

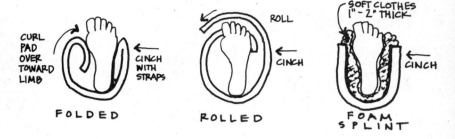

CURL PAD OVER TOWARD LIMB

CINCH WITH STRAPS

FOLDED

ROLL

CINCH

ROLLED

SOFT CLOTHES 1" – 2" THICK

CINCH

FOAM SPLINT

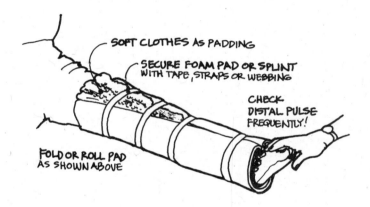

SOFT CLOTHES AS PADDING

SECURE FOAM PAD OR SPLINT WITH TAPE, STRAPS OR WEBBING

CHECK DISTAL PULSE FREQUENTLY!

FOLD OR ROLL PAD AS SHOWN ABOVE

Ankle. It can be difficult to differentiate between a fracture and a sprain to the ankle. The injury can be immobilized with a stirrup of foamlite and wrapped with clothing for insulation and padding. Knee and ankle injuries are also addressed in chapter 6 ("Athletic Injuries").

FINAL THOUGHTS
In NOLS's experience, fractures and dislocations are not common in wilderness activities, but they do occur, and the first responder should be prepared. A careful assessment, traction-in-line, immobilization, and RICE are the cornerstones of our treatment. Most of us, conscious of weight and bulk when we travel in the wilderness, don't carry prepared commercial

splints. We know that we can create what we need from materials at hand such as clothing, sleeping pads, packs, stays, tent poles, bandannas, and natural materials such as sticks. Practice improvising splints from the material you commonly have with you in the wilderness.

Evacuation Guidelines

- Evacuate all musculoskeletal injuries showing loss of function, unreducible dislocations, and any first time dislocation.
- Rapidly evacuate all open fractures and any musculoskeletal injury with altered CSM.

CHAPTER 6

ATHLETIC INJURIES

INTRODUCTION

Living and traveling in the wilderness, carrying a pack, hiking long distances, climbing, and paddling can all cause sprains, strains, and tendinitis. Athletic injuries account for 50 percent of injuries on NOLS courses and are a frequent cause of evacuations.

Sprains, or injuries to ligaments, are categorized as grades one, two, or three. With a grade one injury, ligament fibers are stretched but not torn. A partly torn or badly stretched ligament is a grade two injury. Completely torn ligaments are grade three injuries. Strains are injuries to muscles and tendons. A muscle stretched too far is commonly referred to as a "pull." A muscle or tendon with torn fibers is a "tear." A tendon irritated from overuse can become a tendinitis.

When faced with an athletic injury, the first responder in the wilderness has to choose between treating the injury in the field—possibly altering the expedition route and timetable to accommodate the patient's loss of mobility—or evacuation.

We don't try to diagnose the injury or grade the sprain or the strain. We decide if an injury is usable or not. If usable, we use RICE therapy and may tape for support. If unusable, we immobilize and evacuate.

The most common athletic injuries on NOLS courses are ankle and knee sprains, Achilles tendinitis, and forearm tendinitis. Most of the athletic injuries we experience are minor,

---

Common Causes of Athletic Injury on NOLS Courses

- Playing games such as hug tag and hacky sack.
- Tripping while walking in camp.
- Stepping over logs.
- Crossing streams, including shallow rock hops.
- Putting on a backpack.
- Lifting a kayak or raft.
- Falling or misstepping while hiking with a pack (on any terrain).
- Falling while skiing with a pack.
- Shoveling snow.
- Bending over to pick up firewood.

---

but even a moderate ankle sprain can take a week to heal. It is difficult to rest for 7 days without affecting a wilderness trip.

GENERAL TREATMENT FOR ATHLETIC INJURIES (RICE)

Athletic injuries are generally treated with RICE: rest, ice, compression, and elevation. Allowing these injuries to heal until they are free of pain, tenderness, and swelling prevents aggravation of the condition. Gently rub the injured area with ice, wrapped in fabric to prevent frostbite, for 20 to 40 minutes every 2 to 4 hours for the first 24 to 48 hours, then allow it to passively warm. (These times are guidelines, not absolutes.) Cooling is thought to decrease nerve conduction and pain, constrict blood vessels, limit the inflammatory process, and reduce cellular demand for oxygen.

Compression with an Ace bandage helps reduce swelling. Care must be taken when applying the wrap not to exert pressure on an injury that swells dramatically or to cut off blood flow to the fingers or toes.

General Treatment for Athletic Injuries (RICE)

- **R**est: allows time for healing.
- **I**ce: 20 to 40 minutes every 2 to 4 hours for 24 to 48 hours.
- **C**ompression: elastic bandage to reduce swelling.
- **E**levation: reduces swelling.

Elevating the injury above the level of the heart reduces swelling. Nonprescription pain medications such as acetaminophen and ibuprofen may help as well.

Assessment for Athletic Injuries

A thorough assessment includes an evaluation of the mechanism of injury, as well as the signs and symptoms. Knowing the mechanism helps you determine whether the occurrence was sudden and traumatic, indicating a sprain, or whether it was progressive, suggesting an overuse injury.

Signs and symptoms of a sprain include swelling, pain, and discoloration. Point tenderness and obvious deformity suggest a fracture. Ask the patient to try to move the joint through its full range of motion. Painless movement is a good sign. If the patient is able to use or bear weight on the affected limb, and pain and swelling are not severe, he or she may be treated in the field.

Severe pain, the sound of a pop at the time of injury, immediate swelling, and inability to use the joint are signs of a serious sprain, possibly a fracture. This injury should be immobilized and the patient evacuated from the field.

Signs and Symptoms of Sprains

- Swelling and discoloration
- Pain or tenderness
- Instability and/or loss of range of motion
- Inability to bear weight

Ankle Sprains

Uneven ground, whether boulder fields in the backcountry or broken pavement in the city, contributes to the likelihood of ankle sprains. Of all ankle sprains, 85 percent are inversion injuries—those in which the foot turns in to the midline of the body and the ankle turns outward. Inversion injuries usually sprain one or more of the ligaments on the outside of the ankle.

Ankle Anatomy. The bones, ligaments, and tendons of the ankle and foot absorb stress and pressure generated by both body weight and activity. They also allow for flexibility and

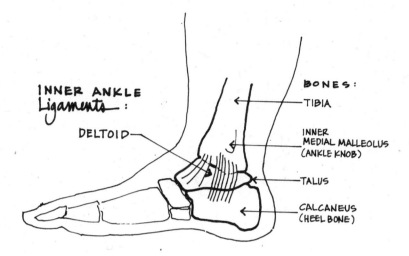

INNER ANKLE
Ligaments :

DELTOID—

BONES:

TIBIA

INNER
MEDIAL MALLEOLUS
(ANKLE KNOB)

TALUS

CALCANEUS
(HEEL BONE)

accommodate surface irregularities so that we don't lose our balance.

Bones. The lower leg bones are the tibia and the fibula. The large bumps on either side of the ankle are the lower ends of these bones—the fibula on the outside, and the tibia on the inside. Immediately under the tibia and fibula lies the talus bone, which sits atop the calcaneus (heel bone). The talus and calcaneus act as a rocker for front-to-back flexibility of the ankle. Without them, we would walk stiff-legged.

In front of the calcaneus lie two smaller bones, the navicular (inside) and the cuboid (outside). They attach to three small bones called the cuneiforms. Anterior to the cuneiforms are five metatarsals, which in turn articulate with the phalanges (toe bones).

Ligaments. Due to the number of bones in the foot, ligaments are many and complex. For simplicity, think of there being a ligament on every exterior surface of every bone, attaching to the adjacent articulating bone.

There are four ligaments commonly associated with ankle sprains. On the inside of the ankle is the large, fan-shaped deltoid ligament joining the talus, calcaneus, and several of the smaller foot bones to the tibia. Rolling the ankle inward, an

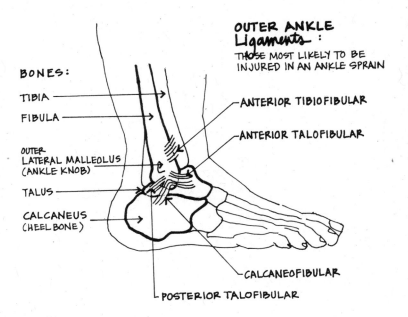

OUTER ANKLE
Ligaments :
THOSE MOST LIKELY TO BE
INJURED IN AN ANKLE SPRAIN

BONES:

TIBIA

FIBULA

OUTER
LATERAL MALLEOLUS
(ANKLE KNOB)

TALUS

CALCANEUS
(HEEL BONE)

ANTERIOR TIBIOFIBULAR

ANTERIOR TALOFIBULAR

CALCANEOFIBULAR

POSTERIOR TALOFIBULAR

eversion sprain, stresses the deltoid ligament. Spraining the deltoid requires considerable force, and due to its size and strength, it is seldom injured. In fact, this ligament is so strong that if a bad twist occurs, it frequently pulls fragments of bone off at its attachment points, causing an avulsion fracture.

On the outside, usually the weaker aspect, three ligaments attach from the fibula to the talus and the calcaneus. Together these three ligaments protect the ankle from turning to the outside.

Muscles and Tendons. Muscles in the lower leg use long tendons to act on the ankle and foot. The calf muscles—the gastrocnemius and soleus—shorten to point the toes. These muscles taper into the largest tendon, the Achilles, which attaches to the back of the calcaneus. The peroneal muscles in the lower leg contract and pull the foot laterally and roll the ankle outward. Muscles in the front of the lower leg turn the foot inward and extend the toes.

Treatment of Ankle Sprains. Sprains should have the standard treatment of rest, ice, compression, and elevation to limit

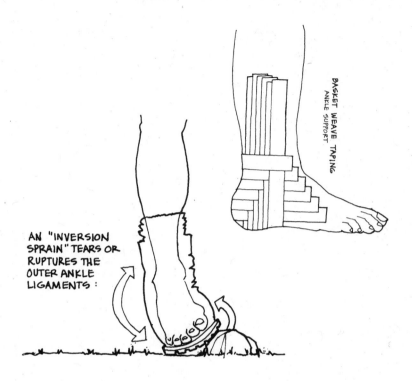

AN "INVERSION SPRAIN" TEARS OR RUPTURES THE OUTER ANKLE LIGAMENTS :

BASKET WEAVE TAPING ANKLE SUPPORT

swelling and allow healing. If a severe sprain or a fracture is suspected, immobilize the ankle. Aggressively treating a mild sprain with RICE for the first 24 to 48 hours and letting it rest for a few days may allow a patient to stay in the mountains rather than cut the trip short. A simple method for providing ankle support is to tape the ankle using the basket weave.

Treatment of Ankle Sprains
• RICE
• Taping for support

Knee Pain
Pain in the knee from overuse can be treated by ceasing the activity causing the discomfort and controlling pain and inflammation with RICE. In the event of a traumatic injury resulting in an unstable knee, splint and evacuate. If the injury is stable and the patient can bear weight, use RICE to control pain

and inflammation. If the patient can walk without undue pain, wrap the knee with foamlite for support.

TENDINITIS

A tendon is the fibrous cord by which a muscle is attached to a bone. Its construction is similar to that of kernmantle rope, with an outer sheath of tissue enclosing a core of fibers. Some tendons, such as those to the fingers, are long. The activating muscles are in the forearm, but the tendons stretch from the forearm across the wrist to each finger. These tendons are surrounded by a lubricating sheath to assist their movement.

Tendinitis is inflammation of a tendon. When the sheath and the tendon become inflamed, the sheath becomes rough, movement is restricted and painful, and the patient feels a grating of the tendon inside the sheath. Fibers can be torn or, more commonly, irritation from overuse or infection can inflame the sheath, causing pain when the tendon moves. There may be little pain when the tendon is at rest.

Tendons are poorly supplied with blood, so they heal slowly. Tendons are well supplied with nerves, however, which means that an injury will be painful. Tendons can be injured by sudden overloading, but are more frequently injured through overuse. Factors contributing to tendinitis include poor technique, poor equipment, unhealed prior injury, and cool and tight muscles.

Assessment for Tendinitis

Tendinitis, in contrast to ankle sprains, is a progressive overuse injury, not a traumatic injury. Common sites for tendinitis are the Achilles tendon and the tendons of the forearm. The Achilles, the largest tendon in the body, may fatigue and become inflamed during or following lengthy hikes, especially with significant elevation gain. Boots that break down and place pressure on the tendon can provide enough irritation in one day to initiate inflammation.

Forearm tendinitis is common among canoeists and kayakers. Poor technique and inadequate strength and flexibility contribute to the injury. Similar tendinitis comes with repetitive use of ski poles, ice axes, and ice climbing tools.

Tendinitis may also occur on the front of the foot, usually caused by tightly laced boots or stiff mountaineering boots. The tendons extending the toes become irritated and inflamed. Tendinitis causes swelling, redness, warmth, pain to the touch (or pinch), painful movement, and sounds of friction or grinding (crepitus).

Signs and Symptoms of Tendinitis
• Redness
• Warmth
• Crepitus
• Localized pain

Treatment of Tendinitis

Treat tendinitis with RICE: rest, ice, compression, and elevation. It may be necessary to cease the aggravating activity until the inflammation subsides. Prevent or ease tendinitis of anterior muscles by varying boot lacing. Lace boots more loosely when hiking and more tightly when climbing.

Achilles Tendinitis. To relieve stretch on the Achilles tendon, provide a heel lift. To relieve direct pressure from the boot, place a 6-inch by 1-inch strip of foamlite padding on either side of the Achilles tendon. The placement should take the pressure off without touching the Achilles.

Treatment of Achilles Tendinitis
• RICE
• Heel lifts
• Pads on ankle to protect the tendon

Forearm Tendinitis. Forearm tendinitis is primarily associated with the repetitive motion of paddling. Pay close attention to proper paddling technique. Keep a relaxed, open grip on the paddle. On the forward stroke, keep the wrist in line with the forearm during the pull and push, and avoid crossing the upper arm over the midline of the body.

Other paddling techniques that may help prevent forearm tendinitis include keeping the thumb on the same side of the paddle as the fingers and switching a feathered paddle

Treatment of Forearm Tendinitis
• RICE
• Taping wrist to limit range of motion

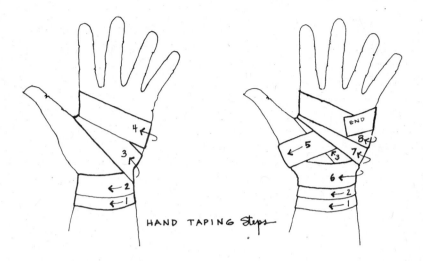

HAND TAPING Steps

for an unfeathered paddle. The feathered paddle requires a wrist movement that can sometimes aggravate tendinitis.

Tendinitis of the forearm is treated with RICE. Also, the wrist can be taped to limit movement that aggravates the condition.

MUSCLE STRAINS

Muscles can be stretched and torn from overuse or overexertion. Initial treatment is RICE, followed by heat, massage, and gentle stretching. Radiating muscle pain, strong pain at rest, pain secondary to an illness, or pain from a severe trauma mechanism is a reason to evacuate the patient for evaluation by a physician.

FINAL THOUGHTS

Errors in technique and inadequate muscular conditioning or warm-up produce injury. Overuse of muscles and joints (when there is no single traumatic event as the cause of injury) generates many of the sprains and strains on NOLS courses.

Jerky movements, excessive force, or an unnecessarily tight grip on the paddle while kayaking contribute to forearm tendinitis. Performing the athletic movements required for difficult rock climbs without warming up or paying attention to balance and form can cause injury. Even the seemingly simple actions of lifting a backpack or boat, stepping over logs, and wading in cold mountain streams can be dangerous.

Steep terrain and wet conditions contribute to injuries. Slippery conditions make it harder to balance and can cause falls. Falls that occur in camp and while hiking are the cause of many athletic injuries. Surprisingly, injuries are just as likely to occur when backcountry travelers are wearing packs as when they are not. Possibly this is because people are more attentive to technique when hiking or skiing with a pack.

You are more likely to be injured when you are tired, cold, dehydrated, rushed, or ill. You're not thinking as clearly, and your muscles are less flexible and responsive. Injuries happen more frequently in late morning and late afternoon, when dehydration and fatigue reduce awareness and increase clumsiness. Shifting from a three-meal-a-day schedule to breakfast and dinner plus three or four light snacks during the day helps keep your food supply constant.

Haste, often the result of unrealistic timetables, is frequently implicated in accidents. Try to negotiate the more difficult terrain in the morning, when you are fresh. Take rest breaks before difficult sections of a hike or paddle. Stop at the base of the pass, the near side of the river, or the beginning of the boulder field. Drink, eat, and stretch tight muscles. Check equipment for loose gaiters that may trip you and for poorly balanced backpacks.

The sustained activity of life in the wilderness and the need for sudden bursts of power when paddling, skiing, or climbing necessitate physical conditioning prior to a wilderness expedition. A regimen of endurance, flexibility, and muscle strength training will help prevent injuries and promote safety and enjoyment of wilderness activity.

Evacuation Guidelines

- Evacuation decisions on athletic injuries are usually based on practical considerations—continued pain, an injury that does not heal, or inability to travel.

CHAPTER 7

SOFT TISSUE INJURIES

INTRODUCTION

Outside the wilderness, we give little thought to the consequences of soft tissue injuries. Our lives are not disrupted by small wounds, and infection is an unusual aftermath. On NOLS courses, however, backcountry travelers take falls while carrying packs and experience lacerations while preparing meals or walking or swimming barefoot. On an expedition, even relatively minor injuries can have serious consequences. Cut or blistered feet can result in litter evacuations, and hand wounds can end climbing trips. Infection is a real and ever-present risk.

Responding with the proper first aid is essential to expedition members' health and safety. Soft tissue wounds are 30 percent of injuries on NOLS courses, but only a small number of these become infected. In addition to controlling bleeding, first aid for soft tissue injuries in the wilderness includes cleaning the wound, monitoring for signs of infection, and making decisions about when to evacuate.

SKIN

The skin is the single largest organ of the body. It protects the internal organs by providing a watertight shell that keeps fluids in and bacteria out. The skin helps regulate body temperature by providing a means of heat dissipation. Sweat glands produce sweat, which evaporates, cooling the body. Nerves near

LAYERS OF THE SKIN:

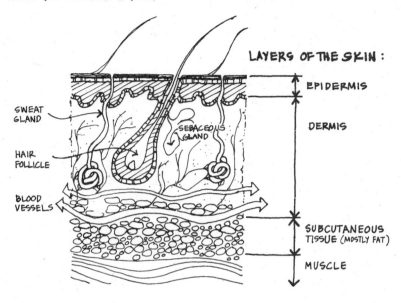

SWEAT GLAND

SEBACEOUS GLAND

HAIR FOLLICLE

BLOOD VESSELS

LAYERS OF THE SKIN:

EPIDERMIS

DERMIS

SUBCUTANEOUS TISSUE (MOSTLY FAT)

MUSCLE

the skin's surface send messages to the brain about heat, cold, pressure, pain, and body position.

The skin is composed of three layers. The innermost layer is subcutaneous tissue, which consists mostly of fat. This layer is an insulator for the body and a reservoir for energy. Beneath the subcutaneous tissue lies muscle.

The second layer is the dermis, which contains sweat glands, sebaceous glands, hair follicles, nerves, and blood vessels. Sweat glands are found on all body surfaces, with most on the palms of the hands and soles of the feet. Sweat glands secrete .5 to 1 liter of sweat per day, and can produce up to 1 liter per hour during strenuous exercise. The sebaceous glands produce sebum (oil) and lie next to the hair follicles. Sebum waterproofs the skin and keeps the hair supple. Blood vessels in the dermis provide nutrients and oxygen to each cell and remove waste products such as carbon dioxide.

The outermost layer of the skin is the epidermis. The epidermis is made up primarily of dead cells held together by sebum. These dead cells continually slough off and are replaced by more dead cells.

Soft tissue injuries are classified as open or closed. With closed injuries, the skin remains intact; open injuries involve a break in the skin's surface.

CLOSED WOUNDS

Closed injuries include contusions (bruises) and hematomas. With both, the tissue and blood vessels beneath the epidermis are damaged. Swelling and discoloration occur because blood and plasma leak out of the damaged blood vessels. With contusions, blood is dispersed within the tissues. Hematomas contain a pool of blood—as much as a pint surrounding a major bone fracture. Depending on the amount of blood dispersed, reabsorption can take from 12 hours to several days. In some cases, the blood may have to be drained by a physician to enhance healing.

Treatment for Closed Wounds

A memory aid for treating closed injuries is RICE: rest, ice, compression, and elevation.

Rest. Rest decreases bleeding by allowing clots to form. In the event of a large or deep bruise, extremities can be splinted to decrease motion that may cause newly-formed clots to break away and bleeding to continue. See chapter 5 ("Fractures and Dislocations").

Ice. Ice causes the blood vessels to constrict, decreasing bleeding. Never apply ice directly to bare skin, as this can cause frostbite. Instead, wrap the ice in fabric of a towel-like thickness

---

Treatment for Closed Injuries: RICE

- Rest.
- Ice 20 to 40 minutes every 2 to 4 hours.
- Compression to reduce swelling and bleeding.
- Elevate above heart level.

before applying to the skin. Ice the wound for 20 to 40 minutes every 2 to 4 hours for the first 24 to 48 hours, then allow the area to passively warm.

Compression. Apply manual pressure or a pressure dressing. When applying a pressure dressing, wrap it snugly enough to stop bleeding but not so tightly that the blood supply is shut off. Check by feeling for a pulse distal to the injured site.

Elevation. Elevate the injury above the level of the heart. Elevation reduces bleeding and swelling by decreasing the blood flow to the injury.

OPEN WOUNDS

Open injuries include abrasions, lacerations, puncture wounds, and major traumatic injuries—avulsions, amputations, and crushing wounds.

Abrasions. Abrasions occur when the epidermis and part of the dermis are rubbed off. These injuries are commonly called "road rash" or "rug burns." They usually bleed very little but are painful and may be contaminated with debris.

Abrasions heal more quickly if treated with ointment and covered with a semiocclusive or occlusive dressing.

Lacerations. Lacerations are cuts produced by sharp objects. The cut may penetrate all the layers of the skin, and the edges may be straight or jagged. If long and deep enough to cause the skin to gap more than $1/2$ inch (1 cm), lacerations may require sutures. Sutures, a task for a physician, are also indicated if the cut is on the face or hands or over a joint, or if it severs a tendon, ligament, or blood vessel. Tendons and ligaments must be sutured together to heal properly. Lacerations on the hands or over a joint may be sutured to prevent the wound from being continually pulled apart by movement. Lacerations on the face are usually sutured to decrease scarring.

Puncture Wounds. Puncture wounds are caused by pointed objects. Although the skin around a puncture wound remains closed and there is little external bleeding, the object may have penetrated an artery or organ, causing internal bleeding.

OPEN INJURIES

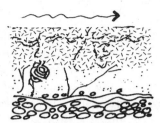

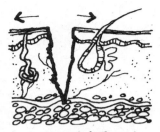

ABRASION
EPIDERMIS / DERMIS
RUBBED OFF.

LACERATION
CUTS PRODUCED BY
SHARP OBJECTS.
EDGES CAN BE CLEAN
OR RAGGED.

AVULSION
THE TEARING OFF OF A
FLAP OF SKIN OR ENTIRE
LIMB.

PUNCTURE
POINTED OBJECT
PENETRATES SKIN AND
POSSIBLY AN UNDERLYING
ORGAN OR ARTERY.

If an impaled object is through the cheek and causing an airway obstruction, it must be removed to allow the patient to breathe. Otherwise, leave impalement in place. Removing the object may cause more soft tissue injury and increase bleeding by releasing pressure on compressed blood vessels. Stabilize and prevent movement of impaled objects with protective padding. Some people argue for removal of impaled objects in situations of long or difficult transportation. This advice usually applies to objects in the extremities, not those in the chest, head, abdomen, or eye. Check with your physician advisor for guidance on this question.

Tetanus is a rare but serious complication. Although tetanus may be more likely to occur in a farm or ranch environment than on a "clean" mountainside, it is a good idea to make sure your tetanus booster is up-to-date before you take off into the backcountry. Tetanus boosters should be given at least every 10 years.

Major Traumatic Injuries. Major traumatic injuries include avulsions, amputations, and crushing injuries.

Avulsion. An avulsion is a "tearing off" that can range in severity from a small skin flap to the near amputation of an entire limb. Skin tends to separate along anatomical planes, such as between subcutaneous tissue and muscle.

To treat a small to moderate-sized avulsion, clean the skin flap and reposition it over the wound. Apply small strips of tape or butterfly bandages to the edges, leaving a space between each strip so the wound can drain. If the area avulsed is larger than 2 inches in diameter, a skin graft may be required for the wound to heal properly.

Amputation. Amputation is the complete severance of a part or extremity. Bleeding may be profuse or relatively light. If blood vessels are partially torn, they cannot constrict, and bleeding may be massive. In contrast, the stump of a cleanly severed extremity may not bleed profusely because the severed blood vessels respond by retracting and constricting. If elevation and direct pressure do not stop the stump from bleeding, a tourniquet may be necessary.

After treating the patient, rinse the amputated body part with clean water; wrap it in moist, sterile gauze; and place it in a plastic bag. Then place the bag in cold water or on ice. Do not bury the part in ice, as this may cause cold injury. Make certain that the wrapped part accompanies the patient to the hospital. Reattachment may be possible if you can get to a hospital quickly.

Crushing Injuries. Crushing injuries can cause extensive damage to underlying tissue and bones, and large areas may be lacerated and avulsed. Always consider what underlying body parts may be damaged, and always conduct a focused exam to find out if any bones have been fractured or if an internal organ has been crushed.

Treatment for Open Wounds

The principles for treating open wounds are to control bleeding, clean and dress the wound, and monitor for infection.

Control Bleeding. Controlling bleeding is the first priority when treating open wounds. Death can come quickly to a patient with a tear in a major blood vessel. There are four methods for controlling bleeding. The most effective—direct pressure and elevation—will stop most bleeding when used in combination. Pressure points and tourniquets are also used.

Controlling Bleeding

- Direct pressure
- Elevation
- Pressure dressings
- Pressure points
- Tourniquets

Direct Pressure. The best method for controlling bleeding is to apply pressure over the wound site. Using your hand and a piece of wadded fabric—preferably sterile gauze—apply direct pressure to the wound. Be sure to wear rubber or latex gloves or place your hand in a plastic bag. If the wound is large, you may need to pack the open area with gauze before applying pressure. Maintain pressure for 5 minutes, then slowly release. If the bleeding resumes, apply pressure for 15 minutes. If a dressing becomes soaked with blood, leave it in place and apply additional dressings. Removing the dressing disturbs the blood clots that are forming.

Elevation. As with closed injuries, the combination of splinting, a pressure dressing, and elevation will help decrease the bleeding. Direct pressure and elevation control almost all bleeding. In fact, it is unusual for a wound to require the first responder to utilize pressure points or a tourniquet.

Pressure Dressings. A bulky dressing, firmly secured with roller gauze, Ace wrap, or a strip of cloth or cravat can provide pressure on the wound and free your hands for other tasks. Check the CSMs to make sure you have not inadvertantly made a tourniquet.

Tourniquets. Tourniquets are rarely needed outside a combat situation. Apply a tourniquet only as a last resort, when no other method will stop the bleeding. Tourniquets completely stop the blood flow and are intended to save the life at the risk of the limb. If the tourniquet is left on for more than a few hours, there is a chance that the tissue distal to the tourniquet will be damaged.

Clean the Wound. Consider any wound, even a minor finger cut or a blister, as potentially infected. On wilderness expeditions wound cleaning is a priority. When you clean a wound, eliminate as much potentially infectious bacteria and debris as possible without further damaging the skin.

Wash Your Hands and Put on Gloves. Wash your hands. Use soap and water to prevent contamination of the wound. Put on rubber or latex gloves.

Scrub and Irrigate the Wound. Scrub the skin around the wound, being careful not to flush debris into the wound. Clip long hair, but don't shave the skin. Then irrigate an open wound for at least 3 minutes with water that has been disinfected with chlorination or iodination, filtering, or water that has been boiled and cooled. Many wounds can be cleaned simply by irrigating with clean water. If the wound is obviously dirty or contaminated, a 1 percent povidone-iodine (usually one part 10 percent povidone-iodine diluted with 10 parts water to approximate the color of dark tea) is a suitable irrigation solution. Medical science tells us that the volume of water is the most important factor in cleaning the wound. At NOLS, we carry 35cc syringes in the first aid kit for pressure-irrigating wounds. Remove large pieces of debris with tweezers that have been boiled or cleaned with povidone-iodine.

Rinse with Disinfected Water. After cleaning the wound, rinse off the solution with liberal amounts of disinfected water. See

How to Apply a Tourniquet

1. Once you've determined that a tourniquet is necessary, apply it as close to the injury as possible, between the wound and the heart. Use a bandage that is 3 to 4 inches wide and 6 to 8 layers thick. Never use wire, rope, or any material that will cut the skin.

2. Wrap the bandage snugly around the extremity several times, then tie an overhand knot.

3. Place a small stick or similar object on the knot, and tie another overhand knot over the stick.

4. Twist the stick until the bandage becomes tight enough to stop the bleeding. Tie the ends of the bandage around the extremity to keep the twists from unraveling.

5. Using a pen, write "TK" on the patient's forehead and the time the tourniquet was applied. Once it is in place, do not remove the tourniquet. It should remain in place until the patient arrives at the emergency room.

6. There are ongoing arguments about tourniquet release in wilderness medicine. Definitive statements are likely to remain elusive. Check with your physician advisor about this issue.

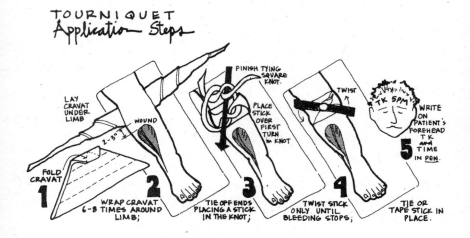

TOURNIQUET Application Steps

LAY CRAVAT UNDER LIMB
WOUND
2-3"
FOLD CRAVAT

1 WRAP CRAVAT 6-8 TIMES AROUND LIMB;

FINISH TYING SQUARE KNOT.
PLACE STICK OVER FIRST TURN in KNOT

2

3 TIE OFF ENDS PLACING A STICK IN THE KNOT;

TWIST

4 TWIST STICK ONLY UNTIL BLEEDING STOPS;

TK 5PM
WRITE ON PATIENT'S FOREHEAD T K AND TIME IN PEN.

5 TIE OR TAPE STICK IN PLACE.

chapter 21 ("Water Disinfection and Hygiene"). Check for further bleeding—you may need to apply direct pressure again if blood clots were broken loose during the cleaning process.

Dress and Bandage the Wound. Dressings are sterile gauze placed directly over the wound; bandages hold the dressing in place. Both come in many shapes and sizes. Semiocclusive (Telfa) or occlusive (Second Skin, Opsite, Tegaderm) dressings promote healing by keeping the area moist. Ointments (such as Polysporin or Bacitracin) serve the same purpose. Dry dressings that adhere to the wound impede the healing process.

Next, apply an antibiotic ointment. The ointment should be applied to the dressing rather than directly to the wound. Apply the bandage neatly and in such a way that blood flow distal to the injured area is not impaired. After applying the bandage, check CSMs distal to the injury.

Do not close wound edges until the wound has been thoroughly cleaned. Generally, the edges of a small wound will

Cleaning Wounds

- Wash your hands with soap and water.
- Put on rubber or latex gloves.
- Scrub and irrigate the wound.
  —Scrub the area around the wound.
  —Use sterilized tweezers to remove debris.
  —Use pressure irrigation.
- Rinse thoroughly with disinfected water.
- Dress and bandage the wound.
- Check circulation, sensation, and movement.

come together on their own. If the skin is stretched apart, butterfly bandages or Steri-strips can hold the edges together. If the injury is over a joint, the extremity may require splinting to prevent the edges from pulling apart. Highly contaminated wounds should be packed open.

Physicians don't agree on how long a wound can be kept open until it is stitched. A wound that will not close on its own or with a bandage can usually be stitched even a day or two later. The need to use sutures to close a wound does not, by itself, create an emergency. Reasons to expedite an evacuation for an open wound include obvious dirt or contamination; animal bites; wounds that open joint spaces; established infection; wounds from a crushing mechanism; any laceration to a cosmetic area, especially the face; wounds with a lot of dead tissue on the edges or in the wound itself; and wounds that obviously need surgical care, such as open fractures and very deep, gaping lacerations.

Animal bites are a concern for infection because of the bacterial flora in animal mouths and the crushing, penetrating, and tearing mechanism of the wounds. In North America, wild animal attacks, while dramatic and often highlighted in the press, are unusual. Worldwide they are believed to be more common, but the evidence is anecdotal, not scientific.

After the Bandage Is Applied. Check circulation, sensation, and movement of the body part distal to the injury. Can the patient tell you where you are touching? Can he or she flex and extend the extremity? Is the area distal to the injury pink and warm, indicating good blood perfusion? Any negative answers to these questions may indicate nerve, artery, or tendon damage that will require evacuating the patient.

Dressings should be changed daily and the injured area checked for signs of infection.

Infection

The newspapers and television media occasionally tell dramatic tales of aggressive and resistant wound infections and "flesh-eating bacteria." But on a daily basis outside the wilderness, we give little thought to the potential for wounds to be contaminated and colonized by bacteria. Before modern medicine understood infection and practiced clean wound care, infections were common and dangerous. In some environments, such as the tropics, they remain quite common and serious. In the wilderness we have less than ideal circumstances for cleaning wounds, but our efforts are essential in preventing wound infection.

Signs and Symptoms of Infections

MILD/MODERATE INFECTIONS
• Redness and swelling
• Pus, heat, pain

SERIOUS INFECTIONS
• Red streaks radiating from the wound
• Fever and chills
• Swollen lymph nodes

KEY POINTS
• A very high level of suspicion for infection needs to be maintained for any soft tissue problem.
• Any area of redness should be watched closely during the first 18 to 36 hours.
• Always think, "Is this an infection?"
• Oral antibiotics should be started early.
• Additional measures including applied heat and elevation / immobilization are important.

Assessment for Infection. Redness, swelling, pus, heat, and pain at the site; faint red streaks radiating from the site; fever; chills; and swollen lymph nodes are all signs of infection.

It may be difficult to decide if local swelling, without an obvious wound, is due to a muscle strain, bug bite, or infection. The possibility of a deep infection is a concern. History may help rule out the muscle strain.

The four cardinal signs of a soft tissue infection are: redness, swelling, warmth, and local pain. The progression in a wound to increased pain, warmth, increased soft tissue swelling, and expansion of redness over 18 to 24 hours suggests infection. Drawing a circle around the swollen area with a pen will help you determine if the infection is spreading or resolving.

Treatment of Infection. An infection that is localized to the

Treatment for Infected Wounds

• Soak in warm antiseptic solution.
• Pull wound edges apart and clean wound.

site of the injury can be treated in the field. If the edges of the wound are closed, pull them apart and soak the area in warm antiseptic solution or warm water for 20 to 30 minutes three to four times a day. If the infection starts to spread—as evidenced by fever, chills, swollen lymph nodes, or faint red streaks radiating from the site—or if the wound cannot be opened to drain, evacuate the patient. If you have oral antibiotics and a protocol for their use, start them early in suspected wound infections.

Blisters

Blisters—a common backcountry occurrence—can be debilitating. Blisters are caused by friction and occur in areas where the epidermis is thick and tough enough to resist abrasion. At first there is a red, sore area called a "hot spot." If the friction continues, the epidermis separates and fluid enters the space, causing a blister.

The First Step: Prevention. Prevent blisters by making sure boots fit properly, wearing two pairs of socks to decrease friction on the skin, checking feet frequently at rest breaks, and stopping at the first sign of rubbing. Apply a solid piece of moleskin or athletic tape to areas that you suspect may cause problems.

Hot Spots. Cut a doughnut-shaped piece of moleskin and center it over the hot spot as a buffer against further rubbing.

Small Blisters. If a small blister has already developed, cut a doughnut-shaped piece of molefoam and center it over the blister. The doughnut "hole" prevents the adhesive from sticking to the tender blister and ripping it away when the molefoam is changed.

Larger Blisters. If the blister is nickel-sized or larger, drain it. Begin by carefully washing your hands and putting on rubber or latex gloves. Clean the area around the blister to decrease the risk of infection. Use a needle that has been soaked in an antiseptic solution such as povidone-iodine for 3 minutes or has been heated until it glows red, then cooled. Insert the needle at the base of the blister, allowing the fluid to drain from the pinprick. After draining the blister, apply an antibiotic ointment and cover the area with gauze. As with an intact blister, center a doughnut-shaped piece of molefoam over the drained blister and gauze. Follow up by checking the blister every day for signs of infection.

FINAL THOUGHTS

NOLS has had great success in reducing the number of people who need to be evacuated for preventable wound infections by focusing on initial wound cleaning, good dressing and bandaging, and recognition and early intervention for infections. It's these simple skills that are at the core of wilderness medicine.

Evacuation Guidelines

- Evacuate an infection without improvement within 12 to 24 hours, or with signs or symptoms of serious/systemic infection.
- Evacuate any patient with a wound that cannot be closed in the field.
- Rapidly evacuate a wound that: is heavily contaminated, opens a joint space, involves underlying tendons or ligaments, was caused by an animal bite, is on the face, has an impaled/imbedded object, was caused by a crushing mechanism, or shows evidence of serious infection.

CHAPTER 8

BURNS

INTRODUCTION

In the wilderness the obvious mechanisms for a burn are the sun, stoves, lanterns, and fires. Improper stove use has caused stoves to flare or pressure caps to release and flame, burning unwary cooks, but the most common cause of a burn on a NOLS course, other than a sunburn, is a scald from spilled hot water.

Minor burns may be no more than a trivial nuisance, yet they represent a potential site of infection. Burns of joints, feet, hands, face, and genitalia, however, can impair these complex structures. A large burn causes significant loss of fluid and may rapidly cause shock.

TYPES OF BURNS

There are four types of burns: thermal, chemical, radiation, and electrical.

Thermal Burns

Thermal burns are caused by flames, flashes of heat (as in explosions), hot liquids, or contact with hot objects. The degree of associated tissue death depends on the intensity of the heat and the length of exposure. Water at 140°F (59°C) will burn skin in 5 seconds; water at 120°F (48°C) in 5 minutes.

Chemical Burns

Chemical burns are caused by contact with alkalis, acids, or corrosive material. Backcountry chemical burns are rare, but burns from leaking batteries, carbide lamps, or spilled gas are a possibility.

Radiation and Electrical Burns

Electrical burns in the wilderness are caused by lightning. The most common burn in the wilderness is a radiation burn, or sunburn.

ASSESSMENT OF BURNS

The assessment of a burn includes the depth and extent of the injury.

Depth of the Burn

Burns are classified by the depth of the injury as superficial, partial-thickness, and full-thickness.

Superficial. These burns injure only the epidermis. A superficial burn is red and painful and blanches white with pressure. There are no blisters, and the wound can be painful. The area heals in 4 or 5 days with the epidermis peeling.

Partial-Thickness. Deeper burns injure both the epidermis and the dermis and can be painful. The skin appears red, mottled, wet, and blistered and blanches white with pressure. Blisters can develop quickly after the injury or may take as long as 24 hours to form. The burn takes from 5 to 25 days to heal, and longer if it becomes infected.

Full-Thickness. These burns penetrate deep and injure the epidermis, dermis, and subcutaneous tissue. The skin appears leathery, charred, pearl gray, and dry (or white and firm if it's a thermal burn). The area is sunken and has a burned odor. The skin does not blanch and is not painful because blood vessels and nerve endings are destroyed. Painful first- or second-degree burns may surround the third-degree area. Full-thickness burns destroy the dermis and, if large, require skin grafts to heal.

Extent of the Burn: The Rule of Palms

The extent of burns can be determined by the rule of palms. The patient's palm and fingers when held together represents

ASSESSMENT of BURNS:

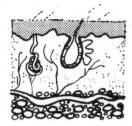

SUPERFICIAL
EPIDERMIS ONLY BURNED
- SKIN RED, PAINFUL

PARTIAL THICKNESS
EPIDERMIS AND DERMIS BURNED
- SKIN BLISTERED (MAY TAKE 24 HOURS +)
- RED, MOTTLED, WET, PAINFUL

FULL THICKNESS
EPIDERMIS, DERMIS AND
SUBCUTANEOUS TISSUE BURNED
- LEATHERY, DRY, CHARRED
- PEARLY GRAY in COLOR

The "RULE OF PALMS"

A PERSON'S PALM REPRESENTS
ROUGHLY 1% OF HIS BODY SURFACE.
USE THIS ESTIMATE TO DETERMINE
THE EXTENT AND SEVERITY OF BURNS.

1 percent of his or her body surface area. Using the palm as a size indicator, estimate the percentage of body area involved.

Location of the Burn
Burns to the face and neck are dangerous due to potential airway problems as well as cosmetic concerns. Burns to the hands and feet are worrisome due to possible loss of function. Burns to the genitals are serious for obvious reasons. Circumferential burns of extremities can produce a constriction that impairs circulation.

TREATMENT FOR THERMAL BURNS
Thermal, electrical, radiation, and chemical burns are all treated essentially the same way. First, the source of the burn must be eliminated. Then, the airway should be checked. The burn itself is cooled, assessed, cleaned, and dressed.

Put Out the Fire. "Stop, drop, and roll" is the sequence to follow if someone catches on fire. Stop the person from running. Make him or her drop to the ground and roll, or roll the person in a sleeping bag or jacket to put out the flames.

Quickly remove the patient's clothing and any jewelry. These retain heat and cause continued burning. Hot water spilled on legs clothed in polypropylene or wool can cause serious burns, as can water spilled into boots, because the boot and sock retain and concentrate the heat.

Check the Airway. Inhalation burns are life-threatening and must be recognized early.

Cool the Burn. Smaller burns can be cooled by pouring cool water (not ice-cold) or applying cool, wet cloths on the burned site. Avoid hypothermia. Never put ice directly on the site, as it may cause frostbite. Ice also causes blood vessels to constrict, which deprives the burned area of blood and thus oxygen and nutrients.

Assess the Depth and Extent of the Burn. Most burns are combinations of partial and superficial injuries. Assess the surface area of each burn type using the rule of palms.

Clean and Dress the Burn. Clean the burn with cool, clean water and apply antibiotic ointment. Embers or smoldering clothing on the surface should be removed; do not attempt to remove melted material from the skin. Dress it with a moist dressing. Keep the dressing moist with disinfected water, change the dressing once a day, and monitor the site for signs of infection. Blisters should be kept intact. If they do rupture, gently wash them with antiseptic soap and water, rinse well, pat dry, apply an antibiotic ointment, and cover with sterile gauze.

TREATMENT FOR INHALATION BURNS

Inhalation burns are caused by breathing hot air or gases and/or particles. The cilia (hairlike structures lining the upper airways) and mucous membranes lining the respiratory tract may be destroyed instantly. The mucous membranes swell, and fluid leaks into the lungs. The body is unable to expel mucus because the cilia are damaged. Mucus collects in the upper airway, decreasing carbon dioxide and oxygen exchange. Oxygenation is impaired when carbon monoxide from burning material competes with oxygen for binding sites on red blood cells.

If you suspect an inhalation burn, check the mouth, nose, and throat for signs of soot, redness, or swelling. Are the facial hairs or nasal hairs singed? Check for signs of respiratory distress, such as coughing or noisy, rapid breaths.

Inhalation burns always require that the patient be evacuated to a medical facility. Signs and symptoms of respiratory distress may not become apparent for 24 to 48 hours.

TREATMENT FOR CHEMICAL BURNS

Flush chemical burns with any available water for a minimum of 20 minutes. Brush off any dry chemical before rinsing the burn. Remove clothing, jewelry, and contact lenses, as these may retain the chemical and continue to burn the victim.

Speed is important. The longer a chemical stays on the body, the more damage it causes. Looking for specific antidotes wastes time. Use plain water to flush, then wash the burn with mild soap and water.

Treatment for Burns

- Remove the source of the burn:
  - —For thermal burns, stop, drop, roll.
  - —For dry chemical burns, brush off dry chemicals.
  - —For wet chemical burns, flush with water for 20 minutes.
- Remove clothing and jewelry.
- Assess the airway.
- Cool the burn.
- Assess the depth and extent of the burn.
- Clean the burn.
- Apply a cool, moist dressing.

Rinse a chemically burned eye with water for at least 20 minutes. After flushing the affected eye, cover it with a moist dressing. After 20 to 30 minutes, remove the dressing. If the patient complains of changes in vision, reapply the dressing and evacuate.

TREATMENT FOR RADIATION BURNS

Most skin damage is caused by short wavelengths of ultraviolet radiation (UVA and UVB). UVB causes more sunburn than UVA, but both wavelengths damage skin. The only known beneficial effect of solar radiation on skin is in the metabolism of vitamin D. Long-term exposure to the sun increases your risk of skin cancer.

Two-thirds of ultraviolet radiation is received during the hours of 10:00 A.M. to 2:00 P.M. At high altitude, the thin atmosphere filters out less ultraviolet radiation, and the skin is damaged more quickly. Snowfields reflect 70 to 85 percent of the ultraviolet radiation. Water reflects 2 percent when the sun is directly overhead, and more when the sun is lower. Grass reflects 1 to 2 percent. Mountaineering at high altitudes, especially on snow, increases the risk of sun-related problems. Clouds filter out infrared heat radiation, and your skin feels cooler, but ultraviolet radiation still passes through and the risk of sun exposure still exists.

Sunburn

People with fair skin, usually blonds and redheads, are suscep-tible to burning. Darker skin contains more of the protective pigment melanin, but does not eliminate the chance of sunburn or provide protection against the cumulative effects of sun exposure.

Unprotected skin can receive superficial or partial-thickness burns from the sun. Fever blisters or cold sores often follow sunburn of the lips. These are herpes simplex (viral) infections and can be quite painful. A patient with extensive sunburn may complain of chills, fever, or headache.

Phototoxic Reactions. A phototoxic reaction is an abnor-mally severe sunburn related to the ingestion of a drug, plant, or chemical or the application of a drug, plant, or chemical to the skin. Certain drugs, such as sulfonamides (Bactrim, Septra), tetracyclines (Vibramycin), oral diabetic agents, and tranquiliz-ers (Thorazine, Compazine, Phenergan, Sparine), increase the skin's sensitivity to sunlight.

Treatment of Sunburned Skin. Cold, wet dressings will re-lieve some of the pain. Aspirin, ibuprofen, or related non-steroidal anti-inflammatory drugs are recommended. Anesthetic sprays and ointments may relieve the pain but increase the risk of a phototoxic reaction.

Prevention with Sunscreens. Exposure to the sun in small doses promotes tanning, which protects the skin from burns. Unfortunately, degenerative changes still occur in the skin, so it is best to use sunscreens or sunblocks and to wear broad-brimmed hats, long-sleeve shirts, and long pants.

Sunscreens are rated by their sun protection factor (SPF). The SPF number is a guideline for the length of time a person wearing the sunscreen can spend in the sun. SPF is based on the minimal "erythemal dose," or the length of time before the exposed skin becomes red. For example, a person without sun-screen may be able to spend 30 minutes safely in the sun.

Applying a sunscreen with an SPF of 10 should allow the same person to spend 10 times as long in the sun, or 300 minutes, before the skin turns red. This system assumes that the sunscreen is not washed off by water or sweat and is used in adequate amounts.

Creams that completely block ultraviolet radiation (zinc oxide, A-Fil, red veterinarian petrolatum) are good for areas that are easily burned, such as the nose, ears, and lips. Use a sunscreen that guards against both UVB and UVA radiation—the label should explain the coverage of the sunscreen. Sunscreens should be applied on cloudy or overcast days as well as on sunny ones. The ultraviolet radiation that penetrates cloud cover is often great enough to burn the skin. Sunscreens work better if applied when the skin is warm and allowed to soak in half an hour before sun exposure. It's a good habit to apply sunscreen well before you are exposed.

Sun Bumps
The itching, red blistered rash we know as "sun bumps" has a real medical name—polymorphous light eruption (PMLE). PMLEs are unusual reactions to light that, as far as can be determined, are not associated with other disease or drugs.

Sunlight in general and UVA specifically is thought of as the causative factor in PMLE, although the overall natural history of the eruption is probably intertwined with skin type, diet, sun exposure, altitude, sensitizing cosmetics, sun cream use, and other factors. It's more common in people from northern climates and affects at least 10 percent of the population (21 percent in Sweden). It's reported 3 to 4 times more in women than men. PMLE typically occurs in spring following ultraviolet radiation exposure reflected from snow. Human skin adapts to UV exposure with time—the hardening phenomenon. This may explain the reduced incidence of PMLE during the summer.

Medical experts say that 30 minutes to several hours of exposure are required to trigger the eruption, which will subside over 1 to 7 days without scarring.

Signs and Symptoms. As the name implies, these eruptions come in different forms. Medically they are described as papules (a raised lesion on the skin) and papulovesicles (small blisters) that can coalesce into plaques and erythema multiforme–like lesions (red or pink raised rash). They can itch miserably and sometimes cause stinging sensations and pain.

Treatment. Short-term management treats symptoms, the prime one being itching. Antihistamines and topical steroid creams are recommended, but really don't work all that well. Unfortunately the reaction seems to run its course, despite our efforts to shorten the discomfort.

Prevention includes wearing protective clothing, using sun block, and ensuring gradual exposure to the sun. We know this does not work for everyone, and the medical literature agrees. There are a variety of drugs that are used for people with recurrent reactions, none of which seen to be particularly effective.

A related condition to PMLE is *phytophotodermatitis* (PPD), a reaction from exposure to certain plants along with subsequent exposure to sunlight.

PPD can occur through ingestion of the plant or, more commonly, through topical contact. Common plants implicated include celery, giant hogweed, parsnip, fennel, parsley, lime, lemon, rue, fig, mustard, scurf pea, and chrysanthemums. Plant oils in perfumes are also implicated in these reactions.

This can look like PMLE with initial burning pain and a raised, red rash, followed by blistering.

Treat mild reactions with cool wet dressings, topical steroid creams, and nonsteroidal anti-inflammatory drugs (NSAIDs). Severe reactions may require systemic steroids.

Snow Blindness

Burning of the cornea and conjunctiva by the sun is called snow blindness. Affected people aren't actually blind, but they're reluctant to open their eyes because of the pain. The eyes feel dry, as if they are full of sand. Moving, blinking, or opening the eyes is painful. The eyes are red and tear excessively. This can

---

Tips for Preventing Sun-Related Injury: Don't Sunburn!

1. Apply sunscreen 30 minutes before going out, and reapply it frequently.
2. Apply sunblock to your lips, nose, and other sensitive areas.
3. Wear a hat with a brim.
4. Wear sunglasses with 100 percent UV protection, even on cloudy days.
5. Minimize sun exposure between 10 A.M. and 2 P.M.
6. Wear a long-sleeve shirt and pants.
7. Examine your skin, and see a physician if you notice a mole changing shape, color, or size or if you have a "sore" that won't heal.

---

happen with as little as an hour exposure to bright sunlight. Symptoms may not develop for 8 to 12 hours after the eyes have been exposed to the sun.

Treatment. Snow blindness heals spontaneously in several days. Cold compresses, pain medication, and a dark environment relieve the pain. Don't rub the eyes or put anesthetics in the eyes. These can damage the cornea.

Sunglasses, especially those with side blinders, decrease the ultraviolet radiation received by the eyes and prevent snow blindness. If you lose your sunglasses, make temporary ones from two pieces of cardboard with slits cut in them to see through. Wear sunglasses on cloudy or overcast days as well as sunny days.

FINAL THOUGHTS

The American Burn Association and the American College of Surgeons classify burns by depth and extent. They recommend that burns greater than 10 percent of the body surface area be treated at a burn center. We often evacuate smaller burns due to patient discomfort, worry of infection, and inability to use the injured body part.

A patient with burns of the face may also have inhalation burns. Partial- and full-thickness burns of the hands and feet may require special treatment to preserve function, and burns of the groin may produce enough swelling to prevent urination. Burns completely encircling a limb may cut off circulation. Burns, like other soft tissue wounds, must be kept clean to reduce the risk of infection.

Burns are serious injuries, more easily prevented than treated. Keep safety in mind at all times, especially when around fires and stoves.

Clothing is portable shade and a simple sunburn prevention method. A brimmed hat shades the face and neck. Long-sleeve shirts and pants protect skin from the sun. Develop the habit of putting on sunscreen early and often.

Evacuation Guidelines
Evacuate all full-thickness burns. Consider evacuating partial thickness burns, especially to the hands, feet, face, armpits, or groin for pain management and wound care.

- Rapidly evacuate any patient with partial- or full-thickness burns covering more than 10 percent total body surface area (TBSA); any patient with partial- or full-thickness circumferential burns, and any patient with signs and symptoms of airway burns.

PART III

Environmental Injuries

CHAPTER 9

COLD INJURIES

INTRODUCTION

On a snowy subzero morning in early November, after 2 days of searching, a lost hunter was found in the Wind River Mountains south of Lander, Wyoming. His nose, hands, feet, and stomach were severely frostbitten, and he showed limited signs of life. After several hours of evacuation by snow litter and four-wheel drive, rescuers delivered him to the emergency room with a rectal temperature of 74°F (23°C).

His ordeal was not over yet. The hypothermia caused his heart to stop, and only after 3 hours of warming and CPR did he begin to recover. His story was presented by the media as one of "miraculous" survival. He was lucky, and he knows it. Today, this man is a strong advocate of hypothermia prevention.

THE PHYSIOLOGY OF TEMPERATURE REGULATION

Humans are warm-blooded animals that maintain a relatively constant internal temperature regardless of the environmental temperature. Human cells, tissues, and organs, and especially the biological catalysts known as enzymes, operate efficiently only within narrow temperature limits. If your temperature rises 2°F above the normal 98.6°F (37°C), you become ill. If it rises 7°F, you become critically ill. If your temperature decreases 2°F, you feel cold. A 7°F decrease puts your life in jeopardy.

Humans are designed to live in tropical climates; our heat loss mechanisms are highly developed. Our insulation mechanisms are less efficient. To adapt structurally to cold, our bodies would have to grow thick insulating hair all over and develop greater reserves of fat. Rather than remaining angular and cylindrical, which promotes heat loss, our body shape would become rounder and shorter to prevent heat loss. This would especially affect our ability to tolerate lower body temperatures and near-freezing temperatures in our fingers and toes.

We gain heat from the chemical potential energy in food and oxygen when we exercise or metabolize food, but this by itself is not sufficient to keep us warm all winter.

As it is, human beings can live in the cold because our intellectual responses enable us to deal effectively with environmental stress. Much of what students learn on NOLS courses is how to live comfortably in extreme environmental conditions by employing skill, disciplined habits, and quality equipment. We compensate for our physical deficiencies with behavioral responses such as eating, drinking, and creating microclimates through the use of clothing, fire, and shelter. The diminished intellectual response evident in early stages of hypothermia, as well as in altitude sickness, heat illness, and dehydration, dangerously impairs our ability to react to the environment.

Mechanisms of Heat Production
The three main physiological means for producing heat are metabolism, exercise, and shivering.

Resting Metabolism. The basal metabolic rate is like a constant internal furnace, liberating heat as a by-product of the biochemical reactions that keep us alive. Metabolism is not an efficient means to convert the energy potential in food into work. As a result, much of the energy from metabolism is lost as heat. Metabolic rate increases slightly when we are exposed to cold for long periods, but not enough to satisfy the body's entire heat requirements in winter conditions. Food is the fuel for metabolism. Nutritionally sound rations and good cooking skills are critical to health on wilderness expeditions.

Exercise. Exercise is an important method of heat production. Muscles, which make up 50 percent of our body weight, produce 73 percent of the heat generated during work. Short bursts of hard physical effort can generate tremendous amounts of heat, while moderate levels of exercise can be sustained for long periods. This valuable source of heat does have its limitations. Physical conditioning, strength, stamina, and fuel in the form of food and water are necessary to sustain activity.

Shivering. Shivering—a random quivering of muscles—produces heat at a rate 5 times greater than the basal metabolic rate. It is our first defense against cold. Shivering occurs when temperature receptors in the skin and brain sense a decrease in body temperature and trigger the shivering response.

As with all forms of work, the price of shivering is fuel. How long and how effectively we shiver is limited by the amount of carbohydrates stored in muscles and by the amount of water and oxygen available. In order to shiver, we have to pump blood into the muscles. Warm blood flowing close to the surface reduces our natural insulation and increases heat loss.

Shivering also hinders our ability to perform the behavioral tasks necessary to reduce heat loss and increase heat production. It is difficult to zip up your parka, start your stove, or ski to camp during violent shivering. Vigorous physical activity, however, can override the shivering response. If we don't capture the heat produced by vigorous exercise in insulating clothing, we can cool past the point of shivering without experiencing the response.

Mechanisms of Heat Loss

The core of the body contains the organs necessary for survival: the heart, brain, lungs, liver, and kidneys. The shell consists of the muscles, skin, and superficial tissues. The ebb and flow of blood from core to superficial tissues is a constant process. As our temperature rises, blood volume shifts and carries heat to the outer layers of the skin. As we cool, less blood flows to the periphery, preserving heat for the vital organs.

MECHANISMS OF Heat Loss

Our mechanisms for heat loss are so well developed that we lose heat in all but the hottest and most humid conditions. On a warm day, if we did not lose most of the heat our bodies produced, our body temperature would rise. The primary means of heat loss is through the skin. Warm, flushed skin can dispose of heat through conduction, convection, radiation, or evaporation.

The circulatory system controls heat by regulating the volume of blood flowing to the skin and superficial muscles. When we are resting comfortably, only a small percentage of blood flows directly to the skin. During heat stress, however, the blood vessels open up and blood flow to the skin may increase a hundredfold. During cold stress, blood is shunted from the periphery to the core, reducing the heat lost to the environment. Constricted blood vessels can reduce blood flow to the skin by 99 percent.

Conduction. Conduction is the transfer of heat through direct contact between a hot and a cold object. Energy as heat moves from the warmer to the colder object. We lose heat when we lie on cold, wet ground. We gain heat when we lie on a hot beach or rock. The rate of heat transfer is determined by the temperature difference between the two objects, the surface area exposed to the cold surface, and the effectiveness of the insulation between the body and the cold surface. The more efficient the insulation, the less heat is transferred. Warm, still air trapped in clothing is an effective insulator. Water, metal, and snow are good conductors.

We reduce conductive heat loss every night by sleeping with a foam pad between ourselves and the ground. If we wake up cold, we add insulation between ourselves and the ground before we put on more clothing. Damp cotton conducts heat, so if we're cold and wearing a damp cotton shirt, we'll take it off. On winter expeditions we place extra insoles in our boots, and in camp we stand on foam pads to reduce conduction between our feet and the snow.

Convection. Convective heat transfer occurs when two surfaces, in direct contact, are moving relative to each other. When we're in direct contact with cold moving air or water, heat escapes from the surface of the body by convection. The rate of heat transfer depends on the temperature difference between the warmer and the cooler body, the surface area in contact, and the speed at which the air or water is moving. Moving air (wind chill), besides cooling us directly, strips away the microclimate of air heated by the body. The loss of this insulating layer next to the body further accelerates heat loss.

To discover the cooling power of moving water, place your fingers in a bowl of cold water. Slowly swirl your fingers. The increase in heat loss is immediately perceptible. Immersion in cold water is a profound threat to temperature balance.

Heat is transferred by convection through the body by the blood. As we cool and the body shunts blood away from the skin, the superficial tissues—especially in our fingers and toes—no longer gain heat from the blood, which increases the likelihood of frostbite.

We reduce convective heat loss by wearing wind-resistant clothes, tight-weave nylon jackets and pants, and hoods to protect the vulnerable head and neck.

Radiation. Radiation is the transfer of electromagnetic energy from a hot object to a cold object. With a normal body temperature of 98°F (37°C), humans are often the warmer objects in the environment, and we lose heat through radiation. We receive radiative heat input from fires, from the sun, or from reflection off snow, water, or rocks.

Radiative heat loss makes clear winter nights colder than cloudy nights. Cloud cover reflects much of the earth's radiative heat back to the ground, reducing the severity of the nighttime temperature drop. Reflected, radiated heat waves bouncing off the walls and snowfields of a cirque during bright sunshine increase warmth—and the possibility of sunburn.

When exposed to the environment, the skin acts as a radiator. Higher radiative heat loss occurs from uncovered skin, commonly the hands, face, and head. Clothing reduces radiative heat loss.

Evaporation. When perspiration evaporates from the skin's surface, the change in state from liquid to gas consumes energy from the surface of the skin. Evaporative heat loss accounts for 20 percent of the body's total heat loss in normal conditions—much more when we are under heat stress or working hard. We use this to our advantage to cool ourselves in hot environments.

Sweating accounts for roughly two-thirds of evaporative heat loss. The remaining one-third is lost through breathing. Inhalation humidifies air and warms it to body temperature. During exhalation, evaporation of moisture from the surface of the lungs and airways uses heat and cools the body. The rate and depth of breathing and the humidity of the air determine the amount of heat and moisture lost. The colder and drier the air and the faster the breathing rate, the greater the heat loss.

We reduce evaporative heat loss by controlling our work rate, by using techniques such as the rest step (walking with flat feet, transferring weight slowly and smoothly from one leg to the other) when backpacking, and by avoiding hard breathing and sweating. Sweating in cold environments is to be avoided. It wets insulation and cools the body.

HYPOTHERMIA

A constant balance of heat gain and loss is required to maintain a stable body temperature. The adjustments the body makes are

---

Signs and Symptons of Hypothermia

MILD HYPOTHERMIA
- Shivering, numb skin with goose bumps.
- Minor impairment of muscular performance: stiff and clumsy fingers.
- Mental deterioration begins: poor decisions, confused and sluggish thinking.

MODERATE HYPOTHERMIA
- Stumbling, apathy, lethargy.
- Obvious mental status changes, irritability, forgetfulness, and complaining.
- Obvious muscular incoordination: stumbling, falling, and clumsy hands.

SEVERE HYPOTHERMIA
- Energy reserves are depleted, shivering may cease.
- Obvious mental deterioration occurs (e.g., incoherence, disorientation, irrational behavior).
- As the body becomes cooler, heart and respiratory rate and blood pressure fall.
- Severe muscular rigidity may occur.
- The pulse may be undetectable, and the patient may appear to have stopped breathing or to have died.

designed to keep our vital organs—heart, brain, lungs, kidneys, and liver—within a temperature range in which they operate effectively. If core temperature rises above normal, potentially life-threatening conditions—heatstroke or high fever—develop. When core temperature drops below normal, hypothermia may be the result.

Hypothermia can develop whenever heat loss exceeds heat gain and is as common during the wind, rain, and hail of summer as it is during winter. Immersion in cold water can cause hypothermia. If body temperature drops as low as 80°F (26.4°C), death is likely.

Signs and Symptoms of Hypothermia

As body temperature falls, mental functions decline and the patient loses the ability to respond appropriately to the environment. Responses are slow and/or improper, such as not changing into dry clothes or wearing a rain jacket or hat. Muscular functions deteriorate until the patient is too clumsy to walk or stand. Biochemical processes become slow and deficient as the body cools.

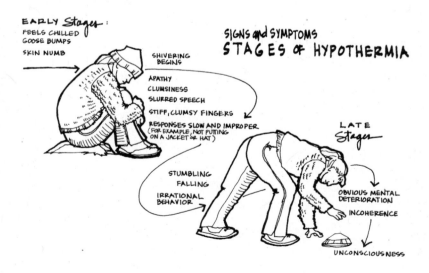

EARLY Stages:
FEELS CHILLED
GOOSE BUMPS
SKIN NUMB

SIGNS and SYMPTOMS
STAGES of HYPOTHERMIA

SHIVERING BEGINS
APATHY
CLUMSINESS
SLURRED SPEECH
STIFF, CLUMSY FINGERS
RESPONSES SLOW AND IMPROPER
(FOR EXAMPLE, NOT PUTTING ON A JACKET OR HAT)

STUMBLING
FALLING
IRRATIONAL BEHAVIOR

LATE Stages

OBVIOUS MENTAL DETERIORATION
INCOHERENCE
UNCONSCIOUSNESS

Recognizing Hypothermia (Assessment)

Hypothermia is easily overlooked. In cities, it has been mistaken for alcohol intoxication, stroke, and drug overdose. It may be associated with illnesses such as diabetes and other metabolic disturbances or with the elderly and the homeless. In the wilderness, hypothermia has been confused with fatigue, irritability, dehydration, and mountain sickness.

You can measure the patient's temperature to detect hypothermia. Choose a low-reading hypothermia thermometer for your medical kit; conventional thermometers read only to 94°F (34°C). A rectal temperature is ideal in the field; oral or axillary (armpit) temperatures may not reflect the status of the core organs. Obtaining a rectal temperature on a cold and confused patient, however, can be awkward. Also, undressing the patient to obtain a rectal reading may cause further cooling, is not practical, and is rarely done in the wilderness.

Early signs and symptoms of hypothermia can be difficult to recognize. The patient does not feel well. You may assume that he or she is tired, not hypothermic. Yet this is the stage at which successful warming in the wilderness is possible.

This patient may not be hypothermic; that is, his core temperature may not have dropped significantly. He may only be wet, cold and unhappy, hungry. Regardless, we need to recognize and address this situation early.

Hypothermia in its later stages may be more obvious. The patient is grossly uncoordinated with a clearly altered mental status. This stage of hypothermia is easier to recognize but much harder to treat in the wilderness.

Assessment of Hypothermia

MILD TO MODERATE

- Awake
- Shivering
- Able to walk
- Alert (altered mental status possible)

SEVERE

- Altered mental status
- No shivering
- Unable to walk

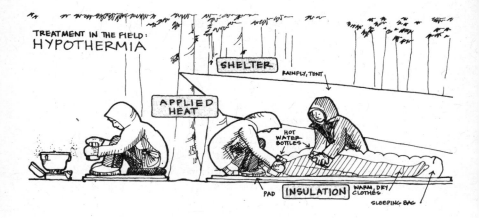

TREATMENT IN THE FIELD:
HYPOTHERMIA

SHELTER — RAINFLY, TENT

APPLIED HEAT

HOT WATER BOTTLES

PAD INSULATION WARM, DRY CLOTHES

SLEEPING BAG

The most important diagnostic tool in the backcountry is the first responder's awareness of the possibility of hypothermia and attention to the patient's mental state. Anyone in a cool or cold environment is at risk for hypothermia. Persons with altered mental status (confused, slurred speech, disoriented) in the outdoors may be hypothermic. Whether you can obtain a temperature or not, if you suspect hypothermia, treat it immediately and aggressively.

Treatment of Mild to Moderate Hypothermia
Prevention of hypothermia is simple. Treatment is not. Warming can be a long and complex process that takes hours, and it may be impossible in the backcountry.

A mildly hypothermic patient may be warmed in the field. In the absence of a serious underlying medical condition, the chances for successful warming are good. Although we can't change the weather, we can replace wet clothing with dry, protect the patient from the wind, add layers of insulation, hydrate and feed the patient, and apply heat.

Dry the patients, dress them in warm clothes, get them to move, give them hot drinks, and everything usually works out fine. If a patient is seriously cold, you place him or her in a sleeping bag "hypothermia wrap" with hot water bottles, build a fire, and take other aggressive actions as necessary.

Prevent further heat loss:
- Dress the patient in dry clothing, especially a hat to reduce heat loss from the head and neck. For mild hypothermia, this and a hot drink are often all the treatment that's needed.

Feed and hydrate the patient:
- Warm drinks are a source of heat, fluid, and sugar. The patient must be alert and able to hold the drink and consume it under his or her own power.
- Warm drinks and simple foods, such as candy bars, can be followed by a good meal after the patient is warmed. A fatigued or dehydrated patient is a strong candidate for another episode of hypothermia. Keep the patient insulated and resting until energy and fluid reserves have been replenished. In our experience, it's best to keep the warmed patient in the sleeping bag for a good night's sleep and to give him or her a hot meal and several liters of water.

The hypothermia wrap:
- A sleeping bag in a "hypothermia wrap" is the backcountry's most tried and true warming tool. Place the patient into a sleeping bag with a foam pad underneath. If you have extra sleeping bags, use them.
- Heat packs or hot water bottles may be helpful sources of heat. Apply the hot water bottles to yourself first to make sure they are not too hot, then wrap these carefully so as to avoid burning the patient. The first hot water bottle usually goes into the patient's hands, which they hold on their chest. This may warm the core, as well as the hands. The next water bottle goes by their feet, to prevent frostbite.
- This whole package is wrapped "burrito style" in a tarp or plastic sheet to insulate from wind and moisture loss.
- If you are without a sleeping bag, dress the patient in dry clothes for insulation.
- Fires are an excellent source of heat. Use a space blanket as a reflector.

Mild or moderately hypothermic patients who can shiver and still produce heat warm themselves if their body heat is captured by warm, dry, windproof insulation.

In our experience, the hypothermia wrap with hot water bottles is a more effective practice than putting another person in the bag. It can be hard to close a sleeping bag tightly around two people. The warmers are not available for other tasks such as setting up camp and preparing food. The warmers can quickly become cold and fatigued. Experts disagree on the amount of heat transferred body to body—some think it's low. The value of a warm person in the sleeping bag may be to heat the insulation, not to transfer heat directly to the patient. If this method is used, we recommend that the warmers wear at least a thin layer of clothing. Feed the warmers to keep their energy levels up. Clothing placed over the opening of zipped-together sleeping bags helps reduce heat loss. Placing several sleeping bags over the patient and the warmers also helps. A humid environment inside the sleeping bag reduces respiratory heat loss, as does loosely wrapping a scarf or other article of clothing across the patient's mouth and nose.

Be Persistent: Warming Takes Time. Individuals such as the hunter described in the introduction have recovered from prolonged, profound hypothermia. Newspaper headlines occasionally describe "frozen" and "dead" people who were successfully warmed. The adage to remember about hypothermia treatment is that "the victim is never dead until he is warm and dead."

Treatment of Severe Hypothermia

A severely hypothermic patient produces little or no heat and, in the absence of external heat sources, may cool further. A cold heart is susceptible to abnormal rhythms such as ventricular fibrillation, a random quivering of the heart that fails to pump blood. Jarring or bouncing, almost inevitable in transport from the backcountry, can trigger this rhythm.

In severe hypothermia, there may be complications from an underlying medical condition or trauma and complex disturbances in the body's biochemical balance. For these reasons, a patient with severe hypothermia needs to be transported to a hospital.

Evacuation of a severely hypothermic patient must occur simultaneously with attempts to prevent further cooling. If you do not apply heat to the patient during transport, further cooling is almost certain. Monitor ABCs and vitals, and carry the patient as gently as possible. Rescue breathing for 10 to 15 minutes before movement may prevent ventricular fibrillation.

It may be difficult to find the pulse or respiration rate of a severely hypothermic patient. The heart rate may be 20 to 30 beats per minute, and the breathing rate only 3 to 4 times a minute. Take your time during assessment. Check the heartbeat and breathing for at least 1 minute, carefully watching for the rise and fall of the chest, listening for any breath sounds, and feeling for the pulse at the neck. Ideally, use a cardiac monitor to assess heart rhythm. If in doubt, withhold chest compression and perform rescue breathing.

FROSTBITE

Frostbite is the freezing of tissue commonly seen on fingers, toes, and ears. Fluid between cells can freeze. The formation of ice crystals draws water out of the cells. Mechanical cell damage also occurs as the crystals rub together. Blood clots form in small vessels and circulation stops, further damaging cells.

A second phase of injury occurs during warming. Damaged cells release substances that promote constriction and clotting in small blood vessels,

Causes of Frostbite

- Cold stress
- Low temperatures
- Moisture
- Poor insulation
- Contact with supercooled metal or gasoline
- Interference with circulation of blood:
  —Cramped position
  —Tight clothing (gaiters, wristwatches, etc.)
  —Tight fitting or laced boots
  —Dehydration

Signs and Symptoms of Frostbite

All forms of frostbite can look similar.
- The skin is cold, waxy, and pale or mottled.
- There can be tingling, numbness, or pain.
- The tissue may be soft if partially frozen, or hard if frozen.
- Blisters may form if the frostbite has been thawed.

impairing blood flow to the tissues. Frostbite is not life-threatening, but tissue damage from frostbite can result in loss of function and amputation.

Frostbite is classified as superficial frostbite, also known as frostnip; partial-thickness frostbite; and deep, or full-thickness, frostbite. Many experts classify frostbite only after it has thawed and the extent of the damage is apparent.

Assessment of Frostbite

With frostnip or superficial frostbite, only the outer layer of skin is frozen. It appears white and waxy or possibly gray or mottled. High winds together with cold temperatures create conditions for frostnip on exposed areas of the face, nose, ears, and cheeks.

After the nipped area is warm, the layer of frozen skin becomes red. Over a period of several days, the dead skin peels. As it heals, the appearance of the injury is similar to that of sunburn, a first-degree burn.

Partial-thickness frostbite has progressed from frostnip into the underlying tissues. It may feel hard on the surface, soft and resilient below. Blisters usually appear within 24 hours after warming.

The most serious form of frostbite is deep, or *full-thickness*, frostbite. The injury extends from the skin into the underlying tissues and muscles. The external appearance is the same as frostnip and partial-thickness frostbite, but the frozen area feels hard. After thawing, the area may not blister or may blister only where deep frostbite borders on more superficial damage.

Differentiating partial-thickness from deep frostbite before thawing is difficult. Blisters containing clear fluid, extending to the tips of the digits, and forming within 48 hours of warming suggest partial-thickness frostbite. Blood-filled blisters that don't reach the tips of the digits, delayed blisters, or the lack of blisters indicates deep frostbite.

Treatment of Frostbite

Frostnip or small areas of partial-thickness frostbite can be warmed by sticking fingers into armpits. Larger areas of partial-thickness frostbite and all full-thickness frostbite should be treated with rapid warming by immersion in warm water between 99° to 102°F (37° to 39°C).

Dangerous folk remedies for frostbite include rubbing the frozen part with snow, flogging the area to restore circulation, and exposing it to an open flame. The treatment of choice for larger areas of partial-thickness and all full-thickness frostbite is rapid warming in warm water.

Delay Warming. Try to keep the injury frozen until warming can be carried out correctly. Many people, including the author, have traveled long distances with frozen feet in order to reach a place where warming could be done once and done well. How long the tissue can be kept frozen without increasing the damage is a matter of controversy. Tissue damage seems to be related to the length of time the tissue stays frozen.

There are several problems with keeping a frostbitten extremity frozen while evacuation takes place. If the injury occurred from exposure to extreme cold, lack of proper clothing, or in conjunction with hypothermia, the frostbitten area may warm as the problem that caused it is corrected. The activity of traveling may generate enough heat to begin thawing, thus increasing the possibility of further injury from freezing a second time or bruising. Unintentional slow warming is common.

If the injury is confined to a small area of the body, such as tips of toes or fingers, slow thawing is likely, and field warming should be started. If the injury is extensive, thawing will be difficult in the field.

Rapidly Warm in Warm Water. Treatment for frostbite, best done in a hospital, is rapid warming in water between 99° and 102°F (37° and 39°C). Use a thermometer to ensure that the water is the proper temperature. For a rough estimate, 105°F (40°C) is hot tap water. Cooler water will not thaw frostbite rapidly. Hotter water is very painful and may burn the patient.

Water temperature should remain constant throughout the procedure. This requires a source of hot water and several containers large enough to contain the entire frozen part. Do not pour hot water over the frozen tissue. Rather, immerse the frozen area, being careful not to let it touch the sides or bottom of the container. When the water cools, remove the frostbitten part, quickly warm the water, and reimmerse the part.

Thawing frozen fingers generally takes 45 minutes. There is no danger of overthawing, but underthawing can leave tissue permanently damaged. A flush of pink indicates blood returning to the affected site. Warming frostbite is generally very painful. Aspirin or ibuprofen is appropriate for pain relief. If hypothermia is present, it takes priority in treatment.

Post-Thaw Care. Air dry the extremity carefully; don't rub. Swelling will occur, along with blister formation. Inserting gauze between the fingers or toes keeps these areas dry as swelling occurs. Blisters should be kept intact. Once the tissue is thawed, it is extremely delicate, and seemingly minor trauma can damage it. Ibuprofen may be helpful for pain and inflammation.

Prevent freezing a second time after thawing. The freeze-thaw-freeze sequence will produce permanent tissue damage. The seriousness of frostbite injury is increased if freeze-thaw-freeze has occurred or if it is accompanied by fracture or soft tissue injury.

NONFREEZING COLD INJURY

A nonfreezing cold injury results from exposure to continued wet, cold conditions—conditions that many outdoor recreationists avoid. Military operations, like NOLS expeditions, rarely have the luxury of choosing their weather conditions and may spend days in weather conducive to the development of immersion injury. Understandably, much of what we know about nonfreezing cold injury—immersion foot, or trench foot—comes from the military. In World War I, when the term "trench foot" was coined, the British Army experienced 29,000 immersion foot casualties in the winter of 1915–16; frostbite and immersion foot casualties for U.S. forces in Europe in World War II totaled 90,000.

Immersion foot is a local, nonfreezing injury that occurs in cold, wet conditions when blood vessels constrict in response to heat loss, reducing

> ### Signs and Symptoms of Nonfreezing Cold Injury
>
> - The skin is cold, swollen, shiny, and/or mottled.
> - Tingling, numbness, or pain, may be present.
> - Capillary refill time is slow.
> - After warming skin may be warm, red, swollen, and painful.
> - In severe cases blisters, ulcers, and gangrene may develop.

blood flow to the extremity and depriving cells of oxygen and nutrients. The ensuing injury may range from a few weeks of sore feet to permanent muscle and nerve damage. In some cases, victims experience months of pain, disability, and even amputation.

It is common to hear that at least 12 hours of exposure to cold, wet conditions is necessary to produce the injury. Our experience, however, tells us that it can happen more quickly, over a long, wet, cold hiking day, for example, or in a multihour river crossing. Murray Hamlet, DVM, an expert on nonfreezing cold injury, says that the minimum exposure is as little as 3 hours, although he thinks it takes 12 hours to sustain a serious injury. These episodes of short-onset immersion foot could be due to individual susceptibility or could be the culminating event of long-term exposure. There are times when our diligence prevents immersion foot, although we have chronically cool and constricted feet. Sadly, as little as an afternoon's lapsed attention can undo our best efforts.

Assessment of Nonfreezing Cold Injury

All these classic signs and symptoms are true. You must be alert, however, to subtle forms of nonfreezing cold injury that do not necessarily look mottled, gray, or waxy, nor do you always see poor capillary refill or altered skin color and temperature. All you may see is cool, pale extremities, numbness or tingling, and mild swelling. Pain is unusual in the field, becoming more common after blood flow has returned to the extremity.

Be suspicious about any numbness, tingling, or pain in your feet in cool conditions. Nerves are most susceptible to injury from reduced blood flow. Many of the long-term effects of immersion foot are due to damaged nerves in the feet: pain, numbness, chronic tingling, and itching.

The patient may not notice the constricted condition of the feet until after the trip. We've learned to advise people returning from prolonged wet and cold conditions to avoid long, hot showers or baths. The rapid warming can surprise the unwary with swollen, painful, and red feet.

Treatment of Nonfreezing Cold Injury
- Warm nonfreezing cold injuries slowly at room temperature.
- Elevate the feet to reduce the swelling.

In serious cases, swelling, pain, and blister formation prevent walking. Bed rest, to avoid trauma, is often necessary until the injury heals. Ibuprofen is recommended because of its anti-inflammatory properties. Aspirin and acetaminophen may also help.

Prevention of Cold Injury
Our experience is that in prolonged cold, wet conditions, some degree of immersion foot is inevitable. The best footwear-gaiter system is of little help. Prevention is based on the consistent daily interaction of equipment, outdoor skills, and habits of vigilance and assessment.

There is no new thing under the sun. In World War I, the British significantly reduced immersion foot casualties (without making major footwear changes) by using techniques that we still follow today: wearing well-fitting boots with heavy wool socks; keeping the body warm; removing wet socks and

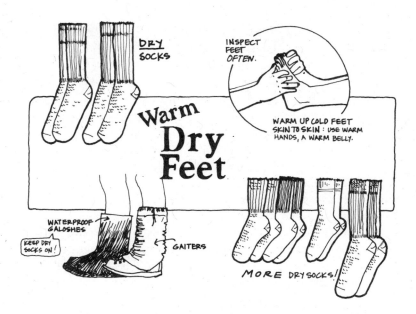

drying and massaging the feet twice a day; not sleeping in wet footwear; drying wet socks against the skin; keeping feet out of water or mud as much as possible; watching carefully and reacting promptly to any numbness or tingling; and keeping footwear loose to allow for circulation.

What follows are suggestions from NOLS instructors that we have accumulated over the years.

Dry Your Socks. Drying socks is a continual activity on wilderness trips. During the day, we stick wet socks under our shirts to dry them against the skin, and at night, we drape them over our chests and bellies in our sleeping bags. We'll hang them in the sun and dry them over a fire. Keep one pair of dry socks in a dry place, such as in a sleeping bag or a small plastic bag.

Sleep with Warm, Dry Feet. Sleeping with dry feet is very helpful, but there is a false impression that this offers complete protection. People coping with prolonged wet, cold conditions have developed immersion foot by hiking for a single day in wet socks. A single night of sleeping in cool, wet socks has undone weeks of vigilant attention. Go to bed with warm, dry feet and keep them that way all night long.

Use the Environment to Your Advantage. Travel early. Stop before nightfall, leaving time to care for your feet. In spring and summer, use the hardened overnight snowpack to stay on top of the snow. Stop when the snowpack becomes wet and soft, and dry your feet and socks in the afternoon sun. Choose campsites with good sun exposure and campfire possibilities.

Look at Your Feet. Local cold injuries are as much a leadership as a medical problem. When the conditions are ideal for trench foot to occur, the leader may need to check susceptible people frequently; visual checks twice daily are often suggested. Visual checking must be part of the routine. Messages sent to the brain from the feet may be faulty due to nerve damage.

Give Your Feet Top Priority. In some places where people hike and ski, it is impossible to have dry feet all day. The best footwear won't keep you dry in soaking wet tundra or through multiple river crossings. On these days, if your socks are damp and your feet cool, stop, warm your feet, and if possible, change into dry socks.

Warming cool feet on a companion's belly or stopping to change socks in the middle of the day should be routine tasks, not impositions. When you get to camp, get out of your wet boots immediately. Change into a pair of dry socks and begin to actively dry your wet or damp socks. Warm your feet promptly. Don't wait until bedtime.

Use Foot Powder. Foot powder does not seem to be helpful in preventing immersion injury, other than as a discipline in conjunction with changing socks. People with a tendency toward athlete's foot (a fungal infection) have found medicated foot powders helpful.

Display Good Habits. For outdoor leaders, role modeling good foot care on the trail and in camp is essential. To many outdoor enthusiasts, frostbite is the cold injury that is most well known. People are not well informed on the subtleties of nonfreezing cold injuries. Novices often assume that some degree of cooling is unavoidable and acceptable, and inadvertently cross a line from extremity cooling to a cold injury.

Keep Your Core Warm. Poor nutrition, dehydration, wet socks, inadequate clothing, and constriction of blood flow by shoes, socks, gaiters, or tight clothing are all predisposing factors.

Use Proper Equipment. Plastic boots and supergaiters are improvements over leather boots but are not a panacea. Rubber galoshes, though unfashionable, are inexpensive, simple, and helpful in keeping footwear dry. Bring multiple pairs of socks; wear two pairs on your feet and have at least two spare pairs.

FINAL THOUGHTS

The possibility of cold injury is our constant companion on wilderness trips. It's a threat not only in the mountains or in winter conditions, but anytime the environment is cool and wet, be it a fall rainstorm in the east, a cold desert night, or immersion in a cool ocean, river, or lake. The most successful and easiest treatment for hypothermia is prevention by choosing effective insulating material such as wool and synthetics and water- and windproof parkas and pants, using these items properly, eating and staying hydrated, and honing your camping and navigation skills to live comfortably as you travel through the wilderness.

A common thread in many nonfreezing cold injury and frostbite scenarios is people who tolerate cold feet, wait too long before intervening, and are surprised when they discover that they have been injured. If your feet are not definitely warm, you're doing something wrong. Novices may believe that they have to tolerate some level of cold extremities as an unavoidable consequence of camping. Although there is some truth to this, a novice lacks the experience to know how much one can tolerate before an injury occurs, and even an expert can be fooled. Don't be one of those people who rationalize not taking care of their feet by saying, "My feet are cold, but not that cold."

Evacuation Guidelines

Hypothermia:

- Mild hypothermia can be treated in the field. Severe hypothermia needs to be gently and rapidly evacuated for hospital warming.

Frostbite:

- Isolated, small (less than quarter-sized) thawed areas of frostbite can be kept in the field if subsequent freezing can be prevented. In general, larger areas of partial or full-thickness cold injuries should be evacuated. The pain from nonfreezing cold injury usually dictates evacuation.

CHAPTER 10

HEAT ILLNESS

INTRODUCTION

Our bodies produce heat constantly. When heat production exceeds heat loss, body temperature rises. Factors that reduce heat loss include high ambient air temperature, excessive clothing, and inability to sweat. To survive in a hot environment, human beings must eliminate enough heat to keep the body temperature within acceptable limits—97° to 100°F (35° to 37°C). Vital organs are irreversibly damaged when the body temperature stays at or above 107°F (41.5°C) for any length of time.

Heat illness is unusual on NOLS courses because we are diligent and aggressive about prevention. Outdoor leaders should be knowledgeable about the causes, recognition, and treatment of heat illness. Preventing heat illness, like preventing hypothermia, frostbite, altitude illness, and dehydration, is a 24-hour-a-day leadership task.

PHYSIOLOGY OF HEAT ILLNESS

The body generates 2,000 to 5,000 kilocalories (kcal) of heat per day. Every metabolic function, blink of the eye, and beat of the heart produces heat. Basal metabolism alone would raise the body temperature 1.5°F per hour if heat were not dissipated.

Organs responsible for heat loss are the skin, cardiovascular system, and respiratory system. As discussed in chapter 9 ("Cold Injuries"), the four main mechanisms by which the body loses heat are radiation, evaporation, convection, and conduction. Of these, radiation and evaporation are the body's primary avenues of heat loss.

Radiation. Under heat stress, the body dilates superficial blood vessels, increases heart rate and cardiac output, and directs more blood to the skin. Normally, one-third to one-half a liter of blood per minute is shunted to the skin and superficial tissues. The body can increase skin blood flow to 4 liters per minute when it is heat stressed.

Radiation accounts for 65 percent of the heat lost when the air temperature is lower than body temperature. In hot environments, radiation is a major source of heat gain. The body can gain up to 300 kcal per hour when exposed to the sun.

Evaporation. Sweating by itself does not cool the body. Evaporation of perspiration cools the body because heat is necessary to change water from liquid to vapor. A heat-acclimatized person can sweat as much as 2 liters per hour for a total loss of 1 million kcal of heat.

Acclimatization. Acclimatizing to heat entails increasing the rate of sweating, decreasing the sweating threshold, improving vasodilation, and decreasing electrolyte loss in the sweat. When acclimatized, we sweat faster and sooner and lose fewer electrolytes in the sweat.

To become acclimatized to a hot environment, the body requires 1 to 2 hours of exercise in the heat daily for approximately 10 days to 2 weeks. To remain acclimatized requires 1 to 2 hours of exercise per week.

Predisposing Factors in Heat Illness. Increased heat production, decreased heat dissipation, and a lack of salt and water are the basic factors that produce heat illness.

Other factors in the development of heat illness are age, general health, use of medications or alcohol, fatigue, and a prior history of heat illness. Patients with underlying problems (illness or injury) may not be able to tolerate heat. Underdeveloped physical mechanisms contribute to the incidence of heat illness in children. Individuals with compromised heart function are less able to adjust when stressed by heat. A study conducted by the U.S. Army demonstrated a correlation between lack of sleep, or fatigue, and the development of heat illness.

Antihistamines, antipsychotic agents, thyroid hormone medications, amphetamines, and alcohol are among the drugs that have been implicated in the development of heat illness. Some interfere with thermoregulation; others increase metabolic activity or interfere with sweating.

HEAT ILLNESS

A continuum of signs and symptoms provides evidence of heat illnesses that range from heat syncope and cramps to heat exhaustion and heatstroke. Symptoms of heat illness, like those of hypothermia and altitude illness, may be subtle and remain unrecognized until a sudden collapse occurs.

Heat Syncope

Heat syncope is fainting due to heat stress. Shunting of blood to the periphery decreases blood flow to the brain through vasodilation and pooling of blood in the large leg veins. Standing for long periods of time (soldier-on-parade syndrome) is a common cause of heat syncope.

Heat Syncope
SIGNS AND SYMPTOMS
• Tunnel vision, vertigo, nausea, sweating, weakness.
• Sudden fainting.
TREATMENT
• Lie flat, elevate legs.
• Hydrate.

Assessment and Treatment for Heat Syncope

Prior to fainting, the person may complain of tunnel vision, vertigo, nausea, sweating, or feeling weak.

Heat syncope is self-limited; leave the patient lying flat, and the fainting will usually promptly resolve. Make sure the patient is hydrated. Conduct an initial assessment and focused exam to check for any injuries that may have occurred as a result of the fall.

Heat Cramps

Heat cramps are painful muscle contractions that follow exercise in hot conditions. We don't know for sure what causes the cramps. They are probably caused by a lack of salt (sodium, potassium, calcium) and occur in muscles fatigued by exercise. People who sweat profusely and drink only water to replace lost fluids are more susceptible to heat cramps.

Assessment and Treatment for Heat Cramps

Calf, abdominal, and thigh muscles can be affected, and muscle spasms in the abdomen can be severe. Treat by moving the patient to a cool spot and replenishing the lost salt. Mix one-quarter to one-half teaspoon of salt in a liter of fluid and have the patient drink it slowly. Tums can be helpful as a source of calcium. Massaging the muscles may make the cramps worse. Try gentle limb straightening instead.

Heat Cramps

TREATMENT
- Rest, lie flat, elevate legs.
- Hydrate.
- Gentle limb straightening.

Heat Exhaustion and Heatstroke

The boundary between heat exhaustion and heatstroke is not completely clear. Some authorities consider heat exhaustion an early stage of heatstroke; others consider it a distinct illness resulting from heat stress, water and electrolyte loss, and ineffective hydration. Sweating, body temperature, and other symptoms may not be distinct between the two illnesses. The prevailing thought is that a patient with altered brain function—bizarre behavior, confusion, delirium, ataxia, seizure, or unresponsiveness—should be considered to have heatstroke.

Heatstroke is caused by a failure of the body to dissipate heat. There are two broad classifications of heatstroke: classic and exertional. Classic heatstroke affects the chronically ill, the elderly, and infants. It develops slowly and is common during heat waves. Exertional heatstroke is more likely to affect healthy, fit individuals and to develop rapidly during exercise or hard physical work.

Assessment of Heat Exhaustion and Heatstroke

HEAT EXHAUSTION

- Heart rate elevated.
- Respiratory rate elevated.
- Skin pale, cool, clammy.
- Alert.
- Headache, nausea, weak, tired.
- Temperature normal or slightly elevated.

HEATSTROKE

- Heart rate elevated.
- Respiratory rate elevated.
- Skin pale, warm, clammy.
- Altered mental status.
- Temperature >104°F (39.5°C).

Assessment for Heat Exhaustion and Heatstroke

The signs and symptoms of heat exhaustion are often caused by heat stress and dehydration. The patient complains of weakness, fatigue, headache, vertigo, thirst, nausea, vomiting, muscle cramps, and faintness. The body temperature is between 102° and 104°F (38.5° and 39.5°C). The patient may or may not be sweaty. Pulse and respiratory rate are elevated. Urine output is decreased due to dehydration.

In contrast to heat exhaustion, the onset of heatstroke is usually rapid. The patient develops an altered mental status. The pulse and respiratory rate are elevated. Prodromal signs and symptoms are confusion, drowsiness, disorientation, irritability, anxiety, and ataxia, as well as the signs and symptoms of heat exhaustion. Heatstroke victims usually have a rectal temperature above 104°F (39.5°C).

Treatment for Heat Exhaustion

Provide a Cool Environment, lay the patient flat, remove excess clothing, and shade the patient or move him from direct heat. Active cooling is not necessary.

Hydrate. If the patient is mentally alert enough to hold the glass and drink, allow him to drink. Water, a dilute solution of sugar drinks with a teaspoon of salt, or a sports drink is fine.

Monitor. Watch the patient. The patient often gets better when you remove the heat stress and assist them in rest and hydration.

Treatment of Heat Exhaustion and Heatstroke

HEAT EXHAUSTION
- Cool environment.
- Rest, lie flat.
- Hydrate.

HEATSTROKE
- Immediate cooling
  (cool water and fan).
- Evacuate.

Treatment for Heatstroke

Treatment of heatstroke is rapid cooling. Both the temperature reached and the length of time it is sustained can affect the long-term outcome of the disease.

Provide a Cool Environment, Lay the Patient Flat, Remove the Patient's Clothing, Cool with Water and Fanning. Shade the patient or move him or her from direct heat. Lay the patient flat and remove his or her clothing. Spray the patient with water and fan the body to enhance evaporation. Apply cool cloths to the patient's trunk, armpits, abdomen, and groin, where large blood vessels lie near the skin surface.

Monitor Temperature. Hypothermia becomes possible with such precipitate cooling, so monitor the patient's temperature for hypothermia as well as rebound hyperthermia. Document how long the temperature was elevated, how high it was, and how long it took to cool the patient. Body temperature may remain unstable even after cooling. Evacuate a heatstroke patient, keeping a close watch on temperature.

Hydrate. Do not give fluids by mouth until the patient is mentally alert enough to hold the glass and drink. If the patient is not responsive, make sure the airway is open and he or she is breathing. If the patient is seizing, do not restrain the patient, but remove objects that may cause harm.

Evacuate. Any patient you suspect of having heatstroke should be evacuated immediately for further evaluation. Internal organ damage may not present itself for several days following the episode of heatstroke.

FINAL THOUGHTS

Prevention of heat-related illness is, of course, the best treatment. Leaders need to be alert for signs of developing heat illness in their groups. Environmental risk factors of high heat and humidity, coupled with dehydration, exertion, the cumulative stress of several days in the heat, and overdressing, should raise caution flags. The vague symptoms of fatigue, headache, weakness, irritability, and malaise should be recognized as indicators of dehydration and heat illness.

Tips for Preventing Heat Illness

- Shade the head and back of the neck to decrease heat gain from the sun.
- Drink lots of fluids: A simple indicator of hydration is the color of your urine. The urine should be clear to pale yellow. Dark urine indicates dehydration.
- Make sure your diet contains an adequate amount of salt. The average American diet contains 10 to 12 grams of salt per day, which should be adequate for exercising in hot environments.
- Wear loose-fitting, light-colored clothes. This maximizes heat loss by allowing convection and evaporation to take place.
- Exercise cautiously in conditions of high heat and humidity. Air temperatures exceeding 90°F (32°C) and humidity levels above 70 percent severely impair the body's ability to lose heat through radiation and evaporation.

Risk Factors for Exertional Heatstroke
• Overweight
• Overdressed
• Fatigue
• Dehydration
• Alcohol use
• Medications
• Exertion
• High humidity
• High temperature
• Not acclimatized
• Young athlete

- Recognize the diseases and drugs that impair heat dissipation.
- Know the warning signs of impending heat illness—dark-colored urine, dizziness, headache, and fatigue.
- Acclimatize. It takes 10 days to 2 weeks to acclimatize to a hot environment.

Evacuation Guidelines
- Heat syncope, cramps, and exhaustion can often be treated in the field.
- Rapidly evacuate any person with suspected heat illness and associated altered mental status.

CHAPTER 11

ALTITUDE ILLNESS

INTRODUCTION

Each year thousands of people trek in Nepal, South America, and Africa at altitudes over 13,000 feet. In the United States, thousands of people climb Mount Ranier (14,408 feet) and hundreds attempt Denali (20,320 feet) each year. Skiers in the Rocky Mountains often ski above 10,000 feet within 24 hours of leaving low elevations. Studies show that symptoms of altitude illness affect up to 20 percent of these people.

Prevention through acclimatization provides some protection from altitude illness, but there is no immunity. NOLS expeditions have managed life-threatening cerebral edema at 21,000 feet on Cerro Aconcagua in Argentina and pulmonary edema at 11,000 feet in Wyoming's Wind River Range. If you travel in mountains, you need to know how to prevent, recognize, and treat altitude illness.

Normally, oxygen diffuses from the alveoli into the blood because the gas pressure is greater in the alveoli than in blood. At altitude, diminished air pressure (barometric pressure) reduces the pressure in the alveoli and decreases the amount of oxygen diffusing into the blood. For example, in a healthy person at sea level,

---

Definitions of Altitude

- High altitude: 8,000–14,000 feet
- Very high altitude: 14,000–18,000 feet
- Extreme altitude: Above 18,000 feet

---

blood is 95 percent saturated with oxygen. At 18,000 feet, it is only 71 percent saturated; that is, it is carrying 29 percent less oxygen.

As altitude increases, barometric pressure falls. Distance from the equator, seasons, and weather also affect barometric pressure. The greater the distance from the equator, the lower the barometric pressure, given the same elevation. For example, if Mount Everest were located at the same latitude as Denali, the corresponding drop in barometric pressure would probably make an ascent without oxygen impossible.

Air pressure is lower in winter than in summer, and a low pressure trough reduces pressure. Although temperature does not directly affect barometric pressure, the combination of cold, stress, and lack of oxygen increases the risk of cold injuries and altitude problems.

ADAPTATION TO ALTITUDE
The body undergoes numerous changes at higher elevation in order to increase oxygen delivery to cells and improve the efficiency of oxygen use. These adaptations usually begin almost immediately and continue to occur for several weeks. People vary in their ability to acclimatize. Some adjust quickly; others fail to acclimatize, even with gradual exposure over a period of weeks.

In general, the body becomes approximately 80 percent acclimatized after 10 days at altitude and approximately 95 percent acclimatized by 6 weeks. The respiratory rate peaks in about 1 week and then slowly decreases over the next few months, although it tends to remain higher than its normal rate at sea level.

When we descend, we begin losing our hard-won adaptations at approximately the same rate at which we gained them; 10 days after returning to sea level, we have lost 80 percent of our adaptations.

Increased Respiratory Rate. During the first week of adaptation, a variety of changes takes place. Respiratory rate and depth increase in response to lower concentrations of oxygen in the blood, causing more carbon dioxide to be lost and more oxygen to be delivered to the alveoli. The increased respiratory rate begins within the first few hours of arriving at altitudes as low as 5,000 feet. The lost carbon dioxide causes the body to become more alkaline.

To compensate for the body's increasing alkalinity, the kidneys excrete bicarbonate—an alkaline substance—in the urine. This adaptation occurs within 24 to 48 hours after hyperventilation starts.

Increased Heart Rate. Cells require a constant supply of oxygen, so the heart beats more quickly to meet the demand. Except at extreme altitudes, heart rate returns to near normal after acclimatization.

Fluid Shifts. Blood flow to the brain increases to provide the brain with its required volume of oxygen (equivalent to that available at sea level).

In the lungs, the pulmonary capillaries constrict, increasing resistance to flow through the lungs and raising pulmonary blood pressure. Dangerously high blood pressure in the pulmonary artery may cause fluid to escape from the capillaries and leak into the lungs (pulmonary edema).

Increased Red Blood Cell Production. As acclimatization continues, the bone marrow contributes by increasing red blood cell production. New red blood cells become available in the blood within 4 to 5 days, increasing the blood's oxygen-carrying capacity. An acclimatized person may have 30 to 50 percent more red blood cells than a person at sea level.

Increased 2, 3-DPG Production. Within the blood cells 2, 3-diphosphoglycerate (DPG) increases. This is an organic phosphate that helps oxygen combine with red blood cells. Production of myoglobin, the

---

Adaptation to Altitude

EARLY CHANGES

- Increased respiratory rate
- Increased heart rate
- Fluid shifts

LATER CHANGES

- Increased red blood cell production
- Increased 2, 3-DPG production
- Increased number of capillaries

intramuscular oxygen-carrying protein in red blood cells, also increases.

Increased Number of Capillaries. The body develops more capillaries in response to altitude. This improves the diffusion of oxygen by shortening the distance between the cell and the capillary.

ALTITUDE ILLNESS

Altitude illness results from a lack of oxygen in the body. Anyone who ascends to high altitude will become hypoxic (the condition of having insufficient oxygen in the blood). Why some people become ill and others don't is not known. It is known, however, that most people who become ill do so within the first few days of ascending to altitude.

Treatment of altitude illness is based on four principles: (1) stop ascent when symptoms develop; (2) descend if there is no improvement or condition worsens; (3) descend immediately if there is shortness of breath at rest, loss of coordination, or altered mental status; and (4) don't leave people with altitude sickness alone. The definitive treatment of all forms of altitude illness is descent.

There are several medications used for the prevention and treatment of altitude illness, including acetazolamide (Diamox)

Factors That Affect the Incidence and Severity of Altitude Illness

- Rate of ascent—the faster you climb, the greater the risk.
- Altitude attained (especially sleeping altitude)—the higher you sleep, the greater the risk.
- Length of exposure—the longer you stay high, the greater the risk.
- Inherent physiological susceptibility—some people are more likely to become ill, and we don't know why.
- Ego, peer pressure, and schedules—if you are not acclimatizing, stop ascent until you adjust.

and dexamethasone (Decadron). Check with your physician advisor for recommendations on the use of these drugs. NOLS brings these medications on high-altitude expeditions for the treatment of altitude illness, but we do not routinely use medications to prevent altitude illness. We focus on slow ascent and acclimatization as the cornerstones of prevention.

The three common types of altitude illness are acute mountain sickness (AMS), high-altitude pulmonary edema (HAPE), and high-altitude cerebral edema (HACE). AMS is the most common. It is not life-threatening, but if not treated, it can progress to HACE. HAPE is less common but more serious. HACE is rare but can be sudden and severe.

ACUTE MOUNTAIN SICKNESS (AMS)

Acute mountain sickness is a headache in conjunction with recent altitude gain and one or more of the following symptoms: nausea, loss of appetite, lassitude, fatigue, insomnia, and unusual shortness of breath.

Signs and Symptoms of AMS

Signs and symptoms tend to start 6 to 72 hours after arrival at high altitude. They usually disappear in 2 to 6 days. Symptoms are worse in the morning, probably due to the normal decrease in the rate and depth of breathing during sleep, which lowers blood oxygen saturation. Symptoms include the following:

Signs and Symptoms of AMS
• Headache
• Malaise
• Loss of appetite
• Nausea, vomiting
• Disturbed sleep

Headache. Increased cerebral blood flow helps the brain maintain its oxygen supply, but the expanded volume causes pain as the system adapts.

Malaise. This uneasy feeling, drowsiness, and lassitude occur because of decreased oxygen in the blood.

Loss of Appetite, Nausea, and Vomiting. Loss of appetite and nausea commonly accompany AMS and contribute to the overall sensation of feeling lousy.

Peripheral Edema. Persons with AMS tend to retain fluid, resulting in edema, especially of the face and hands.

Disturbed Sleep. During sleep, a person's rate and depth of respiration may gradually increase until it reaches a climax. Breathing then ceases entirely for 5 to 50 seconds. This phenomenon is called Cheyne-Stokes respiration.

Treatment of AMS

> ## Treatment of AMS
>
> - Hydrate.
> - Rest (light exercise is okay).
> - Use pain medication for headache.
> - Avoid sedatives.
> - Descend if:
>   —Symptoms worsen.
>   —Signs of HAPE or HACE
>   develop.

Don't go higher until the symptoms resolve. Stop ascending until signs and symptoms resolve, descend if there is no improvement with rest, and descend immediately if signs of severe AMS appear. Light activity around camp is fine as long as the theme is rest and acclimatization, not more fatigue. Stay well hydrated to help the kidneys excrete bicarbonate. Aspirin, acetaminophen, or ibuprofen may ease the headache. If symptoms worsen, signs of ataxia or pulmonary edema become apparent, or there is a change in the level of consciousness, descend.

HIGH-ALTITUDE PULMONARY EDEMA (HAPE)

HAPE is abnormal fluid accumulation in the lungs at altitude. HAPE rarely occurs below 8,000 feet and is more common in young males.

Signs and Symptoms of HAPE

The symptoms of HAPE result from the decreasing ability of the lungs to exchange oxygen and carbon dioxide. The symptoms usually begin 24 to 96 hours after ascent.

HAPE may initially appear with mild symptoms similar to AMS. The patient complains of a dry cough and shortness of breath, and more fatigue than expected. The heart and respiratory rates increase.

As HAPE worsens, the shortness of breath, weakness, and fatigue occur at rest or light exercise. The patient complains of a harsh cough, headache, and loss of appetite. The heart and respiratory rates remain elevated. The nail beds become cyanotic. Rales (rattles) can be heard with a stethoscope. Signs and symptoms may be mistaken for the flu, bronchitis, or pneumonia.

As HAPE becomes severe, rales can be heard without a stethoscope. The patient coughs up frothy, blood-tinged sputum. The patient becomes ataxic, lethargic, or develops an altered mental status.

HAPE, like AMS, becomes worse at night due to Cheyne-Stokes respirations. HAPE is a life-threatening illness. It causes the most deaths at altitude.

Signs and Symptoms of HAPE

- Signs of acute mountain sickness.
- Shortness of breath on exertion, progressing to shortness of breath at rest.
- Fatigue.
- Dry cough, progressing to wet, productive cough.
- Increased heart rate and respiratory rate.
- Rales, sounds of fluid in the lungs.

Treatment of HAPE

Descend to a lower altitude as quickly as possible. Immediate descent is essential. Give oxygen, if available, during the descent. If the symptoms do not improve, descend until they do.

Treatment of HAPE

- Descend at least 2,000 to 3,000 feet until symptoms abate.
- Oxygen may be helpful.

If you are unable to descend but have oxygen available, give the patient 100 percent oxygen at a flow rate of 4 to 6 liters per minute. If the condition does not improve, increase the flow of oxygen. Descend as soon as possible.

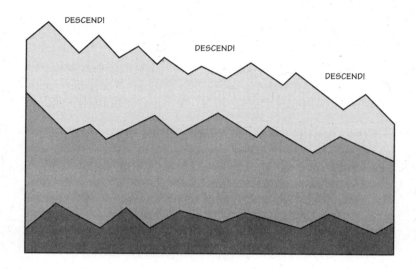

HIGH-ALTITUDE CEREBRAL EDEMA (HACE)

HACE is a severe form of AMS with swelling of the brain thought to be caused by hypoxic damage to brain tissue. HACE generally occurs above 12,000 feet.

Signs and Symptoms of HACE

The classic signs of HACE are change in mental status, ataxia, and severe lassitude. The patient may become confused, lose his or her memory, or slip into unresponsiveness.

Ataxia. Ataxia, or difficulty maintaining balance, is a sign—some experts say the most useful sign—of severe AMS or

---

Signs and Symptoms of HACE

- Signs of acute mountain sickness
- Ataxia
- Severe lassitude
- Headache
- Nausea and vomiting

- Neurological signs such as vision disturbances, paralysis, seizures, hallucinations
- Altered mental status

HACE. The test is simple. Have the patient stand straight with boots together and eyes closed. If the patient wobbles, falls, or has to open the eyes to maintain balance, he or she has ataxia.

Other obvious signs and symptoms may include vomiting, cyanosis, seizures, hallucinations, transient blindness, partial paralysis, and loss of sensation on one side of the body.

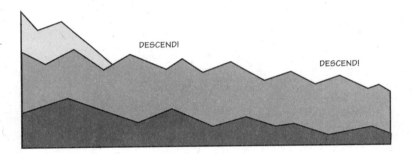

Treatment of HACE
Descend. Do not hope the condition will get better if you wait. Waiting and hoping may be fatal. Descend to a lower elevation as soon as you notice any ataxia or change in mental status. Give oxygen if available.

Hyperbaric Bags. Portable hyperbaric (greater atmospheric pressure than normal) chambers are used in the treatment of altitude illness. These bags, the best known of which is the Gamow Bag, are made of nonpermeable nylon. Inflated with a foot pump to greater than atmospheric pressure, these bags are believed to increase oxygen diffusion into the blood. They simulate a descent of several thousand feet.

Treatment of HACE
• Descent
• Oxygen

Hyperbaric bags are temporary treatment for emergencies—intended for use during evacuation to lower altitudes or if you are unable to descend immediately.

DESCEND!

FINAL THOUGHTS

Acclimatization is key. Start out sleeping at altitudes below 10,000 feet and spend 2 to 3 nights there before going higher. For every 2,000 to 3,000 feet gained, plan to spend an extra night acclimatizing to the new altitude.

Climb high and sleep low. It is best not to increase the sleeping altitude by more then 2,000 feet at a time. Set up camp at lower elevations and take day trips to high points. Ferry loads up to a high camp and then return to the low camp to sleep as you acclimatize.

Stay hydrated. Urine should be clear, not yellow. Over-hydrating does not protect against altitude illness. Avoid sleeping pills, which decrease the respiratory rate, aggravating the lack of oxygen.

Be aware of the influence of ego, peer pressure, and schedules on your rate of ascent. If you are not acclimatizing well, stop, rest, and allow time to adjust. Pushing higher and denying the signs and symptoms of altitude illness is asking for trouble for you and your companions.

Acclimatization

- Ascend slowly.
- Climb high, sleep low.
- Hydrate.

Evacuation Guidelines

- Evacuation and/or rapid descent for patients with severe altitude illness (HAPE or HACE).
- Evacuate any patient unable to acclimitize.

CHAPTER 12

POISONS, STINGS, AND BITES

INTRODUCTION

A poison is any substance—solid, liquid, or gas—that impairs health when it comes into contact with the body. Poisoning ranks fifth in causes of accidental death in the United States, and is responsible for approximately 5,000 deaths a year. Approximately 1 million cases of nonfatal poisoning from substances such as industrial chemicals, cleaning agents, medications, and insect sprays occur each year.

Virtually any substance can be poisonous if consumed in sufficient quantity. For example, vitamins can be highly toxic in overdose. A snakebite that kills a child may only produce illness in an adult. Accidental overdoses of aspirin kill more children each year than substances we commonly consider poisons.

A venom is a poison excreted by certain animals. Venomous animals have specialized glands that produce toxic substances for injection into adversaries and prey. All venoms are poisons, but not all poisons are venoms. Most animal venoms are complex mixtures of toxic and carrier (nontoxic) substances. The toxins in various venoms vary in potency, effect, and chemical makeup. They may impair nerve function, destroy cells, or affect the heart or blood.

Much information has been disseminated about the treatment of serpent, spider, and scorpion bites—much of it inaccurate. Outside the United States, there are snakes, spiders, and insects that carry deadly venoms. In the United States, however, snakes and spiders cause relatively few deaths each year. This is not to undersell the potency of these poisons, but rather to emphasize that ill-informed and misguided treatment can be as harmful to the patient as the venom.

POISONS

Poisons enter the body through ingestion, inhalation, absorption, and injection. In general, treat ingested poisoning in the backcountry by dilution and vomiting. Treat absorbed poisons, if dry, by brushing off the skin and, if wet, by flushing with water. Move the victim of an inhaled poison to fresh air and maintain the airway. As systemic symptoms of poisoning appear, provide the basics of care, including ABCs, continuous evaluation, and evacuation to a medical facility.

Ingested Poisons

Examples of ingested poisons include drugs, toxic plants, and bacterial toxins on contaminated food. The use of poorly labeled fuel bottles as water bottles has led to accidental ingestion of gasoline. Drugs, including nonprescription medications, can be accidentally or intentionally ingested in harmful amounts.

Treatment of Ingested Poisons. Three principles guide the treatment of ingested poisons: dilute the poison, induce vomiting, and bind the toxin with activated charcoal.

Dilute the poison by having the patient drink water. Dilution diminishes a poison's effects.

Drinking white gas, a common petroleum product in the backcountry, usually can be managed with dilution and rarely harms the patient.

Vomiting may help if it is tried early, usually within an hour of ingestion. Do not induce vomiting if the patient has a seizure disorder or if the patient has an altered mental status, as the airway may become obstructed with vomit.

Do not induce vomiting for ingested corrosive chemicals or petroleum products. Vomiting can increase the corrosive damage, as these chemicals burn both on the way down and on the way back up the esophagus. These substances are also extremely harmful if they enter the lungs and can cause a chemical pneumonia.

The wilderness backpacker commonly has to rely on tickling the back of the throat to stimulate the gag reflex. You may find that 2 tablespoons of mild soap or a teaspoonful of dried mustard swallowed with half a liter of water also induces vomiting.

After the patient has vomited, he or she should drink at least half a liter of water to dilute the poison.

If it's available, you can also try to bind the toxins to activated charcoal. Activated charcoal isn't the charcoal from a fire. It's a special preparation, usually packaged in 4-ounce plastic bottles or tubes. It's an over-the-counter product that, because of its weight and bulk, and the infrequency of poisoning in the backcountry, is rarely carried in wilderness kits. You may find it in a well-stocked base camp or boat medical kit. The patient drinks the slurry, which binds the poison and allows it to be excreted without being absorbed into the body.

In the backcountry, people have died after mistakenly eating poisonous plants and mushrooms. An expert should identify any vegetation you intend to eat. If you suspect ingested plant poisoning, treat by dilution and induced vomiting. Save samples for later identification.

Treatment of Ingested Poisons
• Induce vomiting.
• Dilute.
• Bind with activated charcoal.

Inhaled Poisons

Carbon monoxide is an odorless and colorless gas produced from incomplete combustion and is the most frequently encountered inhaled poison in the United States. Automobiles, portable stoves, lanterns, and heaters are all sources of carbon monoxide. Two climbers on Denali (Mount McKinley) died from carbon monoxide poisoning caused by using a stove in a poorly ventilated tent.

Carbon monoxide combines with hemoglobin in the blood, displacing oxygen and reducing the oxygen-carrying capacity of the blood. This can happen rapidly and without warning. At high altitudes, where less oxygen is available, the potential for poisoning increases. Signs and symptoms of carbon monoxide poisoning range from light-headedness and headache, weakness, nausea, vomiting, loss of manual dexterity, confusion, and lethargy to coma, seizures, and death. A cherry red coloring to the skin is a very late sign of carbon monoxide poisoning and may not occur until after the person has died.

> ### Carbon Monoxide Poisoning
>
> **SIGNS AND SYMPTOMS**
> - Lightheadedness, dizziness, throbbing headache.
> - Nausea and vomiting.
> - Irritability, impaired judgment.
> - Altered mental status.
> - Seizures, respiratory failure, coma.
>
> **TREATMENT**
> - Move patient to fresh air.
> - Maintain airway.
> - If possible, administer oxygen.

Treatment of Inhaled Poisons. The immediate treatment for any inhaled poisoning is to remove the patient from the source of the poison. Maintain the airway and move the patient to fresh air. Although not readily available in the wilderness, administration of oxygen is standard treatment. A patient who experiences a notable disturbance in alertness or coordination, complains of breathing difficulty, or becomes unresponsive should be evacuated to a physician for evaluation.

Prevent inhaled poisoning by keeping tents or snow shelters well ventilated during cooking or, better yet, by cooking outside.

Absorbed Poisons

Poisons can enter the body through the skin or mucous membranes. Pesticide sprays absorbed through the skin are a common source of poisoning. Toxins secreted into the skin by sea cucumbers and some species of exotic reptiles can cause serious reactions.

Treatment of Absorbed Poisons. If the poison is dry, brush it off, then flush the area with large volumes of water. If the poison is wet, flush the site thoroughly with water, then wash with soap and water. Exceptions are lye and dry lime, which react with water to produce heat and further corrosion. Do not rinse lye or dry lime; rather, brush the powder off the skin.

Treatment of Absorbed Poisons
• Dry poisons: brush off, then rinse with water. • Wet poisons: rinse thoroughly with water.

Injected Poisons

The poisons that enter the body via the injected venoms of stinging insects and reptiles are often complex systemic poisons with multiple toxins. The injected poisons that most concern us in the wilderness are the venoms of snakes, bees, wasps, spiders, and scorpions.

Bees and wasps cause more deaths in the United States than snakes—approximately 100 deaths a year, usually from the acute allergic reaction known as anaphylactic shock.

Venomous Snakes. Imagine yourself trying to catch a small mammal for dinner, equipped only with a long, limbless body. You might develop the ability to leap quickly to your victim. You might also develop a venom to immobilize the victim. This is how a rattlesnake makes its living: striking quickly and accurately and immobilizing or killing its victims with venom.

Approximately 45,000 snakebites occur in the United States each year, 8,000 of them from venomous snakes. Half a dozen people a year die from these bites, mostly the young, elderly, and infirm. Bites commonly occur on the arms below the elbow and on the legs below the knee. In most cases, the snake is provoked by being handled, antagonized, or inadvertently stepped on.

Prevent snakebite by watching closely where you step. Never reach into concealed areas. Shake out sleeping bags and clothing before use. One NOLS student was bitten on the hand when he attempted to pick up a rattlesnake. Never handle snakes, even if you think they are dead.

CORAL SNAKE

THIN, BRIGHTLY
COLORED

23-32" LONG

ADJACENT RED/YELLOW BANDS

SYMPTOMS:

- *LITTLE PAIN OR SWELLING*

- *NEUROTOXIC VENOM POISONING MAY LEAD TO DROWSINESS, WEAKNESS AND OTHER SYMPTOMS and PROGRESS TO POSSIBLE RESPIRATORY FAILURE.*

There are two families of venomous snakes in the United States: Elapidae, represented by the coral snake, and Crotalidae, represented by the rattlesnake, copperhead, and cottonmouth, or water moccasin. Elapidae venom primarily affects the nervous system, causing death by paralysis and respiratory failure. Crotalidae venom is a complex mix of substances affecting the nerves, the heart, blood clotting, and other functions.

Coral Snake. The coral snake averages 23 to 32 inches in length and is thin and brightly colored, with adjacent red and yellow bands. It is the creature referred to in the old saying "red and yellow kill a fellow, red and black, venom lack." Coral snakes live in the southern and southwestern states, inhabiting dry, open, brushy ground near water sources. They are docile and bite only when provoked. Their short fangs generally limit their bites to fingers, toes, and loose skin folds.

The signs of systemic poisoning by the neurotoxic venom, which may occur several hours after the bite, include drowsiness, weakness, nausea, rapid pulse, and rapid respiration

RATTLESNAKES

GENERAL CHARACTERISTICS:

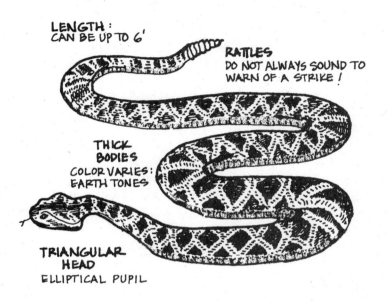

LENGTH:
CAN BE UP TO 6'

RATTLES
DO NOT ALWAYS SOUND TO
WARN OF A STRIKE !

**THICK
BODIES**
COLOR VARIES:
EARTH TONES

**TRIANGULAR
HEAD**
ELLIPTICAL PUPIL

MECHANISMS OF A RATTLESNAKE BITE:

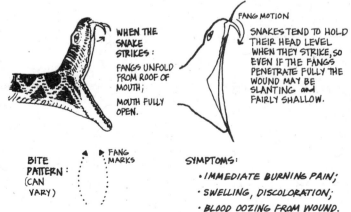

**WHEN THE
SNAKE
STRIKES:**

FANGS UNFOLD
FROM ROOF OF
MOUTH;

MOUTH FULLY
OPEN.

FANG MOTION

SNAKES TEND TO HOLD
THEIR HEAD LEVEL
WHEN THEY STRIKE, SO
EVEN IF THE FANGS
PENETRATE FULLY THE
WOUND MAY BE
SLANTING and
FAIRLY SHALLOW.

**BITE
PATTERN:**
(CAN
VARY)

FANG
MARKS

SYMPTOMS:

• *IMMEDIATE BURNING PAIN;*

• *SWELLING, DISCOLORATION;*

• *BLOOD OOZING FROM WOUND.*

progressing to respiratory failure. Treatment is the same as for rattlesnake bites with one exception—the placing of a wide elastic bandage over the bite site.

Rattlesnake. Rattlesnakes have triangular heads, thick bodies, and pits between the eyes and nostrils. Coloring and length vary with the species. Most are blotched and colored in earthy browns, grays, or reds. Four feet is an average length, although large eastern diamondback rattlesnakes have reached 6.5 feet in length. The number of rattles varies with the snake's age and stage of molt. Often the rattles do not rattle before a strike. Rattles are thought to have evolved as a warning device to prevent hoofed mammals from stepping on the snake.

Rattlesnake fangs retract when the mouth is closed and extend during a strike. Rattlesnakes periodically shed their fangs. At times, two fangs are present on each side. One is potent, the other not. Venom release is under the snake's control. A rattler can apparently adjust the volume of venom injected to match its victim's size. The age, size, and health of the snake affect venom toxicity. The same factors affect the victim's response to the venom.

Multiple strikes are possible, and depth of the bite varies, as does the amount of venom injected. Fang marks are not a reliable sign of envenomation, as 20 to 30 percent of bites do not envenomate. Pain at the site with rapid swelling and bruising is a better sign that venom has been injected.

Signs and Symptoms of Venomous Poisoning. Signs and symptoms of venomous poisoning include swelling, pain, and tingling at the bite site, tingling and a metallic taste in the mouth, fever, chills, nausea and vomiting, blurred vision, and muscle tremors.

Gently clean the wound with an antiseptic soap and apply a sterile dressing. The goal of treatment is safe and rapid transport to a hospital for evaluation. Keep the affected

---

Signs and Symptoms of Pit Viper Poisoning

- Swelling, pain, and tingling at the bite site.
- Tingling and a metallic taste in the mouth.
- Fever, chills, nausea and vomiting.
- Blurred vision and muscle tremors.

limb at heart level or below. Keep the patient quiet, hydrated, and comfortable during evacuation. Activity and anxiety accelerate the absorption of the venom. Ideally, immobilize and carry the victim. Walking is acceptable if the patient feels up to it and if no other alternative is available.

> ## Treatment of Rattlesnake Bites
>
> - Clean wound with antiseptic soap.
> - Remove rings and other constrictive items.
> - Keep limb at or below level of heart.
> - Keep patient quiet, hydrated, and comfortable.
> - Evacuate.

A healthy adult may become ill from the envenomation but probably will not die. The patient is often at greater danger from the effects of treatment by misinformed rescuers. Pressure bandages, tourniquets, electric shock, ice, and incision of the area can permanently damage tissue that might otherwise remain unaffected. Pressure bandages are appropriate treatment for some exotic snakebites but not for rattlesnake envenomations, in which local concentration of venom can cause tissue damage.

Non–North American Snakebite. Snakes outside of North America that are significant sources of envenomation are primarily elapids: cobras, mambas, and kraits; Australian brown snakes, tiger snakes, and taipans; and vipers such as death adders and rattlesnakes. The potent neurotoxic venoms of some of these snakes can result in altered mental status, unresponsiveness, blurred vision, paralysis, seizures, and respiratory and heart failure.

Treatment is the same as for rattlesnakes, with the exception of the use of immobilization and a pressure bandage on the bitten extremity for an elapid bite. To retard venom absorption, the limb is splinted and wrapped distal to proximal with gauze or an Ace bandage. This wrap is firm, but a pulse should still be present in the foot or wrist.

Bee Stings. The venom apparatus of most species of bees, located on the posterior abdomen, consists of venom glands, a venom reservoir, and structures for stinging, or injection. The stinger and venom are used in defense and subjugation of prey.

BEE

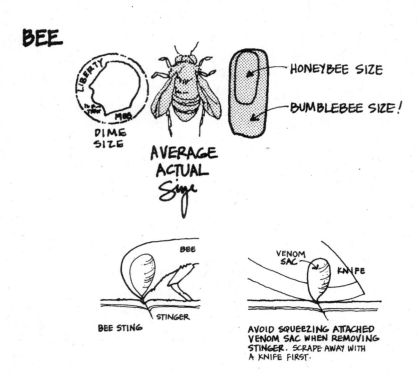

DIME SIZE

AVERAGE ACTUAL *Size*

HONEYBEE SIZE

BUMBLEBEE SIZE!

BEE

STINGER

BEE STING

VENOM SAC

KNIFE

AVOID SQUEEZING ATTACHED VENOM SAC WHEN REMOVING STINGER. SCRAPE AWAY WITH A KNIFE FIRST.

Multiple stings are more dangerous than single stings, and those occurring closely in time are more dangerous than those occurring over a longer duration. Multiple stings, which often result from disturbing a nest, can be life-threatening.

Stings from bees and wasps usually cause instant pain, swelling, and redness. If the stinger remains in the skin, scrape or flick it out. A barb prevents the bee from withdrawing the stinger, so the bee's muscular venom reservoir continues to inject until the stinger is scraped away.

Gently clean the wound with an antiseptic soap. Ice or cool compresses may help relieve pain and swelling. The patient should avoid scratching

---

Treatment of Bee Stings

- Scrape or flick off stinger.
- Clean wound with antiseptic soap.
- Ice or cool compress may relieve pain.
- If necessary, treat for anaphylaxis.

the stings, as this can cause secondary infection. Applying meat tenderizer to relieve the pain is a folklore remedy not supported by any scientific study.

Bees stings cause more anaphylaxis than do the stings of any other insect. Individuals who are allergic to the sting of one species of bee or wasp may also be allergic to that of different species.

Arachnids. Arachnids are mostly terrestrial and wingless and have four pairs of legs. Spiders, scorpions, tarantulas, and ticks are arachnids. There are over 30,000 spider species worldwide. They live in a variety of habitats, and all are carnivorous.

Poisonous spiders inject venom through hollow fangs. The fangs are primarily for subduing and killing prey and secondarily for defense. The venoms are fast-paralyzing agents that contain enzymes to predigest prey, which is then sucked up.

Widow Spiders. The black widow spider has a sinister name, yet kills at most four to six people a year in the United States. A member of the genus *Lactrodectus,* the venomous adult female is 4 centimeters long and is shiny black with a red "hourglass" marking on the bottom of the abdomen. The adult male is not venomous. There are five species of "widow" spiders, all of which have some type of red marking on the underside of the abdomen, but only three of which are black. Black widows are typically found under stones and logs. They are common in desert overhangs, crawl spaces, outhouses, and barns; they are rare in occupied buildings.

The black widow usually bites only when its web is disturbed. The bite is not initially painful—a pinprick sensation with slight redness and swelling, followed by numbness. Ten to 60 minutes may pass before the onset of toxic symptoms. The venom is primarily a nerve toxin that stimulates muscle contraction, causing large muscle cramps. The abdomen may become boardlike and excruciatingly painful. Weakness, nausea, vomiting, and anxiety are common. Systemic signs include hypertension, breathing difficulty, seizures, and, in the very young or old, cardiac arrest.

The pain generally peaks in 1 to 3 hours and can continue over several days. The natural course of the illness is general

BLACK WIDOW SPIDER:

SHINY BLACK

RED HOURGLASS
MARKING ON
ABDOMEN

DIME
SIZE

ACTUAL SIZE OF
ADULT FEMALE
(UNDERSIDE)

- FEMALE ADULTS VENOMOUS;

- LOOK FOR DISTINCTIVE RED HOURGLASS
  MARKING ON THE UNDERSIDE OF
  ABDOMEN!

recovery after several days. Local cleansing and ice may retard pain and venom absorption. Antivenin is available, as are agents to counteract muscle spasm.

Recluse Spiders. The brown recluse spider, genus *Loxosceles*, is rare in the West; it is most abundant in the South and Midwest. It has a violin-shaped mark on its head. The spiders average 1.2 centimeters in length with a 5-centimeter leg span. Unlike the black widow, both sexes are dangerous.

Recluse spiders live in hot, dry, undisturbed environments, such as vacant buildings and woodpiles. They are nocturnal hunters of beetles, flies, moths, and other spiders, and they are most active from April to October, hibernating in fall and winter. They attack humans only as a defensive gesture.

The venom of the brown spider causes cell and tissue injury. Signs and symptoms vary from a transient irritation to

BROWN SPIDER:

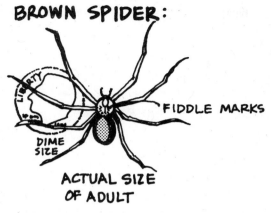

FIDDLE MARKS

DIME SIZE

ACTUAL SIZE OF ADULT

- VIOLIN SHAPED MARKS ON TOP OF HEAD
- BOTH MALE and FEMALE ADULTS VENOMOUS

painful and debilitating skin ulcers. Although the bite can be sharply painful, it is often painless. Nausea and vomiting, headache, fever, and chills may be present. In severe envenomations, redness and blisters form within 6 to 12 hours. Within 1 to 2 weeks, an area of dying skin—a necrotic ulcer—forms and may leave a craterlike scar.

Clean the bite site with an antiseptic soap and evacuate the patient to a physician.

Brown spider bites are rare, especially outside the their home range, yet they are a source of myth and frequent misdiagnosis. Likewise, the hobo spider (genus *Tegenaria*) has developed a reputation, perhaps undeserved, as a source of necrotic spider bites.

Tarantulas. Except for some species found in the tropics, tarantulas are not dangerous. The tarantula's fangs are too weak to penetrate very deeply, and the effects of the bite are limited to a small local wound. Tarantula bites are rare.

Scorpions. Scorpions first appeared on the earth 300 million years ago. Grasslands and deserts are primary habitat for more than 600 species of scorpions, some of which carry deadly ven-

SCORPIONS

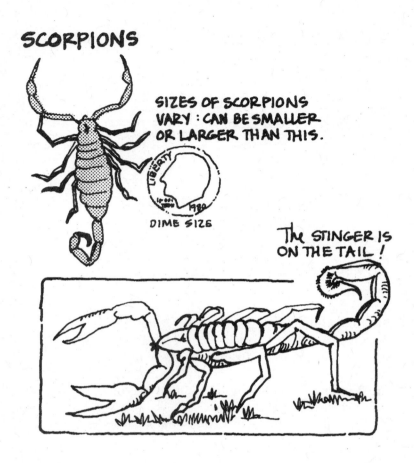

SIZES OF SCORPIONS VARY : CAN BE SMALLER OR LARGER THAN THIS.

DIME SIZE

THE STINGER IS ON THE TAIL !

oms. In North America, most species are relatively harmless, their stings producing effects similar to those of bee stings.

Only one type of North American scorpion, a small yellowish species of the genus *Centruroides,* is dangerous. It lives in Mexico, Arizona, and New Mexico and has been reported in southern Utah. Fatalities from its venom occur mostly in the young and old.

Scorpions feed at night on insects and spiders, injecting their prey with multiple toxins from a stinger at the tip of the tail. Scorpions like to hide in dark places during the day; beware when reaching into woodpiles or under rocks. Develop a habit of shaking out shoes, clothes, and sleeping bags when in scorpion country.

A scorpion sting produces a pricking sensation. Typical symptoms include burning pain, swelling, redness, numbness, and tingling. The affected extremity may become numb and sensitive to touch.

Treat the sting by applying ice or cool water to relieve the local symptoms. Clean the wound with an antiseptic soap. In the case of severe poisoning, signs and symptoms include impaired speech resulting from a sluggish tongue and tightened jaw, muscle spasms, nausea, vomiting, convulsions, incontinence, and/or respiratory and circulatory distress. Immobilize the extremity and transport the patient to a hospital. An antivenin is available.

> ## Treatment of Spider and Scorpion Bites
>
> - Clean wound with antiseptic soap.
> - Ice or cool compress to relieve pain.
> - If systemic symptoms of envenomation develop:
>   —ABCs and supportive care.
>   —Evacuate to antivenin.

Ticks. Ticks are relatives of spiders and scorpions. There are two major families: hard ticks and soft ticks. Most common in the Rockies is the hard tick, genus *Dermacentor*. As with all ticks, it requires blood meals to molt from larva to nymph and from nymph to adult. The various diseases the tick carries are transmitted to the host during the blood meal. These diseases include tick fever, relapsing fever, spotted fever, tularemia, babesiosis, and Lyme disease. Tick season in Wyoming is April through July, although ticks are active throughout the warm months.

Preventing exposure is essential in tick-infested areas. Topical tick insecticide is avail-

> ## Treatment of Tick Bites
>
> - Promptly remove the tick with a gentle, steady pull.
> - Clean the bite site with soap and water.
> - In cases of rash, fever, flu, or muscle aches following a tick bite, the patient should be seen by a physician.

TICKS

DIME
SIZE

**ACTUAL
SIZE OF
ADULT**

GENUS *DERMACENTOR*
COMMON WYOMING TICK

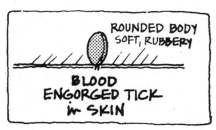

ROUNDED BODY
SOFT, RUBBERY

**BLOOD
ENGORGED TICK**
in SKIN

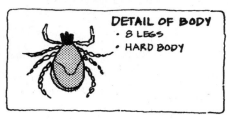

DETAIL OF BODY
• 8 LEGS
• HARD BODY

able; look for the chemical ingredient permethrin. A visual inspection of all body parts at least twice daily is recommended, as adult ticks generally stay on the body for a few hours before attaching. Even after a tick has attached itself, prompt removal may prevent the transmission of disease.

To remove a tick, grasp it as close to the skin as possible with tweezers or gloved fingers. Pull the tick out with steady pressure. Clean the bite site thoroughly with an antiseptic soap. Traditional tick removal methods (a hot match head, nail polish, or alcohol) may induce the tick to regurgitate into the wound.

Diagnosis of tick-caused illness in the field is difficult. If a tick bite is accompanied by a rash, fever, flu symptoms, or muscle aches and pains, the patient should be seen by a physician.

Insects. The bites of mosquitoes, blackflies, midges, horseflies, and deerflies tend to be relatively minor. Usually only localized irritation occurs, although anaphylaxis is a possibility.

LIFE CYCLE
of the TICK:

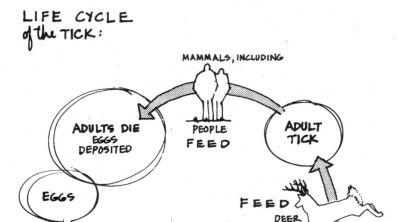

This group is more significant for its capacity to act as vectors of diseases such as malaria and yellow fever. Worldwide, only the mosquito transmits more disease than the tick.

To help reduce mosquito (and other insect) bites, use the following chemical and nonchemical precautions:

- Wearing protective clothing, and avoiding mosquito habitat and times of peak mosquito activity.
- Judicious use of DEET or picardin-based repellents, natural repellents (often made with soybeans or lemon eucalyptus), and products such as Skin-So-Soft.

Controversy persists over the safety and effectiveness of various repellents. The E.P.A. recommends the following general use information for DEET-based products:

- Read the label carefully before use.

- Apply repellent sparingly. Heavy application and saturation are unnecessary for effectiveness. Repeat applications only as necessary and according to label directions.
- Do not apply over cuts, wounds or irritated skin, eyes, or mouth. Discontinue if skin irritation develops.
- Some insect repellents contain a sunscreen. It is recommended that such combination products not be spread as liberally as one might a sunscreen or skin lotion.
- Do not apply to children's hands or allow children to handle the product.
- Avoid DEET use on children under 2, and use only the least concentrated product (10 percent DEET or less).

Poison Ivy, Oak, and Sumac

Poison ivy, oak, and sumac grow in all of the lower 48 states. Poison oak is more common west of the Rockies, poison ivy east of the Rockies, and poison sumac in the southeast. Individuals vary in their sensitivity to urushiol, the oil present on the surface of the plant—some react to very casual contact, others, as they walk through thick patches of these plants, seem immune. Urushiol can be transferred to the skin regardless of whether or not the plant has its traditional shiny three leaves in bloom. Inhaled smoke from burning plants can also cause a significant reaction.

Signs and Symptoms of Urushiol Reaction. This is contact allergic reaction. The skin becomes red and itchy with a blistered rash and scaly, crusting wounds. Contrary to myth, the blister fluid is harmless. The rash spreads over time, due not to the fluid but to the varying time it takes different parts of our skin to react to the urushiol.

Treatment for Urushiol Reaction. We can't stop this rash. Our efforts at best prevent additional contact and treat symptoms. Try to wash the area immediately after exposure with soap and cool water. You may be able to remove some of the oil before you react.

Wash all clothes and equipment that may have been exposed. Urushiol persists on clothing, ropes, and plants for years.

Apply a thin layer of 1 percent hydrocortisone cream or calamine lotion, and try oral antihistamines to reduce itching. In severe cases your physician may prescribe a steroid to help reduce the itching and swelling.

Prevention. Learn to recognize poison ivy, oak, and sumac. Nothing works as well as avoiding contact. Barrier creams for hypersensitive individuals may be considered.

Hantavirus

Hantavirus is found throughout North America but is most frequently associated with the southwestern states. It is carried by rodents, primarily deer mice, pinyon mice, brush mice, and chipmunks. The virus produces a serious respiratory disease passed from the rodent reservoir to humans through inhalation of aerosolized microscopic particles of dried rodent saliva, urine, or feces. You can become infected by touching your mouth or nose after handling contaminated materials. A rodent's bite can also spread the virus.

Symptoms are general and flulike: fever, headache, muscle aches, and sometimes nausea and vomiting. Hantavirus infections progress to breathing difficulty, which is caused by fluid buildup in the lungs.

To minimize the risk of hantavirus infection, follow these precautions:

- Check potential campsites for rodent droppings and burrows.
- Do not disturb or crawl around in rodent burrows or dens.
- Avoid sleeping near woodpiles, burrows, or dens that may be frequented by rodents.
- Avoid sleeping on bare ground; use a ground cloth or a tent.
- Store foods in rodent-proof containers and promptly and appropriately dispose of garbage.
- Don't use old cabins until they have been cleaned and disinfected.

FINAL THOUGHTS
Simple Tips for Preventing Poisoning Emergencies
- Read labels for information on toxic substances.
- Cook outside or in well-ventilated tents or snow shelters.
- Identify plants before you eat them.
- Be aware of foot placement.
- Look before you reach under logs or overhangs or onto ledges.
- Shake out clothing, footwear, and sleeping bags.

Evacuation Guidelines
- Consider evacuation for anyone who has ingested a potentially harmful substance.
- Evacuate rapidly any poisoned patient who has an altered mental status or shows signs of respiratory distress.
- Contact the American Association of Poison Control Centers at 1-800-222-1222 for advice.
- Evacuate all patients bitten by a poisonous snake; expedite evacuation if the patient shows signs of envenomation.
- Rapidly evacuate patients bitten by spiders if slurred speech, difficulty swallowing, blurred vision, seizures, respiratory or cardiovascular involvement are present.
- Evacuate any patient with a history of an imbedded tick who develops a fever, rash, and flulike symptoms.

CHAPTER 13

LIGHTNING INJURIES

INTRODUCTION

According to the Centers for Disease Control, there are 100 deaths per year in the United States and approximately 1,000 injuries from lightning.

Lightning Injuries

Injuries can occur from the high voltage (200 to 300 million volts), secondary heat production, or the explosive force of the lightning. A person can be injured by lightning in five ways:

- Direct hit: Actually being struck by lightning.
- Lightning "splash": Lightning hits another object and splashes onto objects or people standing nearby.
- Direct transmission: Being in contact with an object that has been hit directly.
- Ground current: Receiving the ground current as it dissipates from the object that has been hit.
- Blunt trauma from the explosive force of the shock wave.

Most victims are splashed by lightning or hit by ground current. Very few people actually sustain a direct hit. Although a direct hit can deliver 200 to 300 million volts, the duration is short (1 to 100 milliseconds), and severe burns are uncommon. More likely, a person will suffer internal injuries (cardiac arrest, damage to the brain and spinal cord) and fractures from shock waves.

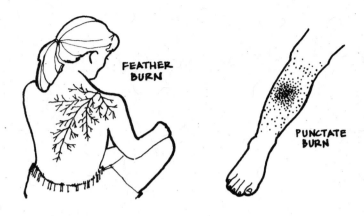

Lightning burns form distinctive patterns. Superficial linear burns follow areas of heavy sweat concentration. A linear burn may begin beneath the breasts, travel from the sternum to the abdomen, then split down both legs; or it may follow the midaxillary line (an imaginary line drawn through the middle of the armpit to the waist).

Lightning-caused punctate burns are circular, ranging in size from a few millimeters to a centimeter in diameter. Also, featherlike patterns, which are not true burns, leave imprints on the skin. Most lightning burns are first- or second-degree, with some of the punctate burns being third-degree.

Most lightning burns are superficial, but lightning strikes may throw victims a considerable distance, causing head and spinal injuries, dislocations, fractures, and blunt chest and abdominal trauma. The respiratory center in the brain may also be injured, causing respiratory and cardiac arrest.

Lightning knocks 72 percent of its victims unresponsive. Some patients will become temporarily paralyzed and have one or both eardrums ruptured. Other signs and symptoms are confusion, amnesia, temporary deafness or blindness, and mottling of the skin. Pulses may decrease or disappear in the lower extremities due to injury-induced spasms of the blood vessels.

Treat cardiac arrest with CPR. The heart may start beating again before respirations begin. Artificial respiration (rescue

FREQUENT STRIKES
EXTREMELY HAZARDOUS

OCCASIONAL STRIKES
HAZARDOUS

RELATIVELY SAFE

LARGE CAVE (NOT SHALLOW) SAFE ONLY IF WALLS / ENTRANCE AVOIDED.

SIT ON SOMETHING DRY and NON-CONDUCTING (FOAM PAD, ROPE, DAY PACK.)

SQUAT WITH FEET FACING DOWNHILL. TRY TO KEEP HANDS OFF the GROUND!

breathing) may need to be continued due to paralysis of the respiratory center in the brain.

Risk Management for Lightning

It's impossible to be safe when lightning is about. It's an unpredictable and immensely powerful force of nature. At best we can manage the risk by reducing our exposure.

Lightning usually hits the tallest object in the area, and water conducts electricity, therefore:

Don't stand under the only tall object in the area. It is better to be in a large group of trees than under the only tree out in the open.

Don't stay at or near the top of peaks or ridges. Head down as quickly as possible.

Don't hide in shallow caves or stand at the entrance of a cave, as you may be in the path of the electrical current.

Avoid being the tallest object near a body of water.

Get out of water and off wet ground. Don't swim!

Get away from metal objects that conduct electricity (metal fences, handrails, railway tracks).

Watch for hair standing on end and a blue ring around objects (Saint Elmo's fire). Listen for high-pitched "zinging" sounds. These indicate that a strike is imminent. Leave the area immediately.

Sit in a comfortable position on something dry and nonconducting (foamlite pad, rope, day pack). This lightning position may help protect against ground current; however, it is a myth that it will help protect against a lightning strike, or that any special position (squatting with feet together, hands off the ground, etc.) is better than simply sitting comfortably.

Stay alert to local weather patterns and cloud buildup. In the Rocky Mountains, the afternoons are generally more dangerous than the mornings.

Monitor approaching storms. Every 5 seconds between the flash of lightning and the clap of thunder indicates a mile. (Every three seconds is equal to one kilometer.) Lightning can strike miles ahead of a storm. When the storm is within six

LIGHTNING Safety

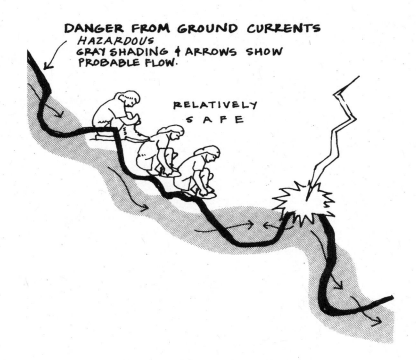

DANGER FROM GROUND CURRENTS
HAZARDOUS
**GRAY SHADING & ARROWS SHOW
PROBABLE FLOW.**

RELATIVELY
S A F E

miles (30 seconds between flash and bang) of your location, begin looking for places to wait out the storm. Wait 30 minutes after the last sound of thunder before resuming activities.

Evacuation Guidelines
All lightning injury patients should be evacuated for further evaluation and treatment.

CHAPTER 14

DROWNING AND COLD WATER IMMERSION

INTRODUCTION

The body's responses to cold water immersion are many. Sudden immersion in cold water causes a gasp for air, constriction of blood vessels in the extremities, and an increase in breathing and heart rate. The initial gasp may result in water inhalation, and the rapid breathing rate makes it more difficult to hold the breath underwater.

Death caused by heart rhythm abnormalities is possible; and as strength and coordination diminish, the chance of drowning increases. What's more, as the brain cools, we think less clearly and may do foolish things, such as removing a personal flotation device (PFD) or swimming aimlessly.

The danger of cold water immersion is widely present in the wilderness environment. Water conducts heat 25 times faster than air. In North America, most water remains below 77°F (25°C) year-round. Lakes in the Rocky Mountains warm only to the mid-50s (13°C) in summer. In Mexico, the Sea of Cortez averages 58°F (14.5°C) in winter. We are unable to remain warm at any of these temperatures unless we wear protective clothing.

DROWNING

Drowning is the second most common cause of accidental death in children, and the third leading cause of death in young adults. A majority of drowning victims are young males. Alcohol is involved in over half of drowning accidents. Freshwater drowning, especially in pools, is more common than saltwater drowning.

Aspects of a Typical Drowning

Panic and Struggle. The victim frantically tries to keep his or her head above water, often using a vertical breaststroke, with the head held back and the mouth open. The victim attempts to hold his or her breath when submerged but eventually gasps for air.

Aspiration. Inhalation of water causes intense vomiting and further inhalation of water and vomit. Approximately 85 to 90 percent of victims experience a "wet" drowning in which they inhale water into their lungs. The other 10 to 15 percent experience a "dry" drowning: spasm of the larynx that obstructs the airway.

Unresponsiveness. The victim becomes unresponsive and stops breathing. Cardiac arrest and death may follow.

Treatment of Drowning

For first aid purposes, the type of water (salt, fresh, clean, dirty) or type of drowning (wet or dry) does not matter. Airway maintenance and, if necessary, rescue breathing and chest compressions are essential to the treatment of unresponsive drowning victims. If you have any doubts about how long the victim was submerged, attempt resuscitation. There are rare case reports of people surviving submersion in ice water for more than 15 minutes, with 66 minutes being the longest documented survival.

Treatment of Drowning
• Remove the victim from the water.
• Handle gently.
• Check the ABCs.
• Protect the cervical spine.
• Perform a focused exam and history.
• Treat for hypothermia.
• Monitor vital signs.

The goals of treatment are to remove the victim from the water, protect the cervical spine, prevent cardiac arrest, and stabilize the patient's temperature.

Remove the Victim from the Water. Remove the victim from the water as quickly as possible. Rescuer safety is a priority. Remember the lifesaving adage "reach, throw, row, tow, and go." First try reaching for the victim, remaining in contact with the shore or boat. Second, throw a lifeline. Third, row or paddle to the victim. Attempt a swimming rescue only as a last resort.

Handle the Patient Gently. A patient who was submerged in cold water may be hypothermic.

Check the ABCs. Assess and check the ABCs. Aggressive initiation of airway, breathing, and circulation is the standard in drowning rescue. If available, administer oxygen.

Protect the Cervical Spine. Unless injury can be ruled out, assume that the victim has a neck injury and use the jaw thrust technique to open the airway. Neck injuries can be caused from surfing, diving in shallow water, or flipping a kayak or decked canoe in rapids.

Perform a Focused Exam and History. A complete patient exam is warranted to assess for injury.

Treat for Hypothermia. Remove wet clothing and dry and insulate the patient to prevent further heat loss.

Evacuate the Patient. Outside the wilderness, any victim of involuntary submersion should be evaluated by a physician, as lung injury from inhaled water may not be immediately evident. In the wilderness, we don't evacuate every asymptomatic person who swims through a rapid or takes a dunking during a river crossing and comes up coughing. Evacuate the victim of a submersion incident if that person required resuscitation, was unresponsive in the water, exhibits shortness of breath or other symptoms of respiratory difficulty, or has a history of lung disease.

The mode of transport and speed of the evacuation should be based on the seriousness of the patient's condition. For example, a patient who is unresponsive following submersion should be quickly evacuated.

IMMERSION HYPOTHERMIA

It's a common assumption that we quickly become hypothermic and drown when immersed in cold water. Dr. Gordon

Giesbrecht of the University of Manitoba, Canada, is a leading researcher into immersion hypothermia. Dr. Giesbrecht's simple message is "1 minute, 10 minutes, 1 hour." We need to control our breathing and survive the first minute. We have 10 minutes to move carefully and thoughtfully before we will become incapacitated by the cold. We have an hour before we will become unresponsive due to hypothermia. Knowing this, while we still need to promptly rescue people and treat hypothermia, we know we should not panic and we have time to plan correct actions.

Treatment of Immersion Hypothermia
Although there may be subtle differences between hypothermia on land and in the water, these differences are not relevant to field treatment. Treat immersion hypothermia by removing the victim from the water. Handle the patient gently, as rough handling may trigger lethal heart rhythm abnormalities. Treat the patient for hypothermia as discussed in chapter 9 ("Cold Injuries"). Dry and insulate the patient; prevent further heat loss; ensure adequate airway, breathing, and circulation; and place the patient in a sleeping bag, possibly with another person or with hot water bottles as heat sources.

FINAL THOUGHTS
Safety around lakes, rivers, and the ocean begins with respect for the power of moving water and the debilitating effects of cold water. Cold water, failure to wear a personal flotation device (PFD), and the inability to swim are, according to the Coast Guard, the most common factors in white-water deaths.

In two out of three drownings, the victims could not swim, had no intention of entering deep water (and thus were ill prepared), and were affected by alcohol or drugs. Most drownings occur 10 to 30 feet from safety; only 10 percent of drownings occur in a guarded pool.

While awaiting rescue, assume the HELP (heat escape lessening posture) position by bringing your knees to your chest and crossing your arms over them. If you're with a group of people awaiting rescue, everyone in the group should face

Risk Factors Related to Drowning

- Age—toddlers and teenage males are at highest risk.
- Location—private swimming pools, small streams, ponds, and irrigation ditches are common drowning sites.
- Gender—males dominate all age groups.
- Alcohol—a factor in one-third to two-thirds of drownings.
- Injury—cervical spine injury, as from diving or surfing.
- Seizure disorder—risk is greatest if poorly controlled; hyperventilation may cause predisposition to seizures.
- PFD—failure to wear one.

inward and huddle with arms interlocked. You must be wearing a PFD to assume either of these positions. If possible, get out of the water onto an overturned or partially submerged boat. It is always better to keep as much of yourself or the victim out of the water as possible, even when the wind is blowing.

Clothing selection for paddling or other activities around water requires finding a balance between overdressing—and overheating—and protecting the body against sudden immersion in cold water. Extra clothing should be easily accessible in the cockpit of your boat or in your pack and should be put on if developing conditions increase the likelihood of a cold dunking.

Well-developed safety and rescue programs exist for swimming, sea kayaking, whitewater boating, and sailing. If you're involved in any of these activities, seek out these programs for further training.

Evacuation Guidelines

- Evacuate any person who required resuscitation, was unresponsive in the water, exhibits shortness of breath, or has a history of lung illness.

CHAPTER 15

MARINE ENVENOMATIONS

INTRODUCTION

Injuries from marine organisms are rarely the result of an aggressive, unprovoked attack. Most injuries occur as a result of accidental contact or when a threatened animal reacts in self-defense. This chapter discusses two broad categories of injuries from aquatic animals: marine spine envenomations and nematocyst sting envenomations. Treatment for these two types of injuries is very different: injuries from spines are treated with hot water immersion; stings are rinsed in vinegar.

Marine Spine Envenomations

Marine animals with venom known to be harmful to people include the zebra fish, scorpion fish, stonefish, sea urchin, and stingray, which deliver venom through spines, and the cone shell, which injects venom through a proboscis. Envenomation may cause life-threatening injury or mild irritation, depending on the species, the number of punctures, the amount of venom, the health of the victim, and other factors.

Signs and Symptoms of Marine Spine Envenomation

Signs of marine venom injury include local discoloration, cyanosis, and laceration or puncture wound. Symptoms include numbness, tingling, and intense local pain. In serious envenomations, nausea, vomiting, paralysis, respiratory distress, heart rhythm irregularities, and shock can occur.

Treatment of Marine Spine Envenomation

Treat marine envenomations by controlling bleeding, removing imbedded spines, cleaning the wound, and controlling pain with hot water soaks.

Immerse the Injury in Hot Water. Immerse the injury in water as hot as the patient can tolerate (usually 115° to 120°F, 46° to 49°C) for 30 to 90 minutes or until the pain is gone. This therapy is thought to inactivate heat-sensitive proteins in the venom. Immersion in a large pot or a plastic bag filled with hot water is best, but hot compresses can also be used.

Clean the wound with irrigation. Remove obvious imbedded spines carefully. Elevate the extremity to help control swelling. Remedies such as meat tenderizer, papain, or mangrove sap are not scientifically confirmed and may irritate the wound.

Removing imbedded spines is against standard treatment for impaled objects; however, the spines are a source of infection and a continued source of venom. Their presence also retards healing and may cause further injury. Removing them is often difficult; the spines are brittle and break easily, leaving a foreign body that may cause infection. Use tweezers or fingers (wear gloves) to remove the spines. If the spine is hard to remove, leave it in place and evacuate the patient. Medications to control pain are appropriate.

Monitor the patient for signs of generalized envenomation. With severe envenomation, signs and symptoms of shock and respiratory distress will develop. In these cases, our treatment is supportive care and evacuation.

Scorpion Fish

There are three genera in this family—stonefish, zebrafish, and scorpion fish—and several hundred species. The stonefish, inconspicuous and possessing a highly toxic venom, is considered to be among the most dangerous of all venomous creatures.

Zebra fish are spectacularly colored; stonefish and scorpion fish are less so. All members of the family are found in shallow waters. Zebra fish are free swimmers; stonefish and scorpion fish often hide in cracks, near rocks, or among plants. The stonefish may bury itself under sandy or broken coral bottoms. A dead stonefish is still dangerous! Its venom remains active for 48 hours after death.

The immediate intense pain of stonefish envenomation peaks in 60 to 90 minutes and can persist for days, despite treatment. Stonefish wounds are slow to heal and prone to infection.

Sea Urchins

Sea urchins are nonaggressive, nocturnal, omnivorous feeders that move slowly across the ocean bottom and are often found on rocky bottoms and burrowed in sand and small crevices. The hard spines protecting their vital organs can envenom victims if the urchin is stepped on, handled, or inadvertently bumped. Their grasping organs, called pedicellariae, can also envenom.

Symptoms are usually local and mild; however, infections are possible if pieces of imbedded spines remain in the skin or joint capsules. Spines imbedded in joints or large fragments left in soft tissues should be evaluated by a physician. Severe reactions are rare.

Spines lodged in the skin often turn it a brownish purple color. This reaction is harmless and can be seen regardless of whether a spine has broken off and remains imbedded or not.

Starfish

The venomous crown-of-thorns starfish is found in the Indo-Pacific area, the Red Sea, the eastern Pacific, and the Sea of Cortez. Starfish are scavengers that feed on other echinoderms, mollusks, coral, and worms. The upper surface of the crown-of-thorns starfish is studded with sharp, poisonous spines that can penetrate even the best diving gloves.

Cone Shells

The shells of these animals, which live in shallow waters, reefs, and tide pools, are beautiful but hide a nasty sting. Cone shells project a long proboscis from the narrow end of the shell and

CONE SHELL:

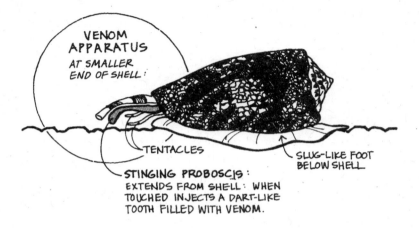

VENOM APPARATUS AT SMALLER END OF SHELL:

TENTACLES

STINGING PROBOSCIS: EXTENDS FROM SHELL: WHEN TOUCHED INJECTS A DART-LIKE TOOTH FILLED WITH VENOM.

SLUG-LIKE FOOT BELOW SHELL

inject venom from its tip. Toxicity to humans varies, but it rarely causes death. Do not handle cone shells. Drop them immediately if the proboscis is observed. Almost all reported envenomations have come from collectors handling the shells.

The injury resembles a bee sting with pain, burning, and itching. Serious envenomations produce cyanosis and numbness at the injury site, which progresses to numbness around the mouth, then generalized paralysis.

Treatment of cone shell stings is largely supportive care. Clean and thoroughly irrigate the puncture wound. The benefit of hot water soaks is unproved, but they may provide pain relief. Likewise, the value of circumferential pressure bandages is unconfirmed, but they may slow the spread of the venom.

Stingrays

Stingrays are bottom feeders, often found in shallow waters lying on top of or partially buried under sandy bottoms. Most stingray envenomations occur when a careless swimmer or wader steps on a buried ray. The stingray's tail whips up, and its serrated barbs inflict a nasty wound. Such defensive attacks

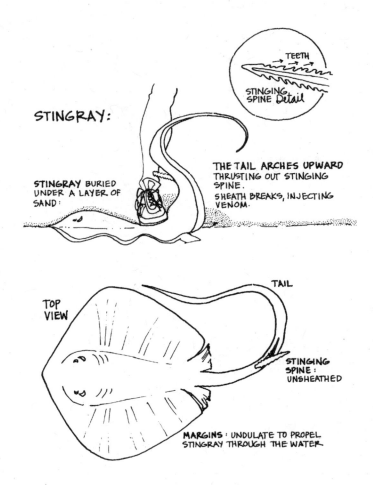

usually cause wounds to the leg or ankle, and pieces of barbs may remain imbedded in the wound. Wounds often take the form of bleeding soft tissue lacerations or punctures. Intense local pain may last up to 48 hours.

NEMATOCYST STING ENVENOMATIONS

Nematocysts are specialized stinging capsules found in members of the phylum Coelenterata, which includes the sea anemones, jellyfish, Portuguese man-of-wars, and some corals.

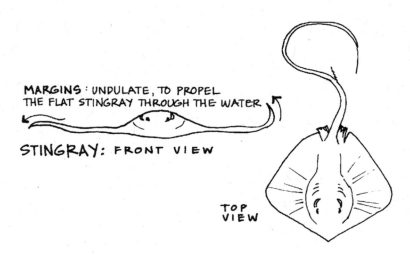

MARGINS : UNDULATE, TO PROPEL
THE FLAT STINGRAY THROUGH THE WATER

STINGRAY: FRONT VIEW

TOP
VIEW

The nematocyst discharges an incapacitating venom, allowing the animal to kill and digest its prey. Some nematocysts produce a sticky venomous substance; others deliver a barbed, venomous stinger.

Nematocyst discharge is triggered by contact with the skin or by changes in osmotic pressure, as can occur when the nematocyst is rinsed with fresh water. Nematocysts are generally found around the animal's mouth or on the tentacles, and nematocysts from dead jellyfish can still envenom.

Signs and Symptoms of Nematocyst Sting Envenomations

Signs and symptoms range from mild skin irritations to rapid death, and vary consider-

---

Treatment of Marine Spine Envenomations

- Control bleeding.
- Immerse the injury in water as hot as the patient can tolerate (usually 115° to 120°F, 46° to 49°C) for 30 to 90 minutes or until the pain is gone.
- Remove imbedded spines.
- Irrigate the wound.
- Clean the wound.
- Elevate the extremity to help control swelling.
- Monitor for signs of infection or envenomation.
- Medications for pain.

ably with the venomous species. In general, contact with a nematocyst produces painful local swelling, redness, and a stinging, prickling sensation that progresses to numbness, burning, and throbbing pain. Pain may radiate from the extremities to the groin, abdomen, or armpit. The contact site may turn a reddish brown-purple color, marked by swelling. In more serious cases, blisters may occur.

Severe envenomation may produce headache, abdominal cramps, nausea, vomiting, muscle paralysis, and respiratory or cardiac distress.

Treatment of Nematocyst Sting Envenomations

Treat nematocyst injury first by protecting yourself and second by inactivating and removing nematocysts from the skin. Rinse the injury with sea water to begin removing remaining nematocysts. Do not scrape, rub, or rinse with fresh water, as this will cause any nematocysts on the skin to release more venom. Soak the injury in vinegar (5 percent acetic acid) for at least 30 minutes. Vinegar should not be used without first testing a small area of the sting for adverse effects—in a few species it may trigger further nematocyst discharge. Alcohol, meat tenderizer, and baking soda are less effective, although a baking soda slurry is effective in treating the sting of the Chesapeake sea nettle.

After soaking, remove all visible tentacles with tweezers. Sticky tentacles may be easier to remove if you first apply a drying agent such as baking soda, talc, or sand. Nematocysts can also be removed with adhesive tape or by shaving gently with a razor and shaving cream. Be careful. Rescuer injury is common both in the water and when removing nematocysts on shore.

Anemones

Stinging cells surround the mouths of these sessile organ-

Treatment of Nematocyst Sting Envenomations

- Rinse with sea water to remove remaining nematocysts.
- Soak in vinegar for at least 30 minutes.
- After soaking, remove all visible tentacles.

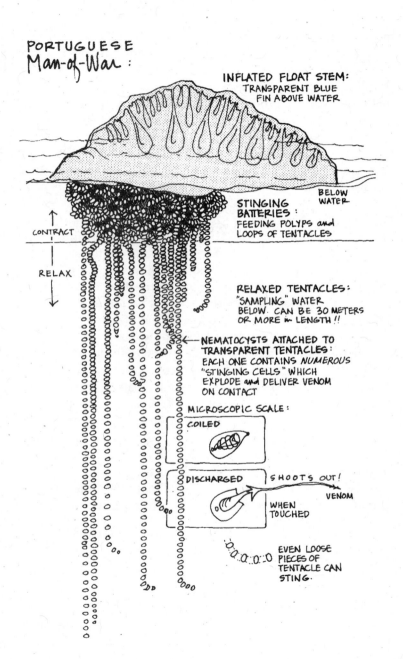

PORTUGUESE
Man-of-War:

INFLATED FLOAT STEM:
TRANSPARENT BLUE
FIN ABOVE WATER

BELOW
WATER

STINGING
BATTERIES:
FEEDING POLYPS and
LOOPS OF TENTACLES

CONTRACT

RELAX

RELAXED TENTACLES:
"SAMPLING" WATER
BELOW. CAN BE 30 METERS
OR MORE in LENGTH!!

NEMATOCYSTS ATTACHED TO
TRANSPARENT TENTACLES:
EACH ONE CONTAINS NUMEROUS
"STINGING CELLS" WHICH
EXPLODE and DELIVER VENOM
ON CONTACT

MICROSCOPIC SCALE:

COILED

DISCHARGED   SHOOTS OUT!

VENOM

WHEN
TOUCHED

EVEN LOOSE
PIECES OF
TENTACLE CAN
STING.

isms. Contact often occurs from accidentally brushing into the anemone. Anemone nematocysts usually produce only very mild local symptoms.

Jellyfish
These animals vary in size from tiny (2 millimeters) to big (2 meters with 40-meter tentacles). Most produce mild local signs and symptoms; however, some produce very potent venom. The box jellyfish *(Chironex fleckeri),* found in the Pacific Ocean off Australia, can cause death within 1 minute.

Portuguese Man-of-War
This large colony of animals usually lives on the surface of the open ocean, its long, transparent tentacles dangling for prey. It is transported by winds and currents, and the animal or pieces of its tentacles can sometimes be pushed into coastal waters. Contact with pieces of tentacle usually causes only mild, superficial reactions. Contact with a large number of tentacles from an intact animal, however, can provoke massive envenomation and cause serious reactions.

Fire Coral
Fire corals are so named because they make you feel as if you've touched hot coals. They are found in coral reefs in tropical waters. Their nematocyst sting causes immediate pain, often described as burning, and small raised red areas on the skin. The localized pain usually lasts 1 to 4 days.

Hard Coral
Hard corals are not highly venomous but often have very sharp edges that can cause abrasions or even lacerations. The wounds heal slowly, especially if pieces of coral are imbedded in the skin. Some species can cause rashes. Vigorous irrigation of the wound is helpful to remove coral pieces. Imbedded pieces of coral often cause slow-healing wound infections.

Sea Cucumbers

These creatures are bottom scavengers found in both shallow and deep water. Sea cucumbers often feed on nematocysts, so they may secrete coelenterate venom as well. They also produce a liquid toxin that causes skin irritations and often severe inflammatory reactions (swelling, raised patches, itching, oozing). To treat, rinse the skin thoroughly with water and soak the injured area in vinegar.

FINAL THOUGHTS

Learn to identify marine animals and to understand their habits. When wading, shuffle your feet to alert stingrays to your presence. Touching marine animals or coral formations is not necessary to enjoy them. When swimming and diving, avoid standing or walking on coral reefs or banging against them. A minimum-impact approach protects not only you but also the fragile underwater environment.

Evacuation Guidelines

- Evacuate any patient with a large soft tissue wound, imbedded spine, unmanageable pain, or systemic signs and symptoms of envenomation.

PART IV

Medical Emergencies

CHAPTER 16

ALLERGIES
AND ANAPHYLAXIS

INTRODUCTION

The immune system is an extensive array of cells, structures, antibodies, and other elements constantly defending us against foreign substances: microorganisms, pollen, dust, food, cat dander—practically all the pieces of the natural world. Normally, the immune system smoothly identifies and neutralizes harmful substances with white blood cells, antibodies, and mild inflammation. It's a wonderful, critical, complex, and efficient system. Among the many things it does is remember a first encounter with a foreign substance, producing antibodies designed to recognize and neutralize the invader the next time it appears.

Normally, this interaction is delicately balanced. An overreaction causes us misery when it triggers an inflammatory response we call an allergy. In an allergic person, reintroduction of the foreign material—an allergen—results in an inappropriately large release of histamine. Histamine causes fluid to leak from blood vessels, resulting in edema and swelling, which can obstruct the airway. It also dilates blood vessels, which can lead to shock.

Signs and Symptoms of Mild to Moderate
Allergic Reactions

Allergic reactions range from mild to severe, and they can be immediate or delayed. For most people, the allergic response is mild, though often irritating. Hay fever is one example of a mild allergic response. Hay fever sufferers complain of a runny nose, sneezing, swollen eyes, itching skin, and possibly hives. An allergic reaction may also be local, the result of insect stings or contact with a plant. The local reaction is red, swollen, and itching, perhaps with hives, but stays near the point of contact.

Treatment for Mild to Moderate Allergic Reactions

First remove the allergen from the patient or the patient from the offending environment. It's hard to treat a pollen reaction standing under a tree shedding millions of pollen grains or to treat an allergy to dust in a dusty cabin. Antihistamines and decongestants are the usual treatment. The antihistamines treat the underlying reaction, the release of too much histamine. Monitor the patient closely for a developing severe reaction.

Signs and Symptoms of Mild to Moderate Allergic Reaction

- Local swelling near a sting
- Runny nose, sneezing, swollen eyes, hay fever
- Flushed and itchy skin
- Hives or welts on the skin
- Mild or no breathing difficulty

Treatment of a Mild to Moderate Allergic Reaction

- Remove the allergen from the patient or the patient from the offending environment.
- Oral antihistamines.
- Hydration.
- Monitor for increased breathing difficulty.

Signs and Symptoms of Severe Allergic Reactions

An anaphylactic response is a massive, generalized reaction of the immune system that is potentially harmful to the body. Common triggers of anaphylaxis are drugs and some foods; people can also react to bee stings and insect bites. Instead of the mild symptoms of hay fever, anaphylaxis produces asphyxiating swelling of the larynx, rapid pulse, a rapid fall in blood pressure, rash, itching, hives, flushed skin, swollen and red eyes, tearing of the eyes, swelling of the feet and hands, nausea, vomiting, and abdominal pain. The airway obstruction and shock may be fatal. Onset usually occurs within a few minutes of contact with the triggering substance, although the reaction may be delayed. Any large areas of swelling, typically involving the face, lips, hands, and feet; respiratory compromise; or shock should be treated with epinephrine.

Signs and Symptoms of Anaphylaxis

- Flushed and itchy skin
- Hives and welts on the skin
- Swollen face, lips, and tongue
- Respiratory distress
- Shock

Treatment of Anaphylaxis

- Remove the allergen from the patient or the patient from the offending environment.
- For large areas of swelling, respiratory compromise, or shock, inject epinephrine.
- When the patient can swallow, administer oral antihistamines.
- Watch for a second reaction.
- Evacuate.

Treatment of Severe Allergic Reactions

If you catch the allergic reaction while the patient can still swallow, administer oral antihistamines. When the reaction becomes severe, the anaphylaxis is treated with immediate administration of epinephrine, a prescription medication, to counteract the effects of the histamine. Persons who know that they are vulnerable to anaphylactic shock usually carry injectable epinephrine in an TwinJect or EpiPen. Trip leaders should be familiar with their use and seek the advice of a physician advisor when responding to this emergency.

Use of the EpiPen

1. Unscrew the yellow or green cap off of the EpiPen or EpiPen Jr and remove the auto-injector from its storage tube.
2. Grasp unit with the black tip pointing downward. Form fist around the unit (black tip down).
3. With your other hand, pull off the gray safety release.

4. Swing and jab firmly into outer thigh until it clicks. (Auto-injector is designed to work through clothing.)
5. Hold firmly against thigh for approximately 10 seconds. (The injection is now complete. Window on auto-injector will show red.)
6. Remove unit from thigh and massage injection area for 10 seconds.
7. Carefully place the used auto-injector (without bending the needle), needle-end first, into the storage tube of the carrying case for needle protection after use.

Use of the TwinJect

Prepare and deliver the first dose:

1. Pull off the end cap labeled "1." Never put your thumb, finger, or hand over the rounded tip.
2. Pull off the end cap labeled "2."
3. Put the rounded tip against the middle of the outer side of your thigh (upper leg).
4. Press hard until the needle enters your thigh (upper leg) through your skin. Hold it in place while slowly counting to 10.

Prepare and deliver the second dose:

1. Unscrew and remove the rounded tip.
2. Be careful to avoid the exposed needle.
3. Remove the red tip.
4. Grab the blue plastic to pull the syringe out of the barrel. Do not touch the needle.
5. Slide the yellow collar off the plunger.
6. If your symptoms have not improved within about 10 minutes since the first injection, you need a second dose.
7. Put the needle into your thigh (upper leg) through your skin.
8. Push the plunger down all the way.

Evacuation Guidelines

- Evacuate rapidly any patient with a severe allergic reaction. Secondary reactions can occur within 12 to 24 hours.

CHAPTER 17

RESPIRATORY AND CARDIAC EMERGENCIES

INTRODUCTION
The topics typically discussed in first aid texts as medical emergencies include heart disease, heart attacks, and congestive heart failure; respiratory illnesses such as asthma, emphysema, and pneumonia; as well as diabetes, epilepsy, and drug and alcohol abuse. These are common emergency runs for ambulance crews but less common on wilderness expeditions, although they do occur. Supported by modern medicine, people with heart and lung disease, seizures, and diabetes are able to enjoy the wilderness.

RESPIRATORY AND CARDIAC EMERGENCIES
A history of asthma, heart disease, or even a heart attack does not, by itself, prevent someone from paddling a river, climbing a peak, or hiking the Wind River Range. The wilderness first responder will see these medical conditions and should be knowledgeable in their assessment and treatment.

Hyperventilation Syndrome
Hyperventilation syndrome is an increased respiratory rate caused by an overwhelming emotional stimulus. The patient becomes apprehensive, nervous, or tense. For example, a person may normally have a fear of heights, and the thought of rock climbing triggers a hyperventilation episode, or a climber may fall and suffer a minor injury but begin to hyperventilate

CARPOPEDAL SPASMS
HYPERVENTILATION SYNDROME :

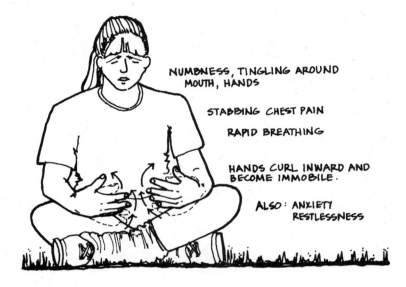

NUMBNESS, TINGLING AROUND MOUTH, HANDS

STABBING CHEST PAIN

RAPID BREATHING

HANDS CURL INWARD AND BECOME IMMOBILE.

ALSO: ANXIETY RESTLESSNESS

out of fear and anxiety. The hyperventilation can quickly become the major condition affecting the patient.

Signs and Symptoms of Hyperventilation. Signs and symptoms of hyperventilation include a high level of anxiety, a sense of suffocation without apparent physiological basis, rapid and deep respiration, rapid pulse, dizziness and/or faintness, sweating, and dry mouth.

As the syndrome progresses, the patient may complain of numbness or tingling of the hands or around the mouth. Thereafter, painful spasms of the hands and forearms—carpopedal spasms—may occur. The hands curl inward and become immobile. The patient may complain of stabbing chest pain. Rapid respiration increases the loss of carbon dioxide, which causes the blood to become alkaline. The alkaline blood causes the carpopedal spasms.

Treatment for Hyperventilation. To treat hyperventilation syndrome, calm the patient and slow his or her breathing.

Coach the patient to breathe slowly. It may take some time before the symptoms resolve. Breathing into a paper bag, once thought to help increase carbon dioxide in the blood, is no longer a recommended treatment.

Pulmonary Embolism

A pulmonary embolism occurs when a clot (usually from a leg vein) breaks loose and lodges in the blood vessels of the lung. Pulmonary embolus is not uncommon outside the wilderness and can be a tough diagnosis. Decreased mobility—lying in a tent waiting out a storm, for example, or long plane flights—may predispose a person to a blood clot. Smoking and a history of recent surgery or illness that kept the patient in bed are also risk factors. There is an increased tendency for blood to clot in arteries and veins at high altitudes. Dehydration, increased red blood cells, cold, constrictive clothing, and immobility during bad weather have been cited as possible causes.

Signs and Symptoms of Pulmonary Embolism. The patient complains of a sudden onset of shortness of breath and pain with inspiration. Respiratory distress may develop, including anxiety and restlessness; shortness of breath; rapid breathing and pulse; signs of shock, including pale, cool, and clammy skin and cyanosis of the skin, lips, and fingernail beds; and labored breathing using accessory muscles of the neck, shoulder, and abdomen to achieve maximum effort.

Treatment for Pulmonary Embolism. First responders can't dissolve the embolism in the field. You can identify the respiratory distress or chest pain, administer oxygen if it is available, and evacuate the patient promptly.

Pneumonia

Pneumonia is a lung infection that can be caused by bacteria, viruses, fungi, and protozoa. The inflammation of the alveolar spaces causes swelling and fluid accumulation. Difficulty breathing can result. People weakened by an illness, chronic disease, fatigue, or exposure are especially at risk. Pneumonia can be a serious infection and is a leading cause of death.

Signs and Symptoms of Pneumonia

- History of upper respiratory infection
- Sweating, fever, chills
- Productive cough
- Pain on inspiration or coughing
- Shortness of breath
- Wet lung sounds
- General illness

Treatment of Pneumonia

- Encourage patients to cough.
- Hydrate.
- Administer oxygen.
- Evacuate.

Signs and Symptoms of Pneumonia. Signs and symptoms of pneumonia are shortness of breath, fever and chills, a productive cough with green-yellow or brown sputum, and pain on inspiration or coughing. The patient may have a recent history of upper respiratory infection and lung sounds, if you can listen with a stethoscope, may be noisy.

Treatment of Pneumonia. Patients with pneumonia should be evacuated. Encourage the patient to cough and breathe deeply to keep the lungs clear. Hydration is important, and oxygen, if available, will be helpful. The patient may be more comfortable sitting up.

Asthma

Asthma is characterized by narrowing of the airways, increased mucous production, and bronchial edema. Asthma's exact cause is unknown. We do know that allergy and environmental (non-allergic) factors such as molds, cold air, chemical fumes, cigarette smoke, exercise, and infections play a role.

Asthma is usually a reversible condition. The airway narrowing can improve spontaneously or in response to medication. A prolonged, severe asthma attack that is not relieved by treatment is an emergency requiring rapid transport. There are other chronic lung diseases, such as emphysema and bronchitis, in which the breathing impairment is persistent because of destruction of lung tissue and chronic inflammation.

Signs and Symptoms of Asthma. Signs and symptoms of mild to moderate asthma are wheezing, chest tightness, and

Signs and Symptoms of Asthma

MILD TO MODERATE ASTHMA
- Chest tightness
- Wheezing and coughing
- Shortness of breath
- Increased heart and breathing rates
- Increased mucous production
- Fatigue

SEVERE ASTHMA
- Use of accessory muscles to breathe
- Decreasing breath sounds progressing to absence of sounds
- Speaking in one- to two-word clusters
- Sleepiness
- Cyanosis

shortness of breath. The heart and breathing rates are increased. When asthma becomes severe, the patient may be hunched over, bracing the upper body and working to breathe. The patient may be able to speak only in one- or two-word clusters. Lung sounds may be diminished or absent. If the patient becomes sleepy or too fatigued to breathe, the situation is dire.

Treatment of Asthma. Usually the patient treats the asthma by self-administering medication, commonly a bronchodilator, with an inhaler. You may need to help the patient relax and use the inhaler properly; shake it first, hold it in the mouth, exhale, and then depress the device and inhale the mist deeply, holding the breath for 5 to 10 seconds before exhaling.

Treatment of Asthma

- Bronchodilators.
- Warm, humidified oxygen.
- Hydration and rest.

To stabilize the initial exacerbation, use of the patient's inhaler 2 puffs every 5 minutes, up to 12 puffs, might be needed. Warm,

---

Signs and Symptoms of Cardiac Chest Pain

- Persistent chest pain: crushing, tight, pressing, viselike, constricting
- Shortness of breath
- Anxiety and denial
- Pain radiating to arm or jaw
- Nausea and vomiting
- Lightheadedness
- Pale, cool, sweaty skin
- Rapid, slow, weak, or irregular heartbeat
- History of angina, heart attack, or risk factors

---

humidified air can help relax airways and clear mucus. Severe asthma episodes may require medications (epinephrine and steroids) usually not available in the wilderness, and such patients should be evacuated promptly.

Chest Pain and Heart Disease

Heart disease is a leading cause of death in the United States. Atherosclerosis, a common form of heart disease, slowly builds deposits on arterial walls that narrow the artery and impede blood flow. The narrowed artery can spasm, constrict, or lodge a clot, depriving tissue of blood. If this happens in the brain, the result may be a stroke. If it happens in the heart, it causes chest pain, also known as angina pectoris, or a myocardial infarction, a heart attack. Angina is pain from diminished blood flow. A myocardial infarction is heart muscle damage from blocked blood flow. Sudden death from a heart that beats erratically, or not at all, can be a result of this disease.

Signs and Symptoms of Cardiac Chest Pain. Cardiac chest pain is often described as crushing, tight, pressing, viselike, and constricting. It is below the breastbone and can radiate into the left arm and jaw. Shortness of breath, anxiety, pale sweaty skin, nausea, and dizziness are also common complaints. The pulse may be irregular. If the pain is brought on by physical or emotional stress and is relieved by rest, it may be angina. If it is unprovoked and persists, it may be a myocardial infarction.

Treatment for Cardiac Chest Pain. Figuring out whether nontraumatic chest pain is a heart condition can be difficult under the best of circumstances. Inflammation of the stomach or esophagus, chest muscle strains, rib injury, lung problems, bronchitis, and coughing can all cause chest pain. To complicate the situation, cardiac pain does not always fit the classic pattern and description. A patient with chest pain symptoms that cannot be attributed to a chest injury, lung problem, stomach upset, or muscle strain should be given one adult aspirin every 24 hours and evacuated.

Treatment of Suspected Cardiac Chest Pain

• Reduce anxiety and activity.
• Administer oxygen.
• Administer aspirin.
• Evacuate.

Reduce the demands on the heart by calming the patient and making him or her rest. If available, administer oxygen. If your patient has a history of cardiac chest pain, he or she may have nitroglycerin, a medication administered by placing a tablet under the tongue.

Evacuation Guidelines

- Evacuate any patient with chest pain that is not clearly musculoskeletal, pulmonary, or gastrointestinal.
- Expedite evacuation for any patient with chest pain that does not relieve within 20 minutes.
- Expedite evacuation if a severe asthma attack is unresponsive to medications. A patient with severe asthma may need treatment with steroids and epinephrine.

CHAPTER 18

ABDOMINAL PAIN

INTRODUCTION

The abdomen contains the major blood vessels supplying the lower extremities and the digestive, urinary, and reproductive systems. A lot can go wrong in the belly, and deciding how serious a problem is can be difficult, even for a physician. As first responders, our role is simple: to decide whether the problem is an "acute abdomen," and if so, to support and evacuate the patient. Knowledge of the location and function of the abdominal organs and some of the common abdominal problems can make this determination easier.

ABDOMINAL ANATOMY AND PHYSIOLOGY

The digestive tract processes food to nourish the cells of the body. Secretions within the digestive tract break down food into basic sugars, fatty acids, and amino acids. These products of digestion cross the wall of the intestine and travel to the liver via the veins for detoxification. From the liver, blood circulates nutrients to the individual cells of the body.

Abdominal and Pelvic Cavities. The abdominal cavity, like the chest, is lined by a slippery membrane, called the peritoneum, that covers the organs. The diaphragm separates the chest from the abdomen.

The liver, gallbladder, stomach, spleen, pancreas, appendix, and large and small intestines lie in the abdominal cavity. The kidneys, ureters, adrenals, pancreas, aorta, and inferior vena

ORGANS OF THE ABDOMINAL CAVITY:

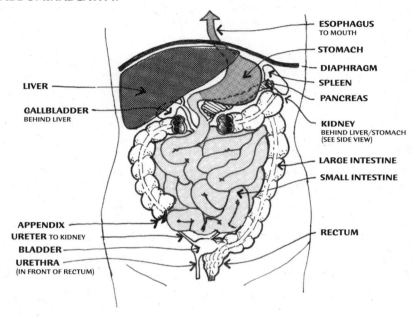

LIVER

GALLBLADDER
BEHIND LIVER

ESOPHAGUS
TO MOUTH

STOMACH

DIAPHRAGM

SPLEEN

PANCREAS

KIDNEY
BEHIND LIVER/STOMACH
(SEE SIDE VIEW)

LARGE INTESTINE

SMALL INTESTINE

APPENDIX
URETER TO KIDNEY
BLADDER
URETHRA
(IN FRONT OF RECTUM)

RECTUM

cava are retroperitoneal. The female reproductive organs, bladder, lower end of the large intestine, and rectum are located in the pelvic cavity.

Digestive Tract. The digestive tract starts at the mouth, where food mixes with saliva—a combination of mucus, water, salts, digestive enzymes, and organic compounds. As food is swallowed, it passes from the mouth into the pharynx. The pharynx divides into the trachea and esophagus. The trachea lies in front of the esophagus. Food could easily go into the trachea, but a thin flap of cartilage, the epiglottis, closes the entrance to the trachea with each swallow.

The esophagus is a 10-inch muscular tube extending from the larynx to the stomach. Contractions of the esophagus—peristalsis—propel food to the stomach.

Stomach. The stomach is a J-shaped organ approximately 10 inches long located in the upper left quadrant of the abdomen. The major function of the stomach is to intermittently store food and move it into the intestine in small amounts. Every 15 to 25 seconds, stomach contractions mix food with gastric juice, turning it into chyme, a thin liquid. Water, salts, alcohol, and certain drugs are absorbed directly by the stomach.

Small and Large Intestines. From the stomach, chyme passes into the small intestine, a tube 21 feet long and 1 inch in diameter. Within the first foot of the small intestine, food mixes with secretions from the pancreas and gallbladder. Ninety percent of the products of digestion (proteins, fats, carbohydrates, vitamins, and minerals) is absorbed in the lower end of the small intestine. Peristalsis moves food through the intestines.

Chyme passes from the small intestine to the large intestine, a tube 5 feet long and $2^1/2$ inches in diameter. The appendix is located just below the junction of the small and large intestines. The large intestine absorbs water, forming a solid stool.

The rectum is where feces are stored. The last 2 inches of the intestinal tract forms the anus, which consists of a series of sphincters that move the feces out of the body.

Liver. The liver lies beneath the diaphragm in the upper right quadrant. At 4 pounds in weight, it is the largest solid organ in the abdomen and the one most often injured. There are 500 known functions of the liver, among them detoxifying the products of digestion; converting glycogen, fat, and proteins into glucose; storing vitamins; and producing bile.

Gallbladder. Bile, essential for fat digestion and absorption, is stored in the gallbladder, a pear-shaped organ $3/4$ inch long. The gallbladder responds to the presence of food (especially fats) in the small intestine by constricting and emptying bile into the intestine.

Pancreas. The pancreas is an oblong organ located in back of the liver. It contains two types of glands. One produces pancreatic juice, which aids in the digestion of fats, carbohydrates,

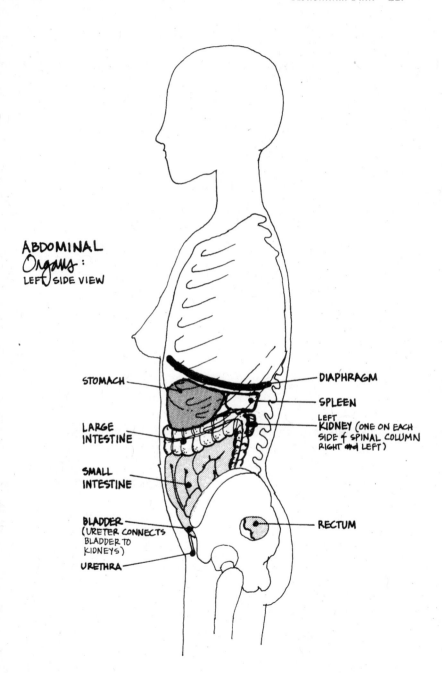

ABDOMINAL
Organs:
LEFT SIDE VIEW

STOMACH

LARGE
INTESTINE

SMALL
INTESTINE

BLADDER
(URETER CONNECTS
BLADDER TO
KIDNEYS)

URETHRA

DIAPHRAGM

SPLEEN

LEFT
KIDNEY (ONE ON EACH
SIDE OF SPINAL COLUMN
RIGHT and LEFT)

RECTUM

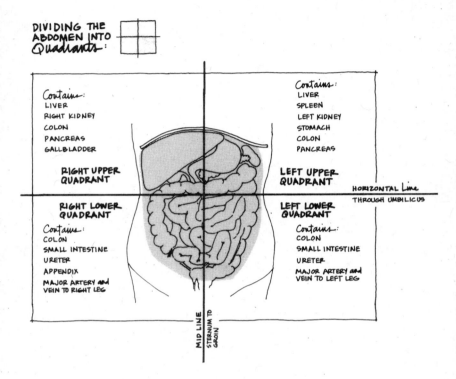

DIVIDING THE ABDOMEN INTO Quadrants:

Contains:
LIVER
RIGHT KIDNEY
COLON
PANCREAS
GALLBLADDER

RIGHT UPPER QUADRANT

Contains:
LIVER
SPLEEN
LEFT KIDNEY
STOMACH
COLON
PANCREAS

LEFT UPPER QUADRANT

HORIZONTAL Line THROUGH UMBILICUS

RIGHT LOWER QUADRANT

Contains:
COLON
SMALL INTESTINE
URETER
APPENDIX
MAJOR ARTERY and VEIN TO RIGHT LEG

LEFT LOWER QUADRANT

Contains:
COLON
SMALL INTESTINE
URETER
MAJOR ARTERY and VEIN TO LEFT LEG

MID LINE
STERNUM TO GROIN

starches, and proteins. The juice flows directly into the small intestine via the pancreatic duct. The other gland secretes chemicals, including insulin, that regulate sugar metabolism.

Spleen. The spleen, located in the upper left quadrant beneath the diaphragm, is the only abdominal organ not involved in digestion. The spleen produces blood cells and destroys worn-out red blood cells.

Urinary System. The urinary system—kidneys, ureters, bladder, and urethra—discharges waste materials filtered from the blood. The two kidneys rid the blood of toxic wastes and control water and salt balance. If the kidneys fail to function, toxic waste will concentrate in the blood, causing death.

Urine flows from the kidneys to the bladder via the ureters. The bladder can hold up to 800 milliliters of urine. At 200 to 400 milliliters, we feel the urge to void. The bladder empties to the outside via the urethra. In women, the urethra is about $1^1/_2$ inches long; in men, approximately 8 inches.

ABDOMINAL ILLNESS
There are many, many illnesses that can develop within the abdomen. This section is by no means exhaustive, but it does cover problems that, in our experience, we tend to see in the backcountry. The most important part of this chapter is the final section, which reminds us not to worry about diagnosis, but rather to do a sound assessment and decide if the patient meets the evacuation criteria.

Kidney Stones
Kidney stones occur when minerals precipitate from the urine in the kidney. Approximately three-quarters of kidney stones are crystallized calcium. Predisposing factors for kidney stones include urinary tract infections, dehydration, an increase in dietary calcium, too much vitamin D, and cancer.

Signs and Symptoms of Kidney Stones. As a stone passes down the ureter, the patient experiences excruciating pain that comes and goes with increasing intensity. The pain usually begins at the level of the lowest ribs on the back and radiates to the lower abdomen and/or groin. The patient is pale, sweaty, nauseated, and "writhing" in pain. There may be pain with urination and blood in the urine. Chills and fever are not present. The duration of the pain depends on the location of the stone. Pain is severe while a stone is passing from the kidney to the bladder and stops after the stone has dropped into the bladder. The pain may last as long as 24 hours, but the duration is usually shorter.

Treatment for Kidney Stones. Drinking copious amounts of water may help the patient pass the stone. Pain medication may help. If pain continues for more than 48 hours or if the patient is unable to urinate, evacuate.

Appendicitis
Appendicitis is an inflammation of the appendix, usually caused by a kinking of the appendix or by a hardened stool

obstructing the opening. Due to the obstruction, mucus builds within the appendix, causing pressure, swelling, and infection. The highest incidence of appendicitis occurs in males between the ages of 10 and 30.

Signs and Symptoms of Appendicitis. The classic symptoms of appendicitis are pain behind the umbilicus (the navel), anorexia, nausea, and vomiting. They usually develop gradually over 1 to 2 days. The pain then shifts to the lower right quadrant, halfway between the umbilicus and the right hipbone. The patient may have one or two bowel movements but usually does not have diarrhea. When you apply pressure with your hand over the appendix, the patient may complain of pain when you remove your hand. This is called rebound tenderness. A fever and elevated pulse may be present. Due to infection and pain, the patient may lie on his or her side or back with legs tucked onto the abdomen (fetal position). There may also be pain when the patient jumps, walks, or jars his or her right leg or side.

Before the appendix ruptures, the skin over the appendix becomes hypersensitive. If you stroke the skin surface with a pin or grasp the skin between the thumb and forefinger and pull upward, the patient may complain of pain. If the appendix ruptures, the pain temporarily disappears but soon reappears as the abdominal cavity becomes infected (peritonitis). If the infection remains localized (abscess), the patient may only run a low fever and complain of not feeling well. The abscess may not rupture for a week or more.

Treatment for Appendicitis. Appendicitis is a surgical emergency. The patient must be evacuated.

Peritonitis

Peritonitis is an inflammation of the peritoneum. Causes include penetrating abdominal wounds, abdominal bleeding, or ruptured internal organs that spill digestive juices into the abdominal cavity.

Signs and Symptoms of Peritonitis. Signs and symptoms of peritonitis vary, depending on whether the infection is local or general. The patient lies very still, as movement increases the pain. He or she may complain of nausea, vomiting, anorexia, and/or fever. The abdomen is rigid and tender. The infection causes peristaltic activity of the bowel to stop, so the patient has no bowel movements. Shock may be present. The patient appears very sick.

Treatment for Peritonitis. Peritonitis is a severe infection beyond our capability to treat in the wilderness; treat the patient for shock and evacuate.

Hemorrhoids

Hemorrhoids are varicose veins of the anal canal. They may be internal or external. Constipation, straining during elimination, diarrhea, and pregnancy can cause hemorrhoids. External hemorrhoids can be very painful. Internal hemorrhoids tend not to be painful but bleed during bowel movements. The stool may be streaked on the outside with blood. The patient may complain of itching around the anus.

Treatment for Hemorrhoids. Apply moist heat to the anal area. This can be done with a bandanna dipped in warm water. Rest, increased liquid and fruit intake to keep the stools soft, and/or anesthetic ointments (such as dibucaine, Preparation H, or Anusol) help decrease pain and bleeding.

Gastric and Duodenal Ulcers

Decreased resistance of the stomach lining to pepsin and hydrochloric acid, or an increase in the production of these chemicals, may result in ulcers. Stress, smoking, aspirin use, certain bacteria, caffeine or alcohol consumption, and heredity are possible causes.

Signs and Symptoms of Ulcers. The patient complains of a gnawing, aching, or burning in the upper abdomen at the midline 1 to 2 hours after eating or at night, when gastric secretions are at their peak. The pain may radiate from the lowest ribs to the back and frequently disappears if the patient ingests food or antacids.

Is it indigestion, or is it an ulcer? Indigestion symptoms tend to be associated with eating. The patient complains of fullness and heartburn and may belch or vomit small amounts of food. Indigestion worsens when more food is ingested. As time passes and the stomach empties, symptoms disappear. Indigestion tends to be related to a single meal.

Treatment for Ulcers. The primary treatment for ulcers is to take antacids an hour after meals; eat small, frequent meals; and avoid coffee, alcohol, and spicy foods, which increase the secretions of the stomach. Long-term treatment includes rest and counseling to decrease stress. If the ulcer perforates the wall of the stomach, symptoms of peritonitis occur.

ABDOMINAL TRAUMA

Abdominal organs are either solid or hollow. When hollow organs are perforated, they spill their contents into the abdominal cavity. Solid organs tend to bleed when injured. Either bleeding or spillage of digestive juices causes peritonitis.

Blunt Trauma. Inspect the abdomen for bruises; consider how the injury occurred to diagnose what, if any, organs may have been damaged. Pain, signs and symptoms of shock, and a significant mechanism of injury are reasons to initiate an evacuation.

Penetrating Wounds. Assume that any penetrating wound to the abdomen has entered the peritoneal lining. Treat the patient for shock and evacuate.

Impaled Objects. Leave any impaled object in place; removal may increase bleeding. Stabilize the object with dressings. If there is bleeding, apply pressure bandages around the wound.

Evisceration. An evisceration is a protrusion of abdominal organs through a laceration in the abdominal wall. After rinsing the bowel you may be able to gently "tease" small exposed loops back into the abdomen. If not, cover the exposed bowel with dressings that have been soaked in disinfected water. Keep these moist to prevent the exposed loops of bowel from becoming dry. Change the dressings daily. Treat for shock and evacuate the patient.

ABDOMINAL ASSESSMENT

The first responder needs a few simple skills to be able to evaluate the condition of a patient with an abdominal problem.

1. Inspect the abdomen. Position the patient in a warm place, lying down. Remove the patient's clothing so that you can see the entire abdomen. A normal abdomen is slightly rounded and symmetrical. Look for old scars, areas of bruising, rashes, impaled objects, eviscerations, and distention. Check the lower back for the same. Look for any movement of the abdomen—wavelike contractions may indicate an abdominal obstruction.

2. Listen to the abdomen in all quadrants. Place your ear on the patient's abdomen and listen for bowel sounds (gurgling noises). An absence of noise indicates an injured or ill bowel. You must listen for at least 2 to 3 minutes in all quadrants before you can properly say that no bowel sounds are present.

3. Palpate the abdomen. With your palms down, apply gentle pressure with the pads of the fingers. Make sure your hands are warm and that you palpate in all the quadrants. Cold fingers or jabbing can cause the patient to tighten the abdominal muscles, thereby impeding the assessment. The abdomen should be soft and not tender. Abnormal signs include localized tenderness, diffuse tenderness, and stiff, rigid muscles ("boardlike abdomen").

4. Discuss the patient's condition with him or her. Ask about pain: Where is it located, where does it radiate to, and what is the severity and frequency? What aggravates or alleviates the pain? Are there patterns to the pain (at night, after meals, etc.)? Ask the patient about his or her past medical history. Any past surgery, diagnoses, treatment, or injuries? Any problems with swallowing, digestion, or bowel, bladder, or reproductive organs?

FINAL THOUGHTS

There are many medical problems that cause acute abdominal pain. Determining the actual source of the pain and the urgency of the condition can be difficult, even for a physician. As the leader of a wilderness trip, your task is not to make a diagnosis;

it is to decide whether the pain indicates an "acute abdomen," a possible surgical emergency requiring further evaluation. Perform a thorough assessment and decide if your patient triggers an evacuation criteria.

Evacuation Guidelines

Evacuation is recommended for anyone experiencing abdominal pain that is:
- Persistent for more than 12 hours, especially if constant.
- Localized.
- With guarding, tenderness, distension, rigidity.
- With movement, jarring, or foot strike.

Associated s/s that require evacuation may include:
- Blood in the urine, vomit, or feces.
- Persistent anorexia, vomiting, or diarrhea for more than 24 hours.
- Fever greater than 39°C (102°F).
- Signs and symptoms of shock.
- Signs and symptoms of pregnancy.

CHAPTER 19

DIABETES, SEIZURES, AND UNRESPONSIVE STATES

DIABETES

Diabetes is a disease of sugar metabolism, affecting, by conservative estimates, 10 million Americans. It is a complex disease characterized by a broad array of physiological disturbances. In the long term, diabetic complications include high blood pressure and heart and blood vessel disease; it can also affect vision, kidneys, and healing of wounds. In the short term, the disturbance in sugar metabolism can manifest itself as too much or too little sugar in the blood.

Diabetes is thought to be caused by genetic defects, infection, autoimmune processes, or direct injury to the pancreas. The pancreas produces the hormones, most notably insulin, that help regulate sugar balance. Insulin facilitates the movement of sugar from the blood into the cells. An excess of insulin promotes the movement of sugar into the cells, lowers the blood sugar level, and deprives the brain cells of a crucial nutrient. This disorder is known as hypoglycemia (low blood sugar).

In contrast, a deficit of insulin results in cells that are starved for sugar and an excess of sugar in the blood, disturbing fluid and electrolyte balance. This disorder is known as hyperglycemia (high blood sugar) or diabetic coma.

A healthy pancreas constantly adjusts the insulin level to the blood sugar level. The pancreas of a person with diabetes produces defective insulin or no insulin. To compensate for this, a diabetic takes medication to stimulate endogenous insulin or takes artificial insulin. Treatment plans for diabetics also include diet and exercise.

Hypoglycemia

Hypoglycemia results from the treatment of diabetes, not the diabetes itself. If a diabetic takes too much insulin or fails to eat sufficient sugar to match the insulin level, the blood sugar level will be insufficient to maintain normal brain function.

Hypoglycemia can occur if the diabetic skips a meal but takes the usual insulin dose, takes more than the normal insulin dose, exercises strenuously and fails to eat, or vomits a meal after taking insulin.

Signs and Symptoms of Hypoglycemia. Hypoglycemia has a rapid onset. The most prominent symptoms are alterations in mental status due to a lack of sugar to the brain. The patient may be irritable, nervous, weak, and uncoordinated; may appear intoxicated; or, in more serious cases, may become unresponsive or have seizures. The pulse is rapid; the skin pale, cool, and clammy.

Treatment for Hypoglycemia. Brain cells need sugar and can suffer permanent damage from low blood sugar levels. The treatment of hypoglycemia is to administer sugar. If the patient is awake, a sugar drink or candy bar can help increase the blood sugar level. If the patient is unresponsive, establish an airway, then place a small paste of sugar between the patient's cheek and gum and diligently watch the airway.

Signs and Symptoms of Hypoglycemia

- Mental Status: Weak, disoriented, irritable. Can progress to obvious mental status changes.
- Heart rate (HR): Rapid.
- Respiratory rate (RR): Normal or shallow.
- Skin: Pale, cool, clammy.
- Breath Odor: No changes.

Treatment for Hypoglycemia

- If you are unable to distinguish between hypoglycemia and hyperglycemia, give sugar until the patient becomes awake and alert.

Hyperglycemia

Diabetics who are untreated, who have defective or insufficient insulin, or who become ill may develop a high level of sugar in the blood. Consequences of this may be dehydration and electrolyte disturbances as the kidneys try to eliminate the excess sugar, and acid-base disturbances as cells starved for sugar turn to alternative energy sources.

Signs and Symptoms of Hyperglycemia. Hyperglycemia tends to develop more slowly than hypoglycemia, but it can come on within a few hours if the patient is ill. The first symptoms are often nausea, vomiting, thirst, and increased volume of urine output. The patient's breath may have a fruity odor from the metabolism of fats as an energy source. The patient may also have abdominal cramps or pain and signs of dehydration, including flushed, dry skin and intense thirst. Unresponsiveness is a late and very serious symptom.

> ### Signs and Symptoms of Hyperglycemia
>
> - Mental status: Restless, "drunken"
> - Heart rate (HR): Weak, rapid
> - Respiratory rate (RR): Increased
> - Skin: Warm, pink, dry
> - Increased hunger, increased thirst, increased urine output, fatigue
> - Breath odor: Acetone, sweet
> - Persistent high blood sugar levels

> ### Treatment Principles for Hyperglycemia
>
> - If you are unable to distinguish between hypoglycemia and hyperglycemia, give sugar.
> - Hydrate.
> - **Do not** give insulin.
> - Evacuate.

Treatment of Hyperglycemia. This patient has a complex physical disturbance and needs the care of a physician. Treatment is supportive: airway maintenance, vital signs, and treatment for shock. Dehydration is a serious complication of hyperglycemia. If the patient is alert, give oral fluids.

Hypoglycemia or Hyperglycemia?

Hypoglycemia usually has a rapid onset; the patient is pale, cool, and clammy and has obvious disturbances in behavior or altered mental status. Hyperglycemia typically has a gradual onset. Often, the patient is in an unexplained coma, with flushed, dry skin, or has a history of recent illness. A fruity breath odor may be present. A patient with hypoglycemia will respond to sugar; a hyperglycemic patient will not, but the extra sugar will cause no harm.

Two questions to ask any diabetic patient are: Have you eaten today? and have you taken your insulin today? If the patient has taken insulin but has not eaten, you should suspect hypoglycemia. The patient will have too much insulin, not enough sugar, and a blood sugar level that is too low to sustain normal brain function. If the patient has eaten but has not taken insulin, hyperglycemia should be suspected. This person has more sugar in the blood than can be transported to the cells.

Most persons with diabetes are very knowledgeable about their reactions and intuitively know if they are getting into trouble. Many diabetics measure their blood sugar levels daily and their urine for ketones. If you're on a wilderness trip with a diabetic, learn his or her medication and eating routines, how he or she measures his or her blood sugar and his or her daily fluctuations in blood sugar level. This can make you familiar with his or her management of diabetes, and helpful if he or she becomes hypo- or hyperglycemic.

When we're sick, we're under stress and we use hormones to fight the infection. Some of these hormones both raise blood sugar and interfere with insulin. The result is that it's more challenging for diabetics to regulate blood sugar when they are sick. A diabetic should have a "sick day" plan, and the trip leader needs to know what that is. The components of a sick day plan include insulin adjustment, food and fluid intake, and decision points for evacuation such as urine ketone, hyperglycemia, and vomiting. Thresholds for evacuation may be: several days of illness without relief; vomiting or diarrhea for more than 6 hours; moderate to large amounts of ketones in urine; blood glucose readings consistently greater than normal despite taking extra insulin; early signs of hyperglycemia; loss of a sense of control of blood sugar levels.

It is important for persons with diabetes to eat at regular intervals. If there is a possibility that a diabetic's insulin could be lost or destroyed—for example, by a boat flipping on the river—make sure that someone else in the group is carrying an extra supply. With control and care, diabetics can participate without problems in any activity.

SEIZURES

A seizure is a disruption of the brain's normal activity by a massive paroxysmal electrical discharge from brain cells. The seizure begins at a focus of brain cells, then spreads through the brain and to the rest of the body through peripheral nerves. This electrical disturbance may cause violent muscle contractions throughout the body or result in localized motor movement and possible loss of responsiveness.

The causes of seizures include high fever, head injury, low blood sugar, stroke, poisoning, and epilepsy. Low blood sugar is a cause of seizures in diabetics. Brain cells are sensitive to low oxygen and sugar levels, and if these fall below acceptable levels, a seizure may be triggered. The most common cause of seizures is epilepsy, a disease that manifests as recurring seizures.

Causes of Seizures
• Overstimulation of the brain
• Eclampsia (a complication of pregnancy)
• High fever and heat stroke
• Brain injury
• High-altitude cerebral edema (HACE)
• Alcohol or drug withdrawal (DTs) or overdose
• Diabetic hypoglycemia

The onset of epilepsy is not well understood. Often it begins in childhood or adolescence, but it can also be a consequence of a brain injury. Most persons with epilepsy control their seizures with medication. Interruption of the medication or inadequate dosage is frequently the cause of seizures.

At one time, seizures were attributed to mental illness. The source of these misperceptions may have been the dramatic visual impact of a writhing, moaning person having a seizure. Educating bystanders and group members about epilepsy and seizures can help alleviate such misunderstandings.

Signs and Symptoms of Seizures. The typical generalized seizure begins with a short period, usually less than a minute, of muscle rigidity, followed by several minutes of muscle contractions. The patient may feel the seizure approaching and warn bystanders or cry out at the onset of the episode. The patient suddenly falls to the ground, twitching and jerking.

As muscular activity subsides, the patient remains unresponsive but relaxed. He or she may drool, appear cyanotic, and become incontinent. Pulse and respiratory rate may be rapid. The patient may initially be unresponsive or difficult to arouse, but in time—usually within 10 to 15 minutes—the patient becomes awake and oriented.

Signs and Symptoms of Seizures

- Aura
- Unexpected and unexplained collapse
- Localized or full body convulsion or temporary disconnection with the present
- Postictal recovery phase

Treatment of Seizures. When the seizure has subsided, open the airway, assess for injuries, and take vital signs. Place the patient on his or her side during the recovery phase to help maintain an open airway.

Treatment for a seizure is supportive and protective care. You cannot stop the seizure, but you can protect the patient from injury. The violent muscle contractions of a seizure may

---

Treatment Principles for Seizures

- Protect from harm, but do not restrain.
- **Do not** place bite stick or any other object in mouth.
- Place on side to maintain open airway during postictal recovery phase.
- Perform a complete patient assessment to check for other injuries.
- Protect the patient's dignity.
- Administer hi-flow/high-concentration oxygen, if available.

cause injury to the patient and to well-meaning bystanders who attempt to restrain the patient. Move objects that the patient may hit. Pad or cradle the head if it is bouncing on the ground. A patient in seizure will not swallow the tongue; however, the airway may become obstructed by saliva or secretions, and the patient may bite his or her tongue.

An accurate description of the seizure tells the physician much about the onset and extent of the problem. In most cases, a seizure runs its course in a few minutes. Repeated seizures, especially repeated seizures in which the patient does not regain responsiveness in between, and seizures associated with another medical problem such as diabetes or head injury are serious medical conditions.

An epileptic patient with an isolated seizure requires evaluation by a physician but does not require a rapid evacuation. These occasional seizures are often due to changes in the patient's need for medication or failure to take the medication as prescribed. After recovering from the seizure, the patient should be well fed and hydrated and assessed for any injury that may have occurred during the seizure.

UNRESPONSIVE STATES

A responsive patient can react to the environment and protect himself or herself from sources of pain and injury. An unresponsive patient is in danger. He or she is mute and defenseless, unable to rely on even the gag reflex to protect the airway. Many conditions cause unresponsiveness: head injury, stroke, epilepsy, diabetes, alcohol intoxication, drug overdose, and fever.

A patient who is unresponsive for unexplained reasons poses a difficult diagnostic problem. The medical history may provide clues; use AEIOUTIPS as a memory aid for common

AEIOUTIPS
• Alcohol
• Epilepsy
• Insulin (diabetes)
• Overdose
• Underdose
• Trauma (injury)
• Infection
• Psychology/Poison
• Stroke

Treatment Principles for the Unresponsive Patient

- Stabilize the spine.
- Manage the airway, consider positioning the patient on the side.
- Search for clues.
- Consider administering sugar.

causes of unresponsiveness. Investigate each possibility and look for clues that either rule out or confirm its presence. Since obtaining a history of an unresponsive patient is impossible, carefully question bystanders for any background information they may be able to provide.

Often, all you can do is support the patient and transport him or her to a physician for further evaluation. Care for an unresponsive patient includes airway maintenance and cervical spine precautions unless trauma can be ruled out entirely. If you are unsure why a patient is unresponsive, place some sugar between the patient's cheek and gum. This will help a hypoglycemic patient and won't hurt a patient who is unresponsive for any other reason.

FINAL THOUGHTS

Persons with diabetes and epilepsy routinely participate in wilderness expeditions. The adverse consequences of these diseases—seizures and sugar imbalances—can be prevented through care and education. Paul Petzoldt, NOLS founder, worked with physicians in the early 1970s to support diabetic students attending our remote monthlong wilderness expeditions. At that time, this was a bold initiative. Since then, NOLS students with diabetes have successfully completed our most remote expeditions.

The physical and emotional stress, new physical and social environment, heavy packs, altitude, sun, and battle against dehydration in the wilderness may be new challenges, but they are ones that can be managed.

Discuss the illness beforehand with the diabetic or epileptic person undertaking the expedition. Make sure that you both understand the disease, the timing and side effects of medications, the appropriate emergency treatment, and any other health needs. It is important to inform the rest of the group—especially the person's tent mates—about the condition and how to deal with it in an emergency.

Evacuation Guidelines
Diabetes.
- Evacuation thresholds for diabetes include several days of illness without relief; vomiting or diarrhea for more than 6 hours; moderate to large amounts of ketones in urine; blood glucose readings consistently greater than normal despite taking extra insulin; early signs of hyperglycemia; loss of a sense of control of blood sugar levels.

Seizures.
- Evacuate all people with first time seizures or seizures of unknown origin. Isolated seizures with brief, uncomplicated postseizure periods are not emergencies and can be walked to the road.
- Expedite evacuation for any patient suffering multiple seizures in a short time period.

Unresponsive Patient.
- Unresponsive patients are usually candidates for evacuation. Prolonged unresponsiveness suggests the need to expedite the evacuation.

CHAPTER 20

GENDER-SPECIFIC MEDICAL CONCERNS

INTRODUCTION

Women have participated in NOLS expeditions since the beginning of the school and take their place among the school's most senior field instructors. Both women and men have enjoyed the challenges and rewards of climbing the highest peaks, paddling the wildest rivers and coastlines, and exploring the world's most remote wilderness.

During these trips, both genders have experienced injury and illness to reproductive and urinary systems. Men can experience epididymitis and testicular torsion. Women, with their more complex reproductive anatomy and physiology, may experience a variety of medical conditions ranging from changes in their menstrual cycles to vaginal infections, pelvic inflammatory disease, and ectopic pregnancy. The wilderness leader should be knowledgeable about the prevention, assessment, and field treatment of these conditions, and know when to evacuate.

MALE-SPECIFIC MEDICAL CONCERNS

The male external genitalia consist of the penis and scrotum. The penis provides a route for urine to be expelled from the bladder and sperm expelled from the testes. The scrotum is a pouchlike structure located to the side of and beneath the penis. The testes lie within the scrotum and are the site of sperm and testosterone production.

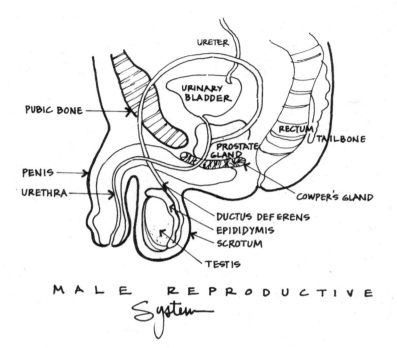

MALE REPRODUCTIVE System

Sperm travels out of the testes via the epididymis, a comma-shaped organ that lies behind the testes. The epididymis is composed of approximately 20 feet of ducts. From the epididymis, sperm travel through the ductus deferens, a tube approximately 18 inches long that loops into the pelvic cavity. Sperm can be stored there for many months.

Epididymitis
Epididymitis is an inflammation of the epididymis and can be caused by gonorrhea, syphilis, tuberculosis, mumps, prostatitis (inflammation of the prostate), or urethritis (inflammation of the urethra).

Signs and Symptoms of Epididymitis. The patient suffers from pain in the scrotum, possibly accompanied by fever. The scrotum may be red and swollen. Epididymitis tends to come on slowly, unlike torsion of the testis, which comes on rapidly.

Signs and Symptoms of Male-specific Medical Concerns

EPIDIDYMITIS
- Usually more gradual onset.
- Scrotum is swollen, painful, and red.
- Testis may be elevated.

TESTICULAR TORSION
- Usually acute pain.
- Scrotum is swollen, painful, and red.

Treatment of Epididymitis. The treatment is bed rest, support or elevation of the testes, and antibiotics. Diagnosis can be tricky. The pain and swelling often prevent any activity; thus, evacuation is recommended. Acetaminophen, aspirin, or ibuprofen may decrease the fever and pain.

Torsion of the Testis

Torsion of the testis is a twisting of the testis within the scrotum. The ductus deferens and its accompanying blood vessels become twisted, decreasing the blood supply to the testis. If the blood supply is totally cut off, the testis dies. After 24 hours without blood supply, the prognosis for saving the testis is poor.

Signs and Symptoms of Torsion. The scrotum is red, swollen, and painful, and the testis may appear slightly elevated on the affected side. The patient must be evacuated for treatment.

Treatment of Torsion. If you suspect torsion in the wilderness, there is little to be lost in having the patient attempt to untwist the affected testicle from the medial to lateral direction—since the testicle will die long before anyone gets to the roadhead. Increased pain is probably a good indicator that you're going in the wrong direction.

FEMALE-SPECIFIC MEDICAL CONCERNS

The female reproductive organs lie within the pelvic cavity. The vagina, or birth canal, is approximately 3 to 4 inches long. The vagina is continuously moistened by secretions that keep it clean and slightly acidic.

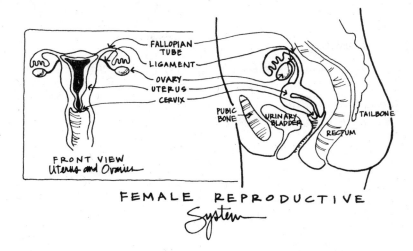

FEMALE REPRODUCTIVE System

At the top of the vagina is the cervix, a circle of tissue pierced by a small hole that opens into the uterus. The cervix thins and opens during labor to allow the baby to be expelled.

The uterus is about the size of a fist and is located between the bladder and rectum. Pregnancy begins when a fertilized egg implants in the tissue of the uterus. The uterus is an elastic organ that expands with the growing fetus.

On either side of the uterus are the ovaries, which lie approximately 4 or 5 inches below the waist. The ovaries produce eggs and the female sex hormones estrogen and progesterone. Each month an egg (ovum) is released from one of the ovaries and travels down the fallopian tube to the uterus. The fallopian tubes are approximately 4 inches long and wrap around the ovaries but are not directly connected to them. When the egg is released from the ovary, the fimbriae (finger-like structures at the end of the fallopian tube) make sweeping motions across the ovary, sucking the egg into the fallopian tube.

The Menstrual Cycle

As early as 12 years of age, a woman starts her menstrual cycle, the monthly release of ova. Hormones regulate the cycle, which continues until menopause, or cessation of the menstrual cycle, at approximately 52 years of age.

The endometrial tissue that lines the uterus undergoes hormone-regulated changes each month during menstruation. The average menstrual cycle is 28 days long, with day 1 being the first day of the menstrual period. From days 1 through 5, the endometrial tissue sloughs off from the uterus and is expelled through the vagina. The usual discharge is 4 to 6 tablespoons of blood, tissue, and mucus. During days 6 through 16, the endometrial tissue grows in preparation for implantation of an ovum, becoming thick and full of small blood vessels.

Ovulation usually occurs around day 14; the egg takes approximately $6^1/2$ days to reach the uterus. On days 16 through 26, the endometrium secretes substances to nourish the embryo. If conception has not occurred, the hormones progesterone and estrogen decrease, causing the uterine blood supply to decrease and the lining of the uterus to be shed.

Mittelschmerz. Some women experience cramping in the lower abdomen on the right or left side or in the back when the ovary releases an egg. The pain is sometimes accompanied by bloody vaginal discharge. This is called mittelschmerz (mittel = middle; schmerz = pain).

Signs and Symptoms. The pain may be severe enough to be confused with appendicitis or ectopic pregnancy, but a careful assessment should allow the first responder to distinguish between the two. Ask the patient where she is in her menstrual cycle. Has she ever had this pain before? Typically, a woman will have had similar cramping in the past. Any light bleeding or pain should cease within 36 hours. The abdomen is soft. Women taking birth control pills do not ovulate, so they cannot have mittelschmerz.

Dysmenorrhea. Dysmenorrhea is painful menstruation (cramps). Possible causes include prostaglandins, which cause the uterus to cramp, endometriosis (inflammation of the endometrium), pelvic inflammatory disease, or anatomic anomalies such as a displaced uterus.

Treatment. Antiprostaglandins such as ibuprofen reduce the pain as well as the volume of flow and the length of the period.

Relaxation exercises such as yoga and massaging the lower back or abdomen help reduce pain. Applying heat to the abdomen or lower back may also help reduce pain.

A change in diet may help. Decreasing the amount of salt, caffeine, and alcohol in the diet while increasing the B vitamins—especially B6 (found in brewer's yeast, peanuts, rice, sunflower seeds, and whole grains)—or drinking raspberry leaf tea (1 tablespoon for each cup) can offer some relief during the acute phase of the cramps. Because exercise causes endorphins (natural opiates) to be released by the brain, many women find that cramps diminish when they participate in strenuous exercise.

Secondary Amenorrhea. Secondary amenorrhea is the absence of menstrual periods after a woman has had at least one period. Causes of secondary amenorrhea include pregnancy, ovarian tumors, intense athletic training, excessive weight loss or gain, altitude, and stress (physical and emotional). Changes in the menstrual cycle are common in the backcountry and may be normal adjustments to unfamiliar stresses.

Vaginal Infection

The normal vagina contains a plethora of microorganisms. Most of the time these organisms are in balance. The normal pH of the vagina is slightly acidic. Vaginal infections can occur when the normal balance of bacteria and the pH are upset. Antibiotics, birth control pills, diabetes, and physical or emotional stress may cause an infection to develop. Cuts and abrasions from intercourse or tampons, not cleaning the perineal area, or not changing underwear can also lead to an infection.

The two most common causes of vaginal infections are candidiasis (yeast) and bacterial vaginitis.

Signs and Symptoms of Vaginitis. Symptoms of a yeast infection generally include curdy white discharge and itching. The vulva may be swollen and excoriated from scratching. Symp-

---

Signs and Symptoms of a Vaginal Infection

- Curdy white discharge or grayish milky discharge
- Malodorous discharge
- Redness, soreness, itching of vaginal area

Treatment of Vaginal Infection

- Gyne-Lotrimin, Monistat 1, or Diflucan.
- Evacuate if symptoms persist for 48 hours despite treatment.

Prevention of Vaginal Infection

- Stay hydrated.
- Decrease sugar, caffeine, and alcohol intake.
- Wear loose-fitting underwear or running shorts for ventilation.
- Wash perineal area daily.
- Change tampons regularly.
- Decrease stress.

toms of bacterial vaginitis include a grayish, milky, thin discharge. The discharge may be malodorous, and the patient may complain of vaginal pain but not itching. For the purposes of field diagnosis, the symptoms are similar, and initial treatment is the same.

Treatment of Vaginitis. Vaginal infections can be treated with over-the-counter medications such as Gyne-Lotrimin and Monistat 1 (vaginal suppository), or with prescription Diflucan (oral pill). If these treatments don't provide relief within 48 hours, the patient should be evacuated. An untreated infection can develop into pelvic inflammatory disease.

Prevention. The best prevention for vaginal infections is education. To help prevent vaginal infections, wipe front to back, clean the perineal area (between the vagina and anus) daily with plain water or a mild soap, and promote ventilation by wearing loose-fitting nylon or cotton underwear or running shorts. Women with a history of vaginal infection should decrease their caffeine, alcohol, and sugar intake.

Urinary Tract Infection (UTI)

Urinary tract infections are common in women due to the closer proximity of the urethra to the vagina and rectum and the shorter length of the urethra. The infection can affect the urethra, ureters, or bladder.

Signs and Symptoms of UTI. Urinary tract infections cause increased frequency or urgency of urination and/or a burning sensation during urination. The patient complains of pain above the pubic bone and a heavy urine odor with the morning urination. Blood and/or pus may be present in the urine. Urinary tract infections can progress to kidney infections. If the kidneys are infected, the patient complains of rebound tenderness in the small of the back and may have a fever.

Treatment For UTI. The best treatment (also good for prevention) is to drink lots of water every day and empty the bladder often. A good way to tell if you are drinking enough is by the color of your urine. Unless you are taking vitamins, the urine should be clear, not yellow. Persons taking vitamins tend to have yellow urine.

The perineal area should be cleaned with water or mild soap daily. Taking 500 milligrams of vitamin C daily and/or eating whole grains, nuts, and fruits may help. Curry, cayenne pepper, chili powder, black pepper, caffeine, and alcohol should be avoided because these irritate the bladder. Vitamin B6 and magnesium or calcium supplements help relieve spasms of the urethra.

Signs and Symptoms of Urinary Tract Infection

- Increase in frequency of urination.
- Urgency and a burning sensation during urination.

Treatment of Urinary Tract Infection

- Increase fluid intake.
- Give vitamin B6, calcium, and magnesium supplements to relieve bladder spasms.
- Change diet.
- Avoid sugar and foods that irritate the bladder.
- Antibiotics.

On extended expeditions, consider carrying antibiotics such as Bactrim or Macrobid to treat urinary tract infections. If an infection persists for more than 48 hours despite the use of antibiotics, the patient should be evacuated. Evacuate patients with symptoms of a kidney infection for further evaluation.

Ectopic Pregnancy

Ectopic pregnancies occur outside the uterus, most commonly in the fallopian tubes. Sperm usually fertilizes the egg in the upper two-thirds of the tube. Due to congenital anomalies or scarring caused by infection, the egg starts growing in the tube.

Signs and Symptoms of Ectopic Pregnancy. The classic triad of an ectopic pregnancy is absence of menstruation because of the pregnancy, abdominal pain, and bleeding. The onset of pain is rapid and on one side of the abdomen. The fallopian tube ruptures in 4 to 6 weeks when the embryo becomes too large for the tube. The pain then becomes agonizing, and signs and symptoms of peritonitis develop. The patient may hemorrhage and die from shock, although slow bleeding is more common.

Signs and Symptoms of Ectopic Pregnancy

- Rapid onset of unilateral lower abdominal pain
- Vaginal bleeding
- Signs and symptoms of peritonitis and shock

Treatment for Ectopic Pregnancy. Treat for shock and evacuate immediately.

ASSESSMENT TIPS

If you're leading or participating in wilderness trips, you will encounter people with gender-related medical concerns. A young male experiencing scrotal pain for the first time may be embarrassed and hesitant to inform the leader, especially if the leader is of the opposite gender. Likewise, a woman with a urinary tract infection may not know the signs and symptoms or that you have the means to treat it in the field, and she may be reluctant to inform a male trip leader.

If a gender-specific medical problem arises, provide a private place to talk. Maintain eye contact; be straightforward, respectful, and nonjudgmental. Use proper medical terminology or terms that you both understand—no jokes or slang. A member of the patient's sex should be present before and during any physical exam.

For female patients, gather information about the patient's menstrual and reproductive history. When was her last menstrual period? How long is her cycle? What is normal for her?

Does she use contraception? Has she had sexual intercourse in the past? Has she experienced this problem in the past, and if so, how was it treated?

TIPS FOR WOMEN'S HYGIENE IN THE WILDERNESS

Wear loose-fitting shorts that allow for adequate ventilation. Cotton underwear breathes better than nylon and may reduce the risk of infection. With washings, two or three pairs of underwear will be sufficient for a 30-day expedition.

During menstruation, change tampons and pads frequently, and remember to wash your hands prior to inserting a tampon.

If you are prone to vaginal infections, consider decreasing the amount of sugar in your diet. Drink tea instead of cocoa, water instead of fruit drinks, and eat nuts instead of candy bars.

Wipe from the front to the back to limit introduction of bacteria into the vaginal area. Wash the vaginal area with water or mild soap daily.

A "pee rag" has become popular among women backpackers to conserve toilet paper. Usually a bandanna, it's tied onto the outside of the pack while hiking. If it gets rained on, fine. If not, women rinse them out every few days. It makes a big difference in staying clean.

Used tampons and pads are bagged and carried out of the backcountry. Having a designated system makes proper disposal of tampons, pads, and toilet paper easier. A small stuff sack with a couple of extra plastic bags allows personal organization and privacy. Some women prefer wide mouthed water bottles or plastic containers for this. Include a small wad of toilet paper in this kit. An aspirin or two placed in the bag or container will help dissipate odor.

How many extra tampons or pads to bring? Bring a little extra for heavier flow, in case your cycle changes and you experience your period twice in a monthlong trip, or if pads or tampons get wet. If each woman in a group brings a bit extra, almost any emergency can be covered by the group without adding a lot of bulk.

An added note: There is no evidence that bears are attracted to women during their periods.

Evacuation Guidelines
- Evacuate any female with signs and symptoms, or the possibility, of pregnancy.
- Expedite evacuation if suspected pregnant patient develops low abdominal/pelvic pain and vaginal bleeding not associated with her regular menstrual cycle.
- Expedite evacuation for suspected testicular torsion, epididymitis, or testicular pain of unknown origin.

PART V

Expedition Medicine

CHAPTER 21

HYGIENE AND WATER DISINFECTION

INTRODUCTION

Twenty-five years ago, we assumed that clear, flowing mountain streams were pristine and clean. We now know that this is not necessarily true. Diarrhea is unpleasant, and it's better to be safe than sorry and assume that all natural water sources are populated with disease-causing bacteria, viruses, and protozoa.

People from developed countries live with the luxury of clean tap water and effective sanitation systems. In other parts of the world, water contamination continues to be a major health problem, and diarrheal illness is a leading cause of death. Wilderness expeditions leave behind modern sanitation and reliably disinfected tap water. Healthy people raised with Western medical standards may not understand the debilitating power of diarrheal illness. For them, maintaining strict hygiene practices in what appears to be pristine wilderness can be difficult. On NOLS courses, and other wilderness trips, diarrhea and closely-related flu symptoms are the most common illnesses. Contaminated water and poor personal hygiene are the two main causes of these preventable illnesses.

WATERBORNE ILLNESS

Worldwide, waterborne microorganisms account for many cases of infectious diarrhea. The microorganisms causing diarrhea include bacteria, protozoa, viruses, and parasitic worms. Diseases that are spread through contaminated water include typhoid, cholera, campylobacteriosis, giardiasis, and hepatitis A.

Although a frequently diagnosed diarrhea-causing microorganism in the United States is the protozoan *Giardia*, other bacteria and viruses are being identified as well. Recently the protozoan *Cryptosporidium* has received attention as a cause of municipal waterborne outbreaks, but it is unclear how much risk it poses in wilderness water sources.

Giardia

Giardia is a microscopic protozoan. It has a two-stage life as cyst and trophozoite. The cyst, excreted in mammalian feces, is hardy and can survive 2 to 3 months in near-freezing water. If swallowed, the warmer internal environment causes the cyst to change into its active stage, the trophozoite. The trophozoite attaches itself to the wall of the small intestine and is the cause of the diarrhea associated with *Giardia* infections.

Humans are a carrier of *Giardia*. It has also been identified in both domestic and wild animals, specifically in beavers, cats, dogs, sheep, cattle, deer, and elk, and in reptiles, amphibians, and fish. It is not clear whether contamination from *Giardia* is increasing or whether it is being diagnosed more frequently as a cause of diarrhea.

Giardia is difficult to diagnose due to the wide variation in symptoms. For a reliable diagnosis, three stool samples should

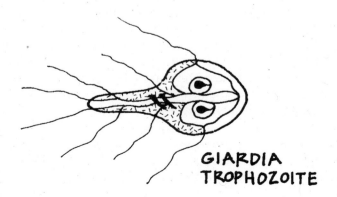

GIARDIA
TROPHOZOITE

be examined. Most infections are without symptoms, and the unwitting patient becomes a carrier of *Giardia*, inadvertently spreading the illness.

The incubation period—from ingestion to the onset of infection—is 1 to 3 weeks. Symptoms include recurrent and persistent malodorous stools and flatus, abdominal cramping, bloating, "sulfur burps," and indigestion. Serious infections produce explosive watery diarrhea with cramps, foul flatus, fever, and malaise.

Although drug therapy is available, prevention through hygienic habits and water disinfection makes much more sense. *Giardia* is sensitive to heat, is easily filtered, and can be killed with chemical disinfection.

Cryptosporidium

Also a microscopic protozoan, *Cryptosporidium* is spread by drinking contaminated water, by eating contaminated raw or undercooked food, or by hand-to-mouth transfer of cysts picked up from fecal matter.

Some people may not have symptoms. Most have an illness lasting 1 to 2 weeks that starts 2 to 10 days after infection and includes watery diarrhea, headache, abdominal cramps, nausea, vomiting, and low-grade fever. In persons with suppressed immune systems, such as AIDS or cancer chemotherapy patients, the infection may continue and become life-threatening.

Cryptosporidium cysts are sensitive to heat and can be filtered but are not reliably killed by iodine or chlorine. People with suppressed immune systems should consider boiling water or using a filtration system to protect them from infection.

WATER DISINFECTION

Purifying water eliminates offensive odors, tastes, and colors but does not kill microorganisms. Sterilization kills all life-forms. Disinfection removes or destroys disease-causing microorganisms. What we commonly refer to as water purification is really disinfection. There are three main methods of water disinfection: heat, chemical treatment, and filtration.

Methods OF WATER DISINFECTION:

HEAT
BRINGING WATER TO A BOIL
IS STILL THE MOST RELIABLE
WAY TO MAKE SURE IT'S SAFE
TO USE.

FILTRATION
REMOVES
GIARDIA BUT
NOT VIRUSES!

CHEMICAL
• IODINE
• CHLORINE

Heat

Incorrect information persists on how long to boil water before it is disinfected. The common diarrhea-causing microorganisms are sensitive to heat and are killed immediately by boiling water. The protozoa *Giardia* and *Amoeba* (which causes amebiasis) die after 2 to 3 minutes at 140°F (60°C). Viruses, diarrhea-producing bacteria, and *Cryptosporidium* cysts die within minutes at 150°F (65°C). By the time water boils, it is safe to drink.

The boiling point decreases with increasing elevation, but this does not affect disinfection. The boiling point at 19,000 feet is 178°F (81°C), sufficient for disinfecting water.

The advantage of boiling is its effectiveness. However, it is inconvenient on the trail, takes time, and consumes fuel.

Chemical Treatment

Chemical treatment is the addition of halogens, either iodine or chlorine, or chlorine dioxide to water. Halogens and chlorine dioxide can reliably kill viruses, diarrhea-causing bacteria, and most protozoa cysts, with the exception of *Cryptosporidium*. The concentration of halogen and its contact time in water determine the degree of disinfection. In general, a halogen dose can be halved if the contact time for the recommended dosage is doubled.

Factors that can affect halogen treatment include pH, chemical binding with material in the water, and water temperature. Halogens are affected by pH, but the pH levels of most natural water sources don't significantly influence the activity of iodine or chlorine.

When iodine or chlorine binds with organic and inorganic particles in water, less halogen is available to destroy the diarrhea-causing microorganisms. Reduce debris before adding halogen; filter murky water with a manufactured filter or use an improvised strainer such as a coffee filter or a clean bandanna. You can also let water sit until the floating particles settle to the bottom or use alum to clear the water. To compensate for halogen bonding with organic matter in cloudy water, increase the amount of halogen (see the recommendations in the table on the next page).

Halogens are also affected by temperature. Cold water slows the chemical reaction. Compensate for a slower reaction in cold water by increasing contact time. On the safe side, wait 30 minutes in warm water (86°F [30°C]), 60 minutes in cold water (59°F [15°C]).

Iodine. Iodine, the most commonly used halogen, is available as a tablet—tetraglycine hydroperiodide—sold commercially as Potable Aqua iodine tablets. Iodine crystals in PolarPure, 2 percent iodine (tincture), and 10 percent povidone-iodine solutions are also effective.

Iodine is affected less by pH than is chlorine and has less effect on the taste of the water. Wilderness medicine experts believe that at the levels used to disinfect water, iodine is safe for most people. Iodine is not recommended for persons with thyroid disease, a known iodine allergy, or during pregnancy.

HALOGEN DOSES PER LITER OF WATER

	Clear Water	Cloudy Water
Iodine		
Tetraglycine hydroperiodide (Potable Aqua)	1 tablet	2 tablets
2% iodine solution (tincture)	0.2 ml (5 drops)	0.5 ml (10 drops)
10% povidone-iodine	0.4 ml (8 drops)	0.8 ml (16 drops)
Iodine crystals, aqueous (Polar Pure)	15 ml	30 ml
Chlorine		
4% to 6% chlorine bleach	0.1 ml (2 drops)	0.2 ml (4 drops)

1 drop = 0.05 ml

Source: H. Backer, "Field Water Disinfection," Syllabus, World Congress on Wilderness Medicine/Wilderness Medical Society Meeting (Whistler, British Columbia: August 1999).

The aftertaste of iodine and chlorine in water can be improved by adding flavoring. The sugar in drink mixes, however, also binds the halogen. Add flavoring after disinfection. An ascorbic acid (vitamin C) tablet, added after disinfection, improves flavor by chemically reducing the iodine and chlorine to iodide and chloride, which have no taste.

Chlorine. Chlorine has been used as a disinfectant for over 200 years. Chlorine bleach (4 to 6 percent) is commonly used to disinfect water. Halazone and Puritabs are chlorine tablets.

Chlorine Dioxide. Chlorine dioxide products such as Aqua Mira, Micropur, Potable Aqua chlorine dioxide, and the MIOX Purifier are newer products that are effective over a broad temperature range and leave less of an aftertaste in the water. They claim to disinfect *Cryptosporidium*, although contact times need to be 4 hours, an inconvenience on the trail.

Ultraviolet Light. There are several products on the market that use ultraviolet light (UV). UV light is a well-established disinfectant. It inactivates viruses, bacteria, and protozoa; does not require chemicals; and does not alter taste. There is no overdose danger, but at the same time there is no residual disinfection power.

Filtration

At this writing there are over 30 different water filtration products on the market. Filtration physically removes solid materials and microorganisms by forcing water through a filter element. Filter elements can be ceramic cartridges, fiberglass, or structured or labyrinth mediums of dense, honeycombed material.

Several types of filters are available with pore sizes small enough to filter *Giardia* and *Cryptosporidium* cysts, as well as bacteria. A 0.2-micron filter (the number refers to the pore size in the filter medium) is a common standard. Most bacteria are removed by 0.2 micron filters, protozoa by 1.0 micron filters. These are believed to be the common waterborne pathogens in the North American backcountry. If you're traveling outside North American, or in areas with a lot of people and poor sanitation, viruses are more of a risk and a purifier may be the better choice.

Viruses are too small to be reliably eliminated by field water filtration. Some filters, labeled purifiers, kill viruses by passing water through an iodine or chlorine impregnated resin or by trapping them in a filter medium that carries an electrostatic charge.

Chemical Water Disinfection Products

IODINE
- Potable Aqua tablets
- Polar Pure crystals
- 2% iodine solution (tincture)
- 10% povidone-iodine

CHLORINE
- Bleach
- Halazone tablets
- Puritabs

CHLORINE DIOXIDE
- Aqua Mira
- Potable Aqua Chlorine Dioxide
- Micropur tablets
- Miox

Filters are more convenient on the trail than boiling water, and filtration may reduce the amount of iodine or chlorine necessary to chemically purify water. Filters can be expensive, costing from $40 to $250. Also, they may clog or develop undetectable leaking cracks.

FOODBORNE ILLNESS

Microbes such as bacteria, viruses, and fungi live everywhere. They're in the soil, in water, on our hands, in our noses and mouths. Many are harmless to us. Some cause illness either through the toxins they produce or as a side effect of colonizing the digestive tract. We can expose ourselves to these organisms by drinking contaminated water or through poor hygiene practices in the kitchen. Bacteria such as *Staphylococcus, Shigella,* and *Salmonella* are common sources of foodborne illness. If we give these creatures a place to live, such as a dirty cookpot, they can quickly multiply or produce enough toxin to make us sick.

With the luxury of modern sanitation, we don't give much thought to hygiene. We're protected by flush toilets, effective waste disposal and sewer systems, reliably disinfected tap water, readily available hot water, and proximity to advanced medical care. Proper human waste disposal, hand and utensil washing, food preparation, and water disinfection need to become habits in the wilderness. A river guide with poor kitchen hygiene was the source of food poisoning for many of the people on his trip. We suspect that most episodes of flulike and diarrheal illness on NOLS courses are caused by poor kitchen and personal sanitation.

Hygiene in the Wilderness Kitchen

These are practices NOLS has found helpful in reducing the incidence of foodborne illness on our expeditions.

Cook Food Thoroughly. Food that is dry or has a high salt or sugar content inhibits bacterial growth. Moist food that is low in salt and sugar is a good medium for growth, especially if it is warm. Protect yourself by cooking food completely; boil your pasta, beans, and rice; cook your meat until it is no longer red (ideally 170°F or 77°C).

Eat Cooked Food Promptly. Heat destroys most bacteria. Cold keeps bacteria from multiplying. Keep cooked food hot or cold, but don't keep it long. The optimal temperature zone for bacterial growth is between 45° and 140°F (7° and 60°C). In only a short period—within an hour in ideal warm and moist conditions—bacteria can multiply to become the·source of diarrhea.

Avoid Leftovers. Storing cooked food without refrigeration invites disaster. Plan meals so that all food is consumed when served. Besides promoting bacterial growth, keeping leftovers creates a waste disposal problem and attracts animals such as bears.

Cold weather trips have the advantage of natural refrigeration. If leftovers are quickly cooled in air temperatures that stay below 38°F (3.5°C) and the meal is reheated completely, your risk of foodborne illness is less, but not zero. It's always safer to avoid leftovers. Heat-resistant toxins and microbes may colonize stored cooked food. If you do eat leftover food, make sure that the food is hot throughout the dish, not just on the surface. A crispy exterior does not mean that the interior has been well heated.

Clean Pots, Pans, and Utensils. Dirty pots, pans, and utensils are ideal surfaces for microbial life. Cleaning grease and food in the wilderness can be a challenge, especially if water is scarce. Plan ahead to minimize leftovers. Use sand or snow to scour pots, then rinse with hot water. Hard work to remove food residue can minimize the water needed for a final rinse.

Dish soap helps clean, but it must be rinsed well to avoid diarrhea and must be disposed of properly to leave no trace. Use a strainer to filter out large food particles, which are packed out. Scatter the remaining waste water widely away from camp and water sources.

Boil cooking utensils daily. Immersing clean utensils in your water pot as you boil the morning hot drink water will help continue the sanitizing process. Bacteria, viruses, and protozoa will be killed as the water is disinfected by the heat.

Large groups frequently use group cooking setups with chlorine rinses as an important step in keeping utensils clean. The three-bucket method begins with a hot soapy water scrub, then a warm water rinse, and finally a 1-minute immersion in a chlorine rinse bucket. Prepare this 100 to 150 ppm solution by adding 1 tablespoon of 4 to 6 percent chlorine bleach per gallon of water or one-quarter tablet of Effersan, a commercially available chlorine tablet. Air-dry the cooking gear.

Keep Kitchen Surfaces and Utensils Clean. Keep the food preparation surface and your utensils clean. Between the grocery store and dinner, your food can be contaminated many different ways. Dirty hands can reach inside, touch, and contaminate the food. Avoid this by pouring food from a bag or box. The spoon used to taste the soup may also be the spoon used to stir or serve. The cook may sneeze or cough and spread germs over dinner. The spatula may be placed on the ground or in a grubby food sack, then used to stir your pasta. An organized and clean kitchen reduces the chance of this cross-contamination.

Rinse Fresh Fruit and Vegetables. The surfaces of fruit and vegetables can be contaminated. A rule of thumb is peel it, boil it, cook it, or avoid it.

Protect Food from Insects and Animals. Insects and animals are vectors of disease. Keeping flies and rodents from your food both protects you from disease and keeps the animal from becoming habituated to humans as a source of food.

Don't Share. Sharing your resources, energy, wisdom, and companionship is good expedition behavior. Sharing your microbes with your tent mate is not. Keep your handkerchief, water bottle, cup, bowl, spoon, and lip balm to yourself. Instead of reaching into a plastic bag for a handful of raisins and contaminating the entire bag, pour the raisins into your hand. Serve food with the serving utensil, not your personal spoon. An ill person or one with open cuts on his or her hands should not prepare food. It takes only one person to be the source of a groupwide illness.

Wash Your Hands. Lastly, but most importantly, wash your hands! Keep nails trimmed and clean. Microbes live on the skin. Hands are an excellent and common tool for transporting these creatures from person to person. Regular hand washing does not sterilize your hands, but it does reduce the chance of infection. Ideally, you should use hot water, lots of soap, and a thorough rinse after using the latrine. Practically speaking, in the wilderness, you'll wash with cold water. At a minimum, you should do this before preparing, serving, or eating food. Large expeditions or base camps often set up a hand-washing station near a latrine or outhouse or in a central camp location. Waterless soaps are an option when water is not available or as an extra precaution after hands have been rinsed of grease and dirt.

Using natural toilet paper—leaves, sticks, rocks, or snow— reduces the paper you use and when done properly, this method is as sanitary as regular toilet paper. But you need to be proficient to avoid contaminating your hands with fecal material. And of course, always wash your hands afterward.

FINAL THOUGHTS

Some people think that contaminated water accounts for most infectious diarrhea in the U.S. wilderness. At NOLS, we think that person-to-person exchange from poor kitchen and personal hygiene practices is also a leading cause. Outside the wilderness, the most common route for infection is believed to be from person to person via hand-to-mouth contact or from contaminated utensils. Infection rates increase with close contact and poor hygiene. Habits of cleanliness and hygiene are essential to health and safety in the wilderness.

Your choice among boiling, filtering, or chemically disinfecting your water will depend on how contaminated the water might be, personal preference, fuel availability, group size, cost, and reliability. None of the water disinfection methods is foolproof. Each has its limitations, and each must be done correctly. They reduce but do not eliminate the risk of getting sick from drinking water. Their benefit is a reduced chance of becoming ill from bad water.

CHAPTER 22

HYDRATION

INTRODUCTION

NOLS instructors constantly harp on hydration, urging their students to drink, drink, drink. They issue liter water bottles and large insulated mugs. They carry water in the desert and melt snow with a passion in winter environments. To the inexperienced outdoorsperson, this appears to be an unnecessarily exaggerated process, when in fact, it is based on need and experience.

Dehydration as the primary cause of an evacuation at NOLS is rare, but many of our evacuations for illness are in part complicated by underlying dehydration. Addressing daily episodes of dehydration on the trail is a fact of life for wilderness travelers.

Dehydration is a contributing factor to hypothermia, heat exhaustion, heatstroke, and frostbite. Dehydration worsens fatigue, decreases the ability to exercise efficiently, and reduces mental alertness. Often the fatigue, irritability, poor thinking, body aches, and headache at the end of a day are the first signs of dehydration. Even by itself, dehydration can be a life-threatening medical problem.

PHYSIOLOGY OF WATER BALANCE

Humans are bags of water. We hear through a medium of water, the brain is cushioned by fluid, and the joints are lubricated by fluid. Blood is 90 percent water, and every biochemical reaction takes place in a medium of water.

Outside the wilderness, we give little thought to hydration. Air conditioning, heating, and lack of exercise enable us to avoid fluid stress most of the time. In the outdoors, we exercise daily at high levels. Exercise causes water loss through sweating, breathing, and metabolism. In the outdoors, we adjust directly to the environment, whether hot or cold. In the desert, we sweat to lose heat. In the cold, we lose water to moisten the cold air we breathe.

In the outdoors, hydration is not as simple as turning on the tap. It's harder to get water in the outdoors; we lose more of it responding to the environment, and we need more of it to maintain health. In the desert, we carry water, ration water, and spend a lot of time searching for water. Our activity patterns may be altered to reduce loss. We rest during the hours of the hot, midday sun; we work in the cool dawn and evening. In the winter, we must melt the water we drink—a time-consuming process. There is always the difficulty of disinfecting potentially contaminated water sources.

Assessment of Hydration

Dehydration is often overlooked as a cause of illness or injury in the outdoors. The signs and symptoms mimic altitude illness, hypothermia, fatigue, heat exhaustion, and shock. Severe dehydration can cause significant mental deterioration, causing us to think that the patient might have a serious brain problem. The key to assessment is suspicion. Dehydration is so common that it must be considered in every patient treated in the outdoors.

General symptoms of a negative water balance are fatigue, heat oppression, thirst, irritability, dizziness, dark concentrated urine, and headache. A seriously dehydrated patient appears to have signs of shock: rapid pulse; pale, sweaty skin; weakness; and nausea. Mental deterioration presents itself as loss of balance and changes in mental awareness. Tenting—in which the skin forms a tent shape when pinched—is a sign of serious dehydration. Normal skin is sufficiently hydrated to collapse; the tent stays in place in severe dehydration.

With a 2 percent fluid deficit, we experience mental deterioration, decreased group cooperation, vague discomfort, lack of energy and appetite, flushed skin, impatience, sleepiness, nausea, an increased pulse rate, and a 25 percent loss in efficiency.

A 12 percent fluid deficit results in an inability to swallow, a swollen tongue, sunken eyes, and decreased neurological function. Dizziness, tingling in the limbs, absence of salivation, and slurred speech may also be present. A fluid deficit greater than 15 percent is potentially lethal. Signs include delirium, vision disturbances, and shriveled skin.

Treatment of Hydration

A mildly dehydrated patient—and all wilderness travelers—should drink clear water to replace fluids. It is the best fluid for hydration. Cool water is absorbed faster than warm water.

Electrolyte replacement drinks can help, although some people find they are too sweet. Sugar increases the time it takes for fluid to be absorbed from the stomach. Coffee and tea contain caffeine, a diuretic that stimulates the kidneys to excrete fluid. Some experts consider this effect overrated, but regardless, coffee, tea, and alcohol should be avoided when rehydrating. Alcohol also increases urine production and fluid loss.

A severely dehydrated patient may have electrolyte imbalances as well as a fluid deficit. Such a patient cannot be rehydrated in the field and must be evacuated to a hospital for intravenous fluid therapy.

Hyponatremia

Just as it's possible to become dehydrated, we can get into trouble by drinking too much water. The scenario is a hot weather hiker drinking lots of water but not consuming enough electrolytes, such as sodium. Your hydration status is good, yet your blood sodium is low and you have a case of hyponatremia, also known as water intoxication.

Signs and symptoms vary among individuals and depend on the patient's hydration and sodium levels. The patient seems to have heat exhaustion: headache, weakness, fatigue, lightheadedness, muscle cramps, nausea with or without vomiting, sweaty skin, normal core temperature, and normal or slightly elevated pulse and breathing rates.

The assessment of hyponatremia versus heat exhaustion or dehydration depends on an accurate history. Be suspicious if the patient has eaten relatively little salty food recently, but has a high fluid intake—several liters in the last few hours.

Patients with an altered mental status should be evacuated. Patients with mild to moderate symptoms and a normal mental status can be treated in the field. Have the patient rest in the shade with little to no fluid intake and a gradual intake of salty foods while the kidneys reestablish a sodium balance. Oral electrolyte replacement drinks are low in sodium and high in water and may not help as much as you anticipate.

FINAL THOUGHTS

There are several cornerstones to good health in the outdoors: staying warm and dry, eating well, resting, camping comfortably, washing hands, climbing slowly at altitude, and, most important, staying hydrated.

How much water should you drink to stay healthy? Probably more than you usually drink. Three to 4 liters a day is the minimum, with another liter added for cold or high-altitude conditions. Thirst is a poor indicator, alerting you to a fluid deficit after you are already dehydrated and indicating that you are satiated before you are fully rehydrated. Urine color and volume are helpful indicators; darker, more concentrated urine is an indicator of dehydration. Again, this is a later sign, appearing after the body has decided to conserve fluid.

Fluids must be forced to maintain hydration in the wilderness. Measure your daily fluid intake. Tank up to buffer your hydration margin. Drink early, anticipating fluid loss during the day. Drink often, preventing the subtle mental and physical deterioration of dehydration. Drink more than you think you need. Oral electrolyte replacement drinks help but may not add sufficient salt to your diet. Eat salty foods while exercising, especially in the heat. Drink before you become dehydrated.

CHAPTER 23

DENTAL EMERGENCIES

INTRODUCTION

Enduring a dental problem in the wilderness, several days from a dentist, can be an uncomfortable experience. There are simple field treatments for broken teeth or fillings, toothaches, and gum irritations that can make life more comfortable during the evacuation. Although we do not experience many dental problems on NOLS courses, they account for 10 percent of problems seen among trekkers visiting the Himalayan Rescue Association clinics.

BROKEN TEETH OR FILLINGS

Lost fillings cause discomfort if hot or cold liquids or spicy foods touch the exposed tooth tissue. Exposure of the nerve, pulp, artery, or vein by a lost filling or a broken tooth causes pain. Various temporary filling materials are available for stopgap treatment of broken teeth or fillings. Cavit is a premixed compound available from your dentist. A nonprescription temporary filling available in many dental emergency kits is a combination of zinc oxide powder (not the ointment) and oil of cloves (eugenol). The oil of cloves is a topical anesthetic. NOLS staff have even had success using sugarless gum and ski wax to cover loose fillings and broken teeth.

Rinse the broken tooth or filling thoroughly before covering with a temporary filling. Roll the temporary material into a small ball and gently press it into the hole in the tooth, sealing the exposed tissue.

A broken or avulsed tooth should be gently rinsed off and slowly and gently placed back in the hole. Irrigate the tooth, but don't scrub it—you may remove tissue that can help the tooth survive. If you can't replace it, save the tooth for replacement. Wrap the tooth in gauze and have the patient carry it between the cheek and gum or in a cool place. For a good prognosis, a tooth must be replaced within 30 minutes and receive the care of a dentist within a week. .

If the socket is bleeding, it can be packed to place pressure on the tissue. A slightly moist tea bag makes an acceptable packing material. In fact, the tannic acid in nonherbal tea promotes clotting.

TOOTHACHES

Exposure of the pulp from a dental cavity can cause pain. In the backcountry, treatment is limited to pain medications, antibiotics, and avoiding excessively hot, cold, or spicy foods. A temporary filling material may protect the pulp and any exposed nerve. Oil of cloves (eugenol) may be helpful for pain relief.

ORAL IRRITATIONS AND INFECTIONS

General mouth irritation is usually due to poor hygiene and can be treated with vigorous brushing and rinses with salt water (a teaspoon of salt per glass of water) 3 to 4 times a day.

Swelling around teeth or gums is an indicator of an infection. On remote expeditions, treatment with antibiotics and drainage of the infection may be considered. Evacuation to a dentist is the best treatment and the only choice on less remote trips in which there is no access to a physician or antibiotics.

FINAL THOUGHTS

Preparation for a wilderness expedition includes a visit to your dentist to identify and treat any potential problems. In the field, brush and floss regularly. Anyone who has experienced the woes of a toothache, loose filling, or dental infection in the wilderness knows that the need for dental hygiene does not cease when we venture into the woods.

CHAPTER 24

COMMON NON-URGENT MEDICAL PROBLEMS

INTRODUCTION

These topics are often mislabeled as "common" and "simple" medical problems. They are indeed common. The data NOLS has been keeping for over 20 years on field medical incidents tells us that flulike illness (colds, upper respiratory infections, sore throat, fever, headaches) and gastrointestinal problems (nausea, vomiting, diarrhea, constipation) are 43 percent of reported illness and dwarf all other reported illness categories.

They are not necessarily simple. These symptoms are common to many different medical presentations and can occasionally be the initial symptoms of more serious clinical conditions. Gastrointestinal symptoms (nausea, vomiting, and diarrhea) are usually caused by a "stomach bug," or "stomach flu." Respiratory symptoms (cough, congestion, runny nose, sore throat) are usually viral upper respiratory infections, a "cold" or "flu." All viral illnesses can also cause a headache, malaise, fatigue, low-grade fever, muscle aches, and body aches.

The challenge to the wilderness leader is knowing how to manage these and deciding when someone is sick enough to warrant an evacuation.

FLULIKE ILLNESS

Often these illnesses (colds, upper respiratory infections, sore throat, fever, headaches) are a viral infection of the nasal passages and throat that causes a runny nose, sore throat, cough, sneezing, headache, mild fever, muscle aches, and malaise. "Colds" are self-limiting, but these infections can linger several weeks, despite all of our remedies. They are most often transmitted by contaminated hands and, less commonly, although possible, as an aerosol. Cover your cough!

Upper Respiratory Infection (URI)

This is a viral or bacterial infection that affects the sinuses, pharynx, larynx, or bronchi. They are uncomfortable for the patient, but usually self-limiting.

Sore Throat

The most common causes of a sore throat are simple dryness due to altitude and dehydration and viral infections such as the common cold. Strep throat, roughly 10 percent of sore throats, is caused by bacteria *(Streptococcus)* and needs a culture to confirm. We can be suspicious if throat is beefy red with white pus spots and accompanied by fever, headache, vomiting, and—less likely—accompanied by respiratory signs and symptoms.

Signs and Symptoms

- Fever
- Headache
- Muscle aches and malaise
- Nasal congestion and coughing

Signs and Symptoms

- Increased mucous production
- Cough, sometimes productive
- Sore throat
- Fever
- Malaise

Fever

Fever is the body's resetting of our internal thermostat triggered by the immune system's response to an infection. It is usually accompanied by other signs and symptoms of illness.

Headache

The most common cause of headaches in the backcountry is dehydration. Other causes include muscular tension, altitude, vascular disorders, trauma, brain tumor, and carbon monoxide (CO) poisoning.

Treatment Principles For Flulike Illness. The management for flulike illness is based on treating symptoms to help the patient feel better while these illnesses run their course. We also need to recognize when this isn't a common and simple presentation and the patient should be evacuated for evaluation by a physician. Hydration is important, as is hygiene, especially hand washing. These illnesses are communicable, and we want to avoid spreading them through the group.

Rest and patience are cornerstones of treatment. Some of these illnesses may respond to antibiotics, but most are self-limiting—they can take a week or more to resolve. People don't like to be sick, and impatience will drive decisions to try treatments or to leave the wilderness. Pain medications (acetaminophen, aspirin, or nonsteroidal anti-inflammatory drugs) for headache and muscle aches are fine. Decongestants (e.g., pseudoephedrine), and anticough medications can treat upper respiratory symptoms. Bland diets are best for gastrointestinal distress.

Evacuation Guidelines

When are these common problems not simple? Evacuation is recommended for flulike illness if:

- Fever persists for more than 48 hours or is high (>104°F/39°C).
- The patient develops a stiff neck, severe headache, difficulty breathing, or wheezing.
- Signs or symptoms of pneumonia develop. This is usually associated with increasing shortness of breath, decreasing exercise tolerance, worsening malaise, and weakness with a predominance of cough.
- The patient is unable to tolerate any oral fluids more than 48 hours, especially if there are diarrhea volume losses, fever, or vomiting.
- The sore throat is in conjunction with an inability to swallow water and maintain adequate hydration.
- The sore throat is associated with a fever and a beefy red throat with white patches.

- The headache does not respond to treatment, is sudden and severe, or is associated with altered mental status.

GASTROINTESTINAL PROBLEMS

Gastroenteritis is an inflammation of the gastrointestinal system. Diarrhea is persistent loose watery stools. These are common backcountry medical conditions. A recent study on Denali showed that a third of the climbers had diarrhea, and that their hygiene practices could use improvement. We may want to blame it on the water, but fecal-oral contamination is probably a more common cause. Wash your hands!

The signs and symptoms of the "mung," as nausea, vomiting, and diarrhea are often called by NOLS students, are familiar.

Treatment of Gastroenteritis. Hydration is a focus of our treatment. Persistent diarrhea and vomiting can cause dehydration and electrolyte problems. If vomiting has been severe, consider electrolyte replacement solutions. Antiemetic medications (e.g., meclizine, Compazine) can be helpful in managing vomiting. Antidiarrheal medication (e.g., Immodium) can be helpful for persistent diarrhea.

Try a bland diet. The BRAT diet works well: Bananas, rice, applesauce, and toast. If you're in a developing country, check current recommendations for antibiotic use and diarrhea.

Signs and Symptoms of Mild Gastroenteritis

- Gradually increasing, diffuse abdominal discomfort, often worse in the lower quadrants.
- Intermittent cramping, usually diffuse and not localized with frequent loose stools.
- Hyperactive bowel sounds.
- Nausea and vomiting, occasionally low-grade fever.
- Usually resolves within 1 to 3 days.

Signs and Symptoms of Severe Gastroenteritis

- Persistent or worsening pain over 24 hours, especially if the pain becomes localized and constant.
- Inability to tolerate fluids.
- Stools with blood and mucus.
- Signs and symptoms of shock.
- Fever above 102°F (38°C).

Evacuation Guidelines

When are these gastrointestinal problems not simple? Evacuation is recommended if:

- There is bloody or coffee-ground vomit, the vomiting persists despite treatment, or the patient is unable to hydrate.
- The diarrhea becomes bloody or persists despite treatment, or the patient is unable to hydrate.
- Abdominal pain persists or worsens over 24 hours; spiking fever, bloody diarrhea, or dehydration should trigger an evacuation.
- The patient is unable to tolerate oral fluids for more than 48 hours, especially if accompanied by diarrhea or vomiting.

EYE INJURIES

Foreign Body in the Eye

Usually eyelashes, tears, and blinking defend the surface of the eye from foreign particles. If a foreign object, perhaps a speck of dust, dirt, or leaf, lands on the eye or inside the eyelid, it can be painful and irritating.

Examine the eye carefully. Don't rub it. Pull the lower lid down and have the patient look up. This allows you to see the lower part of the eye and inside the lower eyelid. Flip the upper lid over a small stick or cotton applicator and have the patient look down. This allows you to see the upper part of the eye and inside the upper eyelid.

Remove foreign material by irrigating with clean water or—if it's on the eyelid and not the eye itself—with gentle use

THE EYE

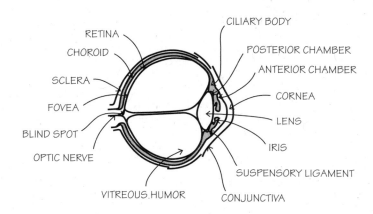

of a piece of gauze. If the object is stuck, leave it in place. Never try to remove something from the eye with force. Close the eye and bandage it shut with a folded gauze pad or sterile eye patch, and evacuate the patient.

The eye may feel irritated. This may be an abrasion to the surface of the cornea. Irrigate the eye. The patient may be more comfortable if you patch the eye shut. If the irritation is very painful or persists more than 24 hours, take the patient to a physician.

If the foreign object is impaled in the eye, do not remove it. The eye contains precious fluids that may leak out, and extracting the object can cause additional damage. Stabilize the object in place with gauze; cover and protect it against being banged. Because the eyes normally track together—when one moves, the other follows—bandage both eyes to prevent movement. Evacuate the patient.

Subconjunctival Hemorrhage
A subconjunctival hemorrhage is bleeding under the conjunctiva, the outer covering of the eye, and over the sclera, the white part of the eye. A subconjunctival hemorrhage may happen spontaneously after hard coughing, increasing blood

pressure, or a direct blow to the eye. Most cases have no specific history and are noticed by someone else. Usually the hemorrhage is on only one side. By itself, it rarely indicates a significant problem and is not a reason for evacuation. If it is the result of a blow to the eye, examination by a physician is advised.

Hyphema is bleeding into the anterior chamber of the eye, often after a blow to the eye. Blood may be seen by looking at the iris or the colored part of the eye. A patient with hyphema should always be evacuated.

Evacuation Guidelines

- Hyphema (blood in the anterior chamber of the eye).
- Any loss of vision, blurred or double vision.
- An object impaled in the eye.
- Acute, severe eye pain.
- A foreign body in the eye that you can't remove.
- Eye irritation that persists more than 24 hours.

CHAPTER 25

LEADERSHIP, TEAMWORK, AND COMMUNICATION

INTRODUCTION

In 1989, the center engine on a DC-10 passenger aircraft with 296 people on board malfunctioned over the Great Plains. Severed hydraulic lines crippled the pilot's ability to control the plane. The three-person crew's response to this crisis was a model of effective communication and teamwork. Working together, and using input from a pilot traveling as a passenger, they improvised a means of controlling the aircraft with the throttles.

Skilled aircrews, rescue teams, and wilderness leaders have found themselves in challenging situations in which communication, teamwork, and leadership are not optimum and things don't work out well. Aircrafts have crashed because flight crews failed to perform a routine task or a team member didn't speak up to report a problem. Ineffective communication of snowpack and terrain observation has contributed to avalanche incidents. Maps and headlamps left behind have embarrassed wilderness travelers caught in approaching darkness. Experts have unclipped from their climbing anchors, avoiding a dangerous situation only when their observant partners noticed the error.

Human error is a prominent cause of many accidents and critical incidents in team activities. NASA estimates that 70 percent of airline accidents involve some degree of human error. The Teton Park rescue rangers estimate that human error contributes significantly to most backcountry and mountain incidents. When the airline industry realized that well-trained and technically proficient crews could crash airworthy aircrafts because of inadequate crew communication or interaction, it developed a series of programs—known as crew resource management or human factors in aviation—to focus on teamwork, communication, and leadership. The DC-10 crew had this training, and they credit it with helping them manage their emergency. Law enforcement, the nuclear power industry, surgical teams, and wilderness rescue groups are beginning to recognize the impact of human factors in risk management.

If you're involved in a medical situation in the wilderness, you will work with the members of your expedition or with outside rescue groups. You may find yourself needing to work fast in an emergency or work slowly to plan a wilderness evacuation. You can use the concepts from crew resource management to enhance how you serve patients in the wilderness by combining medical and wilderness skills with effective leadership and teamwork.

NOLS LEADERSHIP SKILLS

Leadership at NOLS means timely, appropriate actions that direct, guide, and support your group to set and achieve realistic goals. Leadership is a complex blend of skills. For teaching purposes, we organize our leadership skills into seven groups:

1. Competence
2. Self-awareness
3. Judgment and decision making
4. Tolerance for adversity and uncertainty
5. Expedition behavior
6. Communication
7. Vision and action

Crew resource management has identified a number of behaviors demonstrated by well-functioning teams, including:

1. Sharing knowledge and experience
2. Avoiding self-imposed workloads
3. Recognizing and resolving fatigue and work overloads

 4. Using advocacy, feedback, and questioning
 5. Preparing for contingencies
 6. Building teamwork
 7. Setting an appropriate tone
 8. Addressing conflict
 9. Stating decisions clearly
10. Briefing effectively
11. Prioritizing and staying vigilant

In a wilderness medical scenario, leadership may involve assessing and treating a patient, protecting him or her from the cold and rain or heat and dust, and calling for help. Or it may involve leading a litter carry or technical rescue in remote terrain. We can take each NOLS leadership skill area, weave in lessons from crew resource management, and discuss how they apply to leadership, teamwork, and communication in a wilderness medical situation.

Competence

Competence refers to proficiency in technical (outdoor and first aid) and group management skills. Ideally, your outdoor, first aid, and group management skills are sharp, and you train to keep them fresh. The level of technical skill needed is situationally dependent.

The leader must manage the group to capitalize on the abilities of the team. You do not need to be a master of group management or technical skills; however, you must have sufficient skill in both areas to fill the leadership role. For example, in a large rescue operation, a leader may not be the most experienced medical person. He or she can delegate this task. The leader, however, needs information from the medical people to make decisions about the organization of the evacuation. The leader needs group management skills to ensure that communication, decision making, and leadership are effective.

Share Knowledge and Experience. In a crisis, it is common to utilize a leadership style with one person overtly leading the group. A directive leader, however, does not have to act in isolation. Ideally, the leader utilizes the team's skill and experience to make the best decisions. The leader both leads and teaches. He or she takes the initiative and time to make sure that pertinent details on the medical or evacuation plan are shared with team members. Techniques can be explained and practiced before use on the patient. Knowledge and communication strengthen the team. Everyone feels respected and engaged. Higher-quality decisions are more likely to be made.

Self-Awareness

Self-aware leaders learn from their experiences by acknowledging their abilities and successes, facing their limitations, admitting their mistakes, seeking feedback from others, and working to understand themselves. They know themselves well enough to know their bad habits and their tendencies to slip into the procrastination syndrome, the hurry-up syndrome, the do-it-all syndrome, or the perfectionist syndrome. The following are some behaviors that help avert these patterns.

Avoid Self-Imposed Workloads. Self-imposed workloads create stress. A lack of situational awareness when mountaineering (e.g., ignoring building afternoon thunderheads) may self-impose a hasty descent in rain, wind, and lightning. Conversely, watch for a self-imposed hurry-up syndrome—working fast when you don't need to and missing details or failing to complete procedures. Plan ahead, and prepare for the night shift. Will you need to rest, feed people, or find fresh folks to help carry the litter?

Recognize and Resolve Fatigue. Actively plan and schedule for transition and rest periods. In the excitement of an emergency, you tend to ignore the effect of fatigue on your performance. Pilots and rescue personnel have unrealistic attitudes about their invulnerability to stress and fatigue. The author learned a valuable lesson when he was assigned to the night shift on a multiday search. Not wanting to rest when others were working hard, he found something to do. The incident commander noticed this, confirmed that he was on his night shift, and told him in no uncertain terms, "It's your job to sleep. I need you at 100 percent tonight."

Recognize and Report Work Overloads. Avoid trying to fix everything yourself and taking on too many tasks. Leaders need to be able to step back and keep their eyes on the big picture. The culture of emergency services and outdoor leadership can drive a strong work ethic and a sense that it is inappropriate for the helper to ask for help. It's a measure of wisdom and maturity to be able to say, "I'm getting loaded up here. Can you take over?"

Judgment and Decision Making

The best medical protocols and practices cannot anticipate every situation, especially in wilderness. Leaders have to use their judgment by blending their knowledge, experience, character, situational awareness, and the knowledge of other resources into a decision. Wilderness medical teams need leaders who make wise decisions, and who can choose from a variety of decision-making styles. Leaders help a group put vague or complex information into a framework that makes sense. Leaders, regardless of their role as the designated person-in-charge or a team member, seek clarity, question assumptions, solicit input, listen, and thoughtfully share their observations and impressions.

Use Situationally Appropriate Decision-Making Styles. Effective leaders balance authority and teamwork. They choose from a range of decision-making styles, knowing when each is situationally appropriate. They tell others what style they and/or the group will use to make a decision: directive, consultative, a group decision, or a decision delegated to another. As a general principle, they take stands and are directive as needed while working toward maximum team participation.

Use Appropriate Advocacy and Assertion. Foster an environment in which your team can speak up and state their information, until there is resolution and decision. There are sad tales of a team member or leader making a mistake and another team member having the correct information but not speaking up or asserting his or her perspective. For example: "I'm uncomfortable with your delay in starting an evacuation. John has a persistent high fever. I think we should take him to a doctor."

You may need to provide a forum for communicating views. As a leader, model advocacy by checking in with your team and listening to their responses. "Are you getting enough direction from me about what you need to be doing? If anyone disagrees, please speak up."

Tolerance for Adversity and Uncertainty

The common definition of wilderness medicine includes lengthy transport times, arduous conditions, inclement weather, and lack of resources—a test of any leader's tolerance for adversity and uncertainty. Wilderness medical leaders must be able to live with uncertainty, endure hard work and challenge, and make do or improvise what they lack.

Prepare for Contingencies. Weather will turn bad. Helicopters will be delayed. Radios will break. Stable patients will take turns for the worse. Spring snow that's firm and supports weight in the morning can become soggy pudding in the afternoon. Stay ahead of the curve by analyzing your plan over and over and asking, what if? What if one of us sprains an ankle? It's sunny and warm now, but can I keep the patient dry if it rains?

Get Ready for the Long Haul. It's easy to be focused during the initial stages of a crisis. In wilderness medicine, however, the rubber often meets the road when you move into the long hours of work in difficult conditions as you carry a litter or wait through a storm for the helicopter. Leaders understand this change. They stay connected to the group, keeping everyone informed and focused on the task. They make sure that team members are eating, drinking, and staying warm and dry. They keep the process moving and energy and enthusiasm high.

Expedition Behavior

You may be on a wilderness expedition when you have to practice your wilderness medicine. You may be part of a rescue group sent into the wilderness. In both cases, the style of the expedition—the respect the team members show for one another and their work and the effectiveness of the communication within the group—is a critical component of the quality of the leadership. NOLS values good expedition behavior—a balance among teamwork, personal initiative, and responsibility. Team members take care of one another. They watch for fatigue and hazards, lend a helping hand without being asked, yet ask for help when they need it. They treat everyone with dignity and respect and support leadership while they work toward accomplishing the mission. Each person does his or her share; and more. They're honest and polite; they listen, yet they speak up and share their thoughts with the group. They're flexible, take responsibility, and work hard.

Build a Team Environment. Build an environment that acknowledges and respects the skills, experiences, and contributions of team members. Your team members should clearly understand their roles and tasks: "Sandy, thanks for staying alert for hazards. I'll stay at the head of the patient and monitor the airway and c-spine. Jack, finish the head-to-toe assessment and measure the vital signs. Jill, find a foam pad and sleeping bag for the patient."

Establish a team concept and environment for open communication. If there is an urgent need for action, you may need to focus someone who is rambling or talking about a nonpertinent issue. In general, listen with patience, do not interrupt or "talk over," and do not rush through a discussion. Include as many team members as possible in the communication flow: brief and update them as needed on weather, delays, plans, and schedules. Students in outdoor education groups, clients in guided trips, helpful bystanders, and local rescue personnel may all be part of your team.

Set an Appropriate Tone to the Situation. Set an appropriate tone of urgency. If the situation isn't dire, you may need to slow down your team. "Folks, let's take it easy. We've finished the assessment, and the scene is safe. Next we have to splint Bill's fractured leg, then log-roll him onto a sleeping bag and treat for shock. Let's take it one step at a time." Conversely, you may have to remind them to keep conversation and attention on the situation at hand. "Let's worry about dinner later. Right now, let's RICE and evaluate this ankle sprain." Leaders ensure that nonoperational factors such as social interaction or conversation do not interfere with necessary tasks (e.g., small talk does not interfere with climbing signals).

Address Conflict. Disagreements may occur. Personalities may clash. Unresolved conflicts can impede communication and cooperation and contribute to accidents. The leader may need to step in, identify the issue, and ask the team to put aside interpersonal differences until the emergency is over, addressing only immediate issues that are impeding progress. Later, when the crisis has passed, it's important to debrief these issues and emotions, work to resolve the conflict, and increase the team's ability to deal with its differences. A conflict during a crisis often means that expectations, roles, and responsibilities are unclear. People don't know what is expected of them or others, are missing information, or don't have a sense of the big picture. It's the leader's job to clarify structure and expectations.

Communication

Effective leaders master communication skills. They have the courage to state what they think, feel, and want and to listen with openness to different viewpoints. Leaders keep their groups informed and give clear, usable, and timely feedback. They provide a safe forum where each group member can discuss ideas and contribute to the decision-making process.

Clearly State and Acknowledge Decisions. Clearly state and acknowledge operational decisions to team members. Restate communications, clarify, and question to see if everyone understands: "We're going to rig an anchor here and use it to belay the patient to the ground. Let's go around the group and have everyone say what they will do."

Effective Inquiry: Ask and Listen. Foster an environment where questions are asked regarding actions and decisions. If people do not understand, they should be encouraged to speak up, to ask for clarification of unclear instructions or confusing or uncertain situations. For example:

> I don't understand this technique. . . . I'm not sure what you want me to do. . . . Why are we putting a tourni-

quet on this snakebite wound? I thought tourniquets weren't indicated for snakebite. . . . You said you can't hear breath sounds. Do you mean it's too noisy to listen or the patient is not breathing?

Give and Accept Appropriate Feedback. Give positive and negative performance feedback at appropriate times. Make it a positive learning experience for the whole crew—feedback must be specific to the issue at hand, objective, based on observable behavior, and given with respect and politeness. Likewise, accept feedback objectively and nondefensively. Inhibiting communication by having an unreceptive response to feedback has played a role in accidents.

Vision and Action

Leaders assure that the group knows the mission. They keep team members informed about the plan and each person's task. They are decisive when the situation requires decisiveness and patient when it is appropriate to wait or gather more information. They are forward looking and flexible, revising the plan as necessary.

Workload Management: State Clear Expectations of Roles and Responsibilities. Make clear roles, responsibilities, and the big picture:

I'll keep myself visible and in the open in case the rest of the group comes by. John, you're in charge of Fred and Sally. Scout for the best trail through these boulders back to camp. Check back with me before a half hour is up. Allison, you're in charge of patient care. Stay with the patient and monitor vitals. Blow your whistle three times if you need me.

A team works well when people know what they have to do and have a sense of where this fits into the big picture. As well, this prevents people from doing unnecessary tasks or getting in one another's way. Let others know what you expect of them, and what they can expect from you. "Folks, let's splint this arm first, then move the patient to the litter."

Provide Adequate Time for Completion of Tasks. Half-completed tasks—for example, flaps not adjusted on takeoff—have caused aircraft accidents. Backboard straps left loose when a team stops one task to start another are a real possibility on an emergency scene. Identify your key tasks, tell people what needs to be done, allow enough time, and complete each task— one by one.

Brief Effectively. Briefings are clear, complete, and interesting, and address team coordination and planning for potential problems. The team puts aside social conversation or low-priority tasks, pays attention, and asks clarifying questions. If it's an urgent situation, you may need to be concise. Expectations are set for handling possible deviations from normal operations or unusual conditions. For example: "We sent four people walking to the roadhead to ask for help carrying Pete. They should arrive tonight. If we don't hear from them by tomorrow noon, we'll send a second team."

Stay Vigilant during Both High and Low Workloads. Look around, check details, and check in with people when you're busy and when workload is low. It's easy to focus your attention when you're on duty and in the middle of the event. It's harder in the routine situation or when the initial excitement ebbs and the work of a long but apparently routine situation sets in. Accidents can happen when you overlook the obvious, missing the moment when you could have intervened or prevented a problem. How many of us have walked away from a rest break without looking around and noticing the water bottle and map left on the rock?

Prioritize Secondary Tasks. Prioritize secondary tasks to allow sufficient resources for dealing effectively with the important tasks. Talking about whether you will be able to continue your trip in the face of this illness may be the secondary task, the distraction. Feeding your team, having them gather personal gear, and preparing camp may be the primary tasks. Effective leaders keep their teams' eyes on the ball.

A WILDERNESS SCENARIO

Cindy, the designated leader, and her coleaders Pete, Sandy, and Juan were leading ten teenagers on a ski trip. They planned to ski across the pass from Arapaho Basin to Dodge Creek. The weather was warm and blustery, with alternating periods of sun and clouds. They moved as one big group.

Shortly after noon, as the group approached the top of the pass, the weather deteriorated into whiteout conditions. The leaders, concerned about a possible cliff band on the descent route, searched for almost an hour for a route off the pass. The students, in what to them was an exposed, cold, confusing, and new situation, were left alone. Standing around, the students became frightened, wet, and cold.

Cindy told Pete and Sandy to continue to try to find a route off the saddle, but to return in 20 minutes, regardless of their success. Cindy and Juan returned to the group to find several students excitedly pointing out two hypothermic students sitting hunched over on their packs. "They're really cold. We need to get out of here!" Juan began to pull out sleeping bags and tarps to treat the hypothermia. Cindy said, "Juan, first check everyone out. Let's be sure they're hypothermic."

A few minutes later, Juan reported that although cold and scared, everyone could walk and was still alert and oriented. Their hands and feet were still warm. "OK," said Cindy, "let's get everyone together and get extra layers on people. Have them eat some trail food. Have the cold people jog in place. We need to wait for Pete and Sandy before we descend the slope."

Pete returned shortly and said that he had found a good route to the saddle and a decent campsite in the trees. Sandy wanted to dig in on the pass, arguing that people were tired and the descent would take too long. Cindy listened and also asked Pete what he thought. Pete said, "People still have energy. Let's descend to better shelter before it's too late."

Cindy said, "I agree, that's what we'll do—descend to the trees in the saddle."

Cindy clarified details on the route and the campsite, checking the map and Pete's compass bearing. They pulled

Juan aside for a moment and told him this information and the plan—emphasizing the need to stay together and planning what to do if someone was really slow on the descent. Cindy then briefed the entire group. "Let's move. Pete will lead. Juan will be tail person. We will stay close together and not lose sight of each other. The weather is nasty, but we can deal with it. We're doing fine, and we will be in camp shortly."

The group descended to the saddle slowly but without incident and quickly rigged tarps. Within the hour the teenagers were enjoying hot drinks and stories of their adventure.

This incident has several examples of effective leadership and crew management:

1. Appropriate decision-making style. Cindy was directive when needed, and consulted with Pete, Sandy, and Juan before making the plan to descend the slope.

2. Effective inquiry. Cindy and Juan checked the report of hypothermia and thus avoided acting on misinformation. Cindy confirmed the route, compass bearing, and map with Pete.

3. Effective briefing. Everyone was told the plan before the descent. Roles and expectations were clear: Pete in front, Juan in back, everyone staying together.

4. Good situational awareness and an appropriate tone. The leaders knew that they had a challenge but not an emergency.

5. Appropriate advocacy. Sandy spoke up with her plan to stay on the pass, then deferred to the leader when her idea had been discussed.

6. Good preparation for contingencies. Layers and food were accessible, and the group was kept together. The leaders talked through possible problems on the descent.

7. Workloads were managed and tasks prioritized. Everyone stayed together. No one else became lost or cold during the descent to camp.

FINAL THOUGHTS

You may find yourself alone with a patient or in a small team performing wilderness first aid within a larger team of local rescue resources. The quality of your leadership, teamwork, and communication will determine how well you work within your team and with others. People working together add redundancy and synergism; one person may notice something that escapes the attention of others, and everyone can contribute knowledge and experience to the decision-making process. The team members must be effective advocates, and the leader must be an effective listener; multiple perspectives on an event are useless unless the information is shared. As well, we need to understand the impact of fatigue, the distraction of multiple tasks, and the value of effective briefing. Teamwork is enhanced, and many problems averted, when people are clear on their roles, responsibilities, and expectations. Effective leadership, teamwork, and communication are characteristics that lead to excellence.

CHAPTER 26

STRESS
AND THE RESCUER

INTRODUCTION

First aid training has traditionally concentrated on treatment and transport: the nuts and bolts of assessment, splinting, and airway maintenance. The human elements of emergency medical care are equally important. We are beginning to recognize the impact of emergency stress on the rescuer as well as the victim.

Although there is limited data on wilderness rescuers, there is a growing body of literature on the effects of stress on emergency workers. Caring for the ill or injured, having responsibility for the lives and safety of others, is considered a significant stressor. Research is showing that high attrition rates, burnout, and stress-related illness are common in emergency personnel.

EFFECTS OF STRESS

A perceived threat or challenge or a change in the environment can cause stress—a state of physical or psychological arousal. Beneficial stress affects all living creatures and can be a positive factor in change, creativity, growth, and productivity. Healthy exercise that increases your physical capability is a good stress. Continuous hard exercise without rest or adequate nutrition can become a destructive force with negative effects on your health, your family, and your life.

You may be stressed by noises, confined spaces, extremes in weather, and other aspects of the environment. In the social environment, conflicts within a group, and conflicts with the boss or family members are all stressors. You're also stressed by inactivity and boredom.

Stress produces intricate biochemical changes in the body. The brain becomes more active; chemicals secreted by the endocrine system cause muscles to tighten, pupils to dilate, and heart rate, breathing rate, and blood pressure to increase. Protein, glucose, and antibody levels in the blood rise.

·   These physiological changes prepare you to meet a challenge by making you more alert and ready for physical activity. In the short term, they can be helpful. In the long term, or if the short-term stress is significant, the effects of stress can adversely affect your physical and psychological health by wearing you down and making you susceptible to a variety of physical and psychological problems. The surgeon general estimates that 80 percent of nontraumatic causes of death are actually stress-related disease such as coronary artery disease, high blood pressure, ulcers, and cancer.

STRESS ON THE JOB

The job demands of emergency personnel create an environment in which turnover and stress-related illness are common. Emergency situations may subject workers to noise such as wind, rushing water, screams, and sirens; to the confusion of the emergency scene; to having responsibility for the health and safety of patients and fellow rescuers in prolonged weather extremes; to difficult bystanders who may never be satisfied with the rescuer's performance; to equipment failures and inadequate equipment, which add to the difficulty of the situation; and to long hours of hard physical work. Lengthy rescues, rescues in which the patient dies, multiple-casualty incidents, and incidents in which emergency workers or friends are injured are particularly stressful.

Certainly, emergency stress affects an outdoor leader or anyone thrown into the role of rescuer. Experience may help a person cope with these stresses, but it does not make him or her immune.

The leader of a notably difficult expedition experiences significant extra stress when weather, group dynamics, faulty equipment, or complex logistics combine to create a high-pressure situation. In addition to caring for the ill or injured under these difficult conditions, the leader continues to be responsible for the safety and welfare of the group.

ASSESSMENT: RECOGNIZING STRESS REACTIONS

Stress in the short term may produce fatigue, nausea, anxiety, fear, irritability, lightheadedness, headache, memory lapses, sleep disturbances, changes in appetite, loss of attention span, and indecision. These are normal reactions by normal people to abnormal events. A person experiencing an acute stress reaction may wander aimlessly on the scene, sit or stare blankly, or engage in erratic or irrational behavior.

Long-term effects of stress include difficulty concentrating, intrusive images (recurring dreams or sensations of the traumatic event), sleep disturbance, fatigue, and diseases such as ulcers, diabetes, and coronary artery disease. Emotional signs include depression, feelings of grief and anger, and a sense of isolation. Emergency workers suffering from cumulative stress may respond by avoiding emergency situations, taking excessive sick leave, or being easily aroused or startled. It is beyond the scope of this book to discuss intervention for cumulative stress reactions.

TREATMENT: MANAGING STRESS IN THE FIELD

Preparation for stress management includes anticipation of the difficulties of rescue and a realistic appraisal of your ability to cope. Among emergency personnel on the scene of a serious rescue, most will experience at least some symptoms of stress. Rescuers need to remember that a successful outcome is not guaranteed, particularly if the patient is far from modern medical care. Rescue work, especially wilderness rescue, can be long and tedious. Recognition and thanks for the efforts of the rescuer are often sparse, whereas criticism from bystanders is common.

Acute Stress Reactions

PHYSICAL	EMOTIONAL	COGNITIVE
• Fatigue	• Anxiety	• Memory loss
• Muscle tremors	• Fear	• Indecision
• Nausea	• Grief	• Difficulty problem solving
• Glassy eyes	• Depression	• Confusion with trivial issues
• Chills	• Hopelessness	• Loss of attention span
• Dizziness	• Irritability	• Feeling overwhelmed
• Profuse sweating	• Anger	

Delayed Stress Reactions

• Macabre humor
• Excessive use of sick leave
• Reluctance to enter stressful situations
• Intrusive images
• Obsession with the stressful incident
• Withdrawal from others
• Suicidal thoughts
• Feelings of inadequacy

Short-term stress symptoms can be managed by attending to the physical needs for rest, food, and hydration; by briefing the group on the sights, sounds, and emotions they may experience during a long evacuation; and by debriefing the group after the incident.

Acute stress reactions on the scene can be managed by removing an overstressed person from the site. Give simple, clear directions to the stressed person and assign productive tasks that can help shift his or her focus away from the immediate incident. Such tasks might include providing food and drink, building a litter, and setting up tents.

If an emergency caregiver is overly distressed, detached from reality, or disruptive, someone may need to stay with him or her to lend a sympathetic ear. You can help such persons cope by talking with them and offering assurances that their feelings are valid, real, and perfectly appropriate. Provide emotional support with honesty and direct, factual answers to their questions.

FINAL THOUGHTS

The Field Debriefing

Following a rescue, first attend to the physical needs of the rescuers by providing food, water, clean clothing, and shelter.
Light aerobic exercise, such as a hike or a game of hacky sack,
may help relieve tension built up over the course of the rescue.

Provide emotional support to rescuers, staff, and course
participants who experience unusual stress. In wilderness education many of our participants are young and may be experiencing their first real-life stress. Emotional reactions to
accidents are perfectly normal and should be expected but people who don't know this may compound their own anxieties,
making the stress even worse for themselves. The majority of
reactions are short-term, with no lasting consequences.

A simple, voluntary debriefing or a conversation around
the fire with a trusted mentor or friend can help people manage
the emotions of an event, connect people with their support
groups, and identify a person who needs additional help. These
conversations can give people a map to work through the emotional and cognitive wilderness after a serious incident. The
National Association of EMS Physicians, in a draft position
paper on stress in emergency services, recommends "psychological first aid" instead of the more elaborate and controversial
critical incident stress debriefings. Psychological first aid entails
listening, empathy, assessing needs, ensuring that basic physical needs are met, protecting from additional harm, not forcing
people to talk, and accessing family, clergy, or friends for support. Rescuers should understand that their reactions, while
uncomfortable, are natural, normal reactions to abnormal
events and that healing may take time and assistance. For both
patients and rescuers, the emotional first aid we provide is as
important to their ultimate recovery as the physical care.

CHAPTER 27

MEDICAL LEGAL CONCEPTS IN WILDERNESS MEDICINE

INTRODUCTION

There are several medical legal concepts that are pertinent to the wilderness first responder. At first glance these legal concepts can be framed as possible trigger points for a lawsuit. They can also be framed as reminders of the style in which we should provide care. They're reminders that we should do what we have been trained to do (and do it well) and that we should treat our patients with respect and politeness.

WILDERNESS PROTOCOLS

Doing your job well and consistent with the standards and practices for which you have trained is excellent protection against lawsuits, as well as assurance that your patient will be treated properly. Medicine uses the phrase "scope of practice" to describe what care a provider can provide, and "standard of care" to describe the yardstick by which that care is measured. The standard of care by which you will be judged is determined in part by your level of training and the protocols under which you practice.

Most of the care provided by wilderness first responders is straightforward and widely accepted first aid. If someone is bleeding, it's expected that we will apply direct pressure and elevation. If we assess a fracture, it is accepted that the prehospital treatment is to immobilize the limb.

Administering medication, relocating dislocations, doing a focused spine assessment, and making evacuation decisions are examples of a few practices that are outside the normal scope of practice of prehospital medicine, yet are very appropriate and the standard of care in wilderness medicine. To clarify the standards of care you should provide, we encourage all our wilderness medicine students who may find themselves in a leadership position to affiliate with a medical director who can develop a set of protocols. Your physician can review your training and experience and provide support for the context in which you will practice medicine. He or she can develop treatment and evacuation protocols that meet your training and your program's needs.

Documentation. In the chapter on patient assessment we discussed written patient notes—the SOAP report. These serve as a form of communication between medical care providers, and they serve as documentation of what you did, when you did it, and how you did it.

Written documentation can be invaluable if your level of care is challenged in a legal process and you try to reconstruct from memory an event in the past. An axiom in medicine is "If you didn't write it down, you didn't do it." This serves as a reminder of the limits of our memory and the importance of documenting our assessment, our treatment, and any changes in the patient's condition while he or she is under our care.

Duty to Act and the Good Samaritan? As a trip leader, whether paid or volunteer, it can be argued that you have a duty to provide assistance in the event of a medical problem. Your patient is not a stranger; you have a prior relationship with him or her if he or she is a participant in an activity you lead. You would also have a duty if you respond as part of a rescue or ambulance team.

You will be a Good Samaritan in the eyes of your society, and in the legal context, if you provide care voluntarily when you don't have a duty to the patient, e.g., if you stop to help an injured hiker by the side of the trail. To encourage us to provide care in this circumstance many states have some form of Good Samaritan legislation that provides legal protection as long as we are not grossly negligent. Good Samaritan laws vary from state to state, but common elements are that we don't have a preexisting duty to the patient and that the care has to be voluntary—often on an unplanned and unforeseen emergency basis.

Consent

It's simple politeness to ask a person for permission to treat. We do this as part of our initial assessment when we introduce ourselves and ask if we can help. It's also a legal principle that people have control of themselves, and we can't practice medicine on them without their permission.

Informed consent is the process, ongoing throughout our care, where a reliable patient agrees to treatment after being informed about the risks and benefits. The dialogue we have while we assess and treat our patient keeps him or her informed, and again is simply being polite and respectful.

The law assumes that an unreliable patient, one with an altered mental status who is not fully alert and oriented to person, place, and time would want help during an emergency situation. This is the concept of *implied consent.*

Implied consent also applies to minors whose parents are not available to give consent. The laws regarding minors are complex and can vary from state to state. If you're working with minors, which in most cases is anyone under the age of 18 years, it's wise to seek legal advice that is pertinent to your program and your state.

Confidentiality

As you assess and treat a patient you will learn aspects of personal and medical history that again, out of politeness and respect, should be considered confidential. The findings from your assessment and care can be communicated verbally, and in writing, to another medical provider who needs to know to continue care for the patient. Outdoor leaders who learn a student's or client's medical history from a routine pretrip screening process have an obligation to only share this information appropriately and must be cautious when discussing medical history with colleagues. Inappropriate disclosure of medical information would breach your "patient to provider" confidentiality. In addition to being disrespectful, in the legal world you may commit slander, defaming a person's character verbally, or libel, defaming in writing.

Be careful about what you say on the radio or to other members of your program or expedition. On the radio state your facts, avoid identifying the patient unless it is necessary, and avoid speculation. For example, you may note the patient's breath odor and odd behavior as facts, but to state he or she is intoxicated without a blood test can be slander, as well as being incorrect.

Abandonment

Abandonment happens when you stop care too soon or transfer the patient to someone who is not able to provide the care the patient needs. This can arise when a trained medical provider begins care and gives the impression he or she will help the patient, then leaves the patient, or turns him or her over to someone with less training. A scenario for this in outdoor education could be a trip leader turning the patient over to a coleader or a program support person. The trip leader needs to consider the level of care the patient needs and whether the coleader or program support person can provide that care.

FINAL THOUGHTS

Fear of being sued can restrain people from taking training or responding to an emergency. This is unfortunate when it prevents people from helping one another. We can talk about the legal climate in our society, and the details of law, but there is no argument that if we can help and fail to do so, we violate the expectations of medicine and our society. NOLS Legal Advisor Reb Gregg has given us sage advice for years, words that are summarized in the two key points in this chapter: Do what you are trained to do, and treat people with respect and politeness. These simple rules will help you provide the best of care—the key to staying out of court.

APPENDIX A

FIRST AID KIT

These are the contents of a standard first aid kit designed for a group of twelve on a month long trip. (This is the inventory of the NOLS Instructor's Kit.) Obviously, requirements will vary with group size, medical qualifications, trip length, location, and remoteness.

NOLS FIRST AID KIT

General Supplies

Biohazard bag	1
Nitrile Gloves	1 pair
Latex gloves	4 pairs
Micro shield	1
Thermometer (digital)	1
Signal mirror	1
Whistle	1

Wound Care	No.
2" × 2" gauze pad	4
3" × 4" nonstick gauze pads	2
Opsite Transparent dressing	2
4" × 4" gauze pad	2
Band-aids	12

Wound Care	No.
Steri-strips	6
3" gauze roll	1
Tweezers	1
Cravats	1
Oval eye pads	2
Safety pins	2
12cc syringe	1
Bactracin $1^1/_{32}$ oz	10
Cortisone $1^1/_{32}$ oz	10
Benzoin 1 oz	2
Betadine 1 oz	1

Foot Repair Pouch	No.
Scissors	1
Ace bandage	1
1" Athletic tape	2
Moleskin	2 (2" × 3")
Molefoam	2 (2" × 3")
Adhesive knit	2 (2" × 3")
Second Skin	2 (2" × 3")

Suggestions

Protect the sterile dressings from moisture by sealing them in groups of three or four in clear plastic.

If you have a planned resupply of food and fuel, consider including extra tape and blister material.

The kit should be accessible. Everyone should know its location.

Label all containers. Include instructions for all medications.

Thermometers break easily. A strong package is imperative; a spare thermometer a good idea.

The kit should be packaged in a distinctly colored and labeled bag that is durable, waterproof, and not heavy or bulky.

If your first aid kit is too big, you will have a tendency to leave it behind. Many NOLS instructors carry in their summit packs a small package of the most frequently needed items, including tape, moleskin, Second Skin, and povidone-iodine. Others slide a small roll of tape, cravat, and 4 x 4 into their helmet lining.

NOLS first aid kits do not include premade splints, such as airsplints or SAM splints. Premade splints may be carried in the first aid kit or suitable splints can be improvised from foamlite pads.

Keep a note pad, pencil, change for phone calls, evacuation report forms, and emergency instructions with the first aid kit.

EMERGENCY PROCEDURES FOR OUTDOOR GROUPS

INTRODUCTION

This is an outline for organizing an emergency scene and a wilderness evacuation. It is not a checklist; it is a list of considerations we have found helpful in leading evacuations.

Think

1. A wilderness evacuation is a mental as well as physical challenge. Paul Petzoldt's wise advice to step aside and carefully review the situation is always pertinent.
2. Details are important; small omissions in planning can have great consequences. The evacuation team spending the night out because maps were forgotten is a liability, not an asset.
3. Errors in organization and technique have a tendency to multiply over time.
4. Time is an asset and a liability in the outdoors. Rapid transport is not possible. Use the time to think and plan.

Preplan

1. Research possible resources and evacuation options before the trip begins. Under what circumstances is self-rescue an option, and when must outside help be called upon. Know who is responsible for rescue in your wilderness area.

2. Be knowledgeable and proficient in first aid.
3. Prepare for the emergency by carrying water, shelter, matches, and a first aid kit.

Emergency Medical Care

Address the physical and psychological needs of the patient. A thorough patient assessment is essential to making a wise decision regarding method and urgency of evacuation.

LEADERSHIP

In any evacuation, many things begin happening simultaneously. The following topics—organization, decision making, communication, and reports—are presented as related elements rather than as a sequence of events.

Organization

As leader, you must assume the leadership role, delegate responsibilities, consider the circumstances, determine the type of evacuation, and prepare for and execute the evacuation.

Assume Leadership.
1. Review scene safety. Prevent situations that might create additional victims.
2. If the injury or illness is not serious, consider making an educational exercise of the rescue.
3. Organize the members of the group.

Delegate Responsibilities. Keeping everyone purposefully occupied reduces stress. In a complex evacuation there are always more tasks than people. Every task is important. Possible tasks include:
1. Feed the group. Cook food. Prepare hot drinks.
2. Prepare the evacuee's pack.
3. Build a litter.
4. Scout trail; break trail.
5. Find and mark landing site for helicopter evacuation; clear or pack soft ground if necessary.

6. Prepare evacuation and medical reports.
7. Gather and inventory all available gear: maps, first aid kits, food, water, stoves, shelters, technical climbing or boating gear.
8. Feed, shelter, hydrate the rescuers.

Decision Making

Consider the following when determining the type of evacuation:

Severity of Injury. How soon does this patient need to be in the hospital? Does the injury threaten life (ABC systems) or limb?

Distance to Roadhead. What is the distance to the phone or additional help? What are the distance and time of the evacuation considering a 1- to 2-miles-per-hour rate of travel?

Difficulty of Terrain. When will you reach the rough country? In the beginning when you are fresh or later when you're exhausted?

Group's Physical Strength and Stamina.

Group's Technical Abilities and Experience, the Weather. Will you be able to deal with deteriorating weather or technical terrain?

Communication Possibilities. Can you communicate quickly with outside resources by telephone or radio, or must your message be carried by foot?

Outside Assistance. What are available rescue services— horse packers, snowmobilers, etc.?

Transportation Schedule. Who will meet you at the roadhead?

Plan for Mechanical Failures.

Suitability of Landing or Loading Site.

Determine the Type of Evacuation. The following are common modes of evacuation:

Walking or Skiing. For the patient who is able, this is easiest and least complex.

Simple Carries. Whether or not you can carry the patient on your back depends on your strength and the nature of the patient's injuries. Such carries can be faster and easier than litter carries.

Litter. Requires a larger group—at least ten people—and is slow but safe and effective.

Request More Manpower. Consider starting for the roadhead and meeting support en route.

Horsepacking. Injury-dependent but fast; commonly used in Western states.

Helicopter. Fast but expensive; risky in poor weather and mountains; requires special permission in wilderness areas.

Ski Sled Litter. Improvised sled litters can be fast and effective.

Snowmobile. Limited by snow conditions.

Boat/Vehicle (4WD).

Execute the Evacuation. Arrange for the evacuation party:

1. Make sure you have enough people to carry out a safe and effective evacuation.
2. Be prepared with food, extra clothing, sleeping bags, and marked maps.

Communication

Assuming that no radio or telephone communication is available, messages must be delivered on foot. They are generally one-way and must be accurate, concise, and complete.

1. Determine whether messengers should be sent.
2. Designate messengers and leader.
3. Send sufficient number of messengers to ensure safety and effectiveness.
4. Consider: physical stamina, night travel, map, navigation and first aid skills, foul weather experience.
5. Send written instructions including medical and evacuation report form with a time control plan.

Reports

The full evacuation report should include both a medical report and the field evacuation report.

Medical Report. The medical report should include the following:

• Age and gender.

- Chief complaint.
- Physical exam/vital signs.
- Present illness/injury.
- Past history.
- Treatment.
- Medications administered.
- Changes in patient's condition.

Evacuation Report. The evacuation report should include:
- Type of evacuation (walk, helicopter, litter).
- Marked maps showing:
    1. Location of accident.
    2. Present location of group and victim.
    3. Anticipated route out of mountains.
    4. Roadhead destination.
- Estimated date and time of arrival and return.
- Any special requests (doctor, litter, etc.).
- Plans for messengers returning to expedition and plans for the group remaining in the field.

Important! Always include an alternate plan in your report!

GLOSSARY OF FIRST AID TERMS

Anaphylaxis. A hypersensitive reaction of the body to a foreign protein or drug.

Anorexia. A lack of appetite.

Appendicular. Refers to the limbs, the legs and arms.

Avulsion. A forcible tearing away of a body part. It can be a piece of skin, a finger, toe, or entire limb.

Ataxia. Incoordination of muscles. Usually seen when voluntary movement is attempted; e.g., walking.

Axial. Referring to the midline through the skeleton, the skull, vertebrae, and pelvis.

Axillary. Referring to the armpit.

Bacteria. Unicellular organisms lacking chlorophyll.

Basal metabolic rate. The metabolic rate of a person at rest. Usually expressed in kilocalories per square meter of body surface per hour.

Basal metabolism. The amount of energy needed to maintain life when the body is at rest.

Brachial. Refers to the arm, usually the brachial artery or nerve.

Brain stem. The portion of the brain located below the cerebrum, which controls automatic functions such as breathing and body temperature.

Campylobacter. A genus of bacteria implicated in diarrheal illness.

Capillary. The smallest of the blood vessels; the site of oxygen, nutrient, and waste product exchange between the blood and the cells.

Cerebellum. The portion of brain behind and below the cerebrum, which controls balance, muscle tone, and coordination of skilled movements.

Cerebrum. The largest and upper region of the brain. Responsible for higher mental functions such as reasoning, memory, and cognition.

Comminuted. A fracture in which several small cracks radiate from the point of impact.

Congenital. A condition present at birth.

Conjunctiva. The mucous membrane that lines the eyelid and the front of the eyeball.

Convection. Heat transferred by currents in liquids or gases.

Cornea. The clear transparent covering of the eye.

Crepitus. A grating sound produced by bone ends rubbing together.

CRT. Capillary refill time. For example, "Capillary refill time is 3 seconds."

Cyanosis. Bluish discoloration of the skin, mucous membranes, and nail beds indicating inadequate oxygen levels in the blood.

Diabetes. A disease resulting from inadequate production or utilization of insulin.

Distal. Farther from the heart.

Electrolyte. A substance that, in solution, conducts electricity: Common electrolytes in our body are sodium, potassium, chloride, calcium, phosphorus, and magnesium.

Embolism. An undissolved mass in a blood vessel; may be solid, liquid, or gas.

Epilepsy. Recurrent attacks of disturbed brain function; classic signs are altered level of consciousness, loss of consciousness, and/or seizures.

Eversion. A turning outward (as with an ankle).

Giardia. A genus of protozoan, a simple unicellular organism that causes an illness that is often characterized by diarrhea.

Globule. Any small rounded body.

Hematoma. A pool of blood confined to an organ or tissue.

Hyperglycemia. High blood sugar.

Hypoglycemia. Low blood sugar.

Intercostal. The area between the ribs.

Irrigate. To flush with a liquid.

Kilocalorie. A unit of heat; the amount of heat needed to change the temperature of 1 gram of water 1 degree centigrade.

LOC. Level of consciousness.

Meninges. The three membranes that enclose and help protect the brain.

MOI. Mechanism of injury for an accident.

Morbidity. The state of being diseased.

Occlusive dressing. A dressing impermeable by moisture.

Palpate. To examine by touching.

Paraplegia. Paralysis affecting the lower portion of the body and both legs.

Paroxysmal. A sudden, periodic attack, spasm, or recurrence of symptoms.

PFD. Personal flotation device (life jacket).

Plasma. The liquid part of blood.

Prodromal. The initial stage of a disease.

Quadriplegia. Paralysis affecting all four limbs.

Rales. Crackly breath sounds due to fluid in the lungs or airways.

RR. Respiratory rate. For example, "RR is 18 and unlabored," or "RR is 22 and shallow and regular."

SCTM. Skin, color, temperature, and moisture. For example, "Skin is pale, cool, and moist," or "Skin is red, hot, and dry."

Seizure. A sudden attack of a disease as in epilepsy.

Signs. An indication of illness or injury that the examiner observes.

Sprain. Trauma to a joint causing injury to the ligaments.

Strain. A stretched or torn muscle.

Symptoms. Pain, discomfort, or other abnormality that the patient feels.

Tendinitis. Inflammation of a tendon.

TRS. Township, range, and section. A grid system used as a legal description of location. The coordinates are available on many topographic maps.

Varicose veins. Distended, swollen, knotted veins.

Vasoconstriction. Narrowing of blood vessels.

Ventricular. Referring to the two lower pumping chambers of the heart, the ventricles.

Vertigo. The sensation of objects moving about the person or the person moving around in space.

Virus. A microscopic and parasitic organism dependent on the nutrients inside cells for its reproductive and metabolic needs.

Wheezes. Whistling or sighing breath sounds resulting from narrowed airways.

BIBLIOGRAPHY

Benenson, Abram S., ed. *Control of Communicable Diseases in Man.* Washington, DC: American Public Health Association, 1990.

Buttaravoli, Philip, and Thomas Stair. *Minor Emergencies: Splinters to Fractures.* St. Louis: Mosby, 2000.

Forgey, William W. *Basic Essentials of Hypothermia.* 2nd ed. Guilford, CT: Globe Pequot Press, 1999.

———, ed. *Wilderness Medical Society Practice Guidelines for Wilderness Emergency Care.* 2nd ed. Guilford, CT: Globe Pequot Press, 2006.

———. *Wilderness Medicine.* 5th ed. Guilford, CT: Globe Pequot Press, 2000.

Fradin, Mark, and John Day. "Comparative efficacy of insect repellents against mosquito bites." *New England Journal of Medicine* 347 (July 4, 2002):13–18.

Giesbrecht, Gordon. "Prehospital treatment of hypothermia." *Wilderness & Environmental Medicine* 12, no. 1 (2001).

Gill, Paul G., Jr. *Pocket Guide to Wilderness Medicine.* New York: Simon & Schuster, 1991.

———. *Waterlover's Guide to Marine Medicine: How to Identify and Treat Aquatic Ailments and Injuries.* New York: Simon & Schuster, 1993.

Gold, Barry, Richard Dart, and Robert Barish. "Bites of venomous snakes." *New England Journal of Medicine* 347, no. 5 (August 1, 2002).

Gookin, John. *NOLS Backcountry Lightning Safety Guidelines.* Lander, WY: National Outdoor Leadership School, 2000.

Hackett, Peter, and Robert Roach. "High-altitude Illness." *New England Journal of Medicine* 345, no. 2 (July 12, 2001).

Houston, Charles. *Going Higher: Oxygen, Man, and Mountains.* 4th ed. Seattle: Mountaineers Books, 1998.

Hultgren, Herb. *High Altitude Medicine.* Stanford, CA: Hultgren Publications, 1997.

Jong, Elaine, and Russell McMullen. *The Travel & Tropical Medicine Manual.* Philadelphia: W. B. Saunders Company, 1995.

Roberts, James R. *Roberts' Practical Guide to Common Medical Emergencies.* Philadelphia: Lippincott-Raven Publishers, 1996.

Schmutz, Ervin, and Lucretia Breazeale Hamilton. *Plants That Poison.* Flagstaff, AZ: Northland Publishing, 1979.

Setnicka, Tim J. *Wilderness Search and Rescue.* Boston: Appalachian Mountain Club, 1980.

Shimanski, Charley. *Helicopters in Search and Rescue Operations: Basic and Intermediate Levels.* Golden, CO: Mountain Rescue Association, 2002.

———. *Search and Rescue for Outdoor Leaders.* Golden, CO: Mountain Rescue Association, 2002.

Smith, David. *Backcountry Bear Basics: The Definitive Guide to Avoiding Unpleasant Encounters.* Seattle: Mountaineers Books, 1997.

Steele, Peter. *Backcountry Medical Guide.* 2nd ed. Seattle: Mountaineers Books, 1999.

Stewart, Charles E. *Environmental Emergencies.* Baltimore: Williams & Wilkins, 1990.

Sutherland, Stuan, and Guy Nolch. *Dangerous Australian Animals.* Flemington, Victoria, Australia: Hyland House, 2000.

Tilton, Buck. *Backcountry First Aid and Extended Care.* 4th ed. Guilford, CT: Globe Pequot Press, 2002.

———. *Basic Essentials of Avalanche Safety.* Guilford, CT: Globe Pequot Press, 1992.

———. *Basic Essentials of Rescue from the Backcountry.* Guilford, CT: Globe Pequot Press, 1990.

————. *Don't Get Bitten: The Dangers of Bites and Stings.* Seattle: Mountaineers Books, 2003.

Tilton, Buck, and Rick Bennett. *Don't Get Sick: The Hidden Dangers of Camping and Hiking.* Seattle: Mountaineers Books, 2002.

Tilton, Buck, and Frank Hubbell. *Medicine for the Backcountry: A Practical Guide to Wilderness First Aid.* 3rd ed. Guilford, CT: Globe Pequot Press, 1999.

Trott, Alexander. *Wounds and Lacerations: Emergency Care and Closure.* St. Louis: Mosby, 1991.

Van Tilburg, Christopher. *Emergency Survival: A Pocket Guide.* Seattle: Mountaineers Books, 2001.

Weiss, Eric. *Wilderness 911: A Step-by-Step Guide for Medical Emergencies and Improvised Care in the Backcountry.* Seattle: Mountaineers Books/Backpacker magazine, 1998.

Wilderness Medicine Institute of NOLS. *Wilderness Medicine Handbook.* 9th ed. Lander, WY: National Outdoor Leadership School, 2005.

Wilkerson, James A., ed. *Medicine for Mountaineering and Other Wilderness Activities.* 5th ed. Seattle: Mountaineers Books, 2001.

————. "Rabies update." *Wilderness & Environmental Medicine* 11, no. 1, (2000).

INDEX

Italic page numbers refer to illustrations.

Index